Other books by David Fairchild

Circle of Dogs:

The New Paladin
Wolf
Eulogies (forthcoming)

———————

Where's the Blood?
25 Creative Writing Exercises with
Motivational Anthology

THE
EXODUS

FAIRCHILD

Four Doors
Publishing

Four Doors Publishing LLC

Provo, UT 84601

Printed in the United States of America.

Believe me.
I don't like their language either.
Nor do I approve of their choices
and predicaments

. . . but it's not my story,
and I wasn't there.

Prologue

A girl. She liked dogs, had a puppy once. It was a good puppy, grew big, bigger than she. It was a good dog. The girl loved Dog. Dog licked her face. She licked the dog.

"Don't do that," her mother said.

The girl obeyed her mother.

Mother taught the dog to watch the door—all day, watch the door. Dog was watching the door, and a man came in. Dog attacked the man: bit his leg, bit his hand, bit his crotch, tore it out, let him bleed. Mother rewarded him with steak and all sorts of loves.

Dog barked at other dogs. He was protective of his three-year-old girl. Girl loved him. He loved her. Home was good, he got to be with Girl. At night, Dog slept with Girl. Girl held dog; he knew she was safe. He made sure she slept safe.

Mother took Dog to obedience training. Put him in a pen, taught it "bite," taught it "tear." He was obedient. He bit good. He tore better.

"Good boy!"

He got head pet.

"Good boy!"

He got steak.

One day, a bigger pen with a bigger dog, a scary dog. Dog bit the bigger dog, tore the bigger dog. Bigger dog didn't get up.

"Good boy!"

He got steak.

Was happy to see his girl when he got home. Slept well those nights.

Dog went to more pens, bigger pens. More people came then, brought their dogs. Other dogs knew "bite" and "tear" too. Tried to bite Dog. Dog got angry—bit all dogs, tore all dogs. Some people got mad, some people did not.

Dog got steak. Went home to Girl, licked her face. He loved Girl.

One day, Dog go to pen. Pen has Girl in it. He happy to see Girl. He run to be with her. Leash holds him back.

Must get to her. He loves her! He loves her!

She is crying, lost. She holds a silver stick.

His handler lets him pull closer to girl, can almost reach her. He tries to lick her face.

"Stab," Mother says.

Girl cries, drops stick. Mother puts stick back in Girl's hand.

"Stab!"

Girl cries.

Mother slaps.

"What is stab," Dog asks. "What is stab?"

"Stab," Mother says.

Girl cries.

"Just stab," Dog says. "You get steak."

Dog's leash yanks.

"Bite," Handler says.

"Bite," Dog asks. "Nothing to bite. No dogs to bite."

"Bite," Handler says.

"Stab," Mother says and slaps Girl.

Dog angry. "Don't hit Girl. Stop that! Stop that!"

"Bite," Handler says.

"But nothing to bite," Dog says.

"Stab," Mother says. And she helps Girl lift the shiny stick over Dog and pokes down on him.

"Ow," dog says. "That hurts."

He nips at Girl.

"I'm sorry," He says immediately.

"Stab," Mother says.

Girl stabs!

Part One:

First Cometh the
The Son

Chapter One

We marched through the streets with righteous liquor on our breaths and cleansed God with our torches of amendments, soaked in the tears of babies. We sought to incinerate any hope He might have possibly created—or not, we didn't care. God loved everyone, and we bore no responsibility to love Him back. Ours was a life of laughing off such silly notions.

Offense came easy. It was our right. Silencing was our power. Affirmation was our habit. Fault could never be ours. We sat in our bubbles of pomp and fiction and accused them of being common sense. We cried "hallelujah" to people who stirred hate, and crucified higher beings of love over and over and over again.

We pardoned McCarthy. His was the only way to uncover the true poison in our society. The republicans organized the department to flush it out. The democrats extended their committee power to that same department. The republican'ts armed the department. The demoncrats flooded the universities to rally son against mother; daughter against father; students against common sense. They grew, graduated, passed on their lunacy to smaller minds, who, in turn, passed on that anti-critical discovery to the next generation, which finally accepted the belief that political party affiliations were synonymous with scholarship and executive power.

Meanwhile, we discovered the poisons to our society and put bullets in their heads and then ours, and we actually believed we were happier for it. Those who really were happy had no chance because there was nowhere for them to run, nor to hide, when they finally came to the realization that they were not fully content.

They had all run out of places to flee.

For years, mankind had turned its eyes to the stars, to Mars, to billionaires and their wealthy, but poorer, potential consumers. People who would use riches to truly set themselves above the world. Others imagined it as a means to escape, to rediscover freedom, to expand.

If there's anything that the Mayflower and Speedwell taught anyone, it's that the oppressed must flee. The poor fled war. The undesirable ran from economies. The deficient escaped bullies— until the world became a consortium of nations and peoples that all said, "That's enough out of you!"

Everyone built rockets. Rockets needed fuel, and fuel was expensive, so no one went anywhere. The oppressed's only haven was in hiding.

Ernest, for instance, was five-and-a-week years on the Saturday before President's Day. He was playing in his front yard when men and women in black uniforms spilled out of the back of a truck that could have easily passed for an ice cream wagon if it had only been the product of love—real love, not the hate he'd been taught was transcendental of those ideas shared by hillbillies from east to west.

With armed automatic weapons, the soldiers scattered around the house and took root—one broke the gate off the hinges, and two others used their thick, rubber soles to drive the front door into the throat of the two-story house. They dragged Miranda Nelsen out onto the lawn by her wrists, no cuffs. Her husband, Chester, normally a pleasant man, followed screaming, crying for his lawyer. A prosecutor, in his white collar, held high his hands and swore himself under oath on Chester's behalf. He ordered Miranda's husband to sign the paper that waived his rights to an attorney.

Chester struggled back two children, twins and Ernest's classmates, while he argued with the prosecutor. The prosecutor drew his sidearm upon Chester until the husband and father agreed to waive his rights to a lawyer.

When Miranda broke loose and ran back to her husband, one of the soldiers yanked back on her shoulder, dropped her to the ground and drove the muzzle of his weapon into her face. She sat up and smeared the blood of her lips and cheek onto her hands.

The soldier ordered her back to the ground, then commanded her to shut up, and, when she couldn't hear him over her own screaming at the sight of her own blood, he fired upon her.

Ernest remembered the back of her head erupting like the can of his mother's clogged hairspray.

Ernest had been playing on his front lawn alone. People he might have called his friends sought out other places to entertain themselves as usual. He was building a form of castle out of buckets, blankets and yard tools and had barely tapped down a tent peg through a corner of his own blanket when the entire event started.

Ron, Ernest's father, was the first of the neighbors to rush the Nelson's house, identifying himself as a law-enforcement officer. He yelled, demanded a supervisor and even threatened to arrest the crew of unmarked thugs, who he claimed were trespassing in jurisdiction.

He grew silent, then returned home shortly.

"Is Miranda dead," Ernest's mother, Thalia, asked.

"She was a shell," Ron said.

"No," Thalia said in surprise. "What did she have?"

"Compulsive Disorder," Ron replied.

"I had no idea," Thalia announced in shock.

Ron returned into the house, and Thalia asked what Ernest wanted for dinner. He replied with "nothing" and stayed to watch the soldiers leave Miranda Nelsen on the ground while they now forced Chester and his children back into their broken home.

Soon after, Ernie's family sat before dinner trays. Big Bird posed in a "hi kids" wave across Ernest's. Ron prepared to watch the news; the chime of NBC approved media rang out. Thalia focused on her own tofu.

"I can't believe Miranda would do that to her own friends," Thalia said about halfway through her meal.

"She's gone now," Ron replied. "No need to worry."

Thalia snorted contempt. "Is that what you'd say if they shot one of us."

"Yes dear," Ron said. "Wait. What?"

"Well," Thalia blurted. "You never know when or if something's going to appear with someone."

"Oh, God! This is about your mother again, isn't it?"

"I don't know," Thalia replied. "Is it?"

"I'm not having that discussion again," Ron complained. "The last thing we needed around here was a murder-prone psycho."

Thalia locked eyes onto Ernest, and he made the mistake of looking at her when she did. "Remember that, Ernie," She said. "Be grateful we have your dad to lock us away if we ever develop a mental disorder."

"Be grateful for the wall," Ron corrected with his bemused tone. "It's that wall that keeps those drains and mentally-disturbed degenerates safe and away from us."

"How do they get them," Ernest asked.

"Get what," Ron asked before shoving a small floret of broccoli into his mouth.

"The bad brains," Ernie answered.

"Because they let the pharmaceutical companies torture their brains with bad medicine," Ron said.

"I don't' believe that," Thalia replied.

"That's the problem," Ron said. "You don't know. I do."

"Could I get a bad brain," Ernest asked.

He was then sent to his room without finishing dinner.

Ernest's room was typical for an eight-year-old boy. He had his poster of The Vendor from *Carni-land*. It was signed by Tres Special, the actor who voiced him in the game. Vendor dangled from a wire and, with his ice cream cone of justice, snuck upon an unsuspecting shadow.

Mostly, his bedroom walls were bare otherwise. His small desk held his homework. His drawers held a few clothes. None of his ownership was exciting. His floor was clean, his daybed made. He enjoyed cleaning—well, when he could actually finish the job that is. It gave him something to do when his battery was charging or the household's monthly FCC streaming allotment had been spent.

His brick flashlight sat on his chest as he stared past his twisting fingers above his face and towards the smooth, blank ceiling he wasn't allowed to paint. He hated this shade of white. It wasn't even white, it had a tinge of butter to it. If something was going to be white, it should at least be white. That's why Ernest hated this house. Everything was white in this house—not white, butter-white. Still, it didn't stop him from casting shadow puppets upon the ceiling when it was dark enough to do so.

Ernest was in the transition of creating what he was sure was a horse head when he realized the image moved on its own. He dropped his hands to his stomach and watched the shadowy figure of the horse continue to race across the ceiling before him.

Chapter Two

When Monday came, so did school. That, in itself, might seem casual, but it was shopping day. Thalia picked Ernest up in the front, pick-up zone as she typically did. She called out a "hello" to Mr. Cartwright, and he waved her out of the parking lot.

Once on the road, she announced that their food credits were ready, and then drove to the market.

They hadn't spoken about the events of Saturday since dinner.

New California Grocery was stocked on Saturday nights. Thalia had tried many times to move their shopping appointment to sooner in the week. She had yet to draw the lottery, which meant it was still difficult to predict which groceries would be left over after the Sunday rush.

Luckily, they had nuts, which is what Thalia had wanted the most. Any kind of nut was high commodity at New California Grocery. Often, the family settled for bulk peanuts, but Thalia appreciated when she could stock up on almonds and hazelnuts to make spread; pecans for salad; almonds and pistachios for snacking and school lunch; walnuts for bitter flavoring. Whatever was left over, she mixed with pumpkin and sunflower seeds for daily vitamin cocktail.

Ron liked Brazilian nuts for munchies, but they were rare, and expensive. Often, a pound of these were worth nine pounds in any other nut. Thalia pretended many times not to see the Brazilians despite their gargantuan promotional displays in golden, foil barrels. When store employees asked if she needed any Brazilians, she pretended not to hear them. Brazilian nuts went home with Thalia only when she had no other choice, or when she wanted to put Ron in a good mood. Ron thought they came home because Thalia was a good shopper—which she was, better than he realized.

According to Thalia's grocery list, their guide, a forty-ish man garbed in the blue smock of the Shopper's Escort Union, filled a bag with a pound of macadamias and weighed it. He read the weight to Thalia, and she approved. The scale then wheezed out a barcode. The escort attached the code to the clear, plastic bag and tied off the opening with a knot. Then he dropped the bag into the cart.

"Nuts," a small speaker, built into the handle of the shopping cart, announced with a soft and friendly feminine voice. "Macadamia. One-point-one-three pounds."

The guide gathered several more assorted bags of nuts in this manner and awaited Thalia's approval before scanning and dropping each of them into the cart. He reviewed the list that she had provided him.

"Follow me," he ordered cordially and smiling.

As he led away from the produce section, Ernest followed his mother with his hands tucked in his pockets. Thalia directed the escort to the brand of strawberry jam that she wanted. The employee didn't see it at first. He kept reaching for the larger bottle, but Thalia had to keep correcting him.

"I don't believe we have any in this week," he said as he perused the first section of shelving down from the top one last time.

"It's this one." Ernest had found the correct jar two shelves lower. He was confused as to how the escort could not find such a simple object. He dropped the jar into the basket but might not have if he had bothered to look upon the rejection that filled his mother's face.

"Jam, raspberry," the shopping cart announced. "Canderbiggen Farms, twelve ounces."

"Please don't touch the merchandise," the escort said softly. He glared at Thalia instead of Ernest. Thalia shied away and took up Ernest's hand.

Ernest and his mother followed the rest of the shopping spree in silence, Thalia only nodding in approval or denial of the groceries she desired to purchase.

As they finally approached the checkout, Thalia drew her plastic envelope that held coupons, vouchers, store credits and the maximum allowable currency permitted into the store. The escort pressed the cart onto the scale.

A young woman sat at the computer and took Thalia's envelope. She spilled what was inside into a slot in the exchange counter. The counter shuffled and hummed a moment before spitting out the remaining contents that didn't apply to this visit.

Thalia held her hand to the side of the counter and waited for the strip of Smart Film around her wrist to light up with her receipt.

"Does everything look all right," the cashier asked.

Thalia removed the slim bracelet, straightening it, and scrolled through its contents. She nodded back to the cashier and snapped it back into a curl around her wrist.

The escort pressed the cart out of the checkout. Thalia and Ernest followed.

Approaching the doors, a man in a suit stepped out to meet Thalia's group. He was twenty-perhaps and grimacing. He looked over a clear tablet a moment before turning his attention to Thalia.

"Mrs. Aagard," he said.

Thalia nodded and was in the middle of vocalizing a positive answer when he continued on as would an auto-dialer recording.

"As I'm sure you're aware," He said, drawing his tablet behind his back with both arms and taking the stance of one Napoleon Bonaparte, who was too short to reach the power he thought he should have. "We pride ourselves on providing jobs to a great many people. Now, if you do their work for them, they have no reason to remain employed, and this is highly unacceptable and illegal."

"I'm aware of how society works," Thalia replied.

"Uh-huh," the man said, and he puffed his shoulders to announce he wasn't done strutting. "As manager of New California Grocery, I have to inform you that it is your responsibility to monitor your child's behavior. If you cannot do this, I'm afraid we'll have to audit your privilege to shop here as well as notify Family Services. You will receive no more warnings. Do you understand these rights as I have read them to you?"

Thalia stood in silence, rubbed her face with her hands and sighed.

"I need a confirmation," the manager requested. He once again held his tablet out before him.

"He wasn't doing anybody's job," Thalia finally said. "It was a jar of jam."

"It is a violation of union-state law."

"Perhaps if your employees were trained better, children wouldn't have to help them find what's on the shelves." Thalia replied. "Now, am I free to go, or am I being detained."

The manager squinted. He tapped the tablet a few times. "Does your child have a history of acting out."

"Depends on whose twisted definition you're asking about," Thalia almost laughed but didn't want to go too far. "I asked you if I'm free to go, or if I need to notify my husband who, unlike you, is an actual law-enforcement mediator."

"You're free to go ma'am," the manager said and drew out of her path.

"Damn fool managers," Thalia complained.

"Ma'am," the manager said. "You're still in the Trinity of States Union. Your offensive language will be reported to authorities."

"Does your offensive lack of intelligence allow you to spell any of those words," Thalia asked as she directed the escort towards the door, reminding him that the manager had already stated that she was free to leave.

Ron was mad about the incident. By the time Ernest and Thalia returned home, he had already been notified of the infraction and waited, slow-cooking, against the railing of the front porch.

"They didn't waste any time, did they," Thalia asked. She shuffled the weight of her recently-purchased loot so that she could get at the screen-door handle.

Ron glared an instant at Ernest and then pulled on the door that Thalia had already drawn from its frame. Ernest's mother pressed her way into the house.

Immediately, Ernest found himself directed to his room, where he listened to the familiar sound of tones that often tortured the rafters of his home.

"Do you understand how that makes me look," Ron cried.

"Yeah, like a father who raised a son intelligent enough to do a monkey's job."

"Don't use that word."

"Oh for—," Thalia mumbled, then screeched. "Monkey! Monkey! Monkey! Pull your head out and use some common sense."

"Don't use that tone with me," Ron's voice grew. "I'm a member of the law when I'm in this uniform."

"And I'm your wife, and that's your son whether you're in that uniform or not," Thalia replied. The sound of her hand slapping the kitchen table echoed up the stairs.

"You better check that violent behavior," Ron said.

"You don't even hear how ridiculous that sounds, do you?"

"You find my response to violent behavior ridiculous?"

"Oh, I'm so sorry, Mr. Table! Please don't turn me in to the department of Table Protective Services. They might take away our tea cozies." She drummed several more slaps out.

"Don't act like this isn't serious," Ron yelled. "I have a responsibility here. I'm a cop!"

"You're an idiot. Go back to work and come back when you're a human being."

Ron said something after that, but Ernest wasn't exactly sure what; some kids screamed in excitement down the street. The next sounds he heard were his father's footsteps and the front door of the house slamming.

"You better check that violent behavior," Thalia screamed after him. "We don't want someone to confuse our door jamb with a human being and confiscate it before you get home."

The typical sounds of Thalia storing groceries to cupboards didn't come. Her footsteps did, up the stairs. She soon stood in Ernest's doorway, her athletic figure hardly filling the frame at all.

"Come on," she urged, digging her keys back out of her handbag.

"Where are we going?"

"I need to see someone."

Someone had a boring office, and his name was Sigmund Sundry of Harris, Browne and Sundry. His office was quiet with one desk, backed by one office worker and surrounded by fake plants and four chairs where a slender, ghostly receptionist instructed Thalia and Ernest to wait. After some time, one of three office doors opened, and an hour-glass-shaped man, younger than Thalia, appeared. He looked entirely too serious and frightening. Ernest and his mother clenched each other's hands tighter.

When his light eyes locked onto Ernest and then floated to his mother, Thalia could practically hear them roll back into his head. Sundry exhaled and shared some words with the young woman behind the desk.

At one point, Sundry's head snapped back towards Thalia, then to Ernest. Now he walked to greet them.

"Mrs. Aagard." He held his hand out, and Thalia shook it.

"I'm sorry I didn't set an appointment," Thalia said. "I got your card from—

"The consultation is free," Sundry said. "I advise you to not say any more until we can step inside and establish emergency confidentiality."

Thalia fell silent. Sundry shared a nod with her. Ernest's mother stood, told Ernest to stand and began to follow Sundry past the reception desk and through the open door.

They entered a new room, this one large, filled with people, desks and offices made of glass, where more people and desks all appeared to be inhabited by need-to-impress junior associates.

"Before we go any farther, the Mince Act requires me to inform you that unless you pay retainer, my offices will not be allowed exceptional silence," He said. "This means if you have done anything that could be deemed illegal, we are mandated to reveal any confession you are about to make. Do you understand what I have just told you?"

Thalia nodded then stated the affirmative.

"Retainer is ninety-five-thousand bitcredits, are you able to pay," he asked.

Thalia didn't answer, shifted uncomfortably before saying, "Um."

"Mrs. Aagard?"

"I'm afraid I couldn't without alerting my husband who is law enforcement," she finally replied.

"Are you saying that you cannot pay retainer due to privilege of danger?"

"Not domestically, no," Thalia said. "He would never do that, but he would be bound by profession."

"I see," Sundry said. He looked at Ernest a moment. Ernest smiled as best as he could. Sundry did not. His gaze snapped back to Thalia. "Tell me, is this defense for you, Mrs. Aagard?"

"It involves my son, Ernest."

"Has a report been involved?"

Thalia nodded.

"Robin," Sundry called over his left shoulder. A middle-aged woman arose from her desk, dropped a set of fake glasses from her face and approached. She grimaced more than Sundry had done.

"I'm authorizing a class A exception to retainer, please witness."

Robin nodded, retrieved a tablet from her desk. She gestured for Thalia and Ernest to follow Sundry towards a wide hallway. Sundry was already several paces started in that direction.

The hallway led to a conference room where Sundry held a door open to a round table designed to expand and accommodate up to an additional two dozen people.

"Have a seat, please," Sundry welcomed.

Thalia took the first leather chair and instructed Ernest to take the next.

The door closed. Sundry shuffled around to the opposite side of the table, while Robin planted to Sundry's right. She set her tablet between Sundry and Thalia then began recording the conversation.

"Sigmund Sundry, authorizing exception to retainer," Sundry said slowly, clearly. "Witnessing is Robin Brimhall. This is allotment three of twelve as permitted by the Retainer Act. Exception is on behalf of Ernest Aagard, present is his mother," his voice trailed.

"Oh," Thalia realized. "Thalia."

"Thalia Aagard," Sundry picked up his dictation once again. "Hereby, this record is considered a matter of emergency confidentiality."

The attorney continued to introduce the session, carefully and thoroughly. Robin reminded him to state his Juris Identification Number. Finally, he stopped speaking, called for water for Thalia, apple juice for Ernest and cannabis tea for both himself and Robin. Sundry then leaned back in his chair and asked Thalia to explain the events that had brought her into his office that day.

Thalia related all that had transpired previously from the supermarket. Sundry's face revealed very little reaction, except to glance to Ernest every so often. When Thalia finished, Sundry remained in his silence.

"Power-hungry manager or not," Sundry finally spoke. "Even an idiot can make a mess of a pimple."

"Do we have anything to worry about," Thalia asked.

Sundry sipped on his tea.

"Ernest, if you go outside that door there and turn right, at the end of the hall is my intern, William. Why don't you go ask him to show you our shark tank while I speak with your mother a moment." Sundry actually smiled as he said this, almost looked friendly.

Ernest looked to his mother skeptically.

"It's okay," Thalia said.

"We'll come get you when we're done," Sundry added.

Robin helped Ernest through the door and finished pointing him down the hallway towards, William who quickly stood from his desk to answer Robin's gesture to aid Ernest.

"The unions take this business seriously," Sundry said.

"Yes," Thalia replied.

"But you didn't come here to fight a misdemeanor against unions, did you?"

Thalia shook her head.

"Typically, his school will be notified within twenty-four hours. In another twenty-four, he'll undergo a mandatory evaluation by the district psychologist."

"That soon?"

"Mrs. Aagard, what are you afraid they're going to see in your son?"

"I couldn't say for certain."

"Mrs. Aagard," Sundry leaned forward, his elbows kneeling against the table for the first time. "I can't be on your side if you won't let me."

Thalia slumped, defeated, tried to speak, but couldn't bring herself to do so.

"I assume he's never been diagnosed."

"No."

"But you suspect he would be?"

Again, a nod.

"Who did you know who was? Family?"

"My mother."

"What was her tag?"

"Bi-polar," Thalia said, looking into her palms for escape. "She's in a grove facility."

"Anyone else?"

"Gertrude, my sister."

"Where is she now?"

"She took her life before they could enforce facility on her."

"I'm sorry. And you?"

"I get nervous."

"Everyone gets nervous."

"It affects me."

"Anxiety, then?"

She nodded.

"Would it be so bad if Ernest was committed to a safe facility?"

"Because he touched jam?"

"No," Sundry said. "Because of what they'll learn if they speak to your boy."

"Which is why I need your help."

"So, you've kept it hidden all your life," Sundry asked, changing tactic and direction.

"My mother taught me."

"And you've taught Ernest?"

"What I could, but he's not so aware. It's always been a matter of time."

"Is his anxiety?"

"I don't think so."

"Depression, then."

Thalia shook her head.

Sundry wasn't able to ask his next question before Thalia answered.

"He watches things."

Sundry waited for elaboration. None came.

"Such as," Sundry asked.

"Things that aren't there," Thalia replied.

"He told you this?"

"No," Thalia said. "I've seen him. He watches. His eyes scan, you know like when you watch something move. When something's not there to focus on, your eyes jitter, but his are smooth. I've seen it."

"Does he talk to these things?"

"I don't think so—I've never heard him, at least. But it's only a matter of time before someone else notices."

"Imaginary friends aren't uncommon."

"He's five. The school psychologist won't see it that way."

"We'll put an injunction on the school psychologist," Sundry explained. "If they so much as look at your son without your consent, we'll issue misconduct." He drank once more of his tea.

"There is one question, I need to ask though," Sundry said. "Are you undiagnosed as well, Mrs. Aagard?"

Thalia couldn't bring herself to answer.

Sundry nodded as if he knew the response already.

"Why not lease residence in a safe facility, for you both," he asked.

"My mother hasn't been my mother since she took lease in a safe facility," Thalia explained softly. "I don't want to lose myself too."

"Even if we could arrange for you and Ernest to lease the same safe facility?"

"I don't want Ernest to lose me either."

"So, you intend to shell your mental tags," Sundry asked. "You do understand what could happen if you get discovered."

"I do," Thalia said, remembering the gun shot from two days prior. "That's why I'm here."

Sundry leaned back once more. He examined his client for some time before standing. "When the school or anyone approaches your son, most likely in two days, as is common procedure, instruct him to say these words exactly: 'I have Title Thirty representation and injunction.' Say it."

"I have Title Thirty representation and injunction," Thalia said.

"No matter how much they ask him anything, he says, 'I have Title Thirty representation and injunction.' This will ensure our presence is required before they can interview him, and we will proceed to seal the report and event."

"You're positive about that," Thalia asked.

"It was a jar of jam," Sundry replied as if insulted. "I believe I've dropped a jar of jam in the cart myself. Nobody in their right minds are going to make a federal case of that once Title Thirty representation gets involved."

With that, Sundry signaled Robin to have Ernest returned to the room.

Chapter Three

Thalia dropped Ernest off as usual on Tuesday morning. Before getting out of the car, Ernest recited the statement Thalia had caused him to commit to memory. He grabbed up his lunchbox and schoolbag, was soon out the passenger seat and running off towards the front doors of the beige and brown elementary.

Mr. Cartwright waved to Thalia, freeing her for the day. She drove home; realized she didn't want to go there; then drove around aimlessly, doing nothing but wasting energy.

Around 10 a.m., she found herself parked in an all too familiar and neglected lot. She turned the nine keys on their ring over in her fingers, waiting the will to step out of her electric four-door Michigan Liberty. She stopped waiting and soon stood in the parking lot, ensuring her Liberty was locked.

The keys continued to twist to her command as she moseyed her way towards the bronze, facility façade with its four sets of heavy metal doors. The smell of orange grove was sweet and full of spite. The building eventually grew so large before her that she could no longer see the eight hundred acres of orange trees beyond.

The doors opened as Thalia approached.

"Welcome to the Orange Grove Resource Center," An elderly woman greeted from behind distant and unpaid eyes. "May I direct you?"

"I'm here to see my mother," Thalia replied.

"Of course," the woman said, turning, gesturing towards a podium with another elderly woman, this one plumper, more jovial but still distant.

"Please sign in," the plump docent instructed.

Thalia scrawled her name across the white screen of the podium bench. It flashed red.

"It appears she's in the orchard," the docent informed. "You are family?"

"Yes," Thalia replied.

"You are welcome to make your way to her residence. If you have your code, you are welcome to enter."

Thalia exchanged a cordial nod and made her walk to the elevator that would take her to the eighth floor. Here, she journeyed down a hall with carpet of ruby pink and walls of dismal not-white with copper etched wallpaper that was meant to disguise the true nature of the facility. Cherry doors coronated with bright, brass latches stood at attention every 25 feet along each side.

This hall eventually turned left, carried on for far longer than any should have and met at a four-way junction with a yellow chandelier. Thalia stopped a moment and pondered if she had walked far enough. She turned right, went straight through the next junction, then turned left once more into a corridor that curved now with a carpet of a little more wear and grayer tinge. The copper was fading, the wallpaper peeling. Brown portals through the walls replaced the cheery cherry

She finally approached a security door leading into Citrus Wing. A rusty, folding chair propped it open. Thalia crossed from carpet into yellow tile, green floor runners and eggshell walls with bulbous bug-filled light covers. Gray, steel doors with gunmetal latches huddled much more closely together now every six to eight feet.

Room 464CW appeared no differently from any of the other doors now. Thalia slid a small panel beneath the doorknob, revealing buttons. She pressed the code; waited for the door to hum; then let herself into the studio apartment where a mirror, instead of a window, loomed over a kitchen sink.

She dug her folding chair out from behind the 55-gallonless fish tank with projections of humpback whales swimming around its plastic walls. Then she set the metal seat before the polyester recliner that faced the fish tank. Before sitting, Thalia opened the side of the aquarium illusion and drew a serving-sized bottle of cold rice milk from the interior refrigerator. One of the whales sang to her as she closed the fake tank once again.

She drank her milk slowly; it grew warm as it emptied. The Biofoam bottle crumpled in her hand—and she toyed with it for several minutes, feeling the variety of sharp creases that now lined its skin. Several minutes later, the broken bottle found its way into the shredder beneath the sink. Thalia made certain to flush the pieces out of the system with plenty of water.

The door clicked behind her, hummed, then opened.

"You know we have to make up the hours we miss, right," Thalia's mother said, entering the room. She stuffed a pair of leather gloves into a pocket of a red apron around her waist. Then, she untied the apron; drew the top strap over her fading brown hair; and hung it on a hook on the door of a closet beside the front entry. "Try to announce."

"Mom," Thalia said as she fell back into the sink. Her mother had disappeared behind the back of the recliner.

"It's been six months," her mother said. "So? Talk."

Thalia suddenly didn't know how to respond.

"Know what I did yesterday," her mother asked, then, without waiting for an answer, "Oranges. Know what I did the day before that? Oranges. Every day, I do oranges. Oranges in the morning, oranges in the afternoon. I don't even have to eat them anymore to get that wonderful sensation of diarrhea. I just look at them and my stomach starts reciting the Revised National Anthem!"

Thalia sighed inside.

"Imodium doesn't even bother anymore," her mother continued. "I've just learned to hold it. My bowels got nothing on my butt muscle memory. I'm clenching now, clenching and sitting! Now that's control! And here you are now to reward me with silence for such a grand feat."

Thalia found her way back to her folding chair and dropped into it.

"You know, you're lucky I'm here at all," her mother continued. "I'm about ready to use that knife and pfft-pfft, but it took me ten years to earn the responsibility to use one. You never know, though; make me wait six more months and I might reconsi—

Her mother's face suddenly twisted into an expression so livid that her wrinkles frowned a hundred times over. "What did he do," she asked, gripping the arms of her chair and resting deeper into the seat. "Leave him. I told you before, leave him."

"It's Ernie," Thalia said.

"What," her mother asked, face and wrinkles softening.

"They're going to inquiry him tomorrow," Thalia said.

"What happened," her mother asked, suddenly leaning forward.

Thalia slumped. "Doesn't matter," she said. "If they don't take him now, it'll happen later."

"It was something stupid wasn't it," her mother asked. "It's always something stupid that gives it away, like picking your nose or farting as though we were actually some sort of biological lifeform."

"Jam," Thalia said.

"Jam? Are you sure?"

Thalia tossed her a look of ridicule.

"Any story that starts with 'jam' has got to be dumb. I'll bet it was orange jam wasn't it? That damned Mince, wish I'd never voted for him."

"Mom," Thalia cried. "Our attorney says it'll be forty-eight hours. He could be gone tomorrow."

"Then you need to grab what you need and move today."

"And leave you here alone?"

"I'll be fine."

"You were just complaining that I hadn't been here in six months."

"I survived. I'll survive again."

"We're not moving away and just leaving you here," Thalia said.

"Six months isn't leaving me?"

"Besides, Ron would find us."

"In that case," her mother stood quickly. "Let's make the most of today, just in case."

"They're not going to grant you leave, mom."

Her mother waved off Thalia's comment and pulled open the closet door. She pressed inside, parting her hanging clothes to create a gap that she could reach through. After a few moments of rumbling through trite fabric and tolerated cardboard, she stepped away.

Thalia found the box set into her hands while her mother returned to the recliner and then waved her palms out for its return. Upon receiving it, her mother folded back the box lid and began rifling through.

"Before Gertie," Thalia's mother started and then fell silent. "Before Gertie was gone, I purchased some tickets to the hall of mirrors."

Gone? Is that what they called Gertrude's death? Thalia sighed and bit back her response.

"Is the Glass Maze still standing?"

"I think so," Thalia replied after mulling over the thought a moment. "I'm not sure. I haven't really paid attention."

"There we go," her mother said, lifting out two red cards. "We were supposed to go to this, remember?"

"I remember," Thalia replied softly.

"You didn't show. Do you remember why?"

"You don't need your box of reasons I let you down to tell me you resent me, Mom."

"Gertie wouldn't stop complaining that you hadn't shown up," her mother said. "I let her go on ahead. Then you called. You'd learned you were pregnant."

"And we never saw Gertie again," Thalia said. "Hall of glass and a depressed person and all."

This time Thalia's mother seemed quiet on the response.

"Anyway," she croaked and held the red cards out to Thalia. "Maybe these are still good. You might have to ask. Good for one free admission to the Glass Maze and free ice cream at Titan's. If the places are still there."

"Those things are old, Mom," Thalia said. "I doubt they're still good."

"Don't be so sure. There's no expiration date." Her mother closed up the box and set it beside her chair. "It's worth a try if it'll give you one last night with Ernie. Look. If they won't take it, then at least you can go get some ice cream on your own. Titan's is still there isn't it?"

"Yeah, I think so."

"Sorry there's not one for Tom," her mother said. "He'll just have to pay his own way."

"Tom doesn't like that sort of thing."

"I know. Shocker."

"Look, those tickets cost me a lot of money that we didn't have back in the day. Use them."

Thalia shook her head.

"Today," her mother encouraged. "Might be Ernie's last chance at fun."

"If they're still good," Thalia said.

"Promise?"

Thalia's phone rang before she could answer the question. She drew it from her handbag.

Too soon, she thought. "It's the school," she said. "Hello?"

Thalia's mother sat alert in her seat.

"Yes," Thalia said, then, "It's been less than twenty-four hours. Uh-huh. You can't do that, he has Title Thirty representation and injunction. You can't do that!"

"They already questioned him, didn't they," Thalia's mother said.

Thalia ignored her and instead scolded into the phone, "You don't have that authority." Her voice had escalated.

"Have they exercised observation yet," Thalia's mother asked.

Thalia waved her off.

"He has Title Thirty representation and injunction," Thalia continued into the phone. "You don't have the authority to supersede that. What do you mean, you've overruled it? Listen, my husband's a law-enforcement officer, and we have Title Thirty representation. I'm having someone's job."

"Have they exercised observation yet?"

"Mother stop," Thalia snipped, placing two fingers over the microphone.

"If they exercise observation, they'll remove him from the school, and it could be weeks before the courts rule to reveal his location. Stop them now. Ask, if they've exercised observation."

"Mother!"

"Have you exercised observa—

"Have you exercised observation, yet," Thalia asked in defeat, then covered the phone again. "Not yet, he's still in school custody, but the judiciaries are en route."

"He'll be gone before you get there," Thalia's mother said.

"Look," Thalia screamed into the phone.

"Claim Family Medical Leave Section Eighty."

"What?"

"Claim Family Medical Leave Section Eighty."

"What good is that, they ignored our representation?"

"Say it!"

"I don't know what that is."

Thalia's mother jerked the phone away from her daughter's fingers. "You listen here, we claim Family Medical Leave Section Eighty, and if you don't know what that is, you better call your lawyers or kiss something you appreciate goodbye. Now, you call and tell the judiciaries that we've claimed Family Medical Leave Section Eighty."

Thalia's mother ended the call.

"What did you do," Thalia asked.

"Bought you some time," her mother instructed. "Go get Ernie. If you have an attorney, better call him now."

"What did I just claim?"

"They can't exercise observation during time of bereavement, now go!"

"What bereavement?"

"Don't give them time to figure that out. Go, already!"

Thalia rushed. Gathering her bag, she dropped in her phone and managed to get in an "I love you, Mom" before she raced out the door.

Thalia's mother took her apron off the closet door, returned the strap over her neck. She tied it around her waist, then took up the box beside her chair, rummaged through its contents of past memories and returned it to her closet.

An intercom beeped.

"Yes," she spoke gently into the small box while holding down a button.

"Your guest has departed the building, please return to daily activities to complete your quota," a friendly female voice instructed.

"I was just cleaning up," she replied. "I'm on my way now."

She left her apartment; shuffled her way through the halls to the residents' elevator; then continued to the back lot of orange trees. She signed in with her supervisor, then took in a deep breath.

"It's so easy to forget how lovely oranges smell, isn't it," she said.

Her supervisor nodded in patronizing form.

The mother returned to her tree and climbed her ladder to reach the bough she'd been working on prior to her interruption. With a pair of clippers from one of her apron pockets, she snipped a bright, evenly-colored orange from the branch. It was, perhaps, the most beautiful orange she had ever seen. The sweet fragrance she held seemed to emanate more than the entire orchard. After returning the clippers to their appropriate, apron pocket, she then reached into her other, past her gloves, to the knife that only the most reliable and proven of residents were entrusted with. The knife flipped open easily in her hand, and she cut the orange in half. She bit into it and grimaced.

"Do you have any idea what these things taste like," she yelled down to her supervisor. Then, she dropped both halves of her fruit; held the tip of her knife to the top of her head and tucked her body forward. She toppled herself headfirst off her ladder. By the time the first supervisor reached her side, the blade had already punctured her brain.

Chapter Four

Hubbard Elementary administration knew they already had control of the outcome. The school psychologist sealed all of his evidence away in his tan Filson Original messenger bag. He ensured Thalia that he had every right to maintain property of the documents, recordings and other notations he had gathered.

Naturally, the principal, in all good conscience, could not endanger the other children. Ernest was suspended, pending a hearing that was already in favor of the school.

Sundry had instructed Thalia to ask for any and every legal detail she could to buy him time to gather his own team and join her in the school's front office—that is, if he hadn't arrived before she.

He hadn't.

She questioned everything from who authorized the illegal interrogation to the background of the staff member who had decided to confront Ernest about his previous day's events. She asked how recent his credentials were.

She could have wasted more time, but, when Ron showed up, he was entirely too cordial about the situation. He had tried to direct her out of the office, but she screamed at him.

"You're embarrassing me," Ron scowled.

"Poor you," Thalia replied. "How about you think about your son for once."

It was when he gripped her arm and wheeled around to escort her away, that Sundry finally entered and ordered the officer to unhand his client.

"You sought out counsel," Ron asked incredulously.

"Well, welcome to the conversation," Thalia remarked.

Ron snatched his arm away from his wife. He turned to say something cordial to Sundry, only to get brushed aside.

"Did or did my client not identify that he had Title Thirty representation and injunction," Sundry asked dropping a heavy black briefcase atop the pale blue countertop separating visitors from administrative staff. Three other suits filed into the office behind him. Robin took up the rear. With a tablet in her hand, she typed feverishly at the screen.

"Your name," Robin asked, pointing to the district, assistant superintendent.

"And you are," the assistant superintendent asked.

"She's the court reporter and liaison to the Seventh District Legal Ambassador, who just asked you a question under penalty of we're-not-in-the-mood," Sundry explained. "Now, answer the question, or I'll be forced to relieve you of credential."

The assistant superintendent answered the question as did the rest of his party when Robin queried them in similar fashion. The school representatives consisted of the assistant superintendent, the principal, two assistant principals, the school psychologist, an attorney and two secretarial staff.

Once the legal introductions were in order, Sundry turned his attention to his briefcase. The latches released angrily.

"Where is Ernest Aagard," Sundry asked.

The principal moved herself to a door leading to a hovel that acted as a sick room, and holding cell. She opened it to reveal Ernest, who stood confused and already waiting for someone to let him out.

"Let the record show that the administrative staff has unlawfully imprisoned the five-year-old child recognized as Ernest Aagard, who has Title Thirty representation and injunction," Sundry announced calmly and monotonously as a means to protect the integrity of every word.

Sundry removed a folder from the top of a stack of papers inside his briefcase, opened it and began to peruse one of the pages.

"Now," he said without looking up from his folder. "Which one of you geniuses violated my client's Title Thirty representation and injunction?"

"I think this has been enough discussion on the issue," Ron said. He pressed his way towards Ernest and began to lead him away from the nurse's office.

"I don't believe the court recognizes the officer as a bailiff. Stop attempting to remove my client from a counter-action," Sundry continued in his calm demeanor. "The officer will remove his hands from my client, or he will be relieved of duty and detained."

A chorus of steel-clicks burst, and Sundry's three attorneys now stood with expandable batons raised in line with their chests and shoulders as they poised to strike Ron with simple snaps of their elbows.

Ron withdrew his hands. Thalia called Ernest to her side. Ron glared. Thalia didn't care.

"I repeat," Sundry resumed his interrogation. "Who's the genius who violated Title Thirty?"

"I overruled the Title Thirty protections, based upon educational exemption," a round, short man replied. Thalia could practically hear his head puff with arrogance.

"And you are?"

"School district attorney."

Sundry nodded as if he had already known this. "And your court order for an unsupervised psyche evaluation?"

"Not necessary under overrule," the round attorney replied.

"Not according to Magistrate Phillips," Sundry replied. He held a yellow envelope out to the attorney. "You're hereby summoned to appear before the Seventh District Court before tomorrow morning on charges of unauthorized overrule."

"Absurd," the attorney replied, looking up from his subpoena.

"Overrule can only be applied when the minor's parents are present," Sundry replied. "When the child's parents are not present, overrule requires a court order signed by a presiding magistrate. You don't have the authority to overrule. You clearly should not be an attorney for a school."

Sundry pointed at the school psychologist's briefcase.

"You will turn over your bag, all recordings, notes and other documentation from your interview with the unsupervised minor," Sundry held up a sheet of paper with careful type. "And you can report to the Seventh District Court by tomorrow morning for ethics violation."

Before the school psychologist could respond, one of Sundry's associates tore the doctor's leather satchel away from his clenched fingers and slapped a yellow envelope against his chest.

"Why are you doing this, counselor," the school's round attorney asked. "You know perfectly well, you'll be handing that evidence back in seventy-two hours."

"Perhaps," Sundry said. "But only if either of you are deemed certifiable after today's shenanigans, and after we've had our look at the records ourselves, which brings us to—"

Sundry snapped up another yellow envelope from his briefcase. "Which one of you failed to discontinue all legal action after you were notified of Family Medical Leave Section Eighty?"

The school's attorney found a small chair and fell into it. "Please tell me that's not true," he said.

"Who," Sundry asked.

"We had overrule," the principal said.

"Maybe you too will study law in your next line of work," Sundry said, withdrawing a pink sheet of paper from the envelope and snapping it open before the principal.

The principal took the paper and began reading.

"Evidence of Family Medical Leave Section Eighty," the school's attorney asked, defeated.

Sundry fumbled with the last sheet of paper in his folder.

"I have it here, but I have not informed my client of the details yet," Sundry replied.

"She's the one who claimed it, how could she not know them?"

"Irrelevant," Sundry replied. "Proof is here, which I shall disclose once my client is released so that I may inform her hereafter. I'll inform you first as a sign of good faith that you will observe the appropriate window for my client's bereavement."

Sundry motioned to his team of attorneys, and one moved quickly to Thalia and Ernest's side to usher them out of the room. Ron trailed closely at their heels silently. Thalia could see he wanted to rave, but Ron had no choice except to hold onto his badge a little too much.

Thalia drew Ernest close to her, she was too afraid to speak. Ernest tried and Thalia shushed him. Ron, began pacing several feet away.

After some time, another of Sundry's attorneys stepped out of the front office.

"You may return to your vehicle, Mrs. Aagard. Sundry will join you in a moment." he said. Then, catching glimpse of Ron's sudden interest, turned to the other attorney, "See that she isn't disturbed until then."

The associate that had been standing with them in the hallway agreed and began escorting the mother and son down the stairs and towards the front doors of the school.

Soon, mother and son sat in Thalia's Liberty. Ernest had found a seaweed snack left over from his lunch in his backpack.

"I told them what you said, Mom," Ernest said.

"I believe you," Thalia said.

Ernest looked over his shoulder at his dad sitting in his patrol car behind them. "He's going to be mad tonight, isn't he?"

*   *   *

Tears tried desperately to block her view as she drove now. She wiped them away. Ernest was quiet.

Sundry had bought her some time. When he met up with her at the car, he delivered the sad news about her mother, which he had learned, himself, upon calling the orange grove facility. He wasn't able to shake the feeling of what her mother may have been thinking since the moment Thalia had called him on her way to the school and informed him about her claim to Section Eighty. On a hunch, he called Orange Grove and learned of her mother's recent suicide. He broke the news as gently as possible without Ernest hearing.

It was about this time that Ron had intruded upon the conversation. Sundry was about to tell him to leave, when all Ron said was, "I want to talk to you at home when you're done here."

As Ron returned to his patrol car and drove away, Sundry took a state-like stance and made sure Ron knew he was watching him. When he returned his attention to Thalia, he held a small, black fob in his hand.

"This is a tracking device," Sundry explained. "Keep it on your person at all times."

He handed the small device to her.

"I'll have an escort watch your house tonight," he said. "Do you need someone to drive you home."

Thalia insisted that she was fine, but the tears that blinded her several miles later down the road said otherwise.

Ron wanted her home. She'd get there but, for now, wanted to drive. Her first impulse was to return to Orange Grove; recover her mother's body; and start on giving her the rest she deserved. After a few blocks into the city, she decided that she couldn't do any of that just yet. Her mother was right. It might be Ernest's last chance at having any fun.

She drove—nowhere really, anywhere but home. She passed the cinema, contemplating whether anything there would take her mind off the news of the suicide. They stopped a moment to pet a one-eared puppy at the animal shelter. The visit didn't last long, and she was back on the road.

Eventually, she realized there was no dodging it. She pointed the car back towards home.

"I'm hungry," Ernest said.

"Did you eat all your lunch," Thalia asked.

"Yeah."

"There might be a piece of candy in my purse." She left Ernest to rummage through her bag. Even candy would keep him entertained.

"Can we get ice cream," he asked.

That sounded like a decent idea, actually.

"I don't know if I have any vouchers for any," she said.

"What about these?"

Thalia wiped her eyes one more time to find Ernest holding the red tickets that her mother had given her.

"Oh, I don't think those are any good," Thalia said. "Grandma got those before you were born."

"Oh," Ernest replied. He stared at the tickets as one stares at report cards, hoping the grades will change before it gets home. He looked at the backs, found white space and then flipped their faces back to himself.

"One free banana split," they each read.

"Are banana splits good," Ernest asked, already knowing.

"Huh," Thalia asked.

"We never make banana splits."

"Maybe some day."

"Could we still try them?"

Thalia watched Ernest stroke the tickets now under his thumbs as though he'd found a new pet. "Okay. We can try, but if they don't accept them, you have to promise not to get upset."

"Okay," Ernest replied.

Thalia's bag chirped, startling both she and her son.

"The hell are you at," Ron's all-cap text screamed from the speaker, using the imprint of his voice that the device had recorded.

Thalia turned the phone off. She dropped it into the console between the front seats. Here, she ignored the follow-up chirp and "Home. Now!" She ignored the ring that followed. Figures, he'd have it turned back on. She muted the ringtone.

After inspecting one of the tickets, she pointed her vehicle into the direction of an ice cream parlor she had once known from years past.

It was a mid-twentieth century tribute to an all-but-forgotten diner that had stopped serving real soda and ice cream about twenty years ago. One table was presently filled, the rest empty. Thalia let Ernest choose where they would sit: two stools at a gray counter with purple stripes and polished chrome trimmings.

An older gentleman stepped up.

Thalia held up the tickets her mother gave her.

"I know this is a dumb question," Thalia asked. "I don't suppose these are still any good are they?"

The server reached to one of the tickets, confused. He inspected the paper between a thumb and pinky, the only digits remaining on his right hand. Thalia wondered what happened to the others.

"A little old, isn't it," he asked.

Thalia took the ticket back. "I'm sorry for wasting your time."

She reached for her purse.

"I didn't say it wasn't any good," the server said. "Just took your time getting here, didn't you?"

He set two glass bowls on the counter, drew an ice cream scoop and pried it deep into a round tub of white yogurt. One scoop fell into each bowl, followed by a frozen ball of chocolate, then a pink. The server held Ernest's creation under a fountain of hot fudge, then caramel. Ernest saw Mr. Porridge and Sally put on their bathing suits before they each dived from the top of the vanilla ball and splashed into the pooling puddle that gathered in the bottom of the bowl. The man crowned the rim of the bowl with whipped cream from a can, showered the cream with rainbow sprinkles and everything within that ring with chopped nuts. Thalia's bowl soon took on the same decoration. Next, the old server drew out a banana, peeled it, sliced it long ways, then cut these slivers in halves and stuck them into the concoction as though they should be ears. He dropped three strands of thin licorice and placed a cherry at their center.

"Look, Mom," Ernest said. "It's a lion."

The server paused, seemed offended and pushed the bowls of yogurt bunny heads towards the two customers.

"Might I recommend you eat those quickly," he said and pointed his pinky towards his plate-glass window that overlooked the street and a red-brick building, on the other side, with a black and white overhead picture of a labyrinth. "The glass maze closes in ten minutes."

"Can we," Ernest begged.

"Honey, this fine gentleman was kind to accept this," Thalia said. "I don't think they'll be so generous over there."

"Don't be so sure," the server said and left Thalia and Ernest to their desserts.

Four minutes passed and Ernest announced he was done even though he'd only eaten half of his bunny. Thalia was glad, she'd had her fill after one scoop.

They stood, Ernest pulling at her arm and nearly to the door out of the diner.

"That your car miss," the server asked pointing out to her Liberty. A patrol car had parked next to it, and a younger officer, most likely a rookie, peered inside and then looked about the area as if trying to discern which way he should start looking.

"You in some kind of trouble," the server asked.

Thalia couldn't help notice the looks from the customers at the table.

"Just my husband using his buddies to throw a temper tantrum," Thalia pulled at Ernest's hand. "Come on. Let's see if these tickets are still good."

"Stay close to each other in there," the server said. "All sorts of places to get lost in that maze."

Thalia and Ernest rushed onto the street. She was glad she'd left the phone in the car, otherwise the cop would have marched right into the ice cream parlor and made a scene. They were half-way across when the rookie officer spotted them.

"Excuse me, Ma'am," he said.

"Don't you ma'am me," Thalia replied. "You tell my husband we'll be home when we're damn-well ready."

"That's not how it works ma'am," he said, giving chase up to the front of the Glass Maze's front door.

"Oh yes it is," Thalia said.

Before she could press past him, the officers eyes lifted from her to beyond her. The sound of the extension batons clicked in unison.

"Step away from the client," Robin's voice announced standing several feet away from her. "She's under Family Medical Leave Title Eighty protection. Step away, now."

Thalia caught sight of Sundry's legal team standing behind Robin and her stenographer pad. They were armed with batons once more. A car with three doors left open blocked one lane of the road. Sundry stood beside a second gray car behind it.

"Title Eighty only applies to the boy, not to the mother," the officer said.

"Are you sure about that," Robin asked. "Or do you think you might want to call for counsel to verify before you do something stupid?"

The officer stepped back and drew out his phone.

"Meanwhile, you won't mind if she goes about her business." Robin lowered her stenographer pad as the rookie went off into his own conversation with his phone. "We heard the call go out. You didn't go home," she said to Thalia. "Saw where you were though and thought we'd better help you get there."

Thalia nodded. "Under the circumstances, thought we 'd try to cash in on some old coupons."

"I see." Robin glanced at the old, red tickets in Ernest's hand; the gloss coating had aged longer than he had lived. "Better hurry and use them before our young officer realizes he's actually right."

Thalia turned and ushered Ernest through the two-panel and tinted-glass door. They now stood within a dark foyer.

"We're just about to close," a woman roughly Thalia's age announced from behind a black glass counter.

"My mother gave me these tickets," Thalia said. "Any chance they're still any good?"

The woman took the tickets; let her fingers hem-haw against her head; and she turned away.

"Mom," she called, as she disappeared through a narrow, office door.

"Where did these come from," a raspier voice asked, unseen and followed by the woman from the counter's younger, "Just now."

Two women emerged from the office, the older one used the glass counter to maintain her stature.

"A little late, aren't you," she asked.

"I wasn't sure," Thalia said. "The parlor across the street served us and—

The elderly woman looked out the window, past the officer and to the ice cream parlor.

"Just a minute," she said and worked her way deeper behind the counter. She reached beneath and drew out a handheld microphone to an old analog ham radio. "Why you taking these tickets?"

"Because they're paid for," the voice, which Thalia instantly recognized as the server from the ice cream parlor, replied.

"Just like that, huh?"

"Just like that."

"Should have asked first."

"You're not the boss of me."

"Uh-huh." The old lady dropped the microphone.

The elderly woman handed the tickets to the younger, who nodded and disappeared into the office.

"Through that turn-style," the elderly woman said.

"Thank you," Thalia said.

"Thanks," Ernest added. He smiled at his host, and she smirked back.

"Hold each other's hands at all times," the old woman said. "We're closing and I don't want to hunt down a lost child."

"I won't get lost," Ernest said.

"Or parent."

Thalia thanked her once more. The ratchet of the turn-style welcomed them past a doorway of hanging, clear plastic strips that belonged in a meat locker.

Behind them, the sound of the business doors opened.

"Can I help you," the voice of the old woman asked.

"I need you to let me inside," the voice of the rookie cop announced.

"Do you have a ticket?"

Thalia pressed forward around a black corner and found herself in a room filled with glass and mirrors, all cut and placed at angles so that they appeared to exist yet seemed invisible. The ceiling was cone-shaped and silver. The floor was black, reflective tile.

"This way, Mom," Ernest said, finding the edge of a half-inch sheet of glass building the walls directly before them. Thalia had barely noticed it.

"This way," Ernest said again, almost running. She held his hand and tried her best to keep up with him at a pace he seemed pleased with. For an instant, she wanted to tell him to stop or he'd get them lost, but then she realized they already were. And who cared if they were? More time spent in the maze meant more time with Ernest.

After several more this-way-moms, She began to realize that they weren't back-tracking. He seemed to know where they were going.

"Do not proceed any further, ma'am," the rookie's voice called into the maze.

Thalia looked about and saw the officer several yards away, separated by the labyrinth of glass.

"Idiot," she called back. "A smart person would have realized there had to be an exit and just waited there."

As though he'd accepted her advice, he pivoted and suddenly stopped. He felt around, made a turn and found himself stuck in a glass corner.

Thalia laughed. Perhaps, if they got out before he did, they could hop in the car and get away. Then she decided that more of Ron's buddies would have appeared by the time she and Ernest should exit the maze.

Ernest pressed deeper into the chamber, holding his mother in tow. A new section of the maze opened up into black-smoked glass.

"See, mom," Ernest said as he dove into the darker portion of the labyrinth.

The stumbling rookie disappeared from Thalia's sight.

"Attention guests of the maze," the elderly woman's voice announced through overhead and hidden speakers. "This is a friendly reminder that the entrance is now closed. The only way out is through the exit. Thank you for joining us today and come back again sometime."

A sound reached Thalia. It was the cop screaming something from his position. It was a gunshot.

"Firearms are prohibited in this maze, officer," the old woman's voice echoed once more. "As such, we have installed bullet-proof glass, it's very expensive for police departments with destructive cops."

Thalia snorted out a laugh at the response, and felt her arm jerk in a new direction.

"Over here," Ernest giggled.

"Honey, you could be going the wrong way," Thalia said.

"I don't think so," Ernest replied and pointed at the floor. "See?"

Thalia looked down and saw a soft, red light in the black tile. "This way," it read. As they crossed it, another one appeared a few feet ahead.

Eventually, they left the black section of the maze and entered yet another area, this one made of mirrors. They turned three more times, laughed a moment at how many Thalias and Ernests there were and suddenly Ernest stopped.

"Press," an image illuminated from behind the mirror in front of them.

Ernest's hand pushed against the image before him. Nothing happened. He pressed the mirror beside it. Thalia pressed a different wall.

"But it said to come here," Ernest said.

"I'm sure it's there to get you lost, dear," Thalia replied. She turned to lead Ernest back the way they had come, but the path was blocked. She felt around, no exit presented itself. They stood in a cubed-in area with no entrance nor exit.

Suddenly, the floor tilted and continued to slowly increase its declining angle. Thalia sat back, Ernest giggled as he rolled onto his stomach and the two slid out of the maze and into darkness.

Chapter Five

An hour later, officer Tad found his way outside of the maze. He had navigated this place many times before in his youth, but his knowledge helped his exit very little. Anyone familiar with this novelty knew they changed the layout once a month to keep the labyrinth fresh. The business seemed all but dead the past few years, but the family owned the building and obviously continued to generate enough revenue to keep going.

His first call had been to his supervisor, who put him in contact with legal, who then put him in touch with Ron. During his call with Ron, he endured many insults, eventually pointing out that Ron wasn't his supervisor, which, of course, made Ron angry with the rookie.

"She's probably on her way home by now," Tad explained.

"Is her car still there," Ron asked.

"Yes."

"Then she's clearly not on her way home, is she?"

A few of Ron's other fellow officers joined the rookie, offered him verbal jabs, suggested they take over looking for her. It wasn't until Ron finally appeared on the scene, and nearly kicked in the door of the Glass Maze to find out where she was, when an elderly woman with a Taser appeared in the entrance to her establishment. She warned the officers that she knew her rights. As Ron tried to force his way into her establishment, which happened to connect to her second floor apartment, thus making the place her residence, she exercised those rights, tased Ron and immediately contacted her attorney.

*   *   *

As the ceiling hummed shut above their heads, Thalia groped for leverage to pull herself back to her feet, or what she thought was to her feet. The room was pitch, and she had landed in soft memory foam. She called for Ernest. Ernest cheered.

The humming overhead stopped and a soft, incandescent, forty-watt bulb grew into enough of a halo to reveal that Thalia and Ernest now stood in a bin of dusty pillows. The younger woman from the lobby stood before it and offered a hand to help Ernest out of the pile first and then Thalia.

"What in the hell is this," Thalia asked, swatting the woman's hand away.

The woman appeared puzzled.

"This is the way out," the woman said. "I thought that's what you wanted."

"This is the exit to the maze," Thalia asked.

"For your tickets," the woman said. "Yes."

"For our tickets?"

"They're old, but we understand opportunity can be limited."

"Well, I don't understand," Thalia rebuked.

"You didn't buy the tickets," the woman asked.

"My mother bought them years ago," Thalia said. "We never got to use them."

"What about the third ticket?"

"What third ticket?"

"These are tickets one and three of three," she said, handing the red tickets back to Thalia. "Look for yourself."

Thalia inspected the tickets, which hadn't been punched or marked in anyway. They did, in fact, say what the young woman had noticed.

"My mother, sister and I were supposed to use them but never got to," Thalia explained.

"So where's the third one? Is someone else coming?"

"It was my sister's. She died years ago."

"I see," the woman said. She smiled.

"You find that funny, do you," Thalia asked coldly.

"I'm sorry, no," the woman said. "It was a common story." She turned towards the source of the incandescent bulb, which beamed from an old, swing-arm lamp secured to the side of a weathered, wooden desk and its single drawer. She pulled on the drawer, then pushed the desk against the wall behind it.

The wall gave way, allowing the desk to slide in. A small set of shelves with binders revealed themselves.

"Can I see your tickets again," the woman asked.

Thalia dug them out of her bag. The woman thanked her, looked at them and then entered into the small alcove where she muddled through the wall of binders within. Her fingers finally settled on an inch-thick, dusty spine. She drew out the binder, set it on the desk and began thumbing through the pages. She stopped at one filled with handwritten notes. She scanned Thalia's tickets once more and put her finger on the aged paper.

"Was her name Gertrude," the woman asked.

Thalia thought she answered, but she hadn't. She thought she breathed but no. She finally managed to form a soft, "Yes."

"How do you know she died?"

"My mother told me."

"Did you see a body?"

"We had a funeral."

"Was her body at the funeral?"

"Closed casket," Thalia said.

The woman shook her head and smiled again.

"She was here about five years ago," the woman said.

"Not possible!"

The woman returned the binder to its place and pulled down another that sat on its side on the topmost shelf.

"How are you here," the woman asked.

"My mother gave me the tickets today," Thalia answered.

"And where is your mother?"

"She," Thalia looked to Ernest, realizing he hadn't heard the news yet. Thalia hadn't been able to bring herself to inform Ernest. She had wanted to wait until she was ready.

"She passed away today," she finally said.

She looked to Ernest for any reaction. His lip began to quiver, and she hugged him. For several minutes to come, she tried to comfort him. He blew through almost all of the tissues in Thalia's purse.

"Are they going to bury her under the orange trees now," Ernest asked.

"Orange trees," the woman asked, deeply interested in the remark.

"I don't think so, honey," Thalia replied.

"Any other family," the woman asked eventually.

"Husband."

Ernest continued to sniffle into a fresh tissue.

"Does he know you're here?"

"He probably does," Thalia replied.

"Does he know about the tickets," the woman followed up. "Is he going to be a problem."

"He's a walking problem."

"Your mother was in the orchard," the woman asked. She looked to Ernest and knelt towards him. "How old are you, sweetie?"

Ernest ducked behind Thalia. Thalia found herself stepping in front of him.

"Why does that matter?"

"Do you know who identified your mother," the woman said.

"I beg your pardon?"

"They don't just put people into a safe facility unless you've been identified," the woman said. "Who identified her?"

Thalia was ashamed she wasn't fully sure of the answer.

"Dad," Ernest said.

"How do you know that," Thalia asked.

"Grandma told me," Ernest replied.

"Your sister was a shell," the woman said. "I assume you are too. And him?"

Thalia didn't want to reply.

"Ma'am, we're not informants," the woman said. "You still don't get it. Do you?"

Thalia didn't reply.

"You're afraid of your husband," the woman asked.

Thalia couldn't keep this answer off her face.

"You hide your disease from him?"

Again, Thalia tried not to answer but felt the tears swell.

"Why didn't you leave him? Move away? Your mother?"

Thalia nodded. She drew up one of Ernie's used tissues in desperation. "I couldn't leave her."

"And now that she's passed, what's holding you here?"

Thalia shrugged.

"Did she pass naturally?"

Thalia shook her head.

"By choice?"

Thalia nodded.

"She gave you tickets that brought you here; took her life the same day; why the urgency? Were you identified?"

"No," Thalia finally mustered.

"Ah," the woman's eyes fell on Ernest. "That makes sense."

"Can we go home now," Thalia asked.

The woman's face drew itself into a lack of sympathy.

"No," she said. "These tickets cost a chunk of change, and your family started off with three. They are your way out."

"I don't understand."

"You're in a matrix of tunnels that will lead you right out of the Trinity of States Union," The woman said. "They've been used to smuggle hundreds of thousands of people with similar mental disorders out of here. Your sister used them six years ago. I don't know if she's still alive, but I know that she was directed to a refuge in Utah and I know she was alive when she used this tunnel because these notes are in my handwriting, and I'd remember a dead person. When you find the refugee office there, they might tell you more."

Thalia couldn't bring herself to think. A way out? A mother dead? A sister never dead? She suddenly felt safe and in danger at the same time.

The woman stood before Thalia now and took her hand.

"What's your name," she asked.

"Thalia," she replied.

"I'm Gloria," the woman said. "This is a lot to take in, but hear me out. I've seen a lot doing this job. It's been four years since we've sent anyone down this tunnel, thanks to that General Mince and his blasted labor camps. Your mother isn't the first person who pushed her loved ones out of the nest via harm to herself."

Thalia tore her hand away from Gloria's.

"I'm not trying to be cold, Thalia," Gloria said. "I'm trying to help you see that not doing this would mean your mom's actions were for nothing."

"But there's so much to do," Thalia said. "I've got to make arrangements; collect her things; call a funeral home." A new realization hit her. "I've got to bury my mom!"

"Your mother is a ward of the state," Gloria said. "They are required to attend to her properly, even if the family won't. If the day ever comes you can come back to New California, you will be able to find her and pay your respects."

"I'm married," Thalia rejected. "I have a husband. You don't just leave that."

"You trust your husband to keep either of you from making careers picking oranges?"

Thalia couldn't reply. She knew the answer all too well. She knew it since she'd met Ron. Alone, she might be able to keep hiding it. She'd kept it hidden all these years. But Ernest? Ron would believe Ernest would be served better in a safe haven.

"We didn't come prepared," Thalia said. "We have no food, and I can't walk to Utah in flip-flops."

"It's okay," Gloria said. "Your ticket wasn't cheap for a reason. You'll get food; sometimes showers, cold possibly; we have medicine, first-aid. Some of our moderators have medical training. Good idea that if you're going to get hurt to try to do it near one of our safehouses though."

She bent down next to the wall that housed the memory foam where Thalia and Ernest had previously fallen. She pulled up two black backpacks. They appeared worn, not from use but from non-use. They looked as if, until a week ago, they had been layered in dust.

"These have provisions for a few days. Food has a long shelf life, it's been stored in a cool, dark place. Should be enough to last until you reach the food store," Gloria explained. "I strongly urge you to keep moving when you're not sleeping or eating. It's twenty-six miles to the first direction marker. You don't want to starve down here. You could go some time without seeing other people. Be smart about your food and water, don't give yours up for your son. Teach him to ration. The last thing you want is to spend your food on a child who's left to wander the tunnels alone without a mom. Each bag has a small package of hard candy, let him suck on that. Understand?"

Thalia nodded.

Gloria pointed to a wall behind Thalia with a wooden crate.

"We used to drop our lost and found items in there, usually the best of it," Gloria explained. "I know there are some shoes. Grab some warm coats, or make layers with the jackets. If you get too warm, you can always shed some of the layers. It gets cold down here, especially when you intersect with caverns. They can go pretty deep into the ground.

"Unfortunately, the tunnels are dark, this is both to protect them against discovery and to help you hide. You may find some that are lit along the way, but don't get your hopes up here in the west. You each have a windup flashlight. I encourage you to use them sparingly. It may sound like endless power, but they can have a habit of breaking down. Don't worry, you can still navigate the tunnels, but you'll do better if you have a flashlight that works when you really need it."

Gloria drew out her folder, asked a few questions, jotted a few notes and suggested again making way towards Utah. She set the binder away in the hidden library; pulled the desk back and concealed its contents.

In the meantime, Thalia dug through the bin of forgotten lost-and-found and discovered a somewhat fair pair of sneakers, a little big but well-worn. They might help against blisters. She also pulled out a few jackets that fit her and a thick coat for Ernest. She then took out as many shirts, thin jackets or sweaters that she thought they could use. She wadded up what she could and started stuffing them into the pockets of other coats and jackets that she planned on wearing. Gloria acknowledged it was a smart move. She also dug up a pair of gloves that were almost in Ernest's size and some mismatched socks.

"Once you leave here, you're on your own to navigate," Gloria stated and rattled a thumb over her shoulder to the lamp on the desk. "When that light goes out, all you have is this hall and the tunnels it connects to."

Strange. Only now did Thalia realize they had been standing in a hallway the entire time. Its cold, bumpy concrete faded into the depths of darkness beyond the light of the desk lamp.

"You will know the direction you are going by the guides along the walls. The direction you want to go is on your right side of the hall. The nylon rope is soft, you can move the fibers with your fingers, nylon means north. The steel cable is south, it's hard, you can feel the fibers, but you can't move them. If you encounter these, I recommend wearing a sock over your hand. There might be some sharp spots. Let them grab the cloth, not your skin. Don't chance infection getting you down here. The wooden railings mean west. They use a lot of different types of wood. If you're unsure, knock on it, you'll know it by its sound."

Gloria directed them towards the side of the desk where a black, thick conduit of some sort sat. She put it into Thalia's hand. She thought it was nearly as thick as a typical wooden handrail. As she inspected it closer, she could see several severed wires within it.

"Remember this. The smooth surface is electrical cable," Gloria said. "This means you're going east." She put it into Ernest's hand despite that he tried to pull away. "This is what you want to find and use the most. Follow this hall until you find the tunnel that will take you East. One of these items may wrap around another to let you know you're going both directions. When your guide turns to chain, that means you are at safehouse or a signpost. Should be instruction on the wall above the chain. There are no maps of these tunnels. Follow their directions, and they'll get you where you want to go. Good place to use your flashlights. If your flashlights go out, the signs are engraved, you may need to use your skill at reading letters by touch. Believe it or not, you may find traveling in the dark better sometimes but maybe not at the signposts. Just head north for now and you'll see specific locations appear eventually. Head to Utah. So, whenever you're ready—oh!

"One more thing," Gloria continued. "That could have been ugly. Like I said, it's been a while. No one could build these tunnels without some major backing and reason to build them. These are cartel tunnels. While you are down here, if you come across any cartel—you'll know who they are—you will prostrate yourselves on the ground. You will not make eye contact. You will not make a sound. Your tickets are a lease agreement to use their tunnels. They have already collected your residual. If you break any of these rules, should you come across any cartel agents down here, they will not hesitate to dispose of you. If they ask you a question, you answer it. Whatever they ask of you, you give it. Whatever they say, you do. Understand? Whatever they ask. In turn, they will give you safe passage. That's always been the contract."

"I'm not so sure I want to do this anymore," Thalia said.

"The Trinity government shoots anyone who tries to cross the border," Gloria said. "You won't get a second chance, and your son will become a ward of the state. If that's not what you want, you will respect the cartel. However, if it makes you feel any better, your chances of encountering the cartel are next to zero. Although I've heard rumors. I've done my share of upkeeping pretty deep into these things and I've never seen them. I've never actually met anyone who's ever seen a one. So, take that for what it's worth."

Thalia clenched Ernest close to her. She stared at the nylon rope hanging from the wall.

"What do you think, Ernie," Thalia asked.

"It's dark," he said.

"Yeah," Thalia replied.

"I like the dark."

"One more thing," Gloria said and held out her hand. "Your phones or any devices that can track you please."

"I'm having second thoughts," Thalia replied.

"At the risk of sounding cold," Gloria said. "It's really not a choice anymore."

"I beg to differ."

"No, you don't," Gloria replied as apologetically as possible. "We help people here, people who have no other way out. We have records. There's no way out other than through these tunnels. We let you out, and you put us all at risk. You came to us, and we believed you were sincere. I'm sorry, but you're going."

"And if we refuse to go," Thalia said.

"Then you better eat really slow," Gloria replied. "We haven't sent anyone out of here in four years, remember? You have enough food and water for three days, maybe a little more since your son's smaller. Why fight it though? What are you really leaving behind?"

"This all so fast," Thalia explained. "I don't even know what it's like outside of Trinity. Who says it's better there?"

"It's got its own problems," Gloria replied. "But you'll notice this is a way out, not a way in. I really couldn't say though. It's a leap of faith." She checked her wrist for the time and said, "And now your phones. I'll take your wristband too."

Thalia drew out the fob that Sundry had given her, and peeled away her wristband that authorized her to purchase goods for her household in the State of New California. Her phone was in the car still.

Gloria took these and returned to the desk, where she cranked open a steel vice mounted on the end opposite of the lamp.

She inserted and crushed the devices until they broke into pieces. Next, she rummaged through the plastic and glass shrapnel to ensure anything resembling a battery had also been obliterated. She left the broken pieces and squished batteries on the floor to be swept up after she retrieved the broom and dust pan.

"I have to go," Gloria said. "We'll have people with questions about you showing up soon. I'll leave you to your trip. Good luck."

Gloria turned to the swing-arm and turned it off.

"Oh, and when you sleep, keep your shoes on and cover your faces so the rats don't eat your feet or lips," Gloria's voice instructed one last time, followed by the whisper of footsteps and a door of some sort latching.

The underground area was suddenly quiet. The sound of Thalia's own breath seemed to yell back at her to gain control of her faculties. Ernest's breath celebrated the new surroundings, yet whimpered after his mother's discomfort.

"Come on," she said to encourage herself more than Ernest. She stepped in the direction of the desk. She found it, felt her way to the swing-arm and took a little while longer discovering its switch.

Nothing.

She turned it again.

Still nothing.

"Okay," she said. "Let's see what we have."

She knelt to the floor, felt the edges of her bag, found three small pockets on one side, two on another and a larger one on the face, opposite the straps. She squeezed the pockets to discover what might have the substance and size to be a flashlight.

"Mom," Ernest's voice spoke.

"It's okay," Thalia said. "Don't be afraid."

"I'm not afraid," Ernest replied. "Just wondered what you're doing."

"I'm checking my bag."

"Oh. Should I check mine too?"

"Not yet," Thalia said. She found the zippers to the largest compartment in her backpack. She felt in: soft envelopes, some thin boxes, a few cylinders of what she assumed were bottles of water, and then something hard, plastic beneath the scratch of her fingernails.

She drew the object out, felt it. It was cube on one end, round on the other. She felt it over, found a switch that slid back and forth three notches. On one side, a disc raised above the rest of the object's shell. She ran her fingers over it, it twisted and not easily. After more prodding, she popped a small handle from within the circle and used it. The disc turned more conveniently now, its roar garbled out, into the tunnel, a sick siren bemoaning the black hell that thickened around it.

Thalia slid the switch again. The light surged from a ring of LEDs on the rounded end. She wound the generator a half a minute more.

Ernest, appeared calm. The long shadows dug into his temples and corners of his lips. His eyes were deeper. For a moment, Thalia caught herself wondering if this wasn't, in fact, the face of someone who belonged in a safer environment than she could provide.

"Something wrong, mom," he asked.

"No," Thalia replied. She bent over her bag and some of its contents that she'd spilled over the floor. "Here, open your pack. Let's see what we both have."

Olive-green envelopes filled their bags. She took inventory: six packets of fruit, including pears, cocktail and peaches; twelve lunch and dinner entrees: five packages of three different types of pasta, two meatball meals, one chicken stew and two chili macaroni; four packs of rice, six potatoes au gratin, two black bean dinners. Then there were four chocolate chip cookies, four carrot cakes, two corn breads, two pound cakes, six small envelopes of peanut butter, four cheese packages, eight jellies; six envelopes of multigrain bread, six crackers, six hash browns with bacon, twelve packets containing what looked like jerky sticks, four applesauce and twelve tubes of powdered milk. Each bag had three twenty-ounce bottles of water, and a small bag of hard butterscotch candy.

Once Thalia ensured there wasn't anything else in the large section of either of the bags, she stuffed the main entrees, fruit, side-dishes and powdered milk into Ernest's bag. She put the water, candy, cakes, jams and anything sweet or of snacking size into her own backpack. She made sure there was enough room left in the top for easy access to the flashlights. Now, she checked the smaller pockets: two emergency blankets; two small first-aid kits with a dozen bandages each, antiseptic and antibacterial cream and a few packets of hay fever medicine and pain reliever pills. The larger pocket held a large collapsible cup, a box of resealable, gallon-sized bags, and a roll of toilet paper. Another pocket held a hundred-count bottle of vitamins with a note scrawled in fat marker that instructed to start taking them with dinner. The bottle was only half full. Thalia combined Ernest's container of vitamins with her own and stuffed both bottles into her bag. In another pocket she found a foldable knife, a small sharpening stone and two sets of hand warmers. She put Ernest's knife into her bag. In the last pocket she found some peroxide as well as a quartz watch on a plastic wristband. She squeezed a tooth-like button on the side. The watch lit up, and she was certain the time was off by an hour and twenty minutes or so. Perhaps it didn't really matter, so long as Thalia could tell how much time had passed if she needed to know. She checked Ernest's watch. It didn't work.

Thalia sealed the bags back up. Then she returned to the lost-and-found bin and withdrew a pair of pink mittens, in addition to the gloves that she thought would also fit Ernest. After a little more digging, she found another pair of socks. She slipped the mittens into one of the pockets on Ernest's bag, then stuffed her socks into one of her smaller bag pockets. She rummaged a little more for anything she thought might come in useful for a trip into the untold darkness. A purse strap found its way into her hand, a leash of two layers of leather sewn together. Upon closer inspection, two clips, not rings, crimped each end. Thalia, unlatched the strap from two rings at the sides of the purse. Nothing else of importance seemed to present itself in the lost and found. For a moment, she thought about taking some shoe laces, but wondered if that might be a disservice to any other future pilgrims.

Next, Thalia helped Ernest lace his arms through the straps of his bag. She pulled up her own pack, held her hand to Ernest and then suddenly retracted it. She returned to the pile of pillows and grabbed two. Then dropped her own bag and most belongings into the lost and found bin.

"It's a lot to carry, I know," Thalia said, handing one of the cushions to her son.

"I'm fine," he replied.

She hoped so. She extended the purse strap as long as she could; clipped an end to a ring on Ernest's shoulder harness; then attached the other through a wad of the web meshing that lined the outside of her own bag's back pocket. Thalia led Ernest towards the nylon guide strapped to the wall just as her flashlight's energy began to fade. She reached behind to return the light to her bag, then made certain to pull the zipper tight.

She and Ernest belonged to the dark now.

"Remember that we travel with the wall to our right," Thalia said.

"I remember," Ernest said.

"If, for some reason, we get separated," Thalia explained. "Keep following the guide. I'll wait for you the moment I realize we're no longer attached. If we come to an intersection or something, I'll be sure to check. We're both using the same guide. Okay?"

"Makes sense," Ernest replied. "I could go first if you want."

"I want to go first," Thalia said.

Her palm fumbled against the wall, until she found the soft nylon rope.

"Ready," She asked.

"Yeah."

Every vein and artery throbbed throughout her body, her capillaries tingled on the cusp of being numb. Her throat surged as though her right ventricle had become confused and now tried to force oxygen-depleted blood into her brain rather than her lungs.

At the same time, she wanted to throw up.

Yet, her hand managed to stretch farther along her pliable bannister and pulled her along the dark. Her bag tugged only a moment and then the sounds of Ernest's feet shuffled behind her.

Chapter Six

In the beginning, darkness was upon the face of the deep. Then God said, "Let there be light," and there was light. Angels cheered. The devil frowned. The blind man cried out, "What in the hell?" Then God said, "It is beautiful," and, his children committed him to the old folks home: refusing to visit, refusing to pay their bills and concurring that they had created all. There is a story about God escaping to visit his children, but they cried, "We don't serve your kind here," and he was forced to go home, where it is said that the city turned off his power and he now sits by candlelight that he presses himself—and that's okay, because He still loves everyone. For that, his children are grateful, so long as it doesn't interfere with their own agendas. Thus their stubbornness has played a vital role in helping them become adept at navigating the dark.

Thalia prayed. She hadn't before, never had a reason to, but now she did because she couldn't see. She prayed to get her way, to find her way, to make her own way, and deep down she knew that she would stop praying the moment she was out of these tunnels. After all, why pray when one can already see or thinks one can see? As the story goes, God healed the blind to see, and the blind said, "Work your own corner, or I'll gut you like a fish."

Ernest's weight had tugged back on the strap several times. Sometimes, she slowed down, and sometimes she made him pick up the pace. Just now, she stopped and warned Ernest so he wouldn't crash into her like he'd done a few times already. She felt the watch on her wrist and pressed the button until a blinding, blue light revealed the digital numbers on its face. It was eleven now; they'd been walking six hours. They could have stopped an hour ago, but they ate three hours ago, and Thalia wondered if they should wait longer to sleep so their food wasn't so fresh on their breath. She kept thinking about what Gloria had said about the rats.

She didn't suppose she'd crossed any rats yet, but she wasn't sure she'd know if she had. They didn't exactly squeak to announce themselves, if any had passed her or Ernest's way.

"I think we'll sleep here," Thalia said and stretched her ankles by rolling her foot about.

Ernest didn't complain. He hardly said anything. The thud of his pillow told Thalia that he might have fallen to sleep right there. She made sure he hadn't and pulled out her wind-up flashlight to help her begin making a bed. They were on dirt—cold, dark dirt. She began dropping some of the layers of jackets and coats on the ground to create a barrier. She took a shirt and tied it up around Ernest's face, ensuring he could breathe. He complained that he couldn't see.

Thalia let him sleep, and she wrapped her own face in a shirt as well. She set her pillow beside Ernest's and marveled at how much carrying it could cause her hand to cramp. She shoved their bags against the wall and turned off the light.

The first time she awoke, it was midnight. The second time, her watch said it was thirty-five minutes later. She shifted for a while before checking her watch again: one-twelve. She closed her eyes and hoped nature would take its course with her. Five-past-two.

She jerked awake suddenly then checked her watch: Three-fifteen. At four-forty-five, she felt movement.

"Mom," Ernest said. "I'm hungry."

"Not yet," Thalia replied. "Go back to sleep."

"Okay."

At seven-eighteen, her eyes fluttered open. It took her a few moments to realize that they had.

"Mom," Ernest whispered.

"Yeah?"

"I have to poo."

Thalia stirred herself awake and felt for the storage bags. She found one and drew out the flashlight. The light was blinding, but, after a minute, it became bearable enough to locate the collapsible cup. She lined it with a sandwich bag and helped Ernest practice squatting without falling on the cup.

She sealed the bag when he was done, then she wandered a few yards down the hall and practiced the new toilet herself. Unsure of what to do with their waste, she struggled with which of the packs should carry it until they came across a more appropriate disposal area. Eventually, she decided to set both bags on the floor in the center of the hall. Thalia figured if it had been years since someone had left the direction of the maze, she doubted anyone would stumble on them any time soon.

For breakfast, they had peanut butter and jelly sandwiches, and a few swallows of water. It wasn't much, but the food didn't taste that great. Thalia figured when they were hungrier and more tired later, it wouldn't taste so bad.

When they were done, they filled their bags with their trash and gathered their coats and jackets. Thalia tugged at the strap to ensure the packs were still connected. They started their journey once more.

"Mom," Ernest asked, after some time walking.

"Yes, Ernie?"

"Are you scared?"

Thalia checked her watch: eight-twenty-two. She'd been afraid now for about seventeen hours. It was a wonder her heart hadn't burst in her chest. She wanted to say that, but couldn't bring herself to. How would Ernest react if he knew she was afraid? She had a difficult enough time to push herself through her own fear.

"No," she replied. After several paces, she decided she'd better ask. "Are you?"

"No, but others might be," he answered.

"Well, that's good then," Thalia explained.

"Oh."

At ten-past-noon, they stopped to eat lunch: beans, noodles and a half of a cake each. They hydrated. Thalia had emptied one bottle so far about three-fourths. Ernest's first bottle was almost completely empty. Thalia reminded him that when his water was gone there wasn't any more.

As they were cleaning up once more to travel, she felt the breeze from above. Only now had she begun to notice a soft whisper in the air. She'd heard one before but hadn't given it much thought. Now that she felt the draft, she assumed it must be some sort of ventilation to keep the tunnels full of oxygen. Eventually, she decided it must have just been a natural occurrence in tunnels and caves.

The air began to crispen. It felt cleaner. Thalia came to realize how used to the earthy air she had become. On her next step, she felt something straw-like under her foot. A squeal erupted and she jumped, letting loose of her grip on the rope. She kicked out in front of her but felt nothing connect. She returned her hand to the nylon guide.

"Careful," Thalia said. "I may have made us an enemy down here."

"We're bigger," Ernest said. "We can stomp them."

Thalia continued to press forward with leery steps that tended to now kick in front of her. After 9,643 steps—she counted—Thalia decided kicking hadn't served any purpose yet.

The ground fell soft. Since their journey began, the floor had taken many forms. It had started out concrete. Stone followed, then dirt, then a few more stone patches. Currently, the floor felt soft. It didn't tend to hurt Thalia's heels as much.

"Doin' okay," she asked.

"I'm fine."

When she was younger, Thalia had read that there were an estimated 2,500 steps in a mile. The woman from yesterday said that it was twenty-six miles to the first direction marker. Assuming that the average person could walk three miles in an hour, perhaps two with a child, they should reach the marker in twelve hours walking time.

The dark had been a hindrance at first, but she had felt accustomed now walking in it, and Ernest had continued to keep up. For the most part, the ground had been kept clear. Whoever prepared the tunnels seemed to have given special effort to ensuring the walkway was obstruction-free, or maybe it was flat due to being heavily traveled. Considering that she felt their pace had quickened since they first embarked, she figured perhaps eighteen hours tops of travel time to the marker that Gloria had mentioned.

They had put in six hours yesterday, traveled nearly four by lunchtime. If they could cover two miles an hour, that should put them at the marker roughly by dinner. Add in any time to stop for snack, hydrate or to catch breath. Bottom line, 30,357 more steps to go. It would be more for Ernie.

They continued on. She whistled. Ernie asked several times how much farther his mother thought it would be. She called her steps back to him. He asked if he could count. She saw no fault with that, until she realized it was interfering with her own numbers and had to ask him to count silently, which he did.

At 26,240, Ernie decided he hated counting and asked if they could stop to eat. They stopped a moment for Thalia to pull out two of the chocolate chip cookies. They had a little water and started walking again with their snacks in hand.

Potty break came at 32,746 with two more bags left in the hall.

Forty thousand came, and the tunnel began to bend. The nylon rope turned to the plastic shell of the electrical conduit. They were heading east now. Then 41,000 came and went. Gloria hadn't told her about the strange grooves that appeared in the electric cable. She had guessed people who used them before had notched them themselves. Maybe they were mile markers. She'd been counting them as such.

"I'm hungry."

"Just a little farther," Thalia replied.

Ernie spoke to himself for the next 2,071 steps, until Thalia felt the cold large links of steel chain and rust gnaw their way into her fingers. She drew her watch and illuminated the face—11:30 p.m., longer than she had anticipated. Maybe what she had been feeling in the cable wasn't mile markers, just grooves.

Her emergency LED beam panned out into cold tunnels, and her eyes took a minute to adjust. Eventually, the flashlight revealed the rounded ceiling of clay tunnel. It was an endless throat that would resume swallowing in the morning, and, with any luck, Thalia and Ernest would pass without being digested within the earthy belly.

The flashlight drew to the chain and its wall then rose to roughly eye-level to a stone placard. Its lettering had been carved tall against the background of the rock:

N.E. Jct. 1/4 mile

E—NV/UT/CO Store 83 miles

N—OR/WA Rest 73 miles

They needed to pick up the pace.

Chapter Seven

Diana Tan wanted to vomit. Tofu made her want to wrench. She wanted bacon, thick bacon, fresh and juicy with fat pouring out of its sides so that it could scald its meaty veins to crisp perfection.

Amy Frances just had to ask, "Don't you just love this recipe?"

No, Diana did not. She watched Amy dunk the tofu in some sauce made out of what looked like unhealthy cat squirts and avocado. Amy shoved the cube of crap into her mouth and then exhaled in false tongue-gasm.

"Michelle gave me this recipe," Amy said through her food. "It's just about the best thing you've ever tasted!"

No, the best thing Amy had ever tasted was a chocolate doughnut sprinkled in bacon, real bacon. Meat! The stuff real orgasms were made out of.

"Mine's still a little hot," Diana replied.

"That's when it tastes best!"

Of course, that's when it tasted best, Diana thought. All feces probably tasted better if you burned your taste buds off first.

"I'm sorry," Diana lied. "I just haven't been feeling well."

"That's okay," Amy said. "It freezes."

Amy tossed more crap into her face, stretching out her middle-aged, Gerald Scarfe-like lines and chewed. More elation followed.

Bacon! That's what Diana needed. Maybe if she played sick up more, Amy would leave. If Amy left, Diana could have bacon. Why did she do this to herself? Amy had brought a new dish into their home every third Saturday evening for twenty years, and Diana pretended to love it every third Saturday. So far, she had managed never to offend her friend.

She stared across the table to her husband Dwayne who had finally dunked the cube of tofu into the gunk on his plate. With cautious teeth, he wiped the entire concoction off his fork in one grating motion. He swallowed it as one quickly swallows a raw, oyster. He wiped his mouth.

"Wow. That's just a big, old bowl of paper-in-the-crack ass that just keeps on giving is what that is," Dwayne replied, wishing he could push it out just as he had taken it in.

Amy was stung.

"Dwayne," Diana snapped.

"That's rude," Amy replied. "You're rude."

"Dwayne," Diana said. "Apologize."

"Woman poops on my tongue once a month, and of course I have to apologize?"

"Dwayne."

"I don't see you eating any more of it."

Diana complained once again that she wasn't feeling well. Dwayne one-upped that he was dying. Amy slammed her fork on the plate and began to pick up her Eversnap bowls but stopped. She turned cold. She felt their presence, their magnetic shift in polarity, against her flesh, sounds of sirens before they could be heard.

They started softly. Diana and Dwayne drew still as well. Then the alarms grew louder, banshees running rampant through the suburbs. Several sang closer.

Dwayne was to his feet and already out of the kitchen. By the time Amy and Diana had joined him, he was peering through the plastic blinds in the front room. It was still light enough to see, but only barely. Six cars drove into the street and blocked its thoroughfare. A small female officer stood at one blockade, a tall man took up the other. Several more rushed the front yard across the road.

"It's Paul," Dwayne said.

Diana started for the front door, but Dwayne restrained her.

"Don't assume they'll wait to hear you out," Dwayne said. "Remember Torres. Wait for them to come here."

Diana loathingly agreed and returned to peering through the blinds.

The officers moved towards the house across the street from theirs. They knocked, knocked again. When a thin man in his sixties answered his door, four officers forced their way in.

"Did they find it," Amy asked.

They continued to watch in silence, barely breathing. Minutes passed. The thin man stumbled back out of his doorway, his hands cuffed. He screamed, begged, tried to run back to the house. He fell.

The russet Albrecht upright piano squirmed from within the house, following two officers. The antique dropped over the lip of the entry way. Its hidden strings screamed for mercy. Its spruce soundboard cracked. The Maple frame snapped along the top edge.

The officers continued to push the object out of the house until the other side dropped, crying even louder than before. A front leg sprained, and its brass wheel popped like a tiddlywink out into the street. The officers grouped behind the piano and bullied it over the front steps where it fell and regaled one last requiem, it's own.

The skinny man screamed, tears appeared to fall from his lips. His face turned red then blue, under the bright porch light, from the inability to breathe through his torment.

Two officers approached the piano with sledgehammers. They drew their heavy black heads and let them fall against the Albrecht's flesh, and they continued to let them rise and fall until all that remained was a pile of splinters and steel strings.

Paul was released and cited for operating a piano in a noise enforced zone without a license and for promoting anti-STEM values through simply owning it. The officers broke away from each other and set towards the neighboring houses.

"Here they come," Dwayne said.

The three returned to the kitchen table and began to sullenly pretend to be eating their dinner.

The doorbell chimed.

Dwayne stood and walked to the front door, opened it and greeted a stern officer who was two heads shorter than he.

"Sir," she said. "We're just checking with the residents in the area. Do you mind if I ask you some questions?"

"Well, we're having dinner just n—

The officer pressed her way into the house.

"Were you aware your neighbor had a device of artistic design without a permit to offend," she asked.

"You don't say," Dwayne said.

"You never heard him playing?"

"No, can't say that I did. Di?"

"No," Diana replied. "Never."

The officer pressed into the kitchen and seemed to inspect the dinner. Her eyes fell on Amy.

"You both live here?"

"No," Amy replied. "I live next door."

The officer spoke into her headset to let other officers know that Amy's house was empty. "We need to search your home ma'am."

"I beg your pardon," Amy asked.

"With one device in the area, it's quite possible others may be around as well."

"You don't think a band, do you," Amy asked in forced shock. "In our town?"

They often operate in groups," the officer said, turning between Dwayne and Diana. "I assume this is your home, we'll have to search yours as well."

A buzzer griped loudly from down the hallway.

"Someone else here," the officer asked.

"Clothes dryer," Diana replied, startled at the sound herself.

"Okay, well, I'll just take a look around."

"No," Diana said. "And remove your officers from next door as well."

"Are you refusing search?"

"I have life-term, legislative immunity and we own five of the properties in the area, including next door and the one across the street," Diana said. "That's a law maker with five properties and the controlling vote for the home-owners association, which means?"

"This neighborhood is under legislative immunity," the officer replied. Her authority drained from her being, and she seemed to slump down in her uniform.

"I'm ordering you to clear the property and return any devices protected by life-long, legislative immunity," Diana said.

"Yes, your honorable," the officer replied and began for the front door.

"By the way," Diana added.

The officer stopped. "Yes, your honorable?"

"Who ordered the raid on my property?"

"Lieutenant Hopps, your honorable."

"Did he take part in this operation?"

"Gibbs," the lieutenant's radio interrupted.

"Go ahead," the officer said, simultaneously nodding an affirmative answer to Diana's question.

"We found a violin," a voice called over the radio system. "Please detain your residents."

"Leave it alone," Gibbs said calmly. "This neighborhood is under life-long, legislative immunity. We've been ordered to clear the property and return the device."

The buzzer complained again.

"I'll get your dryer," Amy said and disappeared down the hall.

"Order your team who conducted unlawful searches of my properties to lay down their arms and badges," Diana explained. "Those of you who did not seize property upon my protected premises are to take those officers who did into custody and detain them until they are summoned to the tribunal."

"Yes, your honorable," officer Gibbs replied. She called the orders over her radio.

"You are also hereby ordered under legislative judicate to exterminate Lieutenant Hopps for his act of treason upon a life-long elected official of the legislative branch of government," Diana said. "Order to be carried out immediately. Is that understood?"

"Yes, your honorable," Gibbs said. "Anything else?"

"The eighteenth century piano that was destroyed," Diana said. "Your department has two days to have an adequate replacement, under approval of my property tenant, or I will have the remainder of your team incarcerated, and your administrative staff will be replaced. Now, get out of my house, or hand over your badge as you are trespassing."

Gibbs retreated quickly from the home.

"Well," Dwayne said. "Saw that one coming."

"I know," Diana slammed her fork on her plate and stared at the remaining dinner on it. "You're right about the tofu."

Two gunshots popped, signifying the end of the lieutenant who had ordered the raid.

Diana stood from the table and followed her husband out of the dining area. While he moved to the front door to lock it, Diana rushed down the hall, which brought her to two sets of stairs. One led up into a dark second floor and then wrapped back to a third. The other set of stairs carved down with blue carpet into the basement. She quickly made the descent, turned left and traversed a cold tile hall to a bathroom that barely seemed large enough for the sink, toilet, tub and a person to occupy.

Amy, who was kneeling before the tub, looked up over her shoulder at Diana's approach and seemed relieved. "Gone?"

Diana nodded.

Amy turned her attention to the marble basin once more, particularly to a black runner along its bottom edge. She had been pulling at periodic one-inch circular buttons along it, each one turning out to be a marble bolt. Once she had removed all, she set them in the sink where they were too large to fall down the drain. Diana knelt beside her, and the two pressed on the black-enameled, steel bathtub. The entire bathing nook, walls and all, rolled deeper into the bathroom, incovering a dark opening beneath.

Diana reached below the floor and turned a dial. A low watt bulb brightened just enough to open a pit about three feet in diameter.

It dug into the earth about twenty feet, revealing what could have been the face of a woman in her thirties. It was hard to tell from this distance. After a short conversation, she realized there was a second face, a child.

*   *   *

Thalia held tight to the smooth surface of the electric cord. She was angry, frightened and weighted down again. Her shoulders ached. By her calculation, her next stop should take 28,000 steps. That's about where Diana told her where the next marker would be before Amy began to lower food down the hole to Thalia and Ernest.

This time, their packs held about six-days-worth of food. Six packages of pork jerky, six freeze-dried scrambled eggs, two sleeves of Ritz crackers, two squeeze tubes of jelly: grape, mixed berry and, of course, orange. For lunches, they had twelve mandarins and ruby red grapefruit cups; six fresh carrots; six envelopes of mixed vegetables; a jar of peanut butter; four envelopes of tuna and one package of flat bread. Dinner was less lavish, twelve MREs, all chili macaroni and cheese. For snacks, a package of generic sandwich cookies and two freeze-dried ice cream packets. Thist time, they also had fourteen bottles of water, six MRE heaters and another bottle of daily vitamins.

They still had half an MRE pound cake and a few crackers from their previous store of food.

In addition, they received fresh dinner right then, two apples and a large, gallon-sized bag filled with some of the most delicious tofu Thalia had eaten.

"Do you have any sedatives," Thalia called up the long chimney into the bathroom overhead.

"Sleeping pills," Diana asked.

"Or pain killers or hay-fever meds that make you drowsy?"

"Are you injured?"

"No," Thalia replied. "I—I'd be grateful. It's a long walk down here."

Diana dropped down a small bottle of extra-strength Nasadryl and threw in a snack-sized, zipper bag with a few heartburn and anti-diarrheal pills with an apology note from Dwayne. The bottle broke against the ground, and Thalia spent three minutes locating and picking up as many pills as she could. After her emergency light began to fade, she decided she'd searched enough. Thalia quickly swallowed two pills and put her light away. They traveled five minutes more, as requested by Diana, to ensure none of their sleeping or eating sounds came into the house at inopportune times. Legislative immunity still had its limits.

They walked. They ate. Thalia enjoyed the tofu. Ernie was silent as Scat kept begging him in his ear to let him try some of his. He wanted to tell Scat to stop asking but remembered he wasn't supposed to let Scat near him.

They slept. It had been four days now since they had left the maze. On day five, they awoke and started the walk again stopping only for food and bathroom. Three times she swallowed more Nasadryl. It made Thalia tired, but, more than that, her mind felt a little more at ease. She was too focused on staying awake and pressing forward that she didn't care so much about the dark; the earth that could collapse in at any moment; or the responsibility that she had to get Ernie to safety. It wasn't until the end of day five that she even wondered if Ron could be in pursuit.

Chapter Eight

"This is a long tunnel," Mr. Porridge said.

"Are you sure," Scat asked. It was too dark to see, so he drew his fat tongue over the dirt wall. It made a sound much like the first pour of a can of shaving cream. "It doesn't taste long."

Sally snorted. "Do you have to lick everything?"

"I haven't seen dark this bad since the great troll wars," Mr. Porridge said.

"Trolls," Scat asked. "Trolls are real? What do they taste like?"

"Trolls aren't real," Sally replied. "He's making it up."

"Omm. Why you gots to be saying that," Scat asked.

"He's always making it up."

"You don't know that," Scat said. "You weren't there at the big battle of the troll war thing."

"No one was," Sally retorted. "Trolls aren't real."

"Then how come I'm scared of them, huh," Scat asked. "How come I think I know what they taste like, huh? Tell me that Sally Fatty! Tell me that."

"I told you I don't like being called that," Sally said sternly.

"If you two are done bickering," Mr. Porridge said. "I will finish my story."

"They're never done," A silvery, whisper of a voice suggested.

"Oh," Mr. Porridge said. "I didn't realize you were still with us, Anvil."

"Where else would I be," Anvil asked.

"Well, it is a long tunnel," Mr. Porridge replied.

"Hoping I might get lost, old man?"

"He didn't say that, Anvil," Sally said.

"He didn't get to say anything," Anvil said as gentlemanly as a voice could sound. "Someone's big mouth interrupted—

"I don't mind," Mr. Porridge replied carefully.

"Perhaps I mind," Anvil said in his still friendly, yet seductive tone. "How about you, Scat? Do you mind?"

"I'm good," Scat replied softly, wishing he had gotten to taste some of the delicious smelling tofu earlier.

*   *   *

The cavern floor had once again sucked the warmth from Thalia's body during the night. She awoke shivering and felt for Ernie. He wasn't with her.

"I couldn't sleep," Ernie's voice came from below her feet. "

Thalia sat up and let the teeth rattle inside her head for a breath or two. She lit her watch, 6:38 a.m. Might as well get a move on. If anything, perhaps they would sleep all the better that coming, next night.

She drew a heating envelope from one of the backpacks and tossed in an MRE of chili cheese macaroni. As she poured in the water, she could feel the chemical reaction already warming her hands. She continued to hold it until it was too hot to do so anymore.

By the time she was warmed with hot food—only half an MRE this morning for her, the other half for Ernie—she was ready to begin leading once more through the darkness.

At 9:17 p.m., they both agreed that they were tired enough to sleep. At 2:15, she felt Ernest shivering against her. She filled another heating bag with water and cooked two MREs, at once, until they were hot. She slipped one into Ernie's coat and held the other against herself. Eventually, she felt Ernie's shivering stop. He breathed heavily in slumber once more. Thalia's body warmed and she swallowed a Nasadryl, then managed to slip back off into sleep.

Day seven started with freeze dried eggs. A little water gave them some body. They ate in silence. They'd talk later when they needed something to distract their ennui. For now, food accomplished that task.

A sound intruded. It came from the tunnel ahead, softly at first: dirt, stone and rubber sole scraping against each other.

Thalia quietly hushed her son before he could comment. They both held their envelopes of eggs and sat silently.

The scraping drew steadily closer but not quickly.

Scrape.

Ernest's hand crept over his mother's arm. She carefully reached across to hold it.

Scrape.

She dared not reach for a bag. She had a flashlight. She might have been able to blind whomever it was, but she didn't know what the approaching person had.

Scrape, and a slight jingle, not keys, but something metallic certainly.

Whoever it was, traveled west towards them. Thalia and Ernest held their ground. She pulled her legs in tightly. It should leave her enough out of the way to allow whomever was approaching to pass by without ever realizing Thalia and Ernest were there. She felt Ernie tuck up his knees into his chest as well, once he realized what his mother had done.

Scrape and jingle.

That is, unless, for some reason, this somebody should decide to turn on their own flashlight at just the wrong moment.

Scrape and jingle, a metal keychain? But no keys?

Scrape. Jingle.

Ernie's grip tightened.

Scrape.

Thalia held back.

Jingle. Not jingle. A clack! Two zipper-pulls slapping each other? Fat zipper-pulls?

Thalia felt her breath freeze, fall silent.

Scrape. The sound was directly in front of them now.

Clack!

It was one person, but Thalia wondered what kind of person?

Scrape, passing along the opposite wall.

They allowed it to continue, listening to the footfalls scrape, jingle, clack and then creep farther and farther away. Until it was just the whisper of rubber and earth once more.

Thalia breathed in deep relief and decided it was safe to finish eating her breakfast. She reached into her envelope with her trembling fingers to grab out some more eggs.

Ernest's envelope of food crinkled in his own hands. A loud crinkle.

"Summon theh?"

The scraping grew louder once more, drawing back towards Thalia and Ernest. Rustling of fabric followed. A beam of light filled the tunnel, and Thalia recalled Gloria's instruction at the start of this dismal journey. She prostrated herself against the floor and urged Ernest to do the same.

The traveler's footsteps returned to the mother and son.

"Nuh," a raspy and tenor voice called. "Nut mai. Dun boo ta mai."

Thalia drew up slightly and shaded her eyes.

"Ehm Suhrai," the man apologized. He shined his flashlight towards the westward-leading wall to lighten the blare. "Heven't sain anyuhn, doon heh."

"Only the store," Thalia replied, although she wondered if she should have.

"Suhrai," the man said. "Ahm Paydeuh. Gut lust. Tunnal daitud, guh'in Cuhludaduh."

"I'm sorry," Thalia said. "I don't understand."

"Uh, Suhrai," The man said. "Meh nehm's Paydeuh. Wut's yuh nehm?"

"You're Peter," Thalia asked.

The man nodded. "Hahs thuh lattle uhn?"

"I'm not little," Ernie replied.

"Nuh, yah nut," Peter replied. He sighed in frustration.

"I'm sorry," Thalia said. "We've never heard your accent before."

"S'kai." He held out a hand to greet Thalia.

Thalia thanked him and he nodded. Ernest was to his feet before Peter could offer.

"Hey, nu-ut?" He dug into his pocket and drew out something that crinkled. He held it out to Ernie. "Butterscutch. Behn seven et fuh leteh. Et's yuhs. Tehk et." He prepared to drop it into Ernest's hand, then suddenly stopped and turned to Thalia. "Ef et's s'kai weth yah. Puhmess, nut pahsoned. Behn seven es uhl."

"I better not," Ernie said, saving Thalia from having to ponder how to turn down the stranger's questionable gift herself. "I don't really like butterscotch."

Peter recoiled, his shadow remained still a moment as he contemplated the rejection. Then he popped his elbow back and sucked the candy out of the wrapper himself. The butterscotch clacked within his teeth, and then he stood.

"Well, then," Peter said. "Ahl bai hedden aist then." He crossed back to his wall and gripped the wooden railing.

"East is this way," Thalia said. She really didn't want to say it, but she had to correct him.

"Nah," Peter replied. "West is wair."

"West is wood," Thalia said. "Electric cord is East."

"Nah." He laughed nervously to himself and then looked off into the empty black of the path before him. "Yuh suh?"

"We're beneath New California. I'm pretty sure."

"Betch," He said. "Yuh suh?"

"I'm sorry."

"Betch."

"Guess we're traveling companions now."

"Aw wulked uhl from Yaytah," Peter complained. "Betch!"

Thalia took advantage of Peter's flashlight to finish eating and to gather her and Ernest's gear. She cursed herself for not thinking of doing so sooner.

"Uhllwawt. Wai guh tahgetheh then," Peter said. "Aw mawt ehs well laid. Aw behn theh uhllwehdai." He sauntered past the mother and son. His face appeared hollow. Beneath the backsplash of his flashlight, it seemed beaten.

Thalia helped Ernest pull on his traveling gear before applying her own. Peter waited, even shined his light in her direction to help.

"Better save your batteries," Thalia said. She made sure her and Ernest's tether was secured.

"Yeh." Peter grimaced at his light and then disappeared into the dark. "Suppuhs suh. Thes weh then."

With hands on the electric cord, all three began a renewed journey. It started silently at first. Peter tried stirring conversation, but Thalia didn't understand him well enough to make begging his pardon comfortable among them. Ernest simply didn't answer, leaving Thalia to suggest that he was shy around strangers.

Again, lunch, early today, 11:30 a.m.

"Best tah mek uh schedill," Peter said "Helps tah slayp et nawt."

Thalia preferred to press on and eat later. She and Ernest had already developed their own schedule. Ernest grunted his disgust at the intrusion, but she was in no mood for a confrontation with this complete stranger.

They ate, longer than Thalia and her son had liked to do. Peter kept trying to engage conversation. Thalia exhausted her bank of *uh-huh*s and *yeah*s at things she didn't understand.

"Ahm tarwid," Peter said. "Ah could is a nehp." He yawned.

"We should leave you to it then," Thalia said and began prepping her gear for travel. She checked once more: 1:30 p.m. Too much time lost. Whether they walked or sat, Thalia knew the food they had wouldn't last to linger. She had to get Ernest to the next checkpoint.

"Yah," Peter said. "Gehs yah wawt. Gahd Thankehn."

Before long, Peter was back to leading and talking. She wasn't sure, but Thalia thought she had heard Peter saying something that sounded like she'd make someone a good wife some day.

She wanted to puke.

Not long after, they began walking in silence.

At four p.m., Peter wanted to stop again for dinner.

Thalia tried to keep moving.

"Ned to stup noo," Peter said. "Ken't stup leteh."

"What do you mean," Thalia asked.

"Cev up uhead."

"We're in a cave," Ernest said.

"Nuh," Peter replied. "En tunnal. Cuts entah cevuhn. Huhftuh, claim doon. Heffa deh aht layst. Taim tuh ayt. Slayp uftuh claim doon."

They ate.

Thalia gave the stale half of pound cake to Peter in return for a handful of dried peaches, which she gave to Ernest. She later accepted the few that her son decided he didn't want to eat.

Twenty minutes later, they were back to walking.

"Cawful noo," Peter said about an hour after. "Goo-en duhn. Wetch yah step, en wetch yah heds. Gets tayt."

Immediately, Thalia began to feel the wall carve closer towards her, turn left and then disappear entirely. The floor began to slowly decline.

"Hed," Peter warned.

Thalia held up her free hand to discover any sharp or rugged surface that might be the source of unnecessary pain. She felt sharp edges poke out and bite at her flesh. She worked her way beneath the obstructions and warned Ernest to do the same.

For the next six hours, the walls thrust sharp blades and rough edges against the trio of travelers. At first, stone chomped at Thalia's knuckles. Ernest insisted that he was fine. Eventually, the walls grew up slick and ribbed. Then something else stabbed Thalia in the shoulder.

She couldn't bear any more of the unknown. She stopped to draw out a flashlight. It's beam revealed a high ceiling of long calcium teeth, some drooping perhaps a hundred feet, some long enough to stab at the hands and heads of those people using the railing. "Best tuhn it uhf," Peter said.

Before Thalia could question, Ernest cried staring straight down into the chasm, "Look how deep it is!"

Thalia suddenly looked the direction Ernie was pointing and found herself staring down a ledge into a chasm of what appeared to be nothing, and it ate the reach of her LED bulbs. A path perhaps three feet wide had twisted into the wall and crawled even deeper into the chasm. What she thought had been wall, were ribbons of calcium drooping from the ceiling high above her. This alone intimidated Thalia. If their direction had actually been on the wall side of the path, she might not have been so eager to hide the scene away. But they traveled the side of the trail right along the ledge down into the pit of nothingness. The truth is, she'd wished she'd never turned the light on. Despite the steel posts that had been placed periodically along the ledge to string the electric cable-bannister, one misstep and a blind wanderer, which they all were, could slip into the chasm most wretchedly.

"Both hands on the railing, Ernest," Thalia instructed, knowing it would force Ernest to walk sideways. She didn't know why, she thought it seemed safer. She returned her flashlight to her bag, gripped the railing in a similar fashion and hoped they wouldn't cross paths with anyone coming up.

"Yeh," Peter said. "Thes a betch."

The path kept climbing its way down, deeper.

"We could cross the path just for a moment," Thalia said. "Just for this part."

"Nah," Peter said. "Mawt bump intah summon. Mawt fell."

"We could talk, and people would know we're coming," Thalia suggested.

"En, paypul mawt set in the dahk en hup we pess baw withoot nawtehssehn," Peter replied. "Mawt fell."

Thalia felt stung, enough that she allowed her heart to continue to beat higher and higher into her chest until it felt as if was trying to peek up, over her throat, stopped only by the guard of her tongue.

Her foot slipped off the edge. She held the conduit, lurching forward, mostly out of surprise than the command of gravity. The electrical cable stretched away from the path, and the posts it was secured to wobbled under her weight. Peter's hand grabbed at her bag until she had regained her balance.

"Mom?"

"I'm fine, honey," Thalia lied. "Be careful here. Step back a bit from the railing so you don't fall."

"Uhkay," Peter asked.

"Yes," she lied again. Her body lurched once more against the electric cord and she threw up.

Again, she felt her bag pulling her back.

"Dun dah thet," Peter said. "Dun, knoo hoo stahng the cahd is."

That comment didn't help. Until now, Thalia had assumed the electric cord could act as some sort of safety device while traversing the skin of the chasm, but the realization was that it was merely a guide. Suddenly, she found herself traveling a lot more slowly and carefully now of her footing. Likewise, she was constantly reminding Ernest to do the same. He was annoyed at her incessant nagging, she could tell.

At 1:30 a.m., they reached the flat bottom of the chasm.

"Please tell me we don't have to do this again," Thalia said.

"Nah," Peter replied. "Hahd paht's oveh. Tahmahwoo, wai goo up thuh uhtheh sehd uhf thess plehss. Be uhn thuh uhtheh sehd uhf the pehth. Noo mah ledge wuhking fuh us."

Thalia's impulse was to shine her light over the walls to see how far they'd come or discover how many bodies now rested on the floor and in the walls of it. There hadn't been any switchbacks though, so maybe she wouldn't see them. She suddenly thought of Gertie making this trek and needed to not imagine discovering her body here in this cavern.

"Surprising no one's discovered this place yet," Thalia said.

"Summon hes," Peter answered. His light popped on a moment, bright and blinding. Once her eyes adjusted, she realized that she couldn't see any further looking up, now that she was at the bottom of the chasm, than she could see down when they were higher up.

"Better save your batteries," Thalia reminded.

"Ah suhpoos." The light went out.

She was tired. Ernest had yawned several times the past few hours. Peter kept urging them on.

"Slaip uht the buttuhm, nuht hay," He kept saying. "Rahl uhveh edge. Get stepped uhn mehbe."

Out of habit, she began asking if Ernest was hungry. He wasn't, and neither was she. They were tired. In just this moment, she was actually a little bit grateful to have run into Peter. It would have been a much longer time between meals if he hadn't warned them when to have dinner, and she would have probably already tumbled off the path and taken Ernie with her.

Four hundred steps later and, for the first time in a week, she slept comfortably, completely and utterly spent from her day's journey. She might have even dreamed, but, since she dreamt about walking in a black pit of nothingness, she couldn't be sure.

Today, she woke up on her own. Ernest hadn't riled her awake. She was cold, but it hadn't bothered her so much as before. She stirred and checked her watch; it had come loose.

"Mom," Ernest asked.

"Mmm," she said. "Yeah, Ernie."

"Our bags are gone."

Chapter Nine

Thalia felt her wrist once more. Her watch wasn't loose, it was missing. She patted over her surroundings: dirt, jackets and layers for warmth, her tether to her son while they slept, nothing else.

"Peter," Thalia asked.

"He's not here," Ernest replied.

Tears came instantly, though she dared not vocalize them. She sat with her son, far beneath the earth, in a vacuum of black. In one deep breath, it drained her of hope, sapped her joints of strength and tried to squeeze her heart until it burst.

"It's all right," the seductive tongue of her captor, that was the dark, whispered deep into her soul. "It's all right to die here."

"No," She instinctively fought back with her own silent words.

"No?"

Thalia fought back yelling at the dark and his oppressive intentions.

"You're already lost," the dark told her. "It's probably three days to the next store, four because it will take most of one day to climb back up this ravine."

"Then we'll walk it," She debated with her diabolical opponent.

"Yes, slowly," The dark said, almost as though it were agreeing with her, supporting her endeavor. "But, with no food, you'll walk slower and slower. With no water, your brain will dry up. You'll see things even in the dark. You'll forget Ernest, leave him behind."

"Go to hell," she told it. Thalia stood and started dressing herself into the layers that had been her bed. She felt her surroundings to

ensure she hadn't forgotten any of her warm clothes. She helped
Ernest, felt his tether. It seemed well for travel.

"Are we going back," Ernest asked.

"Yes," the dark answered before Thalia could. "Go back. Or stay.
Stay here with me. That's good too."

"No," Thalia told Ernest. "We'll keep going."

"But food," Ernest asked. "What about breakfast."

"You'll starve," the dark said.

"According to the last marker sign, we're about as far from the
next food store as we are to the one we came from," Thalia said.
"Going back means we'd have to climb back up, then come down
again later. If we keep going forward, we won't have to repeat it."

"But breakfast," Ernest said.

"Well," Thalia replied, thinking quickly. "If we don't have to eat,
we can keep walking and we'll get where we're going sooner."

"If you don't stop to eat, you'll die," the dark chided.

Thalia ignored the comment.

"Okay," Ernest said. "We should go then."

Thalia soon felt the electric cord in her hand. She tugged on the
purse strap to ensure her belt loop was attached to her son's. Ernest
announced he was ready, and they began their journey once more.

The cable began to turn subtly as it crossed the chasm over a
spongy floor. Thalia supposed it was a suspended, wooden bridge,
and she would be correct. Thalia didn't want to think about what was
beneath, or, more accurately, what wasn't. After two hundred steps,
they were across, and the floor began to rise again. The familiar
sound of rising chasm echoed their footsteps. This time, they were
on the side of the path closest to the cavern wall. She continuously
pressed her hand out in front of her to verify there was, in fact, a wall
before her, meaning the ledge truly was on the opposite side of their
path behind them. She didn't worry about falling so much here. She
even trusted one hand on the railing again, allowing them to move
forward rather than sideways.

"Perhaps falling, isn't so bad," the dark said. "It's a longer way
down when you get higher."

"Don't be absurd," Thalia fired back, silently.

"Is it absurd? You don't want to be here."

"No, I don't," she agreed.

"Who says the new world will be more accepting of you? How do you know they don't judge people like you more harshly than where you just came from?"

"I don't."

"You belong here," the dark said. "You know you do. You know you didn't make a difference, and you won't again."

"Ernest needs me. I won't do it."

"So, take Ernest with you."

"Shut up!"

"He's worse than you are," the dark said. She could almost feel it hugging her, caressing her matted and gnarled hair. "He'll never find belonging no matter where he goes. He'll kill someone some day."

"You don't know that."

"You know that, my dearest Thalia. You've seen the signs. Remember the bird?"

"That was an accident."

"Was it?"

"Yes," Thalia snapped in her own thoughts.

"They'll be less accepting of him. Don't make him go through that."

"Shut up!"

"When you get higher, just step off the path, you'll take him with you. He can't withstand your weight. You'll both be dead before you hit the floor."

"I'm not talking to you anymore," Thalia replied.

Thalia wasn't sure how long she gave her adversary the silent treatment, but, eventually, the dark confronted her again.

"It's time," the dark said. "You know you're high enough now."

She gripped the cable more tightly. She refused to let the dark pull her away from it.

"Just let go. Take that step."

Her grip loosened. "I can't."

"Why not? You've wanted to all your life. Now you can. No one's watching."

"Not while I still have Ernest."

"He can't see you."

The dark was right. Thalia loosened her grip. She could just go, like the dark said.

Thalia suddenly remembered a time not long ago, a high school field trip to the ocean. She stood in water up to her waist. White carbonation continuously refreshed against her skin with every ocean pulse. Her classmates had begun to exit the beach. To her left some distance, the yellow-orange, school bus honked. Mrs. Porter called through her megaphone that it was time to leave.

Thalia was the last one in the water. In just a few a steps, she could immerse herself, breathe in the sea, let the undertow grab her before any of her traveling companions could.

Then, a hand appeared at her shoulder.

"Come on, Thales." It was Gertie.

Thalia remembered turning, startled to see Gertie and the way she seemed to know exactly what Thalia was thinking.

"You're all alone," the dark's melancholic voice crept back into Thalia's brain, tearing her from her memory. "Now's the perfect time."

Yet Gertie said, "Come on, Thales."

Thalia's hand tightened once more around the cord. "I'm not alone." She kept pushing forward.

"You don't know if Gertie's alive," the dark said. "She could be at the bottom of this pit. This whole trip could be for nothing, and then what?"

"Then screw you, I guess," Thalia replied.

Then the floor began to flatten, and she and Ernest turned away from the sinister cavern. The sound of muffling tunnel began to hide the chasm behind her along with the sound of the dark cursing Thalia's narrow escape.

"I'm thirsty," Ernest said.

Thalia stopped a moment and felt the walls and floor. Nothing. She moved forward a bit, then again. Finally, she found one. She wiped it off in her clothing and found Ernest's hand to place it in.

"What is it," Ernest asked.

"It's a rock," She said. "Suck on it. It'll help you salivate. Don't swallow it. Don't chew it. You'll want your teeth when we get to the safehouse."

Then she set out to find another pebble for herself.

She wished she knew how long they'd been traveling. She'd tried counting her steps, but the dark kept shouting out other numbers in attempts to persuade her to go back to the cavern.

They were a little slower today, the cavern floor had seen to that. She also slowed the pace to help conserve energy, but they didn't have to stop to eat. They stopped to go to the bathroom. Without any supplies, they used the middle of the tunnel. They both fought to ignore how uncomfortable walking had become.

At 50,000 steps, Thalia decided it should be a good day and they set down to sleep.

They awoke, sauntered another 50,000 steps for the day and slept.

They awoke, barely talked to each other, again to conserve energy. There was nothing to say really. They were hungry. They were thirsty. Thalia imagined Ernie walking with his head down. That's how she imagined she was walking. She had given up trying to lift the mood with whistling or singing. It spent energy too.

They just walked.

"Can we stop," Ernie said. "I'm tired."

22,542 steps.

"We need to keep going," Thalia said.

The sound of Ernie's weight crumpling in the cavern brought Thalia back to him instantly.

"Just a nap," Ernest said. "We'll be stronger after a nap."

"All right," Thalia said. She took a nap.

Ernest awoke and riled his mother awake. Again, despite all the energy sapped by the dark and the cold floor, Thalia began her count once more.

At 30,000 they slept again.

Then, somewhere in that sleep, "Hey! Broad!"

Thalia was slow to realize that a beam of blinding light stared her in the face. She let her eyes slap shut.

"Don't die here!" A burley grip shook her shoulder.

She sat up quickly, retreated into the wall and tried to shield her eyes so they could adjust.

"Why are you down here?"

"We're walking," Thalia couldn't finish. She started crying.

A tongue clicked.

A hand slapped her.

"Don't touch my mom," Ernest's voice ordered. It was calm, cold.

Thalia begged not to hurt her or her son.

"What do you want to do." The man holding the flashlight turned the beam away from Thalia's face. It lit up the faces of two other men, a fourth stood and disappeared against the black cone of the flashlight's border.

One of the men, an angry and dangerous face glared down to Thalia. His jaw slid back and forth as if chewing something tough. Despite the dirty surroundings, he appeared well-groomed. His beard and hair were red.

"Where's your food," the man with the red beard asked.

"We don't have any," Thalia replied and then continued to plead that they had nothing.

The man with the flashlight rummaged through their jackets and outerwear that made up the insulation between her and Ernest's bodies and the cold floor.

"Doesn't look like nothing," the gruff voice behind the light replied. He held up the jacket and shined back to the red-faced man.

This gesture revealed a flat-bed hand-truck with metal poles and bungees wrapped tightly around its well-packed cargo. The handle to another truck might have appeared to follow. It was too dark to tell.

A flicker of flame ignited several feet down the cavern. The aroma of tobacco and tar flooded the hallway. The flame disappeared and a red ember remained.

The light snapped to the source.

"Get that damned thing out of my face," complained a short, thin man with long, mangy hair that matched what grew on his face.

The light returned to the red head.

"Are you an idiot," the red-bearded man asked.

"I need it." An ember fell to the earth, scarring the dark in an exclamation point.

"Out," Red said. "Now."

The cherry complained, dropped to the ground and snuffed into nothing.

Again, the light flashed to the smoker, and another face appeared. It was only a glimpse, but Thalia knew she saw him. Peter sat on the smoker's cart, gagged, tied, lying on his side.

"You," Thalia screamed. She tried to jump from her position. She would have attacked him, but whoever held the flashlight before her shoved her back.

"You know this man," the red beard asked.

Thalia nodded.

"How?"

"He stole our supplies," Thalia asked.

"This true?"

Thalia shook her head.

"I'm not asking you." His face had turned slightly away from Thalia. "This true, boy?"

Ernest's face appeared in the light. He nodded his head.

The red beard appeared to consider the information.

"You steal from this woman and her child," Red beard asked.

Peter moaned.

"They're good. Turn the lights back on," Red ordered.

A set of halogen bulbs burst from the lead cart. The tunnels turned white. Thalia shielded her eyes and waited to see again. She almost cheered at the sight of orange paint. Anything was better than black.

The red beard approached Peter and his cart. He drew out two familiar backpacks.

"These yours," he asked.

Thalia nodded.

"What's in them?"

Thalia recited what she remembered after leaving the store. Red Beard handed the bags to the man who had been smoking and gestured towards Thalia. The smoker grudgingly took the bags and tossed them on the ground before her.

Thalia quickly opened one and drew out water, what was left that is. She'd take better stock later, but she could tell the packs were much flatter. Peter had cut into their supplies. She gave Ernest a bottle of water and opened another for herself. She hadn't realized until trying to twist off the lid that her fingers were numb from cold. She found a heating pouch and set it to work on a pouch of food.

"See that," Red Beard asked pointing towards Thalia and Ernest. Then, "Look!" He gripped Peter by the hair and twisted his head to observe the mother and son. "These are our guests." It was here that Thalia finally realized the man was well-enunciated. "They pay for my protection. They pay for a bag each. How is it I have two guests without bags and one guest with three? You stole from Salvo's guests!"

Peter answered in gagged muffles.

"What you did was wrong?" Red drew Peter to a sitting position all through manipulation of the hair on his head. He knelt in front of Peter. "Do you know why it was wrong?" He snapped Peter's gag out of his mouth effortlessly.

Peter burst with apologies and tears.

Red smacked him. Peter continued to apologize, and Red smacked him again.

"My turn," Red replied, taking a full breath between syllables to ensure his command was clear.

"Playse," Peter said. "Eht wuhn't huppen uhghen. Ah sw—

Red pressed the tip of a silencer against the front of Peter's throat. "My turn," he repeated much more poignantly. "Wet yourself, crap your pants. I don't care, but when I say 'my turn,' take that to mean that I will crack your Adam's apple open with the next bullet in this chamber if your vocal chords so much as flap a sigh out of your neck. So, my turn."

Peter closed his mouth and roughly swallowed; the barrel point tried to stop it, possibly bruising his Adam's apple.

"Good," Red said without showing any sign of approval. "Now, the reason you still have your brains in your head is because of the presence of our guest and her son."

Tears streamed down Peter's face.

Red wiped them.

"Everything in these tunnels belongs to Salvo," Red said. "You steal from Salvo's guests, you steal from Salvo, and, for that, we will punish you."

Red turned to Ernest.

"How long since you've eaten," Red asked.

"Forever," Ernest replied.

"Hear that," Red asked facing Peter again. "Forever." He stood and holstered his sidearm and announced to his traveling party, "We camp here. Prepare something for our guests, nothing harsh, we want them to enjoy their much-deserved meal." He looked down upon Peter once more. "Make him watch."

Watch? That reminded Thalia.

"Yes," Red asked surprised at the sound Thalia made upon her realization.

"I'm sorry," Thalia said, and she pointed to the black band around Peter's wrist, and buried partially beneath the layers of twine that bound his arms. "That watch belongs to," she was careful to remember where she was, "Salvo." She did her best to kowtow to the group of men, but she was afraid she'd fall asleep again.

Red smiled, mostly in his eyes. He searched and found the band to Thalia's watch. "Did Salvo give you this to use down here?"

Thalia shook her head. "Came with the bag and his generous tickets.

"Tickets," Salvo asked, much more intrigued now. "What color?"

"Red," Thalia replied.

"Return Salvo's watch to his guest," Red instructed the man who held the flashlight.

The man with the flashlight began to work at Peter's wrists to remove his binding long enough to recover the watch.

"It wasn't enough that you stole their food," Red asked and drew his firearm, once more pointing it at Peter's neck, to remind him that he shouldn't speak.

Thalia received her watch back graciously and quickly checked the date and time. It was 5:00 p.m., and the calendar showed they'd been four days since Peter robbed them.

"Don't eat that yet," one of Red's men said. This one was mostly filthy but shaven. He took the warming pouch away from Thalia and placed a cool tube of yogurt in her hands. "Eat this first."

Thalia turned and handed her tube of yogurt to Ernest. He, as well as the lighting allowed, appeared pale, hollow. She wasn't sure how accurate her perception was, the lights bleached his face yet striped it in shadow at the same time.

Another tube slid into her hands. She devoured its contents, almost threw up, and the shaven man encouraged her not to eat so fast. She finished the tube and thanked the men. Ernest had already finished his yogurt.

Another hand reached down to Thalia holding a sandwich. She took it and thanked the benefactor without looking to his face. She turned to pass it to Ernest, but he already had his face buried into one of his own.

She followed suit: Dry sourdough, wilting lettuce, precooked bacon, sliced tomatoes from a can, butter. Halfway through, she took another drink and realized that Peter was watching her eat. His head was secured between the smoking man's dark and filthy hands to ensure he couldn't look away. Wet fear streaked his grimy face.

Part of her wanted to eat more slowly and draw out his torture, but she was too hungry. She finished her meal. No sooner had she finished her meal that a compulsion filled her: rage. Peter could have killed them, killed Ernest, left them in these tunnels to rot. She took up the warming pouch, ignoring how quickly it burned into her fingers, and threw its hot contents into Peter's face.

The smoking man swore at not getting out of the way fast enough. Red was suddenly in front of Thalia, holding her fists after they had already begun striking at Peter.

"Stop," Red demanded and shook her until Thalia's eyes fell on him. "My turn!"

Thalia broke and felt her arms embracing the man with the red beard. She cried into his wide shoulder, and he let her do it.

Stay this way, she prayed to herself. For once, she wasn't alone. She wasn't leading. She liked not holding the responsibility just now.

Red held Thalia's bottle to her mouth and urged her to have another drink. She did.

"Where did he rob you?"

"In the chasm," Thalia said. "At the bottom."

"Finish sleeping," Red said. "When you wake up, we'll be on our way to take him to the bottom of the divide where he left you."

"Are you going to kill him," she asked.

"I'm going to cut his hands off and leave him to find his way out. Are you okay with that?"

She thought of what could have happened to Ernest because of Peter's crime. She agreed and then laid down. Red made sure Peter was secured to a cart and then shut out the headlights on the lead hand-truck.

Thalia fell back asleep to the sounds of Peter's sobs.

Chapter Ten

On day fourteen, Thalia discovered another button, a simple doorbell, just as the one at the previous store. It was 6:32 p.m. Sounds of footsteps pattered from behind a steel door built into the side of the tunnel.

It opened, and a scrawny man with auburn hair stood. He had a meticulously closely-shaven beard, resembling something from a common logo that Thalia had seen on bumper stickers. He couldn't have been older than twenty-five.

Soft brightness flooded from the other side of the wall, lit as only natural daylight could, from fake blue-ish bulbs.

The man looked over his shoulder to a girl a few years younger than he. She was standing in a stairwell backed by a rectangle of friendlier and more common luminescence. Her hair was wavy and black with unnaturally red undertones filtering through.

"I'll bet you would like a shower," the woman said and stepped down the stairs. She suddenly paused when she realized there was a boy standing behind Thalia. "You poor thing. Well come on, Chuck. Let them in."

"Are you sure," Chuck asked.

"It's just two," she said. "We've done more."

"All right," Chuck replied and ushered his guests through the door. "I'm Chuck, this is my girlfriend Zelda."

Thalia and Ernest politely greeted their hosts.

"We have bath, food and bed," Zelda explained. "Please, this way." Zelda led up the narrow staircase while Chuck took up the end.

They soon found themselves in what appeared to be a basement with a low ceiling and small, blacked-out windows.

"Excuse me," Chuck announced. He helped direct his guests away from the small underground entry and then rolled a large chest freezer over to conceal it.

"Shower is this way," Zelda continued to direct. "If you'll leave what you're wearing in the hall, I'll put it in the wash."

Again, Thalia thanked their hosts.

In minutes, Thalia found herself over a triangular tub. Warm water spewed from a faucet two feet above the rim. It gave birth to bubbles and blasted them into oblivion at the same time. Ernest slapped his hands at the mountain of surviving suds that engulfed his watery world.

"Here's a box of clothes that might fit," Zelda said, popping her head into the bathroom for a moment. "Take what you want. I'm sure you'd like to get out of what you've been wearing. I'll put what you brought in the washer." She turned to leave and stopped. "Oh, and." She dropped a new razor blade on the sink along with a small can of shaving cream and a package of tampons. "I wasn't sure what you might need."

Thalia vocalized her gratitude once more. So far, she'd been lucky, but she took up the supplies. The razor she could use tonight.

Soon the water and suds were gray, but Ernest was clean. He slid into fresh clothes and left the bathroom to discover the kitchen where something savory was waiting for them.

Thalia refreshed the tub with warm, clean water and suds. For a time, she couldn't get comfortable. Strange as it may have seemed, she thought the tub might have been a little too soft for her. She would have liked to have fallen asleep, just as she had in her own tub when she was in need of relaxation, but this just wasn't right. After five minutes of trying to lounge, she finally gave in to conditioning her hair. She also gave use to the razor, mostly out of need to feel civilized again.

Twenty minutes later, she found herself in fresh jeans—a little baggy on her—and a yellow and green flannel that wasn't the prettiest, but probably warmer for going back to the tunnels, if her hosts didn't return her own clothing before she set out again.

She navigated the house until she could set herself at an ebony table in a clean, white kitchen where green marbled through the countertops and the tiled floors.

"I hope you'll forgive us," Zelda said. "We tend to experiment. We're both online culinary students. I hope you'll bear with us."

"It smells fine," Thalia said. "Thank you so much."

She found a platter of meatloaf put into her hands. She dug out two slices and set the dish in the middle of the table where she'd seen it resting before it had been handed to her. She filled her plate with broiled asparagus and mashed carrots with small chunks of baby red potatoes drowned in garlic and butter.

She ate and relayed her journey to her hosts.

"Well," Zelda said. "At least that part's over."

"Can we help you clean up," Thalia asked once the meal and its conversation had fallen to a natural benediction.

"Oh, no," Chuck said. "We'll get this. You didn't come this far to clean up our home."

"How about a game," Zelda asked. She turned to Ernest. "Would you like to do something fun?"

Ernest looked to Thalia for approval. "I guess so," he said with a shrug when Thalia told him it was his choice.

"Oh good," Zelda applauded. "We have a game room." She stood and led the way once more down a white corridor. They passed the bathroom, and the stairs leading to the basement. The hallway re-angled to the right and led to a dead end with a blackened bulb shadowing the farthest corners.

Zelda popped a door open and walked in.

This room was brown and large: plastered in dark 1970s paneling. The floor was hardwood, and a miniature basketball key was painted into it. A hoop hung from an arched ceiling. One wall held shelves of board and electronic games. Another held a large screen, gaming consoles and cartridges. A third wall held a museum of trophies and plaques. A pool table sat deep before it.

"Wow," Ernest said.

Thalia made a note to remember this when they finally reached their destination.

"What kind of games do you like," Zelda asked hunkering down eye-level with Ernest.

Ernest looked around the room, overwhelmed but unwilling to know it himself.

"Too many choices," Chuck asked.

"What's your favorite," Ernest asked.

"My favorite," Chuck appeared amused.

"Ever play Simon," Zelda asked.

"Like Simon Says," Ernest asked.

Chuck laughed.

"All right," Zelda said. "We'll play Simon."

"So soon," Chuck asked.

"Why not," Zelda replied. Chuck walked to the wall of board games and drew out a plain, black box from atop a pile of others with pictures of people smiling and enjoying themselves over more types of table-top entertainment. "Chuck is too proud to admit it, but he was a Simon champion at the, what was it again, Hun?"

"Professional Gamesters," Chuck acknowledged returning to the group. "Paid for this house."

"Okay," Zelda said. "Here's what you do." She pointed at the floor to copper Xs stenciled into silver circles the size of large serving platters. They made two rows of three with the numbers one through six marked in different colored foil dead center of each. A yellow circle separated the two rows. "We each stand on a number." She led Ernest to the diagram in the floor with the number one on it. "You take number one. I have a feeling you're going to give us a run for the money in this game." She kindly directed Thalia to player two's mark which had a red number in it.

By now, Chuck rejoined the group, holding four silver cylinders the size of rolls of quarters with four different color buttons—blue, red, yellow and green—down their sides. He handed one to Thalia, another to Ernest, a third to Zelda and kept the fourth for himself.

Zelda had taken the player circle facing Thalia, which was marked with a five. Chuck took six and faced Ernest.

"Okay," Chuck said. On the yellow circle, in the floor between the two teams of players, he placed a large disc. It was sectioned off into the same colors of buttons as the cylinders held. "Here's what we do?"

"Hold a sec," Zelda said. "Does anyone need to go to the bathroom first."

"Oh. Good thinking," Chuck recognized.

No one had to go to the bathroom.

"Okay, then," Chuck continued. "The lights will appear on the disc. Each one of us plays as one color, and we have to repeat their order as they appear on the game. Every time you get the color right, it will replay all the colors and then add on a new one. Get the order of colors wrong and you lose the round and have to start over."

"What do we win?" Ernest asked.

"Isn't that adorable," Zelda crowed.

"All right," Chuck said and dug into his front pocket. He pulled out a folded knife. "If you win, I'll give you my favorite skinning knife."

"I'm not supposed to play with knives," Ernest said. "I suppose we can just play for fun."

Chuck smirked and put the knife away.

"When I turn on the controllers, you will only be able to play the color button that lights up in your hand," Chuck explained. "But that will change with each round. The last team standing wins. So, for instance, let's try a practice round."

Thalia seemed troubled with the term *last team standing*, but she just assumed it was a gamer thing.

A different colored light lit in each of the player's hands.

"Beep," the disc on the floor chimed, the red quadrant lit up and died.

"So, red lit up," Chuck said. "Thalia, you're standing on the red marker, so you have the red button. Go ahead and push it."

Thalia pressed the red button in her hand. The disc on the floor acknowledge her response by chiming as long as Thalia held the button.

The disc immediately lit up the red quadrant once more and then the yellow, each with its own tone.

"Good," Chuck continued to explain. "I have yellow, so this time, Thalia?"

Thalia pressed her button. Unlike Ernest, she had seen this game before but not with such elaborate game pieces.

"Now, I press my button because I'm yellow, and yellow came after red," Chuck said and pressed his yellow button. "We continue to take turns pressing buttons. If you press your button at the wrong time." He pressed his button to demonstrate, and the disk growled at him. "Or if you forget to press your button when it's your turn, then you lose, and the round starts over. Understand, bud?"

Ernest realized that Chuck was asking him. Ernest nodded his head.

"Okay," Chuck said. "Let's try an easy round for real this time."

The disc illuminated the green quadrant.

Ernest pressed his button. The disc lit up green as he did.

Then it lit green then red.

Ernest pressed. Thalia pressed. The disc illuminated to show they were pressing their buttons in response.

This time, the sequence was green-red-green.

Ernest-Thalia-Ernest.

"Good," Zelda announced.

Green-red-green-blue.

Ernest-Thalia-Ernest, and Zelda cheered as she finally joined.

Green-red-green-blue-red.

Ernest-Thalia-Ernest-Thalia.

The disc moaned with a low-rumbling buzzer, and all the controllers flashed red.

"Oh," Chuck laughed. "Not quite."

"Let's go again," Ernest said, staring at the disc.

"Okay," Chuck said.

Yellow!

Chuck!

Yellow-blue.

Chuck-Zelda.

Yellow-blue-green!

The players all answered.

Yellow-blue-green-green.

Again, all responded correctly.

Yellow-blue-green-green-blue.

Then-yellow-blue-green-green-blue-yellow.

"Oh, Thalia," Chuck said. "Your turn is coming up; I can feel it."

Yellow-blue-green-green-blue-yellow-yellow.

Next round: Yellow-blue-green-green-blue-yellow-yellow-red.

Now, yellow-blue-green-green-blue-yellow-yellow-red-yellow.

Chuck-Zelda-Ernest-Ernest-Zelda-Chuck-Thalia—

"Ow," Thalia blurted. A shock gripped deep into her palm and clenched painfully up past her ankles. She felt it surge up, holding her in place. She wobbled but steadied herself.

"Wasn't your turn," Zelda said.

"What was that?"

"Just a little shock for the weakest link," Zelda said.

"This isn't my idea of fun," Thalia said. "Come on, Ernest, I think that's enough playing."

"I wouldn't—

Before chuck could finish, Thalia had tried to step away from her position and another charge sliced up her heel and almost all the way to her knee this time.

"If you try to leave before your game is over, you will be shocked," Chuck said. "By shocked, I mean electrocuted."

"That's just a warning shock," Zelda added, her face now turned sullen. "Let's play."

Suddenly, Thalia wished to be back in the dark tunnel. "Wait, this can kill us?"

"Only if you lose," Chuck replied.

"Why would you play this," Thalia asked.

"Because it's fun," Zelda said. "Why wouldn't we?"

"I think she means," Chuck said.

"Oh," Zelda realized. "Yeah, because we can, and no one cares if two tunnel rats disappear."

"We didn't even know this place had a secret tunnel until someone showed up about three weeks after we moved in," Chuck said. "At first, we thought, you know, cool, but then we realized. You know, meat is twenty-five dollars a pound now and—well—people are a lot of meat."

"You're going to eat us," Ernest asked.

"Maybe not," Chuck said. "If you win, we'll be dead, and you can leave."

"But I have to tell you, little guy," Zelda explained. "We're both pretty good at this." She pointed to the wall of trophies.

"And remember, if you step off your spot again before the game is over," Chuck said. "You will die."

"You're disgusting," Thalia snapped.

"Says the coward fleeing her own home," Zelda replied coolly.

"Next round," Chuck announced.

Red!

"No," Thalia screamed. "I'm not play—

Her body tensed once more. Her lungs froze and her jaw clenched. Then it stopped and she sucked in breath.

"You play," Chuck said through infected annoyance. "You got a color wrong; you tried to leave the circle; and now you took too long. You used up all our warning areas. The next time, someone will die."

Yellow!

Chuck!

Yellow-yellow.

Chuck-Chuck.

Yellow-yellow-Ernest.

Chuck-yellow-Green-Blue.

Blue again.

Back to Ernest. Now, Thalia. Add Zelda. Thalia again. Yellow. Yellow. Red.

Thalia's body tensed. Her mind blackened. She didn't feel herself hit the floor. The round was over. She had lost.

Except she hadn't.

"Okay, little man," Thalia heard Chuck say. "You're the only one on your team left, so you have to play both red and green now."

Thalia finally realized she was on the floor. She breathed in slowly. It hurt. She had survived the attack. Behind her, the disc beeped out the chorus of memorization. It took a few more moments for her to understand that she was no longer standing on her player mark. She had fallen out of her circle.

Then, she remembered Ernest.

The beeping continued.

"Yeah, kid," Chuck cried. "Nice. Nice!"

Suddenly, Thalia was throwing up her dinner.

"She's still ali—

Thump! Whatever fell was heavy. Thalia turned quickly, unprepared to see Ernest next to have fallen, only it wasn't Ernest.

Zelda lay crumpled on the floor, her fist clenching the controller. Smoke rose from her fingers. Her eyes had popped, and red trails of blood boiled down the sides of her face.

Chuck glanced once at Thalia, then exhaled hatred back into the room. Whatever happened to Thalia, she knew at once, the game didn't do what Chuck and Zelda had expected it to.

"Next round, you little bastard," Chuck said, turning his wrath towards Thalia's son.

The beeping started once more.

"No," Thalia tried to say, but her throat was sore, like it had been strangled a moment ago.

She wanted to drag Ernest away.

She watched him. Her son's eyes fixated on the disc as it continued to spew out random order. Each color painted his face with new lines. Yellow showed a fearful brow, green locked him into inquisitiveness, blue anger. With Red, he was something fierce to be reckoned with. His fingers rolled against the cylinder in his hand as he pressed out the rhythm to the improvisational and visual song that composed before him.

Any moment he would fall before her eyes. Her heart clenched in her chest. This was all for him. This journey, this escape, his grandmother's scheme was all to protect Ernest, and now none of it mattered. Soon, this madman champion at the game would beat her son. He would die and her heart would follow him.

"Not bad, kid," Chuck said. "Not good either."

Unless. . .

* * *

"What is this pretty," Sally asked watching the ground erupt with rain, lightning and a great, big tsunami of moldy frosting.

"It's a storm," Scat cried, and tried to hide under his tongue. "It's a tornado of colors." Rainbow lightning struck in front of him. He licked it. "It's bad!"

"I'm frightened," Sally said.

"Wait," Mr. Porridge said, pointing to the lightning as it danced in and out of the sky. "See it?"

"No," Sally and Scat replied. "We don't see it."

"Well, I do," Mr. Porridge said. "I know how to fix it."

"So, fix it," Sally said.

"I can't," Mr. Porridge said. "I'm not supposed to."

"Well then, Mr. Porridge," Anvil said, stepping out into the middle of the storm. "Tell me how to fix it."

* * *

The round finished. Both survived.

"Congratulations," Chuck said. "Now we get to play endless. This time, we take turns and play the entire sequence alone," Chuck said. Every round will add a new part to the pattern.

The next song of colors started and began to build. The game danced as a disco ball.

The console lit up once more to run the process that would eventually add another color at the end of the string of strobing hues.

"Blue-blue-green-gray," Chuck started spouting out.

"Don't listen to him," Thalia coughed but barely heard herself. She couldn't even remind Ernest that there was no gray.

"So, that's how you want to play it, old man," Ernest asked.

"It's all part of the game," Chuck said.

"Yes," Ernest replied softly and sharply, as the disc finally allowed him to start punching in his turn at the sequence.

"Green," Ernest said while pressing a red button. "Red," he continued while pressing green. He continued to hit the right colors.

Next round. Chuck shouted colors as he had before while the disc spit out the order.

"Green," Ernest said while pressing green. "Green," he said again while pressing green.

Next round.

"Red" when green. "Red" when red.

Next round.

"Yellow" with green. "Blue" with red.

Chuck laughed. "You're going to confuse yourself kid."

Next round.

This time, every color Ernest called out was yellow, but he still hit the correct buttons, and none of them were yellow.

Blue added on, and Chuck answered.

This round, Ernest didn't say anything.

Blue added on again.

"Red," Ernest said. "I mean yellow."

"Oh," Chuck cooed. "Oh! Is this the end?"

Ernest cleared his turn.

The disc spit out the order again, finally adding yellow onto the deadly mix.

Ernest shouted out random colors.

"New record," the disc announced.

"Yeah," Chuck shouted. "Twenty-two."

"Twenty-blue," Ernest asked.

The disc began humming out the sequence again, Chuck shouted different colors to confuse the pattern with Ernest.

"Green, Green," Ernest announced hitting red twice. "Your turn, yellow."

Chuck laughed, hit the yellow instead of the blue. He knew it was blue, but his brain still reached for yellow. Suddenly, Chuck clenched his game remote and other than every muscle in his body clenching, he didn't move. His eyes began to bleed, but they didn't pop or melt as they had with Zelda. Instead, his thumb blasted open, his mouth foamed, and he dropped. Even as he lay on the floor, smoke rose from his mouth.

"Game over," the disc announced. "Player one wins. You may exit your circle."

"I always win," Ernie said, his eyes not Ernie's.

Thalia shrieked no real sound. She couldn't seem to make words. She rushed to Ernest, her joints and muscles aching. She pulled Ernest out of his player one circle.

"Thank God," she wanted to say, tried to say, but nothing.

Ernest hugged his mother back and pulled away only when she allowed it.

She tried to speak but only croaked.

"I don't want to play anymore," Ernest said.

"We should leave," Thalia tried to answer but it all came out as a cough. She knew at once what had happened. She was swollen and knew that electricity burns from the inside.

She had an idea though. When Ernest was even younger than now, he'd thought it funny when his mom would speak in her duck voice. It wasn't always clear, but she didn't need vocal cords for it.

"We need supplies." She said, packing air into her cheek and squeezing it past her gums.

Ernest seemed taken aback. "Does this mean we're not sleeping in a bed, tonight, Momma," Ernest asked.

"Better not," she quacked.

Thalia returned to the kitchen and quickly rummaged for food, anything worth taking. She had one MRE heater left in her bag. She refilled her empty bottles with water in the kitchen sink, found a box of herb rice mix sitting in the windowsill, then moved to the refrigerator. She slammed it shut.

"What is it," Ernest asked.

"Nothing," Thalia mouthed, which would have been true if nothing was a hefty pair of soup bones, skinned, all except for the ankle, the heel, the toes and every bit of human flesh in between. She looked to the table where they had eaten earlier and tried not to vomit at the sight of the meatloaf.

"I'll look for another flashlight," Ernest replied and ran back to the entertainment room to ransack for batteries.

Thalia found Ibuprofen, some amoxicillin, and a few other pills that might be useful. She dumped it all into one of the pockets of Ernest's backpack, all except two Ibuprofen and one antibiotic. She drew a partially empty glass from the kitchen table to wash it down.

It hurt. She should have smashed the pills into her drink.

She turned back to the refrigerator and opened the freezer, this time, hoping for something better than what she found in the bottom compartment. She found a man's hands in a gallon-size freezer bag, not large, clean. They might have been free of scars, but the white frost of flesh may also have been hiding them. A forearm that had split apart filled two more bags, cracked and freezer burned as well.

She found hotdogs under a white towel, covering someone's head. She left the hotdogs under the head but took out two ice cube trays to fill three sandwich bags, which she found in one of the drawers. After, she taped a dish towel lining around them. The dish towel came from a copper ring mounted to the wall besides the kitchen sink. The duct tape came from a drawer next to the refrigerator. She taped the towel and bags of ice around her neck.

"I found these," Ernest said. He held two small flashlights and a package of four AA batteries. "Are these the right kind?"

Thalia realized that she wasn't sure. Thalia checked. They were a fit. She nodded and took the items from Ernest's hands.

"Not enough food here," she said.

"What about the freezer downstairs," Ernest asked.

The three moved out of the kitchen and back into the basement where the long chest freezer covered the entrance into the tunnel.

Unable to find a key, they pried it open with a wedge of wood that had been clumped in a pile of debris in the corner of the unfinished and earthy basement. The lid cracked open: more bodies cut into shanks, steaks and finger food.

"Are we going to eat people," Ernest asked.

Thalia shook her head in defiance and rushed out of the basement in anger. She returned to the kitchen and drew out the frozen package of hotdogs. She scoured the cupboards for containers to hold any leftovers from dinner that wasn't meat. She settled on a box of zipper sandwich bags and another of gallon-sized freezer bags. She took the red potatoes, asparagus and mashed carrots, about two meals worth, if they rationed wisely.

It wasn't much. She found a Snickers laying in the corner of the counter top. She took to ransacking the cabinets. In one, she found another box of rice, Mexican-flavored. In another, was a coffee thermos. She filled two-thirds of it with hot water right out of the kitchen faucet and emptied in the Mexican rice.

She filled two sandwich bags with hot water and the other box of rice in the same manner. She knew it wouldn't work, that rice needed warm to hot water over time to get it to absorb. She wasn't even sure if she could get the MRE heater to make water warm long enough to cook the rice she had brought, but she was running out of options. However, she did return to the fridge and take a closer look to discover that she had missed a half a bag of carrots and a head of cabbage. She dropped both into Ernest's pack.

She stared at their meager findings.

"Damn it," she cursed to herself and snatched up another gallon bag to slide the meatloaf into. Ernest didn't know.

"Would these be good," Ernest asked appearing from the hallway with two cans of food, One of peas, another of mini raviolis. "We just need a can opener."

After a few more moments of searching, they found one.

"Was there anything else," Thalia asked dropping these cans into Ernie's pack as well.

"Yams," Ernest said. "A big can of them."

"Go get them."

"I don't like yams."

"Go get them."

Ernest left, pouting as he did so.

A little more inspection of the kitchen and Thalia found a box with cake baking supplies in it. That is, decorating condiments. She took up a cylinder of chopped nuts and another of rainbow sprinkles. She dug through and found a round container, half-filled with raisins.

She discovered a package of ramen and dropped the square of noodles into a sandwich bag and sealed it with water and its packet of spice. She did the same with the contents of a box of Macaroni and cheese, except put it in a gallon bag. She knew it was all going to taste gross. She found some plastic cups to fold her water-filled, sandwich bags into to protect them from breaking.

She lifted the backpacks and frowned. Water weighed a lot.

Ernest returned with the can of yams.

They sealed up their bags and returned downstairs to the entrance beneath the freezer. They stopped only a moment at the washroom to gather their wet, but now clean clothing and bedding. Once in the basement, they rolled the freezer out of the way.

Then, a clicking sound cried from upstairs. A door opened.

"Hello," a woman called out. The door closed.

"Curfew," the woman called. "Comply?"

Thalia ushered Ernest quietly and quickly into the entrance.

"Comply," the woman's voice called again. This time demanding.

Thalia drew into the tunnel and pulled the freezer so that it covered her escape in time to hear, "Hey! I need some help in here." Thalia guessed the woman had stumbled upon the two bodies in the game room.

Thalia and Ernest returned once more to traveling the tunnel.

She dug out her flashlight. Supposing that the package of batteries Ernest had found were good, she decided they could risk a bit of light in their escape. It's not like they'd had the batteries before anyway. She lit up the tunnels, tethered herself to Ernest and drew again to the electric-cord banister, then, with the light shining the way, they moved quickly down the dark corridor.

"We should save the light," Ernest said.

"I want to get as far away from here as fast as possible," Thalia managed to whisper, this time under her own abilities, weak but clear.

After thirty minutes, she decided they shouldn't be so eager to sleep. If anyone should look under that freezer, it wouldn't take long for that person to get on their trail. There were plans wiser than sleeping now. They pressed forward.

The LEDs continued to burn, turning the walls into a strange white but disappearing into a black portal of unknown. Then, suddenly, the light died.

Again, they were in the dark.

"Mom," Ernest said. "I'm bored."

She stopped a moment to dig out a fresh battery. However, she didn't turn the light back on. This time, she decided, the dark was their friend. If anyone was after them now who didn't know the tunnel operations, they'd use their own flashlights, and she'd see them coming before they could catch up. At least, that's what she hoped. However, then she decided she still wasn't comfortable with that plan and drew out the emergency flashlight. She cranked it to life and followed its beam for twenty more minutes, cranked, and continued for forty minutes. She grew tired of the heavy flashlight, but it was less weight in her hand than on her back. When the light spent its energy this time, she switched back to her battery-operated beam and they continued to walk until it died.

"Can we sleep now," Ernest asked.

"I think we should," Thalia replied and checked her watch. It was 5 a.m., and she realized that she had forgotten to read their last marker for directions.

Chapter Eleven

Day 15—9:02 p.m. Today's breakfast: bloody nose with a side of handcuffs.

Thalia fell, a sharp piece of earth dug under her patella without breaking skin. She screamed or tried to. She was raspy now but still not loud. An automatic rifle muzzle to the back of her head made her stop.

"Move," a woman, younger than Thalia ordered. It was the voice from Chuck's house.

Two men at each side forced Thalia to her feet. Three more followed. Ernest walked ahead of her; a tall man marched beside him with a weapon pointed at his shoulder.

Another armed officer led the way back towards the house they had fled the previous night.

"You shouldn't waste your batteries," Ernest said. "You don't want to get stuck in the dark."

No, Thalia thought. That's exactly what she wanted. Thalia and Ernest knew how to navigate the tunnels; the soldiers didn't.

"Thanks for the input," Ernest's escort retorted. She stopped a moment. The group halted with her as she held her four-lithium-D-cell-powered light out to Ernest.

"See this flashlight," she asked.

Ernest shook his head, she cracked the side of it with the aluminum frame.

Thalia lunged at the woman, croaking a plea to stop. Another soldier's light struck Thalia in the back of the leg.

"See the flashlight now," the woman soldier asked Ernest.

He said nothing, looked to his mother and back to the soldier.

"I'm sorry," he said. "No. I don't."

The group began moving again.

Thalia kept closely to Ernest's heels. His steps seemed determined. Thalia wanted to walk slowly, to take her time in returning to the nightmare home they had just left.

After seven-thousand steps, Ernest suddenly stopped.

"We're not stopping," his escort said.

"I have to go to the bathroom."

"Keep walking, runt."

Thalia wanted to plead.

They kept walking.

It wasn't another hundred steps before the aroma of feces permeated from Ernest's jeans.

Two of the soldiers near Thalia complained.

"What's wrong with you," the female guard asked. She smacked his head with the flashlight again.

"You said to keep walking," Ernest replied.

Another fifty paces and she ordered everyone to stop.

"I can't keep walking with this." She pulled Ernest's backpack from his shoulders. "Take your pants off."

Thalia protested and received a smack to the side of her head as well.

"If you're going to act like a baby, you shouldn't dress like a big boy," the female soldier scolded.

Ernest didn't move.

She held up her rifle and ordered Ernest to take off his soiled jeans once more.

He began to.

"Take off your shoes first, kid," she ridiculed. "How stupid are you?"

Ernest removed his shoes, his socks, then dropped his pants.

"underwear," she said.

"I'll be naked," Ernest complained.

"Think anyone cares," she asked. "You're killing us. Take 'em off."

Afterwards, he put his shoes and socks back on. The officer then forced Thalia to unload three bottles of precious water, rinsing Ernest's backside.

They began moving again.

Two thousand more steps and Ernest said he was hungry.

"No."

Five hundred steps more and one of the soldiers leading point suggested he too was hungry.

They stopped.

Ernest and Thalia hugged against a wall while their captors ate. Thalia took opportunity to remove one of her layers of outerwear to tie around Ernest's waist to help cover his exposed bottom half.

"Shush," one of the male captors suddenly ordered.

The others left their meals and held their firearms cautiously against their chests.

"Who's there," the woman, ranking officer called out.

No answer. Thalia hadn't heard anything.

The soldiers drew their rifles into their shoulders.

"Make yourselves known or we will fire upon you," she called.

Their flashlights filled the tunnels with bright until they faded into a gray mural of a lone figure in front of what looked like a box.

A tongue clicked.

"You shouldn't be down here," a familiarly rough voice followed.

"On the ground, now," she ordered.

Her team rallied into an attack formation.

"You don't give orders in Salvo's tunnels," the rough voice said.

"On the ground," she cried again. "We will fire."

She continued to scream the order. A second figure appeared at the first's side, which seemed to agitate the team of soldiers even more.

"Hands where we can see them." She repeated the order several times.

"Ssshhhh," rolled gently back towards the military team until silence fell. "My turn," Red's voice called down the tunnel.

There was a pop. One soldier's cranium burst into a misty cloud of shade and he spun into a wall before falling, while another officer's back burst with a similar explosion. Two others fell without getting to fire a shot. The woman's body dropped flat, after her knee kicked out from beneath her by an invisible attack. The remaining soldiers gave up their fight quickly and silently.

The commanding soldier rolled behind one of her fallen comrades and slapped her weapon against her shoulder to pot shot a few rounds. Something struck the side of her hand just as she was perfecting her aim. Her hand winced in pain, releasing her grip as something struck her arm this time. She looked up into the lens of a familiar flashlight.

*　　　*　　　*

"Did I ever tell you the about the bickering rams," Mr. Porridge asked.

"No," Scat said. "Please tell."

"There were two bickering rams," Anvil interrupted. "They didn't get along, so I bashed their heads and cut them. The end."

"That's no way the end," Scat complained.

Anvil's dark figure knelt before Scat. His red eyes peered into Scat's blue, fat brain and gave him a migraine behind his left eye.

"I say it is," Anvil said, his silky voice filled with the power of unpredictability. "Keep licking your forehead, and I'll prove it right now."

*　　　*　　　*

"See this flashlight," Ernest asked. Before Thalia could stop him, he drew out a foldable knife, the one he had won for killing Chuck. He had retrieved it after he'd returned to the game room unsupervised, looking for batteries. The little boy had slid it into his shoe so his mother wouldn't know. He thought the soldiers might find it when they made him undress, but he was smart and kept it hidden. He plunged his bladed award into the side of the woman's head.

"How about now," he asked.

She slumped, and he bludgeoned the soldier's head open with her own aluminum wand.

When Thalia finally pulled him away, his face dripped in his former captor's blood.

The sound of footprints and carts approached.

Thalia remembered her instruction and kowtowed, prompting Ernest to do the same.

"Where your pants kid," the rough voice asked. "The hell's wrong with you? Your yankin' noodle's gonna freeze off down here."

"Stand up ma'am," Red's voice allowed. "What happened."

Thalia drew herself to her knees and found Red's face once more kneeling at her side. She collapsed into his arms, and found herself, yet again, sobbing against his chest.

"People tried to kill us," Ernest said.

"These people," Red asked. "How?"

"No," Ernest replied. "The last house. They were bad."

Thalia pulled away.

"Can," she barely squeaked but forced "ibals" to follow.

Red turned to the man with the gravelly voice. "Fix it."

The man nodded and disappeared up the tunnel with two of his allies.

Red turned his attention back to Thalia and realized the dressing around her neck. He peeled it apart to reveal purple and black flesh. He lightly touched and she jerked away.

"Have any meds," he asked.

Ernest dug her antibiotics and ibuprofen out of her bag for her. Red gave her another antibiotic. Then he snapped his fingers and a young, friendlier face appeared from above. Prep a dose of the high-quality."

"What happened to your pants, kid," he asked.

Ernest pointed down the tunnel.

"They make you take them off?"

Ernest nodded.

Did they touch you?

"Hit us with flashlights," Ernest said.

"Anything else?"

"Wouldn't let me go to the bathroom."

Red nodded this time then held a stern finger out to him. "Gentlemen don't hit women, understand?"

Ernest looked to the woman soldier that he had beaten to death. "She started it."

The young face appeared next to Red once more and held a small bungee cord and a slender syringe with a clear liquid to him.

Thalia immediately drew away as Red began to strap the green cord around her arm to fatten a vein.

"Purely medicinal," Red said and gently coaxed her arm back towards him. He popped the vein, and Thalia suddenly fell. Red felt the attack tear at the side of his neck and Thalia's blood backsplashed the side of his face. The gunshot had sped over Red's right shoulder from a wounded soldier who had decided, at that moment, to stop playing dead and quickly rose to shoot the enemy most readily to his aim. He fired off one round before several of Red's allies subdued him.

Red stared at the needle still in his hands. He felt the gash at the side of his neck to evaluate the flow. Hands were suddenly at his side drawing him to the ground, but he waved them off. He found Thalia crumpled now before him. She bled from above the center of the back of her head. An exit wound drooled from the front of her skull.

"Momma." Ernest stood over her then knelt.

Red felt the urge to draw the child away from his fallen mother and would have done save the needle in his hand that he rather not inject the child with.

"Come here, boy," Red coaxed.

Ernest ignored him.

*   *   *

"This doesn't taste right," Scat said. "Doesn't taste right, at all.

"You're licking again," Sally said. "Stop it."

"Fine, you lick it then," Scat scowled. "Why does my tongue have to do all the work, Miss Sally-has-a-caboose-as-big-as-an-alley."

"Mr. Porridge," Sally complained.

"It's so pretty," Mr. Porridge said. "Why can't I see how it works?" So, he reached out to see how it worked.

*   *   *

Red tried to stop him. Ernest had taken his skinny index finger and pushed it into the hole in the front of his mother's head.

Thalia sat up straight and screaming.

Ernest drew his finger out of her head, not startled, more disgusted—not disgusted as in disappointed that his mother was alive but disgusted like when he was eating jellybeans and bit into a licorice one.

Thalia cried and grabbed her face.

"Ernest," she cried and hugged him.

"Ma'am," Red questioned. He expected her ghost to decide once more that it should have left the body and she would fall back to the earth.

Instead, she asked, "What happened?"

"I don't know, but you should really stop moving around," Red said. "Let's get you to a hospital." He ordered his men to get Thalia's head bandaged and then make her stand and keep walking.

By now, Red's men had dragged the soldier that had shot her and dropped him face down on the ground in front of Red.

"And you are," Red asked.

"Goodman, Steven," the soldier replied. Then he added, "Corporal. Seven-two-four."

"Uh-huh," Red replied bemusedly. "Look, Corporal Seven-two-go-fuck-yourself. These tunnels move a lot of income by people who don't care who you are. My father and grandfather helped dig some of them, maybe even this one. Is your father and grandfather still alive?"

"Goodman, Steven," the soldier answered. "Corporal. Sev—

"Very good," Red said and applauded once. "How very Geneva Convention of you. However, we do not recognize the Geneva Convention down here in these tunnels. We are not a form of government. So, I will do to you things that no one will ever know how to train you to withstand, and, if I so choose, you will survive them and wish you hadn't. Do you understand?"

"Good—"

"Please know that if you say anything other than an answer to my question, I'm going to shove this needle into your eyeball and fill it with enough methamphetamine to make it explode inside your head."

The soldier struggled, but Red's allies held the man in place as Red now pressed the tip of the syringe steel to Steven Goodman's eye and laid it gently against his bottom eyelid.

Goodman blinked, and the needle bit in between two eyelash follicles. Red quickly pulled away.

Goodman didn't speak, but his face quivered with false courage.

"It's okay," Red comforted. "You're okay. Nothing got in." He held the needle up close again but didn't touch the soldier this time. "So, I ask. You answer. Do you understand?"

Goodman said nothing.

Red moved the needle back at the soldier.

"Yes," Goodman quickly corrected.

"Good," Red replied, holding back the syringe. "Now we can have a conversation. I don't talk much down here. Mostly, I move product. Today's product is meth, and I kill anyone who tries to stop that. You're stopping that. Are you trying to stop that?"

Goodman shook his head. "We were after her."

"There, good," Red adulated. "See, we're doing so well at becoming friends. Off on the wrong foot, right? You'll like me. I am good, you'll see." He waved his hand back of himself pointing the needle towards his cargo held within trains of flat hand-trucks. "I don't like the stuff, you know, but it makes me a lot of money. It's dangerous. You ever try it?"

Again, Goodman shook his head.

"You don't have to lie," Red said. "It's okay if you have, just tell me."

"No," Goodman said weakly. "I haven't."

"Good!" Red smiled and laid his empty hand on Goodman's shoulder. "It's a filthy, disgusting habit. You lose your teeth, your hair. You look like a raisin. It makes you far too brave. Why, you know, I once watched a video on the Internet of a man who drove his car into a train, and he flew right through the windshield and broke his head open on the side of a passenger car. You know what he did?"

Goodman didn't, and he nodded to signify it.

"He got up and ran fifteen blocks before he just fell dead. He was so full of meth that even his brain swelling out of his cracked skull couldn't stop him from knowing he was dead. Can you believe that?"

Goodman shrugged.

"And another time, I saw a woman so high on it that she ran a red light and was hit by a semi, and she broke both legs then continued to walk on them for an hour before she realized the bone was sticking out of her skin, which it was doing before she started walking on it. Can you believe that?"

Goodman responded in kind.

"It's just amazing what this stuff can do to the human body. I mean, one sniff of cocaine and you think you can do anything, and I mean anything, and this stuff is just cheap cocaine," Red continued. "Geez. Just amazing. Take it from me, my friend. Chemicals that make you feel alive when you should be dead. I still geek out thinking about it."

Red's eyes locked onto Goodman's and he added a friendly smile. "I just wanted to let you know that, because I'm going to put a black bag over your head now and tie you to our cart. If you make a fuss, I'm going to have to cut a hole in your neck and snip your vocal flaps. Understand?"

Goodman pursed his lips, but it still couldn't hide that he trembled.

"Good," Red said. "Now, here's the deal. If that lady lives until I can get her to the hospital, I'm going to take a hammer, not a great, big one but a much larger than your average hammer—a nice blunt

one—and I'm going to bash this side of your head into that side."
He touched one side of Goodman's head and then the other. "If
she dies, first, I'm going to use that hammer instead to smash
your jaw, here and here and then yank it out of your face so
you can't control how much you scream when I start cauterizing
every place blood pours out of your face. Then I'm going to take
that hammer and start breaking other various bones throughout your
body. And, believe me, I'll break a lot of the good ones—ones that
make it hard to stand, ones that make it hard to walk and impossible
to lay down and sleep. But first, I'm going to fill you full of enough
of the stuff I have sitting on my cart here to make you feel that you
can do anything and ignore your pain. Then I'll leave you in these
tunnels to wander around as you'll be wont to do. Then I'll let you
sober up on your own, here, in the dark, with all those broken bones
and no jaw."

Ninety-six hours later, according to, Thalia's watch, Red struck
the side of Goodman's head with a five-pound hammer. Then he
instructed two of his men to wrap the body; take one of the carts and
return to the site of the other dead soldiers; pick up those remains
and return all of the bodies back to Chuck's house, where they were
to assign new tenants to take ownership or destroy all evidence of
any connection of it to the tunnel system.

Chapter Twelve

Day 18—8:37 a.m.—Dr. Markus administered sedative to Thalia. He had no explanation. There was no sign of destruction to Thalia's brain, only one hole in and one hole out from the central canal. He patched the holes shut with thread and plastic then left the woman to sleep.

Ernest, meanwhile, sat at an aluminum picnic bench and squirt ketchup onto a hotdog. Red watched him carefully from a corner of a dazzling room that was filled with all sorts of glittery glass from ceiling to floor. The child lifted the hotdog in his hands and turned it end over end as he tried to decide which side to bite down on. He finally chomped right into the middle.

When a siren erupted and the sounds of coins started falling, he turned slightly in his seat towards them. He'd never been in a casino before. It smelled of smoke and something else he just couldn't put his finger on what it was. Women walked by with trays and offered the people sitting at machines drinks. It was one of them that had brought Ernest his hotdog.

A woman with white hair, before one of the machines, clasped her hands together. She smiled and grabbed coins out of a tray, as they fell faster than she could take them out, and dropped them in a small paint bucket. Then she left, and something remained on the floor.

*   *   *

"What is it," Scat asked. "What's it you finded, Mr. Porridge,"

"It appears to be a shiny," Mr. Porridge replied, holding the item with his foot and pointy finger.

"It's for me," Anvil said.

"That's not fair," Sally complained. "You say everything is yours."

"Maybe everything is his," Scat retorted.

"That's right," Anvil smirked. "Maybe everything is."

"Maybe everything isn't," Porridge debated.

"What's that you say, old man," Anvil asked drawing up close to Mr. Porridge and the shiny thing.

"If it's yours, you should know what it is," Mr. Porridge suggested. "So, tell me, what is it if it's yours."

"That's right," Sally said. "You should know what it is if it's for you."

"Maybe it knows what Anvil is," Scat said. "Maybe Anvil belongs to the shiny."

"Give me the shiny bauble," Anvil demanded in a sinister yet friendly voice. "And I won't have to fold you up and put you in my pocket again, Mr. Porridge."

"Not this time," Mr. Porridge replied sternly.

"Yes," Anvil said kindly and softly. "This time." Then he bent Mr. Porridge backwards, folded him up and began to stuff him into his pocket.

"Then you will not see what I see that you do with that shiny thing," Mr. Porridge's now, small voice said.

Anvil unfolded Mr. Porridge.

*   *   *

No one else seemed to notice the coin left on the floor. Ernest took a large bite out of his hotdog and chewed quickly. He sucked on the straw to his soda until his cheeks felt like they might burst. Then he left his remaining food on the picnic table and hurried towards the coin. He was still swallowing when he finally reached the medallion.

It was a quarter, and he carefully picked it up, ensuring the old lady hadn't suddenly realized she'd dropped it and might be returning to collect it. He looked at the machine he had seen the lady playing at previously. Four windows with small pictures glimmered in blinking lights. The words "Three Wishes" rippled in purple and pink.

He climbed up the stool in front of strange game and kneeled before the four windows. There was writing to the side of them, but Ernest couldn't read it. It was too dark. His eyes turned to the enormous ceiling of dark glass, reinforced with concrete columns that had been painted gold. He wondered if anyone watched him from the other side. Dim, orange globes hung down, giving enough light to see where you walked but not enough to read the rules.

Returning his gaze to the machine, his eyes fell on a slim slot which read, "Insert Coin." This, he could read.

He inserted the quarter.

"1 Credits" appeared in red, square letters below the four windows. A button that read, "Spin" began blinking greenly. He pressed it.

In an instant, his breath stopped in awe, not at the sudden movement of images of gems and genie lamps that were flapping before his face, throughout all the windows, but at the concert of subtle clicks, whirs, hums and rotations that flooded his ears from within the contraption. He could hear the guts of the machine before him clattering against its own windings and gears. A cylinder twinged and a small tick clapped a millisecond before one of the wheels spinning before him locked still in the first window.

He watched the second window, third and fourth snap three more pictures before him, three green jewels and a large "3" filled the face of the machine now.

A white button began flashing before him that read "cash out." Ernest pressed it, and the machine spit out three quarters into the aluminum tray. He took the quarters and climbed down from the stool. Then he began to peruse the row of machines alongside his own, where people played, and he listened to their insides clatter and watched their wheels spin. By the end of his tour down the aisle, he decided that none of these machines had the right sounds. He turned down the next aisle, then another and stopped at one that did.

A fat man with one leg, sat before this machine. One hand held a brown bottle and half-smoked cigar. He huffed, puffed, drank and hit the green spin button, huffed, puffed and smacked the button again.

The clicks and whirrs seemed in harmony. Ernest watched the images flash before him and could see which pictures would appear. The first would be a frog, the second a log. The third would be three cattails. A few seconds later, and these very images painted the front of the windows. The man drank from his bottle and cursed.

Ernest pressed to the side of the man, and the fat oaf looked down from his bottle at the child. Ernest reached up and pressed the cash-out button.

"Where's your mom and dad, kid," the man asked.

Ernest didn't have time to listen to the man. He was listening to the machine stop spitting out more coins. When it finally finished, Ernest shoved one of his three quarters into the machine and slapped the "spin" button. Three frogs on lily pads appeared in the three windows. A pair of white lights on the top of the machine suddenly flashed and a bell chimed loudly.

The fat man choked on the next drag of his cigar.

Ernest hit the cash-out button and the machine pushed out a yellow receipt. Before he could take it, the man tore it off and stuffed it into his own shirt pocket. He sucked in on his cigar and returned his attention to the slot machine, where he stuffed in another quarter and hit the spin button. Ernest held out his hand to the fat man and waited silently.

The man ignored him, and it was in this position that Red found him.

"Whaty'a doing in here," Red asked. "This ain't for young'uns, and I can't watch you when you wander off."

"Watch him better," the fat man said and set the wheels to spinning once again.

Ernest snapped his fingers at the fat man and opened his hand once more to him.

The gambler smacked his own hand against Ernest's.

Ernest continued to hold his open palm out.

"He take something from you, E," Red asked, then turned to the gambler on the stool and asked, "You take something from this kid."

The fat man turned to face Red and set his beer in the machine's drink holder. He shoved his cigar in his mouth and puffed. "He can't cash it anyway."

"Cash it," Red asked. "What did he take, boy?"

"My paper," Ernest said and pointed to the man's shirt pocket.

The gambler stood, smirked and sized himself up against Red. "Children can't play in here," he said. "He must be lying."

Red examined the player's arrogant eyes and drew Ernest to stand behind him.

"My machine," the gambler-thief said, rattling his stogie between his clenched lips and teeth as he spoke. "My ticket."

With an open palm, Red forced the cigar into the fat man's mouth and let him gasp it still farther into his throat. Even as the thief's eyes instantly filled with fear and confusion, Red grabbed the man by the hair on the back of his head and drove his face into the plastic of the slot machine. He slammed the face into the control console then the stool, and again the stool. As the man fell to his knees and looked up to Red through a mask of violent rivers of blood from his forehead, eye, mouth, cheek and nose, Red snapped the yellow receipt from the man's shirt pocket.

"My machine," Red spat, then stepped back and kicked the man up under the chin and let him fall to the ground to choke his last on his cigar.

When he finished, he looked to Ernest who was now approaching the man to watch him die.

"Damnit, Red," he cursed himself and grabbed the fat man's face, then reached into his mouth. With a bit of effort, he dug out the fat stogie. The thief took in a deep, frightened breath.

"You're all right," Red said, helping to pull the man back to his feet. "Walk it off, and don't steal in my casino again."

As the man rediscovered his stool and crumpled against his machine, Red looked to a camera poised to look down this row of games. He nodded and pointed at the man, knowing that in ten minutes a few of his men would escort the gambler from the gaming floor to a nice corner, somewhere out of sight of the child, where they could beat him to death.

Presently, Red looked to the receipt and found the number $7,500 printed on it.

"You win this," he asked as he began to escort Ernest back to the table where the rest of his lunch waited.

Ernest nodded.

"Well, you can't keep it," Red continued. "You have to be twenty-one to play."

Ernest stopped walking and held up his hand.

"Those are the rules," Red replied, turning back to him.

But Ernest still heard the whirrs and clicks, and one now to his left seemed in near-perfect time and harmony. He ran towards it, forcing Red to impatiently follow. He found an elderly lady sitting up straight on her stool but holding herself there by propping up on a black, cane. She saw him at once as he stepped up beside her and held up a quarter to play.

"Well, who might you be," the lady asked.

Ernest retreated slightly at the sudden interest in him. Yet, he still held up his quarter.

"Is that for me," the lady asked as Red finally trudged up.

"What did I say, E," Red asked.

"Aww," the woman said. "He just wants to play."

"I'll find him another game," Red replied.

"Sorry," the woman said. She reached into a plastic cup, pulled out a quarter and handed it to Ernest. "Here, you go."

"Oh geez," Red complained and did his best to ignore the woman's glare.

She turned back to her game and sent her wheels to spinning.

"Kid," Red said, glaring down upon Ernest. "When I say—

The old lady's machine erupted in flashing lights and noise.

"Would you look at that," she cheered to herself.

Ernest couldn't help himself, he listened to the room of spinning wheels, and continued his journey up and down aisles. Red followed in full interest now. Finally, Ernest stopped at a machine that had been larger than the previous ones. It had five windows but could show three pictures in each all at the same time.

A woman, young, wearing a thigh-high sun dress sat frowning at the machine. She mumbled something hateful at the machine's last judgment and reached up to pull a large lever at the side of the box. Ernest had seen the levers before and wondered why she pulled it rather than hit the spin button.

Ernest held up his quarter to the slot and frightened the woman. She blew a stray strand of blonde hair away from her lips and took a moment to understand why this child was here. She looked to Red, who stood behind her, now curious himself. Then she looked cautiously about her aisle, this way then that.

"Let me do it," she said and took Ernest's quarter. She put it into the coin slot and reached for the lever. "Just one line, but I get half though if you win anything, 'kay?"

Ernest nodded.

"That fine with you, dad," she asked.

Red nodded hesitantly.

The woman pulled the lever and the wheels set off like horses, fresh out of the gates. The left-most wheel stopped first. The others followed. When the last one finally halted, the slot machine began to chime.

The woman looked soberly down to Ernest. "You just won half of thirty-two hundred credits, that's four hundred dollars, kid." She printed out a yellow ticket similar to the previous one Ernest had won.

"A deal's a deal," the woman said. "Let's go cash it in."

"No need," Red said. "Thanks for humoring the kid."

"You sure," she asked.

Red nodded and guided Ernest away and towards a corner with fewer players. He knelt before Ernest. "How many quarters you have left, E?"

Ernest revealed two quarters in his hand.

"All right," Red said, holding out his hand. "I'll play for you. Which machine you want?"

Ernest smiled and began a brisk walk back into the aisles, and Red kept up. When Ernest stopped again, a man in a suit and greasy hair cursed at him and then at Red for his etiquette.

"I apologize," Red asked. "He has two quarters. Would you mind if we played just one game?"

"Would you mind licking my ass," the man said.

A woman at the machine next to his turned abruptly and threw her drink on him, then she was off of her stool before he could react.

"In what world did you ever think it was all right to talk that way in front of child," she asked, but she didn't want an answer. She wanted to slap him.

"Oh! You stupid b—

She slapped him.

Ernest reached up and hit the spin button without using his own quarter and interrupted the fight.

The woman laughed, and the man complained. Then the machine chimed and added fifteen dollars to the machine's digital bank.

"You're welcome," Red said.

Again, Ernest set out down the aisles. He was nearing the end of another, when a different type of whir, quieter, caused him to stop and listen more intently. Something began scraping against it, gently, then lost momentum and suddenly clacked. Then it kept clacking, getting faster, softer and suddenly stopped and he could no longer hear the soft whir. The sound was no more. He wandered out of the aisle of machines into an open arena of people hovering and sitting around a sea of tables. The voices were a hindrance, but he waited.

"What is it, kid," Red asked.

The whirling sound began again, the scraping followed. Ernest chased after it, racing to find it before—clack, clack-clackity-clack, clack and stop.

He waited. After a minute, he heard it again. In fact, now he heard more than one, but it was the loudest and closest that he was interested in. He raced off again, barely realizing that Red was having trouble keeping up.

A table, where, on one side, a young woman who was wearing a green vest, black pants and a white shirt with a black bowtie stood and faced three walls of other people wearing normal clothes. They all seemed intent as well on what was making the sound that had caught Ernest's attention.

Ernest stepped up and pushed his way into the group. He tried to peer over the table but was unable to see much. The person to his right looked down and was about to say something when the lady in the vest asked if he was lost. He looked up past the faces towering over him and saw the patch of mirrors overhead mixed into the black, glass ceiling.

"Kid, you lost," the lady asked again.

Ernest shook his head and held up his quarter. The table erupted in laughter. The woman lifted a large yellow phone on a cord to the side of her face.

"I have him," Red said, stepping up.

"Of course," the woman said, her eyes suddenly wide at the sight of Red. "I didn't realize he was with you, sir."

Red nodded his forgiveness and then hefted Ernest up to set on his shoulders.

Now, Ernest could see what made the sound. It was a wheel filled with black and red squares with gold and black numbers painted into each. The table held a magnificent grid of all the numbers. People flooded the felt with chips of all sorts of colors.

"No more bets," the woman announced, and then she set the wheel to spinning. She gently launched a white marble into the cylinder. The Teflon ball sped around and around the inside of the rim.

"Five," Ernest shouted.

The table filled with chuckles. The vested lady looked stiffly to Ernest.

The marble suddenly began bouncing and eventually fell silent.

"Red-five," the lady announced but seemed to be asking instead.

"You come stand by me, kid," a man with a squat glass of gold liquid invited. The table erupted again with laughter.

The woman cleared the chips off the grid with what Ernest thought looked like a little wooden rake without any tines. Then she handed out chips to some of the people at the table but stole them from others.

"Place your bets," she said but didn't need to. The people at the table were already dropping chips.

Soon, she set the wheel in motion again. "No more bets," then she released the marble.

"Twenty-three," Ernest announced.

"Red-twenty-three," the woman in the vest was repeating soon after.

Now the table was silent, its patrons looking to Ernest, the lady on the other side of the table forgetting to clear the chips.

Red pulled Ernest down from his shoulders and drew him away from the crowd once more.

"How did you know that? Where it would land," Red asked.

Ernest shrugged his shoulders. "Easy. I can see it. Can't you?"

"Come here," Red said, pulling Ernest behind him to another roulette table also surrounded by people, including a short man standing on a step stool to reach the spinning wheel. This man welcomed Red's presence with a slight nod.

"No more bets," the casino employee announced before turning to the wheel to let loose his acetal marble.

"Black seventeen," Ernest announced the moment the ball hit the well. He startled the little man.

"The kid's right," the employee announced in surprise, after several seconds of spinning and bouncing.

"Send some of that kid's luck this way," a woman guffawed, watching her stack of five blue chips get raked off to the employee's stash.

"Place your bets," the employee announced.

"Where do you think, kid," a gentleman who appeared too poor to be throwing money at a marble and a wheel asked.

Ernest shrugged. "I don't know."

Then, as the ball set into motion once more, he did know.

"Red one," Ernest said.

"Well, that's about half the table," the woman said then laughed.

"Red one," the employee announced as the ball finally dropped into the wheel below the number one, and no one won.

Again, Red set Ernest down. "You can see all that," Red asked. Ernest shook his head.

This time he rushed Ernest to a far side of the casino floor. Video slot machines rumbled, sang, chimed partial scales and dinged. He stopped and looked to Ernest.

"Anything," he asked?

*   *   *

Mr. Porridge put his ear to the ground, and scat peered down into his black earhole.

"What do you smell," Scat asked.

"Sshh," Mr. Porridge replied softly. "I don't hear anything."

"That's right," Scat added. "I don't see any sounds in there at all."

The ground suddenly rumbled, and Mr. Porridge fell up to his feet. Scat fell on his face. Sally grabbed Anvil for support, and Anvil blew black wisps of smoke from his nostrils.

"This is starting to upset me," Anvil said.

"Maybe you should take a walk, then," Sally said. "To your dark place where you can hide better.

*   *   *

They entered a new room: another cold, not-white hallway with silver tile and steel doors. From here, they followed straight and down a set of stairs. They passed several white doors with no identifying marks upon them. Ernest could hear the ratcheting and flappy flaps of paper stacking at lightning speed somewhere behind one of them. Finally, Red stopped at a door and looked down to Ernest.

"Now, E, it's important you don't leave my side anywhere in these halls," Red said. He donned his wrist to show a black, rubber bracelet. "Without one of these, you could get trapped in here and nobody would know, understand?"

Ernest shook his head.

"So, stay with me, right?"

"Right," Ernest said.

Red opened the door and the repetitive churning that he had heard in the hallways suddenly exploded all around him. The sound kept chiming as Red and Ernest entered. Several faces looked up from behind desks with small, white boxes before them. Ernest watched one man about Red's age set a stack of green bills on top of the machine. A moment later, it sucked the stack in from the top and spit it back out into a tray at the bottom.

"Hiring them young now, are you, Boss," an older, gruffer woman said from the back of the room. She sat at a desk with a computer, ledgers and another white money counting machine. A yellow lamp on a wire dangled less than a foot above her head, a foot or so lower than the similar lamps hanging over the other desks in the room.

Red led Ernest past sixteen rows of men and women who sat counting money, and right up to the older woman.

"Pat's my best money counter," Red said. "Every dollar the casino makes comes through this room. You ever counted money, E?"

"We learned in school," Ernest answered.

"Hand me a stack," Red said.

"Sir," Pat asked.

"Just," and red nodded without finishing what he had to say.

"Your money," Pat said. She reached into a box at the side of her desk, which Ernest only now noticed, and drew out a bundle of bills wrapped in a yellow rubber band.

Red took the bundle and peeled off the band.

"Come stand over here, E." Red ushered Ernest around the back of Pat's desk. Pat quickly accommodated making space for the visitor by abruptly rolling her chair out of the way.

"The money goes in here and comes out there," Red said.

"Uh-huh," Ernest replied.

"I tell you what," Red said, brandishing the stack of bills at Ernest. "If you can tell me how many bills are in this stack after the machine counts them, I'll give you the stack."

Ernest nodded.

Red set the stack on the money counter, and the white box burst to life peeling paper strips from the top of the machine and dropping them out at the bottom.

"Hundred and fifty-two bills," Ernest replied before the machine had finished through half of the stack.

The machine finished its own counting, and Red looked at the digital readout. Ernest wrinkled his nose at the posted result in red numbers.

"Sorry," Red said. "Hundred and fifty-one bills." He sighed as though he had lost a bet. "Well, it was worth a try."

"It's wrong," Ernest said. "Do it again."

Pat smiled through gray teeth and said, "I don't think so, sweetie. I'm sorry."

"No, there's seven hundred and sixty-six dollars," Ernest said. "A hundred and fifty-two bills."

"I'm sorry," the woman said, looking at the machine's small display. "It's seven hundred and forty-six."

"It's wrong," Ernest said. "Do it again."

Red nodded to the woman, and she set the stack of money back into the top.

What Ernest now realized was that the room had slowly fallen silent except for the machine counting his money. When his machine suddenly stopped, Pat rose to her feet and stared down at the readout alongside Red.

"Seven hundred and sixty-six dollars," Red said in disbelief.

Pat tore the wad of money out of the cash counter's tray and began flipping through it by hand. When she finished, she flailed through it a second time.

"Hundred and fifty-two bills," she said. "Seven-hundred-sixty-six dollars."

"You knew that before the machine counted it," Red asked.

"I saw it when you shook the money," Ernest said.

Red took the stack from Pat, returned the elastic band, then reached back into the box of cash and took out another bundle.

"Double the stacks or nothing if you can do it again," Red said, peeling off the rubber band but not flashing the many bills within the stack.

"Two hundred and eighty-nine," Ernest said.

"And how much money is there," Red asked.

"Don't know," Ernest said. "I can't see the numbers, just the paper."

Red set the bills on the machine, and it began eating and regurgitating the stack once more. Red covered the readout.

"Twenty-two-eighty," Ernest said as the last bill fell onto its pile.

Once again, Red looked at the readout, "That's what it says."

"It didn't mess up this time," Ernest said. He pointed off towards the more center of the room. "That machine is wrong too, way worse than this one. Something's slipping inside it."

Red handed the stack once more to Pat. She counted and verified the number. Red reached into the box of money again, and this time concealed the stack he withdrew. He squeezed past Ernest and Pat and, with his back to them, opened a drawer well out of view of the boy. He closed the drawer and returned to the machine, where it now seemed the entire office staff was gathering around to watch.

Red held up his stack.

"Two-hundred and twelve," Ernest said.

Red set the stack on the machine.

It counted, and, when it finished, Ernest was silent. He just stared at the money, confused.

"E," Red asked. "What is it?"

"Do it again," Ernest said.

Red did. The machine counted and Ernest's nose wrinkled once more.

"Well," Red asked.

"I don't know," Ernest said. "Something's wrong with three of the bills."

Red began to grin. "Like what?"

"Well, one bill was blue, another was on different paper and I think one had a naked lady on it," Ernest said.

Red smiled brightly.

"Naked lady? You didn't," Pat shrilled. She snatched up the money and began rifling through. She pulled out three bills. "Even you know better than showing a little kid peepshow fliers!"

"You should try him out on the floor," one of the gawkers said. "Probably clean house at the poker tables."

Red looked the man down. "I should kick you out that door," Red said.

"I'm sorry, sir," the gawker replied.

"Except you're right," Red added. He looked back to Pat. "I believe we may have to consolidate all our counting offices."

"Heh, kid," another employee called out. "Wanna come help me fix the timing on my nineteen-sixty-three Stingray?"

"I hadn't even thought about that application," Red said and knelt before Ernest. "E? Wanna see a spaceship?"

*   *   *

Day 22—11:31 a.m.

Thalia's eyes shook, spasmed radically back and forth, and it frightened her. Eventually, she was able to make out a white ceiling fan spinning above her and behind the glare of three electric bulbs, brighter than perhaps they should have been.

She wanted to sit, but her head was heavy. It hurt. She felt and discovered that all above her chest had somehow been secured to the bed in a gauze belt.

"Ernie," she cried, but what she heard didn't sound as clearly as what she had imagined herself saying. When she called for him again, she wasn't sure if her sound had improved any.

Red's face crept up before her.

"You need to stop moving," Red said. "You've been shot in the head."

Shot? Yes. She knew that. She remembered the moment. She could even recall the sound of the instant pressure as the bullet passed in and out of her skull, the thunder it stirred within her and the sting that seemed to drill even deeper as cool air licked around and then seeped into the fresh holes in the front and back of her skull. Yet, where was Ernie? Didn't she remember walking here?

"We need to talk," Red said. "About your boy."

"Where is he," Thalia asked. Red pressed gently against her shoulders.

"Are you trying to kill yourself? Stop moving around," Red said. "E's just fine."

E? No one called him E before. Why was this man intimate enough to call her son E?

"I want to see him," she said.

"About that," Red said. He loosened his grip on Thalia's shoulders when he realized she wasn't trying to press up and out of her gauze head-restraint anymore. "What's wrong with him?"

"Nothing's wrong with him," Thalia replied, more out of habit and necessity than truth.

Red wasn't buying it. "There's no labor grove here, lady," he said indignantly. "You've done so well to respect Salvo this far, don't lie to him now."

"You're Salvo?" Thalia remembered the custom, that she should bow; that these were Salvo's tunnels; that he killed on whim. She had seen it. Yet, she had to wonder how relentless he truly was. He had brought her to the healthcare that she needed. Wait. Where were the tunnels? Where was she?

Her head! Suddenly it hurt.

Red slapped her hand away as she reached for it.

"Don't."

She didn't.

"About that," Red said. "Why are you in my tunnels? And don't lie to me. It's because of him, isn't it?"

Thalia didn't answer.

"I'll take that as a yes," Red said. He moved down the side of her old hospital bed to the two hand cranks at the foot, which could raise and lower her head and legs. He dropped himself onto a yellow couch, second-hand from one of the casino hotels above ground. Then he kicked his feet into a nearby chair.

"So, what is it," Red asked. "Retarded savant? Hyper-autism? Answer me!"

"I don't know what it is," Thalia answered.

"How can you not know?"

"Takes a doctor to find out," Thalia replied. "Go to a doctor, get a diagnosis."

"Get a diagnosis, go to labor grove," Salvo added. He adjusted his position on the couch to allow the breast pocket of his shirt to cough up a gray cigarette. He flipped the cigarette into his mouth; pressed an electric lighter against it and then sucked a bit of red off its end. "So, you're from New Cali then?"

"Good guess," Thalia replied and listened to Salvo bite a deep breath off his Camel.

"Not really," Salvo replied with the strain of holding in his smoke. "There's only two states that lead to the section of tunnels we found you in. One puts handicapped brains into slave labor, the second support their own and runs others out of town."

"Pardon?"

"You don't need tunnels to escape Oregon, just survive the wilderness," Salvo said as he exhaled his smoke.

"No groves?"

"Of course not," Salvo replied. "It would take work from those who think no one else has a right to, people who live under the philosophy that anyone else who works is taking food off their table. Similar mentality as where you came from though."

"I would prefer that," Thalia said. "The grove took my mother. I hate them."

"They're not so bad," Salvo said. "We do something similar with our lime groves in the badlands of Mexico, except our workers want to be there and we pay them, badly, of course, but we pay them."

Thalia frowned.

"You don't approve? Oh well. I've had no shortage of human resources ever since Mince convinced Congress to pass his asinine put-them-to-death-or-put-them-away laws. A single man who's spent his career devising how to kill people is probably not the person anyone should have listened to about preserving life, and now we destroy it as if it's an expectation not an exception. Even I don't do that, so forgive me if I provide the people who've escaped that practice an opportunity to at least be happier."

"I'm just not used to this," she replied. "I don't typically have cartel friends."

"Yeah, about that," Red said. "A person could use friends in the underground. Do you have any idea where you're going?"

"I'm not sure," Thalia replied.

Without saying a word and with a twitch of his head, he inquired.

"My sister took the tunnels some time ago to Utah. She'd always wanted to go to Colorado. Maybe she's there," Thalia explained. She winced, reached for her head and stopped as Red suddenly lurched forward to launch across the room and smack her hand away once again.

Red watched Thalia a moment and then settled back into the couch. "That must be a burden, traveling with him."

"It's a burden traveling."

"Would it be easier without him?"

"I can't even consider that idea," Thalia replied.

"Why? It's a fair consideration."

"You don't have children, do you?"

"I have several, as a matter of fact."

"Here?"

"God, no," Red laughed. "Their mothers would have my head, I'm sure."

"Where are they?"

"I don't know. Well, that's not true. I know where one is, sort of."

"I can't imagine living like that," Thalia said. "That must be hard."

"Meh," Red said. "They're all fine, I'm sure."

"I'd like to see my son, now. Where is he?"

"About that," Red replied. "He has a mind with a knack that could serve him well in a place like this. What if I asked you to leave him with me?"

"What? No! Why would you even ask?"

"Because I want him," Red said. "I could give him a very profitable life here. Can you say the same?"

"His life is just fine."

"You're running through a tunnel that may or may not take you to a better place."

"You run through these tunnels too."

"Yeah, but I'm also very rich and you are very not."

"The idea's absurd," Thalia said.

"Ten million."

"Ten million? Wait, what? You're not seriously making an offer to buy my son."

"No," Red said. "That's what I'm offering to pay him as a sign on bonus. Then another one million a year after that."

Thalia couldn't even open her mouth to speak.

"Your boy just spent six hours on my casino floor and in my money room and saved me a half a million dollars. I want him."

"That's not going to happen," Thalia said.

"Yeah," Red replied. "It will. It's just a question of whether you want to let it happen with you above ground or below ground."

"What?"

"You're a smart woman."

This time, Thalia was afraid to speak, not speechless.

"You can leave your son, let me take care of him and you can go find your sister," Red suggested. "Or I can take this finger, shove it in that hole in your head and swizzle it around, then keep him here anyway."

Thalia tried to sit again. The bandages reminded her she should not.

She cried.

"Okay, Okay. I'll forgive your hospital charges and give you some travel money."

"Please, don't do this."

"I told you. I want him."

"We'll repay you after we get to Colorado," she said. "Now, I want to see my son."

"Yeah," Red said. "About that."

Part Two:

The Daughters

Chapter Thirteen

Oregon—Portland

Judge Eisley commanded respect, whether or not she earned it. She didn't command it in the sense that she carried herself well nor that she served her fellow neighbors. Quite the contrary, she instilled fear, true fear. Her greatest feat was her façade of genuine interest. Truly, she was not qualified to rule from a bench. That's what the auditors said, yet she continued to get elected because, well, she was a judge, and why would anyone be on a ballot to be a judge if they weren't qualified? Thus, she remained unqualified for twenty-seven years and wallowed in her own importance and lack of compassion and law.

A quiet courtroom was an orderly courtroom. She put pencil to paper just to hear the graphite grate for no other purpose than to remind the court that she was the pulse and breath of this room. She wanted the people to hear her writing, to know they would start when it was finished. With this scribble of nothing, she wanted them to know that it was the stroke, her name, that would ultimately end the day for all in her oversight, and no one, especially the voters who never once investigated her capacity, could ever change that. She marveled at her ingenuity, and set her pencil down after drawing a few lines of what she knew was miraculous poetry:

Thus, is silence once again,
soon pleas, tears,
the enemies of law.
How dare they?

She cast her eyes upon her court clerk of nineteen years, and he knew at once she was ready to begin. The clerk lifted a folder, fat as a candy bar, to Eisley's desk.

"Case JT-seven-six-dash-eight," the clerk said without looking away from the lapel of the folder.

The court recorder put each of his words to paper.

Eisley slid the folder in front of her and peeled back the front cover with a pack of documents attached to its inside. She perused the original complaint and flipped through various collections of documents, more for further reaffirmation that the room would wait on her.

Finally, she flipped back to the front sets of pages.

"This is State of Union Labor vs. Sandra Chevalier," Judge Eisley announced. "Is prosecution present?"

"Nina Argentes for the prosecution, your honor." A stout woman who looked more like a boulder than a human being said, standing, then sat. Her chair whined as she did.

Eisley turned her attention on a second table, smaller than Argentes's. "Sandra Chevalier, I presume."

"Yes, your honor," a woman, athletic and slim, thirty-eight years old, said. She reached to pull thick, dirty blonde waves out of her hair. It was habit but unnecessary. Her hair was pulled straight back and already out of her face.

Eisley scrutinized the woman closely before looking back to her folder. "I see you have decided to represent yourself."

"I was denied counsel, your honor," Sandra said. "I request a continuance so I may have time to acquire it."

"Your honor," Argentes said, hefting herself out of her chair once more and straightening her brown, bulbous skirt as much as she could. "Ms. Chevalier has passed the point of legal option."

"I was never allowed legal option, your honor," Sandra said.

"Your honor, every time we get one of these cases, we hear the same defense," Argentes said. "How much time does the court need to waste with these?"

"As often as you deny legal option," Sandra replied. "That's why it's there."

"Your honor," Argentes disputed in exasperation. She leaned with one palm against the table and rifled through a stack of folders until she drew one from its middle. "Must I cite State vs. Orem?"

"State vs. Orem was a case where the defendant was offered counsel by arresting officers, booking officers, the public defender and a magistrate, and turned them down before asking for a continuance. I have been offered no such offer of legal option," Sandra said.

"Your honor," Argentes started and abruptly stopped as Judge Eisley held up a hand to silence her.

"Ms. Chevalier," Eisley said, twisting back and forth slowly in her chair, while tapping the tip of her pencil against her desk. "You are correct, and I'm inclined to agree. You have clearly done your homework."

"Thank you, your honor," Sandra said.

"But we are here now, and I think your performance has made it clear that you are competent to represent yourself," Eisley said.

"But your honor," Sandra tried.

"Continuance denied," Eisley said and immediately shot out, "That's my decision" when Sandra tried to object once more. "Now sit down or I'll have you thrown out. Your presence here is a courtesy not a requirement."

Sandra Chevalier sat back in her cube, metal chair and clasped her hands in her lap so that only she could know they were pretending to strangle the judge.

Argentes too sat, and Sandra listened as the cushion of her ergonomic recliner cried under her fat ass.

"You are accused of thirteen hundred counts of employment without representation," Eisley said. "How do you plea?"

"Not—," Sandra started.

"Stand up," Eisley ordered.

Sandra stood.

"Now, let's try that again," Eisley said, pointing the eraser end of her pencil towards Sandra. "How do you plea?"

"Not guilty," Sandra said.

"Your honor," Argentes exploded. "Point of reconsideration, I have in my possession evidence of more than one-thousand-three-hundred-and-twelve days that Mrs. Chevalier worked without union representation. I have sufficient evidence to require a guilty plea by proxy of evidence."

"A guilty plea will be entered by proxy of evidence," Eisley said.

"Proxy by evidence was never created to force a change of appeal, your honor," Sandra said. "It was created to ensure that murderers with clear and ample evidence of their crime could not drain the court system of time and resources with a 'not guilty' plea. I was employed before union representation laws were mandated and am protected by after-the-fact laws."

"After-the-fact laws are not binding in a democratic court room, you should have requested a republican court room," Eisley returned.

"How do I do that when I haven't even been allowed legal option?"

"Ms. Chevalier," Eisley replied. "Did I not just declare that you had legal competence? You should have said something then. Now, do you have anything to contribute before I consider this evidence and pass judgment?"

"I did nothing wrong," Sandra said.

"Nothing," Eisley blurted and now stood from her seat. "Food-off-the-table laws were created to ensure that people like you could not take food off the table of hardworking individuals who accepted the responsibility to accept union representation. Because of your immoral employment, a deserving family went without." Eisley now looked into her folder. "You are a teacher. You should have known better than to place yourself above another."

"I didn't place myself above another," Sandra fired back. "I put my daughter first."

"You have a daughter," Eisley asked.

"Yes, I do!"

"She's to be remanded to state custody, henceforth," Eisley said. "You, on the other hand, I find are to be exiled for laboring without union representation, sentence to be carried out forthwith from a location of your choice. Do you have a choice for your point of retreat?"

"I do."

"Let's have it," Eisley said turning her pencil to whatever legal document she was now scribbling her notes upon, this time in ink.

"Warm Springs," Sandra replied.

Eisley stopped writing and looked up from her notations. "Are you trying to make a mockery of this court," she asked.

"No, your honor," Sandra answered. "Your judgment is a location of my choice, and that is my right by your own ruling. I will leave state custody and enter my point of retreat at Warm Springs."

"Very well," Eisley said, and she turned back to her document.

"And I'm legally entitled to say goodbye to my family before exile," Sandra added.

"You are entitled to have a certified message delivered, no more," Eisley said.

"Then I have legal call for receipt of family signature before my exile may be carried out."

"Is it your intention to waste this court's time," Eisley now asked, glowering towards Sandra.

"No, your honor. It is my intention to ensure all the rights and privileges of the sentence you have just passed are carried out to the extent of the law."

"Do I have to hold you in contempt," Eisley asked.

"For what," Sandra asked. "Submitting to your sentencing?"

"That can be amended, right now," Eisley said sharply.

"Very well," Sandra submitted. "I call for representative of the state supreme court and grand jury since they have oversight of all judge-related amendments, and I request prosecution assurance against your honor for charge of laboring in a field without correct union representation. So noted, Madam Prosecutor?"

"So noted," Argentes replied.

"The sentence stands as originally issued," Eisley said from behind a stern face. "The court reporter will now document your message to your family and proceed with all entitlements as requested by defendant. Go ahead."

"Thank you, your honor," Sandra answered. "Begin message. Sweetheart, this doo-doo head judge has exiled me."

"K, that's enough," Eisley interrupted.

"Excuse me, Judge Eisley," the court recorder said. "Your interruption is a federal violation of mail tampering. Please refrain. That is your warning." The recorder smirked at Judge Eisley, founded in the knowledge her own union rep was only a text away. The recorder turned to Sandra.

Sandra nodded her understanding. "Continuing message," she said. "There's nothing I can do about it. This judge's head is up her ass."

Eisley groaned.

"Your honor, please," Sandra replied harshly. "Continuing message: you'd really hate her. She's about as evil as they come. Remember, I love you, and we will see each other again, until then, promise you'll try to find your uncle Austin. I know you think he's weird and off the rail, but he'll always steer you in the right direction. Love, mom."

Judge Eisley, slapped her hands against the desk. "Fine, we'll—

"P.S.," Sandra added, "Forgive the judge for tearing us apart, I don't believe she's been laid since the day she stole her robes."

"That's enough," Eisley shouted.

"Sit down," the court recorder shouted back at the judge.

"Continuing," Sandra replied. "Never mind. She's a cow. Never forget the name that tore our family apart. It's Amara Eisley. End message."

"Any last words to this court before I remand you to the bailiff," Eisley asked.

"I hope you can sleep with yourself," Sandra replied.

*   *   *

Shauna read her message, even though she had read it four times already; new parents were coming today. She sat on the side of her bed with its plastic mattress. The rustling from behind her let her know the child from bed six, which was right next to hers, was reaching for Periwinkle once again. Without looking up from her letter, Shauna reached behind and pulled her pink rabbit to her side.

"I was just gonna look at it," Kola's voice crept innocently, but Shauna knew better.

"It's not a toy," Shauna replied.

"Oh."

Shauna started reading her letter once more.

"What is that," Kola asked.

Shauna drank in a breath of annoyance and let her eyes roll to the four-pane window that looked onto a cloud in the shape of a dying goose. She wished it would break the glass to set her free.

"What are you reading," Kola continued to pry.

"It's a letter," Shauna said.

Kola shifted her weight from her mattress onto Shauna's. Shauna turned and glared at the child.

"This is my bed," Shauna said.

"I just wanted to see," Kola replied, and, although she appeared in retreat, she did not do so. She remained still from time, breathing, trying to be quiet. "Is it a story," she finally asked.

"I told you," Shauna said. "It's a letter. A letter's not a story."

"You're lucky," Kola said. This time, she did retreat to her own bottom bunk. "You can read big words. Those look like pretty big words."

"I'm fifteen." Shauna folded the letter and set it between her blanket and pink rabbit, Periwinkle. She turned back to Shauna. "Of course, I can read big words."

"I'm only seven. I'm almost eight though."

"Whoop de doo," Shauna replied.

Across the room, two of the older girls played a game of Chinese checkers over two top bunks. More had wanted to play, but no one could find enough marbles for more than two players. One of the girls had even commented on the fact that all the marbles were there yesterday—but now, no one knew where they had gone.

"People who don't know how to put things away," one of the girls who had wanted to play had complained. When she couldn't, she and another roommate retreated out to the playground.

Shauna watched closely now so she could challenge the winner when this game was over. She grazed her hand over Periwinkle, pet its head and smacked Kola's hand away from trying to do the same.

"I wish I knew how to play that," Kola said. "Will you play that with me when they're done."

"No."

"Shauna? Kola," Daniella Rasmussen announced entering the bedroom with twelve sets of bunkbeds.

Daniella was a tall woman, not skinny at all, and half her face was painted in white birthmark on light brown skin, which looked more like a disease than a natural skin tone. She was nice, or so the other kids said, but Shauna didn't buy it. She did help take her away from her mother. When Shauna finally looked towards the forty-one-year-old, foster-home director, she noticed a short, thin woman and a heavier, taller man standing behind her. His face was shaven, hers had a black mustache, but her hair was prettier on account that he didn't have any. She smiled. He did not.

"These are the Buttses," Daniella said. "They'll be taking you both in. Get your things."

Kola set to scrambling out of her bottom bunk. Shauna picked up Periwinkle and her mother's letter.

"I don't have anything," Shauna said.

Daniella nodded her head. "That's right. We have someone picking up some of her belongings from her previous home. We can deliver them to you."

"That'd be fine," Mr. Butts said.

The Butts woman approached Shauna and knelt before her. "You have this don't you," she asked, reaching for Periwinkle. Shauna pulled the rabbit away.

"You know," Mrs. Butts said. "You can have a blue rabbit if you want."

"I don't want a blue rabbit," Shauna said. "I have my rabbit."

"I'm just saying, if you want a blue rabbit, you can have that."

"If I wanted blue, I'd have gotten blue."

"Shauna," Daniella said sternly. "Don't be rude.'

Mrs. Butts stood and looked upon Periwinkle disapprovingly.

"Can I have a blue rabbit," Kola asked.

Mrs. Butts looked to Kola as if she were an afterthought. "Why? You don't have a rabbit. Get your things, girls. Let's go home."

Kola leapt from her bunk and drew a thin suitcase on wheels from beneath it. "I'm ready," she said.

Mrs. and Mr. Butts led the teen and child downstairs and outside to a lime-green minivan with solar, side panels. Mr. Butts didn't say a word the entire way. He paused only a moment to grunt as he loaded Kola's suitcase into the cargo area.

"What you got in there," Mrs. Butts asked.

"Two pair of pants," Kola said. "Two shirts; my big box of crayons; my picture bible; my—

"Okay," Mrs. Butts replied. "I get the gist. Well, we don't subscribe to oppressive fairy tales in our home. The bible will have to go."

Mr. Butts closed the back of the van and then made his way to the driver's side.

"You have a really nice van," Kola said, climbing into her seat and pulling her seatbelt on as Mrs. Butts closed her rolling door. "Maybe I can stay with you long enough to learn how to drive it?"

"You've got everything all planned out, don't you," Mr. Butts said, turning in his seat towards Kola.

Shauna rolled her eyes, and Mr. Butts smiled back at her, but she knew this look. She'd seen it before. He turned away and stopped giving it as Mrs. Butts finally climbed into the vehicle.

"Good god," Shauna said.

"Language," Kola scolded

"Koko," Mrs. Butts scolded. "We don't judge."

"Her name's Kola," Shauna corrected.

"She's not offended," Mrs. Butts said. "Are you?"

Kola didn't answer. She looked down into her lap and bit at her lip.

"We answer people when they ask questions," Mrs. Butts said.

"Or what," Shauna asked. "You'll take her parents away?"

"All right," Mr. Butts said. "I would prefer a good first day together rather than one fighting. Can we try that?"

The car was silent. Mrs. Butts opened her mouth to scold once more about not answering questions.

"I'll take that as a yes," Mr. Butts said. Mrs. Butts glared at him for interrupting her. "How about we go for some ice cream after we get you two home and settled in your own rooms?"

"Won't that be nice," Mrs. Butts asked, trying to appear friendly again. "Your own rooms?"

"I had my own room before," Shauna said.

"I did too," Kola added, but much more softly. Her head then popped up, "but I bet my new room will be nice too."

"You get the small one," Mrs. Butts said, now looking past Kola and out the back window. "Your sister will get the bigger one."

"We are not sisters," Shauna interjected.

"Of course, you're not," Mr. Butts said. "But you've both had parents abandon you. Maybe you can become friends at least."

Shauna huffed and slouched back into her seat.

"Problem," Mrs. Butts asked.

"No," Shauna answered.

She lied. It was a problem. She had a mother. She hadn't been abandoned, she'd been kidnapped. Kola probably had been taken too—it was hard to tell though, she only seemed interested in games and talking other people's ears off. She appeared sad but didn't cry, so perhaps that was a sign she may actually have been rescued from a bad situation.

Shauna tried to imagine what that situation might have been. She had a bruise under her jaw, perfect slapping zone. There were straight bruises on her lower arms. Maybe someone grabbed her. Physical abuse could most likely be. Yet, from what Shauna could see, Kola was clean, which most likely meant that she wasn't being neglected. She surmised, despite the bruises, which may have come from misunderstandings, or fights with other kids, that Kola, like herself, had been removed for something stupid.

Her thoughts carried her home, where she found her own room just as Mr. and Mrs. Butts had promised. Hers was a plain room of walls and shelves filled with decorations that tried to anticipate what a teenager might like. Other areas were adorned with nonsense, including a poster with a frog looking into a mirror and grinning. Its caption read, "Leap into a wonderful day!"

Kola's room had a single bed, an empty toy box and bureau as well as eggshell walls. Kola pushed her suitcase under her bed and immediately took to exploring the house.

Shauna stayed inside her room, pretending to be settling in.

"Why would you need rubber sheets," Mrs. Butts's voice erupted from down the hall and stairs. "Oh, good lord!"

A few moments later, Mrs. Butts's feet clamored up the stairs and towards Shauna's door. "We need to get new sheets for your sister's bed. Wanna come?"

"Oh, can I please go with you to buy a bed rubber," Shauna asked.

"I understand. Peeing the bed at seven years old?"

Mrs. Butts left the room, closing the door, and went back downstairs, where she then entered an argument over which of the parents should stay with the kids so they didn't break or steal something. Mr. Butts stayed, and Mrs. Butts soon drove off in the minivan.

Good!

That meant it was just Mr. Butts. That kind of foster parent she could deal with.

She left her room and went downstairs.

Mr. Butts and Kola were in the garage when Shauna finally found them. Along the way, she had also uncovered an apple and a bag of hazelnuts. Kola was wearing a white smock that drowned her down to her ankles. The short sleeves reached almost to her wrists. Half of her face was buried behind a pair of green-framed, safety goggles, which might as well have been a snorkel mask on her tiny head. She held a four-inch buck knife and a piece of dead branch. Mr. Butts knelt behind her, showing her how to stroke the blade away from her while tearing a large chunk of wood off the branch.

"Are you crazy," Shauna cried, nearly inhaling a chunk of apple at the same time.

Kola's head popped up to see Shauna, but the goggles weren't quite so movable. To compensate, Kola lifted her head even more until finally she could see down her nose and past the lens of the goggles. She smiled. "I'm learning to whittle!"

"I have another knife," Mr. Butts said. "Want to try?"

Shauna let her eyes roll and carry her head with them so she could march back into the house, up the stairs and to her room, where she stayed until Mrs. Butts finally returned home. Some time later, Mrs. Butts called her down to the kitchen to eat. The food wasn't that particularly good.

As night approached, Kola bathed. Shauna went next, and when she came out, Kola had already been set to brush her teeth and then head to bed in its new rubber sheet.

Shauna then waited in her own room for the house to fall dark and still. She waited an hour more before sitting up in bed and pulling Periwinkle to her side. She peeled the rabbit's back open at a Velcro patch and dug out a sandwich bag filled with the different colored marbles that she had stolen from the Chinese checkers game.

She opened the baggie, took out three marbles, and proceeded out of her room, down the hall and into Mr. and Mrs. Butts's.

Mr. Butts was on his back and snored loudly. Mrs. Butts slept on her side.

Shauna knelt before Mrs. Butts, gently squeezed her nose to cause her mouth to open a little wider, then, as Mrs. Butts inhaled, snapped a marble into her throat. Before Mrs. Butts's eyes could flutter open and grasp just why she could no longer breathe, Shauna had dropped a second marble into Mr. Butts's mouth as well.

As both parents rose, flailing to seek help from the other, gasping to understand that they both needed it, Shauna watched. Neither fell from their bed, rather they became tangled in their own sheet and blanket. The bedding held the Buttses from understanding how to escape. Mr. Butts was the first to become still. Mrs. Butts stopped fighting perhaps thirty seconds later.

Shauna leaned over Mrs. Butts and stared into her dark, dying and deserving eyes.

"My mother didn't abandon me, you kidnapping bitch," Shauna said, and then she let Mrs. Butts suffocate the same as her husband.

Next, she moved towards Kola's room. She could probably have smothered the seven-year-old under her own strength, but a marble was just reward to finally silencing the brat.

Kola slept on her stomach, her legs sprawled, her bedding was twisted and half kicked off the bed.

That could work to Shauna's advantage in case something went wrong with the marble. The human form wasn't the greatest for swinging arms backwards. She could just shove her face straight into the pillow and mattress.

However, Kola shifted gently onto her side before Shauna could put that plan into motion.

As she had done with Mrs. Butts, Shauna knelt before Kola and squeezed her nose, but Kola's mouth didn't open. Her eyes did, and her whole body moved. Shauna dropped her marble and clenched at her wrist where Kola suddenly sliced with the four-inch buck knife that she was whittling with earlier.

Somehow, Kola had gotten to her feet and readied her blade, as if it were an extension of her own index finger.

She kicked her pillow at Shauna.

"Put pressure on it," Kola said.

Shauna cried but didn't scream. For some reason, she was more worried about Kola's deadly reaction if she did. Despite her injuries, she somehow removed the pillow sheet and clumped it against her wrist to absorb her blood.

"Are you stupid," Kola asked. "Fold it flat and wrap it around the cut."

Shauna folded the pillowcase, while Kola watched her closely and appeared unmoved to help, despite Shauna's excruciating attempts to make her pain-riddled hand work. Eventually, the fifteen-year-old had finally constructed a bandage, wrapped it around her arm and followed Kola's instruction to squeeze it.

"You had this planned from the start," Kola said, her voice plain and soft, frightening.

"Yes," Shauna answered.

"I saw," Kola said, still maintaining her poise which could have passed for casual kneel, or calculated lunge. "I thought about stopping you."

"Why didn't you?"

"They were bad," Kola replied. "I have my own mom."

"So, you understand, then?"

"Yeah, until you tried to do the same to me."

"You're not my sister," Shauna said and finally brought herself to her feet, slightly looking down now upon Kola.

"I didn't want to be."

"I could kill you, you know," Shauna said. "Right now."

"No, you can't," Kola replied.

Shauna became a still shadow within a another on the wall. The streetlamp hidden through fat white curtains, seeped through a slim opening and upon the back of Kola's head, turning her face to near black.

"What now," Shauna asked.

"I don't know," Kola replied without moving an iota. "What do you want to do?"

"Tell you what," Shauna said, her tone shifting into something friendly and false. "If you'll give me the knife, I promise I won't try to kill you again and we can go get some ice cream like we were promised we could do earlier."

"Okay," Kola returned. "Come get it, and I promise I won't stab you in the throat."

"Look!" Shauna's shadow suddenly pointed past Kola, then took more of a lunging stance towards. She crumpled forward grabbing at a new laceration.

"I'm not stupid," Kola said

"I need a doctor," Shauna snapped. "You cut me. Twice!"

"You have no intention of seeing a doctor," Kola said, still in full control of her soft and direct voice, which almost didn't sound at all like a child's. "Because they'd have to call the police and interview the Buttses, and they would find them dead with marbles in their throats, like the one on the floor with your fingerprint on it, and after I say I cut you when you tried to kill me, you'll go to the police and I'll go to a new home and finally be able to get out of here."

"Out of here? Where do you think you're going?"

"Away from here."

"Right, you're seven."

"So."

"Look, I've run away from three foster homes, you don't get far living on the streets."

"You don't get far," Kola said. "And who said anything about living off the streets?"

"Where else you going to go?"

"Where are you going to go?"

"I don't know," Shauna said and began stepping back slightly and taking a more casual stand while trying to pay attention to both of her cuts. "Somewhere."

"I don't plan on living on the streets," Kola said. "My mom was exiled. She's waiting for me."

"Your mom was exiled," Shauna asked, her interest and tone suddenly piqued. "Mine was too. She tried to disband a homeowners association."

"Do you know where she is?"

"No, but I have an uncle in Billings. I know his name. You know where your mom is?"

"Yeah, waiting for me in exile."

"You mean, in the wilderness. Are you crazy? Do you have any idea what kind of people are out there? It's not called exile for nothing. People can kill people out there."

"People kill people here," Kola replied. "You did."

"You won't make it. You can't make it."

"I will. I've lived out there every summer when my mom wasn't teaching. I can survive out there, just need to drive there in the van."

"They exiled a teacher," Shauna cried in exasperation. "Why? Did she teach God might be real or something?"

"She didn't belong to a union."

As the room fell silent again, Shauna leaned back against the wall and Kola climbed off the bed, setting it between her and her would-be murderer. She lowered her knife but didn't put it away.

"You know," Shauna said after some awkward time. "You won't get far in the van. A little kid driving would seem strange, but if I came with you."

"Why would I want you to come with me? You tried to kill me."

"That's because I didn't know," Shauna replied. "Still, we'd get farther with me driving."

"And you kill me in my sleep tomorrow night instead."

"No. No more killing. I get us to exile, you get us through it. Deal? I want out of this place too, but Exile? I'd get lost."

"All right," Kola said. She wasn't silent long to ponder it. "You get us there. I'll get us out of it. But I'll cut your throat if you try that again."

"Great," Shauna's shadow said. She stood away from the wall and moved to the door then turned back. "Can we. . .

Chapter Fourteen

. . . eat first? I'm hungry. Want some eggs?"

It was Shauna's best dish. Eggs had been easy to steal from the supermarket. They were small and could be left out at room temperature, provided they were clean, which supermarket eggs usually were. She could carry them in her pocket for later, so long as nothing bumped into her before then.

She cooked her eggs sunny side up but scrambled Kola's. Kola watched to make sure she didn't try to do anything while cooking them. With her injured wrist, it was a little difficult for Shauna to crack a shell then hold the skillet and a spatula at the same time, let alone palm something dangerous into Kola's food without being noticed.

They ate. Afterwards, Kola found some rubbing alcohol, Neosporin and superglue, then helped Shauna use it to stitch her wounds closed. Following that, they set to filling two backpacks with mostly food items from the pantry. One bag came from inside Kola's suitcase, a school bag intended for a much larger person. She filled it with lighter food, such as freeze-dried apples and envelopes of tuna. They put the bulkier and heavier food items like canned sardines, Spam, vegetables and soup into Shauna's, which was a hiking backpack they found in the garage.

To Kola's bag, she added other items from her suitcase, which she didn't go out of her way to share with Shauna. Shauna, rather than sit by and be offended, ran off to scour the house for anything valuable she could sell if it came to that. She found Mr. Butts's wallet with a credit card that could work or might serve another secretive purpose. She took it anyway. A drawer with Mrs. Butts's underwear had an envelope marked "emergency" with five hundred dollars in it. The rest of her drawers held nothing of importance.

When she returned to Kola, she announced her findings and found the child had strapped a dark blue sleeping bag, which she had also found in the garage, to Shauna's camping pack. To the sleeping bag, she had tied two thin flannel blankets that had been sitting in a basket next to a blue couch in the front room.

"I wish they had a lock," Kola said. "You never know when you might need to lock your stuff down."

"I think I saw something that will work," Shauna said and turned to run back up to the Butts's drawers. She opened a bottom drawer in one of the bureaus and began rummaging through leather vests, underwear and a riding crop. She pulled out a set of handcuffs then dug some more to find the keys.

"Take those," Kola said, pointing to a plastic container filled with colorful wrappers that looked like fruit leather.

"That's not candy," Shauna said.

"I know what they are," Kola replied. "We need them."

"What do you need with condoms," Shauna asked almost protectively, a bit judgmental, mostly out of embarrassment.

"They're useful," Kola said. "How many are in there?"

Shauna looked at the side of the container, which, she did admit could pass for a bin of sweets in a quarter-candy store. "It says two-fifty count and it's almost full I think."

"Bring them."

"How many?"

"All of them."

"We don't need all of these," Shauna said. "You shouldn't be needing one of them."

"Yes," Kola snapped. "We need all of them."

They returned downstairs and Kola squeezed all of the condoms into the side pocket on the camping pack and snapped the handcuffs around the aluminum frame. She pocketed the keys.

"We better fill the van," Kola said. "We'll need a bribe."

"We have five hundred dollars," Shauna replied.

"We may need that for after we cross the border," Kola said. "Besides, they only deal in trade."

"Wait a minute," Shauna said. "Where are we going?"

"Warm Springs."

"Are you crazy," Shauna shrieked. "Everybody knows, you don't go to Warm Springs."

"Well, we are," Kola replied point-of-factly. "So, find anything worth trading and start packing it in the van."

Shauna thought about whether or not Kola was fooling around with her and decided that she wasn't when she started digging through the kitchen drawers and emptying their contents on the countertop.

"I saw a bunch of jewelry in their room," Shauna said. "I'll get that."

"That's good," Kola said. "Food's better, bedding, clothes, not too fancy."

"How about the China?"

"Yeah, and I saw some boxes in the garage, not a lot, but maybe enough to pack anything we find into."

An hour later, the girls closed the back hatch on the van. The cargo area had been filled high but not so much as to block the sight of the rearview mirror. The last thing either of them needed was to not be able to see a cop following them. They had filled the front passenger seat and floor, half of the middle section of seats and its floor too. The third row, like the cargo area, was nearly jam-packed with their trade goods.

"All right," Kola said, standing at the door directly behind the driver's seat. They had already turned off all the lights to the house. "Get us there." She swished her finger at Shauna and then the car to order her inside the driver's seat first. Only after Shauna climbed in, did Kola take her seat directly behind the fifteen-year-old's. She gripped the folded buck knife in her pocket.

"How far is it," Shauna asked.

"Not far," Kola said. "I'm sure Alexa can tell you."

A few minutes later, the green minivan backed out of the garage, and then allowed the automatic door to close, swallowing the interior LED bulbs to a sliver and then to nothing, hiding the Buttses until someone had reason to come look for them. By the time they would be discovered, Shauna and Kola should have already entered the territory of exile.

According to Alexa, the drive was a little under two hours. They had a half a tank of gas and three-quarters charge on the battery. They should have plenty of fuel.

It was 3:21 a.m.

—Mt. Hood Village

It was a dark stretch. Trees draped along both sides of 26. Although street names topped stop signs, they tended to disappear against the black raiment of evergreens and dense brush. There were plenty of power lines. The occasional glow of a business sign or the choir of front porch lights illuminated just enough to show that the electrical poles were strung with guitar strings begging to be plucked, but the poles held no lamps, and all soon fell to black.

A house roof would sometimes peek through the trees and reflect light just enough to let Shauna and Kola know they were still in the land of the living. Fences, trailer parks, signs to exile entrance points and protected campground alike all but disappeared into the black of the forest lining the highway. One might have even mistaken the street for the main drag of a simple town. In fact, they would have been right to assume as much.

The highway was quiet, not quite time for commuters to start for work, not for them to wake up even. Ahead was black sky being bitten into by the gray lower fangs of the forest, littered with houses that didn't belong there, but people being what they are just had to find a place to put a house or two in this jawline. As what was before them masticated the traveling van, the surroundings fell black until all Kola could see of it was the reflection of her own face in her window, even in the dark.

It was here that a bolt had fallen off of a junk truck early the day before. It had bounced around, flipped by other tires for most of the day, nearly damaging many but getting stuck in only the green mini van.

As the vehicle thumped a rhythm of chagrin, Shauna pulled the car to the side of the road.

"Know how to change a tire," Kola asked.

"Think I can change a tire," Shauna replied, brandishing her injured hand. "That's not the problem. We're in a no-self-duty district. We have to call or wait for a tow."

"Or," Kola said. "We change it ourselves before anyone finds out."

"Might as well try," Shauna replied then waved her hand a second time. "Oh wait! You'll have to try."

She and Kola dug out the car jack and the small donut spare from beneath the floorboard under their pile of bribery. The first nut broke easily under Shauna's weight as she bounced on the end of the lug wrench. The other four took a bit more work. They pressed the scissor lift jack under the car, and that's when headlights appeared.

"Maybe they'll ignore us," Shauna said.

They didn't. As the lights drew closer, a set of yellow flashers on the roof of the truck began flickering.

"I need you to stop what you're doing," a male's voice called from behind the set of bright lights. The driver's door opened, shut, and a shadow of a wide man drew into his own headlamps. "You can't self-duty here."

As he neared the girls, he took a long stare into the van.

"Where your parents," he asked.

"Our aunt went back that way to get help," Shauna explained. "her phone didn't have reception."

"I like your mustache," Kola said.

"Huh? Oh," the man said. He twisted at his handlebar mustache that had become more Fu Manchu over the years. "Your aunt left you here by yourselves?"

"She said she'd be right back," Shauna explained.

"I'm scared," Kola added.

"We didn't know what else to do but try to change it ourselves."

"Uh-huh," The man said. "Don't blame ya. Two girls on the road, this time of night." He studied them for a moment. "A-ight, I won't report it. Lucky I showed up."

Now, he pulled a flashlight from his belt and shined it at the work the girls had been doing. "I think we can do better than that."

He returned to his truck and came back, dragging a hydraulic jack. It slid under the side of the van and began hoisting its rear into the air.

"You'd have bent your frame, if you'd have kept doing what you were doing," he said.

A couple minutes more and he had the damaged tire removed.

"That'd do it," the man explained, discovering the bolt buried into the tread. "Give me a minute."

He disappeared back into the beams of his headlights and began making rubber pinging sounds from the back of his truck. It was silent for a while, then a pneumatic chorus sang a few measures. When he returned, he lugged the wheel in one hand. Once the man returned to the van, he dropped the tire and let it bounce a few times. Then he repositioned it back where it belonged on the drum and tightened the lug nuts with his own wrench. He lowered the van and tightened the lugs even more.

"There we go," he said as he withdrew his jack.

"How much do we owe you," Shauna asked.

"What you got," he asked.

"Twenty dollars for gas," Shauna lied. "We're running low on battery."

"You got enough juice to get where you're going?"

"I think so, yes."

"I'll take the twenty," he said. "I can bill your mom for the rest, just need her license when she gets back."

"She could be awhile."

"You could use your license, Shauna," Kola said.

"I don't think that's a good idea," Shauna fired back. "It's dark. I don't know if I can find it."

"Not a problem," the man said. "I have my flashlight."

Shauna led the man back to the front of the van, and she began digging through the front seat and compartments for a driver's license that didn't exist. Kola climbed into the back seat and pretended to search as well.

"Where did I put it," Shauna asked.

"Three of you sat in here," the man asked, shining his flashlight over the seats packed full of the Butts's property. "What's your mom's name?"

"Oh," Kola announced. "Here it is."

The man turned back to Kola just as she squeezed the trigger on her Ruger .22 revolver pointed into his face.

The man grabbed at his nose and fell into the vehicle on top of Shauna's lap.

"Go," Kola commanded, closing her own door, "Before anyone sees us."

"I'm a little stuck," Shauna complained, trying to push the man out of the door.

"He'll fall out," Kola said. "Drive."

"You have a gun," Shauna asked, starting the engine and shifting into gear. "Where'd you get a gun?"

"My mom gave it to me. Now go!"

The van lurched forward, and, just as Kola had said, the man slid out of Shauna's lap. If the van ran over any part of him, neither of the girls noticed.

"The hell is wrong with you," Shauna cried as she watched the darkness swallow the flashing lights of the truck that grew smaller in her rearview mirror.

"Just keep going," Kola said. "And don't stop for anything."

They might not have stopped for anything either, except that a roadblock had sprung up ahead of them, five police vehicles, two cars and three trucks blocked the highway from both directions.

—Government Camp

At the sight of police with firearms all drawn upon them, Shauna slammed on the brakes, but none of their cargo shifted too much to become a nuisance.

"Driver step out of the vehicle," the loudspeaker of one of the police vehicles commanded.

"Start crying," Kola said.

"Crying," Shauna asked. "Oh. Gotcha."

Immediately, even faster than Kola could fake her own, Shauna was bawling. Her window rolled down.

"Help us," Shauna cried.

"Help," Kola screamed as well.

"He's after us."

"Driver step out of the van!"

Both of the girls stepped down from the van at the same time screaming for help.

"He killed him," Shauna screamed. "He's coming."

"I want my momma," Kola cried.

"They're kids," one of the officers announced.

"Help," Shauna continued to cry as if on the edge of an exploding heart that was filled with terror.

A shadowy figure broke from the line of vehicles and other law-enforcement officers.

"Who's with you," the officer asked approaching the girls.

"What," Shauna asked.

Kola started crying and screaming, clutching Periwinkle into her chest.

"It's just you," The officer asked and noticed the splotch of blood on Shauna's clothing from where the tow driver had bled on her.

"He killed him," Shauna shrieked. "He killed him."

"He tried to kill us," Kola added.

"Who did," the officer asked. "How'd you get these cuts?"

"We have to go," Shauna said hysterically. "He's after us."

The cop opened her mouth to speak, and Shauna quickly stole her momentum with, "Help us!"

"Okay," the officer relented. "You're safe now. Pull your van through and we'll help you. He's not going to get you."

Shauna ran back to the van, but Kola ran to the officer and hugged her side.

"It's all right," the officer said, and she hoisted Kola against her chest and began carrying her back to the roadblock.

Shauna steered the van past the police vehicles.

"He had a lot of guns," Kola said. "Machine guns, but he shot him with a little gun."

"It's okay," the officer continued to encourage. They returned to the barricade. "The kid says our murderer is heavily armed."

"All right," one of the other officers said, moving to the woman as she set Kola on her feet. "Maybe this isn't the best place for them to be then right now."

"Right," the woman agreed. She knelt to Kola. "What's your name?"

"Cora," Kola said, she wiped her nose on her arm all the way from her wrist to the inside of her elbow.

"Are you hungry, Cora?"

Kola shook her head.

"Why don't you take them to get something to eat until we're ready for them?"

"Sure thing," the male officer said. He escorted Kola and Periwinkle back to the Butts's van.

"Moving," he asked, looking their cargo over.

"It was for a rummage sale," Kola said.

"Don't make us take it back," Shauna started in. "Please don't make us take it back. He'll see us."

"It's all right," the officer said. "No one's making you take it back. We're going to get something to eat. Leave the van here and we'll get something to eat."

"No, no," Shauna cried. "My mom will kill me if someone shoots it. I said I wouldn't leave it. We need this to pay rent."

"All right," the officer said. "Here." He helped Kola and Periwinkle into the back seat of the van and buckled her in then closed the door.

"Follow me and we'll get something to eat."

"Okay," Shauna said.

"Hey," the officer said, placing his hand on Shauna's shoulder. "You're safe, now. We'll get him. Okay?"

Shauna nodded and wiped her eyes, "Thank you."

"Now what," Shauna asked as they both watched the officer walk away.

"Free food," Kola said.

They followed the patrol car farther down the freeway and into an off road, like the others, dark. However, one light grew brighter than the rest of the dim storefronts that lined both sides of the narrow street.

Dolly's Donuts was now baking. At first, they weren't going to open the doors, but it turned out that Tammy, the morning manager, was also officer Madsen's daughter."

"I can make you some sandwiches, but dough's not ready yet," Tammy said. She allowed them entrance to the small diner with its black and white tables across a blue-tile, floor.

"That's fine, Rockstar," Officer Madsen said.

He ordered a plain tuna sandwich. Both Shauna and Kola ordered ham and cheese on white bread. When the drinks came, Kola began fumbling with the straw wrapper. It took her some tries, but she finally pulled the clear straw, which she was surprised this town had, from the paper wrapper. It was mangled. She took a sip and frowned.

"It's broke," she said, pulling the straw out.

"Not a problem," Officer Madsen said, and stood up. "The nice thing about this place is it has more straws."

As he trudged off to get a replacement from the counter, Kola quickly reached across to officer Madsen's paper cup and emptied a napkin holding white powder, that she had been crushing beneath the table, into his diet soda. Before he had grabbed the straw and started back, she had mixed the powder in.

Fifteen minutes later, he made a deal with the girls that he would let them each have an extra donut if they promised not to tell anyone he was taking a nap.

Tammy rolled her eyes and stayed hidden in the kitchen long enough for Shauna and Kola to get back in the van and drive the rest of the way through Government Camp.

"And if someone stops us again," Shauna asked. "I don't think that'll work a second time."

"Just drive," Kola said. "And this time, when I say don't stop for anything, I mean it."

Shauna didn't stop for anything, not even for the line of flashing patrol cars that had crawled into her rearview mirror. They were gaining on the van.

—Outside Warm Springs

"They're not going to ram two kids off the road," Kola said. "Keep going."

The van's rear hobbled. It could have fishtailed and ended the entire chase, but the officer had executed the move poorly.

"Yeah, well, they did hit us," Shauna complained.

"They did," Kola said, lowering her window. She pushed her Ruger through and fired a shot at the lead patrol car. She didn't care where, the police just needed to see she had a gun and was willing to use it.

The lead car fell back.

"They're coming up the other side," Shauna said.

Kola reached through the pile of cargo in the seat next to her and snapped the door open, then turned herself and kicked at the pile of trade goods in it until they had almost all fallen out and into the path of the other patrol car.

"Border patrol," Shauna shouted, watching the border gates of Warm Springs draw within a mile of their vehicle. "Border patrol. And there's already a line! I have to drive off the road."

"No," Kola replied adamantly. "Do not stray from the road."

"We have to!"

"Listen to me," Kola said. "Dit-dit-dit, Dot. Dot. Dot. Dit-dit-dit. Honk it and get into the emergency lane but do not leave the road. That's reservation land."

Shauna honked out the pattern of horn blasts, just as Kola had said them.

"Again," Kola said. "Keep doing it."

Dit-dit-dit! Dot. Dot. Dot. Dit-dit-dit!

Shauna honked it a third time, a fifth time.

The van swerved off the pavement, lost traction in the loose gravel, but Shauna steered it back into the emergency lane.

"Drive," Kola demanded.

"I should have never listened to you," Shauna yelled.

"Drive!"

The wail of police cars drowned out her voice.

They were nearly at the border.

"The gates are opening," Shauna shouted.

The van cracked and suddenly spun around. The driver's airbag exploded into Shauna's face as the female officer's truck from the previous roadblock slammed into the front of the van now.

Kola's knife cut at the airbag, now pinning Shauna into her seat.

"Reverse," Kola instructed.

Shauna, a bit dazed and unfocused, threw the shifter into reverse and hit the gas without looking behind her.

"Get on the road," Kola quipped.

The van swerved back into the emergency lane, wobbling on its tires and throwing its contents all over both of the girls.

A police truck came from off the shoulder and pinned the front of the van against a barrier. The van halted in a shower of sparks where the vehicle met concrete block. A second truck came from the front.

Shauna stomped the accelerator.

"We're stalled!"

She watched as the second truck drew nearer. She wasn't sure why she did it, only that she did, but she quickly shifted the van into neutral.

The police truck struck. The van cracked, screamed, but was suddenly rolling backwards, pushed from the pincer created by the first truck and the concrete barrier.

The minivan stopped as it was struck once more from the side.

"Run," Kola ordered. She tried opening the sliding side door, but it wouldn't release.

Shauna too, was unable to push her door open for the immovable concrete barrier.

The female officer from earlier that night appeared at the passenger door. It wouldn't open.

"The hatch," Shauna announced. She pushed the button to release the back of the van.

Glass shattered from the passenger's door.

Shauna climbed past the driver's seat into the back to follow Kola, who was quickly trying to push past all that they had packed into the cargo area of the van.

The female officer caught Shauna's leg and pulled. Shauna kicked at the officer to no avail and held the back seat to keep from getting yanked out.

The van suddenly lurched. It rolled backwards only a few feet, enough that the border fence passed from the back of the van to nearly the front of the sliding door. The female officer fell away from the van cursing as the fence squeegeed her away.

Shauna began climbing again for the back and was greeted immediately with several hands taking hers and pulling her through the jumbled mess of stolen property from the Butts's house. She was instantly ushered away from the van, close behind Kola.

A cable attached to a winch on the front of a Humvee drew Shauna and Kola's vehicle farther past the border fence.

"Girls down," a man leading a group of ten border guards decked in body armor and M-4s ordered.

Kola dropped, and Shauna followed suit.

"Oregon officers," the border guard captain cried. "You are on Nation of Reservations soil, turn back or you will be fired upon."

The female officer that once thought she had been rescuing Shauna and Kola stood her ground.

"Those girls are wanted for murder," she said.

"You are welcome to wait and see if we accept their request for asylum, twenty-five feet back that way," the border captain said. "Any attempt for you to do otherwise will be considered an act of war upon the Nation of Reservations and we will respond accordingly."

"Give us the girls," the woman police officer demanded. "You have unlawfully aided fugitives that were on our side of the border."

"You are mistaken," the border captain said. "It is you who have crossed borders."

Two more teams of border guards appeared, one on each side of the Oregon-Warm Springs border fence.

"Our border is twenty-five feet back that way." The border captain said, pointing at the road where yellow paint faded the farther out it reached from the separating wall. You are currently guests on our property," the captain responded. "You are about to be our inmates! And we have no extradition treaty with the state of Oregon."

The female officer reluctantly turned and gave the order to retreat.

"Wait," the captain of the border guards said.

The female officer turned back.

"Impound those vehicles," the border captain said, pointing to the patrol cars that had foolishly driven into the yellow zone in attempt to capture the minivan, which, it turned out, was all of the vehicles. "I don't see that they have reservation tags."

"Now wait a minute," the woman officer protested.

"Start walking!"

The guards stood watch as the officers began their long, slow march out of the yellow zone. The captain approached the girls.

"All right, we got your signal," the captain said. "Talk or we throw you back."

"Passage to exile," Kola said. "Payment's in the van."

The captain looked to the bent and broken van with its contents spilling out.

"For two," the captain asked. "Not enough."

"You have a van, solar panels and everything inside," Kola replied. "Except for our traveling gear."

"For two? Not enough."

"Five patrol cars? More than enough."

"Not. . .

237 left
_____

Chapter Fifteen

. . .the right answer."

"I'm pretty sure six vehicles and all that cargo is worth two people, Uncle Austin," Kola said.

"For two regular people, not two murdering children, one of age," the captain said, insulting Shauna with his eyes then turning his gaze back upon Kola. "And one who will be in a few years. You don't understand the value that adults put on little girls."

"Well, what else am I supposed to do, huh," Kola asked. "We only have what we came with."

Captain Austin pointed a full hand towards Shauna. "You trade her," he said. "If there's not enough for two, get rid of one. You know this! What is she doing here, anyway?"

"Less likely to get stopped driving the van."

"Okay, so you don't need her anymore. So?"

"I trade her."

"Right!"

"Except, we made a deal," Kola explained. "Her mother was exiled too."

Austin scrutinized Shauna a moment. He stepped within arm's reach and stared down at her without blinking for some time. "You have the eyes of people I put in prison. Why?"

"I don't know," Shauna said. "Guess I just do."

Austin's M4 barrel was suddenly against her forehead, and his finger curled around the trigger. "Why?"

"I told you, I—

"Bang!" Austin suddenly yelled, and he thumped the front of Shauna's head with the barrel. She stumbled, stood and tried to focus through a sudden, gray throbbing overtaking her mind and vision.

"She may be a kid, but I'm not," Austin said, this time pressing his weapon against the center of her chest while one of his officers took aim from five feet away. "Three lies and you're out."

"I've done bad things," Shauna replied soberly.

"Like what?"

"Lied."

"Yeah? And?"

"Stolen."

Austin held his gaze on her, twisting his head slightly and pressing closer so to squeeze another "and," out of her.

"I've killed people."

"Who," Austin asked shoving his gun tighter into her chest.

"People who tried to make me pretend they were my family."

"How many?"

"Seven," Shauna said.

Austin shook his head to let her know she had gotten the right answer. He pulled away, and his gaze fell upon Kola with the same serious inquisitive look.

"Yes," Kola answered without being asked. "But she didn't, and I let her live."

Austin shook his head disapprovingly and lowered his weapon from Shauna.

"Your mother will not like this," he said.

"Where is she," Kola asked.

Austin shouldered his weapon. His arms were large, and the rifle strap appeared to belong more to a toy that he had outgrown rather than to a deadly weapon.

"Right," Austin said, gesturing that the girls follow him towards the Humvee with the winch still attached to the van. He ordered his men to dislodge the cable. "It's been ten days since she was vested, and the port of entry snipers didn't give her much of a start. I haven't heard any celebratory events since, so I doubt they've gotten her."

Kola climbed up into the Humvee, waving off Austin's attempts to help her. Shauna followed and did her best to pretend that she couldn't see the distaste in his eyes towards her.

One of the guards approached the Humvee holding two backpacks. Kola affirmed the bags were their travel supplies. Then Austin and a short woman named Collette Martinez climbed into the front seats of the Humvee and began driving them farther into Warm Springs, more than 27,000 acres of impoverished and mostly unemployed reservation.

Since crossing the border, the land had appeared sparse. It could have passed for a desert, was it not for the bearable temperature. Farther in, the land was almost as sparse, but now it had view of a few houses and other buildings in the distance. Kola knew that if they continued down 26, they would pass the casino, but she didn't expect to do that today. Doing so would mean having to re-enter Oregon through New Gateway, an equally impoverished farming community that had become another victim to the subtle, yet sudden, grab of the Oregon Division of Land Acquisition.

The farmers had three choices when the event took place: leave with nowhere to go; stay and turn over all crop yields to state authority; or be exiled. For a people who had been bled of any ability to make a profit, let alone save anything for a new house or even travel expenses, the decision wasn't always as open as it sounded to anyone not living in the community. The people who lived here now made money mostly by capturing strangers in hopes that one of them might have a bounty. They would then smuggle these people back to Oregon jurisdiction. If there was no bounty, they had other ways of making money off the people they found. Young women could be sold to the slave traders. Children could be adopted out for hefty sums. Pregnant mothers were often a two-for profit. Pharmaceutical companies in Florida and Canada were willing to pay for sick and elderly. Able bodies could be smuggled and sold to various oil fields and humanitarian organizations throughout the world. All others could be sent to various groups of traders with more capacity to deal with the odds and ends of human lives left over. In short, New Gateway had become a hub of slave trade.

Naturally they didn't get a lot of traffic and, next to Warm Springs, was the most dangerous port of exile. The sovereign nation of Warm Springs bordered New Gateway's west side; a string of federal villages hedged up the south. The rest of their borders were surrounded by protected federal lands. Any act to remove or attack an individual within these lands, outside those established by the rules of exile treaty, was deemed an act of war. As New Gateway was a city of no legal income and under complete gun control, it could not fight federal soldiers already poised and armed within the guard towers and outposts along those federal land borders. The federal army was capable of marching in and leaving the town in immediate devastation. New Gateway couldn't fight back, not along the borders at least.

New Gateway would not dare to expand their operations beyond the bounds of their neighboring governments. At one time, however, they had convinced state officials to seize federal lands back into state protection, a crime which was met immediately with a federal promise to close down all sea and airports under direction of customs. Then the U.S. imposed travel and trade sanctions that would have immediately destroyed Oregon's economy. As the U.S. wanted to retain Oregon through peaceful measures, it had been cautious never to exert these approaches before. Oregon was quick to relinquish their feigned effort to seize federal land.

Martinez turned in her seat and handed two sets of brown and green camouflage shirts and pants to Kola.

"Better put these on. I wasn't expecting two of you," Austin said.

"Good thing you brought two then," Shauna said.

"The other one's not for you," Austin replied. "But you better put them on for now."

"It's for my mom," Kola explained. "This is what the bribe was for."

"Is that all," Shauna asked. "I think I'll be okay without them."

Martinez rebuked Shauna's ignorance with a glancing stab of her eye. Then she laughed.

"The vest is how they know who to shoot and who not to shoot in exile," Kola said. "Orange for the exiles, camo for the recreationists."

"I thought orange was the correct color for protection," Shauna said.

"Orange sticks out," Austin explained. "Snipers can't see the exiles if they wear camo."

"The camo means you're not exiled," Kola said. "Illegal to hunt you."

"That's barbaric," Shauna said.

"That's right," Kola said. "And my mom's been a target for ten days."

"I never heard anyone say anything about getting shot at from any of the other points of entry," Shauna observed.

"That's because the other points of entry are privatized," Austin said. "The border posts here are government run. One of the many ways your Uncle Sam reminds us who's really in charge. The state and federal governments have an agreement to view any exiles fleeing Oregon as traitors to the state. Soldiers and recreationists have authorization to enter the lands, hunt and kill them."

"If you're not wearing this camouflage, you have no legal protections," Kola said.

"Is there anything else anyone wants to tell me about where I'm going," Shauna asked, and began immediately to pull on a camouflage shirt a few sizes too large for her. "Like, if I should just stay here."

"A pretty non-tribal girl like you here," Martinez said.

"We can't stay," Kola said. "It's illegal."

"That's a bit racist, don't you think," Shauna said.

"So was the genocide of my ancestor's, stealing their land and then imprisoning us in a landlock of limited resources."

"I'm sorry," Shauna said. "I didn't mean—"

"You people never do," Martinez replied. "That's why that kind of person tends to have problems around here when they wander off the beaten path or wear orange."

"But you're her uncle, doesn't that mean anything," Shauna asked.

"I'm a close, family friend," Austin said. "That buys visitation or safe passage. I couldn't even stop the guard towers from shooting at her mother."

"Speaking of which," Martinez said as a checkpoint drew upon them.

The Humvee stopped at a barricade arm that spanned across the eastbound highway. Another arm stretched across the road and walk on the other side of it. Three guards watched each entry.

One of the soldiers climbed up along the passenger's door and peered inside. He was a smarmy fellow with an exploring eye.

"Austin," he greeted.

"Sergeant," Austin replied.

"Thought you were on the wall," the sergeant said.

"Escort to exile," Austin replied.

"Oh yeah," the sergeant asked. He looked over the back seat, his eyes locking onto Shauna, glancing to Kola but returning to Shauna. "A little young to turn loose to exile, aren't they?"

"Lift the gate, Sergeant," Martinez said.

"Where's your point of entry," the sergeant asked looking at Kola.

"North," Austin bit out. "Sergeant."

"You don't say," the sergeant said.

"And they'd better get there," Austin added sternly.

"Sure," the sergeant replied. His brow had turned into something angry. He stepped down from the running bar and ordered the gate arm up. The Humvee steered its way through the arm. Austin tapped out a salutation between his forefinger and right temple of his head to the sergeant. Then he turned left to head north.

"You catch that," Martinez asked.

"Afraid I did," Austin replied. He looked into the rearview mirror to instruct Kola and Shauna to get on the floor and stay there.

It only took a few minutes to reach the next branch in the road and head east, but it felt like much longer to Shauna. Kola had already changed from her simple jeans into the camouflage pants which had been selected to fit her perfectly.

"Why do we have to hide on the floor," Shauna asked.

"Because of you," Kola replied.

Again, the Humvee stopped. This time, the guard approached the driver's side.

"Cap," A woman's voice greeted, friendly and encouragingly.

"Officer," Austin returned.

"Heading east, I take it."

"You take it right."

"All right," she said. "Be careful," She added, in a slightly more concerned tone.

"Planning on it," Austin replied.

The Humvee began moving once more.

"They'll be waiting," Martinez said.

The Humvee slowed, drove across to the other side of the road and parked square in the driving lane pointed back towards the way they had just come from.

"Out," Austin said. "Quickly." He looked to his rearview mirror at the hastily gathered vehicles on the sides of the road, prepared to block it as the Humvee would have approached. The vehicles began to pull off the shoulders and into the Humvee's lane.

"Here they come," Martinez said, and she wheeled around in her seat; positioned herself between the front seats; and took aim with her M4 straight out the back window. "Go."

Shauna, confused at what she was supposed to do, and with her pants halfway down found Kola in her lap, ducking beneath Martinez's gun to reach across and push Shauna's door open. Kola climbed straight out, dragging her bag over Shauna as well.

"Come on," Kola urged.

Shauna followed, hastily pulling her own jeans back up but not buttoning them. She grabbed her bag, turned back to get her shoes and turned to leave once more.

"Don't forget these," Martinez called after her, tossing her camouflage pants out at her. "Good luck."

"Hurry," Kola hollered, several yards ahead of Shauna. "They're almost here."

"Better not keep your mom waiting," Austin said. He moved around the front of the Humvee and knelt by its rear wheel to aim with his own rifle. "Don't be a stranger!"

"Keep up, will you," Kola ordered. She was already running off the side of the road towards the hillside.

"Wait up," Shauna cried, fumbling with her backpack over one shoulder, her shoes in one hand and her pants in another.

"No," Austin shouted. "Put on your pants or guards will shoot you when you cross the border."

"You have to be in full camo or orange to enter," Kola screamed. "Where's the border?"

"Thirty feet in front of you," Austin yelled. "Change already!"

Shauna dropped her gear and began removing her jeans once more. She was halfway done when Martinez's M-4 erupted from within the Humvee and the rear window exploded. Shauna kicked off her pants, fumbled to pull on her camo bottoms and listened to two sets of car tires squeal to her right. More gunfire erupted, this time filling the Humvee with bullet holes. Now Shauna ran, leaving her old jeans and almost forgetting her shoes and pack of survival gear. She quickly spotted Kola several yards ahead of her. The child was now turning on her heels with her own pistol and taking aim on a car that sped straight for Shauna, which Kola's traveling companion didn't notice for fear of what was happening around her. Kola fired one shot at the gray Monte Carlo.

Shauna ran straight past Kola, who had resumed running herself. The car didn't slow once.

"All right," Kola suddenly cried. "You can stop."

"Like hell," Shauna screamed back.

The Monte Carlo skidded to a halt only a few short feet from where Kola stood.

"They can't cross the border here," Kola said.

Shauna stopped and turned back to Kola, who pointed up the mountainside towards a line of tall towers all along the border. Each tower had two shadows of soldiers with rifles all aimed upon the Monte Carlo.

"See," Kola said. "And they can't shoot back neither. It would be an act of war." Kola extended her middle finger to the Monte Carlo but could see no faces for its completely blackened windows. It backed away from the border, spitting rocks up into its own underbelly. Then it joined the rest of the vehicles that were now driving off past the Humvee as though Austin and Martinez weren't even there.

Austin stood, seemingly fine after the attack, then raised and lowered his hand at the girls. "Don't let her get you killed," He yelled at Kola. He moved back around to the driver's side, while Martinez repeated Austin's gesture to the girls, but her arm was bloodied. Their vehicle sped off with lights blazing.

"Now, what," Shauna asked.

"Now, they'll find other people to track us once we get away from the border towers," Kola explained.

"Other people?"

"That's what they do. It's illegal, but that's what they do."

Kola slid her .22 into a pocket at her knee and let the Velcro catch. It had barely enough room to fit. She started walking but stopped upon realizing that Shauna wasn't keeping pace. She was pulling debris from her socks so that she could put her shoes back on, all the while she kept pulling her pants up. They, like her shirt, were just large enough on her to be an annoyance. Kola returned to Shauna and reached into the pocket where she had stuffed all the condoms and drew out a handful of them.

Shauna was too busy working her right foot over. It took nearly two minutes.

A section of ground erupted in a cloud followed by the sound of a rifle in the distance.

"That means we have to move," Kola said.

"I'm not done," Shauna replied. Then yelled, "I'm not ready."

"You better be," Kola said, pulling at Shauna's sock. Shauna took the hint, tore off her sock, tied her shoe back to her foot and began walking quickly to catch up with Kola. She picked at the debris poignantly, motivated by the uncomfortable feel of hard shoe material against the top of her foot. She balanced it all with pulling at her pants.

"Finally," she said, announcing that she had cleaned out her sock.

Kola stopped walking and turned back to Shauna.

"They'll give us two minutes before they shoot a warning again," Kola said. "Fix your foot."

Shauna slid off her shoe, then pulled it back on, this time with her sock. Soon they were moving again.

"K, this is going to be a very long trip if we don't find a rope or something," Shauna said, still trying to manage her pants.

Several yards later, Kola turned back once more to Shauna and instructed her to drop her pack. Shauna did, and Kola handed her a string of colored condoms, opened, unrolled and braided together to make a belt. "Tie up your pants."

"We have twine," Shauna said.

"Not enough to waste on your pants," Kola said. "Less than two minutes, remember."

Shauna fumbled the sticky ribbon of condoms through two belt loops before the ground coughed up another warning of dust. She hoisted her bag back over her shoulders and began marching again. After several more minutes of walking, they stopped again and got the condom belt through the remaining loops just as another warning shot to get moving struck right behind her heel.

"Do they see how close that was," Shauna cried, freezing in realization of how easily Kola could have let her die just by standing there.

"They don't care," Kola said, already walking. "Move or they will hit you."

Shauna grabbed her bag and began walking quickly without pulling it over her shoulders. Despite her best efforts to keep pulling up her pants, they slid from around her waist and she was forced to stop. She dropped her bag.

"I have to stop," she said.

"Not yet," Kola replied. "Pull them up and keep moving."

Shauna did. Several steps later, she dropped her bag, pulled up her pants, grabbed her bag, pulled her pants and then kept walking. It didn't matter what she tried. She couldn't defeat the oversized pants. After several repetitions of this exercise, Kola finally announced they had walked far enough to stop for two more minutes.

Together, they tightened the condom belt around Shauna's waist without tying a real knot into it.

"If you tie it, you'll never get it undone, just loop it," Kola said.

Shauna did just that, not even caring that Kola had used too many condoms to make the belt. Nor did she care, as they started walking again, that the ends of her belt had gotten into a rhythm of flapping against her thighs. Despite all the nuisance, her pants were finally holding in place.

They continued to follow the mountainside, climbing higher above the road that contoured with the border of Warm Springs. It wasn't so much to get farther away from the border as it was to simply get a higher view of dangerous people that may be following.

"Did we think to bring any water," Shauna asked. She had already begun to feel her heavy breath drying the saliva out of her mouth. She sucked some more out of her salivatory glands.

"No need to carry extra weight before we need it. We'll get some here soon," Kola said. "You can always suck your thumb until we get there."

"That's stupid; I'm not drinking my own blood."

"No one said anything about drinking your own blood. Just suck your stupid thumb."

Shauna popped her thumb into her mouth and sucked on it. It was such a dumb idea, but as she sucked on it, and her mouth filled with saliva, it was enough to make her tuck that tidbit of information into the back of her mind in case she needed it later, which she suspected she would but not now. She could already hear the cooing of a creek below and see the approach of a river ahead of her.

They didn't draw close to it though. Kola turned alongside it, keeping distance from the river and a military, guard outpost that had once been a campground.

"They have a vending machine," Shauna observed.

"So."

"So, they might have water."

"We don't have to buy water," Kola replied curtly.

They kept walking until the guard shack had passed behind them. Below was the Deschutes River, and a dirt road meandered alongside it. The only evidence that it had been used recently was a pile of drying horse dung.

"Should we get some of that," Shauna asked.

"Why," Kola replied.

"Well, it burns. We could save it for when we make a fire."

"You know, just because we're camping doesn't mean we have to start lighting every pile of shit we see on fire."

"There's something wrong with you, isn't there?"

"Yes," Kola replied plainly, and she kept hiking.

Shauna followed, and sucked her thumb once more. They continued on as the sun rose with the morning. Then Kola suddenly turned towards the road. They crossed it and began climbing down the ravine towards the river's edge. When they reached the water, Kola set down her bag, which Shauna took as permission to remove her own, and she did. Once more, Kola reached into the pocket with condoms and took out two. Then she dug through her own bag and pulled out a small bottle.

She walked to the bank of the river and crawled down to her stomach so she could dangle over a sharp ledge and reach a condom down to the water's surface. She set the bottle and one of the unopened packages next to her. Next, she opened the other condom, unrolled it, stretched its mouth a bit and dunked it into the current. As she pulled herself up from the river, she held up the condom with about a quart of water in it.

"Hold this," she said. "Don't drink it."

Shauna obeyed, while Kola opened her bottle and took a pill from it to drop into the latex canteen.

"It needs an hour," Kola said. "Unless you want diarrhea, which would really suck out here."

Shauna's face betrayed her disappointment.

"Remember, no knots, just loop it around something or you'll have to puncture it to get the water and it might explode," Kola explained. She returned to the river with the second condom to catch some more of it. She prepped and strapped this one to the side of her own bag, then dug back into the camping pack to rummage through the canned food. She took out some tuna fish and punched two holes in the top with her knife. "Here! Drink this."

Shauna drank it and stopped only a moment to ask if Kola wanted any. Kola took a small amount than handed it back to Shauna who patiently sucked out every drop of water from the fish within.

"That's a waste of food," Shauna said, staring at the can that she couldn't open.

"Oh geez," Kola complained. "Watch!"

She took the can and knelt next to a rock with a somewhat flat edge. Here, she flipped the can over and began scraping the can back and forth over it. After about a minute, the rock had worn the seam of the container down so she could peel off the top. She pinched some tuna between her fingers and ate it.

"That's all you do. Just drink the water first if you're thirsty, or it leaks out." Kola handed the can back to Shauna, who was all too happy to eat and feel stupid about it at the same time. When she was done, Kola handed her back the lid and made her put the empty can into her camping bag.

They zipped up their gear, climbed the hill once more and continued their journey along the river's meandering vein.

Another pile of horse crap appeared.

"See," Kola said. "There's no shortage."

They walked in silence for some time, long enough for the sun to climb into the beginning of afternoon. Shauna guessed it must have been about an hour, but she wasn't sure, and she was thirsty. She hadn't asked because the kid was starting to make her feel a bit self-conscious about her intelligence.

So, she asked, "Think it's been an hour, yet?"

"More like two," Kola replied, pulling something from her pocket, inspecting it and dropping it back. "Two and half."

"You have a watch?"

"Yes." Kola stopped to take a drink from her water balloon.

It took Shauna a moment to figure out how to get a drink from the prophylactic, but she finally did so. The taste wasn't great, and the spout was still a little slick, but she appreciated the hydration more than she didn't appreciate these other details.

"So, where are we going," she asked.

"Lookout Mountain," Kola said.

"How long will it take us?"

"Probably three weeks with the way you're slowing us down."

"Three weeks," Shauna screamed.

"Yeah," Kola replied. "You ready to get moving now?"

Shauna nodded.

"Good," Kola said. "We need to cross the river now."

They climbed back down towards the river's edge. In this place, an island had risen up and cut the river's width in half. The water rushed in white and emptied out the same way, but somehow between these two torrential areas, the water had become calm.

"That's like two-hundred feet," Shauna said. "I don't think I can swim with this on."

"You don't have to," Kola said, taking off her shoes. "You can wade across here."

She stuffed her socks into her shoes, tied the laces together and flung them all around her neck. She crossed, and Shauna did the same. The water was deeper than Kola had anticipated though. She had been here before, when it was only up to below her knees, but this time it was almost up to her waist. She raised her bag above her head and kept moving forward. Shauna too removed her pack and hefted it a little higher while she crossed.

On the island, the girls put their shoes on long enough to march the two more hundred feet across the dry land. Shauna had suggested that they consider staying to get a fire going for lunch.

"And if there's a flood," Kola asked. "Never camp on a river island."

Something about the way Kola also kept looking over the ridgeline suggested there might be another reason for her wanting to keep moving.

The water on the other side of the island was faster, louder, a little whiter.

"But you can still wade across," Kola said. "You might want a walking stick though."

After about five minutes of searching, they each found a branch they deemed sturdy enough to help support either of them across the water, which worked until Shauna's. . .

227 left

Chapter Sixteen

. . . didn't. She forded the river fairly well, a few near missteps along the way, but nothing serious, up until her walking stick became lodged in some rocks, and the shock of the motion was enough that it threw Shauna's balance sideways, and she was on her way downstream.

"Just stand up," Kola screamed after her, but Shauna couldn't hear it over her own panic pounding through her veins and water burying her head as the weight of the canned food in her pack pulled her straight down and across the river-bottom.

Shauna might have been trying to swim, she didn't know. Her arms were flailing, and she was making every motion to stand that she could but only managed to roll against the floor.

It wasn't until she hit a rock with her shoulder that she finally had the thought to try and stand. She stood and held onto the rock, which, as it turned out, was nearly as tall as she was but also awkward to hold.

She caught her breath and heard the patter of footsteps through brush not too far from where she now stood.

"Is the bag okay," Kola asked from the opposite bank.

"I'm fine! Thanks for asking," Shauna yelled, and she tried to shake the pain from her injured wrist, hoping neither of her wounds had reopened.

"You want to tell me how a seven-year-old can walk across this river, but you can't?"

Shauna looked to Kola for help that she didn't know if she wanted for certain. All she knew was that her bag felt heavier now. The good news was that, because of a bend in the Deschutes, she was closer to the bank, but the twenty feet of white water between her and land no longer seemed so simple.

"Think you can handle walking through a foot of water now, or should I build you a boat," Kola shouted.

Shauna looked once more at the water in front of her, and her head began to clear a bit thanks to the rock she had anchored herself to. She realized at once that she reeked of stupidity. Although the water before her was white, she could also see the ground beneath it. Where she stood now, the water only came up to her knees.

"Well, why didn't we come this way in the first place," Shauna roared.

"Because that area behind you has undertow," Kola answered sharply.

As Shauna glanced towards the island they had just left, she could see the water was much darker only a few yards away. It wasn't nearly as white or frightening on the top, but she immediately felt a dark pit take root in her stomach.

"How you're not down there drowning right now is a frunkin miracle."

Leaving a touch of her embarrassment at the rock that had saved her, Shauna began walking once more, carefully. Halfway across, she shouted out, "Kola, your foot."

Kola looked down, somewhat confused until she saw the blood draining onto the ground.

"What now," Kola asked. She sat down and found a large spear of broken beer bottle lodged into the ball of her foot. "That's annoying!" She snatched the glass from her flesh; set it to the side; then dropped her backpack next to it. From inside the largest pocket on the front of the pack, she fished out a red, plastic, first-aid kit and a small bottle of peroxide. By the time she had the medical kit opened and the bottle cap off, Shauna had reached her and also dropped her bag.

"Here," Shauna said. "I can get at it better."

"Thank you," Kola said, handing the bottle to her traveling companion.

Shauna held the bottle to Kola's foot.

"Ready," she asked.

"Just do it already."

Shauna poured all her disdain for Kola into abruptly splashing much of the contents of the bottle onto Kola's foot, eager to see the brat scream when she realized how serious her wound was. It was a deep gash, definitely needed stitches. Even as she poured, the blood spilled out and tried burning into black. However, Kola didn't make a move, didn't react, just stared at Shauna as if to ask if she was done playing around yet. Shauna stopped pouring and found the cap to return to the bottle.

"This needs stitches," Shauna said. "Worse than what you did to me."

Kola Reached down and pressed a medicated surgery prep pad against it. Shauna held it in place while the child then tore open an envelope with a small hooked needle and some clear fishing line.

"You're not serious, are you," Shauna asked.

"Why? Didn't you clean it enough?"

"I'm sure it's clean," Shauna said. "I just can't do this."

"Here," Kola said and then began tying line to the needle. When she was done, she handed it to Shauna. "Down through one side, up through the other. Don't go too deep, I want the stitches to work their way out."

"No way."

"Fine! "I'll do it."

"You can't reach," Shauna said and waved her hand for the needle and fishing line. "How do I tie it.

"Tie it in a bow. Who cares? It only needs to hold long enough for the skin to reattach to itself," Kola said. Then, frustrated, tore out another condom and showed Shauna how to slip a quick two-handed square knot into it.

"K, I think I got it," Shauna said.

She rinsed Kola's foot once more with peroxide then stuck the needle to her skin. It felt rubberier than the actual rubber she had practiced on. The skin was slippery; the bleeding wouldn't stop. She thought the needle had caught a time or two, but it kept slipping off.

"Are you pressing hard enough," Kola asked.

"Yes, I'm pressing har—Ow! Mother fu—," Shauna's thumb went back into her mouth and silenced her immediately. She turned and threw the needle in a sudden fit of anger. The needle and fishing line flew out into the river.

"Did you seriously just throw my needle in the river," Kola asked.

Shauna realized at once that she had.

"Moron," Kola said, then she reached to tear open another surgery prep pad. She pressed it into the wound and opened another package that held a thick cotton wad. She shoved that up against the surgery prep pad. Shauna held these both in place while Kola located a roll of gauze.

"Doesn't that hurt," Shauna asked as she watched Kola wrap the gauze first around her foot, then her ankle and then repeating the process until the entire roll was gone.

"I don't feel anything," Kola said.

"You should be in agony," Shauna said. "You can't walk on that. We have to get help."

"No," Kola replied. "It's okay." She pulled her shoes from around her neck and tugged out a sock, then redressed her feet. After she had finished tying her shoes, she packed up her first-aid accessories and trash and returned them, with the broken glass, into her pack. She stood, hefting her bag back over her shoulders. "See, I'm fine."

She pointed at Shauna's shoes with their socks, the laces had held onto her pack more than they had to Shauna.

"Your shoes are wet. Put some rubbers on your feet before you put your socks back on to keep your feet dry," Kola said.

Shauna took out two condoms and used them to cover her feet.

"Turn them inside out so they don't rub as much," Kola added.

In a few more minutes, they were walking again.

"We'll be able to stop up ahead and dry out while we have some lunch," Kola said.

"Your foot's going to get infected." Shauna said.

"It's wrapped pretty good," Kola replied.

"I don't get it. How do you not feel that?"

"I can't feel it," Kola replied.

"You must have lucked out and missed every nerve. I'd be in a ball crying right now."

"That's because you can feel," Kola said. "I can't."

"No pain? You can't feel any pain?"

"No," Kola said.

"So, you could walk through a chainsaw, cut off your leg and not even know it was cut off?"

"I would when I fell, wouldn't I," Kola asked, "But no, I wouldn't feel it."

"That's kind of sad."

"I don't feel that neither."

"What? Sad?"

"Anything," Kola said. "I told you. I don't feel anything, now can we drop it."

"Wait, nothing? You don't feel anything, no emotion? Nothing?"

"I feel like I asked you to drop it, didn't I," Kola said.

Shauna dropped it. She didn't speak for some time. How long, she wasn't sure, and she was actually a bit afraid to ask the seven-year-old. She followed in silence, expecting the child to start limping or giving into her ego and admitting that her foot hurt, yet Kola just continued walking with no limp, no complaining and no hint that that she even cared. Her sneaker didn't turn red in any way, so Shauna took that as a good sign.

When they reached a spot where a creek joined the river, Kola announced it was a good place to stop and eat. She set down her bag, and together they rummaged through Shauna's pack for lunch. They settled on a can of fruit cocktail and one of ravioli. With her knife, Kola showed Shauna how to punch holes halfway up the side of the tuna fish can that they had opened earlier that day. Then she folded the lid that she had grinded out from it until she had squared it up so it could sit in the can. Now, she pulled a small, clear bottle of kerosene from her pack and squirt some of its contents into it.

Meanwhile, Shauna had set off with the duty to open the ravioli in the same manner that she had seen Kola open the tuna fish before. She'd found a much bigger rock, and, although it took her a few minutes to get the right feel to the process, she sanded the seal off until she could remove the lid.

Kola struck a match and dropped it in the tuna fish can. A yellow film of flame floated across the top of the fuel. She set the raviolis onto the little stove.

"You should take your socks off and let them dry a bit," Kola said. "Blankets too."

She took the can of fruit cocktail and used her knife to poke pouring holes into the top, spending extra time to make them wider for the thicker juice. She produced a small canister, which had also been in her bag, and telescoped it into a plastic cup to hold the liquid. After, she took up a nearby branch about a quarter of an inch in diameter and broke off one of its smaller limbs. With her knife, she quickly scraped the bark off to reveal white, dry wood. Then she carved out a point. By the time she had started working on a second skewer, Shauna had set her footwear to drying on a rock and then took the initiative to open the fruit cocktail.

Kola reached into the container of ravioli with one of the skewers and stirred it. She felt the bottom of the can to ensure it was warming up and used one of her sticks to pull a square pasta out, still cold. She ate slowly, relishing every bite.

"You actually like those," Shauna asked.

"Don't you?"

After about twenty minutes, they had eaten and loaded up their packs again. Their camp left nothing behind. Shauna's socks still hadn't dried, but they weren't nearly as wet as before. Still, she did as Kola suggested and put two more condoms on her feet to keep them from blistering. They felt strange, restrictive in one sense and squishy-slimy in another, but they stayed on her feet. Her socks helped to ensure that. Then they packed up their still-wet sleeping gear and the two adventurers broke away from the river and began to follow the smaller creek.

They found their way to a paved road, overrun with brush and trees that had punched their way through its rocky skin. On the other side of the creek, a Union Pacific slithered past a nearly barren mountain and towards the coast, carefully keeping secrets to itself of what was ahead for the girls. It didn't matter, Kola already knew enough of it, but she was more concerned right now with the man and woman that had been tracking them from the other side of the river.

She doubted Shauna had seen them, and she wasn't certain if they were following, so she'd sit on that information for now. The train had its secrets, and she had hers. As the train rolled by, it carried four people with rifles, roaming the roofs of the cars. None of them seemed interested in Kola nor her traveling companion. Good. That meant, Kola didn't have to waste any bullets. They followed the creek, which snaked under a train bridge that should probably have been condemned. They filled two more condoms each with water from the creek and began a march up a hill instead.

They moved much more slowly going up, but they kept moving, nonetheless. Three hours later, they descended the hillside and rejoined the creek.

"How do you know which stream to follow," Shauna asked.

"It's the same one," Kola said. "Just a shorter walk is all."

Then they followed the creek for three more hours, into a canyon and away from the view of public. The young hikers snaked through the ravine past green and yellow hills, taller than they had climbed before. Sometimes their edges were rounded and easy to climb over a hill, allowing them to shorten time from their trek. Other places, the mountains had sharp walls and the girls had no choice but to take the same windy, lengthy path as the trail of water.

They took a break every hour, but it only lasted a few minutes to take a breath. Kola insisted they move. When the sun finally drew close to the finality of the western horizon, Shauna had just caught view of what had once been a small town. As they drew closer and the sky drew dark, she could see it was worse than that. It was a ghost town. It had been one long before these two travelers had arrived. Some might argue that it was a ghost town when the first scanty was built here.

"These buildings will crush us in our sleep," Shauna said, observing one of the structures already leaning but refusing to collapse on its own. She wanted to walk over and help it topple, put it out of its misery.

"There's a place up here we can sleep," Kola said. "If no one's using it, it should be a bit safer."

Fifteen minutes later, they approached one of the prominent, sturdier buildings. Kola watched the streets for a moment, looking to the windows for any other residents. She saw none, but that didn't mean they weren't there. One way to find out for sure was to send them an invitation. She dropped her bag on the porch. The building looked like it had been built to blend in with the rest of the town, but it was clear it was just a replica. The paint had dried to reveal modern compressed materials for the walls, and these had corroded in ways much worse than the wood from the older structures. Beneath this corrosion was lumber shipped from the average home-improvement yard. A routered slab that once read, "Visitor Center" now hung bare and by two black nails to the side of a doorway without a door.

"See if you can find something bigger than our used ravioli can to boil water in," Kola said. "People leave things behind sometimes."

As Shauna set out to do so, unsure of where to begin looking in this town, Kola set across the street to a structure that had already collapsed. She retrieved some lumber that had broken down into kindling and pieces large enough to sustain a lengthy burn and stacked it all in the road in front of the old tourist center.

She had just finished placing three rocks to begin creating a firepit in what used to be the main thoroughfare of the dead town, when Shauna appeared with a box about the size of two cinderblocks. The awkward manner in which she held the object close to her body, told Kola it was heavy.

"I found this," Shauna said. "It doesn't lock. I think it could hold water."

Kola opened the door on the small safe, found it clean—that is, clean of rust—and she mugged an impressed approval. "We should probably wash it out first."

Shauna's eyes narrowed and told Kola where she could rot, then she set off at a slow pace towards the creek.

"Think you can manage it without falling in," Kola called after her.

By the time Shauna returned, Kola had a fire going in her ring of rocks. Shauna set the safe on a sturdy stone that Kola had placed near the center of the fire. They opened two more containers of food. One was a larger beef stew can and the other was for Spam.

They ate. When they were done, it was dark, and the water in the safe still hadn't boiled yet.

"We should get to cover," Kola said. "We can go ahead and leave this here. It's almost dead. Might as well get some sleep, and it should be ready in the morning."

Shauna submitted to Kola's suggestion. They packed up their empty cans back into Shauna's bag. After the day's travel and five cans lighter, Shauna wondered if her pack had actually lost any weight. Then Kola used a stick to roll the branches in the firepit until the fire doused and coals remained. They'd reignite, for sure, but she needed an illusion right now. Then they carried their bags into the tourist center. The building was wide-open with worn and filthy counters. A room for an office sat open along the back wall. Two more cavities were to the side of it. These were once restrooms. The plastic placards still held the shapes of a man and woman.

Kola moved straight through the building, crouched and signaled for Shauna to do the same.

"Stay close," Kola said. "Stay down. Be quiet."

She set out the back doorway, pausing only a moment to listen and watch the distant dark. Then she moved away from the building and into its wild, vegetative surroundings. She crawled lightly and slowly. About twenty paces away from the structure, she stopped and began slapping the ground until, all at once, the ground changed tone.

She rummaged around the area for a moment until she found a ring-latch embedded in a hidden door. With Shauna's help, she pulled it open enough for them to squeeze through. They climbed beneath the door and down a slope made of earth into a dark cellar.

Here, Shauna could do nothing but listen to Kola's movement. She heard a zipper from about three feet to her left, a wrapper crinkled and plastic cracked. A bead of red appeared in the dark. Kola shook it feverishly and the bead turned into a tube, bright enough to show they were in a small tomb about eight feet by eight feet, and only six feet tall, if that.

"Good," Kola said. "No roommates."

"Roommates?"

"You know, skunks, wolverines, possums, snakes—things that might have attacked us by now," Kola said. She dropped her bag on the ground. Shauna dropped hers and Kola retrieved another condom. She opened it, inserted the glowstick and blew air into it. Before she had even tied it off, the condom had turned into an orange lantern that magnified its original glow.

In a few minutes, they had the backpack and flannel blankets off of Shauna's bag.

"This is why we don't fall in the river," Kola said, feeling the sleeping bag. For the most part, the flannel blankets had dried, but the bag was still damp. She opened and laid out Shauna's sleeping gear. Kola then pulled her own sleeping bag off her pack and opened it. The rubber sheets Mrs. Butts had purchased the day before fell out of the roll.

"What did you bring that for," Shauna asked.

"Oh, you know. For in case we might need a ground barrier or a waterproof tent in the state that never stops raining, or, if say, someone were to fall in the river and get her sleeping bag wet."

Kola opened the sheet to cover the wet sleeping bag, then covered that with Kola's own bag. Next, Kola retrieved a small envelope with a plastic, metallic emergency blanket. She unfolded it and set it out in between the two flannels on top of all the other bedding.

"You try to marble me, and I'll make this your grave," Kola said.

"I believe you," Shauna said.

"Keep it that way." Kola kicked off her footwear and told Shauna to do the same, pointing out that her feet needed to breathe.

In thirty minutes, they were under their covers, but neither girl was asleep, and they listened to the sounds of muffled voices from above ground.

"What if they find us in here," Shauna asked in a hushed tone.

"If they know the cellar is here, they might," Kola replied in an even softer whisper and then held her .22 up from beside her. "Cover your ears if they do."

"Who do you think they are?"

"Don't know. Could be hunters. Could be slavers."

"Why would they be all the way out here?"

"Followed us. Maybe from the reservation, most likely from New Gateway. They probably waited until they thought we were asleep."

"Well they couldn't have gone far," a man's voice shouted close enough that if he looked down, he might just see the cellar door despite all the earth on top of it.

"All right," a woman's voice answered. "I say pitch the tent here. We can't follow them in the dark. We'll head back in the morning and get Goldman. He'll track them down."

"You sure," the man asked. "That's a day there and a day back. They'll have big head start."

"If anyone can catch up to them, Goldman can," The woman replied. "Look, we'll bring horses this time. We know we're dealing with children now. We'll catch up."

Sounds and more conversation followed as the two debated the best place to set up camp, and a fire.

"Stupid," Kola whispered. "They already have our fire burning."

The muffled sound of a hammer driving in tent spikes told the girls that the tent was close to the cellar door. A wooden 'thunk' rattled the door, and Kola sat up with her gun drawn.

"Damn this ground is hard," the man said and went back to hammering. This time with healthy earth sound.

"Come morning, they're going to see that door," Shauna said.

"Perhaps. There's a bit of growth on it." Still, Kola didn't seem convinced herself. She retrieved a handful of condoms from Shauna's pack, as well as three of their empty cans. "Bring the lantern."

They both moved silently up the incline. While Shauna held the lantern, Kola set to opening the condoms and then tied five of them together. She searched the bottom side of the cellar door for some kind of hitch in the surface to secure the end of the rubber string. She found it in a cracked splinter, large enough not to break. She wedged the end of the rope through the splinter and tied it. Then she took what had been the fruit cocktail can and searched the earthy walls and floor for several small stones and quietly set them into it. She slid the open end of the can with rocks into that of the wider tuna fish container and pulled another condom over the entire contraption to hold the makeshift rattle together. She tied it and then used two more condoms to string around the circumference of the rattle. She tied the rattle to the condom rope. The other end she stretched until it was a loosely taut line that rested gently across the incline into the cellar. Finally, Kola stabbed her knife through this end. If the cellar door should open, the condom would slice on the knife and the rattle would alert them rather loudly.

"If we crack the door, they won't see us, we could just shoot them. They wouldn't see it coming," Shauna whispered as they returned to their bed.

"We could," Kola replied. "Or we could wait for them to bring us horses and more supplies."

"Can we do that? Doesn't that depend on them finding us so we can?"

"They'll find us. That's what they do."

They settled into bed, the emergency blanket crinkled between the layers of flannel, but not so much that Kola seemed concerned that the campers above ground could hear it.

"Do you snore," Kola asked.

"No."

"Good. Then I won't have to drop a marble down your throat."

"We have a deal," Shauna said. "Get me through this, and you'll never see me again. You don't have to worry about me."

"I know I don't," Kola said. "I just want to make sure you know that. Goodnight."

Kola, however, did not lay down to fall asleep just yet. She produced a book and began to read it under the glow of their lantern.

"What are you doing," Shauna asked.

"I'm reading."

"Now?"

"Yes," Kola said. "Now."

"What could you possibly have to read that's more important than sleep with two slave runners camping above us?"

"Macbeth," Kola replied. "Now shut up. Lady Macbeth is pretending to faint."

Kola held her gun close, the safety on, and allowed the text of Shakespeare to help her drift into dream. She didn't wake up again until the explosive outburst. . .

211 left

Chapter Seventeen

. . . of obscenities from outside.

"How'd you manage that," the woman's voice asked, laughing.

"It's this stupid tent pole," the man complained and could be heard stomping on the ground.

"It's always the stupid tent pole." She kept laughing. "Come on, I'll put a Bandage on your boo-boo and kiss it better."

"You know what," the man replied. "Go to hell."

The rubber lantern, although diminished, continued to glow softly enough to remind the girls that they weren't in complete darkness. Kola went back to sleep so she didn't have to wait it out. When she awoke again, there was no sound from outside, and Shauna was chewing on hazel nuts.

After a few stretches and morning grunts. Kola stood.

"We forgot to check your dressing last night," Shauna said.

"I suppose we did," Kola said. "How's your arm."

"Oh, you remember that, do you," Shauna said. "It hurts. How do you think it feels? Thank you very much!"

Kola made her way up the slope to the door and carefully listened a moment.

"They're gone," Shauna said. "I heard them leave."

Kola listened, nonetheless. After several minutes, she pressed her back against the cellar door to create a crack of light, which immediately blinded her. She continued to listen and let her eyes adjust before she decided that the man and woman had, indeed, left.

Shauna helped her push the door open, filling their small cavern with blue, waning dawn.

They gathered their belongings and left the cellar.

"They're not entirely stupid," Kola said while patrolling the vicinity where it was clear a tent had been set up. "They didn't leave much evidence they were here."

They returned to the firepit where black and gray coals kissed.

"Good," Kola said after spitting on the side of the safe and watching it sizzle. "It's not cold. You should get some water. I'll stir the fire."

"I want to check that dressing first."

Kola didn't argue. They tended to her injury.

The blood had clotted in the gash of her foot. Fibers from the gauze and padding had dried within it. Tearing either away, brought fresh blood.

"I don't think I realized how deep this was," Shauna said.

"Does it look infected," Kola asked. "Is it red?"

"No. It looks normal, otherwise. I guess that's good."

"Okay," Kola said, thinking. "I need you to dig in and tear out the scab then."

"Are you stupid?"

"We have one roll of gauze left and a long ways to go," Kola explained. "Now that I know it's going to take them some time to go back for horses, we have time to close it, and I can't do that with a scab in it. I need you to pick it out."

"You have another needle for me to sew it shut, too?"

"We have superglue."

"That's going to hurt like a—never mind. All right." Shauna started to reach for Kola's foot. "Why didn't we just do that yesterday?"

"You mean after you threw the sewing needle into the river," Kola asked. "I was afraid you'd superglue your finger to my foot."

Shauna's face sharpened. "I should wash my hands first."

"We should have some alcohol towelettes," Kola said. "In case you wasted all the peroxide yesterday."

Shauna found the towelettes and used one to clean her hands.

"What about these surgery prep pads," Shauna asked. "Should I use one of those too?"

"Yeah, but don't waste it cleaning your hands."

Shauna painted Kola's injury with yellow-brown strokes from a small pad. Then she began tearing out the dried blood from within Kola's laceration. She heaved a time or two when she thought she saw bone.

"I'm sure it's just white tissue is all," Kola reassured.

"That doesn't make it easier."

"Don't be a baby."

Shauna, whether out of curiosity or vindictive behavior—she wasn't sure—stuck her finger in the gash that was about an inch-and-a-half long and had separated about a quarter of an inch. Part of her wanted to see Kola finally scream in pain from the surprise touch.

"I can feel your finger, stupid," Kola said. "I told you, it doesn't hurt. Sterilize it again."

As Shauna continued to work on the seven-year-old's foot. It was evident that this wasn't the first time the child had injured it. It didn't surprise her; it was a soft foot. Any kind of object could have cut her. One scar was the shape of a V on her heel. There was another, a straight line, that reached from her big toe to her heel, breaking only a moment away from the arch of her foot.

Shauna kept gouging dried bits of blood out of Kolas' heel. "There's a lot of bleeding here." Her fingers had become greasy, and she wasn't quite certain that she was removing any more. She scraped out the crevice with her fingernail just to make sure.

"How'd you get this scar, the big one," Shauna asked.

"Oh," Kola said. "I did that. Didn't work though; I still couldn't feel it."

"I think I have it all." Shauna grabbed one of her condoms of water. "Think this is okay to use to wash it out?"

"I'm sure it's fine."

Shauna placed a bit of medical tape over a water-filled condom and punctured a hole in the top of it so she could spray out the bottom of Kola's foot without the condom breaking. She couldn't see any more bits of scab. "I think that's it. It's still bleeding though."

Kola pointed to a small strip of butterfly bandages. "You can use those to pull the skin back together and hold it in place while you glue it shut."

Shauna opened one of the butterfly bandages. "Oh, I see. Okay. Yeah, that makes sense."

She applied three bandages, and they did what they were supposed to and helped draw the wound closed. She rinsed the foot again. Then she took the superglue.

"Just squeeze it over the entire cut and let it dry," Kola said. "Over the bandages too."

"You won't be able to pull them off."

"They'll wear off. It's what stitches do."

Shauna dripped the clear glue over what, thanks to the butterfly bandages, looked like a simple laceration in the skin. They allowed it to dry.

"I think that might have it."

"It's holding?"

"Yeah, I think so."

Kola nodded her head in approval. "Good. I won't have to put my foot in the coals then. I hate the smell of burning flesh." After her foot dried, she wrapped a gauze pad to it with a medical wrap. Finally, she drew on her sock and shoe.

Shauna then took five condoms to fill with water. Kola refueled the fire, and once again marveled at how careful their company last night was to hide their presence. Other people would have either used the fire they had built or put it out. Kola had hoped they would use their fire so she could learn something about them.

When Shauna returned, they boiled the water in the safe, dipped it out with their cans to cool faster, then eventually poured it into the five condoms. Once they had packed away the water and finished eating down a can of peaches, spaghetti rings, and a tin of sardines, they started their journey again, following the creek.

"I should have asked how your feet were," Kola said.

"They're fine," Shauna replied. "Dry. Why?"

"A lot of people get blisters when they're not used to hiking."

"I never said I couldn't walk. I've walked a lot, just not in the mountains," Shauna explained and then added "or with rubbers on my feet."

"You're not still wearing those, are you? You know your feet need to breathe, right?."

"I took them off last night."

"Oh, right. Where are they?"

"I think I might have left them in the ground back there."

"Gross." Kola stopped a moment and kicked a section of tall grass to break it. "We could have used them to leave a trail for them to find us."

"You want them to find us?"

"If we hurry, we can meet up with my mom in eight days, maybe nine, ten at the most. If they bring us horses, we can do it faster, save some of our food for the rest of the trip."

"And then I can trade in my camouflage for my orange target? Or wait for you to decide I'm expendable, right?"

"It won't come to that."

"We have a deal, remember."

"I'll get you to the border," Kola said. "Don't you worry about that."

Here, Shauna realized that Kola had begun to lead them away from the creek that they had followed for most of the previous day.

"Is that smart," Shauna asked. "Leaving the water?"

"We'll find more," Kola replied. "Still, don't drink it all."

They began climbing a hill with open ground and scattered trees that, at once, made Shauna wonder how anyone could get lost out here. Then it made her wonder how difficult it would be for whoever was following to find them.

This hill went up gently then dropped just as such. Another hill, taller, immediately began to carry them up again, and Kola continued to maintain her lead on Shauna. Every so often, the kid would leave some sort of evidence that they had passed through. Here was an intentional trudge through tall brush. A while later, she broke a branch, then began whittling it down to nothing in particular and dropped it on the ground. She dropped one of their empty cans.

Steadily they continued to climb, and Shauna's shoulders increasingly grew tired and sore. Her breathing, at times, became thick with uncertainty of how much farther she could last. When the hills dropped down, it wasn't much easier. Going down, she was more aware of the burden she carried, pushing extra upon her knees every time she pressed forward one more pace.

Still, despite her sore knees, heavy lungs and her parasitic backpack, she continued to keep up with the child forging ahead.

Kola stopped long enough to break a condom and its water over the ground. She left both behind.

As the girls reached the apex of the next hill, this one a bit taller and perhaps a little steeper still, Shauna couldn't help but feel some sort of relief in the far sight of another vein of water. They stopped for a light bite to eat. It wasn't quite lunch time, but they couldn't pass up the opportunity to prepare some more water.

They opened a chicken soup and split it evenly between two cans; filled them the rest of the way with water, and ate. They filled three more condoms and dropped in their sanitizing tabs.

Kola used the larger beef stew can to carry water to cool off their firepit, and then started back into climbing a sharper hill.

"Why don't we use that road," Shauna asked, observing what she believed had once been a highway and was now the beginning of a forest reclaiming what mankind had scarred it with.

"Because less shade and more dehydration," Kola answered. "Not to mention lots of people we don't want watching us tend to observe the roads."

When they reached the creek at the bottom of this long hill, Kola reminded Shauna to take her shoes off to cross. Shauna suggested Kola wear a condom on her foot to protect her wound. While she was at it, Kola tossed the wrapper into the path behind them. Afterwards, the creek was an easy crossing, and then they started up another incline into low grass and hardly any trees.

"Might as well be a desert," Shauna complained.

"Speaking of which," Kola replied. "Don't drink all the water. We probably won't see much again until tomorrow," and she was right, by the time they had stopped for the day, all they had seen were more hills."

"Why is it that it rains all the time here but not for us," Shauna complained. "Oh no, better not rain for us a single drop."

"In this case, I'd prefer to sleep dry," Kola said.

Here, they stopped. It was more of an open area than Kola liked. Anyone could see the tent, even people not tracking them. Kola showed Shauna how to construct a shelter resembling a simple ridge tent out of branches. They set out Shauna's sleeping bag and created a roof out of the rubber sheet. It was narrower in here than it had been in the cellar.

Then Kola found some brush that could conceal them and set up their real sleeping area.

Shauna tried to start the fire, but her choice of large kindling wasn't quite small enough.

"Kindling," Kola said almost in disbelief. "Small stuff to burn the bigger stuff. Look!" Kola opened another condom, unrolled it and slid it into the oversized kindling that Shauna had tried to ignite. "Smaller." She lit the rubber and it lit up like a slow fuse with nothing to blow up. It burned enough that even Shauna's fuel source could ignite. "See," Kola said. "Condoms. The perfect survival gear."

The fire burned until dusk, when Kola had finally allowed Shakespeare to make her tired, and she showered the pit with dirt to kill the flames but not quench the embers.

In the morning, they ate again, packed their shelter and gear and began towards higher ground, where Kola wasn't able to see if anyone was following.

"Maybe they ran into problems," Shauna said.

"Wouldn't surprise me," Kola replied and kept doing what she did best, move forward—up this hill, down the next and repeat until they came to another creek. It was more than that, however. It collected into a small pond, serene, hidden if you didn't know it was there, an oasis in a canyon. They ate once more. Kola threw a fishhook and some thread into the pool and nursed it for about an hour until she decided they couldn't wait anymore for fish to bite.

"You had another hook," Shauna asked.

"Yeah, your point?"

"We could have sewn your foot."

"I didn't want you losing this one too," Kola replied. "Lose this, and we're out fish too."

They journeyed on, back up, down, up again; the rolling, growing hills didn't seem to want to end. Until finally, the next mountain rose and seemed to level out a bit, but they walked down and followed the canyon now.

Here, something caught Kola's attention. It was a lean-to, not a good one but not bad, perhaps, for someone who learned about how to build one from a book.

"Someone might have left something we can use," Kola said as she began her way towards the shelter.

No. It wasn't just a lean-to. Some of the earth had been dug out to give more space for whoever might have been sleeping in it. Kola thought for a moment that if she had a few minutes with it, she could make the roof a little stronger, maybe even flatten it against the earth more and hide it beneath ground clutter so they could wait beneath it.

She poked her head in. A grungy set of old, wool sleeping bags lay inside. There appeared to be more, but she didn't lean in deeper to discover what it all was as she was suddenly aware of other footfalls approaching, trying to sound sneaky. She reached to her pistol.

"There's nothing for you in there," a man said. He appeared far older than he should have and clenched a shotgun, which he held on Kola but turned every so often towards Shauna. He wore an orange outfit. It had been plastered with dirt to make it harder to tell what color it really was. His beard was filthy, teeth were dirty and face may have more cheekbone than skin any day now.

"Food in there," he asked. His wiry arms shook as someone in need of nourishment."

"We didn't take anything," Kola replied.

"Your bag," the man bellowed and stabbed his barrel against Kola's pack. "You have food in there?"

Kola's finger now wrapped around her pistol wedged between her back and the pack it carried.

"Do you," the man yelled.

"Allen," a woman's voice crept from behind Shauna. "They're just children."

She had been quiet enough that Kola hadn't fully noticed her, although she had thought there was someone else.

"Children in camouflage," Allen replied, without lowering his gun.

"Allen, stop!"

"Yes," Kola mimicked, flipping the safety off her concealed firearm without revealing it. "Allen, stop."

Allen snorted angrily and finally stepped back, lowering his shotgun but not removing it from a safe, blasting draw.

The woman stepped out, wearing the same type of grime and filthy orange outfit.

"We're sorry," the woman said. "Someone took our stash. We could use some help. Do you have anything you could spare? We would be grateful for just some water."

"Why are you out here," Shauna asked.

"Why you wearing hunting gear," Allen asked back.

"So, we don't get shot," Kola replied.

"Yeah," Allen asked. "How's that working out for you."

"Allen!" The woman screamed out of frustration.

"Why are you wearing orange," Kola asked.

Allen didn't respond. The woman knelt before Kola, revealing the deep shadows of her sunken eyes and empty cheekbones hidden beneath strands of knotty, brown, but may have been blonde, hair. She bent into the lean-to and pulled back one of the sleeping bags to reveal an even deeper hole, squared and lined in branches. Leaves, stripped away from their twigs, filled the bottom of the hole, and sleeping in them was a baby. A pacifier, perhaps the cleanest object in the camp, lay still in her mouth. She was wrapped in a light jacket. An orange collar from her onesie appeared from within her swaddling.

"This is why," the woman said. "The Mince Act prohibits birth without a permit."

"They exiled a baby," Shauna asked.

"It was that or death," the woman said.

"We have formula," Allen said, trying to change the subject. "We can't get clean water though. Someone stole our bucket."

"Spoon too," the woman said. "Don't have a bottle."

"Well, don't you have milk in there," Kola asked, pointing to the woman's chest.

"Not enough," the woman said, taken aback at the question. "I need food too, water. Tried some bad water, made me sick. That's why we stopped here, so it could pass."

"We were planning to head out tonight," Allen said. "When it was dark and safe to travel again."

"You shouldn't travel at dark," Shauna said. "Doesn't wildlife hunt at night." She set down her pack and peeled a balloon of water from its side.

"Are those," Allen asked.

"Yes," Kola replied, glaring Shauna over.

Shauna handed the water condom to the woman and took the opportunity to look in on the baby, who had a face fuller and healthier than her parents.

"I can't believe they made a baby wear orange in exile," Shauna said. She looked to Kola, ignoring the stink-eye she presently received from her.

"Fine," Kola said, and Shauna watched the little girl's demeanor turn into that deceptive child-like wonder that she had fallen trap to herself. "You know, you could always come with us. We can boil water and fish. I have a hook, and you have a gun. We could hunt." She turned to Shauna. "Please, can we go hunting?"

"Uh, sure," Shauna replied. "I mean, if that's okay with Allen and, I'm sorry, we didn't catch your name."

"Melody," she replied.

"Oh, please," Kola said. "Come with us. We're heading east to the border to meet our mom. She was exiled too."

"I don't see why not," Melody replied then, "Allen! Will you please put the gun down!"

"Oh," Allen replied half-mindedly. "Sure."

"Okay," Kola said. "But we have to leave soon. If we hurry, we can set up camp next to a creek a few miles that way."

Shauna imparted a can of corn and chili to Allen. Kola showed him how to wear the seal off. He ate faster than he should have, without heating it up, and set what he didn't eat, which was most of each can, next to Melody. Melody had opened the loosely tied condom, then mixed several pinches of formula into its water, bit a hole into the tip and was now letting the baby suckle off of it. She held the condom just above the tip to make sure the baby couldn't swallow down any of the soft rubber.

"Oh," Kola marveled at the baby. "She's so cute. What's her name?"

"Riley," Melody said. "Would you like to hold her?"

"Can I, Shauna?"

"That might not be a good idea," Shauna replied. "She needs to eat, and we need to get going."

"Right," Kola replied, but Shauna could see she didn't believe her reasoning, and Shauna knew she was right not to.

Allen folded up their two dirty sleeping bags and tied a rope around each. He slipped a leather belt through the lashings and set them to the side. All that remained beneath the shelter now were two coats, and a box of shotgun shells. He took up those too.

"Well, we're packed," Allen said. "Told you, someone cleaned us out. I guess our bags didn't interest them, or we came back before they could pack them up. I don't know."

Once Riley and Melody had eaten, they all started moving along the canyon. They walked much more slowly now. Allen carried his two bags on his belt, offered to carry Shauna or Kola's bag but gave up trying to convince them. Melody carried Riley, whose face was buried beneath a corner of her jacket swaddling. She made sounds now and then, mostly the gumming sound of her pacifier.

Because they moved slowly, the sky was almost black by the time they had reached the next stream of water.

"I'll start a fire," Allen said.

"Oh," Kola burst excitedly. "We can do what we learned in school. It's really neat."

"What's that," Melody said.

"Do you have a knife or a shovel," Kola asked.

"I have this," Allen said, producing a five inch and slender hunting knife.

"If we dig a hole, we can bury the fire so people won't be able to see us in the dark," Kola replied. "We just dig a pit about two feet down and carve out a chimney."

"I see where you're going," Allen said and went straight to digging out the ground with his knife, dulling his own blade rather than the one Kola kept hidden on her own person.

Instead, Kola took one of their empty cans and used it to help pull out loose soil. By the time the hole was dug out, it was too dark to see the bottom. Allen realized the urgency to start hollowing out a chimney. Ten more minutes, and he had one that reached from the side down to a little higher than the floor of the pit.

"That's okay," Kola said. "My teacher said you can just fill up the hole until it's level with the chimney.

Kola took two more condoms from Shauna's bag, opened and unrolled them, then snapped a lighter under one. The condom began burning and she lowered it into the pit. She set the second condom and both wrappers on top of it, then quickly began tearing tufts of dead and drying underbrush and grass from the area and sprinkling it over the flame. A dim, orange glow grew from the ground. The others helped to bring in more fuel. After several minutes of nursing the flames and searching for wood in the dark, the fire was built. She set a few long sticks over the top of the pit, strong enough to support a can or two.

As water boiled, they ate. The firepit, though glowing with blinding orange, gave hardly any illumination to the area. The people sitting around it were little more than gray-tones under the waning moon.

"So, why, are you two out here," Melody asked. She nursed Riley while she, herself, drank the juice from a can that no longer held pineapple chunks.

"Mom didn't belong to a union," Kola said.

"So, you're sisters, then," Allen asked. He used two forked branches to scissor a can of boiling water off the top of the pit and replace it with another can.

"No," Kola and Shauna replied.

"Have the same mom," Allen said. "Sounds like sisters to me."

"Does it," Shauna asked.

"She was adopted," Kola said. "We don't pretend she doesn't have her own family. We're on our way to find both."

"Then I guess it's a good thing we found you, isn't it," Allen said. "This is no place for kids."

"Perhaps not," Shauna said.

"It's pretty scary out here," Kola added. She set off to begin setting up a place to sleep. Tonight, would be in the open and under a sky of stars. She buried her and Shauna's bags beneath a potentially loud clump of bushes next to where she set up the sleeping gear.

When she was done, she yawned and announced she was going to bed.

"Goodnight, Riley," she said, approaching the mother and daughter and stroking the baby's head. She hugged Melody without stirring Riley, and then hugged Allen. "I'm really glad you found us too. Now we're not alone out here."

She crawled into her bedding and drew her pistol to her chest so she could pull it quickly if she needed. Then she made sure not to fall asleep until everyone else had settled in. When Shauna slid under the covers with her, they looked at each other, silently wondering which one of them should keep watch first. It was Shauna who eventually drifted into slumber.

A couple of hours later, Shauna rustled awake, and allowed Kola to sleep.

By morning, both girls were asleep. When Allen began rustling at the bags, Shauna sat straight up. Kola nearly revealed her gun.

"Just me," Allen said. "I thought I'd start some breakfast. "I got the fire going again."

"I think there was a can of hot dogs in there," Shauna said. "And some powdered eggs. Here, let me find them for you."

Immediately, she regretted the decision. Alan stayed a little closer to the bag than he needed. She could feel his eyes fondling her. She didn't have to look at him to know. No man needed to hold a position this close to anyone unless he was trying to pretend to be looking in a sack when he was really peeping down her shirt.

She rummaged through her bag until she pulled out the hotdogs and eggs. Kola concealed her gun and set to filling up more condoms with the water they had boiled the night before. She set the bladders to the side where they wouldn't explode on the ground. She filled up eight this time, then gave the remaining water to Allen so he could mix and cook the eggs.

"So, what do you say we go south today," Allen asked as he finally set to eating his own breakfast that he had served up in one of the other remaining cans. "There used to be a road down that way. We could use it."

"We should stay away from the roads," Shauna said. "They're traps."

Kola silently approved.

"Well, we can't keep climbing mountains," Allen replied. "It's not safe, wastes energy."

"But that's where we're going," Kola replied. "That's where my mom is."

"Listen, Kola," Melody said. "We discussed it, and we think your mother would agree that she would want you to be safe."

"You don't know my mother," Kola replied, and Shauna watched Kola's cold nature begin to bleed once more into her face.

"The mistake we made was that we left water and tried for higher ground," Allen said. "If we stick with water, we can catch fish, and other animals will come to it and we'll eventually get out of Oregon to the south."

"I can see how that might sound like a solid plan," Kola said.

"But we're not going that way," Shauna replied.

"I think you should reconsider," Allen said, leaning forward where he sat. He tried to hide his discontent over the opposition.

"All right," Kola said. "Let's reconsider. You want to follow a water source that is a magnet to every other living thing in this forest, including the people who want to hunt you. Then you want to find a road that pirates are watching. They have vehicles, we don't. And then you want to retreat to another state that doesn't let anyone out once we get there. Mister, we're going east."

Now, Allen stood. "K, I don't know how your mother lets you talk to her, but we don't talk to adults like that, missy. And I won't stand for it. Not in my camp."

Allen's head jerked to the side and broke open. The gunshot was instant. Melody stood, screamed and fell over a moment later, unable to even grasp at the explosion from within her chest.

"God damn, did you see that," a scrawny man with a fake, orange tan cheered. Kola recognized his voice at once as they had heard it above their camp only three nights before. "Two. Two shots! Bam and damn! Did you see that?"

"Didn't I say wait," another man, taller, devious and wiser than the other two complained. Kola knew at once he was the tracker. His brow was sharp and had hunted enough slaves to make him confident.

A woman appeared from the other side of the camp. "The next time you shoot my way, you better expect a bullet back."

The three entered the camp and looked it over. Riley, hidden beneath her parents sleeping covers stirred and began crying.

"What is that," Fake Tan asked.

"It's a baby," the woman replied, and she peeled the sleeping bag away. She pulled back. "Who puts a baby in orange?"

"Congratulations," Shauna said. "You've created an orphan."

"There they are," Fake Tan said. "Did I tell you, or did I tell you."

"I thought we lost you," Kola said. "How'd you find us?"

"It's simple math," the woman replied. "Horses are faster than feet." She reached to take up Riley.

"Don't touch her," Shauna said and rushed to Riley's side, pushing the woman backwards.

"That's it," the woman drew a rifle on Shauna, and the tracker pushed the barrel away.

"Don't be stupid," he said. "They're worth more than you are right now." He took his time to allow his eyes to taste the new wares that Shauna had to offer. "Yes. Very nice."

"I don't see any horses," Kola said. "You said you had horses. Where are they?"

"Don't you worry," Fake Tan said. "They're safe and sound upstream. You'll see them soon enough."

"Thank you," Kola replied then pulled her trigger twice. The woman fell, the tracker wobbled, disoriented, then dropped.

As Fake Tan raised his rifle at the seven-year-old, Shauna buried a shiv that she had sharpened out of Mr. Butts's credit card into the side of his neck. She drew it out, ripping open his jugular. She got one more straight stab in before the shiv bent and she left him to finish dying on his own.

"That's more like it, again," Kola said, marching up to where Riley lie. She aimed her pistol upon her.

"Don't even think about it," Shauna chided. She'd even thought of taking up Allen's shotgun and unloading it into Kola's backside, but she was more afraid it would just make her angry.

"She's dead weight," Kola replied. "She won't survive."

"She will with our help. God, you really don't feel anything at all, do you?"

Kola turned to Shauna, revealing an even darker intent than she had given off before. Shauna felt her own mask of confidence fall.

"Please," Shauna said.

"I promised to get you across, not her."

"Well then, why did you offer to help them?"

"I needed them," Kola said. "They're wearing orange. They were dead anyway."

"You used them," Shauna realized. "You weren't arguing because you didn't want to go south. You were arguing to make these hunters reveal themselves."

"And we're both alive because of it." Kola returned her gaze to Riley.

"You can't just kill a baby, Kola."

"Sure I can. I have this." Kola pulled the hammer to her gun.

"Damn it, Kola," Shauna roared. "She deserves the same chance you had. You owe her!"

"How do I owe her," Kola asked, her eyes rolling back towards Shauna as if she'd just been introduced to something intriguing and confusing at the same time.

"You made it so she wouldn't survive," Shauna replied. "She's dead weight because of you."

"Yes," Kola said. "Because we need to live, but she doesn't need to anymore."

"You took her mother away from her," Shauna screamed at her. "Just like they took your mom away from you."

Kola's face snapped angrily at Shauna, and, for an instant, Shauna wondered if the gun would turn on her just now.

"But I guess it's okay to make those kinds of choices for daughters so long as you're the one doing it, huh?"

Kola's face curled into a troubled brow, softened into a despised revelation. She studied Shauna a moment, then the ground around her feet, then snapped her attention back up to her.

"You could have said something before all this happened."

"How is this my fault?"

"You know there's something wrong with me." Kola turned her gaze back on Riley and lowered the gun and its hammer. "I'm going to find the horses." She waved a finger over the dead bodies on the ground. "Start carving up some food to take with us. Pack it into the condoms. It should last longer."

"Oh, I am not carving up and eating people."

"Well, it's either them or a horse."

"I'll eat a horse," Shauna replied.

"Don't be stupid? Dead people can't carry our gear." Kola turned and began following the stream upwards.

Riley cried, screamed and cried.

Shauna recovered the formula, it was in a gallon-sized freezer bag, about half full. She rushed to mix some.

Riley didn't wait. She cursed Shauna for not moving faster.

Shauna popped one of the filled condoms, and partially mixed formula splattered her stomach and legs.

She grabbed up another condom of water. Riley shrieked. Shauna held her close and bounced her as she had seen mothers do.

"Please, shh," Shauna begged. She found Riley's pacifier and put it in the baby's mouth. Riley wouldn't hold it, didn't try to hold it, just cried it out through rattling gums. Shauna looked at the gallon-sized bag. It didn't seem like a terribly lot to chance wasting in the rush to silence the baby, but she needed to pacify Riley before anyone came looking for the sound and found the bodies.

Riley had to eat, and Shauna knew what she needed, but her stomach tightened at the thought. She knew what would quiet the baby and she hated it. Shauna looked to Melody. Her lifeless body and red chest filled with warm milk.

"Disgusting," Shauna said.

When Kola returned, leading three horses, two brown and a gray, Riley was just finishing her breakfast.

"Oh, but you're okay with that," Kola said.

"I didn't know what else to do," Shauna said and then held up the bag she'd found. "This is all we have until we get out of this place and find a town or something."

"See," Kola said. "She's dead weight. We should leave her."

"I'm not leaving her."

"Fine," Kola resigned herself. "We'd better hurry then. I don't want to stick around here."

Shauna set Riley in one of the flannel blankets to kick around and then set out to pack up camp. Kola, meanwhile, had drawn one of the brown horses next to a large stone and incline in the ground that allowed her to start searching the saddle bags. In one pouch, she found a small tube of waterproof matches, a half-smoked pack of cigarettes, a paring knife, a mess kit and foldable silverware mess. The other pouch held some MREs, a bottle of vitamins, some jerky and gloves. A sleeping bag was attached to the backside of a black saddle, which was studded in even darker tack. She cinched the straps of Shauna's backpack to the top of the sleeping bag and saddle.

Shauna looked to the sleeping bag and tent that had been attached to the gray horse, which was a bit larger than the other two stallions, and felt a little more at ease, knowing she wouldn't have to lug Riley and her backpack all on her own.

"These horses all have sleeping bags," Shauna said. "Should we take ours too then?"

"These are better than ours," Kola said and sniffed the bag on the horse she had been loading up with her gear. "This smells like cigarettes, how about those?"

Shauna gave them a quick smell test and shook her head that they were okay.

"Then I guess we can leave ours."

Among the other horses' saddle bags, they found a little more food, enough for the slavers to return to New Gateway with their two new hostages in tow. They also found about twenty feet of rope and a shovel with a head that could chop and saw, a hatchet that was probably more roofing hammer than an outdoor tool, and each horse had a canteen lashed around their saddle horns.

"Well, that's a plus," Shauna said, locating two sanitary napkins.

"Save those," Kola said. "They make good kindling."

"They also make good pads," Shauna said.

"What for," Kola asked.

Shauna looked at Kola, and, of all the responses she could think of, settled on, "Don't touch these." Then she took the pads and saved them so she could put them with the box of tampons she had taken from the Butts's bathroom before they started out on a journey that she had no idea of how long it would take.

"You ever ridden a horse," Kola asked while attaching her backpack to the other brown steed that she had decided should be her own.

"No. You?"

"A couple," Kola said. "Look. We'll leave them tied to together and I can lead us until you get the feel for it."

"I didn't think of that," Shauna said. She took Melody's sleeping bag and began cutting off the fabric from one side. She tore out several squares and put them in one of the saddle bags.

"Are those supposed to be diapers," Kola asked. "Cuz she's going to poop right through those.

Shauna grabbed several handfuls of insulation from the bag and stuffed that into a saddle bag as well.

"I suppose that could work," Kola said.

Now Shauna Cut fabric out the other side of the sleeping bag. When she had what she thought was more than enough, she cocooned Riley, then took two strips of the material and used them to tie the infant into an X-shaped harness about Shauna's upper body.

Kola shook her head disapprovingly.

"We're not leaving her," Shauna said.

"The first time the horse freaks out, she's going to slide right out of that thing. You have to use one, solid, bigger piece." Kola cut one of the fleece blankets from corner to corner. "Set her in this."

Undoing what Shauna had just prepared, they tied the half-blanket tightly around her and then cradled Riley into it and cocooned her even further.

"See. Safer," Kola said. "But change her first."

After Shauna had changed Riley, washed her in the creek, then tied a new diaper with wool insulation around the baby, she secured her back against her front.

Five minutes more and Kola rode the lead horse across the creek, with Shauna, the baby, their horses and cargo in tow. They started up the next hill.

"Don't think this is going to be easier," Kola said. "Your butt is going to hurt."

In about an hour, Kola's prophecy came true. In another hour, Shauna was glad Riley threw a fit and needed to eat again. They stopped, let Riley eat, let Shauna complain about how much her rear end hurt, and then they continued on again a few more hours until Shauna suddenly gasped.

"Did you see that?"

"See what," Kola asked.

Then her horse stopped. The others stopped, and she stared off in the same direction as Shauna where a. . .

Chapter Eighteen

. . . head that should not be in a tree appeared and then disappeared. They watched for a moment, and, sure enough, a cow's head bobbed from behind the arrow-shaped top of a tall pine. The tree was bare below the foliage, about forty feet, but was green and poignant the upper thirty. The cow's head pulled back in once more, then appeared again trying to get a mouthful of needles.

The cow lowed and made some continuous whine, artificial and stressed, like a cable panging to be broken, but never actually doing so.

"What the hell," Kola asked. "There's a cow in a Christmas tree."

"Uh-huh," Shauna agreed.

"A cow."

"Yes," Shauna agreed again.

"What the hell?"

"It flew there," Shauna said.

"Don't be stupid."

"I saw it," Shauna said. "It was by the tree, then it was in the tree."

Suddenly, the tree shrieked in a chorus of broken branch. The cow, black and beefy, fell out the bottom of the high, piney arrowhead and continued down about ten more feet before it suddenly stopped. The cow bobbled in the air, hovered away from the tree, steadied, then rose up above the pine tops and disappeared into the distance, lowing.

Kola turned to Shauna. They both shared in the same confusion.

"We don't tell anyone about this," Shauna said.

"Agreed."

"Like ever."

"Uh. Yah think?"

A moment later and the cow was lowing over their heads and flying past the other direction.

Riley began stirring and let out a croak from beneath her binky.

"She needs to eat again," Shauna said.

"Not here," Kola said.

"It's been three hours."

"Not here," Kola replied, staring off into the sky after the cow that had all but disappeared from view. She urged her horse forward once more.

"Yeah," Shauna replied. "There was a cow in a tree."

However, Riley disagreed and started to smell, so they had to stop. They ate dried fruit and jerky, and Shauna changed Riley's diaper.

"Don't waste the water," Kola said. "Just toss the diaper."

"We can't toss the diapers," Shauna explained. "We'll run out. We need to wash them and reuse them."

"Well, do something faster than you're doing, she's screaming like an ambulance, everyone for miles will hear her."

"What do you want me to do, smother her," Shauna snapped then pointed two fingers at Kola and said, "Don't answer that."

"Don't care what you do, just hurry. Throw the poo out and store the diaper in something until we get to another stream."

"In what? A can? We eat out of those. And I'm certainly not putting them in a canteen."

"Use a rubber then," Kola bemoaned. "Geez, haven't you learned anything yet?"

Shauna wadded up and stuffed the diaper into a condom and proceeded to prepare formula for Riley but still wasn't sure how much to mix into the water.

Riley screamed even louder to let Shauna know she was doing it wrong.

"It's three spoonfuls for a mug of hot chocolate, and the formula's only white milk, so it's probably only half of that," Kola said.

"I'm pretty sure that's not how it works," Shauna said. She had poured half a condom of water into one of their empty cans so she wouldn't waste another meal for Riley. Here, she took out one of the spoons they had recently acquired from their new saddle bags. She didn't move fast enough for Riley though, nor Kola.

"Who cares," Kola yelled. "Give her something."

"Well what if we do it wrong," Shauna said. "What if we make her sick."

"Oh geez," Kola complained. "Just put your boob in her mouth and shut her up until your done."

"That's so stupid," Shauna retorted. "I don't make milk."

"She doesn't know that!" Kola snatched up a can. "You keep her quiet. I'll mix the formula."

"Ugh! Fine!" Shauna turned away from Kola to preserve modesty in front of the seven-year-old and prepared to fake breast-feed Riley.

Kola stirred three spoonfuls of formula into the can.

"Ow! Fuck-shit-damn! Let it go!" Shauna continued screaming, trying to remove Riley from her breast. "Stop biting bitch!"

Riley started wailing again.

"Why would anyone let a baby do that to them," Shauna screamed. She had covered herself and was now pacing and glaring at Kola.

"What happened," Kola said.

"What happened," Shauna cried. "I did what you said. I put my boob in her mouth, and, the next thing I know, my nipple was touching diaper. No wonder old ladies have stringy boobs, they've been through a baby's intestinal tract."

"Oh my gosh," Kola scowled. "You're so dramatic."

"My boob will never be the same! I'll have one good boob, and a snake! The next guy who feels me up is gonna call me Medusa."

"Get over it. It can't be that bad."

"Oh, you don't know," Shauna said angrily. "You don't even have boobs."

Kola fell silent. She was about to try and pour the formula into a new condom when Shauna suggested she pull the rubber over the can and let Riley feed right out of it. Kola was angry that she hadn't thought of it herself.

She broke her condom trying to fit it properly, but she succeeded to make the baby bottle work on the next try. She poked a hole in the tip with a safety pin and handed it off to Shauna. Remembering what Melody had done the first time to prevent Riley from swallowing the thin rubber, Shauna monitored the nipple very closely, ready to pull it out in an instant should the baby swallow it.

"Where'd you get that safety pin," Shauna asked.

"My first-aid kit," Kola said.

"Are there any more?"

"A couple. Why?"

"They'd be better than tying the diaper together."

Kola dug out another safety pin and carried them both to Shauna, who did her best to feed Riley. The baby was finally quiet.

"Speaking of which," Shauna said. "It's been a while since we've looked at your foot."

Kola shook her head in agreement and began laboriously undressing her injury.

"Hold it up," Shauna insisted.

Kola did.

From where Shauna sat, it appeared to be in decent shape. The cut was pink but not red. The superglue held.

"It doesn't look too bad," Shauna said.

"I'll wrap it with Gauze again, like before," Kola replied softly and then set to doing so, using their last roll.

Riley finished eating before Kola had completed her wrapping job.

"You should burp her," Kola said.

"Oh," Shauna said. "How do I do that?"

"Like in the cartoons, hold her up so her head's over your shoulder and pat her back until she belches."

Shauna did just that, and Riley threw up formula down her back.

"That's disgusting," Shauna said.

"That's not what they do in cartoons," Kola said.

Then, a cow, out of control, lowing like a poor beast that knew it should never have been taught to fly, fell out of the sky and smashed Kola's horse down. Both animals were instantly dead.

The other horses screamed and pulled, but the trees they were tied to refused to give way.

A strange whine came from the cow and horse's mutilated bodies, similar to a dentist drill, off and on then off and on.

Riley's eyes widened at the sudden eruption. She jerked awake, and Shauna nearly dropped her. Riley set out to show the bovine commotion that she could be louder.

Shauna stuffed her pacifier back into her mouth.

Kola approached the horses, calming the two still tied to the tree. She followed the sound of the whine.

The cow's body suddenly lurched up and off the ground. It raised five feet, the whine screaming in terror of Kola's approach. The cow's broken cadaver wobbled and sped straight for Shauna and Riley. Shauna, luckily, had the clarity of mind to quickly retreat with the infant. The whine stuttered, groaned, popped and died. The cow rose another foot and fell.

Kola and Shauna stood alert, watching themselves and watching the cow.

Riley would have cursed them both, but Shauna held the pacifier against the child's lips.

Kola chanced looking to Shauna.

"Um, excuse me," the cow's body said. "Ladies, pardon me."

A sharp chortle burst from Shauna's lungs. "The cow's talking to us."

"Yes, um, sorry about that," the cow—rather, a man's voice—said. "I saw you with a baby and thought you might need some help."

"With what," Kola asked. "Smashing her?"

"No, please," the cow said. "Do you see the belt that's around this creature?"

Kola cautiously approached and inspected the broken cow as she had started to do previously.

"Yes," Kola said, discovering a matrix of thin black stripes, wrapped around the cow's body, belly and legs. Many of them were stained in blood now or cutting into the beast's avulsion-laden corpse. More than that though, she discovered two chambers, each the size of a football on either side of the cow's torso.

"If you would be so kind as to cut those," the voice spoke from a small box on the side of the strange device. "I would be happy to compensate you if you could bring me back the black canisters they're connected to."

"Now why would we do that," Shauna asked.

"Right," the voice said. It became evident that it came from the black canisters. "You have no reason to trust me."

"No," Kola replied. "We don't."

"Look, if you will bring those to me, I'll give you fresh milk for the baby. I have cows."

"Are they alive," Shauna asked.

"We really don't have time," Kola said. "We need to get east."

"That's great! It's on the way."

"We couldn't find you if we wanted to," Shauna said.

"Look," the voice replied. "I can see the location of my canisters. I can tell you how to get here."

"I'm sorry," Kola started to say.

"I could come to you."

"We won't be here," Kola replied.

"We're not stupid," Shauna added.

"No," the voice replied. "I suspect not."

"Listen, please," the man's voice begged. "My entire life's work is in those two canisters. It's all I have out here. Please."

"Yeah, like you're alone," Shauna said.

"How about this," he said. "It's clear that baby's not yours. You bring me those canisters, and I'll take that baby off your hands."

"And do what with it," Shauna asked sharply.

"Protect it. Keep it from slavers. Keep it safe," he said. "I'm very well protected."

"I don't know about this, Kola," Shauna said.

"Please," the cow's canisters said. "You know it's just going to die out there otherwise. Do you really want to starve that baby?"

Kola wanted to answer, but Shauna quietly pled with her not to give in.

"If I wanted to harm you, don't you think I could have done better than attacking you with a cow?"

"All right," Kola said in her deceivingly friendly tone. "You promise you won't hurt us then?"

"I would never hurt children," the voice said. "I'm trusting you as much as you're trusting me."

"Okay," Kola said. "Because it's really scary out here, and I want my mommy."

Shauna wanted to argue but knew better by now.

Kola cut the canisters loose and moved to her dead horse, which had fallen on her pack.

"Did it smash everything," Shauna asked.

"Of course, it did," Kola replied.

The saddlebag with rope was easily accessible though. So were the buckles on the girth. Kola released the buckles and took out the rope, then tied an end to the saddle horn on Shauna's horse and then that of the smashed one. With a little coaxing, the saddle and its contents peeled away from the corpse.

"Well, better not get hurt anymore," Kola said, inspecting her gear. "The bottle of peroxide is gone. And the dried food is all popped."

"That'll hold until tonight's dinner then," Shauna said.

"Yeah. Suppose so."

"Sorry, girls," the voice from the canisters said.

Kola stuffed one of the canisters into her pack and the other into Shauna's. She took a good look at them as she did. They had the appearance like a small jet engine or a pill.

"Sure these are safe," she asked the canister before she began sealing Shauna's bag.

"I have them turned off, on my end," the voice said. "There is a switch on them that you could turn off, but then I couldn't talk you through how to get here."

"Right," Kola said, noticing a small button under a rubber dot that she hadn't seen until she knew what to look for. She sealed the bag. "Can you still hear me?"

"Yeah," the voice replied, muffled but not gone.

"K, cuz we don't need both on, do we?"

She reached into her bag and turned that canister off. She attached it to the pack horse. She proceeded to move the rest of the gear from her previous horse to both her and Shauna's.

"Don't even think about it," Shauna said, mistaking Kola's attempt to find a place for the roofing hammer in one of her horse's saddlebags as trying to move Shauna and Riley to the pack horse that was carrying the strange flying devices, which could do who knows what at any moment and without warning.

"I'm not taking your stupid horse," Kola said.

By now, Shauna was ready once again to travel with Riley.

"There's just one more thing," Kola said, and she appeared with one of the slaver's hunting knives. "Cow or horse," she asked. "They can't carry anything now."

"Oh," Shauna replied. "Wow. Cow, seems more natural."

Kola approached the cow and sliced into its backside, right before its hip, which had been completely flattened from the fall. She pulled up on the hair and began to use the blade to peel the skin away from the meaty underside near the spine. She pointed a finger at Shauna.

"We need something to put this in," She said.

Shauna returned with eleven condoms. She opened them and held their mouths open as Kola began to stuff in chunks of bloody meat. By the third condom, Shauna couldn't grip the wrappers to tear them open; all the blood had turned to grease. She washed her hands with a canteen, then continued her work once again. By the time they'd filled up the rest of the condoms with beef, she could barely tie the ends together. They stuffed the packaged meat into saddle bags, washed themselves and climbed up onto their horses.

Riley started to stir, and Shauna shushed her. Again, Kola took the lead and they started their path once more.

"All right," the man's voice said. "Just head east until I can see you start moving on my end and can tell you where to go."

"How far," Kola asked.

"About eighteen miles," he replied. "With breaks to feed the baby, should make it by dark if you don't take too sharp of terrain."

"Will your batteries last that long," Kola asked. "A lot of good you'll do directing us if your voice dies on us."

"Should be okay," he replied. Nearly two hours later, they came to another creek, not too wide. They let the horses drink while they stopped to feed Riley once more. She had peed herself during the journey but didn't make any sound over it. After a change and a snack, they followed the canister's voice and began tracing the creek.

"Follow that, about eleven more miles," the voice said, crackling.

"Eleven," Kola said. "Seven miles? That's all we've gone?"

"Follow the creek and you won't—

The speaker crackled out. Kola turned on the other canister.

"That didn't last long," Kola said.

The voice didn't respond.

"We don't have to go there, you know," Shauna said.

"He's right," Kola replied. "You want her to live, she won't do it with us. We don't know how."

"Yeah," Shauna reluctantly sighed.

"Are you there," the voice came back to life.

"Yeah," Kola replied. "Thought we lost you."

"I'd hoped you'd be smart enough to turn the other back on," he said. "Good thing that happened while we were talking, or you might have gotten lost."

"Perhaps," Kola said. "We just wouldn't have found you is all."

"Yeah, um, listen," he said. "Just in case. Try not to stop any more. The cougars like this area and you have meat, horses and a baby. You could be in trouble if you don't get here by dark. You just keep following this creek and we'll meet up, okay? Turn the engine off unless you need direction. I'll listen for you."

When dark came, which was much faster than expected for two horses and three riders meandering the bottom of a canyon, the battery on the second canister had died.

"My butt hurts," Shauna complained. "And she's getting fussy."

"She's really hampering our speed," Kola replied. "We should keep going though. It can't be much more."

"I don't see any lights or anything. Shouldn't we see lights if we were close?"

"Depends."

Kola's horse lulled at her need to sleep. She wasn't quite used to riding herself. That is, it had been perhaps a year since she had been on a horse on a trail near Warm Springs. She relied on the horse's big eyes to navigate the terrain in the dark. Between the slight twist in her forward rocking saddle and the calm song of the creek to their right, Kola took great effort to stay awake.

Riley's fuss turned into a coo.

"That's lucky," Shauna said.

They stayed lucky for another half an hour when they entered a bit of a clearing, and Kola's horse suddenly appeared cautious. His rocking stopped, his head bounced and rebounded in defiance.

"What is it," Shauna asked.

Riley began shifting.

"Shauna? Kola," a familiar voice asked, this time not from the canister.

They acknowledged. A battery powered lantern snapped on through a cheap, plastic and foggy lens.

"It's okay," the shadow behind it encouraged Kola's horse. "Sorry. Hard not to startle you when it's dark."

"Anyone else here," Kola asked.

"No," the shadow said. A face with a dark, fat mustache appeared within the skin of illumination just below Kola's perch.

"How do we know that," Shauna asked.

The shadow sighed. "In this dark? Even I don't know if I'm alone, but I do have soft beds and food, just this way. You don't have to follow, but, if you want to, you're welcome to what I have."

He turned and began trudging away from the creek. Kola urged her horse forward, across the clearing, and to the side of a hill. Here, their guide's lantern painted what became the roof and walls of an entrance to a cave.

"Might want to hop off here," he said. "The ceiling can get a little low."

Kola leapt down. She'd definitely need help getting back into the saddle later.

The man offered to help Shauna and the baby down, and they accepted it.

"It's just up here," he explained and started deeper into the cave. "There's room for the horses."

As they drew deeper, the ceiling came almost as low as Shauna's horse's tall head, but then it began to open and draw higher. They approached an archway-shaped blockade, large enough to pass for an old garage door, that had been constructed into the wall of the cavern. Using a remote, he called one panel open, then the other and the cavern was suddenly filled with light that had been sealed away behind the door.

They led the horses through, and the panels sealed behind them.

It could have passed for a front yard of any house, if that house had no sun but instead ceilings that were twenty feet high and filled with calcified mineral melting from them—not a lot, but enough to draw attention. The front yard had to have been at least an acre open before a plain, one-bedroom house, complete with a decent section of mowed lawn. Beyond that was more, much more.

To the right of the cavern was a pen with about sixteen cows. Several tons of hay lined the wall no more than twenty feet away from this holding cell. Two four-wheelers, a golf cart and a low-profile car, that may very well have been a Jeep chassis with seats and a steering wheel, were parked on the other side of the cavern.

Streetlamps lit up the entire chamber.

"The lights are bright, aren't they," Shauna asked, shading Riley's eyes.

"Sorry about that," the man said. Illuminated now, his face no longer appeared shaded but dark blond. "They have to be to grow anything. You can stable your horses with mine."

It was easy to miss at first. The vehicles hid the fence-line behind them, and the horse within it was almost the same colors as the brown and shadowy walls of the cavern. The fence, unlike the enclosure of the cattle, allowed the horses access to the rest of the cave behind the small house, where the ceiling rose, and a two-story barn stood.

"I put out feed and water already." He suddenly stopped and turned to Kola. In that instant, she almost felt the impulse to stab him in the face. "Can I have my engines?"

"Oh," Kola said. "Sure. They're on the horse."

"Of course," he said. "Duh, huh? Look. I don't get a lot of visitors here. I don't think the best sometimes. Unload and meet me inside when you're ready."

The girls did just that, freeing their tired horses from their burdens and turning them loose into the corral. The lone mustang that previously occupied it appeared curious.

They left their belongings in front of the porch where it didn't appear that they had much to worry about in ways of people stumbling into their camp to steal it. However, they did carry Kola's pack, the canisters, and a few supplies for Riley into the house. Before entering, Kola felt the position of her pistol and knife in case she needed quick access.

As soon as they opened the front door, they found a long staircase that descended before them for a hundred, expanded-steel steps below the façade of the small house. They followed the stairwell right into a warehouse the size of Kola's old school gymnasium. It was filled with desks of all sorts of cleanliness and technological gadgetry and clutter. Computer monitors, keyboards, machine tools all created rows within the shop.

"Back here," their host called from the other side of the facility.

As they marched down an aisle, straight past the rows of tools, desks and other geekly adventures, the room began to clear up as they passed the tables, and the floor and walls turned into clean and shiny aluminum. The overhead fans that filtered air in and out reminded Shauna of the kind of movie where someone with a chainsaw was sure to throw a hidden door open at any moment.

They left this room through two doors that had been propped open and that brandished push bars. On the other side of them was a log-cabin living room that looked like it had come out of a bad Lifemark movie waited. It had shag rugs, wood paneling, a dead bear standing in the corner and a red, green and white plaid couch. It matched a leather recliner which had been sat in so much that white, use-crinkles spread like a circulatory system over its dark brown skin. The windows even had curtains and the light of what could have been the moon coming through.

"It's simulated," the man said from the kitchen area where he was setting dishes out on a square table. "Trust me, being down here alone does a number on you after a while. You just don't realize how much a 24-hour cycle of light can keep you sane."

He turned back to a kitchen filled with every device and shiny, clean surface a grandmother would ever need and took a pair of gray oven mitts off a row of hooks on the wall. Then he grabbed a two-handled pot off the stove and carried it to the table.

"Please," he said, going off to dig a large spoon out of a drawer. "Sit. Eat."

Riley coughed.

"Oh," the man beamed and dropped his mitts on a tan, marble counter. "May I hold her."

Shauna hesitated a moment as he approached. As he was suddenly looking down on the baby's face, while also standing in a way that didn't feel like he was trying to invade Shauna's space, she found herself more willing to oblige his request.

Kola sidled up next to Shauna. "Isn't she cute," she said and brushed Riley's nose.

"She's adorable," the man said. "It's been a long time since I've seen someone so small. May I?"

Shauna peeled Riley's cocoon away from her body.

"She needs to be changed," Shauna said. "I'm sorry. If I could have a minute,"

"Not to worry," he said. "You wouldn't believe some of the things that I've found floating down the creek." He carried Riley to the counter and laid her upon it, curling a hand towel under her head. He urged Shauna and Kola once more to sit and eat, while he produced a tube of disinfectant wipes and cleaned Riley as if she were his own. He left the baby and the room for a moment then returned with a disposable diaper. "See? Never know what you may come across out here."

"Any formula float down that river," Shauna asked.

"Already ordered it."

"You ordered it," Kola asked. "You get mail?"

"In a way," he said. He gestured to a blue, rotary-dial phone on the wall of the kitchen. "I pick that up, and call people to bring me what I need. It's on its way now."

Shauna moaned in satisfaction as she pushed a spoon of macaroni and cheese with baby peas and chunks of hotdogs into her mouth. Kola didn't moan, but she seemed quite content with her own food.

"I imagine you've been eating canned or dried food," he said. "I thought you might like something with a little meat to it."

"We have beef," Kola said. "We carved it off your cow."

The man's face turned quizzical, then seemed to accept the fact.

"Well, where is it," he asked. "We can put it in the freezer if you like."

"In the rubbers," Kola said.

"Rubbers?"

"Condoms," Shauna clarified.

He looked up from the work he was doing on Riley, stumped, then he started laughing.

"That's some funny shit, right there," he said, then appeared suddenly embarrassed. "Stuff! Funny stuff. I'm sorry. I told you, I don't get many people like you."

"It's all right," Kola said. "We know what funny shit is."

He turned to a cupboard and took down a box of corn starch. He floured Riley's bottom with it.

"No wonder she's crying," he said. "She's rashed. Need baby powder. I don't have any, but corn starch works. You were just hurting lots and lots, weren't you, little lady?"

Riley seemed a little quieter but still cried.

Shauna was immediately embarrassed for not realizing Riley might have been in any pain.

"Tell you what," the host said, lifting Riley off of the counter, naked except for her diaper and pacifier. "You eat. I'll feed, what's her name?"

"Riley," Shauna said.

"I'll feed Riley, and then I'll bring your meat in and put it in the refrigerator so you two can relax and settle in a bit. If that's all right with you."

"That's fine," Kola said, paying more attention to refilling her shallow, white bowl with more mac and cheese.

"Um, where's Riley's bottle," he asked.

"Condoms are outside," Kola replied.

"Condoms," he asked, this time not laughing. "Well, I guess whatever works. A little soft though. I think we can do better."

He carried Riley out of the room and came back with a green, dish-washing glove.

"Oh, is that baby formula," he asked pointing to the Ziploc bag that Shauna had set on the table beside her.

She nodded.

"Oh good," he said. "I can mix that with my milk and make it last longer. Make the milk better for her too."

"It's milk," Kola said. "How is milk bad for her."

"Not really great to give a baby straight cow's milk," he said and took up the bag of formula, "But it's better than nothing. This formula will help a lot for now. Until I can get my next supply order in."

"I thought you said you didn't get visitors," Kola said.

"Not outside visitors," he said and set to warming a drinking glass with water, cow's milk and baby formula in a sink of hot water. "My employer makes sure I have supplies I need."

"Your employer," Shauna asked.

"He pays for all of this," he answered. "None of this is mine. It's all Salvo's. He's my boss. What? What is it? You know of Salvo."

"I've heard of him," Kola replied coldly, not aware that she had given herself away. "You ever actually see him?"

"I'm not sure, but I know how to find him if I ever need anything," he said.

"Where is he," Kola asked.

"Why so curious," he asked. He had filled the glove up with baby mix, tied off the end with an elastic, and soon Riley was drinking out of a tooth-pick-pierced finger. "Looking for a job."

"What? No," Kola said. "I just wondered if there was someone else here."

"No, he's not here," the host said. "He sends people through to bring supplies once a month, sometimes twice. I've surmised from conversations with his people that he may live in Vegas."

"Oh," Kola replied.

"Don't be disappointed," he said and gathered a towel from a nearby drawer, while cradling Riley in his arm and managing to feed her too. "He's probably not the kind of person a little kid would like." He moved to the table and sat in a wooden chair closest to Riley. Then he dropped the towel on the floor next to him.

"Oh," Kola said, and she smiled, burying her deadly being: her gun, her knife, the fact that if she wanted, she could use her spoon to puncture everyone's brains at the table this very instant. She hid that she would, had she not given her word to guide Shauna. She would if she hadn't seen a bit of her own situation in Riley's circumstance. She would. A face was just a face. They all looked the same covered in blood. However, it had failed to hide her disappointment. It annoyed her that he had seen through her façade.

What else could he see? Could he see that the mention of the name Salvo raised her pulse? Could he see her hatred and fear of the man at once, bursting in her veins, yet in the process of being tempered. Could he see that she did, in fact, know Salvo? That she had a bullet with his name on it?

"But you never know," the host said. "His people have been known to show up without warning. If that happens, you may need to give up your bed and sleep on the floor tonight."

"So, how do you find him," Kola asked.

The host appeared taken aback.

"Tunnel system," he said. "Runs through a lot of the United States Conglomerate and some of Canada. Comes right to that door." He pointed to a sturdy door capping the end of a darkened hallway off the kitchen.

"You mean, you can get to Vegas through that door," Kola asked.

"And Canada," Shauna added.

"If you don't mind wandering in the dark," he explained. "But I wouldn't go to Canada. You get shot on sight for being American. They're still a little sore about the coast's limited secession destroying their economy. But yeah, if you wanted to go to Vegas, it's just through that door. Read the sign first and you'll be good." He turned his attention to Riley, "And we'll be fine too, won't we?"

"I think I'd like to get some sleep," Shauna suddenly said, trying not to show her annoyance at the situation of leaving a baby with what could be a pervy old man.

"Sure thing," he said and pointed down a darkened hallway that crept out of the kitchen. "Door on the right is a spare room. I've fixed it up for you. You can share the bed. Door across the hall is the bathroom, if you want to take a bath. No shortage of fresh or hot water here! We have a filtration system, feeds off the creek. Use as much as you want."

"Maybe I'll do that," Shauna said and made her way towards the hallway.

"One more thing," the host said. "Stay out of that room at the end of the hall. It's not for you, only Salvo's people. It's monitored, so he'd know if you went in, and so would I."

Shauna went off to take a bath.

"What about Riley," Kola asked. "Where does she sleep."

"I set something up for her in the room with you," he answered. "Might as well enjoy her until you leave."

Kola nodded her illusion of gratitude. She ate a while longer, drank some milk and thanked her host.

"Well," he said, pulling Riley's empty glove from her mouth. "I should go get your things. You can find your room."

He set the near-empty glove on the table, turned Riley's chest into the palm of his large hand and patted her back until she spit onto the towel that he had dropped on the floor beside his chair. Then he gave Riley to Kola and exited the double doors leading back into the warehouse of desks. Riley had already started chowing down on her binky. She looked up to Kola with deep blue-gray eyes. Kola could almost hear her asking if she was going to kill her now?

No. I'm not going to kill you now, Kola would have answered back.

But you wanted to, Riley said with just her eyes.

I changed my mind.

Why?

I don't know. Now, shut up and sleep before I change it back.

Riley sucked on her pacifying metronome, and her eyes began to close.

Kola took her to their room and found what had probably been the wire section of an animal cage that had been turned upside down to hold pillows large enough to comfort a baby. A large bath towel had been folded up within. Kola set Riley inside and covered her in the towel. She watched her, wasn't sure for how long though, listening to their host enter the house a time or two, setting bags on the floor.

After Shauna bathed, Kola took her turn.

As she walked out, wrapped in a towel, she found her host quickly turning away from her as he currently collected dishes for washing.

"I'm not looking," he said. "If you'd like, leave your dirty clothes and anything else you'd like cleaned outside your door, and I'll put them in the washer."

Kola nodded. "Don't have much in our bags, but okay."

Shauna had already settled in on the queen-sized bed.

Kola tightened her towel around her, emptied her pockets from her pants, hid her knife and gun beneath her pillow, then set her clothes into the hall. She did the same with Shauna's, then closed the door and climbed into bed next to her traveling companion.

"I love this bed," Shauna mumbled.

Kola pulled herself under the blanket and reached across Shauna to turn out the table lamp. Then she settled her head against her pillow and watched Shauna's shadow take form in the dark room.

Shauna had started to breathe the long airy notes that announced she was about to stop paying attention to the wakened world.

Here, Kola shifted her hands up to the side of her face, lay silently a while, then lowered them. Slowly, she reached to Shauna and placed her hand on Shauna's awesome breast. Shauna wore a flannel button-up, probably one of their host's shirts. It was clearly too big for her, but Kola could still feel the magnificent—

"What are you doing," Shauna asked suddenly pulling away.

"What are they like," Kola asked.

"What?"

"You said it yourself," Kola replied. "I don't have any."

"You'll find out soon enough."

"Maybe not," Kola said. "Some women don't."

"If your mom has boobs, you'll have 'em," Shauna said. "Does your mom have them."

"No," Kola said. "Mom says I shouldn't get them."

"She can't control that."

"My mom's pretty smart."

"Enough to change your natural biology?"

"Maybe."

"And maybe you'll get them."

"But what are they like," Kola asked. "In case I never get any."

"They're itchy, sweaty and bunch up," Shauna replied, letting her eyes close once more. "Trust me, they're no big deal."

"Boys don't think so."

"Huh," Shauna startled awake.

"Boys, they like boobs," Kola explained. "I heard some kids talking about Miss Ivy's. They like them."

"Yes, they do," Shauna replied. She turned away from Kola and nestled into a fresh position. "Yes, they do." Suddenly, she pushed herself up from the bed and turned to Kola once more. "Wait a minute! Is that what this is about, that I said you didn't have any?"

"You don't have to be rude about it," Kola said.

"So, you do have feelings," Shauna said.

"Oh, come on," Kola snapped. "You don't have feelings about boobs. They're just boobs."

"That's right, and you don't have any," Shauna replied. "And from what you've said, you'll probably never get them."

"You don't know that!"

"Aha," Shauna blurted. "You do care about it. You have feelings."

"Don't make fun of me."

"I'm not making fun of you," Shauna said. For some reason, she felt as though she was being the mean one now. "Yes, boys like them. I like them. They can be uncomfortable. Clearly, you like them. It's okay to be upset that you don't have any yet, but someday you might."

"And boys will like me?"

"Well, yeah, but not because of your tits!"

"They like Miss Ivy because of hers."

"Okay, so maybe boobs help," Shauna replied.

"So, I could go my entire life without people liking me if I don't grow boobs like yours?"

"How many friends do you have, Kola," Shauna asked letting herself back down into the mattress."

"None," Kola replied. "Momma said they get in the way."

"This bothers you, doesn't it?"

Kola didn't answer, but Shauna could tell she was angry about the question.

"Well maybe you and I will be friends one day."

"We're not friends?"

"I don't think you know how," Shauna said.

"Maybe if I get boobs, I'll learn."

"Maybe."

"If I get boobs."

"The nice thing about boobs, Kola, is if you don't grow any, you can. . .

176 left
_____

Chapter Nineteen

. . . always buy some."

"Huh. That's probably what I'll do then. Goodnight."

"Goodnight. And don't grope me again. You're seven. It's weird, and your hands are cold."

Although Shauna fell asleep, Kola continued to think about the plumpness that she had just felt, their warmth tender, yet firm, way they seemed to sink into the palm. If she had her own, she wouldn't have to feel Shauna's to know what they were like.

Also, how could hands be too cold?

She fell asleep on these thoughts, without Shakespeare's help, and dreamed deeply, more than she had in a long time. Even when Shauna climbed over her to get out of the bed and carried Riley out of the room, Kola didn't seem to notice. When she awoke and realized that she hadn't felt any of it, she was angry about it. If her mother had done this in a test, she would have tied Kola to the bed post and either left her until she could escape, or perhaps she would have woken her through waterboarding. Her mother was adamant about Kola being aware of her surroundings at all times.

"You slept your life away," her mother would have said here. "Will this help you remember?"

Kola turned in bed and saw her clothes sitting on brown, shag carpet next to the door. She remembered that she was wearing a towel, which she was only now aware had worked its way off in her sleep. She got out of bed and dressed herself.

A tall mirror on a wall beside a dark stained bureau showed her scar below her belly button, the one her mother used to remove one of her kidneys, then another, and finally a third.

Duplex kidneys, the doctor said she had. People had two. Those were God's rules: two kidneys to a person, but, thanks to the confusion of some people in God's quality control department, some people might only end up with one. Some might be born without any and die. Then God's employees on the assembly line would finish their shift and realize they had extra kidneys left over. Naturally, they don't want to get in trouble, so they just hide their mistake by putting those extra kidneys into someone else who may already have their two standard-issue organs. In Kola's case, the assembly agent had two kidneys left and decided that he or she, or whatever, would stuff both of them into Kola's little body.

The doctor told Kola that a person's kidney can sometimes split into two allowing the person to have three kidneys, and she thought it was cool. She was different, but she peed a lot, which is why her mother took her into see the doctors in the first place.

"Whatever she drinks just passes through her," her mother complained when she was five. "I think she might have diabetes."

Well, no.

"She has four kidneys," the pediatrician said.

Two months later, Kola lie in the back of a tent, not more than a day's journey from where she stood this very moment. She slept, and a nineteen-year-old surgeon and her mother pulled three kidneys from inside Kola. Then Salvo's men gave her mother $225,000 for them, and left Kola with only one.

Kola had many other scars—burns, lashes, home surgeries, punishment piercings—all where people couldn't see them for her clothing.

She dressed and considered whether she should take her gun from under her pillow and decided against carrying any weapons at this point. Having them might tempt her to use them, and she wanted Riley to stay with this man.

She found French toast waiting for her along with sausage, potatoes and a baked apple.

"You can warm it up in the microwave if you want," the host said.

Kola thanked the host and carried her plate to a white microwave next to a tan refrigerator.

Riley was on her belly, on the floor, facing Shauna. She was lifting herself up and laughing at her. Shauna laughed back.

Kola slid her plate into the microwave and set the timer. She hit the start button.

"Kola," Shauna shrieked. "Your foot."

"What now," Kola asked, unsure if she'd heard her correctly. She looked down half-mindedly. Her foot was red, had swollen until the skin around it had turned into a glossy rouge and almost plastic appearance. How had she not seen that a moment ago? It was twice the size it should have been.

"Sweet Raphael, child," the host invoked. He leapt from his chair and moved through the double doors leading into the warehouse area.

The microwave dinged before he returned, and Kola took a chair at the table. She ignored Shauna's distaste of the matter.

Their host returned carrying a brown pill bottle and a white, metal box with its red cross dead center of the lid. He set himself and a chair beside Kola and dropped the first-aid kit on the table.

"All right," he said, slapping the top of his thigh. "Let's have it."

She could have just as easily kicked him for the order, but she decided that he had fed her, given her a place to sleep and was willing to take Riley off her hands. The reality was also that if she wanted to get anywhere alive, she needed to fix the issue. She set her bare foot in his lap.

"I see," he said. "Glue." He prodded her foot gingerly. "Looks like it opened here and closed again, I think. You know, two hundred years ago, we'd have to start worrying about if we were going to cut this off soon."

Kola gasped. "Are you going to cut off my foot," she pretended to fret.

"Uh, no," he said. "Cut it open again and treat it differently, maybe, but we'll try some good old penicillin here first. Being alone and all out here, Salvo makes me keep it on hand. Can't have his scientists dying on him."

"How much is it," Kola asked.

"How much? You mean money," he asked, appearing hurt. "There's no charge." He broke out one pill and handed it to Kola, while sliding a glass of water towards her. "One of these every six hours should do it."

As Kola took her pill and water, he felt her forehead. "You're hot. Are you feeling sick?"

"I feel fine," Kola said, unsure of if she did or not.

"Just to be safe, you should stay here at least another day," he said.

"We can't," Kola said. "We have to meet my mother."

"You go out there in this state, you might not meet up with her at all," he insisted. "Now, I have streaming services and enough to keep you entertained, but I want to wrap that foot in a heating pad for now, and tomorrow, if I see a difference in you, we'll talk about you two going back out. When is your mom expecting you to show up?"

"When we get there," Kola said.

"Then I imagine she'll keep waiting."

"He's right," Shauna said, seeing that Kola was thinking of doing something drastic to their host. "It'll be a burden on everyone, if your foot starts to decay, you know."

Kola turned her attention back to her French toast.

Within ten minutes, she had eaten her breakfast, and was now sitting on the couch. Her host coiled a hot wrap around her foot and secured it.

"Twenty minutes, then we take it off," he said. "It allows the antibiotics to work better."

Kola sat on the couch and stewed. She didn't remember the twenty minutes because, for some reason, her head began to feel heavy and she fell asleep.

She woke up again wet, unsure of how long she'd been asleep. She could hear the voices, mostly in dream than in realization that they were alive. Kola sat then stepped from the couch and followed the voices into the warehouse, where she found Shauna and their host over a table where one of the small engines was open and in pieces.

The host looked up, startled, as Kola crept up. His eyes grew even wider through the magnifying glass headgear he wore over them.

"You're drenched," Shauna announced.

"I'm fine," Kola replied, but she didn't realize her words slurred.

The host pressed his hand to her head one more time.

"Okay," he said, tearing his strange headgear away from his face. He hoisted Kola into his arms and marched her back into the house and down the hallway to the bathroom, where he set her, clothes and all, into the tub. She'd thought about objecting the entire way, but she was still a little too tired.

She heard the water burst from the faucet and felt it slowly creep up over her tiny body. In three minutes, she wasn't even aware that she had slipped back into dream.

The living room was dim when she awoke again, her host was slumped in his chair about five feet away. Kola stirred, dropping several hot-water bottles on the floor, and he jerked towards her as if he'd been faking his rest.

"You hot," he asked, once again feeling her head. He squeezed one of the water bottles. "Probably need to get you some more cold water."

He took up the water bottles and returned to the kitchen where he proceeded to empty them one at a time.

"Where's Shauna," Kola asked. Noticing the silence.

"They're sleeping," he said. "It's nighttime. You've been out all day."

He began to pull crushed ice out of the freezer and fed it into the small hole at the end of one of the bottles.

"I'm thirsty."

"Yes, right." He left the bottles a moment and pulled a pitcher of yellow drink from the fridge. He poured a glass and carried it to Kola. He also held out a pill. "Take this."

Kola took the antibiotic and the glass.

"What is it," she asked.

"Powdered Gatorade," he replied. "Another hour and I was going to stick you with an I.V. again. You got pretty dehydrated. Do you even remember waking up at all?"

Kola downed the pill and a few swallows of her drink. It wasn't a great taste. She shrugged it off. "You mean when you put me in the tub?"

"We woke you several times since to take your antibiotics and some electrolytes. You don't remember?" He returned to filling the water bottle with ice. "You've been here two days."

"I don't remember," Kola said.

"Keep drinking," he said.

She did but didn't like it. She forced herself up and against the arm of the couch.

"Shauna says you keep your promises, that true?"

Kola shook her head and kept drinking.

"If I promise to give your gun back, will promise not to lie to me anymore?"

Kola finished her drink and stared at the empty glass in her hand.

"I imagine you could break that and stab me with it," he said. "But then who would take Riley off your hands?"

She stared at him, angry that he seemed to be able to read her mind, or angry that Shauna had told him too much. She couldn't decide.

"Does that mean we don't have a deal," he asked.

"All right," Kola said. "I won't lie to you anymore."

He looked up from the second water bottle that he was now working on and scrutinized Kola. She knew it was scrutiny. She was prone to do it herself from time to time. Finally, she shook her head—and he accepted the gesture, more out of humanity than faith in the child.

"How many people you killed," he asked.

"I don't know," Kola replied. She clenched and unclenched the glass. She watched the bottom magnify her index finger as she stared down the tubular lens, unsure whether to admire it or throw it. "My mom said if you don't count, you can't feel accountable later."

"It's that many?"

"How many you killed," she asked.

He shook his head. "None."

"Everybody kills," Kola replied unbelievingly.

"No," he retorted, not unkindly, which somehow intrigued Kola. She wasn't sure why. "They do not."

"Everybody kills."

"How'd you get your scars," he asked ignoring her response.

"You saw me?"

"We couldn't leave you in wet clothes, now could we?"

Only now was Kola suddenly aware that the flannel pajamas she wore weren't her own. They were a little small but not much.

"They were my daughter's," he said. "She doesn't need them anymore."

He started on the third water bottle.

"Your scars," he continued to pry.

"Which ones," she asked.

"The clusters on your bottom."

Kola took a moment to think. It wasn't the scar set that she had expected someone to point out. She tried to put those memories out of her mind perhaps the most. She didn't see them like she saw her others, not unless she was purposely trying to find it in a mirror, which she didn't do.

"Dog fighting ring," she said.

"What were you doing in a dog fighting ring," he asked.

"Fighting dogs."

He stopped what he was doing but didn't look up from his work. "I beg your pardon."

"Fighting dogs."

"Why?"

"To learn how," she said.

"Why would you need to learn how?"

"Uh, in case I have to protect myself," she replied and marveled in how stupid he must have been.

"So, it was with another kid," he asked, finally returning to his work with the crushed ice.

"No. Pitbulls."

"Pitbulls?" Ice chunks shot from the rubber bottle's opening as he smacked the bag against the counter involuntarily. "How many?"

"Depended on the night."

"And how many kids?"

"Just me."

"Why?"

"I told you," Kola said. "To learn how."

"How did you end up in dog fighting rings with Pitbulls?"

"I don't know. They put—

"They?"

"My mom and uncle. They put me in, and it was better to get bit in the bum than somewhere else. They always go for the face, unless you turn your butt to them. If they bite your butt, you can stab their brains."

"That must have hurt," he said, and Kola could see he was trying to downplay the extravagance of the issue.

Kola waved her head. "Nothing hurts."

"I see."

"But that did."

"I'm sorry," he said, and began working on the final bag.

"Why?"

"You shouldn't have been in there in the first place."

"How else was I supposed to learn how to fight?"

"You take a karate class with other kids your age. You don't fight dogs."

"There weren't any kids my age," she said.

"How old were you?"

"I don't know," she said. "I don't remember. Four maybe. Three."

The host snatched the bag over to the kitchen sink and began filling it.

"How many people have you killed?"

"I told you," she said. "I don't know. We hunted exiles. There was no shortage of exiles."

He was quiet for some time while he filled the rest of the water bottles. He carried them back to the couch and set them at Kola's feet. He held his hand out for the glass, and she passed it to him, smudged with fingerprints. He took it to the kitchen.

"How many people have you killed this week," he asked.

"Four," Kola answered after thinking about it.

"The tow truck driver?"

"Yes."

"And Riley's parents."

"I didn't kill them."

"How about the people who did."

"I had help."

"And how many last week."

"Just one."

"Who?"

"A judge," Kola said.

"Why?"

"My mom told me to," Kola said, surprised. "Do you need a reason to kill a judge."

"I think so, yeah."

"She took me from my mom," Kola said.

"Your mom," he asked. "Is this the same mom who put you in a ring with killer dogs?"

"Well, yeah."

"Then the judge should have taken you away from her. Any mother who puts her child in a ring with deadly dogs shouldn't have a child."

"Careful," Kola said. "I promised I wouldn't lie to you. I didn't say I wouldn't kill you. My mom loves me."

"No," he shot back. "She doesn't. I should lock all of you here."

Kola leapt to her feet, but before she could charge to the end of the couch and leap at the host to gouge his throat out, he aimed a long finger right at her.

"Sit down." He ordered sternly and without flinching.

She didn't sit but found herself unable to attack him.

"Now!"

She did. She shouldn't have, and she didn't know why she did, but she sat.

He moved to his leather chair, turning himself in it to face her.

"Now you listen," he said. He was angry now, but for some reason, Kola didn't believe it was with her. "A mother who loves her child doesn't let dogs chew on her butt. A mother throws herself in front of the dog, kills the dog, or at the very least takes the attack so the child doesn't get hurt."

"Maybe not all mothers are that stupid."

"It's not stupid. It's selflessness. It's love."

"Kids have to learn to defend themselves too."

"Is that what you're going to tell your kids?"

"I'm not having kids."

"Thank God! Because you shouldn't. They certainly couldn't trust you to protect them, could they?"

"You don't know that."

"I know you were going to shoot Riley, weren't you?"

"Someone has a big mouth."

"Someone knows how to protect a child."

"My mother protected me by teaching me how to fight."

"How many of your scars are because of your mother?"

"How many of your scars are because of your mother," Kola fired back.

"None," he answered, standing up and pulling his shirt up to reveal no scar whatsoever on his torso or back. He lowered his shirt. "Shauna doesn't have them. Riley doesn't have them. The only person in here who has them is you, and you're the only one who can't be trusted with that helpless baby."

"I can be trusted."

"You're dangerous, the worst kind of person there could be."

Kola's face hardened and she knew it.

"Is that what you told your daughter," she asked.

Damn, he was fast!

She didn't even have time to react. His hand was suddenly there. Then her eyes took a moment to refocus while her brain tried to remember what she was doing.

"If you had been my kid, I'd have killed the dog that bit you and everyone else who tried to give you those scars—and if I couldn't do that, I'd make sure he got well fed before he could get to you." He stood and made his way out of the room. "Go to sleep. Put the water bottles under your blanket with you."

Kola sat there, listening to his footsteps disappear down the hallway. A door shut, and she heard the lock click.

She laid down, pulled up the water bottles around her chest and realized they brought more comfort than she realized they could. She ran her finger over her kidney scar.

When she awoke again, her water bottles were warm. Riley, Shauna and their host prepared to have breakfast once more. Kola sat.

The host approached her with a new pill and fresh glass of electrolytes. He looked over her foot.

"Good," he said. "That looks much better. I'll give you some pills to take with you when you leave today. Make sure you take them every six hours for at least another week. It's important you take them until they're all gone, and don't miss taking any when you're supposed to."

They ate breakfast: toast, grits, sausage links and caramelized peaches with whip cream. Riley had formula and milk mix.

Kola took a shower afterwards and dressed into her own clothes. Her host had announced that he and her traveling companions would be out by the creek when she was ready. By the time she had finished, he had already removed all her traveling gear from the house.

Her gun sat on the table next to her knife and the box of ammo that she had buried deep into her bag. A note, folded on top of it read, "Remember. Kill me, and you have to take the baby with you."

She exited the house, the underground warehouse, climbed the expanded steel stairs to the cavern pasture where she found her and Shauna's horses packed up. She decided that their host had started the packing before breakfast had even started. Perhaps he couldn't sleep with Kola in the house. He may have been smarter than she gave him credit.

She was investigating her gear to ensure nothing had been stolen when she heard excited muffled voices, one of them Shauna's, and several popping sounds that echoed through the garage doors into the cavern. These were gunshots, Kola knew these at once, even the types of guns that made them.

"Get inside," the host's voice ordered.

Shauna rushed into the cavern; Riley was crying in her arms. The host followed, clinging to his engine, and when Kola saw the three shadows of intruders appear within the archway of doors, she dodged through the pasture and knelt behind one of the four-wheeler's tires.

The doors started to close, but quickly reopened as three men dressed in suits crossed their safety sensor.

"The device," one of them said.

"Don't have it," the host said, even though he foolishly clenched it in front of him.

"We saw you using it," the trespasser replied.

"Do you know whose land your on?"

Riley cried.

"Take her inside," the host cried. "Lock it behind you."

"That's far enough," a second voice ordered.

A gunshot erupted—a stupid move for a closed cavern, Kola thought. She quickly loaded cartridges into the cylinder of her pistol.

"She's a baby, for God's sake," Shauna rebuked.

"Fine," the first intruder said.

Another gunshot.

Something heavy fell against the cavern floor.

Kola peeked around the back of the golf cart.

Their host lay on his side. He held a black engine into his chest. One of the men reached for it, but the host curled his body over it so they couldn't get at it.

"Really," the intruder asked. "Well, okay." He quickly pointed a silver firearm at the host's leg and blasted a nine-millimeter round into it.

The host didn't scream but continued to hold onto the device.

"You can't be that dumb," the intruder said. He looked down on the host, sighed and then looked to his gun as though asking if he should shoot him again.

He did, in the side of the host's belly. Then the attacker knelt and reached in to tear the engine away from the host's grasp. The host refused to let go.

"It's Salvo's," the host squawked, barely understandable.

"Salvo's not here," the intruder said.

"It's mine!"

The host's eyes locked onto Kola's, and he hugged the small capsule into his chest even tighter despite the thief's attempt to take it. For some reason, she didn't see the engine. She saw something as small as Riley, tucked into him. He wouldn't let go. Why was he so stupid? This wasn't even a person. Is this what he'd do for Riley?

The would-be thief held his gun to the host's head but then fell forward with Kola's knife buried into the back of his neck, where it instantly severed his spinal cord. He crumpled right above the host's body. By the time the other two intruders had the presence to turn their attention to the direction that the knife had been thrown from, Kola had already raced from the four-wheeler and put a bullet into another man's head. From this distance, Kola knew the bullet would enter but wouldn't exit the skull. Rather, it ricocheted throughout his brain. He was dead before he started to fall.

The remaining man seemed confused, perhaps in the surprise of the sudden event, or perhaps at the moral ethics of whether he should return fire upon a child. Maybe it was both. Before he was capable of solving his ethical conundrum, Kola fired a round into his knee, another into his thigh, then stomach, gun-hand, and up into his neck. His firearm fell. He dropped to his knee, toppled to his side and Kola fired her remaining bullet into his eye.

She turned to the host. He opened his hands and the small, black engine rolled towards her.

"Take it to Vegas," he said. "Tell Salvo it flies, but it won't get to orbit yet."

Kola looked to the engine, undecided if she should.

"Tell him I think the blades are knocking at high altitude. It's not cutting like it should. There's drag in the engine."

Shauna knelt down, Riley still screaming.

"I'll take it," She said.

"Take them both." He held out the small remote to the garage doors. "Lock up please."

He groaned, his body tightened, and his skin had paled. He looked to Kola and nodded his head subtly. "What's one more?"

Kola held her pistol to his face, and he suddenly grabbed her wrist.

"Promise me you'll get it there," he said and looked to Riley. "It can get her off this god-forsaken world. Only you two can give it to her. Promise. Please. Give her a better world than the one we got."

"All right," Kola said plainly, and again didn't know why she would do such a thing. "I promise."

Then he nodded, and Kola knew what he was asking.

She held her pistol to his head and pulled the trigger.

The hammer clicked against a spent chamber.

Shauna jumped. The host jerked but cried. Kola reached into her pocket and took out her box of ammo, half full. She put in a bullet, aligned the chamber and tried again. This time it worked.

"He was a good one, you know," Shauna said.

"Was he," Kola asked and looked down on him to see if she could see it.

"He saved your life," Shauna said. "He fed us."

"So, did our last foster parents," Kola said. "But I suppose he did know me better."

She took up the engine.

"You realize we have to take her with us now," Shauna said.

"Or we could leave her," Kola said. "Like we should have done in the first place." Then she reluctantly reconsidered. "That son of a bi—he just made me promise to keep her alive, didn't he?"

She stormed off and towards her horse but then steered herself towards the four-wheelers. She found the keys inside the ignitions. The tanks were full.

"Suppose we could take these instead," Kola said.

"What about the horses? They'll starve if we leave them."

"So will she, if we take them," Kola replied. "There's not enough formula unless we can cover more ground faster, and milk will spoil before we can use it."

"We can take a cow."

"Cow milk's bad for babies," Kola said. "He said so."

"I had actually meant, what do we do to protect the horses if we leave them behind," Shauna explained.

"He said people come here in tunnels every so often. We could open the pens, give them access to the hay. Let the people know they're here."

"We could let them go," Shauna said.

Kola shook her head, "Too much work. You want to try leading all these cows out of the cave? Besides, might advertise the cave is here. Maybe we better not."

"I suppose," Shauna said. She looked over the host once more before turning back to attempt to calm Riley who was still caught up in the energy of bawling. She wrapped Riley into one of the flannel blankets and set her on the floor of the house porch.

Kola searched the area for extra gasoline, she found two five-gallon, metal cans in the strange chassis on wheels.

"How many miles do you think we can go on a tank of gas here," Kola asked, now looking over one of the four-wheelers.

"I don't know," Shauna said. "My friend's motorcycle went two hundred miles on a tank of gas. Those tanks look about the same size."

"Yeah, but they have to move four wheels instead of two," Kola said.

"So? What? Half of that then," Shauna suggested.

Kola's head bounced around as she appeared to be pondering and agreeing with Shauna's assessment.

"It's not enough," she said.

Kola dragged her horse next to the fence so she could climb high enough to start unburdening the animal of her gear. By the time she had started on Shauna's horse, Riley had finally quieted and was sleeping. Shauna set off about the horse pasture and around the side of the house.

"I think I found the hay supply," she called out, but she was too far and too muffled in the cave now for Kola to understand her.

One of the quad-runners had racks on its front and rear ends, so Kola started piling her and Shauna's gear onto the back rack and tied it down with twine. For the front rack, she thought about Riley and how she'd travel. She'd probably be happier if she wasn't strapped to Shauna's stomach, and Shauna would probably steer better without the little body in her way.

Kola opened a sleeping bag and folded it into the front rack. She used horse blankets to line the walls of the bed to keep the baby from falling out. She set Riley inside.

Riley awoke at this and looked to Kola with her inquisitive eyes. Somehow, she had managed to grip onto Kola's trigger finger. Her hold was tight, strong. She was strong. Kola could feel her own pulse pumping through the vice created by the baby's cinching fingers, pumping to the tip of her own finger and then fighting to push back up into her hand.

"You're a nuisance, you know that," Kola said.

Riley kissed her pacifier.

Kola decided Riley needed something to hold her down to keep her from bouncing out, a seatbelt of some sort. With a little rearranging, of the bed, and a few cuts with her knife, she worked the leather straps of the horse bridle through the basket and around Riley's swaddling. She covered her with the second flannel blanket to give her a little more padding against the belts. Then she draped the first flannel blanket over her bed, covering her entirely, and folded it into the padded edges.

"I found some more gasoline," Shauna said, walking up just as Kola was finishing her work. Shauna lifted the blanket and nodded a surprised approval. "Not bad."

"The gasoline," Kola asked.

"Back here," Shauna said, pointing off behind the house. "But I'm not sure how we'll get it out of here."

The gas that Shauna had found was in a rather large tank above ground. Perhaps a thousand gallons at least. The area it stood in was directly behind the house and appeared to be even much larger than Kola had anticipated. She had almost been fooled into believing the illusion that this was all outdoors, had there been no earthy ceiling. It was, in all sense, a grazeland. Grass stretched for a hundred yards, maybe more to a small garden under bright U.V. lights. Beyond that was a barn with a tall mountain of hay bales beside it, all in addition to the pile near the cattle pen. Shauna had opened the gates next to the barn as well as the gates to the pen so all the animals could simply find the food they needed.

"And water," Kola asked.

"There's water coming in from the wall over there," Shauna said. "It's like a spring or someth—you mean you actually care."

Kola glared at her.

"Let's not pretend you've been a saint."

Kola now turned her attention to the large fuel tank behind the house, and realized it wasn't one reservoir but two that were welded together and then bolted atop a concrete slab.

"Well we can't do anything with this," Kola said.

"We could fill condoms with it," Shauna suggested.

"I wouldn't trust it," Kola said. "I put gas in a milk jug once and the jug melted. We need something stronger."

"Maybe we should try checking out the workroom downstairs," Shauna suggested.

They did. Kola checked Riley on the way to see if the new set up was working. Riley was tugging on the blanket and appeared happy. She smiled at Kola and coughed up a laugh. Kola covered her back up.

In the workroom, they found a plastic drum marked "SOLVENT." It was attached to a type of sink with a brush on a hose. Kola pressed a pedal and smelly liquid squirt out of the brush and emptied down the drain.

"What's the point of that," She asked.

"Got me," Shauna said.

"Find some buckets."

Shauna returned with a mop bucket. It took about an hour to empty the tank. Shauna poured the solvent down a drain in what looked like an open shower marked with a sign that read "chemical waste." When the barrel was light enough, they removed the hose and sink attachment and took it to the chemical drain as well. Then they hosed the barrel out and carried it outside.

"Still can't move it," Kola said. "It doesn't have wheels."

"That does," Shauna said pointing to the golf cart. "We can take off the seats and the batteries. We could tow it."

"How do you know that?"

"Me and some friends stole a golf cart from the country club once," Shauna explained. "Remove the seats and the batteries and it's just a big wagon."

"Huh," Kola replied, and she might have been a little impressed. "Think there might be something in the barn before we start trying to make a trailer if we don't have to?"

They checked, and there was a small trailer, attached to a second golf cart, one that looked more like a little pick up truck. The trailer was large enough to carry a couple of bales of hay from the barn to the horse and cow pen. It was narrow but seemed sturdy enough that it shouldn't tip too easily if they were careful towing it.

They drove it out, to the large fuel tank, put the plastic drum on it and filled it as full as they could. They had no lid, so they closed it off with aluminum tape.

When, they couldn't find rope to secure it, they tied it down by creating straps made of more duct and aluminum tape. They found six rolls all together in the workroom, and they used almost all six of them. They towed the trailer and cargo to the other vehicles then switched it from the hitch of the golf cart to that of the four-wheeler that Riley wasn't riding in.

When they finished. They went back into the kitchen, retrieved the formula and fed Riley.

"If we play this right," Kola said. "We should be able to cover enough ground that we can get across the border and find a store to buy some in time."

"Do you really want to chance that," Shauna asked.

Kola agreed. She shouldn't chance it. She turned to the kitchen cupboards and began digging through until she found a half-gallon canister of powdered Gatorade.

"Maybe we can make it last longer if we mix it with this," Kola said. "Water it down maybe."

"Not a bad idea," Shauna said. "But we should take some real milk."

"It's bad for babies," Kola reminded, annoyed that Shauna kept forgetting.

"It will work in a pinch."

"It'll go bad."

"We could pack it on ice?"

They ate and found a cooler that they could pack with milk, ice and some frozen items from their host's freezers. Shauna gathered more material for Riley to wear, as well as their host's stash of diapers, which it turned out, wasn't very large, but any kind of easy diaper was better than sleeping bag cotton and fabric. Then they retrieved the second engine from the workroom and secured it all to the second four-wheeler.

"Do you want to tow gas, or do you want to babysit," Kola asked.

"I'll take care of the baby." Shauna replied with a firm emphasis on exactly who would watch Riley.

Kola allowed it.

The last thing Kola did was gather up the guns from the men in suits. She kept two and handed one to Shauna.

"I don't want it near Riley," Shauna said.

"Then don't let her play with it," Kola replied. She secured her pistol, two Rugers from the trespassers and Allen's shotgun into the trailer of fuel, burying them under the folds of the sleeping bag.

When the quad engines roared to life, Kola wondered if she should feel bad for stealing from their host. Then again, she remembered all this belonged to Salvo, and she was quite interested in meeting up with him now that she knew how to find him. She also wondered if Riley was liking the new sound, she couldn't hear her response. Perhaps the horse blankets that lined her bed muffled her and the engine noise. Maybe that meant they might actually make some ground today.

She drove out first, pulling the barrel of gasoline behind her. Shauna followed to help keep an eye out for any unwanted wobbling of their fuel, she let the remote close the doors behind them.

Outside the cavern entrance, they both stopped.

"What do we do about that," Shauna asked, looking towards the Omniscient helicopter parked a hundred feet away from the cavern entrance.

"Are you kidding," Kola said. "You couldn't tell me we had a helicopter?"

"Do you know how to fly one," Shauna asked.

The girls stepped down from their vehicles and approached it. Kola climbed the steps at the side into what could have passed for a luxurious hotel suite with a leather couch, television, three chairs and a bar loaded with liquor.

"Excuse me," a woman inside sneered from behind a tablet, not from work but from the sound of a video game of some sort. She set the tablet down and moved towards the cabin door to close it. "Don't think you belong in here."

"You fly this thing," Kola asked.

"No," the woman said. "The pilot's not here. Time to go."

Kola shot her with what she guessed could have been the pilot's gun.

"You don't have to kill everyone you know," Shauna said.

"Someone's going to come looking for the helicopter," Kola said. "Won't be hard to find it, don't need her pointing out which way the pilot went."

"Maybe we better get out of here then, before someone else shows up," Shauna said. "They're not going to like your handiwork."

"Wouldn't take them long to find us in that if they do show up then," Kola said. "What were you doing out here before they came?"

"He was showing me how the engine worked, and they just flew down," Shauna explained.

"Did they seem to know where the entrance was, or did they follow you in?"

"Followed us, I think."

"Okay, maybe they don't know where it is then," she said. "I have an idea."

Kola returned to Shauna's pack and opened the pouch with the condoms. She tossed one to Shauna. "Start blowing these up. String them together if you can."

"How many?"

"As many as you can, as full as you can, but don't pop them and leave enough slack to tie them together."

"What are you going to do," Shauna asked.

"Find some glue." Kola unhitched the trailer from her four-runner and drove back into the cavern.

She returned about fifteen minutes later with a shovel, a garden rake and two boxes: one was marked "spray adhesive," the other "black enamel."

Shauna had strung together five lengths of condom balloons, tied end-to-end like giant snakes. Kola broke out a can of adhesive and sprayed one side of the snakes and stuck them together. She continued to lay them out and glue them before the entrance to the cavern, then she helped Shauna blow up more balloons until they had created a large mattress with jagged, bubbly edges.

"That should be enough," Kola announced.

"Good," Shauna said. "I'm lightheaded." She checked on Riley under her flannel canopy.

Riley slept.

Kola took out a shovel and began digging ground around the base of the helicopter. She turned up several scoops of soil and instructed

Shauna to grab the rake and start removing the rocks. After the two had turned soil and gleaned the rocks from the dirt, Kola began to spray the condom mattress with more adhesive, while instructing Shauna to toss dirt over the areas that she had passed over.

Shauna did.

Kola emptied eight cans in the process. Shauna popped one of the condoms when she didn't realize a rock had been in one of her handfuls of dirt. Kola chided her, and they continued with their task. Once they had finished, Kola began spraying once again over the dirt powdered condoms. This time, she had Shauna tear up lush handfuls of grass and leaves and throw them onto the strange canvas. When Kola used up the last of the glue, she broke out the black spray paint to finish the job.

Once they were done, they worked together to heft the mattress up and into the mouth of the cavern, turning it into a wall. Several more condoms popped in the process. They blew up replacements and reattached them with dirt, grass and paint camouflage.

"It stands out, you know," Shauna said.

"If you use the rake, I think you can pull down some of that ivy so it's not so prominent," Kola explained.

"Oh, if I do, huh?"

"You're taller, stupid. You can reach more," Kola said. "And don't pop the rubbers with the rake."

Five minutes later and Shauna had pulled enough ivy and foliage over the mouth of the cave that they had actually created the illusion that there wasn't anything out of the ordinary where the cave entrance should be.

The girls tossed the empty canisters of adhesive and paint into the creek and let the current carry them away. They dumped the remaining, filled cans into Kola's trailer and gathered up all the condom wrappers, so that anyone who found them might not be tempted to question where they all came from, then search the area more in-depth and find their wall. The rake and shovel fit perfectly into the trailer with the fuel barrel as well. Lastly, Kola took several bottles of liquor from the Omniscient helicopter, ones that looked most expensive.

Shauna didn't question Kola's interest in the booze; she'd learned not to do such things by now. Besides, she kind of wanted some herself. For now, they drove away and left the cavern and helicopter behind them.

After fifty minutes of choosing careful terrain that the trailer could handle, the canyon opened, and the land rose up to a flat road. Some time later, Kola stopped and let Shauna pull up alongside her.

A quarter mile in the distance was the old freeway.

"We'll take that for now," Kola said.

Shauna protested. "I thought roads were. . .

17 left

Chapter Twenty

. . . bad!"

"Yeah," Kola said. "But they can hear us anyway, and we're faster now, so we might as well use them while we can."

They took a break to top off their fuel tanks. They didn't need much, but it was a good opportunity anyway.

"If there's a sign of trouble, we still have gas in the cans," Kola said. "And we can barter the drum for passage, maybe."

"Maybe they'll just take it," Shauna said. "Then what?"

"When I say barter," Kola said. "I mean at the first sign of trouble, we drop the trailer and take these off the road. They may have vehicles for the road, but we may do better on the off-terrain. We should have the advantage to get away. Just don't flip over."

They started out again and drove at full throttle over what had once been a bustling, paved street but was now used mostly by exiles, pirates and hunters. An hour later they emptied the contents of both metal gas cans evenly over the tanks. Shauna fed and changed Riley, patting her with corn starch.

She threw a condom over one of their used food cans, and fed then burped her, before remembering she'd brought the dish glove. Then they were on their way again.

They stopped after about an hour. Kola stabbed near the top of the side of the 55-gallon drum and let it pee gasoline. She caught the drizzle in one of the five-gallon cans. When it stopped spurting, she stabbed a little lower and continued to fill the container until it was full, and she began filling the second five-gallon canister. They then used these to fill the quad tanks before stabbing out more gas from the drum to refill the five-gallon cans again.

Kola made sure she slapped pieces of metal tape over the holes she had created.

"That's where we're going," Kola announced, the next time they stopped to fill the gas tanks. She had just swallowed one of her pills, when she pointed off to the distance.

Shauna couldn't tell one mountain apart from the other, but she nodded like she could anyway. What mattered was that Kola seemed to be able to tell them apart. Shauna insisted, however, that she look at Kola's foot to see how it appeared compared to the previous day.

It still had red but was much less swollen.

They were just getting ready to leave again when they saw their first sign of trouble. Two motorcycles and an SUV drove up an old exit ramp and onto the road. Kola had already thought she heard vehicles riding towards them, and Shauna too felt something out of place in the air.

"Hide Riley," Kola said. She picked up a chunk of broken asphalt from the ground.

"Shouldn't we go off road now," Shauna asked.

"Not enough time," Kola said, and she had begun taping the chunk of asphalt to a full paint can. "Think you can handle the biker without a helmet?"

Shauna nodded and slid her gun into a corner of Riley's crib where she could grab it easily, but Riley wouldn't.

The bikes drove up, past, around and back again.

The SUV approached much more cautiously and stopped alongside Kola and her quad. So they'd planned to expose the child as a means to manipulate Shauna, Kola immediately realized. A man drove, a woman sat in the front seat, and two more women sat in the back.

"How are we doing, ladies," the driver asked. He smiled in a way that hid and made his intentions clear at the same time. Shauna knew at once he wasn't nearly as good at it as Kola was.

The woman in the passenger seat's intentions were pasted all over her face, her hand was already resting on a trigger.

"A little lost," Kola replied.

"Where you trying to go," the driver asked.

"Oregon," Kola said. "How far is it?"

The driver smiled. The passengers tried not to laugh. The riders stared as amused sentinels, parked atop bikes.

"It's quite some distance," the driver said. "You're on the wrong road, but we can show you how to get on the right one."

"See," Kola sneered at Shauna. "I told you if we waited, someone would show up."

"We saw a baby," the woman passenger said. "Let us see."

Shauna's hand slid under the blanket and gripped her gun.

"He's sleeping," Kola said. "You can see him when you show us the right way to Oregon."

"Those bikes aren't safe for a baby," the driver said. "If you hit a bump, he could fall out and you'd run him right over."

"He can't fall out," Kola said. "He's strapped in."

"Even still," one of the bikers said. "We better take him in the car. This road has a lot of bad people who would steal from two kids like yourselves." He rocked his bike onto its stand and began to step off.

"No," Kola said. "Don't let 'em. We need this stuff to open our store."

"Your store," the front passenger asked, suddenly more interested.

The SUV driver waved the biker back. "Maybe, if you show us the baby, we'll help protect your stuff for your store."

"You would do that," Kola asked.

"Depends. What kind of stuff you got?"

"Oh," Kola chimed with glee. "I'll show you." She jumped up to the side of the gasoline barrel and tore off the lowest level of tape, to let a small stream fill the Eversnap bowl that she had just eaten leftovers from. She taped the hole back up and shoved the bowl into the driver's hands.

"See," she said. "Know what that is?"

"Is this gasoline," the driver asked playfully. He already knew the answer, and Kola was glad he was so eager to play along.

"Yeah," Kola chirped. "And look what else." She stepped back to her rack and took out a globe of burgundy liquor that she had taken from the helicopter. She excitedly shoved it into the driver's hands as well. The driver handed the container of gasoline to the passenger in the heat of the moment so he could take the liquor without dropping the bowl, but he did spill a bit.

"And," Kola said, turning once more to her stash of supplies. "We have paint." She grabbed the can of paint with the rock taped to it, handed that to the driver too. Again, the driver bumbled the bottle of liquor off to the passenger, who swore as she spilled more of the gasoline into her lap at the abrupt handoff. Shauna realized that Kola must have also known the passenger was sitting with a finger on a trigger. In that instant, Kola had disarmed her.

"What's the rock for," the driver asked, turning the paint can around in his hand, as though he really cared to inspect it.

"Oh," Kola cooed. "For the spark."

She tore one of the nine-millimeters from her basket and shot the can of paint. The bullet sheered through the side-third of the can, which normally wouldn't have done anything, when a bullet hit it, except spew paint everywhere, but, because there was a cluster of rocks behind it, the bullet had a matchbook-like surface to spark itself and it ignited the container's contents.

The can spun loose from the driver's surprised hands, causing a spiral of flames to helicopter within the car. At the same time, the dumb, front passenger, in her absent-mindedness to grab her own gun, dropped the bowl of gasoline and burst into flames. Before she could drop the bottle of liquor though, Kola shot another bullet through it and the alcohol splashed a liquid fireball throughout the vehicle. The SUV became cubicle of screaming and flames licking up and out of only one open window.

Shauna then fired three rounds into her designated biker.

Kola turned her gaze on the second and shot him even as he drew his own firearm.

"They're getting out," Shauna announced.

As the door closest to Kola began to open, revealing the burning driver trying to escape but restrained by his seatbelt, Kola decided he wasn't the immediate threat. She ignored him for the time being and let him earn his scars. At this point, she had already taken up the shotgun and blasted it through the window behind the driver. She then went around to the other side of the SUV where she found the other two passengers fleeing the vehicle. The remaining woman from the back seat was blackened—her back was on fire, but she didn't seem aware as she bent forward coughing. The fireball that was the front passenger ran towards the side of the road.

Kola gunned down one then the other and made her way back towards her four-runner, where she found the driver who continued to scream but still couldn't find the seatbelt release.

"You can't have her," Kola said and then blasted another shotgun burst into him.

She repacked her weapons away into her cargo, started her four-runner and steered the trailer of gasoline away from the flame.

In another hour, they stopped to top off their tanks.

"How do you do it," Shauna asked.

Kola wasn't sure what she meant.

"The stuff you do," she said. "I heard you last night. I know how many people I've killed, more than anyone should, but you don't even think about. How do you do it?"

"I just do."

"I mean, how doesn't it bother you?"

"Does it bother you?"

"Sometimes, yes. Keeps me awake even, but not you."

"It's what people do. It's life."

"No," Shauna replied. "It's not. You're right. You are broken, worse than I am."

During their next stretch between refuels, they had another encounter, nothing big, two people on dirt bikes. They had turned their bikes to act as a roadblock, thinking perhaps that would cause anyone approaching to slow down. Kola shot one and simply ran the other over, all without stopping.

The mountain drew closer, and turned blue, gray, then black against a waning sky until both finally disappeared into night.

"Should we stop," Shauna asked.

"No," Kola said. "Keep going."

As they were refueling, Shauna did her best to feed Riley. They moved again, and the black mountains grew up all around them and their head lamps.

Then, above their heads, a red flare soared and exploded, then another followed.

Kola turned her quad towards the flare and led Shauna into the wilderness as far as their four-wheelers could carry them.

A rock face came up out of the dark, a wall that started inseparable from the sky and black horizon of the mountain. Then, in a blink, turned gray and was suddenly white and blocking their pathway.

Kola stepped off her four-runner and began searching out land that could prove to be a comfortable site to set up camp. After Shauna checked on Riley, she set to helping Kola gather the makings for a fire.

"Who fired the flare?"

Kola shrugged, but not confidently.

The two set up a fire. Rain began to fall, but the fire burned anyway.

Kola and Shauna broke out the tent they had taken from the hunters. They set it up with the door facing the fire, rather, Kola did right after she had laid needles to help insulate against a wet ground. After, they moved in their gear and Riley.

Kola topped off her tank then unhitched the trailer from her quad and reattached it to Shauna's. She removed all her gear from her own quad, collected the shotgun; two of the nine millimeter firearms; and all but one of the bottles of booze. Then she drove all of it a short distance away from their campsite and left it in the distant dark. Then she walked back to camp.

Before she had even returned, her vehicle started, and she spun around to see only its headlight disappearing into the forest.

"Kola?" Shauna's head popped through the dome tent door, and she was surprised to see her. "What just happened? I thought you left."

"They accepted our payment," Kola said and then began cooking some of the flying cow.

When dinner was over, Kola joined Shauna and Riley in the tent for the night.

Riley was in a good mood, a little too good of a mood. She didn't want to have her diaper changed, and she was more interested in laughing at Kola and pulling on her lips than she was in eating. They created her another bed out of the horse blankets so she couldn't slide beneath either Kola nor Shauna in her sleep.

Kola read, Shauna calmed Riley down, told her a story, rocked her in her arms.

"What's your mom like," Shauna asked.

"Why?"

"Is she like you?"

"Do you mean, is she going to try and kill you?"

Shauna was embarrassed to say any more.

"We made a deal," Kola said. "She won't. And no, she's not like me. She's a much better fighter."

Kola settled under her covers and read. Shauna set down a finally-tired Riley on the side of her bed farthest from Kola.

"You think I'd still hurt her," Kola asked.

"I think you'd hurt both of us," Shauna answered.

"What if I promised to keep her safe?"

"You set off a bomb in a bigger bomb next to a fifty-five-gallon bomb right next to her today," Shauna replied. "I don't think you can keep anyone safe. As soon as we're across the border, I'm taking her with me."

"Why," Kola asked. "So she can find out you're not her mom and drop a marble down your throat?"

Shauna froze. Kola couldn't tell if she was about to cry or to start screaming.

"You're right," Shauna said. "But she can't be alone, and she can't be with you. She's mine, you understand? At the border, we'll part ways. Go where you want. I'm going to Vegas with that machine."

"That's probably a good idea," Kola said. "She's probably safer with you."

"I know she is."

"Except, I made a promise to get our little package to Las Vegas for the very purpose of helping her get a better life. So, I don't think that's an option."

"Well, I suppose we'll have to cross that bridge when we come to it."

"I suppose you're right."

"Trust me," Shauna said. "You're the last person anyone should be around, especially a baby."

"Yet you're here."

"We have a deal," Shauna said. "If anything, I believe you're true to your word, but what happens after you keep your promise and we cross that border?"

Kola hadn't actually thought about that. She'd been too intent to make sure they traveled safely so she could keep her word. What was a person without her word, Kola wondered. She fell asleep wondering, and when she awoke, it was still dark, and the tent was a little too quiet for three people.

Shauna and Riley were gone, and the fire outside the tent door cast shadows far bigger than it should have after burning into the night. The rain had stopped.

Had Shauna walked off with Riley? Built the fire bigger to help them pack in silence? She would have heard the four-runner starting. That would have been stupid of Shauna, Kola thought. She couldn't survive on her own. Then a different thought struck her. Had their protectors decided her offering wasn't enough and took Shauna and Riley? All without her hearing them though? Out here? Who could have done that?

She sat up. Reached under her pillow. Gone! Her pistol was gone, her knife too. In fact, the only items she could seem to locate in the dark were her book, shoes and backpacks.

"I hear you moving in there, Kola," Sandra Chevalier's voice said. "Come out here, sweetheart."

Kola obeyed. Upon stepping out, she found Shauna tethered with rope and tape to the barrel of gasoline in the trailer. Her mouth had been stuffed with socks that dripped fuel. Her face, though dark, couldn't hide the streaks of terror.

Riley slept in Kola's mother's arms. Kola's gun and knife were at the side of the rock her mother sat upon.

"I thought I was going to have to start without you," Sandra said. Her orange suit had been disguised black with foliage stains and mud. Her face and hair weren't much different. She might have been more difficult to see, but anyone who knew the style of clothing would have immediately recognized they were those of an exile. She caressed Riley's cheek with an inflated condom.

"This isn't where you said you'd be," Kola said.

"No, it's not," Sandra said. She dropped the condom, and it rolled away carelessly. "I got bored. I came looking."

"You didn't have to babysit me," Kola said. "I can do this myself."

Shauna muffled a scream, barely audible.

"Quiet," Sandra said softly, raising a .357 towards Shauna and without ever looking up from Riley. She lowered it when she had made her point.

"If you could do this on your own, why would I find two people who don't belong here?"

"I was helping her."

"Them. You were helping them."

"Them," Kola repeated.

"She's wearing my clothes," Sandra said. "What am I supposed to wear now?"

"We were going to give them to you when we found you."

"I don't deserve clothes someone else hasn't worn?"

"Yes, you do," Kola said.

"They've dulled your senses. You didn't even hear me remove them nor your weapons." Sandra finally looked to her daughter. "You know the rules."

"Yes."

"What are they?"

"Never let anyone in who's not blood."

"I think you've been listening to a crying baby too much," Sandra explained. "You would have never taken a baby. I assume it was your friend's idea. What's her name?"

"The baby's name is Riley."

"Your friend's name," Sandra said, standing up now.

"I don't have any friends," Kola answered. "That's the rule."

"That's right," Sandra said. Now she smiled. "Good. As long as you're still in there. Come hug your mother, so we can put this behind us."

Kola obeyed and embraced her mother, who continued to gently bounce Riley at the same time.

They pulled apart.

"Except, why would you know the baby's name," Sandra asked. She looked to Riley who was starting to wake up. "She's a beautiful baby, isn't she?"

"I suppose so," Kola replied and squatted on the ground.

"Here," Sandra said. "Take her." She handed Riley to Kola. "No, no, dear. You have to support her head better. There you go."

Kola stiffly held Riley and tried not to look to Shauna.

"She's almost as beautiful as you were."

"Is she," Kola asked.

"Yes." Sandra began tightly wrapping one of Riley's diaper makings around a thick branch. "But you weren't the prettiest either."

"Can we let Shauna go now, Mom," Kola asked.

"Only friends have names," Sandra said. "And you lied to me, didn't you?"

"I promised to help them."

"You shouldn't make those kinds of promises," Sandra said. She tied twine around the fabric, which now looked like a cotton ball at the end of the branch. "What if you can't keep them?"

"But she helped me."

"Did the baby help you too?" Sandra now poured gasoline from the five-gallon can over the tightly wound twine and diapers. She sealed the can, let the cloth drip a bit and then stuck it into the fire to ignite the torch. She touched the flame to the condom balloon and it melted open.

"Okay," Sandra said. "It's time. I have your friend. You take care of the baby."

"Mom," Kola asked.

"You know full well, what I'm talking about," Sandra chided. "Put that baby in the fire."

"But I promised."

"See, this is what happens when you get attached to your leverage. Now throw her in the fire, or we'll give you something to remember this mistake by."

Shauna was now screaming, and Sandra didn't bother to raise a gun to silence her this time.

"She's a baby," Kola said.

"Excuse me?"

"She needs help."

"She's not yours. Now, come on, do as I say," she stepped towards Kola, and Kola flinched backwards.

"All right," Sandra said while nodding her head. "You can have the friend." She held out the torch to Kola with one hand and requested Riley's return with the other.

Kola stepped back. A memory suddenly came to her, a brown puppy, a Pitbull. Dog. She called him Dog. Her mom made her stab Dog. She had forgotten.

Sandra slapped Kola, and the vision of Dog flew out of her head. Kola recoiled, somewhat stunned.

"Don't give me that! We both know you can't feel."

She smacked her again.

"Stop acting like a child?"

"I am a child."

Sandra smacked her again.

"Give me the baby."

Kola recoiled.

"Give me the baby! If you can't take care of her, I'll have to."

Kola screamed like some wild bear cub.

Sandra laughed.

"What are you? A dog now?"

Kola remembered the dogs: the scars, the bites, the blood. She remembered Dog. Dog was hers. Her mother had given him to her. Then made her cut his throat out. Kola clenched Riley. She promised she'd keep her safe. She made that law, her law. Not her mom's law. It was her word. She said what her word was worth.

"Fine," Sandra said and grabbed Riley at her blanket. "I'll do it."

Kola snapped her arm forward. The chain on the set of handcuffs that they had taken from Mrs. Butts's drawer stretched out and cut across her mother's face. Kola pulled Riley as Sandra stumbled back.

The .357 erupted and a spark screamed from a nearby rock.

Kola hurled the cuffs and struck her mother in the face a second time. She turned to run.

"Oh, someone's getting spanked," Sandra said. "Don't even think about it."

The torch struck the back of Kola's head, and the seven-year-old immediately began to smell burned hair.

"Kola Ann Chevalier! Get back here with that baby."

Kola tripped. She caught herself from falling flat on top of Riley, who was now screaming. In that moment, Kola realized that even this baby, this child, knew what Kola didn't: that everything was wrong. Kola was all wrong. Her mother was all wrong.

As Kola tried to stand, Sandra pushed Kola over with her foot. Kola rolled, holding Riley tightly. She caught a glimpse of Shauna straining at her bindings to the barrel.

Kola flung dirt into Sandra's face, then a rock.

"Stop it," Sandra ordered, slapped her and reached in to take Riley. Kola rolled and tucked the infant into her chest, just as the man in the cave had done with his precious engine.

Her mother was too strong. She punched Kola's back.

"Oh, you are gonna get it," Sandra yelled, and punched her again.

Sandra hit again, kept reaching. She was going to take Riley, make Kola watch her burn in the fire. Kola knew what her mother was going to do with Shauna too. It was wrong! It wasn't how things were supposed to be. She believed Shauna now. She believed the man who had saved her foot. Her mother was overpowering her; would overpower her; would punish her; would convince her afterwards that's how life was. She'd go on to be broken forever, like her mother. Maybe Kola would do this to her own child someday.

"Help," Kola screamed. It was against the rules, but it was her only remaining weapon.

"I am helping," Sandra shouted. "Look at what they've done to you. This isn't the little girl I raised."

"Help," Kola screamed and kept screaming.

Riley helped scream, perhaps even louder than Kola was doing herself.

"You took our offering," Kola cried.

Finally, Sandra broke Kola's grip on Riley and pulled her away.

"What's the matter with you," Sandra said and carried Riley back towards the fire.

Kola leapt to her feet and raced after Sandra, scaled up her back using tufts of loose clothing to grip her way, grappled her hair and let her weight fall hard on it. Sandra's head snapped back. Her whole body stumbled, then fell on top of Kola. Riley landed on top of them both.

"That's enough, Kola!"

It wasn't enough though, and the baby that was Riley screamed, "I don't want to die! I'm not supposed to die in a fire! I'm supposed to have a better world. A world where children aren't forced to fight dogs, don't get scars, and have people they can trust to protect them when they can't do it themselves. You promised!"

As Sandra tried to recover, Kola's hands latched around the sides her face, her fingers digging into Sandra's eyes hard enough to bust past her eyelids and crack through her corneas. Her mother cursed, flailed, cursed more. She fired her gun blindly, first in front of her, then back towards Kola, unable to hit her. Riley had rolled out of Sandra's grasp. She screamed, alone in the damp dirt. Kola wormed her way out from beneath her mother, as Sandra rolled now, turning to grab Kola, finding dirt instead. She fired another wild shot.

Kola took up Riley, unable to convince her that she was going to be okay in a minute. She carried her to the place where her knife and gun lay on the ground next to the rock where her mother had been sitting only a moment ago. She ducked behind it. It wasn't large but hopefully enough, in case her mother got lucky. She hunkered down with Riley and was able to reach her .22. Kola shot Sandra until both she and the gun stopped making noise. She took the knife and Riley and moved to cut Shauna free. Upon her freedom, Shauna embraced Kola and the screaming baby.

Kola handed Riley to Shauna.

"She's safer with you," Kola said.

"I don't think that's true anymore," Shauna replied.

Kola didn't say anything. She wanted to believe Shauna, but she was a killer.

"I'm sorry about your mom," Shauna said.

"She's a survivalist. She knew the risks," Kola explained.

"You really don't feel anything, do you," Shauna said.

Kola turned; Shauna couldn't read the expression on her face. Perhaps it was the shadows of the flames, but she seemed something different in this moment. Something not so stone.

"I felt I didn't want her to kill you," Kola said. "Does that count?"

"Maybe. Where there's a drive for something you want or don't want, maybe there is a something to feel buried deep."

"She can't hurt you now."

"She took us both from our beds. How did she do that."

"She's very good," Kola said.

"You never stood a chance, did you?"

"Well, she's dead now," Kola said. "We should go to bed."

"I can help you bury her."

"Why," Kola asked. "She'll feed animals this way."

"We bury her because it's the right thing to do," Shauna said. "It's what the world does."

Kola stared at Shauna, considering her perspective.

"No," she said. "She doesn't deserve the right thing. You were right. You don't put a little kid with dogs, and you don't put a baby in the fire." Then she turned to the black forest and screamed. "I want my payment back! You call this protection?"

She threw dirt on the fire to quench it and keep others from finding them, then went back to bed.

In the morning, her mother's body was gone. The guns had been returned, but the four-wheeler and alcohol had not.

"I suppose a partial payment for a partial night's work is fair," Kola said. They fed Riley.

"You shouldn't be alone," Shauna said.

"Huh?"

"When we get to the border, we should stay together," Shauna explained.

"Why?"

"You need someone to stop you from doing the wrong thing."

"Like you," Kola asked. "Really? You?"

"Like her." She nodded down to Riley.

"She can't talk. How's she going to do that?"

"When you have someone you're responsible to take care of, you think about what your actions might do to them. Look at what you were able to do last night. You knew what your mother was doing was wrong, didn't you?"

Kola was puzzled but shook her head anyway. She stood and began to take inventory of the fuel and the water.

"What are you thinking?"

"I'm thinking we have enough water to go. . ."

15 left

Chapter Twenty-one

. . . back to the cave," Kola said.

"You want to go back?"

"We have no reason to go anywhere else now."

"What about Vegas, to that guy, what's his name?"

"Salvo," Kola replied.

"Yeah. Him."

"The guy at the cave—

"Michael," Shauna replied.

"Who's Michael?"

"The guy in the cave. That was his name."

"Oh. Well, Michael said Salvo owns the cave, and that he sends supplies to it through a tunnel, so there's got to be someone who'll come to us who can take us right to him. We'll be safe there."

"What about the people who might come looking for their helicopter?"

"They won't be safe."

Shauna considered the thought. "We're running low on formula."

"That guy—Michael—said he ordered formula. So, we know some is coming, and he has other food. Maybe we can figure something out like with a blender or something when we run out. He said he has streaming video, that means he has Internet, and we can find out what else we could do to take care of her. Otherwise, cow milk will have to do. Maybe we can mix in some vitamins or something if he has any."

"We only have one vehicle now."

"We have the trailer. We won't go through fuel as fast because we'll only have one vehicle, and we should have about fifteen gallons of gas left plus whatever's still in the tank. That might be enough to top off and fill twice. We won't need the drum anymore once it's all gone. That should get us back to the dirt bikes. We could drain their tanks if they're there, and there's two more motorcycles with the SUV. That gets us back, or close enough that we can handle walking the rest of the way."

"What if the motorcycles aren't there," Shauna asked.

"Then we'll be walking a lot sooner. We may have to trap animals and mix the blood with the formula if we do that, but I think we can still make it."

"Are you sure you can find the cave again?"

Kola shook her head. "I paid attention to the landmarks. We'll ride the road back to where we got on. We find the creek, we find the cave. We'll be good. What's wrong?"

"I'm just wondering if it would be better for Riley if we went to the border, bought formula and just came back."

"I don't know," Kola answered. "I've never been there. My mom has. She'd have known. I'd be guessing. Who knows if there's a town close enough? Maybe you should decide. You choose what to do, and I'll get us there."

"Ok," Shauna said and gave it some thought. "We should go back probably."

They did just that. They made it to the dirt bikes they had encountered the day before. Then they drained both tanks and filled up their own, which got them to the burned SUV and the bullet bikes. The bullet bikes, however, were gone. The SUV, although burned from the inside out, was in pretty much the same place. The bodies were nowhere to be seen though.

"Guess that means we'll be walking soon," Shauna said.

"We've done it before," Kola replied. "But we might not need to."

She walked to the back of the SUV, tried to open the rear door. It didn't open, but the passenger side-doors already were, so she climbed in and, several minutes later, returned with a scissor car-jack.

"What are you going to do with that," Shauna asked. She took the opportunity to feed Riley.

"Raise the car so I can get to the gas tank better."

The car raised, then Kola grabbed one of the empty gas cans and the hatchet. She clubbed a hole into the side and did the same with the other. Then she swung the hatchet into the SUV's gas tank.

"You trying to blow us up," Shauna asked. "Again?"

"You need a spark to do that."

"And you don't think doing that will make one?"

"No," Kola said. She swung a few more times, and finally gasoline began to spit out of a bottom corner of the tank. She slid the five-gallon can beneath the leak, caught the gas, filled it, then slid the other can under, but there wasn't much left for the tank to fill that one. Kola filled the quad tank, and they went on their way again, just as they heard engines in the distance. As Shauna drove, Kola climbed under the pile of gear on the trailer.

Shauna kept driving. Two green bullet bikes raced up, catching the quad rather easily.

They pulled up, one on either side of the trailer. Kola surprised them both—shot one, then the other. They stopped to drain the bike tanks of their gasoline and continued on their way.

They drove off road, found the creek and eventually the mouth of the cave with its untouched wall of rubbers. The helicopter was gone, the wall of rubbers seemed undiscovered. As the night grew dim, they uncovered the cave entrance, removed the wall, drove the quad in, then went back outside to replace the wall and lifted the bottom enough to climb under. Two condoms popped in the process, so they replaced and disguised them once more. Kola had suggested it might be best to keep the camouflage in case others came back to investigate the missing helicopter staff.

"We should bury Michael," Shauna said. "Maybe the others."

"Nah," Kola said. "You take Riley inside. I know what to do here."

Shauna didn't ask any questions, just agreed and took Riley in, fed her, cleaned her, put her to bed. When she returned to the front yard, she found the quad, Kola and the three people from the helicopter gone. Thankfully, the coolness of the cave had kept the bodies from all the bloating and stink that would have come if they had been in the sun. She went back inside so Riley wouldn't wake up alone. She was finishing up an episode of M*A*S*H when Kola's footsteps came down the steel stairs.

"So, they're gone," Shauna asked.

Kola nodded. "Drove them back to the road, gassed them up, probably still burning."

Shauna nodded. "Remember to lock up?"

Kola nodded this time.

"Cooked up some of our beef," Shauna said. "Made some instant potatoes if you want some."

Kola did. She sat down with Shauna to watch Lt. Colonel Henry Blake's face get powdered in soot right before discovering a stash of stolen items in Hawkeye's footlocker.

Then there was crying. Well, not crying exactly, but Riley was babbling to herself. Kola realized she had fallen asleep, Shauna too. Kola removed herself from the couch and found Riley stirring and babbling in her animal-cage crib.

As Kola peered in, she could tell Riley needed changing. She changed her, cleaned her, held her. As soon as the baby was in Kola's arms, she began to fall asleep.

"I may be broken," Kola said softly. "But I promise I won't break you."

When Riley was asleep, Kola set her back in the crib.

They buried Michael the next day about a mile away from the cave, then returned to his home to corral the animals and secure the hay.

"How much you think we should give them," Kola asked.

"I don't know," Shauna replied. "Maybe fill up the hay feeders every day and make sure they don't go empty? We should look online."

They found soy milk in the pantry. It wasn't a large pantry, but it had enough food for a month, Kola figured.

The formula was gone the next day, so they gave Kola soy milk, which she didn't like at first but eventually swallowed down. They mixed in real milk to make it a little better.

For the next ten days, they stayed in the bunker, safe. Kola explored the warehouse, found tools she knew how to use and tools she didn't. She wanted to explore what they could all do, but she'd seen what could happen when people played with things they didn't know how to operate. However, she did create a mannequin out of some brooms and Michael's clothes. She practiced stabbing and fighting it. On day five, Shauna had had enough and insisted Kola do something outside of the house—not the cave, they wanted to be careful.

Kola agreed, but when Shauna found Kola practicing sneaking up on cows and pretending to cut their throats, she interrupted the event.

"That isn't what I had intended," Shauna said. "I meant play or something."

"I don't play," Kola replied.

"That doesn't surprise me."

"Sorry."

"What about tag?"

"You mean where if you get stabbed, you're it until you stab someone else and the last person standing wins?"

"What? No!"

"Hide and seek?"

"Yeah, hide and if they don't find you, you don't get stabbed."

"What is with all the stabbing?"

"For someone who says that's the real world, you're picking all the bloody games."

"They're not bloody."

"Uh. Yeah they are."

"They're not supposed to be."

"You find someone, you stab them. Not in a way that they die all the time, but how isn't that bloody?"

"I mean. You're not supposed to stab anyone."

"Well then, what are you supposed to do when you find them?"

"You touch them and say 'I found you.'"

"Touch?"

"Yes."

"That sounds like a game for creepy, old men, not kids."

"What happens when they find you?"

"You lose the round."

"What do you mean you lose."

"You're out of the game until you all hide again."

"Then why hide at all if no one's going to stab you?"

"Because it's fun," Shauna explained.

Kola's face twisted into bewilderment.

"Okay, so we won't play hide and seek."

"What about kick the can?"

"You mean where you hunt and trap people before they can steal your can? That's the bloodiest of all! That's a game?"

"Well, the rest of the world doesn't do that!"

"Then how is it a game?"

"Because it makes you laugh. It feels good. You have fun."

Kola still appeared confused.

Then a thought struck Shauna. She didn't want to ask, but she did, "When you kill, is it because you feel you need to?"

Kola shook her head. "I told you, I don't feel anything. I don't laugh. I don't have fun. I don't feel a need. I kill because people get in the way of what I need to do, like get you to the border."

"If you played a game then, like say, Chutes and Ladders, and you wanted to win, would you kill your opponent if they were beating you?"

"Are they bamboo chutes?"

Now Shauna appeared confused.

"Didn't you ever do anything because you found it exciting?"

"I trapped a bear once and got the first piece of meat off of it."

Shauna suddenly smiled. "I got it! I'll be right back." She disappeared back into the house and then came back with a metal garbage can lid and some gloves from the workroom. She removed the trailer from the four-wheeler and tied some rope to the quad's ball-hitch. She started it and drove it into the back pasture, then got off and dropped the lid on the ground behind it. "Climb on and get on your knees or sit down."

Kola reluctantly did so.

"Now, hold on," Shauna said, handing Kola the end of the rope. "Try not to fall off."

Kola took the rope. Shauna returned to the driver's seat and drove out slowly until the rope was taut. "K, remember! Hold on."

She accelerated. The garbage can lid, with Kola kneeling on it, lunged forward at once. Kola lost the rope, realizing she would have fallen right on her face otherwise. Shauna drove back and reset the entire setup.

"Pull back on the rope," she said. "It will help you stay up?"

Kola rolled her eyes but nodded that she was ready, nonetheless.

Again, the quad accelerated, and, this time, Kola held on, pulling back on the rope and feeling dirt and growth pelt her in the face as the lid and she trailed after Shauna.

"K! Hold on."

"I am holding on," Kola shouted back just as Shauna turned the four-wheeler sharply to the right and out of Kola's path.

Kola shot past Shauna, felt the rope slack, heard the quad rev up, and, as Kola swung out on the end of the rope, Shauna began pulling her again. She turned sharply right again, and Kola let go of the rope then tumbled off her galvanized sled.

Shauna drove back.

"See, fun, huh," Shauna encouraged.

"Let me get this right," Kola said. "My mom puts me with dogs trying to kill me, and she's wrong, but you giving me a rope and draggin' me around this place, while I try not to break my neck isn't?"

"It's not the same."

"Why not? They both require survival instincts, or you get hurt."

Shauna turned off the bike.

"I guess you have to work up to it," Shauna answered. She started back towards the house.

"Wait," Kola called after her. "If you say it's different, I'll try it again."

"Really?"

Kola nodded. "Would Riley like to try it?"

"No," Shauna blurted. "She's too little."

"Okay," Kola said. "But just a couple more times. "We should check on her."

"Okay," Shauna said, then she climbed up to start the engine again.

On day six, Shauna turned out the lights in the cave, and taught Kola how to tip a cow over. Kola suggested it was silly and that slitting its throat was a faster way to drop it.

"It's funny," Shauna cried.

"Not for the cow."

Day seven, Shauna taught Kola how to play poker with a deck of cards she found in one of Michael's drawers. They played with a bag of peanuts from the pantry.

At first, Kola thought this was silly too.

"It's all luck," she complained. "Anyone can make a combination of cards. How is that fun?"

"It's not just about the cards, though," Shauna explained. "It's about reading the other players in the room."

"They get the same chances at their cards that I do."

"It's like when you burned those people in the car," Shauna said. "They didn't know what weapons you had packed away, and you didn't really know what they had, but you read them and you played them until you revealed what your weapons were. Think of the different hands as different weapons. You don't know what I have. I don't know what you have. At some point, we show each other our weapons and we know whose does the most damage."

"Right," Kola said. "Like when someone gets cocky because they have a knife and they think they have you cornered, and you pull out a shotgun."

"Exactly! But sometimes you have the knife, and they have the shotgun. Or you have nothing, and they have a gun."

"Like with my mom," Kola said.

"Uh. Yeah. Like that," Shauna said hesitantly, but she continued on anyway. "But if they have a shotgun and you don't have anything, you don't want them to know you don't have anything, so you try to convince them to put their shotgun down because you want them to think you have something even deadlier like a canon."

"So, you lie," Kola said.

"Yes."

"Make them think you have the better hand?"

"Yes, but not every time. Because sometimes, they may have a better hand and are just trying to get you to keep piling the peanuts on the table so they can win more."

"So, it's about cards and people."

"Yes, but it's also about knowing when it's okay to lose."

"It's like killing, but you only take their stuff."

"I guess you could see it that way."

"So, it's hand after hand of outwitting my opponent."

"Right, and you don't have to kill anyone."

"A game where you take people's stuff and lie to them? I'm sure someone's gotten killed over it," Kola said, examining the edges of one of her cards. "I'm sure I could kill someone with this if I had to."

"Yeah," Shauna replied. "Don't do that. If you win, and someone tries to kill you after the game to take your winnings, then you can kill them."

"I have permission, then?"

"Well, it's self defense."

"Ok," Kola said. "Let me try again."

Unfortunately, for the reader, the reality of this part of our innocent friends' journey is that it was quite uneventful. The majority of the days were spent exploring the cavern and the house. Perhaps, you would care to know the inventory that they discovered: the second door at the back of the cavern that was locked; the room of servers and two computers just off the workroom; the ice cream maker in the pantry?

Truth is, they were simply bored, and looked for anything to fill the time. They played cards, watched movies. Kola punched hay bales and cows. They fed Riley and tried many a time to figure out what she was yelling about. Despite not speaking Riley's language, things seemed to be working.

On day eight, Shauna fell asleep early and Kola let Riley stay up longer than normal with her while they watched an old re-run of Survivor. Want to hear about that? Didn't think so. Shauna eventually had to wake up and tell Kola to shut up and stop complaining about the stupidity of the people on the island.

On the first day back to the cave, Shauna learned from the Internet that they needed to milk the cows. It had been two days since the cows had been milked. It didn't go well, but they kept trying and finally figured out that if they wanted the cows to stand still, they had to tie the neck, legs and body of the beasts to the fencing. It worked. It worked all the way to day ten too.

They were settling in for bed at the end of day ten when a bell rang in the house.

"What do you think that is," Shauna asked.

The bell rang again.

Riley didn't seem to hear it nor woke up.

"Maybe the front door," Kola asked.

"Think it could be the supplies," Shauna followed up.

"Maybe the helicopter's come back." She let that thought register a moment. "I'll get the guns."

They armed themselves and went up the stairs to the front of the house. They opened the door, guns drawn, and no one was there.

"Guess it wasn't the front door," Shauna said.

They went back down to the living area. A mangy man leaned back against the kitchen sink, bouncing Riley in his arm.

Two more men sat on the couch. One was in the hall, talking to someone behind the locked door, that was now unlocked, at the back of the hallway.

As the girls walked in, the men on the couch drew guns. The man at the sink soon followed suit but took his time.

"Now, who are you two," the man at the sink asked.

More men filed out of the hallway until there were seven in all standing around the kitchen and living room.

"We're guests," Shauna replied.

"That baby's not yours," Kola said. "Put her down."

The men laughed.

"That's enough," An eighth intruder softly ordered from behind the group. He emerged from the hallway, the others in the house gave him room to move.

"This place belongs to Salvo," the man with the red beard said. "If it's in here. It's Salvo's."

"You know where Salvo is," Kola asked.

"I might," the man replied. He pulled up a chair at the kitchen table and sat, crossed his legs.

"I want to see him."

"Where is Michael," Red asked and seemed a little too comfortable in Michael's chair for Kola's taste.

"He's dead," Shauna said.

"You?"

"Men in a helicopter."

"I killed them," Kola said. "Now put that baby down. I'm not telling you again."

The men stirred.

Red gestured to two men, "Go see if you can find this helicopter."

"It's gone," Shauna said.

"Oh? You fly it away did you?"

"No," Shauna replied. "We left it. Someone took it."

"And the men?"

"Gone," Kola replied.

"And Michael," Red asked, his face now hard.

"Buried."

"I see," Red said.

"Times up," Kola said when Riley rose in volume.

"My turn," Red said, holding up a hand to silence the room. "Now, let me tell you what's going to happen. We were asked to bring baby supplies, an odd request for a single, middle-aged man who lives alone in a cave. That made Salvo wonder if it was Michael's way of suggesting he was in danger, and if he's in danger then so is Salvo's work. So, we all came. Now Michael's gone, you're here, the baby's here, and you say he's dead. Which means Salvo inherits the baby."

Shauna protested before Kola could.

"Now, you don't like my friend holding your baby!" Red held out his finger and pointed to a filthy man who wasn't particularly large, but his hands were. "So, here's what's going to happen. That man is going to take Salvo's new baby, and if you say one more word, he's going to break her neck because Salvo doesn't really need a new baby."

The man crossed the kitchen to the other holding Riley, and suddenly dropped sideways from the bullet that burst from Kola's gun. She turned her .22 on Red.

"My turn," Kola said, and she circled about the room, never taking her aim off Red, even when she could reach her bag where she had placed one of the engines. "Now, I'm going to tell you what's going to happen. He's going to put that baby in the sink and step away and you'll leave here only two men less than what you came in with. Or, if that doesn't work for you, I can put a bullet in him and this engine." She slammed one of the engines on the kitchen table.

Red smiled wickedly. Kola recognized he was one who was used to being in control, and probably was.

"You think you can threaten Salvo and he'll let you live," Red asked.

"You saying you're Salvo," Kola asked.

Red smirked. "Maybe. Maybe not."

Kola held her pistol towards Salvo.

"Does my face look like it belongs to someone who appreciates a smartass," Kola asked, preparing to turn her firearm at the first muscle to her side that attempted to try to help Red.

"I can't say it does," Red said, his smirk sobering.

"Are you Salvo or not?"

Red said nothing, not because he didn't want to. Kola could see he was evaluating which answer wouldn't get him shot. He swallowed.

Kola's grip tightened. Her gun fired and one of Salvo's thugs hobbled down to his butt and eventually stopped breathing. She turned the weapon back on Red.

"Okay," Red finally surrendered. "Yes, I'm Salvo."

Kola's finger relaxed.

"Good," she said. "I'd have hated to break my promise to get this to you because I killed you first." She pushed the engine, and it rolled across the table, into Red's grasp.

Red took up the device and inspected it.

"This all," Red asked.

"Here's another one," Shauna replied, and she retrieved the second from another bag and dropped it on the table.

"Michael says to tell you they almost work, but the blades knock at high altitude. It's not cutting like it should. There's drag in the engine."

Red investigated the engine, trying to understand it and finally looked up to Kola.

"Do you know what this is, little girl?"

Kola's face stiffened.

"This is a new kind of propulsion system. It can raise a single person into orbit if it ever gets finished. Do you know what that means?"

Kola held her stance and aim.

"Not too long ago, people paid a lot of money to have others smuggle them into our country," Red said. "Now, people are fleeing their own communities within our country. They pay me to get them out. Problem is, there's nowhere left to go. We've become the land of the flee and the home of betrayed."

"We're fleeing," Shauna said.

"And where will you go," Red asked. "To another state, another town with just as extreme and ridiculous of rules, where the rich and offended dictate the nation and keep you in line? Where people pretending to have scruples attack those who actually do have them, and where people who want to be bigger victims than they are now bully their neighbors? It's the same story in every state, but they all hate different people, depending on your economy. The last time this country was involved in something like that, a bunch of people got on two boats and sailed here to escape the persecution, but now we can't do that. We have only one place we can go."

Red pointed to the ceiling.

He must have been able to see that Kola didn't understand but didn't care.

"Space kid," he said. "This engine is going to help me launch a very large space station and a lot of people into orbit. If the fatcats are going to kill our nation, we'll just have to start a new one."

"Like the pilgrims," Kola asked.

Salvo nodded.

"With this, we can help people escape this place. We can build space stations that can thrive and be self-sustaining in orbit and prevent anyone from robbing that security from us. And if we get too large, we can set off into a grand universe. We can leave all this crap behind and take control of the skies and space and watch from a safe distance, and, as pettiness tears this world apart, no one will be able to touch us. And I'm not ashamed to say I'm going to make a lot of money doing it."

"A better world," Shauna said. "And only people who can afford it can go? That hardly seems fair."

"Fair," Red snapped. "A return to the Constitutional laws that were intended to govern this land before the opportunistic rich, lobbyists, politicians and thin-skinned toddlers imagined ways to overcomplicate the simplest of ideas."

"I promised to give you this so she could have a better world," Kola said, slightly nodding to Riley. "She gets to go there."

"Oh, she does, does she," Red asked, his smirk was returning.

"Yes," Kola said. "And both of us."

Red guffawed.

"Oh, it's just that simple for you is it?"

"Yes," Kola said. "We kept your engine safe from the men who tried to take it. We kept it safe for you."

"That's not how it works," Red said. "You can't afford the trip."

Kola re-purposed the aim of her pistol once more. "I made a promise," Kola said.

"Who cares about your promise," Red replied. "Shoot me. Let's see how quickly that gets anyone into space. You promised? So what?"

"She keeps her promises," Shauna said. "She's already killed two of your men protecting that baby."

"I see." Red pulled a cigarette from his shirt pocket and a lighter from his pants. He lit and puffed. "You think you're a killer, kid because you took out two of my people? When I'm done with this smoke, I'm going to show you what a real killer can do."

"In that case," Shauna said stepping up to the man holding the screaming Riley. "I'll be saying goodbye to that baby now." She took Riley from his hands. He tried to object, but Red waved him down. Then smiled and snickered smoke through his teeth.

As soon as Riley was safe, Kola's gun burst, and the man who had once been holding Riley fell right after his head spit out one of Kola's .22 copper-encased bullets.

"I don't care how good you think you are," Shauna said. "You people were all dead the moment you made the baby cry," Shauna turned to Kola. "You kept your promise to Michael. Show him."

Kola turned on her heels and threw her knife into the first man in a line of heavies standing in a hallway.

"The way I see it," Kola said. "I made your better world possible by keeping your enemies from taking those engines from you." She took bead on another man in the hall and he could have sworn he saw the bullet before it ended his life.

"Okay," Red yelled, but not before Kola had already dispatched one more of Salvo's soldiers. "Stop. I get it."

"I don't think you do," Kola replied. She returned to the table, seated herself in a chair across from Red, and held her gun on him. "I'm broken."

"Sounds like bad parenting to me," Red replied.

"Uh-huh," Kola said. "Funny you should say that, Dad."

Red's face turned from anger to instant confusion and a chilling realization stretched his eyes wide and weighed down his jaw.

"My god," Red said, and Kola interpreted the fear in his face. "You're Kola."

Kola returned her aim on Red who raised his hands as if to surrender.

"Unbelievable," he said. "She looked like you at that age."

"Who," Kola asked.

"Sandra," Red said. "We were in school together."

"You remember my mom?"

"Yeah," Red replied. "We made you, unfortunately."

"What the hell kind of thing is that to say to a seven-year-old," Shauna erupted.

Kola lowered her weapon but not her guard. "Is it wrong to put a three-year-old in a dog fighting ring to teach her how to survive?"

"What," Salvo asked, caught off guard. "It sure as hell is." He suddenly stood. "Your mother do that to you? She always was bat-shit crazy. Told me she was training you to come get me. That why I'm here? So you can finally do the job?"

"She never told me that," Kola said.

"I imagine there's a lot she didn't tell you." Salvo motioned to his remaining men, who had taken to backing out of Kola's line of sight. "Will you stop standing about and get this mess cleaned up before someone slips and falls?"

Several henchmen nodded and set to work, removing the dead men from the kitchen and down the hall towards the door that Michael had warned them away from using. Salvo excused the rest of the crew, and they willingly retreated back to their own door.

"Is it wrong to sit on a garbage can lid and hold a rope tied to the back of a vehicle your friend drives?"

"Hell no! That's fun."

"Why? What's the difference?"

"Because one comes with a thrill of danger. The other is psychotic."

"Oh."

"You going to shoot me," he asked.

"It's possible," Kola said. "You going to threaten me and my friends again?"

Red shook his head. "I didn't know it was you." He turned to Shauna. "Who are you, then?"

"We're friends," Shauna replied. "Practically family."

"But not sisters," Kola said.

"Baby yours?"

"She's hers—," Kola started.

"Ours," Shauna corrected.

"Ours now," Kola continued. "Her parents died."

"If you're anything like your mother, she'd have been better off with them," Red said.

"No, she wouldn't," Shauna snapped.

Red's face turned to her. "I've had enough out of you."

"Don't think she's the only deadly one here," Shauna said.

"Don't think you'd either be alive if she wasn't my kid," Salvo replied. He turned back to Kola. "Where's your mom?"

"Dead," Kola replied. "Tried to burn up the baby."

"You?"

"Someone had to protect her."

"No," he said. "Your mother would have never allowed you to protect someone. Give them up, that's her way. I don't buy it."

"I was there," Shauna said. "She promised, and she does it."

"You kept her alive? You?"

"We both did," Kola said. "I promised."

Red's face tightened into contemplation.

"A promise means a lot to you, doesn't it," Red asked.

"I keep my word," Kola said.

"That true," he asked looking to Shauna.

"She's a lot of bad," Shauna said. "But her word's good."

"All right," Red said. "Then I have a job for you, if you want it."

"A job," Kola asked.

"And you can have a free ride into space, for all of you and more."

"More?"

"I believe I know someone who can figure out how to fix this engine," Red said. "He's very valuable to me. Something in his brain lets him hear and see things other people can't. He can help with this, and he just became even more important to me now. I'd like you to be his bodyguard. This is important work. If I take you home with me, and I give you and your friends—your family—a ride out of this planet, will you keep him safe for me."

"From?"

"From anyone who might try to stop him."

"For how long," Kola asked.

"As long as it takes to perfect that engine."

Kola said nothing, didn't want to say anything. To Salvo, she was studying him. She was unsure.

"He's not a normal, like you," Salvo said. "But not like you. He needs someone to watch over him. He has some strange things going on inside of him."

"Not enough," Kola asked. "I'm the daughter you abandoned."

Salvo smiled and snorted.

"Fair enough," Red said. "How about this?"

He searched the kitchen. When he couldn't find what he wanted, he checked the rest of the house and returned with a pad of paper and a pen. He began scribbling.

Salvo smiled and snorted.

"What's funny," Kola asked.

"You don't know who I am, do you?"

"You're Salvo. You're my dad."

"That all your mom's ever told you?"

"What else is there?"

"That you're also Salvo," Red said. "All of this is your inheritance. Would have been your mother's, but since she can't take it now, I guess that puts you next in line."

"She never said anything," Kola said.

"I'm sure she would have," Red explained as he kept writing. "You see, what's in it for you is that when we get back to Vegas, we show this to someone important, and you get it all when I'm dead."

"Who?"

"Why your grandfather, Micah Chevalier," Red said. "He manages my estate. Once you give him this letter, he'll know who you are."

"Why me? Why don't you give him the letter," Kola asked.

"I have to go hunt down the owner of that helicopter that brought the men who killed my researcher," Red said. "My man Tinker will show you back to Vegas."

"And my grandpa's just going to believe this letter?"

Red smiled in mockery of Kola's intelligence once more. He reached to his neck and drew a gold chain from beneath the collar of his shirt. He lifted it over his head and held it out to Kola. Dangling from it was a black ring, inlaid with rose gold and diamonds. Kola didn't take it as she remained on her guard, so he held it to Shauna, who took it for her.

"That's it," Kola said. "Tinker takes me to Grandpa Micah, and I show him that letter and some ring and I'll be your heir, if I protect this kid?"

"That's not just some ring," Salvo said. "That's my wedding ring from the only woman I ever married. Your mom."

"Just like that," Kola asked.

"That's it." Salvo tore the paper from the pad and handed it to Kola. Shauna collected this too. "Do we have a deal."

Kola turned to Shauna.

Shauna nodded.

"Deal," Kola said.

She held out her hand to shake his. He smiled and shook hers, and Kola didn't have to shoot him for trying to take advantage of the moment to attack her.

Afterwards, Salvo introduced Kola and Shauna to Tinker, a burley, rough man with a beard and all the biker tattoos to show he'd earned Salvo's respect. Then Riley ate once more, and Kola, Shauna and Riley separated from Salvo to their room for the night.

They listened to Salvo plan their adventure for the next day with his men. Some of the voices were clearly upset with Kola's actions, but Salvo reassured them that the fault was his and theirs for taking advantage of their situation. He assured them if Kola acted out, he'd deal with her himself. Eventually, their shadows moved past the door, the voices died down and the house fell silent.

Riley had already fallen asleep. Kola sat up from the bed and rolled off the mattress. She began rummaging through Shauna's pack.

"They're not there," Shauna whispered, cautiously approaching Kola's side. Kola had heard her though, so she didn't respond too hastily. "I threw them out, choking hazards for babies."

"Then I guess we'll need something else," she said, drawing out a handful of condoms.

She and Shauna moved silently and found the rest of the men sleeping across several cots in a room that was lit by dim nightlights. Kola opened a wrapper, removed the spongy donut and found Salvo. She watched him a moment, wondering whether she should revere him or be ashamed of his stupidity. She wasn't sure what either felt like. He exhaled heavily, sleeping on his side. Then she shoved the condom into his mouth, quickly sealed her lips over his and blew in as he inhaled.

His breathing stopped, and his eyes opened.

"It takes two," Kola said as he tried to force himself to find any life-saving air.

He flailed, smacking the walls, stretching for Kola, anything to wake his comrades. Nine shadows of men also flailed in the darkness. Their throats either slashed by Shauna's and Kola's blades, or their airways blocked with condoms—all except one, Tinker's.

"Tinker," Kola called to the one man afraid to move beneath Shauna's shadow that was currently straddling his chest with the point of her blade pressed against his throat.

"Yeah," he squeaked.

"How rich was my father," she asked.

"That's like asking how wet the ocean is," Tinker replied hesitantly.

"Then I have a job for you. It pays double what my dad paid you," Kola said. "You want it?"

Tinker shook his head, more out of interest and less out of fear as he watched Salvo continue to grasp onto his dwindling life.

"Yes," he replied.

Kola drew out the letter that Salvo had written and held it before him.

"I guess this means, I can make that decision now, doesn't it," she said. "I'll work out those details with Grandpa Micah when I get there."

Salvo's body stopped shaking.

Kola approached Tinker as Shauna stood away from his chest.

"Do you think I should have been this evil," Kola asked.

Tinker was afraid to speak.

"It's okay," Kola said. "I'd like to know."

"No," Tinker said.

"Then you understand why I had to do this," Kola asked.

Tinker nodded.

"Good," Kola said. "Betray me and I'll cut your fat belly and turn you loose in the forest."

Something about Tinker's reaction struck Kola.

"What," she asked.

"I think," Tinker replied. "He'd be proud of you."

Kola considered what this could possibly mean, then said, "Tell me everything and take us home."

Red finally stopped flailing.

Part Three:

The Heretic

Chapter Twenty-two

New Manhattan—Diem Estate.

The guard dropped a copy of Merle Dixon's *Huckleberry Finn: Revised* on the metal shelf at Slieve's feet. Slieve stared at the wall. He wanted to stay in that position, staring at the wall. The wall was his friend. It never betrayed him. Never asked him to swallow anything he didn't want to.

He stared at the wall and pretended he could see the sun casting shadows of bars over it. The wall would have liked that. Slieve would have liked that. He was hungry but didn't care and didn't realize it. Did the wall know it? That he was hungry? Or did it know he had work to do?

Frank Lee Morris had escaped Alcatraz by digging a hole through the wall with a spoon, but Frank Lee Morris had a spoon to dig a hole to escape through.

A rat appeared in the sunlight, not real, like the sun. He knew that. Stare at a wall long enough and you know what's real and what's not.

The guard searching through his open metal cabinet, flipped through his journal and ate one of his chips from a tiny bag.

"Your chips are stale," Officer Felman said. "How old this is?"

"How old is this," Slieve corrected.

"Scuse me?" Felman spilled the chips on the ground, stepped on them, kept digging through Slieve's shelves.

Slieve turned his gaze to his ceiling and imagined there was some sort of light fixture hanging from it. Ted Bundy had escaped through a light fixture, but Ted Bundy had a light fixture to escape through.

"God, this room is stank," Felman announced, mostly to get under Slieve's skin. Felman was good at that.

Felman was kind of stupid though. His back was to Slieve. If Slieve had a gun, he could have used it to take Felman Hostage.

John Dillinger carved a fake gun out of soap or wood, or something like that, and marched his way right out of jail. John Dillinger had a knife though to cut that gun. Why didn't he just use the knife to take a real gun from a guard?

Guess it could have been worse, he could have used the knife to carve another knife, but they probably didn't make silver shoe polish back then to make the blade shiny. In any case, Slieve didn't have dumb enough guards for that.

Why couldn't he have dumb guards like Dillinger?

Felman turned to the bed and waved his fingers back at him.

"All right," he said. "Up."

Slieve rolled, sat, stood from the bed, and Felman peeled back the mattress.

"Something funny, offender," Felman asked.

"No, officer," Slieve lied and thought about the prisoner who had made nectarines look like grenades to escape prison, but Slieve had no nectarines.

"Hello," Felman announced. "What we got here?"

He held up a crucifix on a piece of thread. Slieve had made it out of a napkin and spit. The thread was from his mattress and fairly strong.

"Crucifix," Slieve replied.

"I can see what it is," Felman replied. "You ain't supposed to have it."

"I can have a religious object so long as it doesn't pose a security problem," Slieve replied.

"Say who," Felman asked.

"The Supreme Court of the United States."

"You ain't in the Supreme Court. You in prison, and this offensive. You know you can't have anything offensive. You got reprogram."

It's about time, Slieve told himself. *Only took you two weeks to find it, numbnuts.*

A prisoner once strangled another inmate with a crucifix, then used it to stab a guard and take his gun. Slieve thought of doing that, but he figured that would only piss off God.

Slieve was dragged out of his cell, cuffed at the ankles and wrists and escorted down the hall past other inmates inside their own opened, steel cubicles waiting their own turns for inspection. Slieve made no eye contact with them, and knew they made no attempt to even look at him. If they all stuck to the plan, none of them should have anything in their cells to get reprogram themselves. The light concrete floors turned softly into black. A blue door opened before him and he was marched into a small theater with twelve seats before a twelve-foot movie screen, where a woman dressed in a blue-suit pretended to be their friend.

Three of the front four seats held other inmates, chained to individual floor pins before each chair. Two more inmates sat on the rear row. The middle row was empty. The spacing between rows was wide enough to allow the guards to move freely while escorting and securing an inmate.

"Remember," the woman on the screen said at the end of a thought. "Offender's prison can be a place to learn how to say, 'I respect that other people might not appreciate my opinion.'"

Oh good. Slieve didn't mind this one. The videos played on a loop of 24 hours. This one tended to keep him awake the most.

Felman and his fellow guard set Slieve in one of the folding theater seats in the middle row, and the bottom dropped.

"Chair broke," Mason Castleman said. He was a repeat offender—large man, liked to sit in subway stations and compliment pretty women.

"Who asked you," Felman replied.

"Just sayin, it broke."

"I can see it broke."

"Okay, but it didn't look like you knowed it was broke."

"I can see it broke."

"You can't put him in a broken chair," Levi Ausledder, a bald man said.

Felman exhaled his frustration at Levi.

"Hey, not my fault it's broken," Levi said. "You probably threw a prisoner in there too hard."

"You want to stay in here an extra week," Felman asked.

"Why? I didn't touch the damned chair. You touched the damned chair." Levi stretched forward in his shackles. "See, I can't even reach it."

"All right, get up, offender," Felman ordered Slieve out of the chair with the broken hinge. He moved his prisoner to the seat directly next to the broken one.

"That bolt be broke," Mason said.

Felman's partner inspected the eyebolt before the seat to find it had pulled out of the floor.

"It's broke," he said. "How is everything broken?"

"Probably because no one gives a baker's dozen of chairs about offenders as much as the good people of New Manhattan thinks they do." Charles Pidea was an older man, used to be a judge renowned for voicing that his rulings were influenced by the morality of his beliefs. Now, he doesn't judge anymore. That job went to some undergrad who felt she could be nicer and got enough other ignorant buffoons to agree with her.

The guards moved Slieve another seat inward the aisle.

"That one wet," Mason said.

"Why is it wet," Felman asked.

"Jerry what they just took out of here had to go the bathroom."

"Well, it ain't broke, so it works," Felman replied.

"Okay," Mason said. "But you gots to explain to whoever it is takes him back why you made them drag a man smell like old piss back to his cell. Sure they all like that in your world."

Slieve found himself getting shoved onto the next and final seat in the row, which was directly behind Mason's.

"Anything wrong with this one," Felman asked.

"No," Levi replied. "Why would anything be wrong with that seat."

"Hey, if he don't want that seat, I trade him," Mason said.

"No way," Charles snapped. "If anyone gets that seat, it's me. I've been in here longer."

Felman shoved Slieve into the seat and latched his shackles to the eyebolt on the floor at his feet. He held up Slieve's crucifix and crushed it in front of his face.

"Hey, you can't do that," Charles said.

Felman shook his hands of the paper and let it fall to the ground. "Now, there's no reason you can't have it." He and his partner left the room and locked the door behind them.

Mason unhitched his arm rest, and it spun backwards, catapulting a metal key into Slieve's lap.

Slieve's shackles and cuffs began to fall from his limbs until he finally stood.

On the back row, Tevon and his prison wife, Benji, took the key from Slieve's hand, released their wrists and leaned forward to pull back on Slieve's seat. The metal creaked as it bent off of the front bolts holding it to the floor, lifting the commercial rubber tile with it and revealing a hole in the cement beneath it that was just large enough for a person to squeeze through.

Although, Slieve may not have had any nectarines or a spoon, what he did have was a pair of prison slippers made special for him with steel toes, which his old calculus teacher and Petey Jo who ran the commissary then smuggled in. Slieve also had a torch in the welding shop, and Charles had a stash of sewing supplies. Together, they stripped the steel from his slipper and shaped a pick back into the sole of his footwear.

For the past six months, they'd all been taking turns wearing Slieve's slippers and chipping away at the floor beneath them. What else Slieve had was a hyper-metabolism that kept him skinnier than any other person in his wing.

"So," Mason asked. "How it look?"

"Wow," Slieve replied. "Who worked it since I've been here?"

"Jason," Benji replied. "Shoulda used him sooner."

Slieve peered into the hole and pulled back up.

"I think it's time," Slieve said.

"Holy fat damn. It worked," Tevon announced. "You owe me one of your sisters, May."

"Don't be thinking you won anything," Mason replied. "You ain't seen my sisters. Sides, you actin' like you figured all this out."

"Let's not jinx it," Charles said. It was his turn to free himself from his own seat." He pulled his cushion apart from the metal underside.

He couldn't help but to mentally laugh at how the bleeding heart New Manhattan senators had filled offenders prisons with love and safe space rather than practical deterrents, allowing them to hide just about any tool that could cut, kill or be used to escape. Well, it was their own fault for believing a senator could learn all they needed to make a country work in two, short terms better than those senators who spent all of their lives learning to do it faster and more efficiently. Guess there's only so much one could say for proud naiveté.

He held out two coils of stainless-steel, aircraft cables to Slieve. Levi pulled out four cable clamps and a screwdriver from the back padding of his seat. Slieve looped the cable up through two holes in the tile on both sides of his own chair, then into the base itself and back to the tile. He secured one cable into the clamps, cinched it, then repeated the procedure for the other side of the theater seat's base.

"If Jason had been any thinner, I'd have been afraid he might have tried to use this himself and ruined everything," Slieve said.

"Probly why he got so much done," Mason said and then handed a handful of nylon straps to Slieve.

Slieve opened the straps until they turned into a harness that he quickly pulled over his shoulders and tied around his waist. Charles checked his knot to make sure he had done it correctly, then slid the end of one of the steel lines through a cable grab. He attached it to Slieve's vest. Slieve prepared the other cable.

They all looked Slieve over one last time.

"When you offend others, you violate the first amendment," the woman on the screen explained. "You steal a person's right to enjoy their own opinions, and you devalue our diversity. Your time in offender's prison can help you to learn how to allow your energies to selflessly enhance those views and beliefs of your neighbor."

A part of Slieve wanted to find her and knock her teeth out. Offender's prison in New Manhattan. How did that happen? He had come across an old comedian's album that discussed the concept of New Yorkers wearing that fact like a badge of honor. There was a time, according to the comedian that the entire spirit of the city was badass just to live there. Now, it was the biggest club of whiners, intimacy consent contracts and missionary sex. Old, forgotten New York! Missionary Sex! What the hell?

Slieve looked over his friends apologetically.

"I wasn't expecting it so soon," Slieve said.

"Go show that Salvo what you can do," Charles said.

Mason's hand fell on Slieve's shoulder. "Just don't forget us when you're kicking Mince in the teeth."

"I won't forget," Slieve said. He dropped the cable ends down, into the pit and slid in after. Then he lowered through the concrete floor, felt the underside for where they had duct taped the AAA flashlight and pack of batteries.

"You good," Charles asked kneeling over the hole.

"I'd be better if you were coming with me."

"And do what," Levi asked. "Be your beautiful assistant?"

Charles rolled his eyes and groaned before instructing Benji and Tevon to lower the seat over Slieve's exit. The metal holes of the bottom of the chair ratcheted over the threads of the bolts in the floor, and Slieve could hear nuts being tightened to cover Slieve's disappearance.

He flipped on his flashlight to dimly reveal the floor some thirty feet down, past the old, metal structure that had once held ceiling tile but was now bare.

He lowered himself past the ceiling rafters then to the floor of the old subway maintenance hub that no one would have known about, unless they had had parents who once serviced them years ago, like Slieve's father had done.

Once he reached the floor, he pulled his nylon harness free of the cables and immediately searched for the old, tool locker just as his father said would be there. Inside, he found the light switch that was really a battery-operated lamp that had been double taped to the top of the locker. There was a suit hanging on one wall, a briefcase tucked into the shelf. A plastic box that opened into a camping sink was on the floor.

He took out the sink and found a small pouch of sample toiletries. Water seeped up into the small basin the moment he removed the rubber stopper from what would have normally been a drain in a household sink. He replaced the stopper, washed his face and shaved even though he didn't need to really. He shaved every night but figured he might as well start out his journey right. Once he had stripped himself of his clothes, cleaned and bathed himself, then brushed his teeth, and dabbed himself with a cologne sample, he tossed the water from the basin across the floor, then raised the spigot on the side of the reservoir and took a drink. He wiped his mouth. Now, he located the emergency, battery jumper-box and clamped the terminals to the cables that he had just used to rappel from the ceiling.

He changed into his suit, drew a double oxford around his neck and set the non-prescription eyeglasses over his face. From the same pocket that he found the eyeglasses, was also a leather wallet with his new identification and subway pass. In another pocket, he found a deck of playing cards. He was tying his wingtips when he heard the prison alarm sound. He wasn't too worried about anyone finding the exit. Even if the guards were smart enough to know where the hole under the theater seat was, it would take them at least fifteen minutes just to retrieve the wrench they needed to open it up. So, he took his time to check the locker for anything that he might have missed, grabbed his flashlight, turned off the locker lamp and found the door out of the room to a dark and dingy rail tunnel just as a string of R-cars screamed past him.

The train passed, and he followed the narrow walkway to a place that, once he waited for another sub to scream by, he could cross the track to another access that eventually allowed him to meet up with a loading dock filled with people.

It only took about three minutes from here before the next train rolled up, puked out people and allowed Slieve to blend into the crowd that it then ingested.

This car was a little crowded for his taste, so he moved his way down two more until he found a place where he could stand in the aisle and hold up his hands.

"Please folks, if I may," he said after setting his briefcase on the floor before him. He held out his deck of cards and popped one into the air and caught it in his other hand. Then he snapped another into the air and caught it on top of the first card where it balanced for a few seconds before he allowed it to fall back into his hands so he could shuffle it all into his deck once again.

No one applauded.

"That's right," Slieve said. "Card tricks are boring." He threw another card into the air, caught it into his other hand and quickly rolled it down to the size of a pencil. Now, he flipped it into his mouth. With a snap of his fingers across its tip, the end of the card began to give off red smoke. He puffed on it, exhaled long and then pulled it from his lips. "But I gotta tell you, these marijuana decks are so much more fun."

The people around him politely chuckled but didn't laugh.

He returned the cardarette to his mouth and continued to smoke it down, then fanned out the rest of the deck to a small boy to his right. "Hey kid, choose one."

The seven-year-old reached for the cards, now smiling, but Slieve quickly pulled them away.

"You're old enough to smoke a card, right?"

The people now laughed.

"No," the kid replied, embarrassed.

"Okay," Slieve said. "Take one, don't tell me what it is."

The kid pulled a card and then followed Slieve's instructions to put it back into the deck.

Slieve rifled the deck and stopped mid-shuffle.

"Well, it's not in here." He showered his entire hand into the air and drew the card he'd been smoking from his mouth and uncurled it.

"Is this your card," he asked presenting a one-third, smoked-down, four-of-diamonds.

The kid shook his head, entranced. The people on the train applauded.

He handed the burned card to the kid and told him not to smoke it all in place. The small group of passengers applauded. He thanked them and accepted a few small bills from them, then moved down a couple paces to interact with some other passengers whose attention he also held.

"I promise, I won't throw any more cards at you." He turned back to the little boy. "You owe me a deck of weed, kid."

Again, chuckles.

He looked down to a woman in her late thirties sitting next to a teenage girl no more than sixteen. From the bottom of his briefcase, he pulled a yellow plastic line with a small clip attached to it and handed it to the mother.

The train stopped and a small exchange of people happened, but the mother and daughter stayed before the wheels began rolling on again.

"Would you attach this yellow cable to your belt loop there, please," he asked, and then pulled a second one for the teenager to do the same. Once the women had attached the cables, Slieve looked at the lines and said, "Now, I can predict if you are related. If you're related, they'll turn yellow." He looked at the yellow lines. "Tada. Yellow."

Polite chuckles now.

"I know. I know," he said. "Clearly my briefcase is psychic. Oh wait. This isn't the one that tells if people are related. This is the one that tells when people are attracted to someone else. I need some dudes."

He immediately apologized for the use of the word "dudes" at the gasps that followed.

The next cable he handed to a man in his 50s, then one to a woman in her twenties who was riding in the seat beside him. He wore a suit. She wore ear gauges and neck rings. They all clipped their cables to their clothing in some way.

"No, no," Slieve said, "Make sure it can hook through something, like a belt loop."

The man attached it to his belt loop. The woman undid a button on her shirt and clipped through the buttonhole.

"Anyone else want in," Slieve asked.

"Here," a teenage boy said, clearly as an attempt to impress the teenage daughter.

Slieve handed him a line, and the teenager clipped it to a key ring sewn into his pants.

"Okay," Slieve said. "Make sure they're tight so this trick works. Try to unlock those. Can you unlock them?"

The volunteers all tried their clasps and agreed they couldn't remove them from their various pieces of clothing, mostly belt loops.

"Okay," Slieve announced. "Now very important that you don't move." He gripped the briefcase handle. "Because if any of you pull those plastic lines out of this briefcase, it will detonate the bomb inside and destroy this entire train car." Now, he opened the case to reveal several silver canisters, wire and a battery. "And before anyone thinks of taking my briefcase, just know that it's been activated now so that if it leaves my hand, or if I stop having a pulse, it will explode."

The train car was suddenly silent.

"Now, we're all going to stand up," Slieve explained. "Go ahead. Stand up."

The volunteers all began to stand from their seats, frightened yet somewhat eager to appease their captor.

"Careful now," Slieve said. "Don't want to break those lines, do we? So, let's all get closer together, if you will."

The passengers huddled into the aisle.

"Good," Slieve said. "Now, when the train stops again, lead me out the doors. I'll tell you where to go once we're outside."

The train stopped shortly, and the group huddled towards the door with Slieve close behind. He held them as one who was a professional dog walker would.

"You might want to lock arms, so no one pushes past and accidentally breaks your line."

Their arms locked just as the doors opened and people tried to push onto the train.

"It's all right," Slieve announced politely against the angry passengers trying to load. "They don't understand that I have a bomb and should get out of our way."

The murmur of a bomb echoed throughout the crowd and Slieve's group was able to exit the train as people suddenly recoiled.

"That's right," Slieve said, holding up his briefcase. "This is a bomb and if it falls from my hand or I die or any of these people break from its proximity, it will explode."

The train raced away in sudden eruption of steel and electricity.

"Now, would you people be so kind as to get out of our way before you get someone killed," Slieve asked.

The crowd began to clear.

"I can't exactly trust that everyone we run into is going to understand that if anything happens to me, we'll all blow up, so I think you guys should all make a circle around me and we can all walk together. Then if anyone comes close, you can tell them what will happen for me. That way, I don't lose my voice repeating myself."

Immediately the hostages encircled Slieve.

"Why are you doing this," the mother asked.

"Because all you touchy boobs turned what used to be a great state into a safe room, and I'd like to leave now."

"Why," she replied. "I don't understand."

"Maybe you shouldn't imprison voices that could explain it to you then. Now, head to the stairs."

The group began moving and was quickly met at the bottom by police officers who demanded Slieve surrender himself.

"We're a walking bomb, you morons," The woman with neck piercings replied. "We can't leave the bomb."

"Release the hostages," one cop ordered then reached to pull the teenage girl away. The arms of the others quickly grappled her back, and people in the crowd fought the police away.

"What part of 'we can't leave the bomb' did you not understand," the pierced woman yelled at the cop.

"Your gun, please," Slieve said to one of the cops. "Or I will drop this right now."

The cop refused.

"Give him the goddamn gun," the teenage boy yelled.

"Will someone take his gun before I decide to just drop this thing, please." Slieve said to the bystanders.

Several people mobbed the officer and took the gun. One of the men handed it to Slieve.

"I hope you rot in hell," the bystander said.

Slieve frowned.

"And I was going to shoot the cop," he said, then he raised the pistol and shot the bystander through the heart.

"There," he said. "Now, we all know I'm willing to kill people. Clear the way."

Again, the path opened, and the group began climbing the stairs out of the subway. Officers ran up both sides to clear the route.

"I see one helicopter—and I mean one helicopter—we all die," Slieve said, once they reached the city streets, which had been cleared back for Slieve and his group. "Stop," he told the group. Then he turned to another cop, one that had appeared on the sidewalk and hadn't been involved with the debacle underground.

"You don't strike me as an idiot, like the others," Slieve said.

"I just don't want anyone to get hurt," the officer acknowledged.

"I think you should come with us, then," Slieve said. "You know, in case we need an authority figure with a calm head or someone with a radio to call for help if one of these fine people has, say, a heart attack." He looked to the man in his 50s as he said it.

"Don't you worry about me," the 50-ish man replied.

The cop nodded his head then ordered his fellow officers to take up the rear.

"I'm sorry," Slieve said. "I mean just you should come with us. If I see another cop anywhere else, like on a roof or driving by or anywhere, our trip is over. I'll give you two minutes to start getting the word out."

"No," the officer yelled into his radio at his shoulder. "None! No one! Don't look at us from a distance. Don't hide in your car. Don't peek around a corner. We cannot see a single cop!"

"We're going to send you a negotiator," the woman on his receiver announced.

"What did I say?" The cop was now screaming. "No! No cops! From now on, I am the incident commander. Right now, the people are safe, but they won't be. Everyone stays out of our way. That means no cars, no badges, no helicopters."

The radio was silent.

"Understood," it finally replied.

In two minutes, Slieve ordered they begin marching again.

"Nicely done, my friends," Slieve said. "You're all doing very well."

"Can I ask you something," the police officer asked.

"Of course, officer," Slieve replied. "Any of you feel free to ask anything you want. Go ahead, officer. I'm sorry, I don't know what to call you."

"It's Benjamin," the officer said.

"It's nice to meet you, Benjamin."

Ben stumbled in his conflict to respond impolitely to Slieve but finally settled upon, "Why are you doing this?"

Slieve smiled, snickered, and kept looking forward while he and his group continued walking. "Why do people always ask the guy with the bomb when they should be asking the people who made him?"

"We're connected to a bomb, get out of the way," The older man wailed as a three-person group approached, clearly preparing to make some sort of mistake in trying to attack Slieve's little circle of prisoners.

The would-be vigilantes ignored him, until the other members in the group began screaming at them to get back.

"This will go easier if we have police clear the streets for you," Benjamin suggested.

"You are correct," Slieve said. "Tell you what. Catch." He tossed a small black fob to Benjamin, and the officer caught it.

As soon as he did, the fob blinked a green light.

"What is this," Ben asked.

"It read your electromagnetic field when it touched you," Slieve said. "Now it must remain in contact with your skin or it will set off this bomb. So, don't drop it and don't get too far away from our group or your little remote there will upset what's in the briefcase here."

Ben instantly clenched it in his fist, but then loosened his grip when he thought about how it might take his fingers to go numb if he continued to lock his muscles around it for too long. He carefully transferred it to his offhand, ensuring it always touched skin. This made him think about how tightly packed his little group of hostages were here. They had survived one group of vigilantes trying to help. He wasn't sure if they could keep that up.

"We should go to the street, there are fewer people there," Benjamin explained. "We can clear the cars."

The group moved into the street, cut in line of one of the vehicles, its driver honked, yelled.

Benjamin spoke quickly to the driver and rejoined the group.

"What did you say to him," Slieve asked.

"I told him if he didn't organize a group to block all traffic from coming his direction, I'd shoot him myself."

"Good thinking. Maybe you should call in and have the city garbage trucks start blocking the intersections and oncoming traffic."

Ben began calling in the request.

"Make sure they're sanitation workers, not cops," Slieve said. "In fact, just to be safe. I don't think we should see any sanitation workers either, just their trucks."

"What's our route?"

"You know," Slieve returned. "I don't know if I want to say just yet. I guess they'll just have to anticipate, won't they? Better not block our way though. That would be unfortunate."

Ben called in the orders. The right lanes of traffic moved away. The driver did as Ben had instructed. The oncoming traffic was gridlocked.

"Get back in your car," Ben ordered a driver who angrily stepped out and began taunting the group. The driver wouldn't obey, so Ben snapped a retractable baton and smashed the guy in the knee.

An onslaught of ignorant drivers and pedestrians began to rush from their places towards the cop with their phones.

"Oh my god," one woman screamed holding up her hand so her wristband could record the happening and then post it on social media. "That cop just struck that man. Fire the cop! Kill the cop!"

Benjamin approached the woman and stared right into her camera and the other cameras that were now full of bravery at a coward's distance.

"Listen to me carefully, and make sure you post this," Ben said. "This man is holding us hostage with a bomb. Hurting him will make it blow up. Trying to pull any of us away will set it off. If you really want to help, tell everyone to get off the streets."

"You can't be serious," a college punk ridiculed, suddenly stuffing his phone into Ben's face.

"K, stop," Slieve ordered, and the hostages obeyed.

Slieve drew the gun from his pocket and shot the kid in the thigh. "Yes, I'm serious." Then he turned to the crowd and fired another shot over their heads. As the crowd began to scream, run and duck for cover, Slieve yelled, "Post that, you snowflake, Nazi douche bags!"

Ben glared back at Slieve.

Slieve didn't care, just slid his gun into his slacks pocket. He pointed to the first woman who had begun recording Ben's behavior. For some reason, she hadn't fled like the other people. "You," he called. "Come here."

"I'm good right where I am," the woman replied.

Slieve stuck his gun to the teenage boy's head. "Now! Or all your social media friends, or followers or whatever you self-affirming dicks call yourselves now, can all see the true social warriors that you are."

The woman approached the group and soon caught another of Slieve's black fobs, its light turning green in her hand.

"Stay with the group; if that light turns red, you go boom," Slieve explained once again.

The woman froze in this new revelation.

"How much juice you got on whatever you're recording with," Slieve asked.

"It has a solar casing," she did her best to reply.

"Good," Slieve adulated. "You can start documenting for our posterity. How many followers you have?"

"Twenty million," she said.

"Oh no." Slieve shook his head in disappointment. "A boisterous host such as yourself, you should have ten times that amount."

"Well, I don't," the woman said.

"Let's see if we can change that," Slieve said. "You get paid more if you have more followers, right?"

"Yeah," she said hesitantly.

Slieve pressed his gun against the head of the woman who had ring piercings in her neck.

"Let's see if we can't get you ten times more followers in fifteen minutes," he said. "Two hundred million people, fifteen minutes, or her journey ends right here." He nodded towards a clock in the window of a small bookstore. "Tick. Tick."

Heather had wanted to be a graphic design artist. No one thought she was pretty. In first grade, she looked like a cute little kid. By sixth, she looked like an old woman. At school, she was teased and made fun of. You weren't supposed to tease each other in school, but people did. Her recesses were spent sitting on the lawn, alone because no one wanted to play with her.

Heather cooties, that's what some of the kids said they'd catch if they touched her. She told the teacher, no one admitted they did it. No one got in trouble. Then she went home, which was worse.

Daddy wasn't right. The neighbors knew that. The neighbors were nosey, daddy taught that. Daddy taught a lot of things, until Heather's teacher made the police take him away. Then he never did them again.

That's when Heather started to learn, really learn. She learned secrets were bad; people shouldn't bully; people who did evil needed to be exposed; those who did good in the world needed to be seen. She built her life upon that principle.

In her high school journalism class, she uncovered a teacher who blackmailed, manipulated, bullied the under-performing students into his prostitute ring. Her friend Taboo confided in her that she was one. The school silenced the story. High schools are allowed to do that. So, she gave the story to the local news station, and they gave her a scholarship to college.

It wasn't in her nature to let any person hurt another. Not since her father, who died quickly in prison, had she ever let anyone control her. She would have preferred to strip the person in malevolent authority of their power. A bully has none if you're not afraid. A black mailer loses power when you reveal your secret on your own. A person working in the shadows can't handle when someone has a floodlight. However, a person with a gun who can't be shot, or he'll set off an even bigger trigger? How do you take that power?

As Slieve pressed the gun against the pierced woman's head, Heather's mind did two things. First, it screamed and cursed Slieve. It cried. The second thing it did was immediately begin to realize that the way to placate Slieve was to find 180 million more subscribers.

She immediately turned to her camera.

"Hey, it's J.J.J.," she said into the camera with the professionalism of any true field reporter. She begged her followers to start posting her channel, sharing her live-cast. She made sure to remind them of Slieve's warning not to send any helicopters. She begged them to contact their friends in other subnations of the U.S. as well as friends outside.

"Five minutes down, J.J.J.," Slieve said, pointing to the clock in the window.

The number of followers had grown from twenty million to twenty-five million viewers.

Heather showed the briefcase, zoomed in on Slieve's gun poised against the woman's head, begged viewers to contact all their local news channels and pled that news outlets inform their own viewers how to subscribe to her livestream.

"Five minutes left, people," Slieve said into the camera.

The number for viewers read seventy-five million now.

"It's not enough," Heather cried. "Please. I'm begging you."

The woman with the gun to her head asked to speak to the camera.

"It's okay," she said. "If it's my time. It's my time."

"And what if I decide it's hers instead," Slieve turned the gun on the younger teenage girl.

The teenage girl screamed. Her mother cried.

"Three minutes," Slieve said.

The teenage girl screamed in every way that seemed to have emptied all the blood from her heart into her face. Her heart would explode far before the bullet's chamber would.

The clock now read thirteen minutes.

"I don't have a lot of money in my bank account, twenty-thousand dollars. Whoever is the two-hundred-millionth subscriber, I'll give it all to you."

The older gentleman said he could add $32,000 more. The teenager's mother said she could contribute $700,000.

"Time's almost up," Slieve said, and he pulled back the hammer on his gun.

Heather's words began to slur between pleading for anyone to keep sharing her channel and apologizing to the girl.

Finally, Slieve announced that time was completely up, and he turned the pistol towards Heather.

"How many," he asked.

Heather couldn't speak, but she managed to turn her wrist to Slieve. He leaned in so he could read it.

He eyed it, read the number, squinted and made sure he'd read it correctly just to be fair to Heather. His lips pursed, then suddenly popped.

"Told you," he said. Then he gently lowered the hammer and slid his firearm back into his pocket.

He ordered the group to start moving again, and it obeyed, silently, with the exception of the hostages crying and trying to comfort the teenage girl.

Heather, however, suddenly bent forward, hands on her knees, breathing hard.

"You're all right," Slieve said. "Take your time and breathe."

The group continued moving past her. Both sides of the street were empty of cars now.

"But don't take too long. There's not a lot of range on that transmitter."

Ben scooped Heather into his arms and began carrying her, calming her until she could breathe again. After a couple of minutes, he set her back down.

"So, what is your name, J.J.J.," Slieve asked. "Your real name?"

"Heather," she replied.

"How do you get three Js, let alone one out of Heather?"

"It's just a screen name," Heather replied.

"I see," Slieve said. "Well, Heather, try looking at the world with the naked eye for once. Real life is so much better. Heck! Look at this," Slieve blurted, holding up the briefcase with all its yellow leashes to the other members of his group. "This is a bomb! You think your voice is more exciting than this right here? That's a problem you people wouldn't know anything about."

"What do you mean, you people," the woman with piercings asked.

"What do you think I mean," Slieve said. "I mean you bunch of ignorant people who are so set on finding something to be offended over that you can't even let 'you people' mean 'you people who belong to the homo sapien demographic of nescient dumbasses.' Demographics of those looking for reasons to hate doesn't hold the market on what people are. That's what I mean by 'you people.' I mean you people who spend your entire lives talking about the world and how other people wrong you that you can't see beyond your own sky rises or camera frames. You know, maybe if you'd take your own advice and shut up rather than bullying others to do as such, you'd learn just how much noise pollution you jackasses produce."

The streets were now empty of people as well as vehicles, their faces instead peering from inside windows and behind cars.

"Now, Ben," Slieve said. "To your question."

"Huh," Ben asked.

"Why do we ask the guy with the bomb why he's doing it," Slieve asked. "For all that we support in society, claiming that we must help others who are incapable of being responsible for their own actions, we don't afford that same courtesy to the people who get pushed over the edge by that same society."

"Are you seriously suggesting they're the same," the oldest man in the group asked.

"Aren't they? Society puts a person in the poor house and that person goes into debt and declares bankruptcy and no one asks, 'why are you so poor,' because people are intelligent enough to study what's causing unemployment or low wages.

"We don't see the people with money asking the people without it, 'why are you doing this.' They don't ask the poor person, because they're poor, unintelligent, responsible for their own actions but incapable of not being a burden to society. As a matter of fact, we're more likely to ignore the poor person. If that poor person tells elitist people what they need or why they're poor, the policy makers and rich people of the world all shout 'no, that's not what you need. We know what you need, and you'll take what we tell you, you need. If you knew what you needed, you wouldn't be poor.'

"And rich people who used to be poor can be worse with their holier-than-thou 'I got a job and off meth and out of debt, so you should be able to' attitudes. How confidently would they still hold that 'if I can, you can' philosophy if some other person had interviewed better for the job that allowed the rich person to get out of the poor house? See, no one asks the person whose actions led them to being poor why they're doing what they're doing. They ask everyone other than poor people. So, why do we ask the man with the gun? How come nobody asks each other like they do when they're talking around the impoverished."

"How would we know why you're carrying a bomb," the mother asked.

"Why do you have to act so unintelligent?"

"Well, how are we supposed to know that kind of an answer?"

Slieve appeared stunned. "Well, you ask society, don't you? Isn't that the way of things? Society's so intelligent it knows best? Why should it stop knowing best because I'm carrying a bomb?"

"Well what would you have us do," the teenage girl asked.

"Why is it my responsibility to keep you from finding out on your own," Slieve suddenly yelled at her. "Sorry. That was unkind of me. The assumption is we are an intelligent people intrigued by why people behave. Why do we ask the person taking an action, but we can't seem to ask the society that that person belongs to how it could allow that person to take that action? Why would a person escape offender's prison, have a bomb built, take hostages all for the purpose of getting away from this society?"

"Because he's sick," the pierced woman blurted.

"Sick, huh," Slieve asked. "Stop!"

He turned to one of the restaurant windows and made eye-contact with several people peering from behind glass. His perusal finally set on a large man in an apron and grease stains. Slieve pointed to him then mimed drinking from a cup.

The man nodded his head and abruptly left the window. The others on the side of the glass immediately objected, and he waved them off with what appeared to be reassurances. A few minutes later, the man walked out with a tray filled with four pitchers of water, a fifth of ice and a clear, stack of plastic cups.

"I didn't know if you wanted ice or not," he said.

"Thank you," the mother said.

"Quiet," Slieve snapped.

The man followed the cue himself and took a cup from the stack. He crumbled some ice from its pitcher into the cup and then filled it with water. He held the tumbler out to Slieve. The bomber glared at the man.

"It's safe," the server said.

Slieve didn't respond.

The teenage boy held out his hand to take it, but Slieve drew his gun once more, held it on him and shook his head. He looked back to the server and nodded to the glass.

"Okay," the server said. He held the glass to his own lips and drank some to show it wasn't poisoned.

With a simple leer, Slieve told the server to keep drinking. The server did, drank half of it, then all of it when Slieve didn't seem satisfied. He quickly filled up another glass and held it out, forgetting to put any ice in it. The surface of the water rippled as his hands trembled with uncertainty.

Again, Slieve didn't respond. The woman with piercings started to reach for it but stopped at Slieve's silent warning and pointing of his gun. Slieve nodded to the server and the glass once more.

The server hesitated and began to drink it. When he drained the second cup, Slieve gestured for him to fill it once more. He did, then he drank this one too. This time, Slieve waved his gun down to one of the full pitchers.

"What," the server asked.

Slieve knew the man understood what he was supposed to do, so he didn't say anything and didn't allow anyone else to speak.

The server held up the pitcher and began to drink. He drank slowly but still swallowed half of it. When he stopped drinking, Slieve held his gun on the man in his 50s who was linked to his briefcase. The server drank again.

When the server set the pitcher back to the tray, his hands were shaking, and not entirely out of fear.

Slieve pointed to another pitcher.

The server took it up.

"I can't drink any more," he said. "Please."

Slieve returned the gun to the elder in his circle.

The server held the side of the pitcher to his mouth and began to drink. A third of the way down, his eyes began to water. He cried a few gurgles into the pitcher but drank. The pitcher shook. At halfway, he stopped, took control of his swallowing, breathed heavily and then continued. When he finished, he coughed up a mouthful of water. He dropped the empty pitcher rather than set it down.

Slieve pointed to another pitcher.

The server started crying outright. He turned to the pitcher that was emptied of two cups earlier. It was a third full. Slieve shot the pitcher, and the server dropped what remained of it. He understood. He took up the remaining pitcher of water, looked over Slieve's hostages and held the container to his mouth.

"Stop it," Ben shouted. He held out his hand with the fob. "Stop it. Or I'll end this all myself right now. Let's see how far you get then."

Slieve stared at him. His face softened into something bewildered and he finally asked, "Why are you doing this, Ben? You must be sick."

Now, it was Ben's face that turned into something other than that of a man willing to drop his fob and blow his entire circle of traveling companions to their graves.

"Go ahead and throw it up," Slieve said.

At that, Ben doubled up a fist and punched the server in the stomach. The server lurched forward, clenched his face and throat at first, but then water surged from his mouth.

Slieve gestured for the group to start moving again, leaving the server behind.

"I, for one think that's a stupid analogy, and not at all demonstrative of the reality of our culture," the pierced woman said.

"And yet, you people," he sneered out *you people*, "are all tethered to a bomb carried by a man who hates the taste of your Kool-Aid."

"Yeah, and why is that," Ben asked.

"After all that, you're still asking," Slieve replied. "Maybe you are a dumbass after all?"

Benjamin stewed, Slieve could tell he wanted to say something. He let him stew. The blueblood needed to marinate in his anger. Perhaps, if he dwelled long enough without a response, his human brain would do what should have come natural to it, question other things.

"Name calling doesn't accomplish anything," the teenage girl said. Her mother's eyes widened, begging her not to make Slieve angry.

"What's your name, kid," Slieve asked.

"Shashaun," the teenager replied.

"Nice to meet you, Shaun."

"Not Shaun. Shashaun."

"Oh, I'm sorry," Slieve said. "I guess your parents thought having a name that sounded like you were stuttering every time you introduced yourself would help you make a good first impression in any scenario never."

"You gonna harass the young woman now," the pierced lady asked.

"You mean Shashaun?" Slieve asked and looked to the woman with piercings. His brow slanted as if to invite the woman to say something more so he could turn his attention back to her instead. When she didn't bite, he continued. "Name calling doesn't accomplish anything? Are you sure?"

"Nothing productive," Shashaun replied.

Slieve said nothing for several blocks. The faces that had once appeared on the streets and then slinked behind storefront windows now fled out of their backdoors. If he looked up, he might see a curtain move where someone was trying to not look like he was hiding. The alleys were still: no hobos, no boxes, no carts existed. Except for the instantaneous inhale-exhales of the passenger jets somewhere in the distance and overhead, there was no sound of pretty much anything coming from their street.

Without announcing, Slieve stopped before a bistro.

The group followed his lead.

He reflected a moment over the group and his own stomach. He hadn't had any kind of food that didn't come from a mushy, giant, plastic bag in a long time. Most of what they had in offender's prison was vegetarian. Perhaps his favorite meal since his internment of offense was hummus, but only when he was able to eat it as God had intended, off the end of a vegetable that could snap. Because the powers-that-be declared it more cost and space efficient to puree the vegetables than let their natural bulk take up three times their original space on the shipping truck, hummus was impossible to remember ever being part of vegetable dipping. Now it was all more like yogurt. He had almost forgotten what a sandwich looked like, or what meat tasted like.

He wanted meat. When this was all over, he was going to steal a steak. That would be his celebration dinner, he'd already decided. Thick steak, a porterhouse, that blend of old and forgotten New York strip and filet mignon. The only vegetarian item he wanted on his plate were the mushrooms, onions and spices that were special to whichever restaurant made it.

Now that he thought about it, he could go for a baked potato too. All he'd had were mashed, if you could call them mashed. They were too wet to really be mashed either, more smoothie than mashed—if you could call anything that lacked sweetness a smoothie, of course.

He looked at the bistro and decided that even if there wasn't an employee inside, there still had to be food. He turned to Ben.

"Get us some sandwiches, pig," he said.

Benjamin immediately nodded and took out a small tablet to write on. "What kind would you like," he asked as the screen lit into a light orange.

"I want a good, old-fashion hot-ham-and-swiss, how about you, Grandpa," Slieve asked without looking away from Ben.

"Reuben," the 50-ish man replied, "hold the corned beef."

"Well that wouldn't exactly be a Reuben now, would it, you old fart," Slieve asked.

The fifty-something man shrugged off his embarrassment.

"And for you, Momma Stutter," Slieve asked.

"Garden sprouts if they have any," the mother replied.

"How about the little teenage pecker?"

"Grilled cheese with tomato."

"And the two-bit hooker?"

"Chicken salad."

"Look at that," Slieve said, turning to Shashaun. "Nearly an entire order taken to feed us all. Productive, efficient and the pig can bring it all back to us here in a matter of minutes. Now, what do you want to eat, you ignorant little turd?"

Shashaun didn't answer. Her eyes welled with tears.

"There you go," Slieve said. "Standing your morals. Good for you."

She started to cry.

"Oh, don't be like that," Slieve said. "What would you like to eat, Shashaun?"

She didn't answer.

"What does she like to eat, Shashaun's mama," he asked.

"Shasta," her mother answered.

"What kind of sandwich is that?"

"It's my name," Shasta said. "Try using it."

"Well, what kind of sandwich does Shashaun want, Shasta?"

"P, b and j, orange if they have it, otherwise grape," Shashaun replied.

"You know slaves in New California make that right," Slieve asked.

"That's not true," Shasta said. "I saw a documentary on those orange groves. The people love being there."

"You know what," Slieve said, turning back to Ben. "Forget the other orders, just go get Shashaun's."

"Only one," Ben asked and suddenly regretted it.

"Uh-huh," Slieve said from behind an amused brow.

Ben set off to the bistro. The small group moved with him, huddling and scrunching meticulously through the front door so Ben didn't get too far out of range of the briefcase bomb.

Ben found almond butter, which was fine with Shashaun. He also found strawberry jam, which he thought was weird. He wasn't stupid, he'd been to restaurants before. All they ever had was grape, because restaurants seemed to have a difficult time understanding that no one wanted to eat their damned grape. All he could figure was that this particular bistro owner actually understood this part of the business. They also didn't have orange, no surprise there neither.

Ben slathered on the almond butter to Shashaun's approval and then added the strawberry jam to another slice of bread. As he finished up, he looked over the supply of sliced meat, bread and cheeses. He wanted to ask but decided not to invite any more opportunity for saddling behavior.

At Slieve's behest, he wrapped it in a paper towel. Then they took stock of their resources and the mother ended up dropping her wedding ring on the counter as payment for her daughter's sandwich.

They returned outside and continued their journey. Slieve encouraged Shashaun to finish her sandwich while they walked, which she did, but every bite felt like it was filled with more shame than the previous.

"See. Learn from that you people?" He suddenly straightened his posture and announced, "Shashaun was right; name-calling isn't productive."

"Feel like a man now," the pierced woman asked.

"Please," Slieve rebuffed. "We both know that if there's one thing no one's allowed to do in this hell-hole it's act like a man, well, unless you're a woman."

The pierced woman breathed heavily to the beat of a ticking time bomb, but she said nothing so as not to disturb the real detonator.

"Isn't that why you had to become a woman, so you could finally become the sex that allows you to do something masculine with that Adam's apple of yours? Did you really think filling your neck with jewelry would hide it?"

"You're a man," the teenage boy asked.

"So, what is your name, Adam's apple," Slieve asked.

The pierced woman reached into her Louis Vuitton and took out a small wallet. She handed a driver's license back to Slieve, who took one look and immediately started laughing.

"Adama," he asked and couldn't stop laughing while handing the identification back. "Adama! Can you believe that, kid?"

"It's no big deal," the teenage boy said.

"You don't think?"

"That's what makes New Manhattan great."

"No-no-no! New York was great," Slieve said. "Back when people were too intelligent to give a damn that it got its name from the man who sold more slaves to America than any other slave trader, and everyone knew the people who lived there had a God-given right to be an asshole and proud of it. Know what happened to them? Douche bags moved in and ran them all out. Now you're all just douche bags, not even asshole enough to be an enema. It was like one, big haberdouchery moved into to town and you all put on the same damned hat. What used to be a brotherhood of mess with one, mess with all of us is now a support group for douche bags with bruised bums. Does that sound like something you should be proud of, kid?"

"Don't call me *kid*."

"What would you like me to call you?"

"Georgia."

"Okay, George, it's called—

"Did I say George? No. I said Georgia."

"Oh my god!"

"You have a problem with my name?"

"You don't? Between you and Adama here it might just be mercy to drop my case before you make this city anymore sexually confused than it is."

"You know what, fu—

"Hey, hey," Slieve said, pulling his gun. "Don't agitate the man with the gun and bomb. You can still be polite."

"Like you've been?"

"Um, hello," Slieve replied nonchalantly. "Gun. Bomb. Driver's rules. Point being, Georgia," this he said loathingly, before taking a deep breath to calm himself. "I learned a long time ago that the sorer the bum, the bigger the bully."

"Well, I think when you're the greatest city on earth you have a responsibility to act better."

Slieve laughed.

"Oh, please! We could drop your entire city in our beautiful Grand Canyon and people would ask, 'what's that steaming pile over there?' There are numerous cities in this world with bigger buildings, more people—better people, for that matter. What does New Manhattan have? Social media pricks, bullies who think the rest of the world is condensed housing like you have."

"We are not bullies," Adama snapped.

"Oh yeah? Tell me why the stock market moved to Utah. Tell me why the highest-paying jobs you have in your state are run by headquarters in other states. Tell me why you were put on probation as a state in the senate."

"You sum all that up as though you actually think it all happened so simply."

"Your own art Czar censored the Met," Slieve fired back. "How simple was it for him to fine and imprison the Met's directors for showing offensive symbols in historical art? Was it when the senate appropriations committee cut all funding to keep it operational after the State Supreme court forced the government to stop distributing art grants? Can you tell me that? How you went from being one of the most renowned art locations in the world to a place that found it offensive. Tell me that if you're so in-check with world reality."

"It's a new world. We evolved into something accepting for everyone," Adama replied.

"Then why did I just escape an offender's prison? I'll tell you why. You evolved into bullies. You got so proud of how much you had brow-beat your own communities into conforming to one ideology that when your human rights groups began suing churches to remove their holy symbols because they were offensive, you didn't stop to give one thought to the fact that it would lead to shutting down buildings that allowed access to artifacts of humanity and historical significance. Do you even know what used to be on Broadway before you filled it with vegan strip clubs and propaganda tours?"

"We have a better society today without those things," Adama said.

"You have dick, literally, Adama. I'm surprised you people haven't dressed the statue of liberty in a giant strap-on and changed that old sign of hers to say, 'Come here you tired, you poor, you huddled masses and bend over!'"

"You don't know what you're talking about," Georgia replied. "We're a greater place today than we've ever been."

"You're full of it" the 50s man replied.

"See," Slieve said. "Grandpa knows. He was probably here before your mom and dad had to accept you really did have to have ovaries to give you life."

"Ain't that the truth, and it's Severus not grandpa," 50s replied, then turned back to Georgia. "And don't pretend you know which society was better, you've never seen anything other than this, but I have."

"Oh, preach to me, just like the rest of your generation that screwed the rest of us," Georgia said.

"Screwed y—you little bastard. Come here!" Severus started to lunge, but Slieve held the gun at him without pointing it. The others screamed at him to stop. Heather dropped her camera frame to help hold him back.

"Remember the cords," Slieve said.

"Don't even say it," Severus ordered, and a set of silver and gold keys flew out of his hand and struck Georgia in the face.

"You hit me, you prick," Georgia complained. "We're in this together."

"Will you pistol whip him just once," Severus pled.

Slieve smacked the back of Georgia's head with the barrel of the gun.

"Can we not do that," Adama asked.

So, Slieve smacked her too.

The group fell silent for several minutes until Slieve finally piped up again and realized it had stopped shuffling entirely.

"I am addressing the person carrying the bomb," Benjamin's radio suddenly erupted. "My name's Max, I am an FBI negotiator. I'd like to talk if we can."

Chapter Twenty-three

Benjamin detached the handpiece from his shoulder and stretched it towards Slieve. He pressed the button and nodded.

"No," was all Slieve replied.

"If you're not willing to talk, the FBI is going to make decisions neither of us want them to, and I won't be able to stop it."

"I die, they die," Slieve said.

"I just want to be able to tell the FBI that everyone is all right," the negotiator said.

"You have J.J.J.'s streaming channel."

"Please. If it looks like we're making progress, they'll back off."

Slieve and Ben stared each other into the same realization, this man was dangerous to their situation.

"All right," Slieve replied. "One car. Just you. You get fifteen seconds, enough time to look me in the eyes, and take that back to your superiors."

"I'll take it," Max's voice replied.

Almost immediately, a black truck broke from a side street, two blocks down the road. It drove straight and slowly towards the group.

Slieve looked to the storefronts and directed his small posse towards the picture window of a party supply store, now closed. It sat beneath twenty stories of residential apartments.

Heather turned her wrist on the black truck.

"Not one word from any of you," Slieve said. "I don't want to, but I will end it."

The truck stopped, and a short, weasel-like man stepped down from the back seat. He wore a black, protective vest and cautiously approached the group.

"All right," Slieve said, and he dropped open the side of the briefcase to reveal the canisters and reels of yellow line. "You see the situation now?"

"I do," Max replied. "What can I do to get you to let a hostage go? Can we make a trade?"

"Stop bothering me and you'll see them all released when I get where I'm going," Slieve explained, and immediately Max glanced to the truck. Slieve held up the cover to the briefcase and asked Severus to unsnap two of its pockets.

Severus did. At Slieve's instruction, from one pocket, Severus withdrew a silver earpiece—from the other, a black fob with the familiar LED light that would turn green once Slieve activated it for Max's touch. He grimaced, exhaled, but didn't say a word. He mournfully handed both items to Slieve. Slieve held them out for Max, and the negotiator reached into the circle and took them.

Max rolled the items over in his hands as if he were ready to let them fly at a craps table.

"The fob is a microphone," Slieve said. "Give the earpiece to whoever's in the truck." He held up another fob from his suit pocket. "See, I have one too. We all do. Your people will be able to hear us."

Max momentarily left the group and returned to the truck to hand off the earpiece.

Shasta turned to Slieve and slightly raised her hand to speak.

Slieve shook his head. "Don't want them hearing anything that might make me have to drop this."

Max returned to the group shortly.

"Good. Walk with us," Slieve said and then urged his group forward. The hostages kept their eyes off of Max and the road and tried not to think of how the fob now tied him to their fate.

"I would love to walk with you," Max said.

"But the truck stays there," Slieve said.

"Of course."

"If it moves one inch, no one here talks ever again, understand?"

"I understand," Max replied. "Are you sure they can hear you all?"

"Honk if you can hear me," Slieve said.

The truck honked.

"They stay there."

"They stay there," Max replied.

"Good, then we understand each other."

"Can I ask why you're doing this?"

Slieve smiled and shared a quick, overarching, familiar glance with Shasta, Shashaun and even Ben.

Heather carried her camera around in front of Max.

"Shame," Slieve replied.

"Why's that?"

"That you and your traveling buddies apparently didn't subscribe to J.J.J.'s livestream earlier, and that no one apprised you, a negotiator, of our situation. If anyone had, you'd know that little black fob I gave you isn't just a microphone, it's a proximity device. Drop it and blow up."

Max looked to the fob in his hand, realizing what he was the last in the group to understand. He too was a hostage now. Max tried to appear calm even though Slieve wasn't the only one in the group who could tell otherwise. He stumbled over his own feet and Severus caught him. The group continued to press forward.

Suddenly, an eruption a block and half away filled the streets. Slieve anticipated the surprise and moved carefully with the stumbling group to ensure no one snapped their line.

"I told you. One car, just you," Slieve replied coldly. "I see one cop, one car, one helicopter, I set off the bomb, that's what I said, but I get the feeling some of you don't believe that and want to see what limits you can push."

Shasta visibly shook and burst into tears.

Max stopped fully and turned back, once he was of mind to do so, to find what the others found. The black truck had broken in two, its roof torn apart like a popped paper bag. The front half toppled onto its top ten feet away from the back. The rear section sat on its bumper, its gas spilling and burning. The officers bodies were torn worse than the vehicle, and Max was glad he couldn't see them for the flames spewing from within.

"That was just an earpiece," Slieve replied sternly. "Imagine what this briefcase can do. Now, tell whatever genius is listening on the other end of your wire that if they try anything again, ever—and I do mean, ever—we are done here. No more negotiators. No more cops. No more FBI. No more rescue attempts. You got that?"

"We don't have to do this," Max replied.

Adama Screamed. "Stop dicking with our lives, or I'll kill you myself," She instantly apologized to Slieve.

Slieve nodded immediate forgiveness then turned back to Max. "Well, then, get to it."

Max relayed the message, talking to himself, then nodded to let Slieve know the deed was heard.

"Now take that silly vest and hidden wire off. If enforcement agencies want to know what's going on, J.J.J. has a live feed. How are we doing on viewers?"

"We almost have one billion," Heather replied, knowing that since Max had allowed himself to get taken hostage, he'd added a few more to the pot.

Max dropped his vest and bugging equipment on the ground. His hidden gun and holster were now revealed as he rebuttoned his shirt. He looked to Slieve as if he'd been caught in the act of wrongdoing.

"Keep it," Slieve replied. "You may need it to keep back the mobs, Ben did."

"You're not worried I might use it," Max asked.

"You have more reason to be worried I might use it."

Max bent down to set the holster on the ground.

"Pick it up," Slieve ordered.

"I won't be used as a tool to harm someone else."

"Oh, yes you will. You already have. Now, pick it up and put it on, negotiator."

Max reluctantly obeyed.

Shasta suddenly sidestepped and Shashaun caught her.

"You okay there, Mom," Slieve asked.

"Just a moment," Shashaun replied, sitting herself on the ground and holding her mother.

Shasta's body clinched, and her extremities shook. Her head and eyes locked into a strange trance and saliva began to drip from her mouth. She maintained the behavior for about twenty seconds before she started to relax. Slowly, her eyes began to focus on the group, and she blushed.

"Oh no," Shasta replied.

"She's going to get us all killed," Georgia complained. "Another seizure like that and that could be the end of us."

"Where's your compassion," Slieve asked. "She's under a lot of stress."

Slieve held his hand down to allow Shasta help back to her feet.

"Can we get you anything," Ben asked.

"I could use something to eat," she said.

"We all could," Adama suggested. "All of us this time."

"All right, but we still have ground to cover, so I'm thinking delivery." Slieve said and looked to Ben. "Get on your walkie and tell whoever's listening to send us food, and that someone better be a pimply, sixteen-year-old delivery driver."

"They're not going to send you another hostage," Max said.

"Yeah they are," Slieve replied. "Because I'm going to say, 'arm it' right now on J.J.J.s camera here, and, if I say the follow-up magic word, a building somewhere in the state of New Manhattan is going to explode." Now he turned to J.J.J.s camera. "And before anyone thinks of trying to disable J.J.J.s feed, you should know that will be the same as me saying the magic word, so don't do that." He began to look away from the camera but then suddenly turned back. "Oh! And since we'll be heading into the Holland tunnel here soon, you might want to start seeing to it that her service doesn't get interrupted before we get to Jersey."

Now, he nodded to Ben to make the delivery call.

Ben had to be ordered twice to get his head off of the news he had just heard. He knew what Jersey was, a police state that had done all but declare war on New Manhattan. Slieve might as well just blow up the entire group now. Once any of them crossed the border, they'd all be dead anyway.

"You know they have snipers watching the tunnel exit, right," Max said.

Shasta looked forward and kept walking, but Shashaun looked back, not angry, more pleading.

"Don't worry," Slieve said. "I had a mother too. One of the valiant four. You ever hear of the valiant four?"

"Should we have," Adama asked.

"Nobody's ever heard of the Valiant Four," Slieve asked. "Of course, you haven't. It's a Jersey thing. If it didn't happen in New Manhattan, it didn't happen, right?"

"Does that bother you that no one's heard of them," Max asked.

"This is the time where you choose not to psychoanalyze, Max," Slieve replied sternly.

They walked. Slieve tried his best not to look at any of them, and the hostages tried not to invite him to do so.

The Holland Tunnel was closer than Slieve had anticipated. As the group approached, the streets filled with the hums of small, turbine motors.

Slieve turned abruptly to Ben.

"What did I say," he said coldly. "If those are what I think they are—

"Didn't he tell you to send it via a delivery driver," Ben interrupted, anxiously recognizing the sound.

"If I turn around and I see delivery drones," Slieve now yelled.

"Get them out of here," Ben chastised into his walkie.

"Please don't," Shashaun asked. "Please."

Slieve's face, stone, softened at the plea then hardened again.

"I've shot a cop. I've blown up a police vehicle with law-enforcement officers inside. I've warned you about a bomb in the city. I do not think these people are taking me seriously. All right then."

He looked to Heather who was faithfully holding up her camera and clenching her fob, all while supporting her elbow against the palm of her other equally tired hand. Her elbow pinned her supporting hand into her waist. Slieve opened his mouth to speak.

"Please," Heather now pled. "I'm taking you seriously. Doesn't that count?"

Slieve's face softened into a smile now, and he even nodded a little.

"You're safe," he said. "But it's time now."

The hum of drones died, and the air was still once more. Then came the rumbling, crackle, like the sonic boom of a jet, and the group stopped walking, even Slieve. A gray pillow arose into the skyline some distance away.

He looked back into J.J.J.'s live-cast.

"Arm number two," he said, then he encouraged everyone forward once more.

The spelunking entrance walls to the Holland Tunnel had risen on both sides of the group now, and the opening loomed over an empty street. Slieve ordered the group to stop, and they waited here until the sound of crunching tires sneaked down towards them.

A small, lanky girl with her hair pulled through the back of her restaurant-uniform ballcap stepped out.

Slieve snorted contemptuously.

The girl walked towards them, carrying two bulked-up garbage bags.

She walked slowly, nearly tripped.

"I am so pleased that the brave men of this city could step up to send you in their places to serve us," Slieve said.

The delivery driver didn't answer.

"It's okay, Chelsea," Slieve encouraged, reading her nametag as it became legible. "I assure you; you will not be punished for speaking. Did they ask you to come, or did you volunteer?"

She didn't answer, but her eyes were filled with fear.

"Oh, please," Slieve said in a comforting voice. "Do not worry. None of this is your fault. Max? Ben? Please help Chelsea with her bags."

Chelsea handed one bag to Max and another to Ben, both careful not to disturb the contact their fobs had with their skin.

"Max would you kindly and generously tip our driver?"

"Please, you got your food. I'd like to just go," Chelsea said.

"Eat with us," Slieve requested.

Chelsea's eyes reddened instantly.

"See what happens when you become a city that fails to respect women," Slieve said, looking forlornly to Adama. "A man should have come. You disagree?"

"I think you're sexist," Adama replied.

Slieve ordered the others to sit in the road and eat. He encouraged Max to help Chelsea to join them.

Ben began to retrieve boxes of meals and hand them out. Inside each was a sandwich, a bowl of soup, a salad and a bottle of water.

"Could somebody help Max, Ben and me. We only have one hand."

"I," Georgia said.

"I?"

"You said Max, Ben and me," Georgia replied. "It's Max, Ben and I."

"You might find Tobias Wolff's 'Bullet to the Brain' a bit illuminating on the approach you're taking here, and, just like Tobias, you would be wrong." Slieve pushed his lunch box across the gravel road towards Georgia. "Open it."

Georgia opened it and pushed it back.

"Everything is not I," Slieve explained. "See, if Max and Ben were not here, I would be the only object in that sentence and I would not say 'could somebody help I,' would me? I would say 'help me.' Understand?"

Georgia nodded.

"I swear the only people who don't know anything about English are grammar Nazis who think they have a duty to correct people. Does what someone said bother you? Suck it up, welcome to living language."

With one hand, Slieve then pulled off the lid from his container of soup—vegetable broth—and drank from it. He threw the chunkless mixture away, spraying Shasta and her daughter, then turned to

Chelsea and offered half of his sandwich. Before she could reject it, Severus took and handed it to her.

"Tell me, Chelsea. Do you find it absurd as I do that so many women want to prove that they are absolutely so important that they'll demean men to do it, but the moment that a man tries to show a woman how important she is, he's a sexist? Answer honestly."

"I don't need a man to protect me."

"Is that so," Slieve replied.

"Oh shit," said Adama through food.

Slieve smiled. "Who said anything about needing help?"

Chelsea bit into her sandwich and chewed slowly.

"Who here wants to trade places with Chelsea," Slieve asked. "She takes your place and you can go."

"You said I was safe," Chelsea said and tried to climb up to run away.

"One step and you won't live to make another," Slieve said, holding up his briefcase as if he was prepared to let go.

Chelsea sat again, her eyes welling with tears and hatred. "You don't have to do this."

"No. I want to do this." He waited a few minutes for Chelsea to push through a few tears and catch her breath. "I have two, grown men who can trade places with you right now. One of them can go and you can take his place and show how strong you are. All either of them have to do is say the word and you'll stay with me. Ben?"

"No," Ben said, barely audible and nearly silenced by the conflict of freedom.

Slieve turned to the negotiator.

Max said nothing. He looked to the fob in his hand and to Chelsea as he thought about it. If he traded places with Chelsea, he could sleep in his own bed tonight. Not only that, he could serve the entire group better by returning to his comrades to plan how they might diffuse the situation before the bomber could leave their jurisdiction. Plus, there were the buildings with bombs that he could help stop from exploding.

Max slowly closed his fingers around the explosive device.
"No," he said.

"There, see. Did you need him to do that so you could go home?"
Chelsea shook her head. "Yes."

"This would be where you thank them for valuing your life more than their own. Wow! What evil sexist beasts to hold you in such high regard to protect you like that."

"But he didn't protect me, did he," Chelsea replied. "If he was protecting me, this would have ended before I was ever forced to come out, and the only reason I am is because of you."

"Catch," Slieve said, throwing one of his black fobs, and before she could block her instinct, she held out her hands and watched the device sail right into them, but it landed in Severus's as he snatched it out of the air.

"Time for you to go, Chelsea," Slieve said before starting into his half of the sandwich.

Chelsea stood and began walking back to her car before suddenly turning back.

"Do you think things will be different beyond our border?"

"Now that's a question," Slieve replied. "That's a really good question. I hope you're all paying attention to that." He chewed and swallowed another bite of his sandwich then held a bottle of water to Shashaun to open for him. "Maybe they won't be different, but I won't be here."

"Where are you going," Chelsea asked.

"Don't know," Slieve answered. "I guess it can't hurt to tell you now."
Chelsea scoffed and began to leave again.

"It's because I don't know where the person is I want to find. Only that he's looking for brilliant minds to help him build."

"Build what?"

"Whatever he's building," Slieve explained. "That's why I've done all of this, to show what a devoted, brilliant mind can do. Weapons, bombs, manipulation, keeping every single law-enforcement agency at bay while escaping the most naïve and unforgiving state in the world."

Chelsea scoffed more, then laughed. "You want to catch the eye of someone you don't know, so you can accomplish a goal that you don't have, and you think that's a brilliant mind? Do you even know this person's name?"

"There's some truth to that," Slieve replied, and he was starting to appear amused again. "That's why I hope he's one of the—how many viewers do we have now, Heather?"

"We were above a billion, but we dropped some," Heather said. "No one wants to watch us eat sandwiches?"

"What's his name," Chelsea asked.

"Salvo," Slieve said.

Chelsea's nose crinkled as she nodded her head. "You're kidding. What would the American mythological crime lord ever want with you?"

"I wouldn't expect a delivery driver to understand. All right, everybody up." He stood and directed the others to stand. "Time to grow our viewership."

"You know what," Chelsea fired back as the group started moving again. She ran to catch up with it. "It's my experience that the person who thinks he's the smartest individual in the room is usually the most destructive asshole."

Slieve motioned for the group to stop and turned haughtily towards Chelsea.

"Oh, know a lot of intelligent people, do you? Or any?"

"You don't know as much as you think you do," Chelsea said. "Rocky Maddow was my father. Ever hear of him?"

"The father of Omniscient A.I.?"

"That's right. Helped pay my way through college *and* grad school."

Slieve laughed.

"Oh, that's right," Chelsea said. "A delivery driver, right? No, I came because I refused to send my own employees, something my father would have done were he still alive."

"You're not sixteen," Slieve suddenly observed. "I specifically said I wanted—

"I was sixteen when I finished my master's. How old were you when you finished yours?" Then she added, "Slieve."

Now it was Slieve who didn't answer.

"Yeah, that's right," Chelsea said. "Who's the smartest person in the room right now? Me. Member of Mensa at fourteen, two years younger than when my father became a member. My father's Theory of Omniscience paid for my undergrad work, but it was my coding structure, the language of Unknown that allowed my inventions to pay my way through two Ph.Ds. Compared to me, you're a kid with a new box of Legos."

Slieve's face tightened.

"You want to know why I'm here," Chelsea asked. "Because I'm the one that's going to make sure you don't lose your live feed underground. No one else knows how to keep you alive except me. So, you see, you need me." She turned to the car. "Dayanara, come."

The car drove forward slowly. Chelsea reached into the passenger seat, drew out a leather satchel and strapped it over her head and across her chest. "Return home and prepare Little Chubby to extract us when I call."

The car pulled back, turned and drove off.

"Shall we," she asked and started walking past the group.

Adama snickered.

"I wouldn't," Slieve warned, and yelled. "You will stop."

Chelsea stopped.

"Take the fob," Slieve said. He dug into his pocket for yet another proximity device. "You're part of the group now, or boom."

"I'm already part of the group, you ignoramus," Chelsea said. "Which you'd know if you'd been paying attention."

Slieve tossed the fob to, the young delivery driver, and she caught it. Then she dropped it, and nothing happened.

"Please. I deactivated your fobs the moment I drove up and wiped your receiver. My drones scanned your frequencey before I even left to deliver your food."

Ben looked to his fob. "The light's dead," he said.

"Don't think this changes anything," Slieve said. "My dead man's switch and your cables don't work on frequency."

"I'm not leaving," Ben replied.

"I can't go either," Heather said.

Max didn't say anything, but it was clear he was staying too.

"And," Chelsea continued. "Right now, my fleet of vehicles and drones, are swarming the air and streets to locate and shutdown any other remote or wireless devices with your signal signatures. Could take fifteen minutes, could take two hours. Now, you could get angry and do your whole, 'grrr turn them off or I'll blow everyone up now' thing, or you could realize you still have your briefcase, your hostages and about a mile and a half to the other side of this tunnel."

"You think you've beaten me," Slieve asked.

"I know I have," Chelsea replied. "Now, are we taking you to Salvo or not? Because we don't want you."

"Get moving," Slieve said.

Before they even started into the tunnel, Chelsea had reached into her bag and drew out a fist's worth of what looked like silver seeds. She sprinkled some, and they bounced around the pavement. In a few yards, she sprinkled more, then even more at about the same distance.

"What is that," Georgia asked.

"These are micro hotspots for Omniscient service," Chelsea said.

"I've never heard of that."

"You will," she replied. "By this time next year, they'll be mixed into all new concrete, asphalt repair and construction materials. They'll be in bags of fertilizer so they can be spread across every park and front lawn across the Conglomerate U.S. There'll be no more need for towers or modems or server planes. It'll all be here, on this little network, and each one has a life of twenty years. Micro hotspots all networked together. We're still working on the range, but we'll get there. For now, it's just an extension cord."

The tunnel filled with the echo of marching, rubber soles and the occasional clatter of mini hotspots sprinkling around the ground.

"Well, we suddenly got very quiet, didn't we," Slieve observed.

"Did you need us to talk," Chelsea asked staying slightly ahead of the group.

"I'm always up for good conversation."

"Oh. Is that what you've been having," Chelsea asked. "I couldn't tell through all your woe is me-me-me."

"You know what," Severus blurted. "You're just as destructive as his bomb-wielding! Let me tell you something, lady who grew up with a silver spoon. For all your control in social media and communication, you don't know half as much as you think. There's no oppression when you're the one oppressing."

"You think I'm oppressive," Chelsea asked then laughed again. "I'm the one keeping you alive."

"You put us here," Severus snapped back. "He may have a bomb, but he's right. We shouldn't have to ask the man with the bomb why this happened. You're rich. You control the communication outlets. Heck, you own the communication outlets. You can say anything you want to, disagree with anyone you want to. You want to say something, your words get out. I want to say something that people don't like; you can shut down my message. You make your users abide by your own sharing of ideas policies that you've confused them to think that's what free speech is. Tell me that's not you oppressing us."

"You have just as much freedom to share your view as I do," Chelsea scoffed.

"If J.J.J. said something a billion people didn't like right now, tell me you don't have the power to shut her live feed off if you wanted to. You can, right?"

"Well, yeah. We have policies in place to protect against unwanted comments."

"Tell me I can do the same to you," Severus said.

"Well, no."

"Uh-huh," Severus grumbled. "And why do you get to decide what I want to hear?"

"Why would you want to hear what other people don't?"

"Because it's my goddam right! It's my right to use my voice and develop my own beliefs and philosophies in ways that can only happen through discussion with diverse viewpoints! It's my right to say what some people might not want to hear, and have my ideas challenged, and people like you stole it from me."

"I didn't steal anything."

"Your family helped author the freedom of speech restriction act," Severus fired back. "Think about that, the freedom that said no one will put a restriction on, your family created a law that's very name says it does just that."

"I think you're confusing your history."

"I taught U.S. history, you stupid bitch!"

The tunnel fell silent, as if recovering from a nuclear blast.

Now it was Slieve who laughed.

"I," Chelsea spoke slowly, "don't think that's appro—"

"Stupid," Severus boldly enunciated. "Bitch!"

Chelsea stopped walking and had the audacity to appear stunned.

"I taught real U.S. history. Your family, you, rewrote it. You tied me to this bomb every bit as much, if not more than he did, when your family started convincing the American people that terms of use agreements was the same thing as freedom of speech. You did this. You! You don't get it. You're the why."

"Don't put me in the same category as this man. He's the real danger here."

"You," Shashaun squeaked out. "You did say the most intelligent person in the room was the most destructive."

"And you made it abundantly clear you were the most intelligent," Shasta added.

"Might I suggest, you stop escalating the situation before your words get us killed," Max suggested.

"Well, what do you know," Slieve said. "Not everyone here agrees with you."

The group continued walking quietly, with the exception of Chelsea's silver seeds whispering against the concrete surface. The hostages, even the bomber, took to the mundane, such as counting bricks in the walls, light recesses in the ceiling and stripes on the roads; it seemed there was nothing else to do.

"Not everyone agrees with you either," Adama finally added softly.

"That's okay," Slieve said. "That's how it's supposed to be. That's how sharing different ideas works."

They fell quiet again.

"No, let's not do this," Max said. "Surely we can do something with our time. We know Severus is a teacher, what does everyone else do?"

"What a great idea," Slieve said. "Get the bomber to connect emotionally with his hostages and maybe he'll be less likely to blow them up. Go ahead, Shasta, let's see if Max's idea works."

"I'm a pharmaceutical chemist for McBann," Shasta replied.

"Really," Slieve asked.

"Yes."

"Huh. And Shashaun? You want to be a health pirate like your mother?"

"I don't know, I'm only sixteen. I need to finish high school first."

"But you want to, right? Be like your mom?"

"I'd like to study healthcare organization maybe."

"That's not much better," Slieve said.

"Oh, and what do you do, All-high-and-mighty," Shasta asked.

"Besides being a felon," Adama asked.

Slieve smirked.

"I'm a security analyst," Slieve said.

"What does that even mean," Adama asked.

"People paid me to improve their security operations. Sometimes I stole from stores to show how easy it was. Sometimes I broke into buildings. Sometimes I found weak links to get at corporate secrets. There's a lot to it."

"Computers too," Georgia asked.

"Computers too."

"Hm. Ever hear of Topplerone?"

"No."

"Then you must not be that great, because I've never heard of your work until now."

"Why would you?"

"Because that's what I do at Topplerone," Georgia replied. "I break systems worth anything. If you were any good, I'd have broken your system. You would have known my name."

"Perhaps, or maybe you're not as good as you think if you haven't found us yet."

"What are the odds," Max asked. "Two people attached to the same bomb and in the same profession."

"Three," Adama corrected.

"Oh. You're a hacker too," Slieve asked.

"No. I work in security though."

"Computers?"

"Something a little more devastating,"

Heather suddenly stopped walking, and Slieve instantly noticed. "What's wrong? Did we disconnect?"

"You said you wanted a Salvo to see this, right," Heather said. "I just got a post from someone who says they know the way."

Slieve faltered in controlling his appearance for a moment. He looked at Heather as though he had just received something he thought he wanted but, only now, wondered if he really did.

"Yeah," Slieve replied but really asked.

"He says 'welcome to Jersey. Escort en route. Please wait here.'"

"And I'm just supposed to believe that," Slieve said.

A few seconds and Heather came back with, "This person says he doesn't care what you believe. He says you have ten seconds to accept or you might as well set off the bomb right now—Oh, he's posting a countdown, seven now, six, five."

"I'll take it," Slieve replied.

"Good," Heather read from her reply. "Escort will bring you to a safehouse. Prepare to disarm bomb. No one leaves the group until then." She lifted her head. "We did it. We're in Jersey."

They waited an hour in silent anticipation, then the tunnel buzzed to life, softly at first, then obvious that several engines approached.

"Let's—uh—everyone together," Slieve said.

Three electric vehicles appeared: a pickup truck and two Military jeeps with gun mounts. The vehicles stopped.

"Permission to approach," a Jeep passenger asked standing above the windshield of his vehicle.

"Yes," Slieve called back.

The vehicles moved forward, past, then circled back. The bed of the truck squared in front of the group. Four men dressed as militants stood in the bed. Two jumped down to the ground.

The passenger from the jeep stepped out and cautiously approached the group.

"Our employer believes your trip to the safehouse will go faster by car," he said. "If you'll step up, we can help you into the bed to maintain the safe connection of your lines to the bomb."

"Whoa," Chelsea said. "I can't guarantee that I can drop these fast enough in a moving vehicle. We could lose connection."

"Agreed," Slieve said. He turned to the camera. "If we lose connection, give us four minutes. If live streaming doesn't resume by then, detonate one every minute until we reconnect."

One by one, the militants loaded Slieve and his captives into the back of the truck so that they kept their proximity intact. As soon as they were loaded, the vehicles began moving. They picked up speed. The connection dropped.

Two minutes later, they were beyond the tunnel, passing a checkpoint manned by at least a dozen armed officers. Heather took another minute to restart her stream.

For fifteen more minutes, they sped through the streets, turning, turning back, going right, then left, then four lefts, then Slieve gave up keeping track, realizing Salvo most likely didn't want anyone to track the safehouse. Next was an alley, where the cars drew in single file to navigate. Then came another street, then back into the open.

"Wait," Severus said. "This isn't a safehouse, it's—"

A Boeing 927 Defender screamed overhead as it came in for the land.

Newark airport drew close. The vehicles drove to a checkpoint. The soldiers waved them directly into the interior and towards a familiar square jet. To its side was an old military blackbird.

Four people stood near the planes: two men, two women.

The vehicles stopped near the jet. The militants helped the members of the group down now.

The women approached. Monica was 32, appeared professional, wore a tie with her suit jacket, kept her reflective sunglasses on. She frowned, stepped with purpose. Jasmine was older, 47, former law-enforcement until the judges, through the popular opinion of the city dwellers, decided no one who's ever attended a therapy session could be trusted to operate a firearm and took her job.

She was a little friendlier at first glance, locked eyes with Slieve and maintained the hold.

"We were sent to transport you as soon as your intent to reach Salvo was made known," Monica said. Her head snapped suddenly to Slieve, and, for a moment, seemed to shiver. "There will be no bomb—mmbomb—on our plane." She clenched her teeth fiercely as if suddenly in pain and blurted, "turn it off!"

"Not until I have some reassurance," Slieve said. "I don't know who you are."

"We're done—nnnhh, done—here—done here! Done here," Monica explained. Her hand snapped to a firearm but didn't draw it.

"We are not done," Slieve snapped. "You take your hand off your firearm or I drop it."

"So? drop it," she said. "Go on then. Go on then. See where that gets you after coming this far." Her elbow twitched at her side arm but still didn't pull it. "Your hostages are New Manhattaners. The state of Jersey doesn't care if you explode. As far as they're concerned, you haven't broken any laws yet—not yet, yet. Yet-yet. Not yet! You're safe."

"However, you're looking at this all wrong," Jasmine added. "New Jersey is honored to assist the son of one of the Valiant Four."

Slieve felt instantly out of his league and relieved at once.

"Deactivate the bomb and release the hostages, and we can get underway," Monica replied, getting hung up on her W sound for just a moment. "Or were you not serious about Salvo?"

Slieve exhaled and broke into tears. "Finally," he said. He opened the briefcase, wiped his eyes with his sleeve and snapped at a black toggle switch.

"It's okay," Jasmine said. "You're with us now."

"I thought I was going to die there."

"No," Jasmine reassured and smiled to let him know he was among friends.

"Your clips can unlock now," Slieve said. "Everything is unarmed." Now, he set his briefcase on the ground, forced his white fingers to open from their cramped state.

"Gentlemen, you are free to dispose of the ordinance," Monica said, clearly speaking in a hidden earpiece. "Hostages, please stay where you are, and our medical staff will attend you momentarily." Her hand snapped up and pointed twice off towards two ambulances, which were now driving at them without their sirens on.

"This way, sir," Jasmine directed Slieve. She extended an arm for Slieve to follow towards the stairs leading into the private jet.

Slieve eagerly obeyed.

After he passed, Jasmine drew a micro Uzi from beneath her jacket and sprayed a string of bullets up his spine.

He crumpled, unable to move, grasped for shallow breaths, not dead but not far from it.

"He's still alive," Monica said, surprised.

Jasmine knelt down. "If there really was a Salvo, do you think the American cartel lord would trust a selfish suicide bomber like you?" She kissed her hand and patted his cheek. "Welcome to Jersey."

Slieve watched Jasmine stand and listened to her walk off. He was left to ponder the realization of his last few hours, unable to immediately die.

Part Four:

Depressed City

Chapter Twenty-Four

Adama screamed. "He has people watching."

"They're already dead," Monica said. Her head snapped to Heather. "You haven't been streaming since you crossed the border."

Heather lowered her tired arm.

"Your camera, please," Monica said, holding out an open hand to receive it. It spasmed once but flared open again.

Heather removed her bracelet and passed it to Monica.

"Was that necessary," Max asked.

"Yes," Monica replied. "We have enough people who prey on the lives of innocents without the need for suicide bombers. Bastard!"

Slieve continued to allow himself to bleed out and accepted the insult.

"Get on the plane," Jasmine now directed the hostages as she reapproached the group.

"What is this," Chelsea protested.

Jasmine holstered her firearm. "You have Salvo's word. You are safe. This way now."

"Please," Monica added. "You're no longer hostages. There is rest and air conditioning on the plane."

A crew of armed officers had backed up a trailer carrying a large steel sphere on a stand. One of them was currently sliding Slieve's briefcase into it before closing the ball.

The hostages moved to the plane. Even as they passed, Slieve's breath was shocky, and, could he move, would have reached to beg for help. So, they passed him and let him wallow in his success.

Inside the jet, they found recliners, a couch. An airline attendant greeted them with champaign flutes of orange Gatorade.

A second attendant welcomed them to sit and promised the use of a phone to contact loved ones in a moment.

Jasmine moved her way to the rear hallway of the plane. "Salvo regrets not being able to meet you in person."

"Salvo," Chelsea asked. "Salvo's a myth."

"Whore," Monica blurted. Her head twitched.

Jasmine smiled.

"Something very interesting has happened today with consequences that may well intrigue you," Jasmine said. "Normally, we would have let this play out, but, as chance would have it—and it is by chance—a lunatic bomb maker brought an interesting group of people together—and now Salvo wants you, all of you."

"Wants us," Adama asked.

"What does that even mean," Shasta followed.

Monica snorted; her head twitched.

"It's very simple," Jasmine explained. "You're not in New Manhattan anymore. Do you really want to go back?"

"No," Severus replied instantly. "I miss my freedom."

Jasmine smiled to Severus. "How about the rest of you? Can you honestly say you feel safe when you share an idea or say what's on your mind in public?"

Heather was the next to shake her head.

"Heather," Monica asked. "You were put on probation in college for recording a video that supported a professor who presented research that showed students were declining in their abilities to learn. You haven't been able to get into any other school since, isn't that right? You even changed your name so no one could find out who was really running your camera, didn't you? It worked until today, didn't it? Now what happens to you?"

"I don't know," Heather replied.

"And can you two officers honestly say that you are ever able to feel good about the decisions social media forces you to second-think before you can do anything to protect and serve?"

Ben didn't say anything, he didn't have to. His eyes said it all. He thought about how quickly Heather had turned her camera on him after he struck the man earlier with his baton. He saved lives.

Max, however, nodded yes, not yes that he felt good about his behavior but yes that he understood Monica's intent.

"Look at you. A history teacher—a real history teacher—an underground hacker, a medicinal chemist, a diplomat, an honest cop, a media influencer with a scrupled past and who's just gained a very large audience around the world," Jasmine explained. "What if I told you Salvo would like to offer you all jobs and double what you're paid now to help her rebuild the free society that once existed in this very nation? How would you like to help Salvo throw the political crybabies out of the equation and ensure they can't overcomplicate the legal process anymore? I'm talking job security."

"I already make a lot of money," Chelsea said. "I'll just go home."

"I don't think so," Jasmine said. "You're going to volunteer."

Chelsea laughed. "Why would I do that?"

"Because, Salvo knows what happened to your thieving father. All you have is because he stole Omniscient, stole the theories behind it and killed the woman who really developed them," Monica said.

"How dare you," Chelsea fired back.

"How dare you! Your wealth is built on the blood of inventors your dad killed—m-murdering prick—including a man who had been working on an invention that would change the face of transportation forever. Salvo can tell you everything you want to know about why your daddy didn't return home that one day. You can volunteer to work for Salvo, or Salvo can publicly release the documents that prove your family inheritance, your right to education, your livelihood was all paid for in murdering people who had what your father was too lazy to earn himself. After today's experience of murders in New Manhattan, I wonder how much differently your family name would look—like thieves! Like thieves! Mm-bitch! You can redeem yourself, or you can get what your family deserves and rot in hell for the sins of your father."

"I don't believe you," Chelsea said, fighting back tears.

"If you walk down that hallway, you'll find an office and a tablet on the desk with the documents already prepared for you. Pay close attention to the security footage that your father bribed police to hide. Take your time."

Chelsea ran down the hall.

"That was cold," Georgia said.

Jasmine approached Georgia and placed her hand on his shoulder.

"Centuries ago, pilgrims set out from England to America on two ships, the Mayflower and the Speedwell. Only one ship made the journey. Do you know why they left, Georgia," Jasmine asked.

"To expand England," Georgia replied.

"What," Monica asked incredulously. "No!"

Jasmine held up her hand to allow her to finish speaking. "They left to get away from people like her, to escape persecution of the rich, persecution of their leaders, of people who said poor people didn't have a right to worship according to their own beliefs. They came here so they could be individuals. The problem is, we've forgotten that, and it's time for us to escape that conformity again, and Salvo has the way."

"How is that possible? There's no where to go," Severus asked.

"For that, Salvo needs you to make a choice—the right one!" Monica replied.

"You can leave this plane right now and we'll return you to the tunnel," Jasmine explained." Or you can stay and help us rebuild a society and constitution that we should have never torn down, where all were created equal, but not all people were created the same. You can help many, who wish to, escape to a place where individuality is a birthright, voices are unique and the catastrophes from conformity will never be allowed to be forgotten in our history classes."

"That's not a possible society," Severus said. "Any society needs government. You can't have government without the practice of unified parties getting involved, and if there's anything politics has taught us, commercially-driven parties and agenda will create lines that gravitate towards conformity. We'll come right back to this very spot some day and have to escape again."

"And that is why organized political party affiliation will never be legal," Jasmine said. "The manipulation of power-seeking organizations, businesses and lobbyists will never again influence public accord. We are no longer the day where the people can't represent themselves. If we can vote for the best singer on television in a matter of minutes, we can vote on laws without needing representatives to screw them up for us."

"Then we lose check-and-balance. That's a society in the making for a dictatorship."

"The senate will still exist. The judicial branch will still exist. The people will be their own representatives now, no need for a house. The people check the senate. The senate check the people. Both will check the same kind of presidency that we have now."

"And the fourth branch of government," Severus asked.

"Fourth branch," Monica asked. "Oh. The press. I told you, our Constitution will revert to a previous version where rights were protected, and that includes many original and tainted amendments that were never supposed to have been polluted by lobbyists."

"So, just like that?"

"I couldn't answer that without requiring you to make your decision to exit the plane or stay," Monica said, her hand suddenly punching straight out, withdrawing and punching again.

"A warning, if you choose to stay, you must stay. Leaving would put many lives in jeopardy. If you have loved ones who you want to bring with you, give us their names, we will collect them, but they will have to make the same choice as you. You need to decide now."

"Can I ask something," Shasta asked. "I would do better if I understood why Salvo was interested in me."

Monica and Jasmine shared a look with each other. Monica disappeared down the hall and behind a door. A few minutes later, she reappeared. She pocketed a phone and gave an approving nod.

"In creating any new society, you need experienced people. We need ethical teachers. We need medicine. We need diplomats. We need students who are willing to learn how to become leaders," Jasmine explained.

She turned to Georgia. "We need people to help us hide while we prepare to leave this society."

Now, she turned to Adama, "We need weapon designers to create defenses. Yes, we know all about your contribution to military defenses.

"We need moral and steadfast police officers to pass on their values to help us organize our own just and merciful law enforcement," Jasmine said, looking to Ben. "Is it true you took a demotion for whistleblowing on your captain for taking a bribe?"

At this, she turned to Heather. "We need people who many need to speak for us without giving us away. Someone with a past of acting cool under pressure and a respect of reporting truth to others."

Her face squared with Chelsea, who had reappeared in the main cabin and with red eyes. "And we need someone to help us establish a secured network that no one else can break, someone to protect our people and our communication rather than stealing it.

"Salvo has instructed us to tell you that you can all become people of great influence and guidance in rediscovering who we were meant to be in this country," Monica added.

"So, who stays? Who goes," Jasmine finally asked.

Max raised his hand, and Monica nodded for him to answer.

"Will I be starving."

Jasmine smirked. "As with any economy, there will always be uncertainties."

"We can tell you this," Monica said. "Our economy's stronger than yours."

"What can we take with us," Chelsea asked.

"Besides people you trust? Your money. Necessary equipment to do your work. Remember, anyone you bring must make this same decision as you, and going against us after joining will be considered an act of treason. I cannot stress that enough here."

"I'll go with you," Severus said. "I may not have agreed with his approach, but our captor was correct. We have forgotten too many things, and I've been dead inside for far too long."

"A chance to establish law-enforcement," Ben contemplated.

"And our pay is doubled," Shasta asked.

"Yes" Jasmine corrected, pointing to Chelsea.

"Well, I don't care about the pay," Ben said. "I just want to do right by me. I'll do it."

"Well, I care about pay," Max said, and his head began to nod. "God help me why but all right."

Shasta and Shashaun shared a look of uncertainty.

"What if," Shashaun asked, then paused. "I want to go to school."

"We can arrange that," Monica said. "Salvo offers many scholarships for students willing to use what they learn to help us rebuild our forgotten society."

"How many pharmaceutical professionals could they have," Shashaun asked.

Shasta didn't look quite convinced.

"He was right, Mom," Shashaun said. "I don't know anything outside of New Manhattan."

"You sure," Shasta asked. "You heard what they said. If your dad and brother choose not to follow—

"They will," Shashaun encouraged.

Shasta's head began to bob, "I think so too."

"So, I get to do sketchy stuff online and not get arrested for it," Georgia asked. "I can do that."

"I'm not making weapons to attack my own country," Adama said.

"The weapons you made are already being used to attack your own country," Jasmine said. "You'd be making them to stop that from happening."

Adama, whether through being stunned at what she'd heard or the fact that a new life appealed to her, shook her head to suggest she would take on the task.

"Free press," Heather asked.

"Free press," Monica blurted.

Now they all turned to Chelsea.

"I'll give you a list of the things I'll need and the people who I trust will feel the same as I do about what I've just learned," Chelsea replied shakily.

"That's everyone then," Monica observed. She directed the attendants to close the plane; notify the pilot they were ready to depart; and signal the guards outside that there would be no more surprise executions today. After they were in the air, she said, "There's a phone in the office, call your families, tell them you're okay, tell them you've been offered jobs you can't turn down, but that's all. We will send people to escort them to you and give them the same choice as you. Otherwise, there's no going back for them. Understand?"

Shasta moved first to make her call. She came back as though she'd just lost an argument.

"They're not coming," Shashaun asked in shock.

"No, they're coming," Shasta replied. "A car already came for them. They're on their way. They said 'yes' before we did."

Adama went next, took two minutes and came back with. "No one for me. Better to know now, right?"

"I'm so sorry, Adama," Ben said.

"Don't be. I'm not."

The others took their turns. Severus did not.

Ben called his fiancée, his brother and widowed father. He had also dialed his best friend but realized he would most definitely rather stay in New Manhattan. So, he told him he would stay in touch, knowing that he most likely would not.

Max returned from his phone call the most devastated. Nearly made it through his report that his wife and two daughters were angry before he broke down. How could he do that to them? Leave them? The others tried their best to console him.

After all the others had made their calls, Chelsea had her turn and took the longest. Their plane was an hour away from Vegas by the time she had finished her conversations—the ones she could think to make at the time, that is. When she came out of the cabin, the others were deep in discussions, getting to know one another.

"I assume you can tell us what's going on now." She took a seat in one of the recliners.

"Soon," Jasmine replied.

Within twenty minutes, the jet had touched down. The hatch opened and an old, black-chrome, army-personnel truck waited for them.

The group loaded into the back, which had been decked out with far more comfort than the original design would have allowed. The seats were soft benches, and a mini bar beneath a retractable television was secured to the back of the truck cab.

The truck coughed up smoke and began moving. The lighting within the bed was dim. It was only after bright, recessed streetlamps flooded out the night that it was suddenly apparent the truck had entered a tunnel. It started out wide enough for one vehicle. Then it ran into a check point. Several personnel approached and drew automatic weapons upon the people in the bed of the truck.

"We're back," Jasmine explained.

After she took a few minutes to speak with them, and they spent a few moments to inspect the people and truck, the soldiers made a phone call. After all this, the guns lowered, the men dispersed, the truck proceeded once more.

The single lane turned into two and then a parking structure within a steel and concrete dome ceiling. The entire descent beneath ground took fifteen minutes. When the trucks stopped, Monica began leading the group towards a convex wall with accordion doors that stretched from floor to ceiling, about fifty feet in height. Monica, however, opened a single steel security gate to side of these.

Inside, was a hallway that bent with a shallowcurvature of a wall and ramped down. They followed the decline and passed a door to the left, then another, a third, fourth and a fifth, but they ignored them all. Then a viewing area to the right suddenly opened up to a twenty-feet-tall and at least fifty wide wall of glass that looked into a brightly lit and vast silo 200 feet across and 1,200 deep. The window looked into the silo to the top of a cylindrical structure where an aircraft with sharp edges sat pointed towards the ceiling, awaiting an abrupt order to launch.

Severus approached the glass and stared in awe.

"If I didn't know any better," he said, pointing to the plane that topped what appeared to be a massive and fat rocket. "I'd swear that was an old B-2 Bomber."

"With some modifications," Monica replied.

Severus followed the nose of the object into the chasm as far as the glass would allow him to see. For what he could view, the body was a tube that held the same kind of stealthy, cold edges as the head.

"Is it a space station," Georgia asked.

"No," Monica replied. "The heart of a space nation."

"This is one of eighty-three modules we have throughout America," Jasmine explained. "What you're looking at is the central hub and command structure of it all. The people who work in there, literally rule the world. Or will rule it."

"It'll never fly," Adama said, she had been scrutinizing the strange object just as Severus had. "The rocket fuel it would take to propel this is—and I don't see that it even has any fuel tanks or thrusters installed on it yet."

"It won't need rocket fuel," Jasmine said. "We have something new."

"How? It's got to be at least five-hundred feet."

"Eleven-hundred currently, not our smallest. Our grazeland and agricultural modules are far larger.

"Still, with the weight of this and the people it would take to pilot it, it's just not possible to achieve lift off," Adama observed.

Jasmine smiled, not afraid to reveal that she knew a secret that Adama did not.

"Yes, it will. We're going to pop it out of here like a champagne cork and then let it keep flying."

"Then how—

"We can almost send a single individual into orbit with an engine smaller than a football," Jasmine explained.

"Almost," Adama asked.

"That's something Salvo hopes you and Chelsea can help us figure out," Jasmine said. "To help us complete the trip."

"And hopefully create some defensive weapons along the way," Monica added.

"There is that too," Jasmine said. She pressed her finger against the glass to direct everyone's attention at a set of silver letters, that almost disappeared against the black of the body paint.

The silver letters read "Mayflower."

"The original Mayflower was successful because it had a place to flee to," Jasmine said. "There are no more hidden continents for us, so we're building one. Once we get up and take control of orbit, we begin efforts to let the earth know we are a sovereign nation, trade will follow."

"Trade," Georgia questioned. "How? There's nothing in space to trade."

"The boy has a point," Ben suggested. "We're going to break down eventually."

Again, Jasmine smiled to announce that she knew more than the others.

"Oh," she said. "Space has plenty that the earth wants and needs."

"What does that mean," Shasta asked.

"Manufacturing and tourism, of course," Jasmine said. "Our technology just made getting into orbit as simple a matter as getting on a bus. And we're going to have places for everyone to go."

"You're talking about terraforming," Georgia said. "That's awesome."

"No. Sci-fi bullshit! B-bullshit!" Monica erupted, gained control of her outburst and started again. "To terraform an entire planet takes a long time. Humans would be more likely to evolve to the planet before they could make it livable for their current state."

"They're not going to let you just take orbit, you know." Max said. "They'll shoot you out of the sky. That's not a small target."

"Again, that's where techs and weapon engineers come in," Monica said looking particularly to Adama.

"Right," Adama replied.

"This way, please," Jasmine said. Then she turned and began walking down the hallway once more.

They followed but didn't move much farther beyond the wall of glass before reaching an elevator. They all fit inside. It may have appeared cramped, but many more could have fit.

"Something on your mind, Ben," Jasmine observed from a troubled brow that had been crunching tightly into his face.

"Huh," he asked as if being caught in a deception. "Are we safe going deeper. Seems like a—

"He's scared," Monica said. "Thinks the ground will squish us in here."

"And other things," Ben replied.

"Oh," Monica asked.

"I'm starting to feel a little cornered. You're asking a lot of trust of me right now."

"Tell me about it," Jasmine said. She nodded to Ben's hip where he was suddenly aware of how much his hand had been tapping his side arm. It was only now that he realized Monica had been standing behind him the entire journey, and Jasmine was directly to his right, which is where he kept his weapon. If he had tried to pull it, this was the place to be. With her so close to his drawing hand, he would have never been able to draw and turn upon her before she could disarm him.

"Oh," he realized and allowed himself to see how much of the trust they had already been trading.

"The earth's not going to fall on you," Jasmine said.

The elevator doors opened into an underground nightlife. A city of paved roads and nine city blocks stood beneath an earth ceiling supported by dome braces, which, in turn, were supported by upright supports that doubled as posts for streetlamps.

The tallest building—mostly offices and labs—stood five stories in the center of the grid, but delved another 200 feet below ground for ten more floors of research and development. It was surrounded by four story-condos, a hotel and a park. Four city blocks held houses. Three blocks together made up convenience supermarkets, a movie theater, a recreational arcade, restaurants and more on the opposite side of the city from the houses. There was enough for a decent community of employees to live and keep sane.

The sound of life filled the entire chamber, muffled it even as the outside world could not.

"This is what Salvo has done underground. Imagine what we can do when we send this all and more into space," Jasmine said. "And this is just our capitol." She hailed a yellow golf cart with three rows of seats. The taxi pulled up from its place among three others. "This is the industrial side of the complex. Network access and security offices are on the other. Don't try to enter there, you will find yourselves very unhappy if you do." She pointed to the hotel now. "That's for guests. We'll set you up some accommodations, should be ready in an hour. You've had a long day. Until then, please, visit the city. Trust me, we all know who you are. You're very popular today. If you see something you'd like, put it on Salvo's tab. Oh, and I'd stay out of the residential area. They like their calm."

"Hold up," Max said. "You're seriously just going to turn seven traumatized victims loose into your city."

Jasmine smirked. "This whole city's traumatized. You'll blend right in."

The members of the group had mostly loaded into the taxi. Shashaun was the last to enter and was just taking her seat when Monica held her hand in front of Ben.

"I must ask for your weapon now. Belt! Naked! Show me your—she relaxed again. I promise you'll be safe without it. I'll return it later."

Ben removed his tactical belt and cautiously handed all of his defensive gear to Monica. She smiled and acknowledged his action. Then she waved the taxi towards the city, and it started off with the day's hostages for a street where a crowd had started to recognize who they were and gathered to see them. There were so many people down here.

Monica and Jasmine set off to prepare accommodations at the hotel.

The taxi drove straight down the street. Adama and Ben stepped out on the first block—Ben because he wanted to get a lay of the land and a feel for the people, Adama because she needed a stiff one.

Georgia asked where the best place to blow off steam was; the taxi dropped him off at the rec mall. The taxi drove again and suddenly stopped when Max decided here was as good as any place to start exploring. The taxi continued on once more to eventually release

Shasta and Shashaun to a strip of food stands. Chelsea asked to ride around and see the town then be returned to the hotel.

As Max tried to take in his surroundings and decide which direction to try, he was greeted with nods from people on the street.

"I know you," one man said. "I saw you."

"Leave him be," his wife said, pushing the man forward. "So sorry. He's a fan."

Max nodded off the action as affably as he could.

He turned left, nearly knocked down a group of people taking a selfie with him in the background and quickly apologized. They jived with him a moment and let him go on his way.

He felt he should have been taking in more of the sights, but he found himself more interested with the people on the streets. There were so many: groups of friends, friends of groups, laughing, interacting, minding their own business and living together. Where were the cops to break up these gangs? He had seen this kind of lifestyle and jubilation in old photographs, and, like that, he suddenly realized that he'd been strapped to a bomb.

He needed to sit and think or sit and not think. He needed to scream, yell, punch something, but not here. He needed a corner.

As he approached a dark alley, he followed the sound of a drum and applause. At the end of the brick corridor, he stumbled into a small club with cobblestone walls and no ceiling. A man sat with a white, five-gallon bucket and beat out a song he knew he was familiar with but couldn't place from where. Maybe it was Huey Lewis.

Max decided he could use a drink and walked in to find a place at the bar. He quickly surmised the bar was filled, so he found a seat at a table hardly big enough to act as a dinner tray.

All at once, the drumming stopped.

"You," the drummer called into a microphone, which he hadn't been using for anything vocal until this point.

Max took too long to realize the drummer was actually speaking to him.

"Me," Max asked by pointing to himself.

"Your drink on me, welcome home," the drummer said and then led the audience into applause. They stopped, and he asked, "Where the leash bomber?"

"He, uh, won't be joining us," Max replied.

"Where he at?"

"Stuck in the muds of Jersey," Max replied.

The audience stared at him as if waiting for him to finish explaining something alien.

"He ended up doing the Jersey bounce," Max added.

Still, nothing.

He reminded himself he wasn't in New Manhattan anymore. Was his captor today correct? That his world was made of people who felt they couldn't be honest, or they'd go to prison? With this thought came a glint of another. At first, he shoved it down. That's what you did, pushed down thoughts that could offend someone. Wait a minute. Why was he shoving this down? He let it up. It was uncomfortable. What the heck, let it talk for you. See if it's true.

"Where is he, my man," the drummer asked.

"Let's see," Max said, pretending to look at a watch that wasn't on his wrist. "We left him in a puddle of blood about eight hours ago, so I imagine by now, he's asking God if he has any toilet paper."

The room didn't respond. Then there was a chuckle, a few more, some people explained the bad joke to others around them, and a few polite laughs filled the room.

"Oh, that stank," the drummer said. "But we forgive you, you had a long day."

"Forgive me," Max said. "I'm from New Manhattan. Apparently, we don't have humor."

A few more people laughed.

"But can you blame us," Max asked. "It's hard to laugh when your head's up your ass!" He shoved his face into the crook of his elbow and made some strange muffle laugh mixed with farting noise.

Now, even the drummer smirked, didn't laugh though. He shook his head in pity towards Max.

"All right, all right, Manhattan, you gonna send yourself into shock tryin' do somethin' you ain't made ta do," the drummer said.

"Oh, but I'm better now," Max said. "Apparently it's a requirement when you leave to pull your head out. Though, you all might not want to kiss me, cuz that smell just don't go away." Here, he noticed a woman lost in confusion and disgust regarding him. He pointed to her, "You know what I'm talking about. That stink never leaves your upper lip, does it." Her group of friends bust up laughing at her expense. She glared.

The drummer picked up his bucket and gave it a quick "ba-da-BUM," and the people in the room laughed harder at that than they did Max. "Next time just say he dead."

Max sat and ordered the cheapest whiskey they had. When it came, he choked on it. He watched the drummer perform to the end of his act. The drummer thanked everyone, and the stage, which was only about ten square feet, was suddenly empty.

A few people acknowledged Max as they left the small club or café. He couldn't quite decide what it was. He stayed though, couldn't bring himself to stand. In fact, his muscles had all seemed to have grown into his wicker bucket-chair.

He couldn't quite figure out what the smell was that had been tempting his taste buds for the past fifty minutes, but he decided it must be bakery goods and melted sugar. Sugar wasn't banned in New Manhattan, but it was rationed—a fight against diabetes, policing how people chose to eat. Dang! There was that concept: choice. He liked doughnuts, but he had only seen those that were under glass before they were cut with a pizza wheel into small bites. You were allowed one a day, provided you had earned enough points on your app for showing you were active enough to burn the calories. Nothing had made a better treat, Max thought, than that morning doughnut bite.

He pulled a puff-pod charge from his pants pocket, and his pipe piece from his shirt. He snapped the AAA battery-sized pod into his pipe piece and let it pop cannabis into his lungs. He instantly relaxed. Then he peeled off the empty cartridge wrapper and ate it. The caffeine from it flooded his blood, and he felt his senses quicken once more.

His daily cleanse was complete. He stood and immediately located the bartender.

"Do I smell a bakery around here," he asked.

"That you do," the bartender replied. "Back out the alley, to your right, next alley over."

Max thanked the man and went on his way to follow the directions, which led him right into a similar hovel as the café's, only this one was a little brighter, both in light and color. The tables were pastel triangles. For a moment, Max let the aroma trick him into thinking the tables looked delicious. Each one could seat three people and were bolted to the ground so they absolutely could not be combined for larger groups. It appeared to be slow right now. Only three of the tables had anyone sitting at them.

The sweet scent roped his tongue and pulled him towards a glass counter with far too many choices of beautiful round cakes with a hollow heart.

Glazed, that's what he wanted. His eyes fell right to the silver platter with a pyramid originally built out of a baker's dozen but now only held two.

"A bite of glazed please," he asked the teenager who seemed uncomfortable in her pink and white striped uniform with its light-green, balloon, baker's hat.

She twisted behind her and took up a glossy, white plate, then returned to the glass display counter and used a piece of wax paper to pull one of the golden doughnuts away from the diminishing pyramid. After setting it on a white, Formica counter with what appeared to be rainbow sprinkles, she reached beneath and drew up a pint-box of milk.

She slid the plate and pint towards him.

"No, no," Max said. "I just want a bite. I don't want the whole doughnut."

"You just want a bite," she asked confused.

"And do you have any rice milk," he asked, frowning at the carton of 2%.

"Rice milk and one bite of a doughnut," she asked.

"Right."

"I'm sorry. You're lactose intolerant. I should have asked."

"I'm not lactose intolerant."

Now, she was really confused and did little to let her face hide it. "You want one piece of a doughnut and rice milk."

"Yes."

"Rice milk?"

"Yes."

"With a doughnut?"

"Is that really such an odd request," Max asked unpleasantly.

"Yeah," she said and then pushed the plate and milk at Max once again. "Eat the doughnut. Drink the milk. Learn how to eat a damned doughnut. Six bucks."

Max drew his bank stick out of his pocket.

"You must be new," she said. "We don't take bank sticks."

"Oh," Max said. "Um, they said to put it on Salvo's account."

"Salvo's account," she asked. "How stupid do you think I am?"

"Look, I'm sorry," Max said. "I'm not doing this right. They told me to put it on Salvo's account. Everyone was expecting it."

"They?"

"The women, they—you know I don't know their names come to think of it. Huh. They flew us all the way from New Jersey, and I didn't even learn their names."

"Jersey," she asked. She snapped her finger at Max. "You're the leash bomber!"

"What? No. I was a hostage."

"Just a moment." She left the front of the store through a swinging door. A minute later, she returned with an Omniscient screen in her hand.

"Okay. Okay," she said, looking over the cream-colored screen. "Salvo's account. Sure. Sorry about the misunderstanding."

Max chose a purple table in a corner. It was darker here, but the cobblestone seemed to have more character from the cuts of shadows, and he seemed to enjoy that little bit of darkness. His eyes drifted upwards, along the brick walls enclosing the small alcove, then beyond and into a black ceiling where LED lights had been strung and programmed to resemble familiar constellations from the true sky.

He tore his doughnut, aware that he should have asked for a toothpick. As he glanced to the counter area, there was no toothpick dispenser in sight. He took his piece of torn doughnut, and bit. It was, perhaps the best doughnut that he had tasted. The flavor was thick with sweet that glued to the outlines of his mouth, and his salivatory glands immediately leaked celebration. The sound of elation he made was involuntary, but he was aware of it at once and quickly apologized.

Now, he tore open his milk box, took another bite of his meal, appreciated the moment even more and took a swallow of the cold milk. It was, perhaps the most abominable action he had taken, drinking that which came from an animal, but he drank and just couldn't bring himself to stop. Before he knew it, his carton was gone, but he had eaten only two bites of his doughnut.

"May I get another milk, please," he asked, momentarily returning to the counter.

The cashier smiled and dropped another carton before him. "And you wanted rice milk," she said, laughing.

He retreated, somewhat ashamed. As he returned to his seat, a young child, four years old perhaps, sat in his chair. His doughnut was in her hand, her mouth pleasantly masticating the piece she bit off. She smiled as she ate it and her feet kicked contentedly at the pole holding up the three-sided table. She looked up to him and instantly recognized that she had been caught. She slid down shyly from the seat without taking her eyes off of Max and quickly retreated.

"Stop right there, young lady," a woman's voice shrilled, now standing in the alley entrance. She was young, attractive, more than she should have been perhaps and barely into her 20s, if that.

The child stopped, trapped in the shock that she was dumb enough to get caught.

The woman marched in, her finger held straight before her, drawing her path to the doughnut in the child's hand.

"What is that," she asked.

The little girl startled and hid her hand with the doughnut behind her back.

"You don't have any money," the woman said. "How did you get that?"

"Found it," the child said.

"Riley Michael Chevalier-Matheson, where did you get that?"

"I'm sorry," Max said, unsure of whether or not it would be wise to speak up. "It's my fault."

"Is it now," the woman asked.

"I'm sure she thought I had discarded it when I left my seat."

"So, you stole his doughnut?"

"No," Max intervened.

"Was it yours?"

"Well, yes."

"Were you done with it?"

"No, but that's entirely be—"

"Then she stole it."

"Please," Max said. "I've had a really bad day, and if it ends with a little girl having a happy treat, then I'll at least have succeeded in doing one thing right in all of it."

"I see," the woman said. "All right, in that case, thank you, and we should go." She held her hand down to Riley and the child took it. The two began to walk off when the mother stopped and turned slightly to Max.

"Are you coming Maximillian," Shauna asked. "We need to talk."

Max, mostly out of being caught off guard, quickly followed Shauna and Riley out of the alley and into the street where they were met by two men who Max had thought stood with a bit more purpose than any of the other people around. After Max, the mother and child passed, the men began to follow.

"This way," Shauna instructed, and she led Max across the road to a plain white building, and down a small side street wide enough for two passing bicycles or one golf cart. Once beyond it, they continued towards the tallest structure in the center of the city. The park they passed through was mostly quiet, but they didn't march to the building. They walked to a gazebo where an old man was talking to a young girl. Another guard stood at the bottom of the steps leading up to the platform. As Max's party approached, the old man stood from the bench, nodded to the pre-teen and then disembarked from the gazebo and walked off.

"So, did he hang her out to dry," Kola asked. She smoothed her pleated slacks and crossed her legs. Had Max been as alert as Shauna, he would have known Kola was merely aiming a slim .22 caliber pistol at him, which she could fire off by squeezing the trigger through the fabric of her pocket. Her other arm rested on a red lunch cooler at her side.

"No," Shauna said as she sat upon the bench as well. "He was pretty nice about the whole thing. Stuck up for her and everything."

"Is that true, my beautiful little girl," Kola asked. "Was he nice to you?"

Riley nodded and smiled and bit another piece out of her nearly finished doughnut.

"Is it good?"

"M-hm," Riley said, smiling and nodding and chewing her sticky mouthful.

"You know, I bet if you ask him nicely, he might let you have that milk too," Kola suggested.

Riley scrunched her nose and shook her head. "I have my own milk at home."

"Ready to go home," Kola asked.

Riley shook her head as she continued to chew.

"Okay," Kola said. "Give me and your mom a kiss and we'll be there in just a little bit."

Riley jumped up on the bench and hugged Kola, kissed her and got annoyed that some of her glazed doughnut had attracted some of Kola's long, straight hair.

"Your hair won't get out," Riley said.

"Well, it's hungry too, can't you tell," Kola said. "Like this! Nom! Nom! Nom!" She started making biting motions at Riley's neck.

Riley pulled away, laughing. It tickled. Max made note of the bizarre sparkle in Kola's eyes as she played with the child. As Riley finally got away, the doughnut came free of hair. She ran to Shauna, hugged her. Shauna embraced her and kissed her head.

"Be home soon," Shauna said. "Love you."

"Love you, moms," she said.

Riley bounded down the steps of the gazebo, and one of the men, who Max had assumed were bodyguards, turned and followed her at a distanced but quick pace. Max watched the child run off towards the tallest building smack in the center of the park and city. When he returned his gaze upon Kola, the girl's face had become something unsettling towards him. He was strangely and suddenly worried that he should be afraid of her.

"So, you're the shrink, yes," Kola asked, now poignantly.

"Well, yes," Max replied. "But I mostly profile. I haven't counseled in, well, since grad school. I'm a negotiator now."

"Not a very good one, are you," Kola said. She tapped the top of the cooler with her fingers.

"I'm an excellent one," Max replied.

"How many hostages did you free today," Shauna asked.

"None," Kola answered for Max.

"In fact, you added another hostage, didn't you," Shauna added.

"I don't intend to be rude, but can we berate me some other time. I've had a little bit of a really long and very bad day."

"That's right," Kola said. "The reality hasn't quite set in yet that you were strapped to a bomb, has it?"

"I'm sorry, but why exactly am I here? Is this level two of some trial? First you test me on how I act with her daughter, then your parents observe how I interact with you," Max said. "Well, let's just cut to the chase and get mommy and daddy out here now."

A strange flash of something grave flushed through Shauna's face. Kola's countenance was an empty canvas. Max felt himself instantly reminded to be still. "I'm sorry," he said. "I'm not proud of today. It's new for me."

Kola didn't seem to be moved. She took in an evaluative breath.

Shauna spoke now, "Among the many unique services that Salvo provides—

"You mean drugs," Max asked then.

"I haven't let anyone talk that way to me in a very long time," Shauna said.

"I'm sorry, again," Max said. "I'm sure you and your sister—

"Friends," Shauna said.

"Best friends," Kola echoed.

"But, yes, drugs, crops, pharmaceutical redistribution, casinos, among other things," Shauna replied, unashamed of any of these sources of income. "And when I say you're on thin ice, right now, I mean you should be worried about if you'll leave this podium by walking down the steps or falling down them."

"Is that a threat," Max asked.

"Yes," Kola replied in a direct voice that was calm, commanding and frightening all at once.

Max looked back at the two guards standing at the bottom of the gazebo.

"I wouldn't worry about them," Shauna said.

"Would you like to see who you should worry about," Kola asked.

Max understood now that this child sitting on the bench, and who couldn't be older than twelve, before him, was someone he should heed a little more respect to. He thought back on the past ten minutes: the child at the table, the mother, the manipulation to direct him to this gazebo to speak to this woman and this child. Had he been more awake to his situation, he might have been in the right mindset to notice that the pre-teen had not once shifted in her bench except to interact with Riley. Something about her said he should pay more attention to her than the mother.

The child was young but appeared confident. Not the leader, not Salvo—too young, she couldn't have built this place—but she was likely a relation to whomever did. Right now, she was probably the gatekeeper to Salvo. That was important. Gatekeepers had jobs to evaluate before potentially placing whoever was in charge in danger. Teens wanted to be taken seriously, gatekeepers wanted more recognition and authority than they had, both of these added up to needing to stroke her ego by showing he respected her authority. Do this, and the child would reveal more than she realized.

"If I have offended either of you, I apologize," Max said.

Kola stared at him and said nothing. She didn't blink, barely breathed and was so calm in her current position that Max finally understood, for the second time in twenty-four hours, that he had no leverage. If he had, she'd be rigid. He was not in charge, and she was evaluating him in this very moment, perhaps better than he was doing with her. Once again, he was a hostage. All right, he could handle this. He'd finally started paying attention, believed he understood enough about this girl to know how to connect with her. Time to build a rapport.

"I'm truly, sorry," Max apologized again. "You ever have one of those days where no one listens to you?"

Kola's face tilted and her lips drew in as she now gave him an unimpressed look. She shook here head side to side in warning.

"Sorry. It's habit. I'm sure you know what I mean."

Kola inhaled, plainly bemused.

"I promise you; I mean Salvo no harm. Is there any possibility you could let him know I'd be grateful if we could talk," Max said. It was a dangerous move jumping into trying to influence the other negotiating party, but he was confident the tactic would work on a child. He'd shown her he was aware of who she was but also let her know she wasn't in charge. That little subconscious reminder could have a lot of power."

Kola's eyes turned to Shauna, it was enough to tell him she was on the hook, but then her eyes darted back to him. They were insulted. No. Wait. They were not insulted, and now he saw something he'd failed to see before, nothing. She'd shown some emotion earlier, with the child. It was there. He saw it. He saw she had something she loved. No, he realized—not love nor emotion, purpose. The child gave her purpose. The sparkle was an act. He was onto her now. He understood the lack of insincerity from before.

"Let's get something straight, you're here because you made a choice to help," Kola said. "Have you changed your mind?"

Max couldn't help noticing that she stroked the side of her pants pocket. She was far too young to be dressing so professionally. Her suit alone would have cost several tens of thousands of dollars at a New Manhattan tailor. He decided that she wasn't just any relation to Salvo, she was a prominent relation, an heir most likely, and she knew she was grooming herself to take power. What wasn't adding up though? He needed to know more.

"You're here to make sure you trust me near Salvo, aren't you," Max asked. "The old man that left, just now. That's him, isn't it?"

"He's my grandfather," Kola said.

"I assure you; I have no intention to harm him. I want to help."

Kola said nothing, but she scrutinized him.

Max knew this tactic. Let the other person talk. Only, it occurred to him, he'd been the one doing most of the talking, apologizing, asking questions. A more experienced opponent would have used this against him already. He needed to wake up. Don't treat her like a child. Treat her like a serious adult.

He waited and said nothing. She said nothing. They stared at each other for some time. She tapped incessantly at the cooler. He started tapping at the railing behind him. Her eyes locked onto the action, and she locked eyes with him. Again, no emotion behind it.

Oh god, he thought. *She's not right.*

Her eyes narrowed to slits and he reacted.

"What can I do to prove myself," Max asked and then cursed himself for being suddenly manipulated by the girl.

"Oh, this is about me now," Kola asked. "It was hard to tell through all that bullshit I've been smelling the last ten minutes."

"I don't know what you—

"I dare you to finish that statement," Kola said blandly, clenching at the side of her leg.

They sat in silence once more.

"All right," Max finally relented. "What do you want me to do."

"I have a dilemma," Kola answered at once. "It seems I have a group of people who've just joined us from the outside world. Now, I want them to feel part of the community, and we want there to be a mutual trust, but one of their hackers has already betrayed that trust, used our own Internet café to breach our firewall and try to send a way to trace our location to the outside world."

"Georgia," Max realized at once. "Please, whatever he's done, it doesn't represent us. Let us talk to him, we'll straighten this out."

"All right," Kola said. She swatted the lunch cooler to Max's feet.

Max eyed the cooler a moment before he realized he had been invited to open it. He was going to ask if it was safe but decided this might be the time to show trust instead. He opened it.

Georgia's head stared right out at him, trapped in surprise. Max snapped the cooler closed, and, before he knew it, drew his firearm, only to find Shauna's own weapon to the side of his head, and Kola's guards with guns to his back. The girl on the bench didn't even flinch.

"Do you see our dilemma," Kola asked.

"I'm sorry," Max said and safely allowed Shauna to take his weapon. Why didn't she flinch? He wondered, and he thought he knew. "You took Ben's gun. You let me keep mine, didn't you?"

"Did I," Kola asked.

Max looked to Georgia's head staring up at him. "Did you have to—

"Yes," Kola answered. "I have eighteen-thousand people in this city alone depending on that space module you saw and others just like it. What your friend did would have been a death sentence to everyone here, including you, had he been smart enough to know he was communicating with our own techs. Luckily the message did not get out. You know what he did next? He roamed the arcade, found a girl and took her off and attempted to rape her. We stopped that. Treason brings the penalty of death, and on top of that he's also going to attack these people after we invite you into our home? We have never had to execute a single person in any of our cities for crimes against our own.

"I do not appreciate that a member of your group, who I saved from becoming human shrapnel today, did this in my city less than two hours from being allowed in. So, how do you think we should proceed?"

"You can't show this to the others," Max said.

"Why not," Kola asked. "I can do whatever I want here."

Max shuddered at this revelation, more at how much he'd misread the child and her importance.

"If you show them this, they may help you achieve your new society, but it will be out of fear instead of genuine interest. Fear corrodes loyalty."

"Are you afraid," Kola said.

"Very much so," Max said. "But I understand. However, he deserved a trial before this. You can't build a society without a fair justice system."

"We're working on that," Kola said. "But rest assured, he was guilty, so his sentence was carried out."

"I'm not assured," Max said. "But in your shoes, I would have probably done the same thing."

"Despite your oath to uphold the law," Kola asked. "Cop!"

So, that's what it was. He was a cop. He could work with that.

"How was your call to your family," Kola asked.

"Excuse me," Max asked.

"Your family," Kola replied. "You called them from the plane."

"Not happy," Max replied, suddenly sullen.

"Yeah," Kola said. "I imagine Captain Brimley isn't too happy that you took an impromptu assignment, was he?"

"I'm sorry, Capta—

"Brimley," Kola said. "The man you called from the plane. How could you possibly pass up infiltrating a Salvo terrorist ring?"

Max suddenly couldn't reply.

"Maybe the whole undercover approach wasn't the best," Shauna said. "Although, the whole sad act after was top-notch."

"You're out of your jurisdiction, Doctor," Kola said. "If you didn't want to be here, you should have said so."

"So, it's my head now," Max replied.

"It's possible," Kola replied. "Why didn't you try to negotiate just now, or try to shoot me?"

"I had guns to my head," Max replied. And what did she mean? He'd been trying to negotiate this entire time with her.

"I don't think so," Kola said. "I've had guns to my head and I'm not a negotiator."

"I think the bigger question is really why didn't you shoot me," Max replied.

"Good," Kola said. "Because we have a very important job for you, and you're going to have to make similar decisions as the one I made to execute this man. Harder decisions. It requires a diplomat and we're going to pay you a lot of money to do it."

"I just pulled a gun on you. How do you know I'll do the job?"

"Because if you betray these people again, I will have you dragged back here by your teeth and hang you up like a fish on a very big hook. If you don't do your job, there will be a war and many innocent lives will be lost. We could use you."

"Just like that, huh? Willing to forgive me," he said.

"No," Kola said. "But I read your file."

"That's classified," Max said, insulted.

"And still, I read it and your medical files," Kola replied. "When you put yourself between the Broadway Sniper and Maudra Halifax, did you really think you could stop his bullet?"

Max was stung and silent. "No," he answered weakly.

"Yet you still blocked it," Kola said. "Why?"

"Sometimes people need help," was all he could think to say. "I just did it. Anyone would have."

"And now you have an artificial heart, don't you?"

Max nodded.

"And the very next year, you threw yourself at a man struck by a broken power line, damaging your artificial heart, and you knew your insurance wouldn't replace it, would they?"

Max shook his head this time.

"And you're still putting yourself in harm's way."

"Who else is going to do it."

"Are you sure it's not because the heart was damaged, and you know it's only a matter of time before it goes out now?"

Max was silent.

"Didn't tell the guys on the force any of this, did you? Now you have a bit of a death wish. Even chose to come here, knowing your doctor wasn't here to tune you up when it went out."

Max nodded.

"A bomb going off could at least put an end to your needless wondering if one of those little circuits was going to finally give out," Kola continued, then asked "Why doesn't anyone know about your malfunction?"

"I'd be reassigned."

"You wouldn't be reassigned. You'd be forced into one of those early retirement homes where people treat you like you're going to die every day, isn't that right?"

Again, he nodded.

"The reason no one's shot you is because you're the kind of person this place is for, only you don't know it. You're hiding just like these people all had to do before they came here. You don't have to do that anymore; we will not put you in a facility nor forget you. And when you die, we'll take care of you. So, here's the deal I'll offer right now. I'll give you a new heart, and you'll help us."

"You can do that," Max asked. "Repair my heart?"

"I can," Kola said. "But I can do better than that. I'll give you a real one again. I'll put the word out."

"I can't pay for that," Max said.

"Call it a sign on bonus," Kola said. "But you try to betray us again, and I'll take it back myself."

"What do you want me to do?"

"I have no diplomats with clean bills of mental health down here. These people are going to need an advocate out there, and I want you to help me change that."

"Just like that, you're going to trust me to do that."

"Again, no."

"So, what do you want me to do?"

"One of the particular services that Salvo provides is the rental of our network tunnel to help a very particular people escape their societies. These people tend to have a very special need for therapists and counselors who care, and you happen to have a hefty professional background in psychology, don't you?"

"You want me to, what? Start giving therapy sessions," Max asked.

"Yes," Kola said.

"You can't advocate for someone you see as less than human," Shauna said. "Maybe it's time you start seeing them for what they are."

"You need practice," Kola said sternly. "And I'll fix your heart."

Max was taken aback by Kola's response, but he strangely didn't argue with her.

"Okay," was all he could bring himself to say. "That's very kind of you both."

"No," Kola replied. "It's not, and you can sign me up for five sessions a week. My current therapist has been helpful, but she could use a break."

"You need that many sessions," Max asked.

"Who says they're all for me?"

She nodded to the guards. They moved up to the gazebo and began to lead Max away.

"You'll be shown your permanent residence tomorrow, you'll have space to practice there."

Max suddenly turned. "Whose name should I write in for our weekly sessions?"

Kola seemed surprised. "What name do you think you should put down?"

"I suppose, Salvo," he replied.

"Welcome home," Kola said then added, "Perhaps you'll pass your test after all."

"So it is a test?"

"Everyone gets tested down here, didn't they tell you," Kola said. "How else could we ensure our safety?"

"And if they pass?"

"They get to stay."

"And if they fail."

"Then they don't get to stay."

It was the "don't" that suddenly frightened Max.

"Welcome home," Kola said again. "Good luck."

Chapter Twenty-five

Max found his way back to the hotel where Jasmine and Monica had promised to find him accommodations. The guard followed him only to another side street that led out of the park. Once he found his way to the hotel entrance, a man in a black and white tux held the glass entrance open.

"Good evening, sir," the doorman greeted. "Welcome to The Little Underground. Main desk is just across the skywalk."

Max thanked him and passed through, even though he had an urge to adventure through the nearby rotating door instead. He stepped onto a glass floor that spanned the entire lobby. Every panel was cracked into frightening spiderwebs, and forty feet beneath was a casino. Although Max was certain the casino was alive with noise, the lobby above it was no more than what should have been expected for a five-star hotel. In the center of the hotel lobby was a round concierge desk made of fine granite. He was almost afraid to approach it for adding more weight to the surrounding floor area.

"They say it's just the top layer of glass that's cracked," Shasta said from an aqua, plastic-looking and glossy armchair in a sitting area to his right. She appeared frazzled. She hardly seemed present.

"Where's Shashaun," he asked.

"I'm not sure," she said.

Max, however, seemed particularly alert for someone needing sleep, therapy and a lot more booze to help him nod this day off. The mother seemed more on edge than earlier. Maybe the P.T.S.D., but something deep down told him it was more than that.

"What's wrong," he asked.

"Well," she stumbled. "I don't know. We had stopped to get something to eat, but we barely sat down when we noticed this little girl crying and looking for her mother. Shashaun thought she saw a cop and took the child to him, but she ran into another girl—her sister, I think. She seemed happy to see her. The three girls came back and asked if Shashaun could join them in the park. I was going to go too, but the mother showed up and promised they'd be okay and asked if she could keep me company. What? What is it?"

"Was the mother young? Maybe twenty, if that?"

"Yeah."

"And the little girl about four? Her sister maybe eleven or so?"

"How'd you know?"

"What did the mother say to you," Max asked.

"Well nothing really. That's what was odd. She asked if she could have a bite of my burrito. I figured she might need help or something, so I was 'okay.' She was polite. She used the fork and knife from Shashaun's plate to cut off a piece and then she ate it.

"She said, 'Tim makes the best burritos, don't you think,' and I told her I didn't know, I'd just gotten here. So, she held the burrito up to my face and insisted that I take a bite—but isn't that weird?"

"I'd think so too," Max said. "So, what happened?"

"Well it was just right there in my face and I, well, I wasn't comfortable and I took the burrito and, I know it sounds crazy, but I thought what if this woman is scamming me, what if she's put something in my burrito. What if she's trying to drug me? So, I inspected the burrito. I looked at it, wiped my finger through the hole she had cut open."

"And?"

"And nothing, but she was offended. She was all, 'You think I'm trying to poison you,' and I felt bad. She was probably just trying to make a friend and I made her out to be some bad guy."

"Understandable after today," Max said. "I take it she left then?"

"No. She got concerned. Asked if I was okay. And I was honest with her. I told her I wasn't, that I'd had a bad day, and she knew at once who I was when I mentioned that I'd been a hostage earlier. She was very nice to me."

"I had similar experiences."

"The next thing I know, she's offering me a Valium."

"Did it help?"

"I didn't take it," Shasta said. "I didn't know her."

"So, she was offended again?"

"I don't know. She just got up and left."

"And Shashaun?"

"I don't know," Shasta said, and now the appearance of stress was dominant. She picked at the arm of her seat, and Max had only now realized that she hadn't looked away from the hotel, entrance doors once. "I looked for her, and I told someone who looked like he might be a cop, and he said I should come back here in case she showed up."

She suddenly started to cry. "I can't take anymore. Where is she?"

Just then Shashaun ran past the front windows and through the door that was held open for her.

"Mom!" Shashaun screamed. She was disheveled. Tears ran down her face, and her clothes had grass and dirt stains.

"Shashaun?" Shasta stood and was only to her feet when Shashaun reached and hugged her. "What's wrong?"

She cried. "I've been looking everywhere for you."

"What happened?"

"That girl's sister. We got to the park and she threw me. I tried to get away, but she was so strong. She kept telling me to fight back. She insisted I knew how. Then she started asking me questions about you," Shashaun explained.

"What kinds of questions," Shasta asked.

"What you were like. If you loved me. If you were good to me. Did you ever slap me or try to make me fight other kids or animals? She kept asking, and I kept telling her you weren't bad to me. Then you came to the park, calling for me and she pinned me behind this gazebo and put a gun to my head. She said I had a choice. If I called you for help, she'd shoot you, but, if I was quiet, she'd shoot me dead right there instead."

Shasta's face burst into tears as well. "How did you get away?"

"I didn't call your name, and she let me go. She said I should be proud and to go after you."

Shasta suddenly pulled away, determined. "Who is she. I want you to show her to me."

"I wouldn't," Max said.

Shasta snapped a scolding look to Max but dropped it. "You're right. She's armed. We should call the police."

"It's not that," Max started to explain.

"Good Lord," Shasta cried towards the front doors.

Ben was hunkered over, his face beaten, bloody. Adama strapped his left arm over her back and helped him walk. Max ran to take up Ben's other arm. As soon as he did, Ben's body collapsed and Adama screamed as she realized they were standing on a broken glass floor.

"It's fine," the doorman said, stepping inside long enough to calm everyone. "The top layer's broken, the other five are not. We're fine."

"Oh, we are not fine," Adama snapped.

"Is there a hospital around here," Max asked.

"Emergency medical services are already on their way, ma'am." The doorman said, then he returned outside.

"What now," Shasta asked.

"We wandered too far. A man said we were out of bounds and we apologized, but he asked for our papers. When we didn't have them, he detained us. He directed us out of the city where his friends were waiting. They put a gun to Ben's head and told me they'd let us go if I, you know, serviced all of them."

"Did you," Shashaun started to ask. "Did they—"

"No," Adama said. "The guy forced me to my knees and Ben threw himself over me. I was going to just yank the son of a bitch's balls off the second they were there, but Ben was over me and I couldn't move. He's kind of heavy when you're crumpled beneath him. The men beat him. They kept trying to tear him off, but he held me there and wouldn't let them pull me away, and they just kept kicking him. Finally, he rolled off because they'd knocked him out."

"What did they make you do," Max asked.

"Nothing. I snapped, I guess. I stole one of the men's guns and beat him with it. He got away though and I tried to shoot the man we first encountered, but the pistol didn't work. The hammer fell, but nothing. Before I knew it a ZD 436 was in my face and he asked if I knew what would happen if he pulled the trigger. I told him nothing, then I struck the gun. If you hit that automatic weapon on the side just right, it resets the on-board computer and won't fire for seventeen seconds. So, I did that. Then I disengaged the barrel lock and before I could strike him with it, he had run off. I would have gone after him, but Ben started to come to. So, I helped him, and we got the hell out of there. We snuck through the residential area and came back here."

"This isn't what I signed up for when they asked us to choose," Shasta said.

"Where's Chelsea," Shashaun asked. "And Georgia."

The front doors opened once more, and a team of men scrambled through with a stretcher and medical equipment. Behind them came Kola and Shauna with their guards posting themselves just outside and inside the hotel entrance. Only, Adama recognized many of them at once as the same men that had attacked her and Ben. She suddenly stood ready for a second round.

The men stopped and stepped back.

"It's them," Adama explained.

"It's her," Shashaun added, pointing to Kola.

Shasta and Shashaun both stepped in front of Ben. Max was the last to join as he found himself understanding what was happening.

"You're safe," Kola said. "Let them help."

"Like hell," Shasta said, her rage visibly building. She stepped towards Kola to let her know just how wrath could manifest itself in an angry mother, but she stopped short, frozen by Kola's unflinching eyes and unwavering stance.

Kola stepped towards Shasta, and it was the mother who retreated a step, nearly falling over her daughter. Kola had made her point.

"We understand that this is difficult, especially after the day you've had, but we don't have the luxury of taking chances. We don't give our trust lightly," Shauna explained, then waved the paramedics to Ben. "Most of you have proven yourselves tonight."

"This was a test," Shashaun asked in disbelief.

"What else would it be," Kola asked.

"And if we didn't have people relying on us to protect them, we wouldn't have," Shauna said. "But we did, and you succeeded."

Shasta suddenly came to her senses and slapped at Kola. Shauna caught her wrist, but it was the barrel of Kola's .22 in her face that caught her cold.

"I wouldn't," Shauna said. She waited for Shasta's strength to expire before letting go. Then she waited as Kola slowly lowered her weapon.

"Not in my city, lady," Kola said coolly. "Don't piss me off."

"You're Salvo," Shashaun observed. "Aren't you?"

"Sure, why not," Kola replied. "And I don't care if you're angry. I'm not apologizing for testing what kind of people we trust."

"There are other ways you could have handled this," Adama said.

"Yes. I could have let you all blow up in New Manhattan," Kola said unapologetically.

"It's unfortunate this is what your society requires us to do," Shauna explained. "But you need to know two things. One, you're safe here. Bruises heal and there may be many more to come. Two, zero tolerance when it comes to acts of treason." Her eyes flashed at Max, and Max suddenly felt a heavy debt upon him.

"I needed to know you were a good parent," Kola said. "That she would protect you, that you were an alert person with your child."

"What gets to make you that judge," Shasta asked.

"Because I need my chemists and key assets not to be addicts nor so eager to let their guard down. I have important work for you. I can't be worrying that someone can take advantage of your position with us. We have a specialist who will help prepare you for your new job, and then you'll understand."

She turned to Shasta, "The best schools are up there. I need to know when the time comes to let you loose, that you're the kind of person willing to put good people first."

"And you," Kola said, looking to Adama. "I needed to know you weren't a fraud. I'd expect the engineer of that top-secret weapon to know how to disarm it. Well done."

"By trying to force me to—

"What exactly did they force you to do," Kola asked. "Get on your knees?"

"And him," Adama asked, holding Ben's hand as his stretcher raised.

"I'm about to put the lives of many people who can't fend for themselves in his care. I need to know if his morals are as good as his records say."

"This isn't to bully you," Shauna said.

"Where's Georgia," Shashaun suddenly observed. "And Severus?"

"Has anyone seen Chelsea or Heather," Adama asked.

Kola looked to Max as if to warn him she might not be able to withhold the information about Georgia from the rest of the group, and Max begged her, as best as he could with his eyes, not to give in yet.

"This will be difficult to hear," Shauna said.

Max surrendered himself to the aftermath of what Kola was about to reveal.

"Heather was attacked tonight by an extremely dangerous man," Kola explained.

"What?" Adama asked.

"Is she okay," Shashaun followed.

"She's in the hospital. We were able to stop the crime. She's not hurt, but we thought she could use a good night's sleep, as do you all. By now, she should have been given something to help her rest. Severus is with her. He saw her with the paramedics and insisted he stay with her."

"Well, did you catch who did it," Adama asked.

"My god," Shasta scolded. "What kind of a place is this?"

"This is a good place," Kola said.

"Oh yeah," Shasta said. "We can tell."

Kola's face turned steel.

"It was one of your people who attacked her," Shauna said, stepping in before Kola couldn't contain herself. "Georgia attacked her, and we stopped him. We protected her because that's what we do here. This crime happened because we allowed you here."

"I don't believe it," Shasta said.

"You can ask Heather in the morning," Kola suggested.

"Where is Georgia," Adama asked. "So, I can kill him."

"Oh he's—," Kola started, then caught Max's pleading eye. "Been removed from our premises."

"I think I'd like to go to the hospital," Shasta said.

"Of course," Shauna said and signaled the doorman to call a taxi.

Adama, Shashaun and Max all chose to take it.

"We'll send you word regarding your permanent residence in the morning," Shauna said.

"Until then," Kola said. "Behave rightly."

The remaining members of the party exited the hotel.

"That leaves only one," Shauna said.

"Yeah," Kola replied. She moved towards a wall of three elevators with copper doors, nodding to the woman behind the concierge desk as she passed. "Where is she?"

"Room 407."

The rightmost elevator carried Kola and Shauna up four floors.

"You've had to restrain a lot tonight," Shauna said. "Is this going to be too much?"

Kola drew her pistol, mini Uzi and three knives from her person, then handed them all to Shauna. Shauna concealed the weaponry about her own person.

"As if this would matter," Shauna said.

"I know," Kola replied. "I promise, I'll rap my knuckles on something if I think I might kill her so you can stop me."

"Well, remember, we told Riley we'd be home soon, and you know how much Mrs. Jenner enjoys working late."

"What's wrong," Kola asked.

"I don't like her with Riley," Shauna said.

"Ah," Kola said.

"What's that supposed to mean?"

"It means, 'ah.'"

"I'm not kidding," Shauna said. "One step out of line with Riley and she'll disappear."

"Agreed."

"I'm just saying—

"That she's not your family," Kola said.

They left the elevator and found 407 in just a short walk. They knocked.

"Will this be too much for you," Kola asked.

"I'll rap my knuckles," Shauna said.

"Maybe you should see Max too."

They knocked on the door again.

They heard Chelsea groan from inside, then her heavy footsteps grumbled towards the door.

"What," Chelsea demanded, throwing the door open, revealing herself in a bathrobe and wet hair. Now that she wasn't made up to look like a teenage, delivery driver, she looked a bit closer to her upper twenties. Her eyes were beaten with red and tears. "Well?"

"I'm Salvo," Kola said plainly.

Chelsea straightened up. "Tell Salvo to grow a pair, and don't send a kid to do his dirty work."

"I changed my mind," Kola said to Shauna.

"Don't," Shauna said.

Kola pounded her fist dead to Chelsea's chest. Chelsea yelled in pain and grabbed at the area that would be a bruise come morning.

"Shut up, or I swear the next time I'll punch a tit flat," Kola said. "I just came here to tell you that there'd be a taxi waiting for you to meet me at eight a.m., but you just convinced me to change my mind. Get dressed we're going to work."

"Kola," Shauna said. "Riley."

Kola clenched her jaw. "You go, I'm showing this bitch who's boss."

"That's not a good idea."

"I won't kill her," Kola replied, then she added, "I promise."

"I'll see you at home," Shauna said and returned to the elevator. "And I'm taking all your shit with me, so be careful."

"Yeah, yeah," Kola replied and finally spoke at Chelsea again. "Well. You going to dress or what?"

"You're telling me you're the one that killed my dad," Chelsea asked.

"No," Kola replied. "Your dad killed your dad. I just helped him make sure he did the job right. He and some others drove their *Omniscient* helicopter to an old man's home and shot him. So, I killed them, all of them. I can't tell you how exactly your dad died, either a knife to his head or a bullet I'm sure. What I can tell you is I dragged their bodies through the woods and let them burn on the side of the road. They lived like dogs, they deserved to die like dogs. Ever since I figured out who your dad was, I've followed your family very closely. Now, if you want to see what he was willing to kill for, get dressed and be out here in two minutes."

Chelsea retreated silently into her apartment and returned two minutes later. Another three more minutes and they were hailing a taxi. Ten more minutes and they were ten floors below the ground floor of the centermost building in the city.

Chelsea held the strange engine with a gunmetal-like housing.

"So, it's real," she asked. "And it works?"

"For the most part," Kola said.

"What does that mean," Chelsea asked.

"I'm not a scientist," Kola elaborated. "So, I don't assume to be explaining this correctly. The staff here are smarter and know the math. We know we can get the engine to orbit. We know the composite shouldn't tear while on our modules. We know it can carry the weight. Part of the problem is the regulator. We haven't been able to figure out how to ensure that every engine can deliver the appropriate punch for wherever it launches from and for however much weight it carries."

"So, a smarter regulator that can adapt to geographic location and any atmospheric and environmental variables," Chelsea said. "Okay, that should be simple enough. How far apart are you planning to pace your individual launches?"

"No spacing between launches," Kola said.

"Okay, so a chain launch, one right after the other," Chelsea said. "Whew. That's a tall order. Um." She scratched her forehead with her french tips.

"No," Kola corrected. "No chain launches."

"What do you mean no chain launches," Chelsea asked. "How else are you going to do it if you're not going to space their timing out?" Chelsea had been looking past the Brilling zests and to the insides of the small turbine within her hands, then pulled away in realization. "You want to do one mass launch?"

Kola shook her head.

Without thinking, Chelsea flipped the engine into the air and let it crash down.

"Hey," Kola said. "Those aren't cheap."

"You might as well get used to it, because that's what's going to happen if you try a mass, simultaneous launch. Do you have any idea the problems you'll be running into? The flight paths you have to plan. One launch is difficult enough, but how many are you sending up?"

"Currently? Seventy-five thousand."

"Are you out of your mind?" Chelsea cried. "You're not just talking geographic and environment, you're talking making sure no one flies through a passenger jet or something else in the air," she breathed and finally exploded with "Seriously? Seventy-five thousand people?"

"And eighty-three space modules."

"Oh, fuck me with five minutes to live, right now." Chelsea found a chair and fell backwards into it. She held a hand up. "Okay, let me think."

Kola remained quiet and watched as Chelsea thought her way through the endeavor that had just been dropped into her lap.

It only took about thirty seconds before Chelsea said, "Okay. You need a central processor that can handle communicating with every engine at once and can simultaneously configure and adapt all the flight plans while being aware of every little bit of traffic in the air."

"And missiles," Kola said.

"Missiles? What?"

"You don't think the U.S. militaries are going to just let a whole bunch of modules and humans fly off into space do, you? Especially if they get wind of it? We can get out of firearm range quickly enough. Missiles are a different story."

"I suppose that means we need to be ready for any possible fighter jets as well."

"Can you do it," Kola asked.

"If we use Omniscient, we can, but we're going to need a lot of processing power to hide ourselves. We'll have to piggyback the current Omniscient network without being revealed, which is near impossible. I know, I added the security features myself. It would be easier if we shut down all air space."

"Would that make you feel better," Kola asked.

"Maybe," Chelsea said. "Can the engine go in reverse? Shut off? That sort of thing?"

"Yeah," Kola said. "But you lose a lot of headway trying to make the corrections."

"Okay. That's a start."

"So, then you can do it?"

"I believe so, yeah," Chelsea said. "If I can get the right crew here, I can get your processing hub ready."

"We'll need two," Kola said.

"Two?"

"We need to put it one in the command modules, and we should have one here."

"Right," Chelsea said. "You'll want a back up. That's a lot of servers, a lot of weight."

"So, we'll make more engines."

Chelsea picked up the thruster once again to inspect it. She lowered her head, and it took Kola a moment to realize that she was staring at the floor.

"You read the files I sent you," Kola asked.

"Yes," Chelsea replied, her voice frigid.

"Then you know he deserved it?"

"That's a horrible thing to say," Chelsea said, snapping her angry face towards the eleven-year-old.

"It was a horrible thing that he did," Kola replied, and she held her gaze in return.

"What?"

Kola examined her for some time to clearly make Chelsea feel uncomfortable. If Chelsea could have walked out, perhaps she might have, but the reality was that she didn't know where she would have gone.

Finally, Kola inhaled deeply.

"I killed your dad because he deserved it," Kola said. "The man he killed was good and did not. What you hold in your hands is his work. It was almost added to your profitable heritage, and you'd have never known your father killed an innocent man to get it, just a few more lavish shoes in your New York closet. Your dad stole a lot of heritage that should have belonged to someone else, so you could have pretty things and nice schools, but you know the truth now, and you have a chance to redeem that. Help the man that your father murdered complete his work, which was to take these people to a better place. Do something right with that education of yours that murdered people paid for."

"I'm willing to redeem my name, but I need you to know something," Chelsea said. "I'm not okay with you. Murderer or not, you took him from me."

"We gonna have a problem then," Kola said.

"I've been wondering all night what I would have done in your place, but I had every intention to kill my captor today. So, I guess I get it. I will not betray you, but you did take something from me, and I want you to know that. And I also have to wonder if it's the best thing to do, to create a society of people with mental instabilities."

"And you get to decide that all on your own, do you," Kola asked. "You're not just a technological genius, you're a prophet and executioner as well. These aren't all people with disabilities or illnesses. Some are people who are persecuted in other ways. We have all kinds here. Yes, the majority are people with mental obstacles though. Most of them have problems with names: ADHD, Depression, dissociative disorders, personality disorders, schizophrenia, anxiety, people who are creative, gay people who fled states that outlawed homosexuality, straight people who have been locked up in heterosexual ghettos. My own daughter didn't have permission to be born."

"You're not old enough to have a daughter," Chelsea asked.

"Careful," Kola replied.

Chelsea chose to be.

"Then there's me."

"And what's wrong with you," Chelsea asked.

"That's none of your business."

"Perhaps you owe me. You killed my father."

"I killed my own father. Think I feel some kindred regret for killing yours?"

"You want to trust me? Give me a reason to trust you. This is your town. How do I know that once I help you, and you leave, that you won't kill me too?"

"Will that help you trust me?"

"It's a start."

"Okay. I'm a psychopath," Kola said. "I'm an emotionless person who can't feel physical pain."

"What does that mean exactly," Chelsea asked.

"It means if anyone in this city ever finds out, I will attach one of these engines to each of your limbs and turn them on, and I won't give any of it a second thought. If that's not enough for you, then there's this."

Kola dropped the red cooler at Chelsea's feet.

"What's this?"

"Georgia's head," Kola answered. "He tried to rape Heather."

"Oh my god! You're just now telling me this?"

"I was told not to because you might only be loyal out of fear."

"So, why did you tell me," Chelsea asked.

"Because your head's not in a cooler too," Kola replied. "And as long as you don't put this place, its people or my family in danger, it never will be. You'll always have a place with us no matter where that is, and you'll always have my protection from anyone who would take it away. You have my word. I may not feel, but I have my word."

"He really try to rape Heather," Chelsea asked.

"Yes."

"The others know?"

"Max."

"I hope you put his balls in there too then."

"Then we have an understanding, I take it," Kola said.

"Yes, but I just want to be sure," Chelsea said. "I get to go up when you launch, right?"

"Lady," Kola answered. "Not only do I expect you to go up, once you get your tech into my toys, I'm probably going to need you to command the entire launch."

"Then, I can start now?"

"No," Kola replied. "After you visit your friends. They all went to be with Heather and Ben at the hospital."

"Ben? What happened to Ben?"

Kola nodded. "We should say goodnight. The elevator will take you to the ground floor. You can go back to the hotel or ask the doorman there for directions to our hospital."

With that, Kola left Chelsea on her own, unconcerned that she would do anything harmful. The cameras watching this particular lab would tell Kola if Chelsea would stay and remain interested in the technology of the engine; leave to be with her friends; or go back to her hotel and fail her test. Two options would show she cared about the people she had interacted with that day. One option would show selfishness and lead to a bullet to the head after Chelsea did her work. Kola was certain she'd never forget her contribution whether she was alive or dead.

Kola would have to wait until she returned home to the penthouse at the top of the administration and laboratory building to find out what choice Chelsea picked. Kola took a shower, changed into a long nightshirt, then checked in on Riley who was already asleep.

Riley hugged a green plush puppy to her side and heaved into its ear. The puppy didn't seem to mind. Kola watched her a moment in the light of the bulbous lamp with the image of a clown painted on it. She leaned down and lightly stroked Riley's head. Riley stirred and mumbled the tired sound of "I love you," but she was too tired to realize she had done it.

Kola wondered how she had ever held her in her arms.

"You're supposed to say you think you love me to too," Riley said groggily.

"I think I love you too," Kola whispered back and kissed her head. She turned off the clown, which Shauna had said was too creepy for a child, but Riley liked it, and Kola suspected she only did because Kola gave it to her.

"Well," Kola asked, after walking to the living area, which was a wide, open room with windows on two walls that overlooked the south and east sides of the city. "How did she do?"

Shauna came out of the bathroom, brushing her teeth. She walked to the kitchen sink, spat then washed it down.

"She stayed in the lab for twenty minutes then went to the hospital," she explained.

"Good. Cuz I'm tired."

"Maybe you can start sleeping more now that she's here," Shauna said. "You work too hard."

"Maybe."

The two made their way to a bedroom which had a wall of glass that also looked out over the city nightlife.

"You did good today, Kola," Shauna said, peeling back the covers to the bed and climbing in."

"Did I," Kola asked climbing in from the other side. "It's hard to tell when people only see an eleven-year-old girl."

"I'm proud of you, and what kind of luck was that," Shauna yawned out. "I really thought we were going to be stuck with that jackass bomber."

"I was afraid we were going to have to kill all three engineers today," Kola said.

"Go to bed," Shauna said and began massaging Kola's head until she had fallen asleep.

When Kola awoke four hours later, it was to the telephone at the side of her bed.

"What is it," she asked.

"The engine's not where I left it," the nineteen-year-old boy's voice said from the other side of the line.

"It's gone," Kola asked drowsily sitting up in her bed.

Shauna moaned and rolled at the opposite end of the California King.

"No, it's here, just not where I left it. I left it on its side, so it was facing due west, and it is facing northeast."

"Ernie," Kola said. "It's fine. I moved it."

"Why would you do that?"

"I was showing our new tech."

"We have a new tech?"

"Yes."

"Why?"

"She's going to help."

"Well, tell her to stop touching my things."

"I'll tell her, Ernie."

"You really shouldn't move things unless you're going to put them back."

"Ernie?"

"Yes."

"I'm going back to bed." Kola fell back against her pillow.

"Fine. You can help me put it back together when you get here."

"Huh? What," Kola said, now fully awake.

"I'm going to have to check to make sure she didn't cause any internal damage."

"Don't you dare."

"I'll to have to check the others too probably. Did you touch the others?"

"Damnit, Ernie," Kola complained. "I'm coming down. Don't touch a thing."

"I've already touched it, what am I supposed to do? Turn back time and not touch it."

"Ernie! Don't touch it again. I'm coming." Kola slammed down the phone. "God! Damn it!"

"I told you he'd go ballistic if you showed it to her."

Kola jumped into a pair of tight jeans and tucked her nightshirt right in as she buttoned up. "I should have asked if he was retarded before I promised to protect him."

"Mommy said a bad word," Riley said, suddenly standing at the bedroom door.

"You're right, angel," Kola said and then smiled to the little girl. "I'm sorry. I shouldn't have called him the R-word in front of you."

She gathered up her weaponry from the top of the bureau where Shauna had placed it all, then she pulled a suit jacket over her shoulders and rushed off to the lab.

When she stepped off the elevator to Ernie's lab, she immediately heard the screaming and ran to find Chelsea backed against a wall while Ernie was yelling at her.

"This is my stuff," he said, holding the engine in her face. He was taller and larger than Chelsea in every way, hardly the stereotypical appearance of a genius. "You don't touch my stuff."

"It's my stuff," Kola said.

"But I built it," Ernie yelled.

"We've talked about this, Ernie," Kola said, and she pressed a small red panic button at the side of the door.

"This is mine," Ernie said. "I can't build these right if everyone keeps touching them."

"Well, if you give that to me, then it will be mine," Kola said.

"It's not for you."

"Oh, it most certainly is."

"Who is he," Thalia's voice suddenly startled over the speaker system in the lab.

"I think it's Scat," Kola said.

"Don't make me come down there," Thalia's voice ordered.

"But they touched my stuff."

"You have to share," Thalia replied.

*   *   *

"If it's mine, how come I have to share," Scat asked. "Huh? Tell me that Mr. Porridge. How come I have to share if it's mine?"

"Did I ever tell you the story about when I had to share my apple with Mr. Anvil," Mr. Porridge asked. He hunkered over his cane and pet its fur. The cane purred and licked itself.

"That's a lie," Sally said. "Anvil doesn't share. Anvil takes. Anvil always takes, like that time he took my hair."

"Well he can't take my apple," Scat said. "It's my apple."

"You don't have an apple," Anvil said slyly.

"Yes, I do. I do so. I have an apple. I found it underneath that big rug that keeps barking at my curiosity. It's my apple. Only I can have it so only I have it. You can't have it."

"You do not," Anvil said.

"Then what do you call this, Mr. Can't Have My Apple," and Scat turned holding the engine.

So, Anvil took it.

*   *   *

Kola held Ernie by his throat, her gun barrel under his chin.

Ernie laughed. He was on his back with Kola's knee in his chest.

"It's the bitch," Ernie laughed.

"Let him go," Kola ordered.

"You never pull the trigger," Ernie replied. "Never pull the trigger." He laughed.

"Maybe today I will," Kola said and pushed hard on the barrel.

The change was sudden and subtle.

"Ow," Ernie said, and his eyes rose to Kola. They immediately filled with tears. "Don't kill me. Please stop."

Kola drew away.

*   *   *

"Looks like the monster beats Anvil again," Mr. Porridge said.

Anvil kicked the ceiling and stomped down on the wall.

Scat laughed.

"What happened to you Anvil," he asked. "You used to be scary, but now you're not."

"That other monster is scarier than you," Sally laughed. "You're a great big ha-ha now."

"You're a nobody, Anvil," Porridge said. "No one's afraid of you anymore. They're afraid of her. She's stronger than you."

"Anvil's not the scariest person anymore, is you," Scat added. "He's just a scaredy cat now. Scaredy cat of a little girl."

"Then I guess, I'm going to have to do something about that," Anvil said and then pulled out a chalkboard to start drawing a plan to destroy the monster who was bigger than he was.

*   *   *

When Ben awoke, Adama was the one holding his hand, even though she was uncomfortably asleep in her chair.

Up until an hour ago, Chelsea had been asleep on the couch, but now Heather was.

"How long," Ben asked.

Adama and Heather both became alert quickly.

"You're up," Adama said.

"How long have I been here?"

"Not long," Adama said. "In and out a couple days."

"You okay," Ben croaked, but his voice resurfaced.

"Are you okay," Heather mused stepping up to the side of Ben's bed. "He's the one beat to hell, and he asks if you're okay."

"That's a sign of a good cop," Kola said. No one had noticed her sitting in the cushioned armchair just outside of the room. She had been there the last fifteen minutes listening.

"I know you," Ben said. He tried to sit up but let the button on the side of his bed do it for him instead. "I saw you somewhere."

"This is Salvo," Adama said, more as warning than an observation.

"Good," Kola said. She approached the bed. As she drew near, her eyes somehow held Ben's. He couldn't look away. There was something about her, something he'd seen in other people's eyes. He saw it in people he had arrested: thieves, burglars, the leash bomber, but there was something worse about her, more dangerous, more frightening. She leaned over him and stared deeply into him.

"Isn't that close enough," Adama asked and immediately retreated as Kola's gaze now snapped to her.

When her eyes returned to Ben, he was certain he feared this child. He was sure his eyes weren't awake yet. He thought the girl looked like she had two different colored eyes.

"Do you know why my men beat you to a pulp," she asked.

"You did this to me," Ben asked.

Kola didn't answer, but she appeared perturbed.

"I don't know, no," Ben replied.

"My officers aren't like any you've dealt with," Kola said. "Beneath these so-called United States, I have many tunnels. Sometimes, I let people use them to escape their horrible lives and come here or someplace like here. Sometimes I get messages that someone is in danger and they are unable to escape without help. As you can imagine, the mail can be a little slow down here." She donned a filthy envelope. "We received this letter the day you arrived. It's dated two years ago, from the Alabama Nation."

"The nation of Alabama," Ben asked, stunned. "Are you sure."

"We're sure," Kola replied. It says there is a little girl there hiding in an old abandoned prison, waiting for someone to come rescue her because if law-enforcement officers catch her and find out she has issues that their laws don't agree with, they'll kill her on the spot.

"Two years is a long time to expect her to hold out," Ben said.

"Why not use the tunnels," Heather asked.

Kola appeared to have almost forgotten that Heather was there.

"That's the plan," Kola explained. "We need people to help her through, people I can trust never to abandon her."

"You want me to extract her from a hostile country," Ben realized.

"That's only a part of the issue. The prison is in an area where we don't actually have a tunnel system, but there are some that were used by another cartel many years ago. We're trying to connect ours to those, but we don't know them well. Going to Alabama's been a risk that hasn't been worth it before."

"That seems like a lot of work for one little girl," Adama said. "Why the risk now?"

"Other than the fact that someone asked me for help, and she's been in hiding for the past two years, the letter says she's also a physics savant. As you can imagine, we could use that here. It wouldn't be right to ignore her or what she can do for these people. I need you to go get her and bring her back. If you get caught, Alabama law-enforcement won't be kind to you, if the stories are true. You can't afford to get caught. The reason I had you beaten is so I can ask you this. Will you give her the same devotion as you gave Adama?"

Her eyes pierced him. He was afraid to answer. Truth was, he didn't know, but something about her drew out the truth, maybe it was the additional drug that he wasn't aware he had been receiving for just this conversation.

"So, this is a test," he asked. "No, you shouldn't trust me," he eventually said. "But that's because I've learned I shouldn't trust anyone. However, if there's a little girl in trouble, then I'll get her."

Kola examined him closely. She looked into his eyes, his soul, searching for that one deceitful sliver hidden within his brain.

"All right," Kola said, without withdrawing. "You go get her, bring her back, and I'll give you reason to start trusting me and what we're doing here."

"That sounds fair," Ben said.

"Many people come here because no one else will protect them. If you are caught or tortured, will you withstand worse than this?"

Ben was silent in thought for some time.

"I don't like your approach," Ben said. "You don't take someone who's already suffering from what we went through and throw more trauma at them."

"Oh waaa! If your only trauma in life was being strapped to a bomb, then you're the luckiest people down here," Kola said. "Look, before my test, you didn't see one thing out of place with this city."

"You mean, other than it's an underground city, created by a drug lord who has spaceships in her garage?"

Kola's eyes grew cold.

"But you're right. No. I didn't."

"Your answer, then."

"I already said I was in, didn't I," Ben asked. "That was before I knew this was a safe haven for so many people. I'm more in now, but don't beat me up anymore. What am I without my word?"

Kola waved a finger between Adama and Ben. "I'd like you two to go pick up that girl as soon as possible. She's a VIP, and we need her. I've set you both up in a condo in building three. You can move out of the hotel until then."

"Wait," Adama said. "The same condo?"

"As you can imagine, we don't have unlimited space. And you never know when we might have a group of guests who need a home. We'll be adding more housing soon, and I'll make sure you get the first pick of the bunch, but, for now, that's what I have, and that's what you get."

"Can't I go with one of the women," Adama asked. "I need privacy."

"Why," Kola asked. "Are you worried he'll be a voyeur now after he took a beating for you? The mother and daughter and Heather get one of the one-bedrooms. The teacher, the shrink and Chelsea are all sharing a place. You two get a studio, or we have tents in the next cave over, if you'd prefer that."

Adama and Ben shook their heads more out of no choice than acceptance.

"I put you together for now, because you both have military service, and," she said focusing on Adama, "I understand you speak the same language as the girl, we need you to retrieve. I assume you can design weaponry and travel at the same time?"

They all agreed to their different commitments.

"Um," Ben asked. "You said she was a VIP, a physics wiz. What can she do?"

"It's classified."

"It's always good to know everyone's skills when you're planning a retreat," Ben said.

"Good thought," Kola said. "If what we've been told is true, she's going to help us have babies in space. Get her here, and you might just ensure we have a future once we get there." She turned to leave and made it to the door before turning back. "A lot of people are putting their trust in you. Don't make this about me. I don't want to have to hurt you."

Ben realized he didn't want her to either.

Chapter Twenty-six

Straine sat in the dark. She was fourteen and sat in the dark. She had a candle; it had three inches left on it. With the flame, it had four. But, without it, it had three, three inches of paraffin to see her to bed when it grew dark. When the shadows of electric lanterns flickered on the walls and drew to her corner of the maze, the flame would be two-inches, two inches to help her retreat through a two-foot wide hole. The hole led through a stone wall that had once housed a clay pipe where water, long ago, flushed when the streets backed up with rain. Soon, the candle would be one inch, two with the flame, but mostly one inch, and would lead her into the end of the corroded clay, down the tube to where no light could reach her nor her bedding, water and boxes of food that Mister Cistern would refill from time to time.

Sometimes, he was late. Today, he was a week late. Today, she had no more candle. She felt through her box, found an envelope of cheddar-flavored, mashed potatoes and mixed in a little bit of cold water, stirring with her large spoon until they reached a consistency she liked. She ate.

Someday, she thought, this portion of the storm pipe would break too. Someday it might break on her in her sleep, maybe fall in or drop her through the bottom. Maybe it would cave in while she was outside and cut off her food, water and shelter. She supposed she could try to dig it out if that happened. She ate and shimmied her way out of the pipe, felt the wall and jumped, jumped in the dark, careful not to stray too far from her hole.

She had done sixty-two jumping jacks when she watched the eye of a cheap, five-and-dime flashlight crawl towards her cell. She fled through the wall and down the pipe once more until she was certain no one knew to look for her. Who would? It appeared that there was only pipe and earth behind this wall.

However, this electric beam stepped through the hole and peered down the tunnel towards Straine. It blinked as it did when Mister Cistern cupped his hand over the lens to signify it was his. Straine withdrew herself from the pipe once again and found a fresh box of food and two gallon-sized jugs of water. It wasn't much this time. He must have planned on coming back, but she couldn't tell because he also brought another box of twenty-four candles.

She asked him if he was coming back, but she didn't understand what his answer was. He tried to fingerspell but made even less sense then. His fingers were old, and he had been trying to learn from a book that could get him arrested. It wasn't working, so he put his finger against the dusty, stone floor and wrote, "18."

Let's see, eighteen candles usually meant about—all right, an inch an hour roughly, and don't forget the four hours of light that came through some of the windows that weren't boarded up, divide by— wait a minute! The water he brought wouldn't last that long.

She held up one of the jugs of water and asked with a look. He held up his hands, as if to tell her to stop. He left, and fifteen minutes came back with a box of four more gallons under each arm. Meanwhile, she pulled the previous jugs into her pipe and put them with the rest of her supply.

When she first moved in, Mr. Cistern had brought her some steel wool to keep the rats out of her stash. She filled the emptied water jugs with dirt, then used them to wall in the tube and create a barrier several feet beyond where she slept. Then she used the steel wool to fill in the gaps. He brought more wool. The idea was because they thought it could build a fire if she needed. It wasn't a bad idea if they could have found a more ventilated and hidden place for her to burn anything larger than her candle. She had pressed the steel wool against the jugs until she built an entire wall of the metal rolls. Then she put more jugs and more dirt against the wool.

Cistern said the rats couldn't chew through it. That meant only the end of the pipe she accessed could let any critters in. To prevent this, Mr. Cistern cut a circle out of quarter-inch plywood. It was the circumference of the pipe, and he hinged it to fold at the side. Straine glued more steel wool to it, particularly around its edges and over the hinged area. It allowed her to lock herself and shelter away.

Cistern didn't come back after dropping off the boxes of water. Ten gallons of water, that's what she got this time. That could last about twenty days, forty if she rationed herself and didn't eat anything that needed water. The box of food he brought was mostly canned or shrink wrapped, which should help her there. That was okay actually, but she didn't want kidney stones again. Sometimes he brought more food than others, and she had conserved a pretty decent store to keep her going longer for just in case he stopped coming all together. Today, she received three tubs of long beef and jerky strips and a case of Spam, but he also brought her far more vitamins and nutritional supplements than she'd go through any time soon. The vitamin bottles alone had 500 pills and he brought her two of those because they were buy-one-get-one-free online. She had lots of vitamin D as well. Although water and candles were scarce, because who used candles anymore, and water was heavy, water was much more difficult for her to conserve and have delivered.

You couldn't just walk across abandoned prison grounds carrying heavy, bulky loads without careful thought and long periods of waiting and watching to see if someone might be waiting and watching for you. It meant Mr. Cistern didn't always get to make his full deliveries.

Fifteen candles later, he brought his backpack of surprises, which he emptied onto the ground at her feet. A box of baby wipes—good, now she could bathe. There was also a bunch of green bananas and a bag of apples; he hadn't brought fresh fruit in a while. He even restocked her with a 48-pack of AA lithium batteries. These were for the handheld game console he had given her two years ago, when he had first brought her here. It was an older console, needed an outdated Wi-Fi connection to download anything beyond a cartridge. It helped her pass the time and some of the boredom.

The item she was perhaps most excited for was the set of colored pencils that she had asked for last time, but she worried he didn't understand her. The last few times she had asked, he just brought her ordinary, gray graphite pencils. They were boring in a gray place. She wanted some color. Today, he brought colored pencils but no paper. That's okay. She had a few sheets left still. Well, they weren't really full sheets, she had almost filled both sides of the remaining paper in her sketch pad, but she still had a few pages to get her by if she budgeted herself wisely. Her calculator had run its own battery out, and pencils were more reliable. She needed trustworthy numbers. She asked for another pad of paper the next time he brought a bag of goodies.

Really, supplies didn't worry her too much. The water always did. Even so, if water ran out, she had a means to slip out and get some in an emergency, but Cistern really tried to keep her from having to do that so she couldn't be spotted. He looked at this new supply and then signed ten candles, which Straine immediately took to mean five or seven candles because Cistern didn't seem to understand that she didn't burn candles for every minute of the day. She also slept; she was human after all. Cistern probably thought he was being smart measuring out one candle per day, which would have been roughly twelve hours, but his math was never great. The time before last, he'd left her 36 candles and told her he'd back in 32, which was a completely opposite direction in the term of guesstimates.

She wanted to tell him that, but she doubted he'd understand. Perhaps she should ration her candles more this time and start rebuilding a stockpile. As it turned out, flashlights weren't as good as candles for her. They could be dangerous as they had a distinct light, steady, artificial and easy to spot through cracks in dark places. It was also powerful, meaning that they made it difficult to see other light sources approaching. A candle wasn't strong enough to overpower any kind of trespassing LED; intruders were less likely to notice her light in comparison to her own. When she first used the hinged door-plug, she thought she could at least have a flashlight or electric lantern on when she was tucked away in her hole. Yet, when she tested it, the light still leaked around the edges. She just couldn't chance it.

Hiding out here seemed like a good idea, like no one would want to come down, beneath the catacombs of the prison, but that wasn't true. Teenagers appeared mostly, looking for a good scare or make-out spot, or both. Of course, it wasn't a secret that the high school kids did this, so the police would make their rounds as well, just looking for anyone who didn't belong there. This could also include the occasional hobo that lurked within the halls. These were the ones that frightened Straine the most. They were sneaky, like her. That's how they survived, but most of them used flashlights. One time, she did have someone take camp right outside her hole in the wall. He was a mean man. Straine would watch from deep within her pipe for his light to go out, then she'd wait an hour and crawl out. He had a knife, often hunted.

The one detail that saved her was that down the opposite side of the hole in the wall was the continuation of her collapsed pipe. When she had first arrived to the prison, she thought she might need an alternative escape path, so she followed the conduit down two sharp bends until she found another collapsed section of the pipe. She dug the rubble and earth out until she found more of the brick and mortar wall, which she'd hoped could create a backdoor. During one of Mr. Cistern's visits, she took a chunk of the clay pipe and tapped at the wall for three inches of candle until Cistern could hear her and break through with a hammer. He left the rubble for Straine to clean up, so she'd have something to occupy her time.

This new opening led to a room that was larger than most here, perhaps a storage room at some point. In the far side, was some kind of a chimney that dropped down about thirty feet. The only reason she knew the measurement was because Cistern tied a pebble to some kite string and lowered it until it slacked up. Then he pulled it out and they guesstimated. So, they figured, with a few safety preparations to make sure she wouldn't fall down the hole, it would make a good toilet. They threw two-layers of one-inch plywood over the chimney and cut in a hole. Then they bolted it to the floor just enough so it wouldn't slide off and allow Straine to fall in.

They made sure to seal the wood and paint it, so it appeared filthy like the rest of the environment. Then they shoveled on some of the particles of decay that had fallen all about the prison. Now, someone would really have to look to discover what it was.

It was a simple enough set up now—her food-store and bed at one end of the pipe, access to the toilet at the other. Up until that time, she'd had to use a bucket and lug it down one of the halls so it wouldn't stink up her hovel so much. Cistern came around a lot in the beginning to make sure the toilet cover hadn't broken beneath her, and it seemed to be sturdy.

Then that particularly mean hobo came and set up camp outside her hole in the wall. He ate a litter of kittens. Straine had to wait for him to fall asleep or leave before she could sneak out and go to the bathroom. She had hoped he'd go away, but he never did. On the fifth day of his stay, when he went out to find his next meal, she gathered up his travel bundles and pushed them all down the pipe to the room with the chimney. She'd thought of dropping it all down the toilet but then wondered what would happen if any of it plugged up the hole. So, she pushed it well past the break in the wall and left it all there.

The hobo was mad. She wasn't sure how long he stayed and searched for his belongings, but he looked in the hole, shined his flashlight down both directions of the pipe within and then disappeared.

That would have been the end of it, she'd thought, but then he came back some time later. If it wasn't him, it might as well have been. He got up to wander the halls to find a place to relieve himself without spoiling his camp, and, by the time he got back, Straine had already disappeared with his gear into the pipe. She left it with the other hobo belongings. This second hobo must have thought he was lost because he wandered the old prison hallways for hours before disappearing for good from the building.

There would also be, from time to time, groups of homeless who would take up camp within the old cells but hadn't done so near her tunnel too much. She was still cautious when she moved about though. After two years, she had learned not to take anything for granted within these walls.

She thanked Cistern for the water and supplies today. They hugged, and she felt her shoulder vibrate as it often did whenever he said his goodbyes to her. Then he was gone. She carried the jugs of water and supplies down to her alcove and organized them with her store ahead of her sleeping area. It made her little tubular room feel cramped, but she'd been cramped before. It was worth it. Then she put up her wall and played some of her old handheld, game console, careful to keep the screen turned down to its lowest brightness. The speaker icon was crossed out, which meant no sound. She had to be careful about checking that most of all. After about two levels of her favorite plumber, and several attempts on the third, she decided that it was time to turn it off.

Sixteen candles later, sooner than she expected, Cistern returned. He gave her 48 candles this time, more lighters, a bit more food, three plastic canteens and a can of powdered milk, all of which fit into a new backpack. It had been a while since she'd had milk. She was happy about that, but the most exciting item he had brought came in a white envelope. She opened it. It stated "Soon. Watch here for a light, August 2 to August 6." It also had a crude drawing of a floor plan from the main cellblock. She and Mr. Cistern recognized the general area at once, having been there a few times during early explorations when looking for the best place to hide Straine. A line crawled from the central cellblock through a matrix of halls and ended in a room, where an edge of it was circled. It was a simple note and unlikely anyone could decipher what it meant or where it was, unless they knew what to look for. All they'd have to do was follow the line on the map to the circle. At the bottom of the note was a scribble that turned out to be the word, "burn."

Cistern looked happy but sad. He also looked thin and tired.

Today was July 30. In as little as 72 hours, Straine could be out of this place. She asked if Mr. Cistern would go with her, but he shook his head. He seemed to understand. He had to stay behind. They hugged. She didn't know if she would be there when he came back. Then they both set out to follow the map. They left the old cell and wandered into a short hallway with corroded doors, some with flaky steel, some barred. Her cell, as far as Straine could tell, wasn't like the others in the prison. It was isolated for some reason. Maybe it was an old infirmary, or a place for prisoners to meet with lawyers. The only detail that really said it was a prison cell at all was the rusted, heavy door fallen off its hinge and laying on the floor. To the right of this room, were old restrooms, stairs up and the exit to the grounds overrun with tall grass, barley and trees. To the left was this area's old cell block, and beyond that another maze of halls, which, it so happened, appeared to be where the line on the map showed they should follow.

They found the room that the map directed them too. It was a familiar one. It should be. It was the room with the toilet. In fact, the part of the room on the map with the small circle on it was right where the toilet was.

Cistern and Straine both shared looks with each other, ones mixed with disgust and I-should-have-known realizations.

It had been a little over two years since they had adopted the hole in the ground for the toilet. Today, they were both surprised to find a heavy chain in the corner of the chimney that they hadn't noticed before, or, if they had, didn't seem to think it overly interesting enough to pay attention to. It was pinned into a groove in the wall by the very plywood covering they had placed over it.

They shared their annoyances again with each other and set to removing the toilet seat. Once they had, Cistern grabbed the chain and began dragging it out. Towards the end, he realized what the note was asking. He left and an hour later returned with a bucket, then waved Straine off from using the chimney anymore for the bathroom. He bid her goodbye and held up one finger.

That evening, he came back. He had a sledgehammer. On his hip was a belt, and at his waist was a tethered camera. He straddled the hole and lowered his camera a few feet down the chimney. He pulled a small tablet from his belt and a dark image appeared on the screen of the carved walls in the hole beneath him. From this tablet, he was able to lower the camera, until the walls disappeared, and a tunnel opened up. It was small, not just narrow, not wide enough for two people, but it also didn't seem to be tall. The camera lens turned towards the ground, and Mr. Cistern frowned. He let the camera reel back up and onto the spool at his side. He took up his sledgehammer and left once more. Three hours later, he returned and shined a flashlight down the pipe, towards Straine's living area. It was night now, early morning. He flashed twice, twice more then three times to let her know it was him.

When Straine emerged from her tubular apartment and joined her friend again, she found him with a two-wheel dolly and a large barrel of water strapped to it. He wiped his forehead, out of breath or trying not to look like he was out of breath. He had tried once to bring a water barrel for her permanently, but they couldn't find a place where it could be installed without being discovered. It couldn't fit through the hole in the wall, and she had come to prefer anything that could be dragged down the pipe.

She took his shoulder and asked if he was ok. He held up a hand and pretended that he was, but she didn't quite believe him. Together, they returned to the room with the chimney where Cistern turned the barrel on its side next to what had been Straine's toilet. He attached a five-foot garden hose to the spigot; removed the cart; opened the plug on the top and finally let the water flow.

It poured from the hose and he signaled for Straine to aim the stream down the chimney. Cistern took the cart and left while she did this. An hour later, he returned with another barrel, and they repeated the act. He left again, taking the empty barrel. When he came back, he had a tool bag, a thick board and a plain, cardboard box filled with hardware attached to the cart. He walked slowly and still pretended to be okay, but his shoulders were slumped.

She asked if he was feeling well again, but he just brushed her off with a smile and dug into his tool bag to draw out measuring tape and a pencil. The tape, he used to evaluate the hole opening. The pencil he attached to a string, which he then measured out, cut and tied to a nail. He drew a perfect circle onto the two-inch thick board. His measurements were off though, and she had to correct him. She usually didn't, because he liked to follow through on his own projects. She understood that, she didn't like people interfering with her own work.

Now, he began cutting down the board with a simple handsaw. He wasn't through his first cut when he wobbled on his feet. Straine took the saw and motioned for him to let her do the work. He drew her several straight lines to follow and shave the board down to an oddly shaped star. Then she trimmed it down again. Finally, he handed her a coping saw and she whittled the board to the circle that he had drawn.

Next was a drill. He drilled out four holes from the board, large enough to shove one-inch eyebolts through. Washers and nuts cinched them into place. Within another two hours, he had the board attached to a cable and pulley system that ran a counter weight up through the ceiling and over a section of structure that appeared it should be strong enough to handle the task a few times. Straine stood on the platform, clenched the cables as Cistern instructed and felt herself lower into the pit and stench of more than two years of her own feces and urine.

He pulled her back up, loaded his gear onto his cart, hid the small elevator as best as he could in the rubble of the room and then held up one finger.

The next day, he returned with two more barrels, then two more the day after that. Then he dropped his camera once more and viewed the bottom of the chimney. He didn't seem happy, but he didn't frown neither. He shrugged at Straine, signed "24 hours," which he did correctly, and then hugged her. He held her, vibrated against her shoulder and kissed her head, which he never did, but she understood. This might be the last time; tomorrow, he might come in to find she was gone.

As they pulled away, it was clear the old man was crying, happy but also sad. He held an envelope to her. She took it. It was for Salvo. She nodded that she understood. The last item he gave her was a shopping bag filled with a change of clothes, more diaper wipes and some toiletries.

Then, he left.

After she returned to her nest, she cleaned herself with a diaper wipe and set the new clothes and even a pair of shoes to the side. Then she dug through her stores and filled her new backpack with food, her game, batteries, the sketch pad with more than just drawings and a couple of candles—things she thought she might need for a long journey.

Once she was satisfied for the umpteenth time that she had everything she would need, Straine carried it, along with a gallon of water, towards the pipe section near the toilet so it would be ready for quick pick up in case she had to escape in a rush. Now that she knew they were coming, she felt more anxious about being all the more prepared. She had always believed Salvo would come for her. Cistern said he would send for him, but now it was real, and she was sick of living in a pipe.

The potty-bucket wasn't so great to work with again. It wasn't safe to navigate the old prison halls alone. When Cistern was there, she didn't feel so afraid, even though it was still dangerous. Anyone could have stumbled upon them while they were working, but she still felt safer with him. He could hear things she could not.

She hoped he was all right.

Straine couldn't sleep at all that next night, she was too excited. She watched the hole for most of the next day; fell asleep next to it and caught herself nearly rolling into it. That was when she decided she'd have to trust she'd see their light sometime from August 2nd until the 6th, and that they'd leave it on long enough for her to find if she should need to sleep. She needed to sleep. She couldn't afford to fall asleep and fall down the chimney—or worse, get discovered sleeping by someone she didn't need to be finding her.

The second day, there was nothing. The third day, she was disappointed. That following night, however, she actually slept through uninterrupted. She wasted several batteries the next day, sealed off her pipe with her steel wool door and played all day. She didn't even take a break to exercise. She'd checked the hole once but nothing. Twice revealed nothing as well. She threw her bucket at a wall and didn't care, went home, closed the door and played a racing game.

Tonight, she slept. When she awoke, she reinvigorated herself to have a better attitude. She bathed everywhere and finally changed into her new clothes. Whether she saw the light or not, she deserved to wear new clothes.

Underwear! Cistern had remembered underwear. It was folded into her new jeans. That was better than tampons! She had no shortage of those. Cistern had misjudged how much a girl should go through and brought two or three boxes every single visit for the first year she'd been there. If you were wondering what all those other boxes were that crammed up against her water jug and steel wool wall? Tampons, all tampons about a million boxes of male-overestimation tampons, and not the good ones either. She had more tampons than food. Mr. Cistern took her request to stop bringing them in good spirits. After she dressed, she ate, crawled out to do jumping jacks, then hauled past the room with the chimney to toss her old clothes into the pile of hobo belongings. Now, she returned to pee in her bucket.

As she crawled through the wall into the room with the chimney, two flashlights on semi-automatic rifles fell upon her face. Two sets of hands came in from her sides and threw her to the ground. They grabbed at her hands. She kicked, bucked, somehow found herself running for the chimney. She reached the elevator platform, threw it into the chimney and immediately stepped on. She had no choice. It was the only way out. She lowered into darkness, clenching cables as her only security.

The elevator stopped dropping though, and she swung back into the wall of earth, then forward into another. Somehow, she maintained her grip on the wires. Then the elevator rose. Straine and the elevator flew upwards, out of the shaft. Three officers each pulled on a cable, the fourth grabbed her and threw her back on her face.

They piled on her. One kicked, one pressed her face against the rotting floor. Cold steel cuffs clamped around her wrists. One officer yanked her to her feet, hard enough that Straine twisted her ankle upon the landing. Another yelled in her face, snapped his fingers at the side of her head and kept yelling.

None of them saw the movement that Straine noticed though. Perhaps if they too had been deaf, they might have seen him. He leapt out of the chimney, scaled the entire wall as one who had been certified in parkour pursuit. Once he was out, he hurled a rock-climbing hammer, its spike sank into one of the arresting officer's backs. Then he fired a small sidearm once, twice. Another officer fell. Straine's savior fired again, a third intruder crumpled.

The fourth drew his own automatic weapon upon the assailant, but the man from the chimney disarmed him and strangled him in the strap of his own rifle.

All four of the intruders had fallen. The man detached a flashlight from one of the officer's weapons and then knelt before Straine. She started to back away, but he began to talk to her, or tried to. His fingers moved but not in a way she fully understood. He didn't make sense, but he was trying, and that must have meant he wasn't all bad.

Maybe he thought his glove was in the way because he tore it off and struggled. The "C" came out clearly. That one seemed to be easy for him, but the "P?" What was "cp?" He kept signing "cp" over and over. Frustration filled his face as he realized he wasn't connecting, and he turned for the hole and appeared to yell. When he turned back to Straine, he'd finally realized she'd been cuffed, so he searched the officers for keys and released her.

He pointed at the elevator and made some dropping gestures. He was clearly an idiot, but she pointed out the counterweight system, and, together, they dropped the platform into the ground. When it returned, a woman stood on it. Her face opened to surprise at the sight of the four fallen officers. First, she listened to the man, then she approached Straine. She, like the man, knelt before her so she didn't appear threatening. She asked if Straine was okay.

Oh! Duh! Not C P. It was O K. Was she Okay? The man really was dumb.

Yes, she was okay. The woman explained her name was Adama, and that the man was Ben. The woman asked if Straine was ready, and she was. Straine collected her backpack and gallon jug of water.

At the sight of the jug, Ben, became excited. For that matter, so did the woman. They wanted to know if she had more. After explaining that she did, the woman asked her to retrieve what she could, and they would take it with them. She led them back to her hovel and spent about thirty minutes retrieving her food stores and other supplies, leaving mostly her bedding, some of the water and a bit of food behind. She didn't take it all because she had wanted to leave some for in case Mr. Cistern had to bring someone else to the prison, and they didn't know they should build a store. Over several trips in and out of the pipe, they took all Straine pulled out and used the elevator to lower everything into the shaft. Adama rode down with a load and then rose as Ben added his own weight to the other side of the system to bring her back up. They dragged the bodies of the officers out of the room next and swept over their trails with their feet. They couldn't hide all the evidence. A nice dark corner, one hallway down, made for a nice diversion spot though.

Adama was just asking Straine if she was ready to go, when Straine remembered the letter that Mr. Cistern had given to her. She handed it to Adama, who opened the envelope, and passed it to Ben. He instantly transformed from the image of a bumbling oaf to that person with focus that had first appeared. Her rescuers both seemed excited, argued but more with the letter than with each other.

Finally, Ben left. Adama asked how long she could hide with the supplies she had in her bag, and Straine answered that she could for a few days, especially with the supplies that she had left behind for someone else to possibly use. Adama instructed her to stay hidden; they would be back in a few days, seven at the most.

Straine was disheartened, reticent even, but Adama reassured her that they weren't going to leave her. Ben returned wearing one of the officer's uniforms and all the weapons to go with it. He brought another for Adama. She changed into it, asking Straine to put their previous clothing somewhere safe. Adama then took one of the rifles, checked herself for other gear and ammunition and promised Straine once again that they would be back in a week at most.

Ben unfolded a large sheet of paper and shined a flashlight on the map printed upon it. He stepped into the hall, studied the map and pointed off towards the direction that Straine knew was the entrance to the corroding facility. Adama and Ben disappeared.

Straine spent that first day feeling like she was right back where she had started, the same as when Mr. Cistern had brought her here and promised he would send for help and be back. She did what she did that day too, crawled into the pipe and took inventory of how little she had once again. This time, she had a door for her pipe. She lit a candle and used up one of the blank sides of paper in her sketch book. That night, she didn't sleep. She played her game. She slept the next day instead but forced herself to stay awake the next night and day, which was much more difficult than she had anticipated it would be. It took a lot of game playing, jumping jacks, four more empty sides of precious paper, but she pulled it off.

She continued her familiar routine after that.

On the fourth night, a hand broke her sleep. It gripped her ankle and tugged her. A flashlight was in her face, and she started kicking. It took a while for her to realize that the light had settled on Adama's face. Adama had climbed in to retrieve her, and she appeared cramped in the pipe. They both retreated from within and took the long way through the prison, avoiding the second section of clay conduit, back to the elevator where Ben awaited. With Ben, now huddled Mr. Cistern and three other children, no older than five years old any of them. The flashlights moved feverishly about the room and cast mostly shadows, but she knew Mr. Cistern's frame.

Suddenly, Straine was thrown onto her stomach, Adama on top of her. Cistern had stepped defensively in front of the three children. Ben raised his weapon and a burst of light erupted from its barrel and towards the doorway. Adama rose to a knee, then poised herself and pointed her own weapon upon the doorway.

Ben directed Mr. Cistern to the elevator and then lowered him. The platform returned to the top and Ben helped a child down.

Adama's rifle exploded with light towards the doorway once more. Straine noticed two bodies laying on the floor near it.

A third officer quickly poked his weapon around the entryway and fired at Adama, but Adama shot too and forced the attacker to retreat.

Ben hadn't pulled the elevator back yet to load a second child.

Straine ran for the hole in the wall. She was quickly in the pipe that led to the hobo's stash and her own traveling supplies. She dug through and found the lock blade. Now, she returned back towards the hole near her sleeping area. There was no one outside here. She watched the hall, saw no one, but she couldn't be certain. It was dark. She ran most of the way down the old corridors back to the room with the chimney. There was a man hunkered against the outside of the doorframe to the room with Adama and the others. He turned around its edge and fired off a few shots before quickly pulling back.

Straine crept upon him slowly, she wasn't sure what of her approaching sounds might give her away to the cop who could hear.

He leaned out again to fire his weapon, and Straine rushed. He was caught up in the monstrosity of sound that his rifle made that he didn't hear her. She drove the knife into the back of his leg. He stumbled forward, into the doorway, and small geysers burst from his back, as the room flashed with light once again and he finally fell.

Straine waited a moment and carefully revealed herself to the others inside the chimney-room. The flashlight fell on Straine and suddenly flew up to the ceiling. Ben's light turned on Adama, and Adama held up a hand to let him know she was okay. She stood shouting something at Straine but seemed more relieved than angry. Straine realized she, herself, should also be relieved that Adama had the wherewithal not to shoot her. Adama came to the doorway to inspect the fallen officers, while Ben lowered the children, including Straine with all her traveling supplies, down the shaft. As they waited in the dark, Ben and Adama took a while longer to return. Straine knew what they were doing, hiding the bodies as they had done before to keep anyone from noticing the elevator.

The tunnel smelled of toilet but could have been worse, Straine supposed. How much worse would it have been if Cistern hadn't had the sense to try washing some of it away. Perhaps, the only good the barrels of water did was make the bottom of the shaft a little better of a landing.

Straine ignited her flashlight, afraid a candle might ignite them all. She found the children clinging to Mr. Cistern. He was filthy. Wait—no, not filthy—he was bloody, bleeding from his head. His arm was bandaged, blood had seeped through that as well.

Adama came down the shaft. It was only now that Straine seemed to realize how tight the walls were. Adama ushered the others farther along.

Ben joined them. He pulled on the platform, deeper into the tunnel, then broke into a frenzy of stronger, harsher yanks. Adama and Cistern joined in to help him. For three minutes, they maintained this until they could all finally drag the rest of the line, as well as the counterweight, down the chimney so no one could use any of it to follow their trail of retreat.

Ben moved his way to the front of the line of refugees, and Adama took up the rear. Their flashlights lit up the brown earth all around them. It was tight. It was cold. It stunk of Straine's sewer. It hadn't all washed away. It was worse than living in the pipe. In a few paces, they were at a type of a wagon that was barely narrow enough to fit in the tunnels but large enough to hold the supplies that had once been Straine's food storage, plus whatever Ben and Adama had brought with them. Ben and Cistern spoke. Cistern took hold of the wagon handle, and Adama instructed Straine to let the children hold her hand and follow behind her. The children, all girls it turned out, came to her. One took her hand. As the others moved to fall in line, single-file and hand-in-hand behind her, she realized that they were blind.

They moved forward. Straine turned out her flashlight. She knew Ben's and Adama's batteries couldn't last forever, so she'd wait to light it again.

She wasn't sure how long they had walked, but it felt too long to her. She was tired. They hadn't eaten. The children were restless. Mr. Cistern's own balance appeared more wary. The air became cleaner.

Then the narrow tunnels, drooped to half their height and they had to crawl. Cistern and Ben repacked the wagon to decrease its height. It wasn't a long crawl, three hundred feet perhaps.

The children that Straine had been leading, now moved forward by grasping an ankle of the person in front of her. At first, it was awkward, took some coordination, but Straine decided it was a nice break from her previous monotony. Better, was that there was something up ahead that she hadn't seen in over two years. Real, artificial light, not from a flashlight, a game console or a candle but from authentic lightbulbs.

After three hundred feet, the tunnel opened up again, not to the narrow corridor they had been in before but into a wide roadway with a concrete street, marked with black trails where rubber tires had traveled in two directions over them. Curved streetlamps posted in both ways as far as Straine could see. A yellow, Cushman flatbed waited silently for them. Its tires appeared largely out of proportion from the rest of the vehicle. It pulled a light trailer, half its size with a few pieces of traveling and sleeping gear as well as a small supply of food, a very small supply of food. Straine understood why they were interested in her stores.

They loaded Straine's inventory into the trailer. Ben took the steering wheel of the cart, Adama the passenger seat. The others huddled into the truck bed and they all drove off down the tunnel. It didn't seem like they had gone too far when Straine spotted a trailer similar to the one they were pulling at the side of the underground roadway. They pulled over, moved all the cargo from the trailer they had and loaded it into the new one they had just come upon.

Ben unhitched and unplugged the trailer, which Straine had ascertained was really the batteries for the cart. He attached the new trailer into the Cushman and their used one into an electrical socket within the wall of earth. Then they were on their way again. This time, they traveled for several hours before they came across another trailer of batteries. They continued their journey this way for several days, stopping to change charges only.

Adama and Ben took turns driving and sleeping. They stopped for bathroom breaks at places along the trail. The cart would stop beneath some door in the ceiling and a ladder. One of them would press a doorbell, and someone would open a hatch in the roof to let the party up to use a real bathroom.

The first time they stopped, Straine got to use a shower, an honest-to-god, real shower. Straine knew her excitement about a real shower must have been what others might consider loud, but no one came to tell her to keep it down. That was when she realized that nothing was the same for her anymore. Afterwards, they returned to their cart.

Despite how cramped it all seemed for the others, Straine thought the back of the golf cart had been more comfortable than the pipe. Along the journey, they passed against four other golf carts and their drivers. One cart was another Cushman, and three like Straine had seen in advertisements for sports magazines.

In a few days, the cart pulled into a large underground parking arena filled with multiple electrical vehicles of many sizes and shapes. Adama stepped from the driver's seat. She and Ben both stretched and helped the others from the bed. They then led everyone through the cavernous parking lot towards two guards dressed in black and holding automatic weapons. Ben spoke with them, they seemed confused. Adama spoke. The guards' faces softened, their heads shook, and they opened the heavy doors behind them. They smiled at the children as they walked past. One of them, a fat man with a beard, gave each of the little children a peppermint candy disc. He didn't have enough for Straine, but that was okay. She wasn't really a little kid.

Dang! Peppermint candy though.

They walked through the doors and a bit more tunnel, right into Salvo's underground city.

Chapter Twenty-seven

By the time Ben and Adama had hailed a couple of taxis and escorted their new guests to the hotel, Shauna was already waiting in the foyer and rushed to greet them.

"Whatever you do, be submissive," Shauna warned Ben and Adama in a whisper. "She's not pleased that you just brought these people here."

"What do you mean these people," Mr. Cistern asked, unable to restrain himself after such a tiring journey.

"I mean these people who want to live through the next five minutes," Shauna replied sharply. "Now keep your mouth shut and behave agreeably. You're welcome here, so long as you understand you're about to get vetted."

"What is vetted," one of the blind girls asked, she was blonde.

"It means they don't trust us," Cistern replied.

"Yet," Ben amended.

The fourteen-year-old Straine reached up and took Cistern's hand. She could tell something didn't settle well with him, but more, she knew if the glass floor broke beneath her, he'd keep her from falling.

"Is that her," Shauna asked.

"Yeah," Adama replied.

"When I said, 'bring her back,' which one of you heard 'plus a pedophile and his underage harem?'" Kola had approached silently. Her tone, however, was anything but serene. It wasn't angry, nor friendly. It was a calm, an unsettling quietness like that of an ocean that pulled its water from the shore, but never sent it back in. Forceful.

"Pedophile," Mr. Cistern replied, insulted, and stopped as something in Kola's eyes told him he should have listened to Shauna, or maybe it wasn't her eyes so much as how quickly her pistol drew and took aim on him.

Now, Ben's mistake at this moment was that it was instinct to react when someone with a gun drew it, and he reached out to smack Kola's out of her hand. He missed the gun. Kola dropped, spun on the floor and kicked Ben's feet out from beneath him, and the glass floor shook in unnatural, brittle silence. Her wrist cocked back a knife to snap at his throat.

The faces looking down on him were that of shock.

"I'm sorry," Ben said. "It's habit. You did want me to protect these people."

"Now that, I can understand." Kola's face nodded. She returned her knife to its sheathe and held a hand to help the officer up. "Perhaps we could both remember this better."

Shauna leaned in to whisper something to Kola, and Kola's attention turned to the children and she nodded to Shauna.

"Forgive me for frightening you, children," Kola said, hiding her pistol away in her pocket. "I'm very protective of anyone who lives here. If you live here, I'll be that protective of you. My only concern is that all our residents know they can count on me to keep people who would harm them out. I just don't know you, yet."

"Surely, you don't think we're capable of—," Cistern started to say and might have wished he hadn't.

"You bet I do," Kola interrupted and held up her hand, warning Cistern to hold his tongue as he opened his mouth to speak again. "I'm not one of those people you want to test words with. Nod your head if you understand."

"We should have stayed back—

"Listen to her," Ben erupted. "Don't you get it yet? She's why you're here."

Cistern's eyes widened in realization.

"Better," Kola said but glared at Ben, as though he should have known she knew how to maintain her own authority. "Ben? Who are they?" Suddenly, she was aware of Ben and Adama's new uniforms they had taken from the Alabama officers. "And what are you wearing?"

Ben reached into his pocket and drew out the letter that Straine had given to them when they first encountered her.

Kola took the paper and read it. She looked to the three young, blind children and passed the letter to Shauna.

Kola waved her hand in front of the youngest child's eyes, a pudgy little girl with a round face and strawberry hair, not even long enough to get a good grip to pull on.

"This is the same handwriting that was on the other," Shauna said.

"Who wrote this," Kola asked Cistern.

"I did," Mr. Cistern replied.

"You wrote to us more than two years ago," Kola asked.

"Mail is slow over there," Cistern said.

"I've heard mail is nonexistent over there, took us three months to bribe the Georgia postal service to get one to you." Kola corrected. "How did you get it out?"

"Used my resources," Cistern said. "Worked round-the-clock, mortgaged my house, bribed a diplomat."

"What do you do for a living?"

"Cleaning contractor. My company cares for all government buildings, including the programming and corrections facility in the Florida territory of Alabama Nation. That's where I hid these three."

"Programming and corrections facility? What does that mean?"

"It's a campus that's part school, part courthouse, part detention facility for troubled youth."

"And you continued to care for these kids even when you didn't know if we'd be coming or not?"

"I only had Straine at the time I wrote you. The diplomat I bribed brought the others to me later. I could never get them all in one place though."

"Did you have help?"

"Just the diplomat."

"Hid them in your home?"

"No. These three I smuggled into the corrections facility basement. No one ever knew they were there. Straine lived in a prison. It was safer there."

"Your letter says they were found though."

"Yes," Cistern said. "One of the teachers snooped where she ought not to have been and notified the chief justice. They were taken into custody, placed in youth detention, awaited—," he couldn't finish saying it.

"They were going to kill them, weren't they," Shauna asked.

Cistern nodded.

"Yes, ma'am," the fat girl replied.

Now, Kola turned to Ben and Adama. "You stormed a government detention facility to bring these kids back here?"

They nodded.

"And what about him," Kola asked.

"He was there when we arrived," Adama said. "Waiting for us."

"Good thing too," Ben added. "We were going in blind. He got us where we needed to go."

Kola turned on her heels to the concierge ring in the middle of the foyer.

"Put them in the family suite. Arrange an escort to take them to town and feed them. Then contact Max at once," she instructed.

The concierge signaled to a bellhop to lead them to the elevators and then their rooms.

"One moment," Ben called after Mr. Cistern. "Could we all speak in private, Salvo?" Mr. Cistern assured the children that they would be all right to go with the bellhop. He and Straine stayed behind.

"Is this her," Kola asked looking upon Straine. "The smart one."

"They're all smart," Mr. Cistern replied disturbedly.

"Are they all scientific savants," Kola asked.

Cistern nodded so the blind children who were still in earshot could not hear his response.

"I'm sure they're all geniuses," Shauna said, stepping in and noticing Cistern's predicament. "I imagine they'll all have ideas that will help us do better down here."

Kola agreed and realized her mistake without having to announce it to the room. She wondered how she might react if someone had suggested Riley wasn't the smart one to her face.

The three blind children exited with their escorts.

Kola approached Straine. "Talk for me," she instructed Adama.

"People call me Salvo," Kola said.

"Straine," the child replied.

"What's your favorite food," Kola asked.

"Banana."

"Really," Kola asked. "Just a plain old banana?"

"How else would you eat a banana," Straine asked.

"More than pizza?"

"What's pizza?"

"When you have to hide your entire life, you don't get some of the luxuries," Mr. Cistern said.

"I think we can find you a banana," Kola said. "That's one of the crops in my control."

She stood and turned to Ben. "What did you want to say?"

"There is a danger of us being discovered," Ben said. "Our people were able to attach our system to the other tunnels. But it's a simple climb down a shaft to access them. With the resources and time we had, we didn't have the means to cover our tracks fully."

"It's just an abandoned prison, right," Kola asked Cistern.

"A very old prison," Mr. Cistern replied. "It was federal land, but when the three lower east states seceded, it was left to ruin."

"And no one's re-opened or bought it?"

"No one's been able to."

"How much do you trust your diplomat friend?"

"She's a good woman."

Kola nodded and nodded more as her wheels set plan to motion. She turned to Shauna. "If we could secure a line into that territory, we could broaden our customer base. That nation has been closed off for too long."

"All right," Shauna replied, understanding that Kola was thinking out loud more than discussing anything with anyone. "We couldn't rescue the entire state. Just people in imminent danger."

"I'm thinking we buy the land, build something on it, a private school or something. Figure out how to get Severus or someone else knowledgeable down there to run it so it seems legit. Get the diplomat to support it."

"Should you meet with the department heads," Shauna asked.

"They won't sell to anyone who's not a citizen," Cistern interrupted. "You won't be able to just steal someone's identity. You need to prove you originated there."

"I need you to tell me everything about your identity system." Kola said. "Is it just a matter of forging documents?"

"You need a birth certificate, the social security number—

"They still use those?"

"Yes, for in—in case they rejoin the union."

"What else?"

"You'll need the silver record."

"Which is?"

"It's a 3-D scan of your hands and feet prints from when you're a toddler, your debtors card, and a baptismal certificate—

"A baptismal what?"

"It's a Christian territory."

"Whether you want to be or not, right," Adama asked.

"Why wouldn't you want to be," Mr. Cistern asked.

"Because it's a freedom to choose," Kola said sternly, then chose to move on. "How reliable is your diplomat friend?"

"She could have turned any of these children or me in at any time over the several years, and she didn't."

"That doesn't mean anything."

"She's a diplomat without a country. She can't leave. She can't go home. She hasn't seen her daughter since the walls went up twelve years ago. She wants her country back."

Kola thought for a moment, or appeared to think. She excused herself for a moment and retreated a few paces with Shauna so they could speak quietly. They returned shortly.

"How do they control immigration," Shauna asked. "I don't imagine they have a spotless record of people not getting in or out."

"No one gets in. No one gets out of Alabama Nation," Mr. Cistern said. "The beaches are lined with snipers. Most people don't get across their own territory borders. I have exception."

"Why is that," Kola replied.

"My contracting company is national. It grants me permission."

"How does that work," Shauna asked.

"It means I'm used to being searched thoroughly every time I cross a border."

"How'd you smuggle the children in then?"

"I didn't," Cistern replied. "They're all natural born in Alabama."

"Rumors say that's not possible," Shauna said.

"Rumors say a lot of things don't they," Cistern replied.

"I've decided you're annoying me," Kola said. "I didn't send my people across the country to answer your letter just so you could come into my home and be a dick to my best friend."

"Perhaps you should get some sleep and you'll be more agreeable in the morning," Shauna suggested.

"You may be right," Cistern said.

Kola gestured to the concierge, and a bellhop in a white tux offered to lead Mr. Cistern to his room. "Give him his own room."

"Leave Straine," Kola said.

Mr. Cistern seemed hesitant.

"We did just do all this for her," Kola reminded him.

Mr. Cistern agreed and did his best to convince the deaf child that it was all right, then he tried just as well to wish his hosts goodnight before he took the elevator to his room.

"I need to send you two out again," Kola said, turning to Ben and Adama. "I have a forger stationed in Salt Lake. I need you to go get her and bring her back. If we're going to do this, we'll need her insight. You can head out in the morning. We'll let her know you're coming."

While Ben and Adama turned into their condo for the night, Kola found herself home early for once, same time as Shauna, and tonight they brought a guest.

As they entered, Riley's head popped up from what she was drawing at the mocha coffee table, while Libby was reading and humming.

"They're home," Riley gasped to the white-haired Libby Jenner who looked entirely too young to have white hair.

Libby was a little woman. Her lower leg had been severed during a military excursion during the great secessions, and her face was scarred from the Klansman who tried to leave a much more memorable mark before she cut his throat open. Her leg now was prosthetic. She pretended it didn't exist, but it was obvious. She'd had a son of her own once until the brain cancer took him at the age of six. Kola liked her because she knew how to protect a kid and would protect Riley to her death. Riley liked Libby because she knew how to sing. Shauna still did not trust her.

Libby had been humming something Venezuelan when Kola and Shauna stepped through the door for the evening.

"Just a minute," Riley said when she saw Straine, and she rampaged through four crayons and some harsh rounds of scribbling to finish up her art. When she finished, she left her drawing on the table and rushed to hug Shauna then Kola.

Libby apologized for not realizing they had company coming. Kola and Shauna assured her it was fine. They thanked their nanny and let her go for the night; she was happy because that meant she just had enough time to get to a film she had wanted to see.

"Hi," Riley said, looking up to Straine. "I'm Riley."

Straine, of course, didn't understand her, but she signed back.

"Sign language," Libby asked.

"Do you speak it," Kola asked.

"Some, alphabet mostly," Libby said. "But that was a long time ago, it seems."

"What does it mean," Riley asked, confused.

"It means she can't hear," Shauna said.

"Oh," Riley said, a little disappointed. She ran back to the coffee table, grabbed a blue crayon and wrote her name on one of the pieces of paper. She handed it to Straine.

Straine smiled, then dropped her backpack and took out one of her pencils. She wrote her name and handed it back to Riley.

"I only know how to write my name," Riley said through a frown. "You're lucky. You know how to read."

Shauna and Kola shared a look. Shauna smiled. Kola remembered.

"It says Straine," Libby said as she gathered the last of her belongings and looked over Straine's shoulder at the paper. She crumpled her nose. "Who named this child. She ought to be slapped." She asked if Kola and Shauna were sure they didn't want her to stick around.

"We have paper," Kola said.

"Go to your movie," Shauna said, smiling slyly. She'd knew what Libby was off to do. Everyone knew Libby loved movies every chance she got.

After Libby left, Kola turned to Riley.

"How about we take Straine to get some ice cream," Kola asked.

"Okay," Riley said, excited and ran to put her shoes on.

In fifteen minutes, they took a seat in Tappy's Mmm! Tappy, a round closet-broney in his 30s stood with an old-style ticket book.

"Hi, Salvo," he said. "Riley."

"Hi, Tappy," Riley greeted happily.

"Hello, Shauna," Tappy said, and tried to look like he wasn't trying to be extra nice to her, even though it was clear he was.

Kola felt a sudden desire to smack him out of that stupid. "Banana splits," she said. "For everyone. But the big ones."

"The Big Banana or the Monster Split," Tappy asked.

"What's the difference," Kola asked. "I can never remember."

"Big Banana has banana, ice cream, chunks of banana in the topping. Monster split has an additional scoop of sherbet," Tappy explained.

"Big banana," Kola said.

Tappy meandered off to fix the order.

"I don't want a banana split," Riley said. "I just want ice cream."

"It comes with ice cream."

"Oh, yeah," Riley realized. She looked at Straine and asked, "Why can't you hear?"

"I don't think you're supposed to ask that," Kola said.

"Why not?"

Straine pulled out her sketch pad and looked for a blank page.

"What did she ask," Straine wrote.

Shauna held her hand out for Straine's pencil then wrote her reply. Straine scribbled and handed back to Shauna.

"So I can't hear when someone says I'm in trouble," Shauna read. "If I can't hear it. I can't be in trouble, can I?"

"Moms, can I be deaf too," Riley asked.

"No," they both replied.

"You're lucky," Riley said.

Shauna lost grip of the pages she was holding back, and the images drawn into the book flipped before her. She shuffled back through to find her place in strains sketch tablet. There was a drawing of a dingy hobo hunkered against a brown wall eating something green and gray. His hat was ratted, shirt torn and underwear stretched too large for his wiry frame. There was another of a man sleeping on the other side of a broken brick wall. Here was one of Mr. Cistern, and another of a jug of water with a small mirror to the side of it and a part of Straine's face in it.

"These are really good," Shauna said to Straine, and assumed the blush she had stirred meant that the teenager knew what she meant.

Then she came across a series of diagrams and strings of numbers, equations and angles.

"Kola," Shauna said, holding the pad before her and slowly flipping through.

"Is that," she asked, pointing to one of the pages, "a laser system."

"Deflects laser guidance systems," Straine wrote on a napkin.

A few pages later and they both suddenly stopped. Kola turned back to their sheet of conversation and asked, "What is this?"

Straine looked at the image then took her pencil and answered, "Artificial gravity." Then she added, "In theory."

"What are these arrows," Shauna asked.

Again, Strain looked. She turned a few pages to one that provided a much more detailed diagram of a specific cut-out from the previous sketch.

"Air flow," Straine wrote. "A vacuum. To push you down and stimulate muscle use to stay up."

"Better than centrifugal force," Shauna asked.

"For temporary back up, just in case primary artificial gravity goes out. It's not enough for child development though. Just muscle use."

"What is this," Kola interrupted pointing to a new set of pages and equations that all appeared to connect one thought.

Straine looked.

"Ozone neutralizing shielding," she wrote

"What does that mean," Kola asked.

"It means, in theory, you can stop space radiation naturally and have babies when combined with primary artificial gravity."

"So it's true," Kola replied. "She solved the problem."

"This makes it so we don't have to get pregnant women back to earth," Shauna said.

"How is that possible? How does it work," Kola asked.

Straine began to explain as best as she could until Tappy announced their Big Bananas were ready. Shauna handed the sketch pad back to Straine and gestured to join her to retrieve their desserts from the counter.

"Is she smart, momma," Riley asked as Shauna and Straine walked away.

"She is," Kola said.

"Smarter than me?"

"What? Why? Does that bother you?"

"She can draw too." Riley pulled up the drawing she had been working on at home earlier.

It had been rolled up in her hand. She showed it to Kola. It was simple, not pretty at all. There were three objects that looked like fat blobs with thick scribbles for skin tone, black dots for eyes and red for fat lips. Then there was a brown one with four lines for legs. It was horrible, for sure. Kola knew that, but she also knew what it was. It was Riley and her moms, Kola and Shauna. Kola didn't even need real letters, in place of the blue scribbles, that were beneath each image to say that's who they all were in Riley's illiterate illusion. Kola ignored the brown blob that was also in the picture.

"Are you looking for a better daughter than me," Riley asked.

"No," Kola said and turned to the child. "No one would be a better daughter than you."

"You don't know that," Riley said.

"What's this about, Riley," Kola asked.

"You never brought another kid home before," Riley said. "Are you leaving 'cause you don't want me anymore?"

"Don't be absurd. I will always want you."

"You don't know that," Riley said again.

"She's older than you, huh?"

"Yes."

"I don't want another older mom," Riley's eyes teared up.

Kola wiped them.

"Riley. I want you to listen to me," Kola said, imitating the softest voice she could recall from listening to other mothers. "The day we got you was the day my life got better. It was the best thing that ever happened to me. I will never leave you or let anyone take you from me, and if they try—"

"You'll stop them?"

"I will absolutely destroy them," Kola said.

Riley hugged Kola. "I love you."

Kola hugged her back, and before she could say she thought she loved her too. Riley said, "I think you do to."

"Yeah."

"Yeah, but you don't know," Riley said sadly. "Other moms know." Then she added, "Momma?"

"Yeah?"

"Could we get a puppy if it was a little one?"

The scraping of Formica and plastic bowls with ice cream, bananas and appropriate toppings broke the conversation.

Riley cheered, and Kola couldn't help but notice Straine appeared unprepared for the dish that sat in front of her.

Straine scooped up a chunk of banana, whipped cream, chocolate syrup and a cherry with sprinkles and put it into her mouth. She sat a moment, taking it in, staring at the dessert, almost oblivious that the others were watching her. Suddenly she began crying.

"Did we mess up," Kola asked.

"I don't think so," Shauna replied, but she wasn't fully sure.

After some time, Straine cut her spoon into the mountain before her. This time, she was smiling.

"See," Shauna said.

"I see Tappy gave you extra sprinkles," Kola said. "Again."

"So," Shauna said. "I like sprinkles."

"And Tappy likes you," Kola observed.

"Tappy? Him," Shauna asked. She looked across the restaurant to Tappy who was working behind the counter to make a caramel sundae for a lovey, young set of teenagers. She turned back to Kola. "He's too old."

"Tinker's older than Tappy," Kola said.

"No," Shauna said, looking Tappy over in consternation. "Besides, he's fat."

Once they had all finished their banana splits, they walked Straine to the hotel and signed her into one of her own suites on the second floor, next to the room they had assigned Mr. Cistern and across the hall from the room of her blind traveling companions. They promised that tomorrow, they'd take her to get pizza.

*   *   *

Cistern was in the shower when the concierge knocked on his door. He didn't answer it in the happiest of moods. He had been enjoying his overdue quiet time. For the first time in two years, he didn't have children counting on him to keep them alive.

"Your host is waiting for you in the lobby sir," the morning concierge, Phillip Barstow explained. "Hurry and get dressed, please. Your presence is required."

"I'll be out once I'm ready," Cistern replied.

"If I may, sir," Phillip replied before Cistern could close the door. "Your presence is required, not requested. I have four doors to knock on now. If you would like to enjoy the rest of your stay with us, I would encourage you to be by the elevator when I am done."

Cistern looked as though he wanted to say something on the issue, but instead he nodded, dressed and was waiting before the concierge returned.

They rode down the elevator and found Kola sitting in one of the couches speaking with her grandfather, Shauna and whoever's face appeared on her tablet.

Kola ended her current conversation, stood and directed Cistern to follow. She and Shauna, shadowed by two bodyguards, led Cistern out onto the streets and to a taxi. They rode back to the entrance that allowed Cistern into the city the night before. As they drove past the set of large doors into the golf cart parking, Cistern discovered that he had become suddenly unsettled by the silence of the conversation.

They drove farther down the tunnels than Cistern had traveled previously and passed a series of lower-ceiling caverns filled with tents, lean-tos and shelter pods. It didn't appear to be a lower-class of people, nor a poor section, just a community within itself too large for the city to handle. Children ran to see the golf cart pass and Kola waved to them and blew them kisses. Shauna tossed out pieces of saltwater taffy to them.

Parents waved in appreciation and then ushered their children back to their chores or play. When the cart stopped, they were in front of a metal shed that looked like it had been forced to fit inside the height of this part of the cave, which was lower than that of the city. Inside the shed, was a bustling office of paperwork and red tape to accommodate all the residents and people who desired to be.

"This way," Kola said, leaving the guards at the front doors and leading Cistern towards a set of stairs that went up to another floor. Kola, Shauna and Cistern climbed a total of three sets of stairs.

Men in traditional police uniforms littered these gray walls. As Kola approached a counter with a door built into it, the officer behind it buzzed it open for her.

"How's Dolly, Herbie," Shauna asked.

"Says I'm a bad cook," he laughed.

Kola stopped to take a clue from Shauna. She was still learning. "And the baby," Kola asked after taking only a moment to remember his daughter's name, almost calling her Claudia.

"Stacie walked yesterday, ma'am," Herbie replied. "Took a video. Want to see?"

No, she really didn't, but Shauna's nod told her otherwise. So she did, and Herbie showed her a thirty-one second clip of a skinny, little girl smiling like there was nothing in the world to frown about and stomping out four convoluted steps, if you could call them steps, before falling into a young woman's hands.

"She's beautiful, Herbie," Kola regurgitated. "Go home early today and play with her."

"Yes ma'am," Herbie said pleasantly.

They continued forward.

"You're smiling," Shauna whispered. "Did you know that?"

"Am I," Kola said. "I can't tell sometimes. Just, remember when Riley did that?"

Shauna nodded and smiled back to Kola, and Kola knew it had more to do with Riley than with Herbie's baby video. In this moment, she wanted to take Shauna's hand, but Shauna would think that was weird for sure. Kola thought about Tappy and wondered what would happen to her family when Shauna decided she wanted a better parenting partner than some child like Kola.

These thoughts lingered as they entered a door, and inside was a dark room with two-way glass that looked into an interrogation chamber.

The only items normally in the interrogation room were a steel bench with locking rings and seat belts. There was no table. Today, four people sat, cuffed and secured to the bench.

"Those are Alabama Nation uniforms," Cistern said, taking notice of the strange black and white logos on their shoulders.

"They followed you into our tunnels shortly after you left, but they were taken into custody before they reached the first checkpoint. I wanted your input."

"About?"

"One moment please," Kola said, then she left Cistern alone in the room with Shauna.

"That one could use a good slap, couldn't she," Cistern said.

"I don't know," Shauna replied, summoning intentions she hadn't had in years. "Maybe you could try giving her one."

Kola entered the interrogation room, closed the door then approached the man sitting second from the left.

"What's your name," she asked him.

"Where's my phone call," he asked.

Kola drew her pistol and fired it off into his groin. He screamed, leaned forward and started bleeding to death.

The other officers began yelling at Kola but fell instantly silent as she pointed the gun at the only woman officer in the group. Now, Kola walked around the back of the officer and pressed the gun against her lower spine.

"I'm going to ask a very important question," Kola said. "And before you decide to say the wrong thing, I'd just like you to consider how many limbs you'd like to have use of for the rest of your life."

The officer bleeding out cried.

Kola ignored him but turned her head to one of the other detained men. "Name?"

"Tyson. Tyson! Now help him, please," Tyson replied.

"No," Kola replied and then nodded to the officer with Kola's gun against her back.

The dying officer tried to hold his pain in but couldn't.

"Whose idea was it to come into my tunnels?"

"Mine," Tyson said.

"Who did you tell you were coming down?"

"No one," Tyson replied.

Kola revealed a knife as simply as a magician might reveal a bouquet of roses and flipped it in Tyson's thigh.

"Who did you tell?"

"We didn't tell anyone," the third man replied.

A second knife flew into Tyson's other thigh.

Kola leaned in close to the woman officer's ear.

"Did you decide yet," Kola asked, and pushed the barrel hard against her lower vertebrae. "Who did you tell?"

"We were afraid to tell anyone," the woman stammered through tears. "If we had told our superiors, we couldn't have kept anything we might have found for ourselves."

"Do you do that a lot," Kola asked, and she slid the barrel up to the officers mid-back. "Hide things from your superiors."

The woman nodded. "I'm telling you the truth."

"Why would you hide things from your supervisors?"

"Why," the woman asked and immediately realized her mistake as Kola raised the weapon a little higher and snapped the hammer back on her pistol. "You don't know what it's like there: the indoctrination, the hate, the punishment that comes if you don't pretend to hate as much you're supposed to. We followed the drag marks from the bodies and found the tunnel. We thought if it went somewhere, we could sneak out whenever we wanted to."

"Drag marks," Kola asked.

"We covered them up," the woman replied.

Kola looked up to the mirror, and nearly startled at her own image of her deadly brow. She didn't look like that when she was brushing her teeth after returning home to her family. Perhaps if she could feel, she might be afraid of her reflection as well.

"Does that ring true to you, Mr. Alabama," she asked.

Static popped through a speaker in the corner of the ceiling.

"Lots of people would leave if they had the opportunity."

"People in power too?"

"Depends."

"On what?"

"How many people they've killed and why."

"How many people have you killed," Kola asked the woman. "Three."

"Why?"

"They tried to kill me."

Kola looked to the man who was dying from his groin and whose face had turned to the early stages of white death. "And how many have you killed?"

"Screw you, psycho," he mumbled.

Kola shot him and put an end to his suffering. He slumped forward and tried to hang off the bench.

The woman started to scream but stopped herself.

Kola pointed her weapon at the remaining uninjured man who had been ignored and silent until now. "How about you?"

He nodded yes.

"Black people? Mexicans?"

Again, yes.

"Kids?"

Another yes.

"Blind kids? Deaf kids?"

He shook his head in the negative.

Kola twisted the knife in Tyson's thigh. "How about you, Tyson?"

"Yes," he screamed.

"Why would you do that?"

"I don't know," he said. "They're better off dead."

"But not you," she asked the woman.

"No."

"Why?"

She flushed and looked at her fellow officers as though she had betrayed them.

"My daughter had Spina Bifida," she said.

Kola looked to the mirror. "Spina Bifida?"

"The spinal cord bunches up and develops outside of the spine," Cistern's voice explained. "Her daughter would have been put to death."

The woman cried.

"That true," Kola asked.

"Yes," the woman croaked while gently nodding.

"How old is she," Kola asked.

"Five. They found her when she was five."

"And you didn't try to protect her?"

"I couldn't. I was running errands." Her voice trailed off. "Left pocket."

Kola checked the woman's back left pocket and drew a wallet that held very little: a money clip with ten dollars, identification papers, and a photo of the woman, a man and two children, one not much older than Riley. Kola couldn't tell from the photo that anything was wrong with either of the two blonde girls. They looked happy. They looked free.

"So, you have other family?"

This time, the woman shook her head no, "Like I said, I was running errands."

"Dead," Kola asked.

The woman sobbed.

"Shauna," Kola requested. Then Kola turned her pistol and shot the other two officers. She hid her pistol and moved around to the woman's side. "What's your name?"

"Bailey," she said.

"Do you have anyone you'd like to let know where you are," Kola asked.

Bailey shook her head again "no."

"Do you want to go home?"

"No," she said, barely audible. "Please, no."

The door opened into the room. Shauna and a uniformed officer waited to enter. Kola waved them in. The officer moved to uncuff Bailey.

"Bailey, I can offer you asylum, give you a better life and take you away from that place and people who robbed you, and I will protect you from people like this. I will not let any outsider harm you ever again, and you can remember your daughter freely in conversation and on the streets here with others who have also lost. Will you stay and help me find other people who want to escape?"

Bailey's red and swollen face raised. Her eyes were bloodshot. She was afraid. Kola knew fear when she saw it.

"Do you work for Salvo," Bailey asked.

"Bailey," Shauna said, kneeling down beside her. "This is Salvo."

Bailey unleashed a new torrent of tears. "You're real. She told me you were real. She said I'd find you some day."

"Who told you? Your daughter?"

Bailey nodded.

"Bailey," Shauna said. Her voice was gentle, soft and inviting. "I'd like you to meet a friend of ours. His name is Max, and he helps people like us."

"A shrink," she asked.

"A psychologist, yes."

Bailey wiped her face, but the tears came faster than she could clean them.

"There's nothing to be ashamed of," Shauna said.

"Until this Max says I'm crazy, and you put a bullet in my brain, right," Bailey said.

"What," Kola said. "No! Not here."

"I'm not going to no shrink."

"Bailey," Shauna started again with her gentle tone. "I'm beginning to understand what psychologists are like where you come from, but they don't sentence people to death here for being different. They don't put you in camps. They don't take you from your home. They help you learn to live with all the bad that can happen."

"You have my word," Kola said. "I woul be more inclined to shoot Max before I shot you."

Bailey visibly shivered and looked to her dead fellow officers. She flew to Tyson next to her and tore out one of the knives.

Kola drew her pistol and took aim on her.

"Wait," Shauna said, placing her hand over the firearm.

Bailey began stabbing Tyson and screaming at him and didn't stop until Kola finally shot another bullet into one of the other corpses. Bailey turned without realizing that she was holding the knife in a threatening manner.

"If you keep that up, the knife's going to slip, and you'll cut yourself. What did he do to you?"

Bailey turned back to the man and slashed the blade across his throat.

"They all did it," she said. She dropped the knife. "All right, I'll see this Max."

Shauna began to lead Bailey out the door when Bailey suddenly turned back. "Do you mean what you said? About helping other people escape?"

Kola nodded.

Bailey shook her head. "Would I have to go back to Alabama?"

"No," Shauna replied. "There are other jobs."

Kola followed the others out of the room. Three people in white hazmat suits waited in the hall so they could clean up the dead bodies. Kola retrieved Cistern from his little viewing room and instantly recognized the all-too-familiar, fearful respect in his eyes that she usually came across in people once they saw how deadly Salvo could be.

"You're going back," She said.

"I'm not going back there," Cistern said. "You don't know what it's like."

"I'm going to make it better."

"Not possible!"

"Would you like me to prove it to you?"

Kola proceeded to escort Mr. Cistern to the rocket viewing area, and, before the week was over, Mr. Cistern, Ben and Adama were in a golf cart on the way back to Alabama Nation.

Chapter Twenty-eight

Nelson Markus sat on his swing, and it swung. Forward, back. Forward, back. The chain pinched itself and grinded against the eyebolts holding it into the ceiling of the log cabin porch. Nelson spurred the motion with the tapping of his toe. Tap. Forward. Tap. Back. Forward and back. Tap. Tap.

His corn had grown in well this year, tall, swaying in the wind—forward and back, side and back. Farmers know, you can hear it grow. Stretch and grow. Forward and back. Stretch! Side and back. The stalks were playful, relaxed. They always were before their deaths, unaware that the sounds growing in the distance were the respirations of grain combines, gathering like hunting dogs, excited to make their next kill.

The corn didn't know this though. Corn was stupid. For acres in every direction, the corn played. The corn swayed—back and forth, side and forth. This morning, the corn was tall. By tonight, all that stood before his cabin would be mowed down. Nelson Markus had watched the corn play and lose this game for more than sixty years.

He had no driveway at his home, just places where the front lawn had died from having vehicles parked on it: three pickups, a Peterbilt tractor without its semi trailer, a Ford sedan and a Winnebago. His six vehicles were old, heavy, made in the U.S.A., from back when there was a made in the U.S.A., and they stood proud and tall. He'd kept them all running himself. Other than leased delivery trucks, they were the only vehicles that ever traveled the road to or from his farm. No one ever had any reason to visit him, which is why, when he saw the black of the BMW crawl towards his house in the distance, he decided today wasn't going to be his favorite.

Two silver Suburbans crept behind the Beamer, blooming dirt in places that didn't settle too right with Nelson Markus. He stopped his swinging and swigging of his blend of imported Cuban coffee and tossed the liquid off to the side of the porch before setting his mug on the railing next to him.

The three vehicles drove onto his lawn and parked invasively before his porch.

The passenger door to the BMW opened, and a tall man in his more-dangerous-than-you black suit stepped up from within. His black hair must have been slicked back in one stroke, and he straightened a pair of reflective sunglasses over his pointed face. More doors opened and all three vehicles began to unload.

"Y'all first mistake was parkin' on my lawn," Nelson Markus said, setting himself at the top of his four steps leading from his porch. He crossed his arms and leaned against the post.

"Nelson Markus," Slick Sunglasses asked.

"Y'ain't got no business here," Nelson Markus replied. "Y'all can go back down that road."

Slick Sunglasses didn't go though. He pressed up the first step, and Nelson Markus stepped down to remind him whose porch the intruder was standing on. Nelson Markus wasn't as tall as Slick Sunglasses, so when Slick Sunglasses stepped up one more step right below his and still looked down on the old farmer, Nelson made sure the years of military service and memory of his dying brothers showed he shouldn't be underestimated.

"We're lookin' for homosexuals," Slick Sunglasses said through a fake smile that told Nelson Markus that's what made this man more dangerous than most.

"This a Christian home," Nelson Markus said matter-of-factly.

"Of course it is," Slick Sunglasses said, climbing up to Nelson Markus's step, and then past him. He crossed the porch to the faded, green and wooden, screen door then peered inside. "Your Christian home got any fags?"

"Faggon's a sin," Nelson Markus said.

"Yes, it is."

"Burn in hell, they do," Nelson Markus said. He spit on the ground.

"Yes, they do," Slick Sunglasses said. He abruptly turned on his heels, startling Nelson Markus. "After we burn 'em here of course." He now stepped back down the steps straight towards Nelson Markus, taking up the middle ground just to force the farmer all the way to the bottom of his own porch. When he reached the last step, he looked long and hard upon Nelson.

"So," he finally asked. "You got any?"

Nelson Markus puffed up and pressed back into Slick Sunglasses. "No, we don't!"

"Well good. Then we know we have nothing to worry about here." Slick Sunglasses smiled to him, but Nelson Markus knew the sound of horse shit when it fell.

"Do it," Slick said. He circled a finger in the air to his companions.

"You got your warrant," Nelson asked.

Slick moved to hover over the farmer again.

"You got a reason we should have one?" Slick stepped out of the way so two of his suited men could pass, into Nelson's house. A pair of officers passed along either side of the residence. Another group of four started off towards the barn. The remaining woman began scanning the front yard for who knows what kinds of clues.

"See," Slick said. "We're looking for some very specific people." He held up a tablet with a drawing of a woman. The artist hadn't done her justice, turned her into a psycho killer just like every sketch artist does. He flipped from this picture to another woman's face, and then turned through three more. "Anyone look familiar?"

"You musta missed where I said this a Christian home, huh?"

A log fumbled from the side of the cabin, and Nelson's eyes darted towards the sound.

"For the love of—," he cried and moved quickly to the side of the house where the two officers here were prodding at a wall of firewood stacked against it. "Y'all have any idea how long it takes to stack that? Now, leave that alone!"

The two officers looked up from their search to Slick. Slick nodded, and the partners pulled at the wood until the wall, three cords thick began tumbling to the ground, revealing a bare side of the cabin.

"What did I tell you," Nelson chided. "There's nothin' here."

"I believe you, Nelson Markus," Slick replied, and he kept on believing Nelson until the sun had all but gone down, when the officers packed back into their vehicles.

Nelson didn't even see them off his land. They didn't deserve that courtesy. He found himself looking over his home, a disaster now. Anything on a shelf was strewn across the floor. Everything that was on the floor had been turned over. Every painting on his walls, plaques, awards, military honors, framed articles hung crooked now or had been dropped. The cupboard under the stairs stayed open, and its contents, including his war medals bled out into the hardwood hallway.

He just didn't even know where to start here, so he went back out to his porch swing and watched the taillights of the cars disappear past the field of corn, which still stood because Nick had halted all production for the day. Once he could no longer see the car in the growing dusk, he left his porch, took up his coffee cup and returned inside to locate his pot and maker. Once he had brewed up another batch, he returned to his swing and drank his coffee until the night was nearly black. The corn had eluded the dogs today.

He drank the last swallow of his coffee then refilled his mug and waited for it to turn cold.

He left his swing and moved to the side of the house to his fallen pile of wood, chose a spot to begin picking up and stacking again. As the earth revealed itself through the fallen wall, so too was the rope tied to the cellar door, if anyone had thought to see what it was tied to.

He opened the door and found his six guests huddled around a table, playing cards beneath a dangling incandescent lamp.

"Where's What's-his-bucket," Nelson asked.

"Jackson," the woman, Roueghta, who looked much prettier than her psychopathic-killer, pencil illustration on Slick's tablet had demonstrated.

"I imagine he found a hiding spot, Roueghta" Nelson replied. "They didn't haul anyone out, but we should start thinkin' of gettin' y'all outa here. Place is on their radar for some reason."

"Might as well be burned," Clayton Hammond said. He had hardly looked up from his cards, since Nelson entered the cellar. "Lotta good coming all this way did."

"Don't be like that, Clay," Chuck Amos said. He squeezed Clayton's hand.

"Before we do," Marley Donovan said as she placed her cards on the table. Yes. That Marley Donovan, the one whose brothel was burned to the ground, and everyone hoped she had been consumed with all her girls. Except, she had run out to a call with Roueghta and Trinity, and they had all three escaped the peaceful-protestor-sponsored attack. "Can anyone beat four eights," she asked.

"Again," Clayton complained and surrendered his three jacks. "Every time!"

"Maybe if you knew how to play," Trinity said. She was small. Her game was in-your-face. It worked.

"How bad was it up there," Peter Hoskins, an overweight man with a sweaty brow and rectangular glasses, asked. "Sounded bad down here."

"It's a mess," Nelson answered.

"Well," Roueghta said as she pushed herself away from the table. "You heard him. Let's clean it up."

They began to clear away from their game. Marley gathered up her winnings and stuffed them into the pockets of her long shirt that could have passed for a trench coat on appearance, no doubt used to hide a suit of lingerie or two or none at all.

The cellar emptied.

"Well, that was lucky," Peter said, climbing out of the ground to the fallen pile of wood that had once covered the entrance to the cellar.

"Not really," Nelson replied. "That's what it's there for." He abruptly smacked the life out of a mosquito that had decided it was dark enough to try its sneak attack on the farmer's arm.

They continued on to the house and had mostly made it to the porch when the area filled with spotlights.

"Hello, Nelson Markus," Slick's voice called from behind one of the spots. "We felt so bad about leaving your house in a mess that I told my crew we should do the respectable thing and help you clean it up, but it looks like you already found help."

Peter bolted for the side of the house, a gunshot later and his head spit, then he fell.

The others froze.

"What is wrong with you," Nelson yelled. "He didn't do anything."

Slick stepped into the spotlights and his silhouette drew towards the group. The electric vehicles from before drove out from the corn field.

"That's a fair question," Slick said. "He looks an awful lot like one of the men that we're looking for, which is unfortunate because he's a criminal. He was one of them bum drummers."

He held up his tablet and began looking through the police sketches, along with their driver's license photos.

"And this one looks a lot like you, sir," Slick said, pointing to a picture of Chuck. He flipped to the next picture. "And who do we have here? Is that one you?"

Clayton and Chuck said nothing about Clayton's resemblance, but they gripped each other's hand and pulled closer together.

"Yeah," Slick said. "You're little deviants too, aren't you?" He flicked his finger over the tablet and past several more photos until he stopped at Marley's. "Madame M! So lovely to see you survived the fire, and who are these magnificent ladies. I don't seem to have any record of them."

"They're my daughters," Nelson replied and wrapped his arms around Trinity and Roueghta, pulling them tightly to him. as a protective father would.

Slick examined Roueghta, then Trinity, then Nelson, then started the process over.

"Yeah," Slick said. "I can see the family resemblance. Okay. Okay. You have very beautiful daughters, Nelson Markus."

He pulled away from Nelson and pointed at both Chuck and Clayton. Two officers in black moved in and forced Clayton to the ground.

Chuck turned on the officers and found Slick's firearm in his face.

"No, no," Slick said. "They know how to do this."

They dropped Chuck and cuffed him next, then stood both up and dragged them some distance away.

"Let's kill the lights," Slick ordered. "We want to see this."

The flood lights that were aimed directly at the porch turned dark.

Nelson's eyes hadn't fully adjusted. He was barely able to see the two, black shadows of Chuck and Clayton against the backdrop of corn and night.

A small light appeared in the dark, flickering like a camping lantern, and drew towards Clayton and Chuck's figures.

"Clayton," Chuck cried. "Clayton. What do we do."

"Shut up, Chuck," Clayton replied. "This isn't funny," he yelled as the flickering light stopped about ten feet away from him.

"What are you doing," Nelson asked.

"You said it yourself," Slick said. "Faggon's a sin." He raised his hand towards the officers hidden in the dark. "Light 'em up," he announced.

Before Nelson could demand that Clayton and Chuck get a fair trial, the small flame exploded into a long, straight pencil of white, and a continuous storm of red and orange blisters grew and exploded from within. The geyser waved over the two men and began to erase them from existence.

Roueghta screamed at the sight. The others turned away as Clayton and Chuck ran only a few steps, fell, rolled, screaming the entire time. The scent of their sudden burned flesh wafted instantly to the porch, and Nelson and his guests cried out because they couldn't stop it.

The flame thrower continued spitting red fire at the two men until they were unmoving piles of burning debris.

"Sorry you had to see that," Slick said.

"You're not a judge," Nelson said.

"Who says," Slick replied. He turned his gaze on Marley. "Guess you're up next."

Roueghta and Jasmine quickly clung to Marley, begging not to harm her.

"Your daughters sure do love this woman, don't they," Slick asked. "Are they, you know, active with her sexually?"

"No," Nelson said, pulling back Roueghta first and then grasping at Trinity's arm. "We've just grown fond of her."

"Oh good," Slick replied. "In that case, we should get moving."

Trinity was thrown down and cuffed next.

"Wait," Nelson objected. "Why?"

"Harboring fugitives, especially them gay kind, is a felony," Slick said, enjoying his job entirely too much at this moment.

The officers pushed Nelson down and the cold cuffs swallowed tightly around his wrists.

"Burning is excessive punishment," Nelson yelled. "This is an unlawful act."

"Don't worry. Whores get stoned, not burned," Slick said, amused. "But first you get a chance to repent."

Their cuffs were now shackled together. Then slick marched them away from the house to the back of a black Suburban where they were all forced into the cargo area. As he tucked his knees against him into one of the corners of the back of the truck, Nelson watched his farm grow to life in flames as more fiery geysers sprayed into various places throughout his remaining cornfields. Clayton and Chuck continued to smolder less than twenty feet from him now, and the officer that had set them ablaze climbed up Nelson's four porch steps and released a jet of more burning gel into his house. He moved to one of the two front windows and threw Nelson's coffee mug through a small pane before stuffing the barrel of the thrower through the broken glass and igniting Nelson's living room ablaze.

He didn't break the other window, rather blasted the porch swing with one flaming exhale.

As the Suburban drove away, everything Nelson had known grew into a burning monument of disrespect.

"Sorry about your farm, Nelson Markus," Slick said from the front passenger's seat. "It really didn't deserve to end like this."

The truck drove into the early morning. No other vehicles joined it. They had stayed behind to reap destruction on anything that proved Nelson had once made a mark on the world.

It wasn't quite two a.m. when the vehicle pulled into the bondsman parking camp where five tractors and their 45-foot trailers waited patiently for their turns to move out with fresh inmate cargo.

The Suburban pulled to a checkpoint leading into the chain-link-enclosed parking lot, rich in bright spotlights and streetlamps. They stopped only a moment for Slick to present his ID and identify that he was collecting bounties. The vehicle was waved through and directed to a rig and its trailer at the farthest end of the arena. When the truck stopped, guards in white military garb opened the back door and began to draw the linked criminals from the positions that had held them for the past two hours.

One of the men wearing a beret and captain's bars walked with Slick along the line of Nelson and his group. Together, they verified the image of Marley.

"These are the harborers," Slick said.

"You ain't the law," Nelson yelled.

"Quiet," the captain ordered.

"We have a right to a—

The captain held up a taser and fired the two leads into Nelson's chest. The old farmer's body clenched, and he dropped. Those attached to him didn't drop, but they felt it.

In a moment, Slick was helping Nelson to stand.

"Sorry about that," Slick said.

"Yeah," Nelson said. "All sorts of sorry, I'll bet."

"All right," the captain said. "Fifty thousand for the chief harlot, five thousand a piece for the rest. Although I'm sure them's is sluts too."

"What's the goin' rate now for regular sluts," Slick asked.

"Ten thousand, twenty if you can prove they're whores. Can you prove they're whores," the captain asked.

"They're not whores," Nelson yelled.

The captain squeezed the trigger on his taser, and Nelson fell once more.

"They're whores when I says they're whores," the captain replied.

"All right," Slick said. "Whores then. No way they dress like that without being the type of person who's asking for patronage."

"Not good enough," the captain said. "I'll give you seven thou a head but no more."

The ladies helped Nelson to his feet again.

Slick waited for the captain to touch his tablet to his own. Slick thanked the captain and left.

"Truck two," the captain said flashing two fingers to his right. He yanked on the leads of the taser and tore them from Nelson's flesh and clothing.

Nelson and the four women were instantly rushed off towards one of the diesel trailers. A woman at the bottom of a ramp poked her pencil into each one's person as she counted, "One. Two. Three. four." Then she turned around and yelled "four" up to a podium with three guards sitting around a computer console. They nodded.

Another white-suited soldier appeared before them. He threw a leash around the first person in the chain of prisoners, which happened to be Roueghta and began leading her and the others up the ramp.

Inside, the trailer was darker. Two other people, a young man and a woman appeared to be asleep on the floor, all the way to the back of the otherwise empty storage area.

They aroused themselves only after each member of Nelson's group had been secured to the wall and the guards had left.

"Polygamist," the man asked.

"Farmer," Nelson replied.

"Figures," the man said. His eyes fell on Trinity. "Whore?"

"Daughter," Trinity replied.

"Same thing," the man replied. He looked her over. "You any good? Show me."

"Are you kidding me," Trinity asked.

"Gonna die here soon anyway," he said. "Why would I be kidding you?"

"Just mind your own side of the trailer with your girlfriend," Marley said.

"Not my girlfriend," he said.

"I'm his wife," the woman said without attempting to move from her sleeping position in any way.

"I'll avoid the bondage and voyeurism for now," Trinity said.

"At least give him a show," the wife said. "He can do the rest from here."

"What's wrong with you," Trinity asked.

"Look," the man said. "We've been waiting five days. You might as well show something because you're going to later anyway."

"You presume a lot, don't you," Roueghta said.

"I have five hundred dollars. They didn't find it," he said. "I'll give it to you, ya pop something out."

The doors to the trailer shut tight and sealed everyone with the darkness. The hum of the tractor started. A few minutes later, it lunged off towards the next destination.

"You owe me five hundred dollars," Trinity said.

"For what," the husband asked.

"You said five hundred if I popped something out."

"I ain't seen nothing," he said.

"Not my fault you can't see in the dark," Trinity said.

The trailer swayed, slowed, sped up, swayed, slowed. The doors opened again. Another man in white garb held up a clipboard, peered into the trailer with a flashlight. He looked down at his clipboard and rummaged through a pile of papers.

"All right," he said. "Take 'em south."

The doors shut again. The tractor began moving.

"Wait," Nelson yelled. "We haven't had a trial yet."

The husband laughed. "There ain't no trials anymore. Don't need 'em unless you're gay, in which case you don't get one anyway. You just don't have to worry about the monastery."

"The what," Nelson asked.

"Where you been?"

"Hiding," Marley replied. "What's the monastery?"

"New place," husband said. "A place for everybody that ain't right. Pick you up, take you down, have your trial, burn you."

"Just like that," Roueghta asked. "Hardly seems right."

"I hear if a work position opens you can take that," the wife said. "If not, burn. Or worse."

"Worse," Nelson asked.

"It's a house of torture," the husband said. "Endure your torture, take your pain, get forgiveness, meet god with a clean conscience. Fix you if you're gay—you see—burn you if you don't repent, drown you after you do. Either way, fix you of what you done wrong."

"And that's just the gays," the wife said.

"Believe me," Nelson said. "Gays don't make it to be fixed."

"I heard they use the guillotine," the wife said.

"Public beheadings," Nelson asked.

"Amputation of that which offends," the wife said. "For deformities, remove the deformity. They only do beheadings if you're deaf, blind, something wrong with your head. That is, of course, as we said, unless they have a work opening."

"You never answered," the husband said.

"Answered what," Nelson asked.

"Polygamists? You the pimp?"

"He's not a pimp," Roueghta snapped.

"Girls," Marley said calmly.

Roueghta and Trinity apologized.

"My five hundred dollars is yours, you tell me why you're here," the husband said.

"Your five hundred dollars is already mine," Trinity said.

"Doesn't count," the husband said. "I didn't see it."

"Not what you said," Trinity replied. "You said five hundred dollars I pop something out. Why would we trust you to give us the five hundred if you're going to squelch on your first bargain?"

"We shouldn't," Nelson said. "Don't talk to him anymore."

They rode another five minutes in silence. Marley said she had to pee. Nelson had been sitting for about thirty minutes and his hands were beginning to feel numb from being shackled to the restraining bar above his head. He stood.

"Tell you what," the husband started at the sound.

"Will you shut up," Nelson replied.

"Not talking to you," the husband said.

"We're not talkin' to you," Nelson snapped.

"I'm just trying to pass the time," husband said. "You tell us what you did, and we'll tell you what we did."

"No one cares what you did," Marley said. "No more talkin' now."

Nelson hushed the couple for the rest of the trip. When the truck stopped some time later, muffled voices crawled up through the walls of the trailer. They seemed purposeful, more commanding.

The truck drove a short distance and stopped. The doors opened and three guards wearing uniforms that appeared more corporately ironed instead of garbed militarily attached a ramp and climbed into the compartment. One approached the group and began to uncuff them individually from the walls. The other two stood with automatic weapons aimed, ready to fire upon anyone who tried to bolt or attack the guard releasing their restraints.

As the three guards retreated from the trailer, two women in rubber suits appeared in the opening with a firehose.

"Undress," the woman at the hose nozzle ordered.

"We demand attorneys," Nelson yelled.

They fired off the hose, shooting foaming, stinging water at the passengers. After the walls and prisoners had been sufficiently buried in foam, the hose shut off.

"Undress."

"Lawyer," Nelson demanded.

The hose blasted again, for longer this time, then shut off.

"Undress," the nozzle operator ordered again.

They undressed.

The nozzle opened again, and the foam stuck like butter to their skin. The spray shut off.

"Scrub," the woman guard said.

The prisoners scrubbed.

"Told ya, you was gonna do it anyway," husband said.

The women at the doors retreated. Showers overhead suddenly burst with cold water and began washing the foam away. The water and foam flowed out of the open doors. A large fan at the deep end of the trailer, suddenly blasted them dry.

The women returned to the doors holding cloth satchels. They tossed the bags deep into the trailer.

"Dress," the commanding woman ordered.

Each of the prisoners recovered one of the satchels and dressed in a pair of thin slippers and a set of paper, pale-blue coveralls.

The women guards disappeared again and the three previously-armed officers approached. The one that had unshackled them now re-shackled all except for the husband and wife.

"This way," he said, motioning for the group to exit.

The group marched down the wobbly, metal ramp.

"What about them," Trinity asked, nodding to the married couple.

"They're police," Marley said. "They wanted a confession."

Nelson's group now stood in what appeared to be a prison compound. It was barren land. A six-story building with a sniper tower at the top of a three-hundred-foot elevator stood in its center. Only the top floor had any windows.

The sun was already breaking the new day in, enough to reveal the jagged razor wire along the outline of the roof.

A man in a black trench coat met the group at the side of the trailer. He looked through a clipboard, scanned through a tablet and then went back to examine it more deeply.

"I am your public defender," he said. "You will follow me."

"Where," Nelson asked before the public defender could turn away and start walking.

He stopped, turned to Nelson.

"Wherever I and my bailiffs tell you to," the public defender replied. Then he nodded to his armed guards and began walking away once more. The officers with guns, who, now that they were in the light more, were definitely privatized prison guards. These bailiffs urged the group forward.

The group followed the man in the trench coat, towards the building.

"Hold up," Slick's voice called from behind the group.

The public defender stopped and turned in agitation.

Slick jogged up to the man holding the clipboard.

"I need this man," he said, pointing to Nelson. "Release him."

"For what purpose," the attorney asked.

"Because I said," Slick replied, standing behind his aura of authority. "Now release him. You can have him when I'm done interrogating him."

The public defender seemed unmoved.

"This man is linked to smuggling undesirables," Slick said. "During our search of his premises we discovered evidence to suggest he knows others who are involved. Release him."

"How did you get in here," the bailiff asked.

"I am an Alabama Nation marshal," Slick said, donning his badge. "I order you to release this prisoner back into my custody."

An expandable baton burst from the public defender's hand and cracked Slick in the side of the skull.

Slick buckled to all fours, wobbled on his arms but held himself.

"I am," he slurred. "A marshal."

"Article Seventeen of the Process of Elimination Act," the public defender said. "Any attempt to interfere with the process of internment of undesirables is an act of treason and subject to the same classification as terrorism and tyranny. You are out of your jurisdiction."

He nodded to two of the armed guards. They drew Slick to his feet and forced him into the back to the truck trailer. The prisoners waited for the sound of firehose and shower before Slick reappeared wearing the same blue prison uniform. The guards cuffed and chained him to the rest of the line. His stature still wobbled some.

"Hello again," Nelson said.

One of the guards shoved the barrel of his rifle against Nelson's head. "Remain silent."

"Shoulder that firearm," the defender ordered. "He's in cuffs."

The soldier withdrew.

The public defender returned to leading the group to the building again.

There was only one door into the structure. Before it, stood a fifty-foot walkway enclosed by two walls of chain link with two feet of spacing between them. Before entering the hall, they passed by a glass booth with two guards. One requested to inspect the prisoners, the defender and his paperwork. The other scrutinized a set of computer monitors linked to a scanning machine. The one at the scanner nodded his head. The one inspecting the paperwork acknowledged the contents.

"The fence is electrified, people," he said, handing a clipboard and tablet back to the public defender. "Unless you want these next fifty feet to be your grave, I wouldn't let anyone in your chain within an inch of it."

The steel door leading into the electrified pathway buzzed open. The defender led the group in, leaving the bailiffs behind. A yellow light flashed over the top, and a siren announced the arrival of more prisoners. At the end of the walkway, a black door buzzed as the first had. A yellow light flashed here as well. The door opened inward.

Behind this was a plain white hallway with a single line of fluorescent lights, which ran straight along the center of the ceiling to the opposite end where an equally bland door awaited. The floor was concrete. The walls and ceiling surface were matte, and there was nothing else. It echoed the shuffle of the inmates low-quality, throw-away booties.

"Someone's job is mine, if you don't release me at once," Slick ordered.

"No more outbursts," the public defender said. "Or I'll initiate the chloride gas." He drew a thin mask over his face.

They continued in frightened shuffles. The bland door opened, making no sound. The defender removed his gas mask. Here, they entered a courtroom like any other. Its rows of benches were empty, however. An older judge sat in the highest seat in the room, behind the tallest desk. A woman to his left stood with her hand outstretched. Both looked like they had just woken up, which they had.

A man against a far wall typed at a stenography machine. The bailiff in here was a small guy with thick glasses and a lot of hardware around his belt. He approached the public defender. The defender handed him the clipboard and tablet. The bailiff, in turn, handed these towards the clerk. The clerk tapped her tablet against the public defender's, then tapped hers to the judge's before passing him the clipboard as well. The bailiff returned the defender's tablet to the lawyer.

Meanwhile, the public defender directed the line of prisoners into one of the benches and motioned they should sit.

The judge took the clipboard from the clerk and flipped through the papers while he also read over whatever was on his tablet.

"Let's see," he said as he read. "Hiding undesirables, Mr. Markus?"

The public defender signaled for Nelson to stand. Nelson did.

"Yes, your honor," Nelson said. "And if I may, your honor, we have not been afforded our attorneys as requested. We have been denied."

"You have an attorney right there," the justice replied without looking up from his studies.

"Yes, but—

"But nothing, Mr. Markus," the judge said. "I assume you plead not guilty to the charge of aiding and abetting of criminal behavior in regard to hiding undesirables?"

"No sir," Nelson replied.

"No," the judge asked and looked up from his clipboard. "So, you're guilty?"

"Yes, sir."

"The court will view that confession with mercy," the judge replied. "What is your background, Mr. Markus?"

"I'm a farmer, sir."

"What do you grow," the judge asked.

"I can grow anything."

"Learn it all on the farm?"

"And the military, sir. I was an agricultural engineer."

"So, you have some schooling, I take it?"

"Yes sir. I have degrees in botany and agriculture," Nelson explained. "Give me a seed and I can make anything grow, anywhere, any time."

"Sounds like you had a pretty good career," the judge said. "Why would you throw that all away to hide degenerates?"

"I didn't hide degenerates, your honor. Degenerates don't have to hide."

"All right then, who did you help?"

"People in need."

"Such as?"

"The disabled."

"And?"

"People on the run."

"That all?"

"Gays. These women."

"And who are these women," the judge asked rifling through the papers again. "Ah yes Madame Marley Donovan. You're a very popular person. Congratulations on being alive. Are these your Jezebels?"

Marley stood. "Yes, your honor."

"Mmm," the judge said. "And would you do it again, Mr. Markus?"

"You bet I would," Nelson said and knew he was signing his death warrant. Who'd care? No one. Yet, it was the right thing to do, and he would do it again, and he wasn't going to lie about it to a judge. Someone had to act appropriately in the legal system. Maybe someone, an intern perhaps, would see the transcript of this trial and question procedure all because of Nelson's moral fiber.

"I see," the judge said. "Hookers stand."

Trinity and Roueghta stood.

"Why would a couple of young, pretty things like yourselves want to spread your legs for money and sin?"

"We can't all be born with nice, golden gavels, your honor," Trinity replied.

The judge smacked his golden-plated gavel against the desk. "There'll be none of that."

"Forgive her, your honor," Roueghta replied. "When there's nothing for you, you do what you can or you starve. For me it was prostitution or staying home and getting raped by my stepfather. Miss Donovan provided a shelter for abused runaways. Either way, I was getting screwed. At least this way pays for me to go to school."

"What are you studying," the judge asked.

"Public administration, sir."

"And you," he asked Trinity. "You goin' to school too?"

"Criminal Justice, your honor," Trinity replied.

The judge laughed. "Law? What could a prostitute want with law?"

"I studied at the academy. I wanted to be an agent."

Slick Sunglasses laughed.

"That's enough of that," the judge smacked his gavel. "Why do you want to be an agent."

"Ethics, your honor," Trinity replied. "Someone needs to bring 'em back to law enforcement."

"I see. So, runaways come to you, Miss Donovan and you whore them out. How gracious of you," the justice said. "And how much income do you let them keep?"

"All of it," Marley replied.

"Oh, come on."

"It's true, your honor," Trinity said. "We help pay bills and room."

"So, she doesn't profit off of you, market you, sell you for sex," the judge asked. "That what you're saying?"

"We are not slaves," Roueghta replied. "She's better at the marketing than we are. Well, until our place burned down."

"So, you sought out Mr. Markus here," the judge asked.

"A friend told us how to find him," Marley replied. "He helped us."

"And gays, and other undesirables," the judge spat.

"Shame on you," Nelson blurted. "Guess they don't teach humanity where you studied law, huh?"

"You're pushing it, Mr. Markus," the judge said.

The public defender's baton appeared again in his hand.

"No need for that," the judge proclaimed, then turned to Slick. "So, why are you here, marshal, other than the trespassing issue?"

"That's a good question," Slick replied.

"I'm so happy you think so," the judge retorted.

"I am an Alabama Nation marshal. I arrested these people earlier and seized their property. We found a per—

"I'm sorry." The judge held up his hand to interrupt the testimony. "What do you mean you seized his property?"

"He burned it to the ground, your honor," Nelson announced.

"This true," the judge asked.

"Without a warrant!"

The judge struck his gavel. "Mr. Markus, please!" He turned once more to Slick. "This true? You didn't have a warrant?"

"Didn't need one."

"Marshal, are you aware that when this facility went online, it was assured that all crime related to undesirables would be decided and sentences passed by the jurisdiction of this court?"

"Well, we didn't have time for that, your honor," Slick said.

"He burned two men alive, your honor," Nelson blurted again.

"All justified," Slick said.

"Are you telling me that you took it upon yourself to deny this court access to two criminals?"

"I was in my jurisdiction; they had not been warded to this facility yet."

"And what made you think for a moment that you had the authority to carry out execution judgment," the judge asked.

"I'm FBI licensed, sir."

"FBI licensed? Here? In the great Nation of Alabama?"

"Yes sir, our esteemed Alabama president sent some of us out to train and bring that training back to our own country."

"So, you just left to train and came back? You never actually worked for the FBI," the judge questioned.

Slick nodded, then, "Yes, sir."

"Is there anyone at the FBI who can verify that?"

"Just teachers. I came right back after licensure."

"I see," the judge said, deeply in thought. "So, you have no one to corroborate your licensure is what you're saying?"

"The president's office of Alabama could sir."

"But no one outside of Alabama," the judge questioned.

Slick shook his head. "Just teachers."

"Very well," the judge said. "I'll need to question everyone involved in the raid tonight to verify your testimony. I need all names, or I will have no choice but to charge you with obstruction. Do you understand?"

Slick immediately began to recite the names of his fellow officers from the previous night.

"Well, I have enough to rule," the judge finally said.

"I find you all guilty for the crimes set before this court," the judge announced. "Bailiff see Mr. Nelson and his whores to the site of internment. See that the marshal is formally reprimanded."

The bailiff nodded his understanding as the judge struck his gavel.

The public defender gestured for the five inmates to follow after the bailiff.

"A lot of good you were," Roueghta said as she passed him.

The bailiff led the group to another door. This one, on the side of the courtroom, opened into a series of halls filled with empty prison cells.

"Where is everyone," Nelson asked.

"Haven't filled this wing yet," the bailiff replied.

They passed another block of empty cells before arriving in a blue and black tiled shower room. The bailiff began releasing cuffs. "You four against that wall," he instructed.

Nelson and the women obeyed the order while wishing their goodbyes to each other.

The bailiff released Slick Sunglasses from the chain.

"In accordance with the judge's order, go and sin no more."

The bailiff drew his sidearm and shot Slick through the chest. Slick dropped and bled onto the shower floor. The bailiff spoke into his radio piece, "Four for internment."

A section of tile in the floor pulled down and slid to the side.

"Can you really grow anything, anywhere," the bailiff asked.

"Yes," Nelson replied in confusion, "What is this?"

"We do what you do, we're just bigger." The bailiff pointed to the hidden exit. "And our boss is really going to want to meet you."

"This isn't a prison," Nelson asked.

"Not today," the bailiff replied. "It's the way out. You're done here."

The bailiff searched Slick Sunglasses and located his I.D. and wallet.

"You really want to be an agent," the bailiff asked, turning to Trinity. "We can make that happen, and you'll be working for us, but you need to decide now."

"You can do this," Trinity asked.

"If you can," the bailiff explained. "You heard him. No one really knows this agent outside the Alabama Nation. We'll make you him, and get you to work. Otherwise it's time for you to go, and they do need to go."

Trinity looked to Marley and Rhoueghta for help.

"This is what you wanted," Rhoueghta said.

The four hugged, and Trinity watched Nelson, Marley and Roueghta disappear down the hole. The exit sealed back up.

"Disposal of one needed in internment," the bailiff said into his mouthpiece then turned to Trinity. "Come with me."

Trinity followed the bailiff once more down a hallway. This one shrouded in doors. The bailiff opened one and stepped through. The room was filled with about fifteen desks, all filled with either piles of work or people.

"Ah," the judge said, approaching. He smiled, shook Trinity's hand. "Good! Good. You can help a lot of people."

"Thank you, your honor," Trinity said. "I'm a bit confused still."

"Please," the justice said. "Call me Cistern. I work for Salvo." He took the agent's wallet from the bailiff.

"Salvo," Trinity asked. "What's that?"

Cistern simply smiled and led Trinity past the desks and through another door. Here was a woman, a photo booth, three desks with different materials on each, and a strange machine that took up one-third of this entire room.

"This is the eye," Cistern said. "The eye is Salvo's best forger. We'll talk when you're done." Cistern set the wallet next to the eye's workspace and then left the room.

The eye continued what she was doing for another couple of minutes. Her face was pressed against an ocular lens, and she was operating a piece of machinery that reminded Trinity of something a surgeon might use for meticulous operations. The machine laser etched fingerprints onto a small metal hand that was the size of a newborn infant's.

Trinity had tried to speak at some point, but the eye shushed her. After about three minutes of this, the woman finally pulled away from her work.

She was a squirrely woman, perhaps thirty-two years at most. Her body was thin and hunched forward, and her smile was border of crooked and unsettling.

"Hello," She said and then took up the wallet beside her. She nodded approvingly. "How fun will this be? Ready to see the U.S., Agent?"

Chapter Twenty-nine

The priest was unusual in every way. He made no sense. He had no logic. Every week, Kola wondered why she insisted on attending his sermon. Each time, she sat in a new spot in the chapel and thought about whether she could hit the preacher between the eyes with a hymnal. Mostly, she wondered if God would protect him.

Riley smoothed her dress. She wasn't fooling anyone, and Kola knew it. Jordan Brunson had just made eyes with her and she was trying to look her prettiest, that's precisely why she asked to sit on the end of the pew. Kola looked past Riley and made eye contact with Jordan. He looked away in shame. He should have run.

"You're twelve," Kola said.

"Huh," Riley asked.

"You're too young for boys."

"But I—"

"Shh," Shauna hushed. She gripped Kola's hand, which had been tapping her sidearm that was hidden within her handbag. "It's okay. Twelve-year-olds flirt."

"I didn't," Kola replied.

"That's right. You didn't."

Kola believed Shauna. She cupped her other hand over the top of Shauna's and let her head fall on her shoulder. From here, she sought out the scar across Shauna's wrist and found herself tracing it with the tips of her middle and index fingers. She wasn't sure why. It fascinated her. It was part of her and Shauna, something they'd made together.

"And now," the priest said. "If anyone would like to say a few words about Steven, please feel free."

The congregation looked to Kola, and she wasn't sure what she thought about that. If she had something she wanted to say, she'd say it.

"Will you come with me," Riley asked.

Kola consented with a nod, while Shauna encouraged with another. Riley gripped Kola's shoulder and tugged at her until Kola took her hand and stood behind her. Kola, likewise, dragged Shauna out of her seat.

They all three approached the casket at the front of the chapel. Right below the pulpit, Kola's grandfather had been dressed in his favorite brown suit, and peach-colored bouquets of roses sat at his head and foot.

Riley led Kola and Shauna up to the pulpit. She reached to the microphone and bent it towards her mouth, and her face tilted towards the congregation.

Kola had seen it only crying for the past two days. Riley's cheeks were streaked with black tears even now. Although Kola reached to her bag for a tissue, Shauna held one out to Riley first.

Riley turned to take the tissue, and Kola awkwardly reached to begin wiping her face. Riley took control of the tissue and finished the work herself, then she returned to the microphone.

"I don't know who my real grandpa is," Riley said. "But Great-grandpa never let me know he wasn't mine, and I'm sad he's gone. He was my best friend, like my moms. He loved us."

The words didn't settle too well on Kola. That is, they were all true. She knew they were all true. She also knew, though, that there was more to Riley's relationship with Shauna and Kola's grandfather that went beyond what Kola had with him. Kola trusted him. She even found appreciation in his presence as he helped her learn to navigate the politics of her leadership role. She was surrounded by people she relied on to make her Salvo syndicate work, but that didn't mean she trusted everyone involved. Her grandfather helped her to understand why. Kola missed him. She didn't know how, but she wished he was still here, and she understood that she didn't feel but knew Riley did.

If Kola felt this way without emotion, she understood that Riley must feel it at an extreme level. Kola believed that what she lacked in feeling, Riley more than made up for.

Kola looked to Shauna and realized she had been crying too. Shauna had come to call the man grandpa, even before Kola could allow herself to do it. Kola squeezed Shauna's hand because that's what people who love each other do in their time of support.

Then Shauna's face opened into surprise, and she began to move. Her eyes darted through Kola and towards the pulpit, she took one step, pushing Kola backwards. That was when Kola saw him—Ernest, or rather Anvil's sharp brow. He had stepped out from his pew and drew a firearm.

The cathedral cracked with a single gunshot. A wooden pimple burst from the ledge of the pulpit. The bullet punched through Shauna's back and into Riley's shoulder.

Kola leapt from the stage and over the coffin. She heard Riley cry instantly, and that's all that mattered. Kola's knife was in one hand. Her other clenched at her small purse but couldn't find the trigger within well enough to fire due to her fingers fumbling too much, and she couldn't understand why. Ernie turned his weapon towards Kola.

"You took him from me. I took her from you," Ernie shouted.

That little bastard. She had sworn to protect him, to keep him safe, he knew that she had promised him that. She never broke her word, and yet—and yet nothing. He attacked Riley.

She threw her knife. Ernie fired. The shot flew threw her hair, past her ear. Where he had missed, she did not. Her knife sank into the base of his neck, and he smiled and re-aimed his firearm.

She dropped to her knees, just before the gun fired and missed her a second time. She finally drew her pistol, but a gunshot burst from the podium first, and his chest dimpled. Ernie's arms floundered in front of him, throwing his gun, and he stumbled. Another gunshot burst from within the cathedral and Ernie's head snapped backwards, taking the rest of his body with him straight to the floor.

Kola turned quickly to the stage and found Riley's arms extended in front of her just as she had taught the child to do—both eyes open and looking down the stainless barrel of her Springfield EMP, lining up the three green dots that glowed in the dark. The oversized beaver tail intimately cupped her thumb and made the squeeze of the trigger natural to Riley's small hands. Two shots, both in places where Kola had taught her to finish someone quickly, struck their marks near perfectly. More than that, something in Riley's countenance settled unwell with Kola. Riley had Kola's brow, but then it suddenly softened and looked to Kola.

"Mom," Riley cried.

Kola's guards, having been posted outside the chapel and under the assumption it would be safe in the church, had finally pressed their way into the cathedral.

They nodded that Ernie was dead.

Kola, sure the threat was over, climbed to her feet and scrambled back to the stage, through some of the parishioners, the priest and two of Kola's guards.

Riley was over Shauna, crying. Shauna's beautiful blue dress turned black from the wound that punctured out of her chest. She clasped at Riley's and Kola's hands.

"Did you get that son of a bitch," Shauna asked. Her words wheezed with blood.

"Riley did," Kola replied.

Shauna appeared surprised and looked to the twelve-year-old with tears running down her face. "Good! Now get me to the hospital. I don't want to die on the floor of a god-damned church!"

*   *   *

Shauna awoke in her own bed. Kola had demanded if she was going to die, she should do so in her own room. Kola knelt beside Shauna, asleep. Her make-up had run into the gray blanket. Her wavy, beautiful hair was knotted with tears, drool and no sleep.

Shauna lifted her hand upon Kola's head and drew her fingers over her scalp.

Kola aroused and interlaced her fingers into Shauna's.

"What are you doing down there," Shauna asked.

"I don't know," Kola said. "Praying."

"Well, knock it off. You don't pray." Suddenly, her eyes widened, and she jerked up and the pain pushed her back down. "Where's Riley?"

"She's fine," Kola said.

Kola quickly turned to the phone at the side of the bed and picked it up. She informed the doctor that Shauna was awake. When she hung up the old, rotary-dial phone, she made it easy for Shauna to tug her into bed with her. They hugged each other. Kola kissed her head and Shauna gave one to the top of her chest.

Suddenly, Shauna pulled back and looked upon Kola, puzzled.

"Don't look at me," Kola said.

"You're crying," Shauna said.

Kola's hand wiped her face, and she stared at the tears it had collected.

"I am," she replied in disbelief. "How the hell did this happen?"

"This is big, Kola," Shauna said.

"I know," Kola replied and then burst into sobbing. "I can't stop."

"Oh sweetheart," Shauna said. She did her best to hold Kola even tighter, except it pained her and she couldn't.

"You can't do that to me," Kola said.

"Okay," Shauna replied. "I won't"

"Yeah," Kola said. "Well, you also said when I grew up, I'd grow boobs like yours or I could buy some, and here I am, nineteen, with small boobs and no plastic surgeon."

"Ow," Shauna replied. "Don't make me laugh."

"I'm sorry. You know I'm broken."

"I know," Shauna said, looking into Kola's eyes again. "Doesn't mean you're not perfect though."

"I don't know how you can say that," Kola said. "We know I can't love you back."

Shauna smiled and wiped Kola's eyes. "This is what love does."

"It is?"

"Yeah."

"I'll take your word for it," Kola said.

"You should," Shauna said, sliding her hand beneath Kola's shirt while she kissed her neck.

Kola exhaled into her ear and held her back. "I'm not sure you should do that. You were shot, you know."

"Was I?"

"I'm just saying," Kola said then felt her breath shudder before she could bring herself to say, "You've been asleep for three days."

"Three days?" Shauna pulled away. "Riley must be starving!"

The floor creaked.

"Damn," Shauna said and gave Kola another caress before the drumming of footsteps could reach the bedroom door.

"You're up," Riley announced as she pressed inside.

Shauna smiled and tried to sit up but thought better of it.

"What do they have me on," Shauna asked. "I feel like I should be in more pain than this."

"Morphine drip," Kola said. "Lots of it."

"I don't want that," Shauna replied.

"Well you were shot, Mom," Riley said.

"And I didn't die," Shauna said. "So can we not let the morphine finish the job instead."

"Look," Riley said, unbuttoning her nightshirt and peeling her pajamas off the side of her shoulder to reveal a bandage. "We're both going to have a scar."

"You were shot," Shauna cried and sat straight up in bed, ignoring her pain this time. As best as the tubes would let her, she began searching Riley for any further damage. "You said she was fine!"

Kola couldn't speak, only trace her kidney scar through her clothes. It never went away.

Riley wriggled away. "I'm fine."

Shauna pulled Riley to her and let her own tears well. She kissed the top of her head and looked to Kola. "I'm so sorry."

When the surgeon arrived, he immediately chastised Shauna for sitting up, and she chastised him for the morphine. He checked her, listened to her lungs, then checked Riley's stitches.

"Will there be a scar," Riley asked enthusiastically.

"Yes, there will be a scar," Dr. Wright replied. "A big ugly scar."

"Cool!"

He removed the tubes and the morphine as Shauna had requested, warned her about the pain, and left her with some Tylenol.

"I want to know if the pain gets too bad," Dr. Wright said. "It doesn't have to be torture. We can monitor the drugs."

"I'll keep that in mind."

"And you," Dr. Wright said, suddenly turning on Kola. "I can see you still haven't slept."

"I got some," Kola replied.

The phone rang.

Riley ran to it before anyone else could reach. "Hello? Uh-huh." She handed the phone to Kola. "It's Max."

"Is he out of his mind calling here," Kola screeched and took the phone. "Yeah, what? We didn't send you topside to blow everything for us!"

The doctor took his leave and gave a friendly nod before bowing out of the room. Kola returned the nod while Shauna verbalized a "thank you." Riley walked him to the door.

"We're all fine," Kola said into the phone. "Why ask me?"

"Give me that," Shauna said, holding her hand up for the phone until Kola gave it to her. "She's been crying, Max. Yes. Crying." She handed the phone back.

Kola glared. "Yes," she said coolly. "Well, I guess because I must have lost my goddam mind, Max.

"Go talk to him," Shauna said.

Kola nodded that she would and kissed Shauna before she disappeared into the bathroom, as far as the phone cord could reach, just as Riley returned to the bedroom.

Forty minutes later, she came back to find Riley asleep in Shauna's arms.

Kola crawled into her side of the bed and looked across Riley to Shauna.

"What did Max say," Shauna asked.

"He said he thinks I love you too," Kola said.

"I could have told you that," Riley said from her sleep.

"And what did you say," Shauna asked.

"I said he was under too much scrutiny to be calling here, and if he risked us by doing it again, I'd have to send someone to put a bullet in his brain."

"Okay, good."

Kola allowed Shauna to fall asleep first so she could tell she was still breathing. For the first time in days, Kola would have finally gotten a full period of sleep if the phone hadn't rung to wake her. Shauna, that stubborn woman, had taken Riley into the living room to watch some old 80s Saturday morning cartoons. It was their weekend ritual. It wasn't Saturday, but Shauna believed there was an exception to the rule since they had missed Saturday on account of Shauna sleeping through it.

"What time is it," Kola asked.

"Did you finally get some sleep," Chelsea asked from the other end.

"I think so."

"How's Shauna? We heard she's awake."

"She is."

"Well, I hate to do this, but Ernie left us a little going away gift. He breached our security and sent out a little, delayed message."

"How little?"

"He told everyone how to find us."

Kola was suddenly getting dressed.

"I was able to use Omniscient to catch most of them, but several got through to some people and places that might ask questions."

"What did he say?"

"He gave addresses to our safehouses," Chelsea said. "Not all, just one in each state that we have safehouses."

"What about our prison," Kola said.

"Prison too."

"Can we fix it?"

"Heather's already working on something to make it look like a conspiracy theory," Chelsea said. "She's thinking she'll head out to one of the places; do a live feed; tear apart the floor to find nothing beneath it."

"Can you prep that fast?"

"It's become an engineering priority."

"All right," Kola said. "Call an emergency meeting with the heads, and make sure Heather's there. I'm on my way down right now."

"Are you getting dressed," Chelsea asked.

"Well, I'm not coming in naked," Kola replied.

"I was just going to suggest you shower first, please. It's a small room."

Kola held her cursing, showered and dressed again.

"Should you be out of bed," Kola asked.

"I'm okay," Shauna said. She was watching an old dog cartoon with Riley: Rooby Roo, or something like that. "Want me to come with you?"

"No, you've been shot," Kola replied.

"Like that's ever stopped you."

"Excuse me?"

"Seems I remember a seven-year-old walking for days on an injured foot."

"That doesn't count."

"How old are you now, mom," Riley asked.

"Nineteen," Kola replied.

"Don't ask that," Shauna said.

"Why," Riley asked. "Afraid I'll ask how old you are next."

"Don't even think about it," Shauna answered.

"I'll try to be home soon," Kola said and kissed Shauna goodbye, then kissed the top of Riley's head. "She's twenty-seven."

"Want me to come with you," Riley asked. "Be your bodyguard?"

"Not a chance."

"Oh," Riley said. "Well, then."

"Yeah," Kola asked, knowing Riley had something on her mind.

"Well, know how I was shot too," Riley asked.

"Uh-huh," Kola replied.

"Well, I really think an emotional support animal would help me feel better," Riley said. "Can we get a puppy?"

Kola was silent. Riley deserved everything she wanted, but Kola couldn't say yes. She couldn't say anything Riley would like.

"I have to go to work," she said and then walked out the door.

In the hall, Kola met up with her bodyguards. Her next stop was one floor below to the administrative offices where her secondary secretary, a woman ten years older than she, rushed to her.

"They're in the conference room now," the secretary said. "Madden is on one?"

"Madden is always on one."

"Coffee?"

"Yes, please," Kola replied and then added, "See if you can find any doughnuts. We might be awhile."

"Of course," and the secretary was already picking up the phone to place an order.

Kola's guards posted themselves in the front lobby, and she entered the conference room that was surrounded entirely in glass walls. The table within was oval and had a one-seat's-width area that was a few inches taller than the rest—not enough to be pretentious but enough to afford respect to the person who sat there, which, was Kola's grandfather's seat until now.

She drew into her usual chair and then changed to the taller area of the table, as if taking up a mantle of more than just leadership. She was already in charge, but she thought her grandfather should sit there as homage to his experience. She also had thought there was something to her adviser being high enough to observe everyone at the table.

On the lower end of the table sat nineteen different people. These were the ones who helped direct the city and their space program. Along one wall sat a row of five attorneys and Heather.

"All right," Kola said. Her eyes fell upon the man she had appointed to be head of the education department. "Severus?"

"Yes, Ma'am," Severus responded.

"My grandfather thought highly of you, and I've come to trust your judgement and ethics," Kola replied.

"Well, thank you," Severus replied. "He was a good man."

"Will you sit here from now on and advise me in all things?"

"Me? Are you sure?"

"I think perhaps one of the more senior members should fill that role," Madden suggested. He leaned back in his chair and tried not to look like he was sighing at Kola's stupid suggestion.

She heard Shauna's voice in the back of her mind yelling, "Don't kill Madden."

Madden was the head of Kola's casino. He had been around since her father was in charge. He had helped to create the underground gambling establishment, accessible to the outside world, but entirely oblivious for the most part to the hidden city that encompassed it. She didn't want Madden here, but her grandfather had taught her his value, acting as a firewall against the rest of the city of Las Vegas. He wasn't the friendliest of people, but he had developed a hatred against outsiders ever since he watched public health enforcement officers take away two of his best friend's daughters who had cystic fibrosis for "voluntary" scientific prevention research, which was just a fancy way of saying "legal dissection." Three months later, they imprisoned his wife for her depression that followed. Three days after that, his best friend was shot as he tried to visit his wife.

Madden wasn't a friend to what had happened with his country, but he also wasn't a friend of Kola's, and the only reason she assumed he was tactful towards her was because he knew she didn't particularly care for him neither.

"Madden," Kola said abruptly. "If I give you the role, you'll have to leave the casino, and no one can do what you do down there."

"There are plenty of senior staff members who could fill this role for you," Madden said.

The voices around the table began to contend with each other, all except one: Severus.

"Stop," Kola demanded, and the table fell silent. "I do not need counsel from people who think this is the topic we should be quibbling about today. We have more pressing matters."

Her thoughts turned to Riley's request, and how she couldn't bring herself to grant it. She'd let Riley down, hadn't she?

"Severus will you act as my adviser-in-chief," she forced herself to ask.

"Perhaps we should vote on it," Venice Kroger suggested. She was the head of housing for all of Salvo's underground cities.

"Why," Kola asked. "It's my adviser."

"Salvo," Severus said. "If we're going to restore the ways of our old republic, we shouldn't forget their most important tenets of representing the voices of the people."

"Anybody think that's not the type of adviser I should have," Kola asked, pointing to Severus.

Venice smirked. "All in favor," she asked.

Eighteen people raised their hands.

"All opposed," Venice said.

Madden's hand went up.

"Then with that," Thomas Hilton, the oldest man at the table now, and man designated as lead counsel said. "The director of the board of education forfeits his vote, and we have another empty chair on the board. Do you have anyone in mind?"

"I do," Kola replied and pointed towards Heather. "I imagine you all know Heather."

Many of the heads around the table nodded in mid-to-positive approval.

"Well, we have two departments without heads right now," Kola explained. "After today, head of education and, of course, our public relations director is on assignment. Hopefully, for a long time. That means we need to fill the PR seat. I'd like Heather to do it."

"And you think our resident blogger should be deciding how things work around here," asked Tinker Vox. He was the head of smuggling operations under Kola's father and now under her. He was what he was because he had to be.

"No, I think I make those decisions." Then it occurred to Kola, "You don't know why I called this meeting, do you?"

"We had assumed to discuss security matters after the attack on you and your family," Venice replied.

"Chelsea," Kola invited to speak.

"Right," Chelsea said from her own department head seat. "Ernie exposed us and got some messages to the outside with addresses to one safehouse in each of our operational states."

"How could you let that happen," Venice cried.

"Aren't you supposed to be the one who stops that," Tinker asked.

"Yes, but you all know how Ernie is, was. You've seen what he can do," Chelsea answered. "It's impressive we caught him at all."

"Well, how bad is it," Thomas asked.

"They don't know where we are," Chelsea replied. "But the addresses are pretty good clues to find out."

"We have to seal the tunnels," Ford Nancy, head of underground records, suggested. She preferred Nancy or Ford. She was usually quiet, but when she spoke, she was heard.

"We've already got a plan to deal with that," Arron Phelps, the head of the corp. of engineers said.

"Well, we need to start evacuating," Venice said. "I'll notify the other cities at once to—

"Heather," Kola tactfully interrupted and directed Heather to an empty PR seat at the table. "What can you do to fix this?"

"I've already contacted the safehouses and we should be able to obtain floor plans and photos of their layouts, videos of the exterior and of the owners. That part's easy. We just need our fastest couriers." Heather said. "If we build some quick sets, I can get some of our techs to create some hoax videos showing idiots going into the homes and showing there's nothing to be found. From there, I can link to my conglomerate of fellow bloggers above and below ground to saturate the Internet with evidence of misinformation."

"Should work," Chelsea said. "Give it a week from there, and I should be able to locate and delete any remnants of the message, then we delete Heather's videos, and we're out of sight out of mind."

"Except for those people who save that info to some sort of file outside of your reach," Madden said. "Such as government officials."

"And until law-enforcement kicks in the safehouse doors and starts digging around," Tinker replied.

"If we need, we can seal the entrances with some quick concrete and reopen them later," Arron replied.

"Or law-enforcement can," Venice said.

The table burst into debate.

"Salvo," Madden's voice called loudest from the table. "Salvo! Regardless of our plan, we have no choice but to consider evacuating and heading south."

"That's almost as bad as above ground," Nancy protested.

"And abandon everything we've built," Chelsea asked.

"Don't talk to me about building," Madden yelled. "I was here before there was a here."

"There may be another option," Severus said.

Kola silenced the people at the table.

"Go on," Kola said.

"Let's send some more messages out," Severus said. "Let's spam it. Tell them where all the safehouses are—

"This is the counsel you want," Madden cried.

"Plus," Severus exclaimed, demonstrating he wasn't finished. "The address of every other place in the nation. Say every building is a safehouse. Start with government buildings, they'll become national security priority. Identify addresses around those government buildings, addresses of government employees. Clusters of addresses around nothing, clusters around our places, and keep going until the messages become a nuisance and every single property is identified."

"Accuse all the people," Chelsea said.

"Yes," Severus said.

"Get all government security manpower searching those houses, and every person with a camera breaking into every home to uncover its hidden tunnels, and you have a law-enforcement crisis," Tinker said calculatingly. "They'll spend so much resource safeguarding the government addresses alone, they'll have no choice but to see it as a drain on human resources. They'll give up before they even consider searching the houses of citizens."

"Combine that with Heather's plan, and you'll no longer have a threat. You'll have a hoax," Severus finished explaining.

"It's a sound tactic," Thomas said. "Lawyers have been dumping excess information at each other for years to bury one damning nugget of information. It works."

The table was silent and looked to Kola.

"Can you make that happen," Kola asked Chelsea.

"Yeah," she said through thick contemplation. "We can. But we'll be on their radar from here on out."

"Yeah, as a conspiracy theory," Thomas said and laughed silently.

"I think we can handle on their radar," Kola said.

"Okay," Chelsea said. She had been working on her tablet feverishly ever since the idea came up. "I'm starting to send out press releases now to every media outlet possible, as well as every government agency and office, that begin to identify federal and state buildings. I've copied Ernie's original message and have inserted the address for one federal building in every state. Let's see. It's been Three hours since Ernie's message went out. If I put this message on repeat every three hours, rotating addresses with each message. We can overload every media and government outlet. After four cycles, we'll double the entries and then send them out each hour, on the hour, until every address in the U.S. is named. It will hit the news cycle, become huge news, by tomorrow at this time. If we gradually decrease the increments that we release information and keep doubling the entries, we can have every address in the U.S. identified within 48 hours and we can end it all with a great big follow up message that says, "Ha! Ha! Suckers.""

Madden suddenly grinned, "What about advertisements to some of our products instead like, 'Brought to you by Vegas's only Underground Casino.'"

The table burst into laughter.

"Ooh, I like that," Chelsea said.

"Any company we advertise is going to get investigated," Severus said. "Do we want that."

"You're right," Madden conceded, then smiled again. "So, let's list our competitors."

"You don't think that would be odd," Kola asked. "All our competitors but not us?"

"Not all of them, just one or two across our conglomerate. Shut 'em down for investigation, send some of their profits our way for a bit."

"I have a question," Nancy said, looking to Chelsea. "Why every three hours? Why not all at once."

"Creating a pattern based on the first message will camouflage that first set of addresses in case anyone down the road decides to pay more attention to them," Chelsea explained. "People remember what is most recent. I've already been cluttering the media with fake news stories that should keep others from looking too closely at Ernie's release for now."

"Maybe Max can help us in that department, if it comes to that," Severus said.

"If it all lines up, maybe," Kola replied.

"Might I recommend that we arm the safehouses for in case they do get breached," Tinker asked.

"What do you mean?"

"I'm thinking build reservoirs of chemical warfare in the walls of the homes, then release them if anyone really does come searching. If anything, it would make for a safe escape for out hosts if they were uncovered."

"Do we have the supplies," Kola asked.

"Maybe Adama has something," Chelsea said.

"We wouldn't need it," Tinker explained. "We could show the gatekeepers how to install something as simple as thin reservoirs in the walls and fill some with bleach and some with toilet cleaner. Put them in front of a vent. Hit a button, let them mix, knock intruders out while our people escape. Maybe even buy some time to seal the entrance."

"That's a lot of weight to dispose of in case they have to exit quickly," Kola said. "Let's put that on the back burner for now." She thought a moment and finally leaned forward in her chair. "Thoughts, legal?"

Thomas nodded and tapped his teeth with a gold pen.

"I'm all for burying a needle in a bigger mountain of dirt," Thomas replied.

"Doesn't sound like we need our head of PR now, does it," Madden said.

"Sure we do," Kola said. "Heather, can you influence any of your dumber, useless followers to start trying to investigate some of the empty addresses. Start flooding idiocy at its finest but nowhere near our places? Send some of your conspiracy theorists to a government building, let them start getting arrested? Raise exposure to the stupidity."

"Oh. Easy-peasey!" Heather was already typing away at a laser keyboard that her bracelet now printed out on the table for her. "We can put some of our own people into making fake vids for all the safehouses that have already been revealed so no one would try those again. I'll be subtle so I don't lose my own viewers over it."

"That's one problem down," Kola said. "Gues that means we can move on. Polls are not shaping the way I'd hoped."

"How do you know that," Aaron, the space-aeronautics engineer department head, asked. "We don't even know that."

"You're not Salvo," Kola said. "We need to start looking for another potential senator."

"Well, there's another eight years at least," Venice said.

"You realize that maniac's going to load this nation up with so many armaments that we'll never get a single module off the ground," Tinker said.

"Yes," Kola replied. "I do realize that. But it's important to remember that this has always been an event of patience. Let's stay focused. The time's coming. We can all see that. We're not completely ready yet for launch anyway. We're at least two years out before we can even test a completed module. If we have to wait another eight, we can do it."

"You know," Severus said. "We could do the same thing there."

"What do you mean," Kola asked.

"What we just did here, dumping too much information," Severus said. "Saturation can work in other places."

Kola's secretary entered the room now with Kola's coffee and three boxes of donuts.

"Um, Madam Salvo," she whispered into Kola's ear and handed her a small note.

Kola read the note, and decided she was not the right person to read the news it brought. She handed it to Severus.

"We've just been handed some more unfortunate news," Severus said. "Thalia's head secretary, who you may remember was Ernie's mother was discovered in her home. She hanged herself."

The table was again quiet.

"I think we've come to say what we needed to," Kola said.

"I'd like to propose that we put her in the freezer with her son," Madden said. "She deserves to go too."

Kola had wanted to reject the notion. Freezers and bodies took up weight. Ernie had helped make the engine possible, so they had decided he deserved to make it to space, but Thalia knew they couldn't send every single person who died there. However, she also knew why Madden asked and why he strained to keep his face stern. She knew about them. She also knew an opportunity to gain loyalty when she saw it, and, if there was anyone she could use more loyalty from it was Madden.

"I agree," Kola said. "They didn't make people much better than Thalia."

The table agreed.

Then they exited, taking doughnuts and drinks with them. Kola stayed behind, which meant her chief adviser stayed.

Kola looked to Severus.

"Why do you think she did that," Kola asked. "She always seemed so in charge."

"Sometimes, when you lose purpose, you lose your control," Severus explained. "Maybe she lost purpose."

"Oh," she said, "Well, I'm tired." Then she stood and made her way to leave the conference room. "I'm just glad that little bastard finished the work before he died."

With that, she excused herself and returned home to finish her rest.

Shauna had gone back to bed.

"You should talk to your daughter," Shauna said, pretending that she wasn't in as much pain as she really was.

Kola acknowledged. She found Riley sitting on the floor, leaning against the side of her bed, in a pile of pillows and reading a copy of King Lear. She put her book down and began to stand but then stopped, as Kola knelt then sat next to her instead.

"I should have given you a better answer than I did earlier," Kola said. "About the dog."

"It's okay," Riley said. "Mom told me."

"She did?"

"I never knew that happened."

"I never wanted you to."

Riley hugged Kola and began sniffling. "Why did your mom do that to you?"

"I don't know," Kola said. "Because it's all she knew, I suppose."

"Kind of like you?"

"I suppose, kind of like me."

Riley pulled away and looked up to Kola with swollen, red eyes. "It's not fair, Momma."

Part Five:

The Trial

of

General Mince

Chapter Thirty

As the polls flashed across the screen, President Munger cracked a pistachio in his teeth without sucking the salt off.

"West Washington will go to Senator Wilkissey," the news anchor said, barely able to contain his approval.

"There's a surprise," Munger said, then spit his shell halves across the floor.

"Mr. President," Assistant to the President of the United States, Lucero Eleo said, staring at the paper in her hands and thinking she should tear it up. "It might be time to start thinking of practicing your other speech."

"Don't need it. Already have it memorized," President Munger replied.

"All right," Lucero said. "Let's hear it."

"My favorite Amorons," President Munger said. "Congratulations! You elected a Jackass. Get used to kissing it."

"Mr. President, I'm being serious."

"So am I," he spit out another pair of shell halves.

Lucero slid a glass of whiskey into his hand, and he drank it down.

"We can now project that Wilkessey will take the state of Washington," the anchor said.

President Munger hurled his glass at the television. Cracks immediately rippled over the screen. "Can you believe this garbage? I create a bill that gives them control over all courts in their sub-country and they still turn their backs on me."

Lucero held up another paper from her hand, and President Munger took it. He was able to get through reading it twice."

"We are now ready to make a large prediction," the anchor announced again.

"Gee, I wonder what that's going to be," Munger said.

"I'm sorry, Mr. President," Lucero said.

"It looks like President Munger will take New California," the television announced.

The room was silent.

"Son of a bitch," said the intern finally.

"No, Jake," President Munger said. "Son of two bitches."

He tore the speech and handed the remnants back to Lucero.

The phone rang.

Mckenzie Sorenson, President Munger's assistant campaign manager picked up the phone. "Yes?" He turned to Munger. "It's for you, Mr. President."

"This is president Munger," he said. "You are correct. This was close. Well, thank you sir. That's very gracious of you, and might I say—" He hung up.

The room applauded.

The hotel door opened, and Chief-of-staff Tyresa Oppenhalmer entered with her hands empty, which only meant one thing. She didn't want to write down any record.

"Tyresa, I just won again, do we really have to do this now," President Munger asked.

Tyresa let the remark glance off as was her job.

"Mr. President," she said, more as a teacher chiding a student than as a chief-of-staff. "It's Salvo."

"When did I become the president who would be brought down by an imaginary drug lord," Munger replied.

"The Philadelphia P.D. found a tunnel," Tyresa nonchalantly dug her hands into her finely pressed black slacks.

"Who hasn't found one of Salvo's tunnels," President Munger asked. "It's been, what? Four years? Five years? Since that prank!"

"Last election," Lucero reminded.

"Right," Munger said. "Is there any evidence this actually belongs to Salvo, or is it another nut-job do-it-yourselfer like all the others?"

"There was an exchange of gunfire in the tunnels."

"Oh goodie. Any casualties?"

"One civilian and two Philadelphia police officers were shot and killed, Mr. President."

Munger chewed on this new information.

"So, no evidence it was Salvo," Munger said.

"But we should support the local, law-enforcement."

"Why? I'm sure Philly can handle this one on their own."

"Mr. President," Tyresa replied. "You don't need another reason for the people to hate you. Dismantling of the Interstate Trade Agreement is still fresh on everyone's minds."

"Not that fresh."

"You had how many secret service try to kill you?"

"Now that's a scandal. Why didn't anyone care about that?"

"They don't like you sir."

"And yet, I won the presidency again, didn't I?"

"Twenty-two percent of the vote isn't winning, Mr. President. With respect."

"God bless my sixteen last-minute opponents."

"Mr. President. We really should send P.P.D. assistance."

Munger nodded. "Notify the FBI. If there's someone in those tunnels, Let's find them."

"Of course, Mr. President," Tyresa turned to leave.

"Oh, and Tyresa? Let's not mention Salvo until we actually have reason to believe it *is* Salvo and not some gangbangers being where they're not supposed to be. The last thing we need to be remembered for is resurrecting a hoax."

"Some say it's not a hoax," Lucero say. "Remember the leash-bomber?"

"Yes, I certainly remember the leash bomber," Munger said. "There's another reason we don't need this. Bring me evidence or keep a lid on it."

"Yes, Mr. President," Tyresa said.

President Munger turned for another door leading out of his room, into a different section of his presidential suite where flashbulbs and questions quickly erupted as well as cheers and applause. Fourteen secret service officers escorted him out of his suite and down to a conference hall with a stage separated from the rest of the room by bullet-proof glass. The room applauded, and Munger victory-danced a few steps before he stepped up to the podium and microphone.

Cheers!

*   *   *

The Jergensens were good people, friendly, favorites in the community to hero any who needed help. They prayed a lot, gave a lot, exercised a lot and screwed a lot, not necessarily each other, but who cared? They paid their tithes and gave of themselves, so they were righteous.

They had married after courting through high school, loved each other. He went to college to study ethics and business. She averaged $12,000 a night and had the curves and implants to make more on the weekends. The senators loved her, and she lobbied them hard.

Separate, they were brilliant. Together, they were unstoppable. The flight was only half an hour between her place and Washington, and sometimes she traveled round trip two or three times within a day. She was reliable, some might say sturdy. He stayed at home and orchestrated his stock and the stock of others around him. He was great at devaluing others' money, spending his own on what he caused others to lose, and then made it valuable again at higher rates for himself. She made sure regulations allowed him and his brilliant team of economic geniuses to continue their rape of the working class and those who would soon be demoted to the working class.

They had a garage of cars, owned a pastor, and helped fund an orphanage with just enough passion to build loyalty for future employees who would love them back and ignore how little their pay would be. He understood the game of perception. She knew the one of discretion, sometimes.

Their first house was a leaning heap. They knew no one would ever purchase it. Yet, with enough money to the right city officials and building inspectors, a person who never planned to move could create all sorts of floor plans, building permits and other documents to suggest they had added upon the house, built a guest house right off the garage. Then when stacks of lumber burned down having never built what they were intended to, a note from the fire marshal and a quick declaration of emergency clean up would leave the insurance company no choice but to payout. He'd had a plan to retaliate if the insurance company refused to write a check for ten times the value of the little, one-bedroom house, but he didn't have to take the action.

He took his honest money, gave one-tenth to his church and kept the rest to build a one-bedroom house that he then turned around and sold for twice what he paid for it.

Then he took that money and started taking other people's— and when laws said he couldn't, she'd take one or two of her thirty-minute flights to find the right senator to lobby into submission. Together, they had managed to take control of lives, commerce and an ability to interfere with Salvo's capacity to operate some of her own properties, including safehouses. Unwittingly trying to bribe a city to foreclose on one of Salvo's safehouse properties was not Mr. Jergensen's wisest decision. So Salvo simply had to put an end it.

When the Philadelphia Police showed up to the Jergensen's five-hundred-million dollar mansion with a warrant to search the secret room in the basement and behind the wine cellar, where she kept her collection of blackmail photos and videos from the hidden camera in her clutch, Mr. Jergensen was relieved and dismayed to discover that all of the records had mysteriously disappeared. What confused him even more was the tunnel that had appeared in the back wall of his safe that led into an underground tunnel. When the police moved the safe and found the hole in the ground with the ladder leading down, both he and she protested that they had no idea how it had gotten there. When the strange rifle barrel poked out from the safe and hinged so the camera on it could view the room, only she noticed before it unleashed enough bullets to kill everyone in the room except for her.

A gas grenade knocked her out, and when she came to, what had once been a room filled with filing cabinets and office equipment now held two bunkbeds and a small food storage, everything to suggest that the Jergensens had been hiding people and selling orphans.

Now, Agent Lim sat in front of a computer monitor segmented into four parts and watched the gray and white hand-shoveled edges of narrow, dirt tunnels pass the lens of the small rover's peripheral.

"Switch to night vision," Agent lim said and sucked static out of his teeth.

The walls of the caverns turned from gray and white to black and green. The rover crawled for another two minutes and then stopped.

He nodded his head as if to agree with someone who had suggested some sort of action that no one else had made. Then he stood and signaled his squads of armor-vested agents with automatic weaponry to follow him into the basement.

They descended into the tunnel and Lim split them into two groups. The second group made it a quarter of a mile before they entered a circular dead end. As they announced their findings to the first group, the alcove burst with heavy, expanding foam concrete. It took all of ten seconds to spray and another twelve to expand enough to disorient every soldier of the group. In another minute, the foam had hardened, trapping, suffocating and crushing them. The first group was Lim's. They followed their tunnel for a quarter mile before he decided they needed more equipment and gear to sustain a longer search. He was also concerned with losing his radio contact with his bravo team. As they were making their way back, bullets came at them from behind, piercing their body armor and destroying every remaining member of the squads.

*   *   *

President Munger stared at the report in his hand. Eight agents dead, it said. Seven bodies were missing.

"We believe the other seven were encapsulated in a quick-setting cement," F.B.I. Director Gordon Feinstein explained. We have excavators on their way now to begin digging.

Munger closed the file and tossed it back to director Feinstein. "Do we know it's Salvo?"

"We don't know who it is," Feinstein replied.

"I want to know who did this," Munger said. "How do you recommend we approach?"

"The tunnels are booby trapped. We're on their turf," Feinstein replied.

"So, your recommendation is to avoid answering the question," Munger said and turned to General Mince. "What do you think?"

"I think we send rovers in to start mapping the tunnels. We send them a hundred feet before a team of our men, let it spot the booby traps," Mince explained.

"Mr. President," Tyresa spoke. "What about sound measuring?"

"General," Munger asked.

"Thought about that," Mince replied. "But there is an issue with whether we can or not."

"How so?"

"Only one house has tunnel access," Mince said. "To track the tunnel means we have to conduct searches beneath other properties, and we could end up needing a lot of warrants. We can't hide that act from the public."

"Better not upset the public," Munger said. "We don't need another state threatening secession. Send in a special ops team and a robot."

*   *   *

Other than walls, the only other thing the robot noticed was the flashbang that blinded its night vision. There was no gunfire, but when the robot's sensors came back online, the tunnel behind it had collapsed and it had no escape route. The robot was quickly seized upon—its sensors confused, and its cameras blocked with strips of black duct tape.

Two hours later, the robot was blindly patrolling through a residential district, bumping into curbs, scratching cars, sounding an alarm for people to find it.

A police officer discovered it. He recognized at once that it was a little more expensive than what his own law-enforcement could afford.

Overall, it was a precision piece of machinery. Its artificial intelligence was second to none, except duct tape. The officer tore off the tape. The robot stopped; its camera flipped to the cop.

"GPS tracking, not connecting," the robot said. "Attention! You are in vicinity of United States military equipment. Step back twenty feet. The officer stepped back and called his supervisor.

"Are you sure it's not a hoax," his Captain asked.

"If it is," the officer replied. "We can't ignore it. It has a sign taped to its back saying 'President Munger has entered our tunnels. We are coming for him.'"

Naturally, when word reached Munger, he flew into a rage.

"That's three teams of different enforcement agencies and now a robot with a death threat," Munger shouted. "Who's doing this?"

"Salvo, Mr. President," General Mince said. "No doubt."

"And your evidence," Munger asked.

"Does it matter," Mince said.

"And what are we supposed to say to that when the press asks," Tyresa asked. "A robot with a 'kick me' sign on his back told us."

"Don't let them ask," Mince said. "The Mince Act allows that discretion."

"And how do you think that's going to look for the president, General," Tyresa asked.

"I want everything we have on Salvo," Munger said.

"We don't have anything on Salvo," Clinton Myers, secretary of defense replied.

"How don't we have anything on Salvo?"

"He was a hoax four years ago. He's never attacked. He's never threatened. He's never been anything more than a waste of resources."

"And yet, everyone seems to know who he is."

"Everyone knows who bigfoot is too, Mr. President."

"Didn't that leak tell us he was in every state," Tyresa asked.

Now, a door opened to the oval office secretary's quarters.

Marcy Hamilton, personal assistant to Tyresa respectfully waited to be waved into the room. She approached and handed another file to the chief-of-staff.

Tyresa thanked her, looked through the file, frowned and handed it to the president. He too perused the documents.

"Are you serious about this," Munger asked. He threw the file at General Mince. "The tunnel doesn't go anywhere."

"How can that be," Mince asked.

"You tell me," Munger shouted. "The tunnel goes two directions and has two dead ends. Tell me, how does a supposedly prominent cartel lord like Salvo operate any kind of business from a solitary tunnel with two dead ends?"

"Well, there must be more."

"Does it attach to any other house or structure," Munger asked Tyresa.

"Just this one house."

"We sent a special ops team to die in a wine cellar!"

"There must be more."

"Then show it to me," Munger said, snatching up the file again and drawing out images that looked like sonograms more than maps. One by one, he threw a photo of the map at the General. "Show it to me!"

"We could revisit the scanning option," Clinton suggested.

"I thought we had ruled that out," Munger said. "How do you propose we pull that off."

"Fly over the whole country if we have to. We know there are tunnels. Scan our own land."

"And violate every American's personal privacy. I'm sure some advocacy groups will have a problem with that?"

"So, don't tell the people."

"Are you prepared to go to prison then," Munger replied. "Because that's exactly where you're proposing we buy a summer home if we do that."

"What should we do then, Mr. President," Clinton asked.

Munger sat back and stared at the ceiling. He reached into his suit pocket and pulled out a blue rubber ball. He tossed it a few feet into the air and let it fall back to him where he caught it. He did this for nearly two minutes before finally sitting forward in his chair and pocketing his ball.

"Back some four years ago when the defense department first got the tip about addresses that accessed these tunnels, how many addresses did it provide," Munger asked.

"All of them," Clinton replied.

"What do you mean all of them?"

"They released every address of every home in every state, including Alabama Nation's, sir."

"What are we supposed to do, check every address in the contiguous states," Clinton asked.

"Well, except Rhode Island."

"Every state but Rhode Island?"

"The letters only listed federal and state facilities there, no residential addresses."

"Why?"

"Don't know."

"Did we investigate this in any way."

"The government buildings were cleared."

"Don't you think it would make sense that the reason they didn't list any addresses in Rhode Island could be because it was the one place that might actually have something we could find?" Munger asked.

Munger chewed on what he'd suggested for a moment. He played with his ball, and no one interrupted him. When he was done, the ball slid once more into his pocket.

"Maybe we can't search every state," Munger said. "But I think we could cover the smallest. Let's mobilize a division to Rhode Island and test the waters. Have all soldiers unarmed and dressed in civvies so as not to turn this into a threatening event. Sweep door-to-door, provide our military personnel with a set of questions to ask to help screen the process. If we receive certain answers, record the address, we'll follow-up with a more in-depth investigation of the premises."

"I'll organize the military operation at once," Mince asked.

"A survey," Tyresa replied quickly.

"Excuse me," General Mince asked.

"Mr. President. When the press gets wind of this, we don't want the public thinking that you've sent the military into your own country to search people's houses. We do as you suggest, prepare a door-to-door survey, a 'President Munger is interested in what you think he could do to improve relations with you and your community' type of thing. We'll add in some prodding questions such as, 'Do you ever feel unsafe with people you don't recognize hanging around your or your neighbor's houses?'"

"That sounds like it would take a longer time to perform," Munger said.

"Yes, Mr. President," Tyresa replied. "But it would be for great public relations."

"I like that idea," President Munger said. "How soon can you have a survey?"

"End of the day, sir."

"Let's be careful," Munger replied. "Let's at least invest a couple of days into developing this if we're going to do it."

"Of course, Mr. President."

"Well, we have somewhere to start," Munger said. "All we need is one way in and we can see if this Salvo is a ghost or not."

*   *   *

"All right. Let's see if we can finally make something launch this time," Chelsea announced. "Initiate pre-flight check."

"Master Navigation server online," a woman said, watching her screen and the progress report now flooding it.

"Earthbound Navigation server online. Mock self-destruct parameters initiated," he said, directly to her left.

"Initiate thruster registration," Chelsea said, from the center of a completely spherical room, nicknamed *the marble*. Her podium climbed like a tall, cylindrical monument from Arches National Park and looked over everyone and everything else in here. The inner curved walls, floor and dome ceiling appeared as a single, continuous viewscreen. The segregation of smaller screens along the wall were pre-programmed segments to help each department monitor their numbers data better. The ceiling currently presented a satellite image of the earth floating in a sea of black. Satellites floated through its orbit as if it were more of a junkyard than it should be a glorious heaven.

"Never ceases to amaze me how much junk is in space," Riley asked staring up at the ceiling from the designated observation deck to one side of the room.

"Some call it junk," Kola said. "I call it natural resource."

"Wow," the 19-year-old man seated at Riley's right said. "That's brilliant."

"Jim," Shauna said, noticing the flash that crackled across Kola's brow. "Sshh. It's not your turn right now."

"Mom," Riley protested but saw the impatience in Kola's eyes as they snapped towards her and quickly away again.

"One step at a time," Kola replied.

The inventorist looked up from his console; surveyed his personal screen in front of him; and then checked it against his section of the wall. "Test thrusters one through fifty-three are 'at-ready' status. Contiguous state testers are standing by."

"Omniscient meters," Chelsea asked, turning towards the left side of the ringed stage that she stood in, leaning over its railing and looking below to the lowest curve of the marble, directly at the base of her podium.

Three people in a blue alcove checked their work and then each other's.

"Omniscient is holding steady at ninety-nine-point-six percent connection across the board," One of them called through her headset, and the view screen itself vibrated without altering its imagery to ensure the entire room could hear the message.

"And response lag," Chelsea asked turning slightly to her right in her stage.

"Pings show a point-oct-aught-four millisecond delay, Ma'am," a twelve-year-old girl replied.

"Initiate onboard piggyback," Chelsea instructed. She turned back to her central observational position. She watched a grid of the forty-feet wall turn a list of fifty-three state names from red to green."

"All fifty-three onboard piggyback are initiated," this sector supervisor replied.

"Piggyback meters," Chelsea asked.

"Piggyback meters are holding a ninety-six-point-nine percent connection," a woman five feet from the supervisor's left announced, and the viewscreens echoed.

"Response lag?"

"Point zero, zero, zero, zero, zero, zero, zero, two, six, three millisecond," another young girl, perhaps nine replied.

"Hept-aught will work just fine, Angela," Chelsea replied. Now, she turned 180 degrees to look towards a section of twelve people all dressed in white. "Omniscient response?"

"No faults detected," said a woman.

"No security pings," replied another.

"No traces detected, Ma'am," said an older man with shaky fingers but refusing to let go of his passion.

"Temporary rewrite of additional omniscient nodes integrated and prepared for reversion upon module loss of contact," said another man.

"Ma'am," announced another after consulting with the remainder of his department and their screens. "We are omniscient."

"Display air traffic control," Chelsea asked, turning to the left.

The ceiling turned from a black, starry view down from space to the current, consistent and cloudy sky over the U.S. typical of the weather forecasts for this week. Maps of airline routes speckled the sky, with small dots showing where every commercial, private and low-flying vehicle currently tracked through the skies.

"Overlay military solution."

Another grid, placed blue lines and splotches for military bases, weapons and response vehicles.

"Weather consortium?"

The skies added a representation of info from weather balloons, satellites and monitoring stations over and across North America.

"Show only radiosonde data on the dome," Chelsea ordered, and the ceiling applied a layer of gray weather currents. She looked to the western wall, which she knew in the moment because of the large W engraved in her rosewood handrail, and examined the rest of the weather imagery and data on that section of screen as did the department of twenty meteorologists.

"Search and display potential local and auxiliary obstructions," Chelsea now requested. Purple dots appeared throughout the map where events like hot air balloons, carnivals, fires, public gatherings, etc. were currently taking place or reported to be taking place.

"Verify with satellite."

Some purple dots disappeared while other new ones appeared.

"Give me a go-no-go."

The individual departments began to reply with "go" until Chelsea completed turning a full 360 degrees above the crew beneath her high-rise stand. Then she stopped.

"I know I'm going to regret asking this, and I'd really like to be able to finally launch these things," Chelsea said. "Laser guidance scrambler?"

"Umm," the male translator said.

Straine raised a thumb's up sign from her two-seat sector.

"Are you kidding," Chelsea asked.

"No," the translator spoke. "We're good."

"I'll be damned," Chelsea said, then announced, "We are good to go. Finally!"

The room erupted with applause.

"Knock it off," Chelsea said. "Don't jinx it."

"Do you have any doubts, Chelsea," Kola asked.

"Oh yes," Chelsea replied.

"Should we hold?"

"No."

Kola nodded approval to move forward.

"Initiate activation warning for test modules," Chelsea announced.

The room filled with an alarm.

"Attention," a simulated man's voice called over the speakers. "This is a test for the emergency broadcast system for the," silence for four seconds. "This is only a test." The room filled with an alarm again. "This has been a test for the emergency broadcast system. If this had been an actual emergency, instruction related to your emergency would have been posted. Thank you for taking part in this emergency broadcast test."

At every quadrant in the wall, a five-minute counter appeared.

"Recite the emergency script," Chelsea ordered.

"This is an alert of the emergency broadcast system," a matter-of-fact, middle-aged woman with her hair pulled back began to read from her tablet. "This is for the, insert location. Military ground forces have been spotted in your neighborhood. Please seek immediate shelter in your homes and stay away from all windows and lock your doors. Repeat. This is an alert of the emergency broadcast system. Military ground forces have been spotted in your neighborhood. Please seek immediate shelter in your homes and stay away from all windows and lock your doors. Again, this has been an alert of the emergency broadcast system for the, insert location."

"Initiate test texts to our module sector leads and respond," Chelsea said.

"Test successful," one voice called from somewhere behind Chelsea after several seconds.

Others validated this.

"Ping the thruster counters."

"Counters are synchronized and visible on modules," another voice announced.

The counters on the walls now read three minutes.

Again, the EBS alarm went off, Chelsea asked for the script to be read again.

"Ping operator presence," Chelsea said immediately afterwards.

"All operators checking in."

"Ping suit-safety-check and initiate personal instructions to correct any faults," Chelsea said.

"Instructions sent."

"Lift offs in T-minus 60 seconds," the counter captain announced taking priority and volume over all other conversations.

"Mock a set of random test faults for fifteen of our engines," Chelsea said.

"Test engaged," a previous voice called. "Instructions to correct faults are being delivered."

"Make two uncorrectable," Chelsea said.

"Set," the voice replied. "Instructions on how to evacuate suit if take off does not initiate and how to destroy module are being delivered."

"Ten," the countdown voice announced.

"All departments," Chelsea continued speaking.

"Nine."

"Mock emergency."

"Eight,"

"Test pings,"

"Seven."

"Now."

"Six. Five."

"Report."

"Four. Three.

"Ping again."

"Two."

"One. Initiating lift offs."

Fifty-three bright gray dots appeared on the ceiling, representing the thrusters that would hopefully carry individual people into orbit someday. The walls turned into a 3-D view of the upper hemisphere, allowing the room to visualize invisible, non-existent trails of the engines as they shot towards the heavens.

"How are our two irreparable faults," Chelsea asked.

"Delivering messages now."

"Fix the faults. And launch."

"Faults cleared; launch enabled."

"Initiate military response test," Chelsea instructed.

The screens suddenly filled with simulated missiles, fighter planes and other weapons fire. The thrusters affected by attacks reacted, changed courses, fell even, then resumed their climb after the dangers had passed.

Over the next eight more minutes, Chelsea ordered the same test three more times and similar tests four more times, always with different modules. She even mocked an unidentified flying object suddenly appearing on a collision course for all fifty-three modules at the same time. They all dodged the obstacle and survived the test.

"Orbit obtained for all fifty-three thrusters," another department's voice announced.

"All right," Chelsea finally said. "Let's not leave any evidence to chance. Cut trajectory, and let 'em fall and burn, except for two."

One by one, the gray lines and dots representing the engines, bent back towards the earth and disappeared from the dome, all except for two.

"Send our two stragglers into orbit and maintain for ninety minutes to simulate low orbit collection time," Chelsea said. "Then bring them down."

"Yes, Ma'am."

"I do believe we can call this a success," Chelsea said.

The room erupted into applause.

"Keep monitoring our stragglers." She began climbing down the long, narrow set of stairs from her podium and towards Kola's observation sector. "You know the drill. Gather your data, check in with your field leads, return and report tomorrow morning."

She approached Kola, who, as always, seemed serious.

"That was so cool," Riley said.

"That was badass, wasn't it," Chelsea said, unable to contain her full excitement.

Kola nodded and faked a smile. "Well done."

Chelsea's face now puckered into preparation for bad news. "I know that look. What is it?"

Kola turned to Jim.

"I'll wait for you outside," he said, knowing Kola's intention, and then kissed Riley before leaving.

Kola's face didn't betray her disdain. She didn't care if Riley was barely seventeen, she was too young to be serious with a boy, especially Jim.

Jim left the room.

"The military has been dispatched to Rhode Island to start searching for kinks in our armor," Kola replied. "They're looking for safehouses."

"Oh shit," Chelsea replied, and the blood drained from her face. "They're ahead of schedule."

"Right," Kola agreed.

"We can't afford to lose that hospital module," Chelsea said. "It would take ten years, at least, to regather the equipment to build another. And we haven't finished building a test module yet."

"If we needed to, could we use our hospital for the test module," Kola asked.

"If it fails, we'll suffer a major setback. We may lose our leverage to ever launch again. That's our only hospital module," Chelsea said.

"Then we better make sure it succeeds. If it does, can we keep other astronauts hands off of it until we can get to orbit ourselves?"

"Are you suggesting giving it defensive capabilities?"

"I am."

"A weaponized hospital? Oh, our medical administrator is going to love that."

"Can you do it," Kola asked.

"I think so, but I'm going to need Adama's help."

Kola turned to Riley. "Sweetheart, will you recall Adama and have her report to Chelsea."

"Of course, Mom," Riley said then started to turn.

"Wait," Shauna said.

Riley stopped.

"Probably should recall Shasta as well and have her report to the hospital administrator," Shauna said.

Kola looked inquisitively to Shauna.

"If we're talking sending it into orbit, we should think about stocking the pharmacy and chemical plant," Shauna suggested.

"Right," Kola replied. "And that has nothing to do with the fact that Shashaun's the administrator there, which might upset our pharmacy smuggler if we don't send her up as well."

"If Shashaun's going to potentially get caught, her mother's going to want to be there."

"If the module can sustain life," Riley said. "And we're thinking of sending it up. It might need a crew. Shasta and Shashaun won't forgive us if we keep the rest of their family out of this one."

"That's good thinking, Riley," Kola said. "This issue though is that, on its own, that module is not prepared to sustain a crew from bone and muscle loss."

"So, you are paying attention to our engineering professor," Riley joked.

Kola rolled her eyes. "I should have never agreed to take an online class with you."

"I'm sorry," Riley said. "I know you pay attention."

"The question is, how long can they live in space before it's too late for us to help them," Kola asked.

"We could follow the same regiment as American astronauts enlist until we can launch the other modules," Shauna suggested.

Kola turned to the phone in her section and requested the operator track down her other physics advisers. Within an hour the faces of two older men and three women, not one of them much older than Shauna, appeared on the wall behind the observation section. Kola relayed the previous discussion.

"You do that, and you've just put a launch date on all of this. People can't live in space if their muscle mass, bones and organs fail," Kola's physics professor, Martin Gad explained. He was the oldest and most experienced of all of the other faces on the wall. "Are you prepared to do that?"

"Depends on the launch date," Kola said. "What would we be looking at?"

"From time of launching the hospital module, I wouldn't go leaving them alone in space any more than a year," Gad said.

"Or nine months," one of the women, Ona Lyons, Kola's biology professor said.

"Or seven," another woman, Kelcie Kunz added.

The others agreed.

"Seven would be ideal," Gad said. "But we could go a year, a little more if we had to."

"The longest we've gone with a person in space is five-hundred-and-one days, and it didn't end well," Burt Craven, the other man on the screens added.

"That was without gravity," Kola said.

"We don't know if your simulated gravity will work," Ona said.

"It will work," Straine's translator said as Straine crept up into the conversation, which she had learned Chelsea and the others expected of her. "The vacuum artificial gravity will force them to work muscles, and we can give them supplements for bone conservation. They just have to know, no babies. It will be enough to help them maintain muscle use until we can. Plus, I think we can get enough spin out of the module to affect blood flow, not enough for full gravity or child development, but enough to sustain organ health. It would be a mix of both artificial gravities. They'll need to follow a strict exercise routine too though."

"If she says it will work, I believe it will work," Chelsea interjected.

"Could they live five to ten years without us getting there?"

"I'm not comfortable with it, but if they followed a strict routine then perhaps," the translator said. "If they don't all go Jack Torrance on each other, that is."

"Can we have the hospital module ready in seven months," Kola asked Chelsea.

"If we move now, stretch our manpower thin, we could, but I'd feel better with a year," Chelsea explained.

"Can we hold off authorities for a year if they find a way in though, mom," Riley asked.

"You know," Kola said. "I think it's time we got ourselves a military adviser."

"I'll notify Adama," Riley replied.

"No," Kola said. "We need a real strategist."

"A dozen would be better," Shauna said.

Kola looked to the screens. "I think we're going to need you to get more involved down here," she said. "I can get two of you with the jet, can the rest of you get to your safehouses for extraction?"

They agreed. Then their screens went black.

"I'll get Shasta and Adama recalled," Riley said and began walking towards the stairs leading away from the observation deck.

"Riley," Kola said. "I don't need to tell you this isn't for Jim's ears."

"I know," and Riley was gone.

"Well, then," Shauna said. "What stateside options do we have for military leader potential?"

Chapter Thirty-one

Gerbil Mainstay stood in his doorway and recognized hidden agenda in front of him.

"Look," he said, holding up a hand to interrupt the survey. "I'm going to save you the trouble right now and tell you I still have the pull in Washington to make two soldiers' lives difficult if they don't get off my porch right now."

The soldiers dressed in jeans and t-shirts that said "Volunteers for Munger and Community" began to scribble down notes on their tablets.

"Be sure to write in your notes that if Colonel Whoever wants to follow up, he can contact his General and his General can run a background on me, and if the new director of the Central Intelligence decides he's authorized, then he and I and the director of the CIA can all sit down and discuss whatever it is he has a concern about. Now, get off my porch before I decide to learn who you two are."

The soldiers smirked at each other, made their notes to report the address for follow up, and then they left.

Gerbil turned back into his house and locked his door.

He walked to his couch where a black foldable dinner tray sat in front of it. His bowl of beer-cheese soup and a turkey sandwich waited for him. He sat down to eat, taking comfort in the soft shade cast by the dim, brown curtains from his living room drapes. With the remote, he snapped the television to life. It was an older television. He had kept it running ever since his grandpa said he could have it after he found it buried in a basement when he was seven years old. The old world of diodes and tubes had fascinated him ever since. Parts went out, but, so far, he'd not done too terribly in finding replacements. They could get expensive, but it was the first treasure he'd learned to build, so he kept it alive.

It was this skill that saved his regiment while he was in the Argentinian War. When all technology fails, never underestimate what may lie in the basement of the house you're hiding in. Chances are, it has an old radio that no one knows how to operate anymore.

The television snapped on and the colors gently warmed over the screen until they could blaze no brighter. He flipped through his streaming channels and settled on something old. He'd first thought about going with some old-school, black-and-white show. Then he decided on something old but not quite as so. He turned on *Die Hard*. He thought he had seen it when he was little when his grandfather came across it during a visit.

"This was my dad's favorite movie," his grandfather had said.

Gerbil finished his soup, ate his sandwich and then stretched out to watch his movie.

If Alice had been here, he couldn't have stretched out, but she was off to a better place now. It was difficult without her, but it was so much more difficult to watch her suffer. She wanted him to let her go. So, he did, and now he had the whole couch to himself. Before the movie was over, he fell asleep.

The phone woke him up. It was an old rotary dial, loud, retro, another marvel of technology of its time. It had cost him three thousand dollars, and, to date, he had changed the mouthpiece twice and the receiver three times over the past twenty years. He reached over and took up the handset mid-ring, and the chime lingered until he held it to his head.

"Hello," he said.

"Mr. Mainstay," the young man's voice said.

"Yup, I'll hold."

"Director Tra—oh—okay. One moment please."

Gerbil sat up on the couch and turned off the television.

"Gerbil, you dick and a half, how was *Die Hard*," Director Travis greeted.

"Not bad," Gerbil replied. "You ever see it."

"Not yet, but there's some magic to those old pieces aren't there? Listen, I got a flag across my desk, seems some low-ranking stooges tried to run your background."

"I told them to let their high-ranking stooge run that background," Gerbil replied.

"What you want me to do about this?"

"What do you think? Two weeks of grunt work enough time to help them to reflect," Gerbil asked.

"I mean about their commanding officer?"

"Who's that?"

"Their sergeant wants to follow up with you."

"Oh. You can tell him I don't follow up with anyone less than a director or cabinet member, you know that."

"I do," Travis said. "But they don't."

"Okay, give the sergeant kitchen detail too. Hell, give it to the colonel. I don't care, but no one gets into this house without proper clearance."

"I couldn't agree more," Travis said. "That's why I just spent the past hour pissing on a colonel and then a general."

"I'm sure they liked that."

"Not really, because now they called their boss and he's ordered you to meet with the general."

"Where?"

"Hartford."

"I don't go to Hartford unless I'm buying art."

"So take your wallet. Look. Go. Answer two or three of their dumbass questions and intimidate the general so they know to leave you alone and not waste the president's time, then leave."

"You got security for my house then? I'm not in the mood to find Alice's stuff thrown all over. I might have to kill someone."

"They have been duly informed that under no circumstance does anyone go inside that house if they don't want to be court-martialed."

"All right, I assume I'll get my ticket at the airport."

"Helicopter's coming for you, should be able to hear it about now."

Sure enough, Gerbil heard the blades of a familiar and important piece of machinery drawing closer to his house where it would set in a two acre back lawn and then carry him off to the very meetings he had been promised he'd never have to take part in again.

When the helicopter arrived in Hartford, he was immediately met by a Bentley.

"Mr. Mainstay," the driver said. "I'm to take you to your destination." She was polite, yet he assumed not to be underestimated.

The Bentley carried him to his meeting in a large house behind a gated driveway. The meeting itself lasted about fifteen minutes and consisted of Mr. Mainstay telling General Mince, who should have known him better, how much of his ass he could kiss, and if he ever attempted to investigate him again he would own him. Then he answered his questions.

"Have you ever noticed any strange comings and goings with your neighbors," Mince asked.

"I'm a former director of the Central Intelligence Agency, trained to see only strange behavior, what do you think?"

"Have you ever noticed people in your neighborhood who should not be there?"

"Yeah, two little bastards came to my door earlier today and wanted me to take a survey."

"Are you going to give me a straight answer?"

"Depends, what do you want to know?"

"Does your house accommodate any relation with Salvo?"

"No. Are we done? Good. Next time leave the inquisition to intelligence." He stood to leave. "I think serving two terms as a senator made you soft, General."

"We are not done. I ordered you here, I say when we're done. We are not done."

Gerbil glared at the general and knew at once he intimidated him in that moment. "Oh yes, we are. I came at the request of the president, not yours. And now we are done."

Gerbil left the office into a hallway that led to a foyer, which then led through a front door out of the house. Three soldiers and Gerbil's driver waited in the foyer.

"Detain Mr. Mainstay." General Mince ordered from behind Gerbil.

The officers moved towards Gerbil.

It was here that Gerbil's driver drew a silenced weapon, fired three shots and dropped all three soldiers before turning her firearm towards Mince.

"The hell is this," Gerbil asked turning suddenly to his driver.

She drew a second weapon and fired a blue dart filled with tranquilizer into Mince's chest.

"Your ass is mine," Mince said and then slowly dropped.

The driver retrieved the spent dart and sealed it safely into the pocket of her sports jacket then she withdrew a fresh one.

"So, what should we do with you," the driver asked.

Gerbil tried to read her but decided he couldn't. Something about her was off, not fully evil, although perhaps she might have come from it. He acknowledged his vulnerability with a nod and held up his forearm. "Will this do?"

"I'd prefer to do it in the car after you help me move him," the driver said.

He did as the driver requested and took a back seat in the Bently, where she finally shot him with the second tranquilizer dart.

When he awoke four hours later in the back of a golf cart surrounded by earthy walls, he was mystified. When he saw General Mince cuffed and bound while he himself was not, he began to take inventory of his surroundings. Then when a familiar hand set on his shoulder from the front seat, he no longer cared.

"Alice," he cried, and the golf cart stopped so the hugging couple wouldn't injure themselves. "I thought we agreed don't ever come back."

Alice was older than Gerbil. Her hair was silver, and she was happy, happier than he'd ever seen her. He'd heard of the safehouse, kept this secret to himself, killed the agent who brought him the news of it to his office; then eliminated all the other agents who knew anything about it. He destroyed the agency evidence and then stole his wife from the hospital that the judge had allowed their neighbors to force her into. After this rescue, he then weaned her off her over-medication. Then he delivered her to the safehouse, and she was gone. He never followed because he would be tracked. After he retired, his tracker was finally removed. Now, she was here and more the person he remembered from so long ago.

"It's better here," Alice said. "Safer."

The cart drove through the underground roadway, from Connecticut to Rhode Island, to show both Gerbil and Mince the hospital rocket.

"Why are you showing me this," Gerbil asked peering over the squat, fat module through its viewing area.

"I'm not showing you," Alice said, and she gestured towards the golf cart driver, who had also been the Bentley driver and had killed three soldiers. "This is the person who took me in. This is Salvo."

After remaining silent and focused on driving the entire time, Kola approached the couple at the window and exercised every bit of courtesy, without neglecting reservation, and held one hand to Gerbil and the other hand to her favorite pistol.

"Now that the military is snooping a little too closely, we could use some of your unique insight to help us complete our task," Kola said.

"You were there when we needed you," Gerbil said. "Whatever you need. I'll help."

"That's what I had hoped," Kola said. "Then we don't need him." She drew her pistol upon Mince who was still restrained.

"Wait," Gerbil politely begged.

Kola held her execution.

"If I'd have said no, would you have kept him?"

Kola didn't nod, but he assumed her answer was yes.

"Give him time," Gerbil said. "It's always good to have a second opinion. Maybe given time."

Kola turned to Mince, "That true. Are you willing to atone for the world of hurt you've caused?"

"Mince, General," Mince replied.

"Oh, shut up," Kola pistol whipped him then stuffed her silencer against one of his nostrils. "I'm not asking you for state secrets. I'm asking if you have it in you to help protect the Americans down here."

"Mince—

Kola pulled the hammer on her pistol. "Oh, we know very well who you are down here, General. Author of the Mince Act. Baby killer. Assassin. One might say you helped build this place." She held the barrel of her gun to the side of Mince's nose. "Now, is it worth losing your nose over refusing to answer the very simple question of whether you would help us or not?"

"Is 'go to hell' sufficent,'" Mince said. "Or do you need a 'no.'"

Kola drew the pistol away. "See, that wasn't so hard."

"They'll catch you. You're traitors and terrorists," Mince said.

"Doubt it," Kola replied, holding up a little baggy with a metal sliver inside. "We learned how to deactivate your tracking chip. But you made us. You might as well see what your handiwork could do." She left him tied in the back of the cart. Then they returned to a safehouse in Connecticut, one that had a helicopter waiting for Kola and her party in a field. The helicopter took them to a private jet waiting in another field in Pennsylvania. By morning, Kola had returned home. The moment they entered the city, she called two guards to General Mince's side. They released his bindings.

"Your jacket," Kola insisted, bending a hand to signal Mince to give it to her.

He hesitantly removed his coat filled with stars, insignias and awards. Mince almost didn't take it off but decided to against his better judgement.

"How long you're here is up to you," Kola said. "Try to leave, you'll be treated as a potential threat and killed on the spot. Try to hurt anyone, and you'll wish you'd have tried to leave instead. Say anything that upsets the peace and I'll melt all the metal on this jacket and pour it down your throat. You'll be given a room and some bedding."

"Careful," Mince said. "I could hang myself with a blanket."

"So," Kola replied. "Who'd care?"

"What good would I be to you then," Mince smirked.

Kola slipped her knife from her hidden sheath and moved on him. Mince's left pinky fell to the ground and he grabbed at his fresh wound. As he began to curse, Kola's knife was at his jugular.

"You're no good to me now," Kola said. "It's up to you if you decide you want to be. Until then, see our surgeon. Tomorrow, you start work."

"Work," Mince forced out. "With this?"

"Things aren't free here," Kola said. "The streets need sweeping."

She allowed Mince to pick up his finger and she nodded the guards to direct him off towards the hospital and stay with him. Then she went home.

"So, you decided to go anyway," Shauna said coldly as Kola entered the apartment. She was just washing her dishes from the day's use.

"I wanted to see it done right," Kola replied.

Shauna looked up from the sink and pointed a sudsy, white finger at Kola. "You don't get to do that, not without me you don't."

"I didn't want you to go."

"And what gives you that right? Huh? And don't even think of saying because you're Salvo."

"I'm sorry."

Shauna suddenly glared disapprovingly at Kola. "Don't you dare play me like that."

"It was not my intention to hurt you," Kola corrected.

"Better."

Shauna set her remaining glass on a dish towel to dry and began draining and cleaning the sink.

"I don't like almost losing you," Kola said.

"Oh, but it's okay for me to lose you," Shauna replied. "What are those standing outside our door right now? Bellhops? No, they're bodyguards. Your bodyguards. Not like you need them."

"It is okay for you to lose me," Kola said.

Shauna turned and started to prepare a rant, but Kola was now standing in front of her with her heterochromia eyes. Rare eyes and Beautiful, one was brown, the other green. They were dangerous and exciting eyes.

"Riley cannot be alone," Kola said.

Shauna's face softened into confusion.

"You're the better mom. You're the one that can love her. I'm the broken one. This mission was too important to ask anyone else to do. It's better if something happens to me than to you," Kola explained. "It can't happen to both of us. It can't happen to you."

"She loves you, and you've taught her to be strong."

"No," Kola corrected. "No, I teach her."

"That's enough!" Riley stood at the front door seething.

Neither Shauna nor Kola had even heard her enter, which naturally bothered Kola, reminded her that she must have felt too safe at home.

Riley turned to Jim who was standing right behind her. He was a nerd mostly: bad eyes, bad teeth, shorter than any respectable male specimen should be.

"Jim," Riley said. "Wait outside."

Like the loyal lapdog he was, he agreed, and Riley calmly closed the door after him.

"Neither of you get to die on me, do you understand," Riley dictated with a finger that hovered between her two mothers. Then it settled on Kola, "And you don't get to go running off without discussing it with us anymore, is that understood?"

"Riley, you know there are things I have to—

"Ever again!" Riley now stood before Kola, perhaps six inches over her but an inch less than Shauna. "You think I like wondering if my mom is going to come home from one of her soldier-of-fortune outings?" She lowered her finger and embraced Kola. "I don't know what my parents were like before you came across them, but I'd like to think they could have supported me half as much as you do, and from what I've been able to tell, they couldn't."

Kola clasped Riley back and, although she may not have realized it, the shame of her actions looked up to Shauna as if waving a white flag.

"I'm sorry," Kola said.

"Now, that one I believe," Shauna said and continued her work about the kitchen area.

"From now on," Riley said, "We make decisions about outings that can affect our family together. If you have to go somewhere, I'm going too."

"Like hell you are," Shauna said sternly.

"Either I get to go too, or no one gets to go," Riley said and then pulled away. "That's a more than fair request. Either its all of us or its none of us."

Shauna leered towards Kola.

"All right. That's a fair deal," Kola said. "I don't go unless everyone's going."

"Guess that means you're never going anywhere," Shauna said.

"Guess so."

Riley hugged Kola again and then Shauna.

"And just so you know," she said, returning to Kola and taking her hands. "You are more important to me than you will ever know. Your emotions may be invisible to you, but they're not to me. And I know my happiness is one of the most important things to you."

"Ah crap," Shauna said, realizing what Kola's face also showed it realized.

Riley recoiled in embarrassment of getting caught.

"Bad at emotions, good at reading them," Kola said. "I told you, I don't want a dog in the house."

"It's not that," Shauna said, squeezing Kola's arm.

"Huh," Kola asked. "What else could it—

"Jim wants to ask you if I can marry him," Riley said.

"Oh, no," Shauna replied. "You're seventeen."

Riley shot Shauna a look and said, "Really? And how old were you two when you got married?"

"Older than you."

"I'm almost eighteen, and I'm pretty sure since my birthday didn't start until the day you found me, I probably am eighteen."

"Is this really what you want," Kola said.

Riley nodded. "It's either him or a puppy."

"That's not funny." Kola began stripping the weapons from her person and handing them to Shauna, which Riley knew meant one thing.

"Thank you," Riley said, embracing Kola but stopping from hugging Shauna as she now held firearms and knives.

"Two years," Kola said.

"Huh?"

"You haven't known him long enough," Kola explained. "I'd really hate to have to kill your husband when this honeymoon period is over, and he decides he didn't really want all this luggage. So, two years and you will have my full support."

"Mom," Riley complained, looking to Shauna for support.

"Don't look at me," Shauna replied. "If it were up to me, you'd wait until we got to space."

"That could be ten years!"

"Two years," Kola said. "And I promise, I'll give you any kind of wedding you want."

Riley contemplated for a moment.

"He's also your first boyfriend," Shauna said.

"Everyone's afraid to date me," Riley replied sullenly.

"Who's afraid to date, you," Kola visciously inquired.

"I'm the next Salvo. Everything about me screams *death wish.*"

Kola guffawed, and it frightened Riley and Shauna. Kola caught herself, confused.

"Do not call Max!" Kola regained her composure. "I think what your mom's point is, is what if you realize you don't want to be with him."

Shauna nodded.

"Then we'd have to kill him, so you could be with who you really wanted to be with, and it wouldn't be Jim's fault," Kola said.

Riley looked stunned but not surprised. Then she agreed to the logic. "Two years," she said. "But that's all."

"I'm good with that," Kola said.

"Me too," Shauna said. "But no sleepovers, no babies."

"And no sex," Kola added. "Ever."

Riley chuckled to herself and relented. "No sex, ever," she said. "Unless someone better comes along in two years."

"Good," Shauna said. "Go get Jim so we can tell him 'no.'"

Riley returned to the door to retrieve her boyfriend who she'd met because he vacuumed the floors in their building.

"This is worse than a puppy," Kola said.

"If he calls me mom," Shauna whispered but didn't have to finish.

"We have two years," Kola replied. "If we can get to space by then, maybe he'll have a fault with a piece of his equipment." Then she suddenly turned to the door and released her phony charm. "Jim," Kola announced, gleefully welcoming him into their home. "Are you hungry? Have you had lunch yet?"

*   *   *

Ethics and press went out the window long before discussions on viral videos became what used to be known as above-the-fold stories. When it became a popularity contest, people stopped paying attention to free speech and prior restraint. They didn't exercise it, so they didn't know it. The media with the agenda that supported the politicians got the greatest freedom to publish.

Since the media did not support Munger, he had no qualms with walking into the press room that afternoon and spitting on the floor to let the reporters know what he thought of them before he stepped up to the podium of microphones.

Two reporters out of nineteen present held up recorders. Another took out a small notebook, while one more took a moment to look up from the crossword puzzle on his tablet before deciding there was nothing to get excited about. The others barely gave him any notice. It was okay, the unions said they only had to pay attention once a day.

Munger stood at the microphone, forced a fart and leaned against his elbows.

"A military general and a former CIA director disappeared yesterday, and several military personnel were found dead," Munger said. "Not that you care. Why would you?" He drew back from the podium and began to exit.

"Wait. What," a reporter from the back of the room who had not been paying attention asked.

"Go back to your circle-jerk," Munger said, shaking a loose fist at him.

"Are you serious about the kidnappings," the young reporter with the notebook asked.

"The deaths too," Munger said. "Oh, and I said 'disappeared' not 'kidnapped.'"

No more questions came, so Munger returned to the podium and kicked it off the stage.

Now, everyone paid attention.

"Can I get a copy of that video, Mel," one of the reporters asked, the one who had been solving a crossword on his tablet and who had decided he might as well start recording but didn't know why.

Munger walked off the stage and met Tyresa in the hall.

"A high-ranking official and a former one disappear, and the top story tonight will be President Munger throwing a temper tantrum," Munger said.

"Bad press is good press," Tyresa said.

Marcy Hamilton and Lucero Eleo, the two most important assistants in the White House, next to Munger's personal secretary, walked purposefully towards the president and his chief of staff.

"Please tell me Congress is going to start another war to spike the stock market," Munger said sarcastically.

"You need to come to the oval office, Mr. President," Lucero said.

"Of course, I do," Munger replied, then he led the way himself.

He entered the oval office and found Clinton sitting on a couch. He stood at once and waved a folder in Munger's face.

Munger took the folder and opened it to photos that he had seen a few weeks earlier of the earth. Fifty-three U.F.O.s leaving earth's atmosphere over the U.S.

"I've seen these," Munger said.

"Yes, Mr. President," Clinton replied, and he waited for Munger to sit in his usual, brown chair with bronze, decorative tacks. "But I have an idea."

"I believe I said let the local law-enforcement deal with it," Munger replied.

"Yes, Mr. President," Clinton said, but he leaned forward in the couch to speak anyway.

"What?" Munger knew he wasn't going to get any peace until he listened to his defense secretary.

"I was thinking about that message we got about Salvo with all the addresses," Clinton said.

"I'm getting a little tired of hearing that name, considering we don't even know if he's real," Munger replied.

"I noticed something in those messages we got years ago," Clinton explained. "It said, Salvo plans to conquer the heavens."

Munger stared unmoved at Clinton.

"We know these fifty-three images were flying objects, and we know they made it to orbit and burned up upon re-entry. What if this is Salvo trying to conquer the heavens," Clinton said.

Munger fell back in his chair and rubbed his temples.

"Mr. President, we can see a general vicinity of where they took off from," Clinton said. "We could check these areas faster than we could the entire state of Rhode Island."

"Have we found anything in Rhode Island," Munger asked.

"No sir."

"And if I send more military out to search these fifty-three vicinities, how many more resources will we need to expend?"

"A squad each should do it sir," Clinton said.

"That's what we said before." Then Munger gripped his rubber ball in his jacket pocket and thought about beaning it off Clinton's head.

"Finish searching Rhode Island first, and, if we find anything there, then we can talk."

"American soldiers were killed, sir."

"Then call their department heads and let them investigate, and when they come back with something definitive, we can talk again. Other than that, we have nothing telling us why the White House should be involved."

"But Mr. President—

"No more goose chases! Finish Rhode Island."

"Of course, Mr. President," Clinton said and then allowed Munger to excuse him.

Munger stared at the photos in his hands now.

"You know the media loves anything Salvo," Tyresa said. "Salvo and bigfoot, two legends that never die."

"If you can find a way to kill it, I'll endorse you to be president next term," Munger said.

"I'd rather have an endorsement from bigfoot," Tyresa replied.

"Well, if we find Salvo, maybe I'll feel lucky enough to track him down too."

"This will come back at you at some point, Mr. President," Tyresa said, reminding Munger of his reality.

Munger sighed, closed the folder and handed it to Tyresa to begin preparing her magic to respond to whatever came from it.

"Do you think if Salvo's real, he has to go through this crap," Munger asked.

"What crap would that be sir," Tyresa asked.

"Just wondering," Munger said, mostly to himself.

"Mr. President?"

"What do you think you'll do when my presidency is over," Munger asked.

"I suppose I'll have to get a real job, sir. You?"

"I don't know. We both know what the unemployment rate for former presidents is, and that's if you're a good one." Munger said.

"Maybe we could find Salvo and punch him in the face for ruining our options, Mr. President."

"Why do you assume it's a he," Munger asked.

"Don't you," Tyresa asked.

Munger sighed in the entire room. "I don't assume anything with fairy tales." He rubbed his eyes and leaned forward in his chair. "Why can't I get caught up in a good, old-fashioned intern scandal? I hear those were good days."

"Would you like me to find you an intern, sir," Tyresa asked.

"No. Just, if there's anything you can do to let me rest for thirty minutes, I'd appreciate that."

"Unfortunately, you have a meeting with Senator Winchessle in ten."

"Can you just tell him to go to hell for me," Munger asked.

"I'm afraid not, Mr. President," Tyresa said. "But I'll get on this Salvo issue at once, sir."

"Yay," Munger replied. He called to his secretary Miss Bamberger that he was ready for his next meeting when it came.

"I could cancel your meeting with the People for a Better People Society," Tyresa said. "Give you an hour nap."

"That would be great," Munger replied and sighed some expected relief. "See you then?"

"Well, I'm certainly not sending the intern," she saw the fatigue in his brow. "Mr. President?"

"When this is all over, let's take a vacation," Munger said.

"I'll schedule it as soon as our term is up," Tyresa said. "I'll pencil it in between looking for a job and re-evaluating what I want to be when I grow up."

"I'm serious," Munger said. "You and me. Nevermind. You don't want to."

"No," Tyresa said. "I'll go, but not now. You have a meeting," Tyresa left the room just as Miss Bamberger walked in to announce his appointment.

*   *   *

Salvo and her department heads looked to one of the glass walls that had shaded into a monitor and was now showing a map of the tunnel system beneath all of North America. Gerbil held a tablet and sat at the conference table.

"Currently your main defenses in the tunnels are your safehouses, smugglers and the simple fact that no one knows where to dig," Gerbil explained. "If anyone gets in the tunnels, you have your foam bombs, which although annoying, aren't difficult to dig through. You have rapid concrete filler, again only slowing down the inevitable if someone finds it, and you'll block off your own potential escape routes. Then there are your western tunnels."

"What do our western tunnels have," Tinker asked. "They're run down."

"They're dark," Gerbil said.

"We're getting there," Kola said.

"No. Gerbil said. "That's always a good defense. Intruders won't understand the coding. They won't be able to navigate."

"Except for anyone with night vision, right," Venice asked.

"Possibly," Gerbil replied. "But only until batteries run out. Depending on where they entered, they could be left wandering the tunnels for days, and its my understanding that the majority of this western section of network doesn't get used nearly as much for escape as they used to, due to the efficiency of the coastal state's early identification laws. This is where the foam bombs and rapid concrete filler would serve us the best; trap them in the tunnels, let their supplies run out, they'll be too weary to use any tools they bring that could help them get out."

"They could radio," one of the lower-ranked attorneys on the wall suggested.

The heads of the departments all turned unapprovingly to the man who spoke out of turn.

"Yes, they could," Gerbil said, not realizing that the attorney was considered out of order. "But there are ways to jam or interfere with that too."

"And VLF," Heather asked.

"You can interfere with very low frequencies too," Gerbil said. "Stronger LED lights in the powered sections can do that. So can a variety of jamming equipment and noise makers strategically placed throughout the dark sections. Foam bombs or rapid concrete at bottlenecks can also interfere with signals."

"Can we do that," Venice asked. "Do we have the manpower?"

"It would take a lot," Nancy said, quickly scanning her records of available residents for such a project. "But I think we could do it."

Kola looked to Heather and Chelsea. "Can you two hash those details out with Gerbil later."

They all three agreed.

"Keep going," Salvo invited.

"I would also recommend that we start training more of our own police force," Gerbil said.

"We can't ask the people we protect to start fighting," Thomas said. "We'd lose faith in the people."

"I think you underestimate the people," Severus said.

"We may not need as much as you think," Gerbil said. "Although they are some of our most obvious vulnerabilities, the safehouses are also strong defenses. Combined with any of our other defensive measures, they could resist invading forces long enough for one of your security squads to provide additional support in time."

"Our security squads are a little busy escorting people here who need us," Venice said.

"I'm sorry," Gerbil said, turning abruptly on Venice. "I don't know how everything works down here, yet, but I do know that independence is synonymous with loss of life. American soldiers will come here. One of our greatest weapons to stop them is to keep them from sharing any information they learn. That means prisons, death or give them nothing to see, which do you prefer."

"We can't spend our resources on prisons," Venice said.

"I agree," Ford added.

"Well, perhaps enemy soldiers will be sympathetic of that shortfall," Gerbil replied. "Otherwise, your defenses can deal death or give opposing forces nothing to see."

"Well, that's easy then. They don't see us now," Thomas said.

"Yes, they do," Chelsea said. "That's the problem. They saw us the day Ernie revealed some of our entry points."

"We keep them from seeing more," Gerbil said.

"Police training at our entry points, closing down some of these places, putting up radio jamming tools—all of these will help."

"That's not going to stop them all," Venice snorted.

"Exactly," Gerbil said. "And this is why we need to train a police force. While entry points can choke enemy forces, even an inexperienced sniper in the right tunnel can take out the best special forces wearing night vision because it paints the perfect target on the person's head wearing it, if you know what to look for. The advantage of tunnels is they can turn our enemy's technological weapons useless in them. We can fight with fewer numbers."

"Until they decide to nuke us," Thomas said. "Or bring in their own lights."

"Then we don't let them do that," Kola replied abruptly.

"We all know full-well that President Munger isn't going to authorize a nuclear strike on his own soil, not Munger anyway," Severus said. "He's a lot of things, be he's not a mass murderer."

"How will we train our police force," Venice asked. "We have security, but do we really have anyone who can train to military grade."

"We have more than you might think," Tinker said. He had been cracking corn nuts with his teeth and glaring mostly at Gerbil.

"I can check our records," Ford said.

"I mean we do have an army," Tinker said. "If we wanted it."

"I would prefer not to go back to my father's tyrannical system," Kola said. "These tunnels should be a place for refugees to feel safe, not a place to kowtow every time our smuggling crews pass." She, however, didn't want to downplay Tinker's ideas. He was rough around the edges ever since she'd met him the night she'd killed Salvo and his crew. Likewise, he never had fully forgiven her for being more important to Shauna than he was. "Do you think we should bring them here, Tinker?"

Tinker's face softened, but his jaw clenched then relaxed. "No, but maybe we should start thinking of how to implement them into any contingency operations. They are soldiers after all, and they are loyal to Salvo."

Kola shook her head, simply acknowledging she was willing to start such considerations.

"Speaking of plans," Gerbil said. "I think it's time to start thinking about your planetary withdrawal."

"We're not even close to being ready to launch yet," the engineer head, Aaron protested.

"How soon can you be?"

"We're not sure right now if the engines can sustain the module weight yet," Aaron said. "We've barely gotten 50% efficiency out of them for our simulators on our hospital module in Rhode Island, and if that thing fails, we will be absolutely buggered."

"It will work," Chelsea said.

"You don't know that," Aaron replied.

"I think I have some idea," Chelsea replied coolly.

"Regardless," Kola interrupted, then gestured to Gerbil to finish.

"As it stands, your current plan is to schedule a mass launch date," Gerbil said. "That's a huge risk to keeping the military from knowing more. If that plan leaks, the military could already be prepared to respond. So, I think it's important to keep a launch date under wraps."

"We currently have almost a hundred thousand thrusters on a list to be shipped to individuals throughout the United states. That's above and below ground," Aaron said. "How do you suggest we coordinate a blind launch and get to everyone?"

"You don't worry about everyone," Gerbil replied.

"That's not an option," Kola sounded off.

"What I mean is, I've been briefed on what these engines can do. You don't worry about everyone the first time. Instead of a date, you send a signal to the devices to let their passengers know the time is coming. Something simple like red, yellow and green. If it's green, they put it on. If they miss the green, they miss the launch, but they can get the next."

"It wouldn't work," Kola said. "Our plan requires all hands-on deck to help the assembly process once we have everyone in orbit."

"And that's exactly why I recommend that we prepare a proper evacuation protocol and proper contingencies, such as being able to assemble your station with a skeleton crew if needs be."

"How Skeleton," Madden asked.

"A tenth of what you're using now," Gerbil said. "Just in case."

"A tenth?"

"And that's just a start," Gerbil explained. "We'll need more."

"Such as," Kola asked.

"Phase one: seal off half of your tunnel entry points now but continue to allow in refugees, supplies and any mandatory personnel that you need for operations until enemy forces enter your underground. When these points are fully breached, start phase two, which would be a complete withdrawal of all personnel from the safehouses and seal off large sections of tunnels, recalling your people into individual communities or underground pods. That includes completely closing off your capital here. Phase three is a complete evacuation of all pods to their appropriate transport locations until launch is initiated. Red, yellow, green."

"If we close down our tunnels, our smuggling income can't continue," Tinker said. "We are going to need revenue even on our station until we can establish our own trade operations. We are still going to need an operational commerce down here."

"We could review the tunnel system to turn over the operations to your own cartel militaries after you've stopped bringing in new refugees. Seal off what tunnels we can survive without to protect your cities, while letting the cartel continue to operate your smuggling in the rest. Let your armies do what they do, while you do what you do and keep these people separate from them," Gerbil said.

Kola turned to Tinker. Tinker nodded.

"Should we consider shutting our doors to new refugees all together," Madden asked. "If they got caught underground before they got to one of our havens, the military would most rather kill them than carry them out."

"I actually agree with that," Gerbil said. "They'd be safer never coming in here right now, except—"

"Except a people seeking freedom are willing to face that death," Severus said.

"Just like I know anyone here would be willing to die to help another person escape," Gerbil said. "I know because I was willing to do that for my wife when I helped her come here. Which brings us to the casino."

"What about my casino," Madden said and quickly caught his error. "Salvo's casino."

"It's still an entry point, and immediate threat. If soldiers breach it, they'll be in the city faster than we can organize defensive measures. We need to implement a tactic to buy us time for escape or prepare defenses. I recommend either preparing the casino and hotel with explosives so military forces will have to dig through months of rubble."

"And bodies," Madden replied sternly. "And potentially the part of our city that falls in on it."

"Absolutely not," Kola said.

"Option two is to flood as much of the casino and hotel with concrete foam, while creating better evacuation measures for guests so they don't get trapped. Either way, people die if they don't get out of the building fast," Gerbil explained.

Madden groaned in displeasure.

"You have a choice," Gerbil said. "Protect your hotel guests or protect your people."

"Then let's hope it doesn't come to that," Madden said.

"If it comes to making that decision, I'll make it," Kola said.

Madden nodded his sullen gratitude and may have even appreciated Kola's role in this moment.

"Prepare the cement bombs," Kola said. "And whatever we do. We still need to consider how we can continue operations down here, in case things don't go to plan, and we can't launch. We still have a people to defend no matter what."

Kola turned to Severus, and he knew it was his turn.

"It sounds on the right track," Severus said. "But I'm concerned about the reality of a possible timeline. What is it?"

"Four to ten years to full station launch," Aaron said. "Four more months prepping the Rhode Island module alone."

"Three," Chelsea said. "We could achieve three years for full launch and four months prepping the hospital module."

"If you can call it a hospital module anymore," Aaron replied.

"You're on their radar, even if they don't know where to start. They'll be here well before then," Gerbil said. "And I would say you should have your hospital module prepared within a month, just in case someone gets lucky in Rhode Island or you get infiltrated."

"A month," both Chelsea and Aaron protested.

"That's our only hospital module," Aaron said. "We can't play roulette with it."

"Then I suggest you make sure you know which chamber has the bullet when you pull the trigger," Gerbil said. "It should be ready in a month, but that doesn't mean launch it in a month. It means minimal readiness in a month, they will be searching that vicinity of Rhode Island, and if they find it, they will stop it."

"So, we don't let them find it," Chelsea said.

"That's possible," Gerbil said. "We could bury the launch port, but if they scan it, and we need to launch it or lose it, we'll have all that debris to fly through, which I'm sure could damage chances of that module's survival. Or you could send a military force to intervene, which would severely speed up your calendar. At least if that one module launches, we could confine its specific tunnel network. Give the government something to study for months, possibly thinking that's all the tunnel there is. Get them focusing all their searches there and not somewhere else." He turned to Kola. "One month. We can interfere with military operations for one month once they stumble upon your module."

"How can you be sure," Kola asked.

"I think he's saying that's for my team to get to work on," Thomas said. He excused himself from the table and beckoned all but one of his staff of lawyers and legal aides to follow so they could start learning about any legal blocks they could put up if the military reached the land their module was hidden beneath.

"It's still not possible to be flight-ready, even stocked in a month," Aaron said.

"We could if we made it a priority," Chelsea replied. "Pulled everyone who could get to Rhode Island from their current construction and put them to work on the hospital module.

"Stop construction on all other modules for one," Madden asked.

"If we brought in the other site directors, it could help them all thinktank how to speed up their own module construction," Severus said to Kola. "We just have to be able to launch in a month. Doesn't mean we'll have to launch in a month."

"We could forgo on some of the construction the crew could perfom themselves in orbit," Aaron suggested. "That would help."

"It couldn't be anything big," Chelsea said. "We don't have time to write a construction manual, and the crew doesn't have extra time to add to their training as it is."

"Anything they can do up there, lightens the load here," Gerbil said.

"One month it is then. Make it a priority," Kola said. "And how long from hospital launch would you give us before we could no longer mass launch?"

"Conservatively speaking, she's right," Gerbil said, nodding to Chelsea. "Three years. Closing the hospital section of tunnels, forcing them to map them. They would have no reason to suspect more modules, but they could learn how to discover more."

"We can do three years," Chelsea said.

"But I'm not conservative, and neither will the president's advisers be, once you launch that hospital," Gerbil replied. "You should plan on two."

"Two years," the majority of the table groaned.

"At most," Gerbil said. "One would be better."

The table erupted.

"Friends, please," Severus said calmly, breaking the incredulities. "I think we agree that I'm not a rambunctious stallion anymore," and he was right. He was gray. His wrinkles ran deeper, many owed to Kola. "But if there's one thing I've learned, sometimes the only way to keep from blowing up is to stay with the bomb. Look what we've built so far."

"All right," Chelsea said. "Two years, but we'll think more on one."

Kola somehow felt a sort of solace in this number.

Chapter Thirty-two

Typically, nothing interesting happened with or at Pelosi High School. The teachers complained more than any group of educators in the state, and they complained about everything. Any time anyone tried to take advantage of their little, overpriced and superficial institutions, the underinformed teachers all barked and gnashed teeth. Of course, if anyone offered any kind of benefit to their tiny, pompous and ingratiating institution, the contentious teachers all barked and gnashed their teeth then too. The fact is, it didn't matter what anyone offered in ways of ideologies or tools for teachers or students, the entire institution had to bark and gnash their teeth at everything they heard. Because everyone knows a Pomeranian must bark and gnash teeth at absolutely everything that passes its front door, it was only obvious that their school mascot should be a Pomeranian, and it was no surprise that the fans of the opposing teams brought shock collars to wave from their seats,

Naturally, Pelosi High officials complained about that, but the other schools didn't care, they actually had lives. Pelosi High passed on grants to fund new computer labs. It fought against students who wanted to raise funds to buy new books. It resisted new desks, better lunches and just about anything else it needed. Then when there were no grants offered, the teachers fought for more money. Whatever the school needed or didn't need, it barked and growled and left everyone wondering why it was still standing.

This was why it gave President Munger great pride to ride past Pelosi High in the beast and know he was not speaking there. He thought about flipping it off, or better, mooning it, but that wasn't the type of person he was. In truth, the school just brought that kind of response from anyone who had to deal with it. Everyone walking past it wanted to drop their pants, smack their butts and blow an anal kiss in its direction. The students wanted to, but they had to attend. The parents wanted to, but the school had the power to become a prison if you made the administration mad. It made the president mad because he couldn't tear it down. No matter what he tried, it just kept operating and barking.

"Don't look at it," Tyresa said.

Munger looked at Tyresa shamefully, then down to a book in his hand, *The Yappy Snappy Puppy.* He bust up laughing.

Tyresa took the book from him and buried it into her own briefcase.

The beast pulled into the smaller parking lot for Session Heights Elementary. Three hours earlier, the small lot with its tight roundabout in the front of the two sets of doors was packed full of vehicles dropping off students. Now, the entire parking area was empty. The cars that would normally have filled it were moved to the streets or crammed behind the school.

The first SUV led the string of three security detail vehicles and the beast into the roundabout until President Munger's limo sat directly before the front doors.

Secret service stepped out, scanned the courtyard, the playgrounds, the parking lot. The special-agent-in-charge checked with those who had been assigned to monitor those sectors. She checked with the teams at both ends of the street, the teams monitoring the other side of the city block. She ensured the security detail on the school roof, and those watching from the highest floor windows of the surrounding residential houses were all in accordance that it would be safe to help Munger exit the vehicle. The final agents to check in were the two snipers above the school whose spotters hadn't stopped scanning, with their binoculars, even once over any spot that could hide an enemy gunman. The lead agent pulled Munger's door open.

Munger hated this part.

"Is this where a bullet finally hits me in the head," he always asked himself.

He followed his protocol: stayed behind the door; kept himself between an agent and the beast; and walked around the vehicle while his detail tried to make him appear natural and friendly to the public. Only there were no cameras today nor journalists or even people out front of the school. Still, there would be a story about something he did wrong with the way he climbed out of the car or the direction he positioned his toes as he walked.

They entered the school. Tyresa followed the detail and made a call to ensure that Munger's exit and next appointment would be on time.

The school foyer was large and doubled in its role for student assemblies. It was filled with children who all stood and cheered at the sight of the president. The teachers applauded, one or two of them authentically. A tall lanky man welcomed the President and introduced himself to the students.

"What do we say to the president of our country," Principal Vause asked.

"We love you, President Munger," the children announced.

"If you love him so much, why don't you marry him," nine-year-old Fabian Roscoe followed-up.

"Fabian," Principal Vause reprimanded. "Office now."

"I was only joking," Fabian said.

"Office, now."

Fabian walked off and turned to his two friends, Russ and Dennis. "Thanks for getting me in trouble guys!"

"Fabian."

"I'm going," Fabian groaned. "Gosh!"

"I'm sorry about that," Principal Vause said. "Please, this way."

He led Munger to the side of the Foyer to a small stage with two folding chairs. The president took the seat on his left, which was the wrong one. Watching his security throw their signals to each other, while the lead agent began speaking into her sleeve, reminded him that he had made his mistake, and decided he didn't care. This area of the foyer was blocked from view of anyone who might snipe him from outside.

Tyresa smiled at the children as she sat in the other chair, and then smiled at Munger, but he could tell when she was hiding her disappointment in his absent-mindedness. The foyer filled with shuffling of children as they all sat down on the bare floor according to their classroom sectors outlined on the glossy tile.

"Well, hello," Munger said. "How is everyone today?"

"Fine," the younger children replied in unison and the response petered out the older the classes became towards the back of the room.

"Are you having fun today?"

"Yeah," again, the kindergarteners led the charge in enthusiasm with their answers.

"Do you know why I'm here today," he asked.

"Are you gonna start a war," one of the kindergarteners, a tiny girl with thick-round, glasses asked, and Munger couldn't even get mad.

He laughed.

Tyresa smiled but shook her head in that subtle manner that told him that was the wrong way to respond.

"I'm here because this school has recorded listening to more audiobooks in the entire state than any other school."

"How neat is that," Tyresa asked.

"Are you his wife," One of the kindergarten boys asked from the first row.

"No," Tyresa replied. "I'm not his wife."

"Do you have sex?"

"Fabian!" Principal Vause marched towards the back of the auditorium in that way that all students knew someone was in trouble.

"What," Fabian asked innocently.

"I am the president's chief of staff," Tyresa answered, without skipping a beat, doing her best to hide her blush that she was sure only Munger recognized.

"Do you know what that means," Munger asked.

Tyresa smiled and, this time, used it to tell him not to ask these kids any more questions.

"Are you a native-American," one of the first graders asked.

"No," Tyresa said. "I'm in charge of all the people who work in the White House."

"I thought you were in charge of everyone," the little girl with large glasses asked president Munger.

"Well, I am the president, but it takes a lot of people to help me do my job, and Tyresa helps me make sure everyone does that," Munger replied.

Just then, Tyresa's phone buzzed, and she held it up to show it was ringing.

"See," she said. "Because I'm here, I can answer his phone and President Munger can keep talking to you. Excuse me, I'll be right back." She turned in her chair and began whispering.

"So, she's your secretary," some boy asked from the back.

"No, but I do have a secretary," Munger replied.

Tyresa leaned in close to whisper into Munger's ear. "Someone has just launched a rocket from Rhode Island into space, sir, a very large rocket."

Munger didn't even hear all the teasing gasps breathe through the children.

"Clint says it happened during their search for Salvo. They believe its Salvo. They found an abandoned network of tunnels. We should go."

"We can't just leave," Munger said.

"This will look bad to the people if you just stay here," Tyresa said.

"What do they think I'm going to do about it? Lasso the rocket and pull it back down? Let our people do their jobs. They don't need me in the way."

"You sure?"

Munger nodded, and pretended the children were more important at the moment.

*   *   *

The city streets erupted with cheers at the news. Friends clasped each other's backs, offered to buy beer for each other; and paid no attention to General Mince, who was trying to enjoy his one day off with a cheeseburger that he knew he shouldn't be eating but really wanted right now.

He wasn't sure, because he couldn't exactly remember every single burger that he'd had, but this joint may have possibly made the best one he'd ever chomped down on. It was greasy, messy greasy, just like he was told to stop eating right before he'd turned 57. Six years had been a long time to go without a piece of meat with cheese as beautiful as the one he held right now in a bocca bun.

The pat-pat, pat-pat, pat-pat, pat of the orange-head, push broom passed through the gutter. Ancel Dingle, an old man with a slow walk and an elbow that seemed locked into place, even when he wasn't pushing a broom, seemed the perfect fit for his job. His back curved just right over the handle, and his elbow slid back and forth to the rhythm of a pool shark lining up his shot at the table. He nodded to general Mince, didn't smile but noticed the prisoner's existence more than anyone else on the street seemed to regard Ancel's. A teenager, Nicky, followed behind with a rolling garbage can and shovel to help scoop up the large piles that the street sweeper would leave behind. He glared at Mince, would have killed him if he could. Mince could see that. Yet Nicky couldn't do it, not with Mince's bodyguards poised to protect him ten feet away.

Mince didn't have time to care really. It was his day off. So far, he had only taken one bite of the burger that the menu called Kay's Favorite, but he chewed and savored it as if it would be his last.

"I'm glad you approve of something around here," the young woman in her late twenties asked. She wiped a bench that curved around a yellow table. The way she bent catered to her pregnant belly, making her apron appear sharper than it really was.

"This is all I have to look forward to in this cesspool. I don't care if you're my favorite person here, Bayla. Don't ruin this for me," General Mince said.

"Oh," she cooed. "I'm your favorite person?"

"The only person I don't take pleasure in thinking about killing in this hell-hole of a prison," Mince said. "Now, let me enjoy this. I've earned it."

"Have you," Bayla asked. She took a paper cup that was half-filled with lemonade from the table and tossed it into the street where it exploded and rolled into the gutter.

"Not my shift tonight," Mince said. "Throw all you want out there. I'll probably toss this out there when I'm done too."

"You really are something, aren't you, General," Bayla said and started wiping the table with her wet hand towel.

Mince bit off a second bite of his burger and enjoyed this as much as the first, if not more.

"I don't get it," he said as he rudely chewed.

"Get what?"

"You're normal."

"Thanks? I think."

"I mean—look—you're not rude, don't treat anyone badly. You don't spout some of the nonsense politics I've heard others blather around here. Clearly, you have good upbringing."

"Where are we going with this," Bayla asked.

"How can a family like that turn their backs on the good old U.S. of A. and still make the best damned burger I've ever had?"

"I guess it had something to do with Kayla," Bayla replied.

"And who, pray tell, is Kayla," the general asked.

"That would be my twin sister," Bayla replied.

"Oh, there's another one in your wonderful, treasonous family?"

"No, a week after our fifth birthday, she had an operation, a present that her entire community worked so hard to make happen. During the operation, a nurse that we trusted notified local law-enforcement of our illegal behavior, and a detective under authority of your Mince Act put a bullet in Kayla's head before she could come out of anesthesiology."

"I'm sorry to hear that," Mince said.

"Are you," Bayla asked.

"It's unfortunate on so many when we have to realize that it's inhumane to force any individual to grow up knowing they'll be a burden on society. The Mince Act was intended to lighten that burden. I had to oversee many releases myself, and it was never easy. What kind of operation did she have? What was wrong with her?"

"Oh," Bayla said. "She had a sister attached to her hip. See?" Bayla lowered the side of her pants and raised her shirt enough to show the scar, then covered it again. "My treacherous parents brought me here so I wouldn't be a drain on society." She finished wiping her table and turned to Mince. "Let me know if you need anything else and enjoy your burger. It was Kay's favorite. We'll see you tomorrow."

She smiled, squeezed his shoulder in friendly demeanor, and returned to the kitchen to help her parents take orders and slave over a grill.

Mince stood. Suddenly, his burger didn't taste so great to him. All he could see was another Bayla. He'd come here every day off for this burger. He swept its street all the other days, and didn't care to eat with the masses after. She waited on him because no one else would. There was always more trash in the streets on his shift than the others, yet he still watched her throw trash in the receptacles. In fact, today was the first he remembered that she ever threw garbage into the street for the sweeper. She was also kind enough to bring him a cup of water to keep him going, and he was certain she didn't spit in it. Before coming here, he had personally authorized, overseen, even carried out the execution of many who didn't deserve to live life knowing they couldn't perform in society. He tossed what was left of his dinner into the trash can and decided to turn in for the day.

He was mostly home, made it into the hotel lobby.

"Good evening, Mr. Mince," the young concierge said politely. "I see you got a new guard. Hope our general isn't giving you too much trouble."

Mince suddenly stopped in front of the concierge desk.

"Can I help you, Mr. Mince," she asked.

"Why you here," he asked.

"It's my shift, sir," she replied. "Have I done something wrong?"

"No, I mean, why are you here. What brought you here? Here, to this place."

Her face tried to maintain a smile, but he could tell she was uncomfortable.

"Please," he said. "I'd like to know."

"Of course," she said, mostly stuttered, and kept trying to smile. "I'd like to not think about it, if that's okay, sir."

"I'm sorry," he said. "It was someone close to you, wasn't it?"

She started to cry but tried holding it, which only made her appear that she wanted to cry even more.

"It's okay ma'am," she said, trying her best not to show her emotion to whomever approached the desk. "I'm sure he doesn't mean any harm by it?"

Ma'am? He turned to see the guest, but he and his guards, both men, were the only other ones in the lobby, two of the same ones he'd had since he arrived. He turned back to the concierge, and she looked like she'd been caught doing something shamefully wrong.

"You don't have a female guard, do you," the concierge asked.

The general shook his head.

"Will there be anything else, sir."

"I don't understand."

"My apologies, Mr. Mince," she said politely.

"Help me understand, please," Mince said.

"Sir, please," she said. "I like my job."

"I'm sorry," Mince said and turned to leave.

"I see people who aren't there," she said reluctantly. "And there was nowhere for me to go."

"What about a hospital or a—

"Or an orchard?"

"You're from New California," Mince said.

"I escaped," she said. "A security guard helped me, even drove me and my mom across state lines. He was shot, but we got away. You may know my mother. She manages the hotel." She stopped and appeared unsure of herself. "Is that what you were looking for, sir?"

"I'm not sure." He thanked her and walked back out of the hotel. He stood there a moment. He no longer knew where he wanted to go and turned to one of the guards assigned to babysit him.

"What," the guard asked.

"What brought you here," Mince asked.

"Dyslexia," he said, taken aback by the question. "I was holding back the rest of the class. They labeled me as clinically unable to learn and gave my parents an order to sterilize me so I couldn't have children."

"So, you don't have children," Mince asked.

"I have three."

"Do they have dyslexia too then?"

"No, they're smart. Real damn smart."

The second guard joined the conversation with an annoyed sigh.

"What about you," Mince asked him.

"I was an anesthesiologist and worked from time-to-time in the newborn abortion ward," he said. "You know, told to kill babies born with obvious mental incumbrances or without life approval. One time, I put the gas to a little girl, and I could see that even she knew what I was doing was wrong."

"So, you brought her here instead," Mince observed.

"No," the guard said, hurt. "She'd already breathed in the poison. I foolishly tried to save her for five minutes, and she died terribly asking me why she had to. No government should tell any person to do that kind of a job. You know, the one minute of pay I earned on that job was more than enough to buy me a cheeseburger combo meal and a strawberry shake to help me cope with my conscience."

"Did it work?"

"No, but I went to the family, and, despite what I had done to break it up, they helped me. We worked together and eventually came here."

"Why don't you work in the hospital here?"

"I'll never work in a hospital again," the guard said. "People like you got me to violate human ethics."

"Why the questions," the first guard asked. "Feeling righteous?"

"No," Mince said. "I'm not. I'd like to talk to some more people here."

"Good luck with that," the second guard said.

"Will you help me?"

A six-seated taxi filled with shouting teens turned a corner. They shot cheap streamers from the ends of party poppers. One of the kids held a large, plastic tub of the tiny champagne bottles and they all kept pulling them out to fire them off.

"Hey!" The first guard stepped out into the street and stopped the cart. "Where'd you get those? You know explosives of any kind are forbidden down here."

The teens jubilation suddenly died down and they turned sheepish.

"I want some," he said.

The teens held up the plastic tub, and he pulled out three. Then he thanked the kids, laughed at them and fired one of them off and let them start cheering again.

He returned to Mince and the other guard and handed each a party-popper.

Mince took his and heard the soft pat-pat sound he knew he'd never be able to forget. As he turned towards the whisper of bristles, he watched Ancel turn his broom and start back into the street of celebration.

"Excuse me, we'll pick this up later," Mince said and chased after Ancel. He handed Ancel the popper and took his broom. He told Nicky to run along too and enjoy the celebration. He set brissle to street, built a small pile of streamers and returned to fetch the can and shovel. After he scooped up the streamers, he started building another pile.

The garbage can began wheeling behind him, and when he heard it over the smack of his broom, he turned to find one of his guards towing it. The other pulled the spare broom from the cage on the can and started sweeping next to Mince.

"We'll get done faster," the first guard said. "Then we can introduce you to some people."

Mince nodded his *thank you* and continued his work into the crowd of joy and mess-making.

*   *   *

The satellite turned towards the module that had risen into high orbit without the use of combustion, fire or fuel. This satellite tattled all it saw about the module down to earth. Its human controller back on the ground wanted to tell it to draw closer to the cylinder, but the most he could do was instruct it to turn its camera lens. This wasn't the only satellite that had turned its eye away from the world.

While Munger watched the video feed of the floating spaceship, he found himself secretly sad that he had missed what must have been a most spectacular launch.

"How big is that," he asked.

"We believe it to be more than 900 feet, sir," the voice on the phone said. It belonged to the Gangri Mallister, the director of American Space Program, currently vacationing in Toronto.

"How is this possible," Munger asked. "As far as we can tell, no combustion? No fuel?"

"Well, sir," Gangri said. "ASP's best guess is whoever built this developed some sort of anti-gravitational device."

"Anti-gravitational," Munger asked.

"Yes sir."

"No shit," Munger replied. "A frisbee is an anti-gravitational device! Show me why you're in charge of the largest scientific organization in the world?"

"I'm sorry, sir," Gangri replied. "What I meant is, someone's invented something we haven't seen before."

"What about those images we saw a few months back," Clinton asked. "Do they tell us anything more?"

"You're referring to the coordinated small rocket launch where they all burned up in orbit," Gangri said. "There's no way something that small could lift something this large."

"Can we get a more close-up view of it," Munger asked.

"Those photos should be on their way to you, Mr. President."

"I'd like to get some people on board, Mr. President," Clinton said.

Munger turned to his new staff member, General Hayden. "What do you think?"

"I can order an air to orbit launch immediately sir," Hayden said.

"Make it happen," Clinton said.

"Excuse me," Munger asked.

"I'm sorry, Mr. President," Clinton said.

"Mr. Mallister," Munger said poignantly. "What kind of danger could this thing pose to our troops, if we sent any up to investigate?"

"There could be many dangers, sir," Gangri said. "But from what we can see, we can't tell. We can't even see any evidence of what lifted it into orbit, sir."

"Mr. President," Hayden suggested. "I believe it is important to discover if this is a danger. I suggest a scouting party, sir."

"You want a potential suicide mission," Munger asked. "I refuse to allow that."

"We do need to learn, sir," Clinton said. "If we're going to launch an attack and reclaim that technology."

"Reclaim that technology," Munger asked. "It was never our technology. What you mean to say is steal that technology. You want to board someone else's invention and steal that technology."

"Yes, I do," Clinton snapped. "That represents a threat to the United States, which you are sworn to protect."

"I am also sworn to defend the Constitution, and the Constitution is very unclear on this matter," Munger replied.

"Mr. President, if you will not uphold your oath, I will have no choice but to notify the vice president and exercise—

"I would think very carefully with the threat you are about to make about over-throwing this presidency. There is a process here. If the government is seen just going out and taking other people's intellectual property, we lose faith in the people."

"So," Clinton said. "Screw the people. What do they know about defending the United States?"

"They just invented a way to launch a rocket into space that we haven't seen before. Strap that technology on a missile, and I'd say they know quite a bit about defending a country," Munger explained. "What you need to understand is we don't make our country safer by tearing down the little trust we do have with each other."

"And what you need to understand, with all due respect, Mr. President," Clinton shouted. "Is that if they decide to turn that technology against us—

"Then they'll be less likely to do so if we don't go about trying to steal it by attacking them," Munger returned sharply. "We absolutely do not know if they have any more of this technology. Are you confident that we could defend against that, if there's more? Because I'm not. Sometimes, you have to play the long game."

"So, we let them get away with it?"

"At some point, they've got to come down, and then you can write them as many citations as you want," Munger said. "Until then, we don't just go blindly shooting people at them in space."

"What about our military shuttle, then," Hayden asked.

"And what if that's a military shuttle up there? Are you ready to blow 40 billion dollars up? Do we have any reason to believe it's capable of posing a threat right now, Mr. Mallister?"

"Not as yet, Mr. President," Gangri replied.

"We observe for now," Munger ordered.

"Yes, Mr. President," Clinton said hatefully.

"However," Munger said returning to his conversation. "I am not against a scouting party, but I will not back a suicide mission. So, find another way. We have satellites. Can we use one to learn more."

"There is a problem with that," Gangri said. "The module seems to be positioning itself in geosynchronous earth orbit, Mr. President."

"What does that mean?"

"It means, it's really high up. To get to it, we would either have to lose some form of important communication with one of our satellites in the same orbit, or we'd have to steer a satellite from a lower orbit on prayers," Gangri said.

"And you want to send men up there," Munger said looking to Clinton.

"Sir," Gangri's voice crept from the phone. "We could use robot vacs to do it."

"I'm listening."

"With simple modifications, we could prepare some cheap, consumer robot vacuums to glue themselves to the hull of the vessel and map it for us. We could get a better idea of how its constructed, how to approach it more fully. We could prepare a few quickly and send them up with a satellite."

"And we can hit the mark?"

"If we plan it from launch, yes. It would be faster than building our own robots or sending up expensive scanners."

"How soon," Munger asked.

"We have a launch scheduled in seven days. We can have it all prepared and loaded by then."

"If we can do that, we can put men on it, right," Clinton asked.

"Sure," Gangri said. "If this was a suicide mission, but not if you wanted them to come back, not with this type of a rocket."

"I always said you should have never cut Astro Force funding," Hayden said.

"Hindsight's always twenty-twenty, isn't it," Munger replied. "Besides, everyone cut it."

"Yeah, well, everything seems stupid until you need it," Hayden said. "And now we need it."

Munger agreed.

"Mr. President," Tyresa announced from where she had held her silent post. "The rest of the cabinet is here."

Munger nodded. "Mr. Mallister, prepare the rocket."

*   *   *

The park was always peaceful, no matter what time of day it was. It was that one spot where people expected tranquil clarity. Security may have had to enforce it a time or two with newcomer teens, but, overall, it was expected that there would be no disruptive behavior. There were other places in the city for such outbursts.

Mince sat on a bench next to a small pond and tossed in some food pellets that sank to the bottom and awaited a blind cavefish to stumble across it. He'd met the man who found the fish. The man thought the city would enjoy them. He had come across creatures in one of the caverns on his way here and went back for them after the pond was built. He had no tools nor hooks, just his hands and Parkinson's.

The woman who dug the pond had lost her husband to cancer. He had once been a firefighter who was recognized by the governor of Texas for rescuing a mother and a daughter from an apartment complex above a shopping mall. He was a town hero. However, town heroes were not immune from cancer diagnoses nor the mandatory compassionate, doctor-assisted suicide that came with it. He was given more than enough of his dose of Compassion-elixir by a young twenty-four-year-old who had spent her young, adult life learning humanity from her cell phone rather than climbing trees. The inexperienced youth had finally figured out how to rebel against her elders without having any moral obligation to consider what they could learn from them.

The interesting part about this entire story was that the firefighter had actually been misdiagnosed. Another young person, a twenty-seven-year-old oncologist who graduated college and high school at the same time, and immediately went off to an online medical school without ever having to gain any real-world life experience, confused the records of a twenty-two-year-old woman with those of the firefighter's. That young woman is alive today, only because the wife of the firefighter used her own human and life-long connections to help her escape. They had purchased passage into the tunnels.

They dug and prepared the pond themselves shortly before the young woman died. She didn't leave much behind, just a pond that would ever contribute to her society any time someone needed a place to meditate upon the concept of life and lives.

Mince stared at a small placard, placed on a concrete, observation platform that jettied into the pond. He didn't have to read the sign anymore. He knew what it had said from reading it so much. He didn't have to, but he couldn't stop. Yesterday, alone, he had reviewed it for nearly two hours, and the day before that, three. It was a monument to all who had given their lives unnecessarily for those who didn't deserve it. Today, he read it from the bench, its words were engraved in his brain.

The "For those who could not" gave him pause. It seemed everything that he had learned in just these past few days had given him pause. Everyone he spoke to had a story. The lawn to this park was mowed by a man who was imprisoned for five years in Ohio for speaking out against the arrest of an entire family for refusing to get Macca-virus shots and an electronic tracking implant. The woman who planted the trees, had provided one for every child that the state of Washington had taken from her when she had given birth to sextuplets. Since parents were only allowed two children in Washington, her other four were euthanized at birth. After that, she had been forced to have three more abortions before her husband had died from complications to the mandated sterilization. She planted a tree for each of those people in her life as well.

The flowers were communally planted, placed by those who had lost loved ones. The UV lights overhead were maintained by a company owned by two brothers whose father had died in a car accident. Their mother was arrested for singing opera and annoying the neighbors. After her third offense, the three-strike law required imprisonment where her fellow inmates smothered her for snoring, and they used the Mince Act to successfully defend their actions. Every day, a group of young blind women watered the park flowers.

The gazebo was designed by a woman from Chicago whose son was beaten to death for being a cop. It was built by a man whose life the cop had saved a moment before mob-mentality said the cop behaved badly. It was cleaned daily by a man who had been doused in gasoline and then lit on fire by his students because he had the audacity to demonstrate how two opposing viewpoints could have merit.

Still, Mince stared at the plaque that stood twenty feet away and couldn't shake the "for those who could not."

"Are you all right," Riley asked, sneaking upon him.

He startled. "Oh yes, I'm fine."

"You're the general," she said.

"Yes," he replied.

"You were here yesterday and the day before, and the day before that," Riley said. "Are you sure you're okay?"

"I didn't realize my actions were so important that everyone needed to watch," he said and then began to excuse himself.

"Not everyone," Riley said. "I saw you once from the gazebo, another time from under that tree, twice from up there." She nodded to the top of the building in the center of the city park.

Mince followed the gaze and turned it back to Riley.

"I've seen you," he said.

"Most likely," she said. "My mother's, Salvo. She's not a fan of yours."

He appeared pained, felt pained—not because of the statement, but because he was beginning to feel the same way.

"Can I show you something," she asked.

He wanted to say "yes," but he was afraid to. He looked for his guards and realized he couldn't see them.

"They're still there," Riley said, then she motioned to her mothers who were in the gazebo. Shauna sat on the bench. She had an easel in front of her, a palette in her hand and a brush, which she angrily stroked across her canvas. Kola stood at the top of the steps and watched Mince closely, alert, deadly.

"I still wouldn't try to leave or do anything to hurt anyone," Riley continued. "I'd especially be careful not to do anything to look like you might try to hurt me. My mothers wouldn't like that very much."

"I wouldn't do anything," Mince said.

"Then can I show you something," Riley asked again. She started walking and turned back, "Come on."

Mince followed. Riley led him to a rosebush before the steps leading into the central, administration building and her home. The roses were a peach and white and the thorns were fat.

"This is mine," she said and pulled out a pair of hand-clippers. She snipped a few leaves that had grown outside of the smooth, vase-like shape that stood about three feet high. Two of the roses were allowed to sprout and fully bloom from its top, but a third had bloomed just that morning. Three buds stretched and prepared to open as well. Several small buds began to blister or had already cracked to allow more colorful petals to burst some day soon. She pointed to the other side of the administration building steps, to a similar bush in the same shape but which held pink and brown roses instead. "That's mine too. I planted these to remember my parents, even though I can't remember them."

"How's that," Mince asked.

"They were murdered by men in a place above ground where it was legal to hunt other humans. That's the gist of the story anyway," she explained. "I never had a grave to pay them respect. Didn't have an urn neither, so I planted these and shaped my own. I have a place to remember them and to know that something good came from them." She leaned in and smelled the new rose. "I got two new parents that day. They protect me and could have left me to die, my mom and my mom." Again, she gestured to both of her bushes with their roses blooming from the tops.

"Why are you showing me this," Mince asked. "I don't deserve it."

"I heard you were asking people their stories," Riley replied and then clipped the oldest rose, which happened to be white, from the top of her bush, so that only two bloomed roses stood above the urn. She began to snip away the thorns. "There are many ways to become deserving." She handed the rose to Mince. "One of them is to heal."

"Some wounds can't heal," Mince said.

"No," Riley said. "All wounds can heal. It's just some take far longer than others." In that moment, she couldn't help glancing to her mothers—specifically Kola—and taking some pride in her. Riley smiled to Mince and nodded a farewell. "Perhaps we'll talk again some time." She left him.

Mince stood at the bush for several minutes. When he turned around, the gazebo was empty except for Shauna's canvas, and Riley was gone. He'd thought that he should respect the privacy of her mother's art and even began to leave the garden with no plans to step foot onto the gazebo, but as he passed it, he was drawn to it. He had to look, first from a distance and then in closer. He glanced around for his guards. They were gone. Salvo was gone. No one seemed to be watching him. There were a few people lounging, walking, meditating in their own ways but none with eyes on him—at least, none that he could see.

He looked upon the canvas, which had been left sitting on the bench. It wasn't a great piece of art, he thought, but better than what he could do. The details weren't remarkable, but the image was clear: the back of a bench with a beaten, old man sitting in it. His shadow was blood across the ground. Before him was a pond of ghosts, and the blood spilled into the pond. Behind him was a child, no more than two or three, with her hand on his shoulder and handing him something, a flower. In the foreground stood a woman atop the gazebo steps, smiling, free, wearing a yellow sundress. She had gorgeous, bare legs and a straw hat in her hands. It didn't have to be beautiful to him, it was beautiful to the person who painted it. Yet, it was beautiful to him. He left the painting where it was.

Then he left the park, rushed mostly, maybe ran, he couldn't be sure. He found himself standing before the counter on the street that he had come to find that small amount of joy in every day off for dinner.

"General?" Bayla appeared astonished and waddled that familiar pregnant woman maneuver around the counter to him. "Mom," she called, and her mother knew exactly how to respond to step in to take over her daughter's absence.

Bayla led Mince to a table.

"What's happened," she asked. "Are you okay?"

She helped him to the only empty bench on the street. "Are you in trouble?"

She had barely sat down on the other end of the bench and asked if he wanted some water when he turned on her and hugged her, crying. The other tables watched now. A week ago, perhaps they wouldn't have cared, but today his endeavors to learn about them had become known.

"I'm so sorry," he cried, over her shoulder, and he kept saying it until it no longer sounded like any kind of language.

She didn't really know what to say, so she held the old man and patted the back of his head to let him know he wasn't alone.

At this point, two things happened. The first was that the third person involved in the embrace decided that she wanted out of her mother's belly. Bayla's grip tightened a moment around Mince, and he wasn't sure how to take it. It took him a moment to realize that if she'd wanted to kill him, she could have thought of something better than clenching his head and shoulder. He'd never had children, nor a wife. His career had been his wife. Women, sure, he had women in his life, but none important to charm him into matrimony nor motherhood. When her grip loosened enough to let him pull away. He realized she was in pain and that their bench was warm and wet.

"I'm sorry," she replied painfully.

"Wait. Now," Mince asked, then stood and, "Hey. Help. Uh! Baby." He waved to Bayla's parents. "You grandpamama. Hey! Help!"

Bayla's parents took immediate interest in what was happening and began to abandon the kitchen. The father started shutting off the grills and announced that they were closed.

Others began to gather close to the situation, but, before anyone could offer any aid, Mince had hefted Bayla into his arms and began turning on his heels. Once he gained his bearings to the direction of the hospital, he began marching off with her, her mother close behind now.

"Are you crazy," her mother called after him. "It's two blocks. Let me get a taxi."

A taxi abruptly jumped the curb and onto the sidewalk. Mince turned and placed Bayla inside. Her mother climbed into the seat behind hers.

"Okay, go," Mince said.

"What about dad," Bayla struggled to ask.

"He's not perfect, but he can find the hospital," her mother said.

"K, go," Mince said.

The taxi drove off even while Bayla did her best to thank him for his help, and Mince, for a moment, felt like something good had transpired that day.

Now, the second thing that had happened was that a particular pain had begun to build inside the old general. It was a cramp in Mince's arm that reached into his neck and chest, but he ignored it as he had assumed it was excitement of the moment and the consequence of having Bayla's weight in his arms. When he dropped her into the taxi, he had thought the pain was residual from the exertion. As the taxi drove off, and his chest tightened, and his heart clenched into a painful mash that paralyzed his every nerve, he knew it was something worse. He grabbed at his chest before he stumbled sideways and fell into the gutter.

He had dreams but didn't remember what they were. They were mostly voices and shapes that sometimes reflected them and sometimes didn't. Sometimes it was just black to him with sounds. When he awoke, he was in one of the dark hospital rooms, and he was alone.

Once he had the awareness to do so, he started searching the side of his bed for a button to call the staff but then wondered why he couldn't swallow. He sat for about ten minutes before he finally realized there was a tube in his mouth and decided to press the button to the side of his bed that would call help to him.

"Hey," a nurse called from down the hall. "Hey," he called again. "The general's up."

A doctor, a woman with one arm and in her thirties came in and placed her stethoscope into her ears.

"General," she greeted. Two nurses followed in behind her and moved about his bed to help make sure he was comfortable. "You're not supposed to go lifting pregnant women when you're having a heart attack, General," the doctor said. She listened to his chest, pulled away and glowered. In a few minutes, they removed the tube from his throat.

"You're not supposed to be eating cheeseburgers either, are you," she asked.

"Who says, it's cheeseburgers," Mince was able to say.

"Everyone knows it's cheeseburgers," she said, giving a scolding look. He let his shame show.

"Mr. Mince," Doctor Corona said. "You've suffered a severe heart attack. We had to perform some bypass surgery, but we can discuss that later. You're going to need to stay in bed for a few more days."

"You did this," he asked. "Why?"

"There's no law saying I can't treat patients who need me down here." A knock came to the door as she was checking his incisions.

"Is it true," Bayla asked peeking in from a wheelchair.

A male nurse pushed her in.

"She's been checking in constantly," Corona said.

It was only now that Mince was aware of the small, white bundle in Bayla's arms.

He tried to move, was forced down again.

"Can I at least turn to see the baby," Mince asked.

"General," Corona chided. "No."

Bayla stood and held the baby to him.

"Should she be standing," he asked.

"She's fine," Corona replied. "You're not."

"I'm fine," Bayla said.

Mince raised his hand to the baby and touched hers with his little finger, the only one not encumbered by the way a wire or hose tangled over his hand, the finger with a still fresh and tingling scar that had been married to him since the day it had been reattached after Kola cut it off. His pinky struggled to match the behavior of the rest on his hand, but it was the one that touched the baby's tiny arm before the others could.

"What's her name?"

"Kayla," she said.

Mince smiled.

"Kayla Mince Clarke."

Mince frowned.

"Nope," Bayla said. "No frowning. It's a good name, after two people who risked their lives so she could be here."

"It shouldn't have been any."

"No," Bayla said. "But it was."

Bayla sat back down in her chair. "Come see us when you're able. And no more cheeseburgers!"

The nurse wheeled her out of the room, just as another visitor appeared in the doorway.

"Aww," Riley said at once, upon seeing Kayla. "She's so beautiful. Congratulations, Bayla. I left something for her in your room. They told me you'd come in here, so I assumed he was awake."

"Let us know if you need anything," Corona said and recoiled her stethoscope around her neck.

"Can I have some water?"

Corona nodded, and one of the nurses who had been assisting him started to fill up a bottle in his sink for him.

Riley drew up to his bedside.

"When I said heal, I didn't mean go out and find a new way to injure yourself first," Riley said through a friendly smile that turned into a concerned purse.

The remaining nurse began to feed a straw to him, but Riley took it from her. "I've got it, thank you, Susan."

Susan left the room after making sure Mince's call button was in a comfortable reach for him.

Mince took a drink and, for a moment, thought he wanted to throw up.

"She needed a doctor," Mince said.

"Yes," Riley said. "But you're not a doctor." She offered him another drink, only to have him shake his head.

"She wouldn't have been allowed to have that baby outside because of me, you know," Mince replied.

"I know," Riley said. "I didn't have a permit either when I was born."

"That's why your parents were hunted, wasn't it? Because of you," Mince asked.

"No," Riley replied. "Because of you."

Mince winced at the remark. "Why are you here," he asked.

"I don't know," Riley said. "I figure I should at least get to know you before I start hating you like everyone else."

"And have you?"

"Not yet," Riley said. "Heal. Okay?"

"I can't pay for this, you know."

"Yes, you can." Riley said. "We transferred all your assets to our own accounts. It's standard procedure for anyone who comes here. Don't want the government or banks taking your money because they think you're dead, while we can put it to use instead."

"How? All my assets?"

"All of them. Don't worry. We have them and they're accruing interest. They'll be there if you ever need them, such as for surgical supplies. Allows us to put them to better use if we need."

Again, he started to feel like crying.

"Good," Riley said, placed her hand on his shoulder and nodded to add assurance. "Keep at it."

He nodded back and gripped her hand with his and painfully wished he hadn't.

"Can you ask your mother if I can have something from topside?"

"You want us to go shopping for you?"

"Something for the park," he said.

"All right." She held her tablet down to him and he wrote down a short list of requests. She drew the tablet up and looked it over then looked to him. "I'll see what I can do."

"He up," a familiar voice asked. It was one of Mince's guards.

"I'll talk to you later," Riley said then left, instructing the guard to let Mince rest.

"We'll come back tomorrow," the guard said.

Mince barely waved as Riley and the guard left, and he didn't have to wait long to fall back asleep.

*   *   *

Today, was the day they said he could go outside again, and he knew exactly what he wanted to do. He took his pills and stared his chest scar over before pulling his shirt on. He took the elevator down to the lobby and looked over to the casino beneath his feet.

"No," the young concierge said. "Smoke and alcohol, no."

"Actually, I was just wondering what's going to happen when there's no more casino in space," Mince replied.

"Who says there won't be a casino," the concierge said. She gestured to the front doors. "Your escorts are waiting for you."

"Escorts?"

His two guards stood watching for him. They waved through the glass front of the building.

"Someone needs to make sure you don't do something stupid on your first day out of the hotel," she said.

Mince made his way to the doors and met his guards on the street. They called a taxi and took it as close to the park as its tires were allowed to get.

He spotted Riley at once at the edge of a picket fence on the side of the garden closest to the residential district. A patch of ground had been tilled for him and she held a shovel.

"Good morning," she said. "Thought you would want this today."

"You got it," Mince asked. He saw the three plants with their roots wrapped in burlap sacks and reached for the shovel.

"You stop if anything feels wrong," Riley instructed. "Your babysitters tilled the ground to make it soft for you." She handed him the shovel.

Mince set to digging. He took it slowly, unsure of what to expect, but he kept at it. Once he started to sweat and breathe slightly heavier, one of his guards took the shovel and finished digging the first hole. The other guard dug his second. Mince insisted he dig the final one, which he did. The cavities were all set about three feet apart.

With help, he knelt and took in a deep breath.

"I'm good," he said. He then set to unwrapping the burlap from a bush with a blue lilac burst and planted it in one of the two backside holes. He filled in the soil and packed it down. The second bush held buds for a small pink lilac. He pressed it into place too. Lastly, for the one pit in the foreground, he placed a white and pink bleeding heart that currently bloomed a single bead of blossoms.

When he was done, he sat back on his knees, and finally felt he might actually have done something to build a people rather than tear it down.

"What's it mean," Riley asked.

"They say lilacs are great for helping people remember," Mince said. "Maybe if people smell them, maybe someone can remember a person I helped take away from them, all the men and women, and boys and girls and little babies."

He broke into sobs.

Riley knelt next to him. "And what's that?"

"Not enough," Mince said. He wiped his face dry and asked his guards to help him to his feet. He turned to Riley and, with some help from his guards, stood straight. "If your mom's interested, I'd like to help now."

Riley smiled. "All right," she said. "I'll go tell her."

Chapter Thirty-three

General Mince was allowed to keep his title with Salvo, and she granted him an advisory seat alongside Gerbil Mainstay. They had a seat at the table only when they needed to speak. Otherwise, they sat in row with the lawyers.

Kola now needed Mince to speak, and he took a place with the department heads.

"Are you even fit anymore, General," Tinker asked. "I mean this is a bit outside your expertise of killing us all off."

Mince was instantly stung.

"I'd like to hear it please," Kola said.

No one objected.

"Thank you, Madam Salvo." Mince could see Kola's head tilt, not much, but enough that he could tell that she'd been displeased at the comment. The average person wouldn't have seen it, but Mince had been an interrogator for ten years of his military career. She probably didn't even know she'd done it. "I apologize, I've been trained to—

"Not necessary," Kola interrupted. "Continue."

"Of course, uh, ma'am. I've seen the defense plan laid out by Mr. Mainstay, and it is good, but um, with utmost respect to his work, it's not great," Mince said.

"Excuse me, Salvo, you know every single one of us supports you at this table, but do we really want to trust this man," Venice asked. Some of the others in the room agreed.

"If I may," Gerbil requested, and waited for what appeared to be approval from the majority in the room to continue. "I've discussed this in depth with Mince, and I do agree with him. I understand your reservations towards him, but he is a general for a reason, and I do have a history with knowing his work. I do not get the sense that he is trying to mislead us. He is, I promise you, one of the best tacticians I've ever studied."

After, Gerbil took back to his seat, the others gave Mince a silent permission to continue.

"Mr. Mainstay's plan is effective to buy you time to hunker down long enough to find an escape door out of your sanctuary. The problem is that when you lock the doors to your castle so the mob can't get in, and they light the place on fire, they're already outside when you climb out the window," Mince explained. "Our defense strategy needs to be an escape strategy. We need to let them peek in while we're sneaking out."

"You're suggesting we let them into our house," Kola said.

"Yes," Mince replied, and the table erupted with objections. "But-but. Please," he tried to speak. "On our terms so we can control it. If we control it, we can direct it."

"How," Venice asked. "We know it's only a matter of time before they get here."

"Yes," Mince said. "But I know the players who will develop and authorize the plan to attack when the time comes. Just as I know that Director of Defense Clinton Myers takes a nuclear solution approach, I also know President Munger is conservative and calculates every little move. He won't do anything unless someone can actually put evidence pointing to you in his hand. Myers and Munger will keep each other in check, at least until Myers or someone threatens a vice-presidential intervention.

"Knowing Munger, his attention is on the module that was launched not long ago. He'll drag his feet to investigate or authorize a manhunt if he has no evidence to tie to Salvo, but he'll spend another month analyzing the tunnels connected to the silo. The first tunnel that he came across ended in dead ends, and that pissed him off a little. This system from Connecticut to Rhode Island is larger, but you've sealed it off, so it's also a dead end. I believe he'll question whether he's dealing with domestic terrorist cells.

"If that happens, he'll call for an intelligence briefing on any and all domestic cells that the government can say for certainty exist. They'll study and discuss this for some time. Honestly, we could have probably manipulated events to keep the White House away from us until Munger left office, but you went and launched a module into space and now we have no choice but to join it before your crew runs out of willpower and supplies."

"They have gardens and small animal livestock. If that ever becomes a problem, we can always send up another module for supplies," Venice said.

"And we've prepared their module to defend against physiological problems," Chelsea added.

"Yes, but once you send a second module, Munger won't have any reason to behave so conservatively with the military anymore, and they'll be forced to adapt defenses to take any future launch attempts down. Right now, they most likely think that there is no way any other rocket could exist. The cost is too astronomical. Launch a second, however, and they'll put money into artillery that can bring anything next down. I promise, some of your personal engines will get to space, but there will be no modules to pick their passengers up because they'll all be blown out of the sky."

"Unless," Kola asked.

"I recommend we prepare every entry point to your underground railroad as laid out in Gerbil's plan, but we only put up enough of a fight to keep insurgents out of the tunnels long enough to make it appear as if we're a weaker ragtag group of revolutionists who are giving up ground. A few ammo clips, some flash bangs and booby traps can slow the military down, but allow our people to reach safety."

"You mean our people," Madden sad coldly.

"Yes," Mince surrendered. "And I think we should let the military get their hands on enough of a map of the tunnels to let them see just how big of an investment this operation would cost Munger."

"He means to convince us to let them walk right in and take us all," Thomas screeched.

"If we only give them an entrance, they'll only send small groups of soldiers and they won't send enough," Mince replied. "We need hordes of military in here. We show them every possible escape route, every entrance in every state and they'll have to coordinate the largest military movement to prevent us from using them. That's the only way we can get them to swarm. They can't bury us in, because they know we can just dig our way out. Our only escape routes can be the modules and engines."

"Our only escape routes," Madden erupted. "You make it sound as if you think you're coming with us."

"Madden," Kola warned. "Stop."

"They could use a bunker buster," Tinker said. "Take out an entire one of our cities."

"They could do more than that," Mince explained. "They could drop super bunker busters and gas these tunnels."

"And you think that's what we should gamble with," Madden asked.

"That's why we need to let them in as their first option. They're not going to gas or bomb their own troops. Even if they didn't have troops, they won't fire on American soil," Mince said. "Munger would be branded a war criminal, but even that has limitations to being upheld."

"I don't like it," Chelsea said. "Letting them see where we are?"

"We put faulty maps near every tunnel entrance," Mince said. "We show them enough of the tunnels to get them get lost. And if we do it right, by the time they actually get deep enough to catch on, our modules and engines will be ready to launch. By the time they got out, we'd be out of range, and to bomb us would mean to bomb their own military. We can remove our cities from the maps entirely. They'll never find us."

"It's a death warrant," Aaron said.

"Everyone here has already signed that warrant," Mince countered. "Death warrants are central to revolution. This way, there will be far fewer executioners to carry them out."

The table was silent, angry too. They turned to Kola.

"Severus," Kola asked.

"During World War II, a small squad of black U.S. soldiers sat in a house directing artillery at German forces that had overrun a village in what used to be Italy," Severus said after a moment of contemplation. "This is significant because Hitler had convinced his nation that these kinds of people were less than human and cowards because of the color of their skin. They radioed artillery bombardments on the enemy, and, each time they did, the Germans retreated closer to the house. As the German forces continued to gather near the American outpost, this small group of soldiers decided the only way to stop the Germans was to call the artillery right down upon themselves. The last command from these soldiers was "fire it." Because of this sacrifice, German forces were destroyed, and Americans were able to retake the village for Italy.

"I think if General Mince wanted to betray us, he could come up with a better plan than think we'd be so stupid as to let him march captors in and take us. I think it would be wise to consider that we may very well have to put ourselves in striking distance of destruction if we really want to escape."

"That doesn't scare the hell out of you," Venice blurted.

"We've been scared before. We'll be scared again. It's part of the package," Severus said. He looked inquisitively at Mince. "But I think we'd feel better if you demonstrated some good-faith on your part."

"Like what," Mince asked.

"Perhaps if we could get our hands on something that would deliver a particularly attention-grabbing bang to fight back with."

"You mean missiles," Mince asked. "It's possible. What kind would you like?"

"The kind we would never build," Kola said.

"And the kind you'd never want anyone getting their hands on," Severus added.

"You'd never be able to access them," Mince said.

"Try me," Chelsea replied, her voice crackled as she realized that she had just helped administer General Mince's true test, possibly his death warrant.

Part Six:

Armageddon

Chapter Thirty-four

Majesty VII launched as was planned from Cape Canaveral. Its cargo contained supplies for the International Space Station, four satellites and four robot vacuums. Their suction motors had been removed and replaced with thrusters and enough fuel to direct them to the hospital module. The wheels had been coated with a sticky adhesive to allow the robots to roll over enough of the module surface and help understand its construction better. Each robot had been fitted with sensors and fuel. The original plan was to put small explosives within them, as Clinton Myers had thought it best to have an emergency response in case the module appeared to be a threat.

Munger, however, did not approve of sending an explosive device to any space capsule holding American lives. This was, as he put it, an act that could be deemed as an attack on the U.S. people by their own government, and he wouldn't allow that. When Clinton threw one of his tantrums, Munger threatened to have him removed from his post permanently. The department of defense, therefore, withdrew his plan of attack. Instead, he instructed ASP to imbed drills into the rotor housings so they could puncture the hull of the space pod. This, he did not inform the president about, believing the president would yet again kowtow to the petty, potential concerns of the public.

When the ASP rocket reached low orbit, it separated into its various cargo compartments, which all sped away to their appropriate destinations. As the ninth hour since take-off transpired, the pod carrying the modified vacuums approached the hospital module. Here, the ASP on-board navigational computer guessed the distance and speed of Salvo's space vehicle, then it adjusted its course appropriately.

What it did not account for was the variable known as the plastic pipe that was in the housing of the hospital module, and that this tube was guided under the direction of its own defensive operating system. When the hospital-module computer became alerted to the approaching capsule holding little robots, it told a dart to enter the tube. The pipe extended and took aim on the approaching pod of vacuums. After the operating system ran its math, an impressive puff of air from the oxygen generators shot the dart from the pipe.

The dart followed its 700-mile course and punctured into the approaching robot-filled pod, sealing the hole it had created upon entering it. Simultaneously, a needle within the dart punctured a small, heavily pressurized canister within itself. The gaseous contents of Salvo's little barb abruptly filled the inside of the ASP pod, and, after five seconds on its timer, the dart exploded. Within the pod, the explosion was an intense wave of heat and pressure that instantly melted all internal plastics and contents. Outside, the explosion was hardly noticeable. One moment, the pod was secure and sure in its heading towards the hospital module. The next, it looked like an exhausted firecracker.

*   *   *

Clinton Myers seethed at the president. It was all he could do to keep from throwing his briefcase at the man.

"Something you want to say, Myers," Munger asked.

"Oh, I've got plenty I want to say, Mr. President," Clinton said. "If we'd have done what I suggested in the first place, we wouldn't be in this situation."

"If we'd have done what you wanted," Munger said. "Those would have been dead soldiers instead of vacuum cleaners. Rule number one of negotiation, don't force yourself into the room."

"Rule number one of facing your enemy," Clinton said. "Dominate with the very first move."

Munger's blue rubber ball bounced off Clinton's head, surprising Clinton.

"See that," Munger said. "I just dominated, and it wasn't the first move. Shall I demonstrate again?"

Tyresa had followed Munger's ball and handed it back to the president—not because she was his lapdog, but because she actually wanted to see him bounce it off Clinton's head again.

"Well, we know one thing don't we, Mr. President," General Hayden replied. "We know these are dangerous people."

"Damn straight they are," Clinton said. He was more cautious as he realized he caught Munger's eye. "They have attacked us."

"They defended themselves from us in orbit," Munger said then turned to Alex Pardo, U.S. Attorney General, who had been sitting quietly. "You want to take this one?"

"Space isn't sovereign," Alex said. "Launching a pod into space with the intent to study a spacecraft and destroy it is open to consequence of space law, and space law, as far as any country on Earth is concerned, is that no one can lay legal claim to any part of it. Your intrusion could very simply be viewed as a threat to the people on that rocket. You invited this, and any complaints need to be taken up with the sovereign nation to which the spacecraft originated, which would be the United States of America. In other words, you have conspired to attack your own country contrary to the orders of your Commander-in-chief. I'd personally shoot you for treason, and, yes, we know about the drills."

"And as President of the United States of America, which you are not, I have decided that I don't want a national incident funded by our own taxpayer dollars over a spaceship that has to come down some time," Munger said.

"So, you're not going to do anything," Clinton asked.

"If you want to go up and try talking to them, go ahead," Munger replied. "But you have to pay for the fuel."

"Can we at least continue our investigation of the Rhode Island tunnels we found linked to the launch point," Clinton asked. "We should at least be thorough about what's going on in and below our own soil."

Munger approved General Hayden to overlook a continued investigation of the Rhode Island underground, and put on a deadline of two months to complete it.

"I don't want this eating resources anymore, if we don't find anything in two months, I want our military returned to where they can actually do some good."

When the two months had finally passed, Munger ordered that the military withdraw all operations above and below ground. Their search of Rhode Island had turned up no other tunnels except those connected to the barren launch tube and Connecticut. Because they too led to dead ends, there was nothing for them to find, which naturally pleased Clinton Myers almost as much as the nail he'd once had go through his big toe. To celebrate, he went to a high-end bar.

Myers drank. He tried to hide that he had been drinking, but he was a bit of an amateur in that arena. Salvo had preoccupied his mind nearly every second of the day, it seemed. A rocket in space! They sent a rocket into space and the United States put up not one single bit of a fight to stop it. He knew it upset Hayden and the other generals as well. Munger was worthless, and that's what Myers told himself as he continued to drink himself a little angrier with each swallow. Perhaps it was time for a good old presidential assassination.

He leaned over the black bar, saw his reflection in the onyx countertop and realized the sight of himself made him sick. He would have thrown up, but he needed to drink more to do that.

A fat woman squeezed beside him and asked the bartender for a boiler maker and a godmother. While she waited, she turned to Myers and smiled the kind of confident smile he didn't want to see from that kind of a woman with that many hidden rolls because he just knew she didn't have any hot friends. Both of those drinks were hers.

"I'm Wanda," she said.

He nodded back, the kind of nod with a smile that said, "fuck you," all while he was trying to not say "fuck you." She took her drinks and slid away. He tried not to watch her, but he did, and her date wasn't half bad looking. Part of him wanted to march over to the guy and punch him just to make sure he could still tell what ugly coming his way looked like. He downed his black Russian, ordered another and stared at himself in the bar some more.

None of this Salvo nonsense would have gone on as it had if Myers had been given a longer leash. He knew it was Salvo. He knew Salvo was real, and that Munger just needed to see that, but there was nothing, and the bar revealed nothing new to Clinton.

Another woman slid beside. This one wasn't bad, the perfect combination of fake and silicone from head to toe, and she didn't order a drink.

"Go ahead, buy me what I like," she said, squaring up the line of her cleavage with the longitudinal fissure in his brain that separated intelligence from "duh, your boobies has pretty."

"Hey," Myers called after the bartender. "Give the lady a—

"Screwdriver," she said, not a bit subtle about the screw, nor who she wanted the driver to be.

"Ah," Clinton said. He got the hint. That's all he needed, get the cow out of his way and start focusing on what he could do with this beauty who clearly got enhancements to hide what had once been a smaller but very real set of ta-tas. Why else would a woman get silicone if not to cover up the real ones that came first? Then, he felt his facetious brain take over. "Ah damn it!"

He stood, signaled to the bartender to tab his drinks and he stormed out. A cab took him to his office in the pentagon where he had the authority to search for any document or history of documents that he wanted, and he definitely sought a particular set of them.

When morning came, he was sitting back in that oval room debriefing the president on the previous day's analyses of events.

"Mr. President," he said—smiling as he did, so much that it unnerved Munger.

"I would like to recommend a new plan of attack on Salvo," he said.

Munger disapproved instantly, and was ready to quash the idea, but Clinton was prepared to move faster.

"It occurred to me last night that maybe we're going about this all wrong. When we received the messages identifying every single address in the world as possible safehouses, they came in a string of them and spread out in intervals," Clinton explained.

"We still can't do anything with every address in the nation," Munger said.

"We won't need to, Mr. President," Clinton continued. "What if the string of messages was meant to cover up the real ones."

"Why would they reveal any of them," Munger asked.

"Maybe someone on the inside of Salvo's crew didn't like him," Myers said. "Maybe the only way Salvo could think to bury the evidence was to saturate us with more."

"I'm familiar with the tactic," Munger said.

"That would mean the first message containing addresses was correct," General Hayden asked.

"I believe so, yes," Clinton replied.

"Except, if I remember correctly," Munger remembered. "Every vlogger near these addresses broadcast that they were frauds, broke into their houses, stirred a commotion. Law-enforcement took a stand and notified their locales that the string of addresses were hoaxes."

"I think that was the hoax," Clinton said. "Salvo didn't just bury the addresses; he has his own mass media control. If they lied, then we not only have suspects with relation to Salvo, who can be questioned, but we also have real addresses of safehouses still."

"And if you're wrong, it's another wild goose chase," Munger said. "I've had enough of those."

"One agent. That's all I'm asking," Clinton said, holding a good, old-fashioned piece of paper to the president. "You pick one address, and if our person doesn't find anything, you'll never hear me utter another word about Salvo again."

Munger thoughtfully took the stack and began to peruse them. He turned to Tyresa and asked if she had a pen. Of course, she did. He circled one of the addresses and handed the papers back to Clinton, who was all too happy to receive them and begin his work.

"Meanwhile, we'll start gathering background on any vlogger that had something to do with broadcasting these houses were empty," Clinton replied.

Munger denied that particular action until they had actually verified the address was a safehouse.

*   *   *

In Boulder Colorado, Tammy Englewood and her husband Jerry went for a run at 5 a.m. on a Wednesday morning. They tried to put in a ten-mile day on Wednesdays before their lives started.

There was nothing out of the ordinary for the day. As usual, Jerry forgot his water pack and had to unlock the door to run back inside the house and retrieve it. Tammy avoided chiding him as the effect had worn off by now. They saw no one on the streets at this time of morning, no one on the trail that broke away from the city boundary and looped through a park. As always, they circled the park twice, stopping to refill their water once, before heading back home.

It was a good day, a solid run as usual.

What wasn't usual was that, upon returning, an unfamiliar sedan sat in their driveway in front of their garage, and the front house door was open. They continued running past their own residence, hoping no one would notice them. They passed, jogged another two miles to a park-and-ride lot at a nearby bus station, and activated the Salvo, home-intrusion alarm within a vehicle that had been maintained and reserved for their escape, just as had been set up for every other home on that list of addresses that Ernest had sent out. Then they drove to their emergency house in Grand Junction.

While they were escaping, Agent Olivia Patterson had tried to serve her search warrant, only to find the residents not at home. She began her search with an x-ray scanner in the living room and found nothing. There wasn't anything in the kitchen, nor in the two bedrooms and one bath on this floor.

In the basement, she had the same outcome, every wall was solid. Anything that could move had nothing secret hidden behind it. The floor offered no hollow betrayal. In case there was something faulty with her scanning equipment, for an hour more, she peeked behind pictures, moved bookcases, lifted beds and couches. The attic was empty. She scanned all interior walls again. No reason to bother X-raying exterior walls. The mere fact that windows were in these demonstrated they were too slim for people to hide within them. The fact the tunnels were underground suggested any hidden passages should be in the basement. In the end, she decided that the house was empty.

She checked the yard next, no hidden cellar, no playground equipment to hide a door beneath, just lawn and flowers. She strolled the entire enclosure with her x-ray machine and found no sign of a hole or covered cellar. Using a sledgehammer, she trekked the full yard a second time while dropping the hammer every two feet to listen for any sort of hollow sound that could suggest any kind of hidden entrance.

There was nothing.

Four hours later, she dialed the pentagon as she roamed the back house exterior one last time to contemplate if it was possible that she missed anything. As the phone began to ring, she looked up to the house and cursed how it had wasted her entire morning and afternoon. Now she'd have to write a report on the entire event of nothing happening.

She felt somewhat badly now for tearing into such a simple, yet beautiful home. It was open inside, airy. It had brick, which wasn't her favorite, but it was an attractive green stone that she somehow found settled well with her. She didn't care, however, for the white brick that trimmed the windows the foundation and the chimney of the house. White brick was nasty and got filthy easily—and this house didn't have fireplaces!

So, why did it have a chimney?

Olivia returned to the inside of the house, scanned the exterior wall, and realized that the hollow of the chimney appeared just as the empty space of house exterior. The wall over the chimney on the main floor showed nothing to access it. Downstairs was a complete concrete wall. On a second scan, she realized that the reason the x-ray didn't pick anything up here was because the basement, on the chimney side, had been purposely recessed seven feet from the rest of the house's structure so as to hide whatever was behind it from scanners. That left the top floor, again.

Back to the top, what she had assumed wouldn't reveal an entry, was a piece of white wood paneling that held itself to the wall with a magnetic seal. After prying it away, she found the entrance to the chimney and a ladder down.

She retrieved a flashlight from her vehicle then descended the ladder. Sixty feet down the chimney, she found herself in a cavern strung with bare incandescent bulbs that traveled in two directions. Her first instinct was to follow the tunnel, but she had read the report from those who had entered trenches before and were sealed in concrete and foam. She decided better of the situation and searched only the immediate vicinity beneath the entrance.

A map on the wall drew her attention quickly. It presented a system of passages that spanned about three miles from where she stood. She snapped several photos of the map, whole and in sections, then made a video of it before returning to Tammy and Jerry's house. She had thought about tearing the map down entirely and taking it as evidence, but she didn't want to tip the owners off that someone who shouldn't be in the tunnels had just found a map to them. Yet, something about the map called her to look behind it, which was where she found the small shelf-sized alcove engraved into the earth. Within the shelf, was a binder that contained what she believed was every house that connected to this tunnel system in Colorado.

She notified the Pentagon at once and cleared out of the house before its owners could discover her.

Clinton Myers returned with her discoveries to the president, informing him of all Olivia had learned. He presented her photos and video of the map.

"We can send in troops now," Clinton said.

"We need to be careful," Munger explained, examining the photos that agent Patterson had taken of the map. "Think of the technology we've seen them use and look at all these exit points. If we handle this wrong, they could simply slip away."

"We have tunnels beneath our soil," Clinton said. "That's a very real and immediate threat to our national security."

"Yes, and if anyone escapes those tunnels, they could still be a threat but from somewhere else. I don't want to take any chances on this," Munger replied. "Where are the homeowners?"

"The residents weren't home," Clinton said. "We're looking for them now."

"Prepare some possible scenarios," Munger said. "Play it right, don't rush it. They don't know we know. We have time to plan. Let's verify this addresses on that Colorado list. Be stealth. No clues." Munger circled an address in one of Olivia's photos. "If there's another tunnel here, see if they have a similar record of Colorado addresses. If there is one, let us assume then that we should find similar binders of entry point locations for each state within the original addresses that first leaked out to the public. If we have those, we may discover every entry and potential escape point, and more maps. If this is Salvo, I want to take these tunnels and every entry point—all of them, no chance for failure here, no chance to let these people escape."

"That's going to require a lot of men, sir," Clinton said. "The soldiers it would take to storm these tunnels, across the entire nation."

"What? After all your complaining, now you don't want to be aggressive?"

"Of course not, Mr. President," Clinton objected. "I'm just saying it will take a lot of resources, more than what Rhode Island took."

Munger threw his ball for several minutes, then suddenly stopped and returned to the conversation smiling.

"When it comes to our own soil, we should withhold no military power," Munger said. "I won't have terrorists dwelling beneath us. I think it's time we show Salvo our full American military strength."

"Yes, Mr. President," Clinton said. "I should suggest that we can seal tunnels with explosives to limit our manpower."

"No," Munger denied. "No explosives of any kind under our people or lands. I will not detonate bombs on our soil. Find these people and arrest them or kill them. Besides, they'd probably just dig their way through anything we collapsed anyway."

Chapter Thirty-five

The tunnel entry points sustained gunfire on an average of ten minutes, enough time for those who monitored the safehouses to escape. As the stewards had been prepared for the invasion, their exits went mostly well. Residents and business owners who were present during the invasion got out. Those who were not retreated by various methods to other safe areas to await possible launch. Salvo's automatic turrets bought another half a day as American troops were ordered to withdraw until specialists could measure just how to go about disarming them.

Flashbangs, it turned out, prevented the turret at each entry point from seeing the intruders, and military personnel were able to use that weakness to disable the machine guns. One hundred troops, armed with silenced weapons entered each safehouse and filed into the black tunnels, separating into various clusters of mazes. Another fifty troops entered each area to secure any possible exit that any sneaky terrorist might try to use to escape.

In every city where a safehouse had been located, troops amassed for nothing short of invasion of their own land. Munger had ordered that they secure the tunnels with every possible soldier, robot and dog. Clinton Myers and General Hayden suggested they consider the entire scenario could be a trap and that it might be wise to keep half of their resources outside to catch any that might try to escape.

Munger agreed it was a wise decision for now.

Operation: Ant storm was under way. The hunt for Salvo and his cartel began.

Meanwhile, the hospital module high in Geosynchronous orbit fired another dart.

*   *   *

The young woman approached the security gate with her military grade pack over her back. It was heavy, bulky, entirely conspicuous.

"Ma'am," the guard said, stepping out of the gate, his hand open to stop her. "Can I help you?"

"Yes," the woman said. "I have vital information for the military operations taking place right now beneath American soil. I need to speak to the president immediately."

"What is your name," the officer asked.

"My name is I speak only to the president of the United States," she replied.

"That's not happening," the guard said. "Step away from the gate."

"Oh, I think it will happen," she replied and then revealed two six-inch cylinders in her hands. She flipped the metal cap on each one up and slid her thumbs over the buttons they concealed. A string of green lights flared up the sides of the canisters, and she placed her fingers over some of them.

The officer drew his weapon, and the woman knew she already had more rifles aimed upon her than they were ready to reveal. Perhaps two dozen guards and special agents appeared over the White House lawn and driveway, all prepared to open fire upon the woman.

"Ground! Now," Officers began to order, and several came up from the sides of the walkways and from behind her on the streets. Cars sped to the curb, squealed to stops and parked. Doors opened, officers and secret service agents continued to command her to her knees.

The time to speak her demands was not now. Any one of these officers could decide to mistake her actions as an immediate threat and shoot before it was time. She slowly knelt. From here, she followed the instruction to lay flat on her belly.

The officers hovered over her bag, inspecting, careful not to touch it.

"Suspect is in hand," one of the agents said. "Possible explosive device on premises, secure Bruce Wayne."

One of the agents knelt beside the woman and inspected the devices in her hands.

"What are they," he asked.

"Dead man switches," she replied.

"What kind of explosives are you carrying," he asked.

"None on my person," she replied. "But I am currently in control of explosive devices if I don't see the president. What's in the bag is for him. I told you, I have vital military information concerning operations underground right now."

"Scan the bag for explosives and remove it," the agent ordered.

"I wouldn't do that," she said. "It's on a switch too."

"What do these switches control," the agent asked.

"A variety of missiles and nuclear warheads aimed at locations all throughout the United States, including the White House, the pentagon, seven state capital buildings, three residential areas and one Canadian province, currently hostile to the U.S. right now," she said and then announced, "And you're going to relay that information to the other officers, then you're going to put your guns away, and I'm going to stand up."

"You're going to stay down," the officer said.

"I understand," she said. "I was told you'd need proof." She pressed her pinky against one of the green lights.

"What was that," the agent asked pressing his sidearm against the side of her head.

"A small verification that you want to remove your gun from my head right now," she answered.

"Call them off," he ordered.

"Can't."

"I will shoot you!"

"Then my entire sampler of missiles will launch, and I do have them."

The roar of rockets rumbled overhead.

"I'd tell your officers to remove their aim in case the explosions make their trigger fingers twitch and inadvertently cause my grip to loosen here," she said.

"Those are Gerrymanders," one of the secret service said.

"Better hurry," she said. "It's about to get loud."

"Fingers off the triggers," the agent shouted. "Fingers off the triggers. Lower your weapons. Deadman's switch. Repeat! Fingers off your triggers. She's on a dead man's switch."

The first missile struck the Lincoln Memorial Reflecting Pool blasting water, mud, and mortar over the park, harming no one with anything other than blast and noise trauma. The second missile, however, struck the base of the Washington Monument, and the devastation did take lives of people in and around the falling structure and debris. The third Gerrymander struck the back lot of the D.C. Zoo, disabling the *Seal and Walrus Hologram Arena* and destroying the *Oceanic Animatronics Exhibit* where two real leatherback turtles were having sex.

As the explosions echoed and distant screams began to flow towards the streets, the woman looked to the secret service agent beside her. "I'm standing up now, and you better make sure I'm safe."

"Stand down," the agent said. "She's standing. Repeat stand down. She has dead man switches attached to multiple missiles. Do not. I repeat, do not shoot her."

She stood and turned to the gate officer.

"You will not point a gun at me again. I am not here to kill the president," she said. "But if I don't see him, I'll use my entire arsenal, including thirteen nukes, to send large groups of people to a place where they won't need a president, and I'll send another to start a war you won't be able to win. Now, are you going to let me in, or would you like me to try opening the gates myself while I'm holding these things."

Sirens rang from the distance: police, fire, ambulance.

"That's the sound this entire country's going to hear today, if you don't make the right choice," she said. "That is, if there's anyone left to turn those sirens on. I've still got plenty more button combinations I can push."

Just then, the canisters in her hands screamed.

"You should know," she said. "This dead man's switch is also a dead signal switch, jam it, the signal stops. Try to hijack and it's over. As I stand here, the receiver is constantly checking fifty-three verification points to ensure I am still in control. One of these is DNA verification, another is my pulse. Might want to tell your tech staff trying to disable my signal that that's strike two."

The second set of missile rumblings came from the sky. The first struck the Lincoln memorial dead on.

"No reason to pay tribute to a president who abolished slavery anymore in this country," she said. The second missile struck the front façade of the Library of Congress, while the third struck a half a mile down Pennsylvania Avenue.

"I would seriously tell your people to stop trying to voodoo my triggers, because next time I call a nuke."

The agent nodded as if he had just heard something in his ear to suggest the voices in his head had responded to her threat.

"Might I point out that twice you've activated my defenses, so open the gate because I only want to speak to the president and save your military."

"Tell you what," the agent said. "You deactivate the triggers and I'll see what I can do."

"That's sweet of you," she said. "But we can't build a relationship on lies."

The officer redirected his weapon on the woman once more, mostly out of frustration in not knowing what else to do.

"I told you not to do that," she replied. "I'm so sorry."

At this, the agent's body crumpled beneath him as a bullet lobbed by a sniper a mile out came in down through the top of his cranium and peeled it apart upon entry.

"Are you starting to get this," she asked. "Do not exercise any potential threat at me, and that includes the sniper on the roof who's about to end up like him if she doesn't put her gun down now."

The agents and guards suddenly stood back, reacting less to her than to the authority figure on the scene. The gate began to fold open, and a woman dressed in a white suit made her way down the steps and then towards the bomber at the gates.

Tyresa approached.

"The president will see you on the south lawn, if you'll follow me," Tyresa said, but she didn't quite start leading the woman away yet. "Trust, right?"

The bomber nodded. "I have no intention of killing the president. I just need to show him what's in this pack. It will save many lives."

"What is it," Tyresa tactfully asked.

"President only," the woman replied.

Tyresa was still hesitant.

"Trust," the woman said. "Right?"

Tyresa conceded and began to lead the woman along the north drive of the White House. Neither spoke. The looks of fear and hatred from the agents they passed made it clear that the bomber had disarmed the staff, as they had to listen helplessly to the continued rise in screams of sirens and people in the streets. The guards at the front gates had, in fact, been forced to turn their attention towards the frightened public and away from the woman in control of thirteen nuclear missiles, even as she approached the very person they were sworn to protect. The officers were resigned to the fact that this had become the only way to protect him.

*   *   *

After the initial 100 troops entered each of the 247 safe entry points into Salvo's tunnels, and then an additional 50 troops followed to secure control, Salvo's automatic turrets intiated a firefight below ground that required the withdrawal of forces until specialists could examine the defenses and develop a plan to disarm them. This added several hours to the operation, but the U.S. forces did take control of all defensive turrets at each entry point.

The U.S. military then released gas, which did very little because Salvo had suggested the installation of fans and ventilation to blow fume attacks back towards the entry points.

Like the turrets, they forced the military to locate and disable the fans as well, delaying their incursion, for another six hours.

General Hayden dispatched another 50 HAZMAT troops to each entry point to specifically track and disable ventilation measures.

Along the southern and northern borders of the U.S., using the maps that the Central Intelligence Agency had provided, government leaders were able to track down the locations of the fifty-seven additional entrances that led in and out of the country. In a concerted effort, military engineer teams smashed these in with heavy equipment then dug their own entry positions towards the United states.

Within 36 hours, the military excursion had spread throughout every entry sector of the catacombs. Within forty-eight, the first report of a potential underground encampment had been found. In reality, it was one of Salvo's smuggler camps, and this one was armed with gas, automated weapons, grenades and trained cartel soldiers. It was enough to turn the sector into a kill box, wipe out an entire invading squad and send waves of emotions throughout the entrenched military. It was enough to drive U.S. soldiers' need for revenge to prevent them from thinking the best. Hayden, under authorization from Munger to take over the battle, gave the order to send in the additional 500 to 2,000 troops at each entry to join the hunt and swarm the caves. If Salvo wanted a fight, he was going to get one.

Once Salvo's own snipers began shooting out military lighting and using the white targets painted across the faces of soldiers wearing night-vision goggles and glasses, the military scrambled to avoid the attacks. This reaction caused many militants and their bands of brothers to forget which tunnels they had previously used and the directions they had followed to get to where they were.

Salvo's snipers retreated to their appropriate communities, using tunnels that weren't on the maps.

At the reports of the attacks, Hayden sent in an additional 100,000 reserve officers to bolster his own confidence. Enemy gunfire meant they were close to pinpointing a specific place of impact where a single deep-earth, bunker-buster could echo a message throughout Salvo's communities that surrender was the only option. The explosion underground would be massive but controlled. Any damage to civilian property could be easily repaired, once the residents had all been evacuated from their homes above the blast zone.

*   *   *

President Munger awaited his nuclear guest on the south lawn. Marine One's blades were already spinning, in light of the missile attacks. He was in the process of being rushed to escape the White House when he finally ordered that the presidency would continue whether he was that president or not, and it wasn't worth the cost of the threat.

"You want to try negotiating with this terrorist," Tyresa had asked.

"We negotiate with terrorists all the time," Munger then replied. "Especially when they've just climbed the ranks of domestic superpower."

"Then I'm staying too," she demanded. "I go where you go."

"I was hoping you would," he replied before sending Tyresa to escort the woman onto the White House grounds.

As Tyresa and the woman with the missiles approached, Munger tried to hide the fear, but she saw it. He was nervous. Tyresa knew him. She was every bit just as frightened, watching him await the intruding guest. Yet, something in the way he looked at the woman with the bomb suggested he wasn't nearly as afraid of her as he was of the situation itself.

"Tell your lady friend on that roof to take her hand off the trigger," the woman said.

"It's not aimed at you," Munger said. "The bullet is for me."

The missile-wielding woman nodded her understanding. "Well, then, if the president dies, I have no reason to hold these anymore, and the need to preserve government secrets won't very much matter after that."

Munger held his breath a moment at the reality.

"Did you hear that," he finally asked.

"Stand down all arms on Bruce Wayne," he heard the command through his own earpiece.

Next, the missile-toting woman ordered all personnel off the roof and lawns except for Tyresa and President Munger. The woman directed themselves closer to Marine One, where the helicopter blades blasted white noise upon them.

"Are they able to hear you now," the woman with the bomb asked, yelling.

"Can anyone hear me," Munger asked. "Can you hear me? I'm asking, never mind."

He turned to the woman and said, "no they can't." Suddenly, his face widened into realization. "Riley? They sent you?"

"New rule. Mom can't come alone anymore," Riley replied. "Sorry for the theatrics. You kind of forced our hand."

Tyresa turned to president Munger, "Mr. President." She dropped from formality into intimacy. "Max? You know this woman?"

"I bought her a doughnut once," Max said. "It's a long story. Will you trust me, T?"

Tyresa found herself nodding that she would, although she didn't know why. Actually, she did, but she still thought it was a foolish reason to.

"Will you come home with me," Max asked.

"Home?"

"Help a lot of people rebuild what should have never been broken," Max explained.

"I don't understand."

"It's okay," Max reassured. "Will you come with me."

Tyresa found herself nodding.

Riley now turned to Tyresa and instructed her how to disconnect her pack without setting off any booby traps. Tyresa did so by first entering the proper code into the number pad midway up Riley's shoulder strap.

"Inside this bag are two suits, please put them on," she continued to yell over the chopper blades, then, seeing Tyresa's distrust added, "This technology will protect you."

Munger nodded his approval and took a golden, sheer clump of plastic-like fabric from the bag—somewhat rigid, yet also soft and foldable.

"Might want to take your shoes off," Riley said.

President Munger removed his black, cap toes, then opened the golden one-piece and stepped into it. As he did, he further encouraged Tyresa to do the same. Tyresa immediately kicked off her white stilettos and drew her own golden suit. The clothing zipped up, and a magnetic strip covered the zipper and held to the fabric. The sticky substance on this magnetic surface immediately began fusing until it had become airtight.

"There are three attachments in that bag," Riley instructed. "We each need one."

"Don't you need a suit," Max asked.

"Already wearing mine," Riley pressed her fist at her collar to show the strip of gold beneath it. "But I'd appreciate if you could help me strip my outerwear off."

Tyresa and Munger helped to undress Riley down to her gold inner-wear, which wasn't too difficult as they found all that she had been wearing over it had been crafted with Velcro to pull apart for just this point in their discussion.

Riley instructed Tyresa to pull out one of the attachments, an oval device with straps. It was about the size of a tall beer can.

"It's not a bomb," Riley said. "I promise, all of this is strictly for your protection."

Tyresa acknowledged and continued following Riley's instructions, attaching the device to a strange belt within the suit that felt more steel than plastic.

Riley then reached back and pressed at the device latched behind her. It split into two halves, an upper and lower. The top half separated and slid around her waist on the belt so that she now had a circular thruster at her front and back.

Riley then asked Tyresa to draw a hood from a small pouch in the back of Riley's own collar. It zipped and the magnetic strip began sealing. The plastic window over her face started to turn a yellow shade. Munger and Tyresa pulled their own hoods over their faces, then attached and prepared their own engines as Riley's had been.

Now, Riley pointed to Marine One.

"Can we get rid of the chopper blades," she asked, and her voice spoke clearly through the small speakers in Tyresa's and Max's hoods.

Max waved at the pilot and the marines who had been forced to retreat back inside the chopper at Riley's orders to clear the lawn. Marine One lifted slowly and departed.

Riley then pointed to the device in front of her.

"See the lights," she said. "Press the green one."

President Maximillian Munger pressed his.

Tyresa felt something she hadn't before, anxiety. She'd heard about it. She'd seen it. She felt her chest tremble and her breaths started to shoot out but only pretended to draw back in. Perhaps it was the mask, although closed spaces never got to her before. She was fearless, always had been. Give her a room of terrorists with guns pointed at her, and she'd speak well enough to leave the room alive. She couldn't bring herself to press the button.

Max placed his hand on hers.

"Max," she asked. "How do we know these will stand up to a nuclear blast?"

"It's okay," Max said. "Trust me. I've been attached to a bomb before. Besides, that's not what these are for."

Tyresa pressed her button but fumbled in trying to do so.

Finally, Riley hit hers.

"Riley," Max asked.

"Yes, Mr. President?"

"Where is your mother?"

But Riley didn't get to answer as the devices attached at all three of their waists burst with power and tore their feet away from the earth, building their speeds up to the 18,000 miles per hour necessary to lift them out of their world's atmosphere.

As they climbed higher, Munger could see other sparse, golden reflections over the D.C. area climb towards the heavens. The suit had clenched along his spine and neck, preventing him from shaking or snapping his bones. What he could see of skies over Delaware and Pennsylvania all held scattered specks of the same flecks of gold glitter that were other flight suits, climbing with him.

*   *   *

"Thrusters are away," the man announced from his sector.

Here, Chelsea, like all the others within the marble and throughout the various places within the command module, sat strapped with her back towards the gravitational pull of the earth. She stared at the curvature of the ceiling over her head with the images of sky and potential obstacles, which were far fewer now. Commercial airlines had immediately been grounded to the nearest airstrips after the attacks in D.C.

Military craft scrambled, but their armed forces had mostly been called to infiltrate Salvo's tunnels. Only enough pilots remained behind to rally to the unlikely defense of American airspace from foreign attacks, particularly near the coasts and boarders. These pilots that remained didn't provide nearly the obstacle count as the remaining commercial airlines that now all flew in for their nearest airports. Chelsea's eyes flashed to the thin glass to the right of her chair that spit out technical data at her.

"One hundred percent of those pinged have launched," a woman beside the man announced. "That's eighty-two percent of all modules."

"We'll have to get the rest later," Chelsea said. "Initiate mass module launch, now."

A countdown of ten started.

"Ma'am," the man said. "There is a problem with one of the personal engines."

"If it's just one, that's a good day," Chelsea said.

"But ma'am, its—

The module moaned from below its pressure launch plate and whined all throughout the walls. The command center it carried suddenly launched upwards, along its launch tube, through its airtight seal, out of the earth and into the sky nearly three-thousand feet. Once it had cleared the tube, its launch pressure exhausted, it began to fall back to the earth.

"Oh shit," Chelsea said, unable to hide it as her stomach was suddenly lunged into her head, which was okay because half the people in the marble had all said it too.

The nearly four thousand small engines extended instantaneously from their various compartments over the command module hull and caught the capsule from crashing back into the Earth's crust. The module jerked violently upwards a second time to an extent that Chelsea feared she wouldn't be able to command efficiently. The launch continued.

"Please, God," Chelsea prayed. "Let our composite hold."

The marble's walls flashed red.

"Military defense systems reported," a woman near the defense monitoring sector of the circular room announced through serious strain.

"Types," General Mince's voice warbled over a speaker system.

"Heat and pursuit, sir," the woman replied.

"Rain flares and ignore heat type," Mince's voice announced.

"Proportional navigation incoming," a man called from the same defense sector of the room.

"Here we go," Chelsea called.

The entire module slowed, then suddenly thrust the module back towards the planet.

The room filled once more with people who couldn't help themselves curse.

"Missile trajectories are misaligned," the man groaned.

The module jerked upwards again.

"God," Mince groaned. "Damn!" This time, he didn't need the speaker system to relay his message from his post twenty feet away from the base of Chelsea's command podium. "I don't know how much more of this I can take."

"Come on General, it's not that bad, is it," Chelsea replied.

"Tell that to my spleen that just played pat-a-cake with my balls," Mince replied. "Oh, I'm so sorry. That was crude."

"Yes. But amen, general," a man in pre-launch cried out.

"All right, people," Chelsea called.

"I'm going to need those baby grabber spoons to fish mine out when this is over," another man called.

Chelsea tried not laugh with the others but couldn't stop from snorting.

"How are those incoming missiles performing," Chelsea forced out through it all.

"They've missed modules so far," a woman replied. "The laser redirect is working. All defensive measures are working. I'm receiving reports of additional launches now."

Again, the module dropped, then continued its climb.

"High-altitude fighter jets have been launched ma'am."

*   *   *

"We never should have let her go," Kola said, allowing her suit below the neck to seal.

"They had a gun on her," Shauna said.

"It shouldn't have been on her at all," Kola said. She kicked her sniper rifle case. "It should have been me."

"Who else could have lobbed that kind of a potshot at that agent if it had been you," Shauna asked. "I sure couldn't have done it."

Kola began fumbling with her engine, so much that she could no longer tell if it was upright or not. From the roof of the building that she and Shauna stood upon, she watched out towards the White House where Riley followed Tyresa onto the south lawn.

"Damn it," Kola screamed.

"Kola," Shauna said.

"What," Kola replied sharply.

"She's fine," Shauna said.

Kola stared at Shauna and could speak only breaths that had said more about how she felt than she, herself, could do.

"You taught her," Shauna said. "She has the best of all the suits and all the gear. She has more people paying attention to her than they do to us. The launch doesn't even start until she initiates her own engine."

"A mom who loves her child doesn't let dogs chew on her butt," Kola complained.

"What?"

"It's something Michael told me," Kola explained. "A mother throws herself in front of the dog, kills the dog, or at the very least takes the attack so the child doesn't get hurt."

"You remember that," Shauna asked.

Kola didn't need to say anything to answer, and she didn't know what to say. Something inside of her stirred. She knew what death looked like, how easy it was to pull a trigger, slice a throat, drop a body and never give it a second thought. She knew all the weapons that were upon Riley now, and none of them would give her face a second thought if they painted it with death. Kola couldn't stop hearing Michael's voice in her head.

"Oh my god," she sullenly cried. "What have I done? Shauna?" She held her hand out for Shauna to take. "Shauna? What have I done? I did what my mother did. I sent her into a dog pen. Shauna? I did it too!"

She could no longer move now.

Kola heard Shauna's voice, felt her hand on hers then on her shoulder. She felt Shauna shaking her. "Kola!" Shauna looked strangely frightened, which she never appeared.

"Shauna," Kola kept muttering. She gasped in breath shallow enough to get the next repetition of her name out.

"Kola," Shauna shouted and shook her extra hard until Kola finally remembered to breathe.

"A mother also knows when to let her child fly," Shauna said. "That's different than making her fight dogs. She wants to fly. Let her."

"What if she falls?"

"She won't."

"You don't know that."

"She won't," Shauna said sharply, and Kola saw the fear in her eyes too.

Kola hugged Shauna and clenched.

Shauna cradled Kola's head a moment and then held her away.

"You going to be okay," Shauna asked.

"I'm not sure," Kola replied. "Depends on if I get to orbit alone or not."

"If that happens," Shauna said. "I love you, and Riley loves you."

Kola peered through sniper scope and could see that Munger was putting on his flight suit now.

"She's almost ready," Kola said, and she found the nerves to finish dressing herself.

She watched as Riley now stood in her suit with Munger and Tyresa fully dressed as well. Kola and Shauna pressed their ready buttons. Thirty seconds later, after Riley activated her own ready button, Shauna and Kola lifted off the roof. Only, while Shauna raced towards the skies, Kola's engine hefted her ten feet then spun her out of control, flew her off the building, across trees, over devastated and burning parkland, then down Pennsylvania avenue before slamming her into the black iron-wrought fence of the White House.

"Engine malfunction," the automated message rang through Kola's ears. "Suit seal is complete."

At once, she began to climb to her feet. She suddenly heard her mother's voice tell her, "When caught off-guard by a surprise attack, always get back on your feet so you can fight back." She folded the top half of her two-part engine away from her front and around to the other half on her back.

Secret service caught sight of her at once and drew in.

"Don't you dare leave me," Shauna's voice crackled into Kola's ear. "You're not the only one who's bro—n," and her voice petered out.

She thought she could hear Riley's voice crackle as well.

The closest officers drew on Kola, ordering her to her knees, hands on her head followed by, "The hell is that," as one of the smaller space modules erupted from the earth, about two miles out, surprising the armed men. The entire earth shook under the instant release of millions of pounds of pressure into its atmosphere.

In the officers' shock, Kola twisted, grabbed a secret service weapon from the agent closest to her, fired a bullet through his spine, another through a different agent's head, then one into the man between her and the iron fence. As this one fell, she used his corpse to launch herself to the fence, where she scrambled over, shot another agent at her pinnacle then scrambled to find shelter behind a tree from the sniper that had turned her aim on Kola. However, the rooftop sniper rushed her shot at the surprising intruder and missed.

Kola wrapped her arm around the tree, fired another shot, didn't kill the sniper but watched her recoil in pain. Kola charged across the lawn, where she fired upon two more agents, and took one of their automatic weapons.

From here, she climbed the steps of the White House and ducked inside, shot four security officers and sought shelter behind the first door she could find. She fired several more times and screamed for the staff to get out.

From here, she took up anything that she could throw, wield or use to fortify herself at any agent who would try to enter the room. Then she felt her suit for any holes.

"Engine malfunction," the automated message repeated. "Suit seal is complete."

Meanwhile, the dart that the hospital module had fired finally reached its intended target, a communication satellite some distance in the same orbit and ahead of the hospital. The dart penetrated the satellite, released its gas and exploded within it.

*　　*　　*

"U.S. missile guidance is down," the voice announced from the defense sector of the marble. "High-altitude jets have no satellite direction."

"They can still fire manually," Chelsea said.

"One of our modules has been engaged," an older man's voice announced, then, "Module defenses have succeeded."

"Yes," several voices cheered.

"Generals," Chelsea asked.

"Let's not do that again," Gerbil suggested.

"I agree," Mince added. "We don't have to hold back anymore. This is the defense of our people and way of life now."

"You know," Chelsea said. "You're right. Tactical, initiate fleet-wide full lock-on of any high-altitude military enemies and launch mini-seekers."

Several minutes later, the gravitational force began to lighten against the crew's seats, and continued to lessen.

"Ma'am, command module has reached low orbit," one, young man reported.

"Ping all modules," Chelsea said.

"You did it ma'am," a woman's voice called from directly behind Chelsea's seat. "Our electronics, smelting, chemical bay and cathedral modules have all taken damage, but their flight captains are reporting that repairs are already underway, and that we've lost nothing critical. You got Omniscient to bring them all up."

Cheers across the room erupted.

"Quiet down," Chelsea ordered. "Ping engines."

"Ma'am," a male voice from earlier said. "Ping shows a ninety-eight percent response of those launched."

"Keep pinging," Chelsea said.

"We did expect there could be a problem if passengers didn't assemble their suits correctly," Heather said from her seat in the observation area. "For a first-time massive run, I don't care what you're selling. That kind of product launch just isn't heard of."

"Agreed," Gerbil said.

"Ma'am," the male voice called again.

"Did Riley and Max ping," Chelsea asked. "I don't want to answer to Salvo if she didn't."

"Riley, Max and Shauna have all pinged," he said. "Salvo did not."

Chelsea unbuckled her seatbelt but maintained her tether. She gripped the handrails on her command stage.

"There's no way she didn't suit up properly," Chelsea said. "Where is she?"

"She strayed from launch path, ma'am."

"Where is she?"

"According to this, the White House."

"How long until we intercept Riley and Shauna?"

"Forty minutes, Ma'am."

*   *   *

Forty minutes came. Fifty passed. At fifty-five, riley and Shauna, followed by Max and Tyresa floated into the operations room.

"What the hell happened," Shauna screamed.

"Where's my mom," Riley demanded to know.

"She's on earth still," Chelsea said. "It was Ernie."

"How could it be Ernie?"

"We didn't catch it, I'm sorry," Chelsea explained. "He embedded a virus for Salvo's engine to fly off course so she wouldn't make it to orbit."

"Well, fix it," Shauna demanded.

"We're working on it. It's a worm, and it's currently attacking Omniscient," Chelsea said. She tried her hardest not to let it show that she believed she'd never solve the problem. "We've already had it trying to shut down systems across all our modules."

"Meanwhile, where's my mom," Riley asked again.

"She's in the White House."

Riley grabbed her mother's hand, and they both clenched.

Chelsea frowned her agreement that it wasn't likely Kola could have held out long enough in the presidential palace. "What would you like us to do, Salvo," she asked.

"Don't call me that," Riley said.

"Your mother's not here. According to your parents, that officially makes you—

"She's not dead yet," Riley started to say but had to force into a crying scream to finish getting it out. She wiped her face. "Call her."

Chapter Thirty-six

The desk held a letter opener, one with a jade handle and black rivets. The blade was silver but turned red as it dug into the neck of the agent that had the nerve to peek in through the secret entrance.

She wasn't quite sure how she'd ended up here. She emptied the previous four rooms she'd been in of anything she could throw or smash someone with. Before this guard could fall out of the doorway, she took his sidearm, pulled the letter opener and threw it into the forehead of the officer who was next in the hallway. As the woman behind him opened fire, Kola had already vanished from the entryway and turned her weapon on the man who took a bead on her from the secretary's reception area. She fired, dropped him and knelt behind the desk.

A gas grenade rolled into the room, she threw that into the secret hallway and returned to fire bullets at anyone who coughed. At the sound of the main office doors opening, she grabbed a book off of a nearby shelf and threw it, just enough to make the next officer in line hold up an elbow to deflect.

Kola held her gun to his exposed armpit and fired a round through it. Then she grabbed his sidearm as well as his hidden knife in his belt buckle. Four men filed into the room, overestimating where they had thought Kola to be. By they time they realized, Kola slipped behind them, slit one throat, sliced a thigh open then shot the remaining two agents in ways that caused one to gurgle himself to death and the other to hobble until he stumbled over an end table. Then she put a bullet in the head of the agent whose thigh she'd cut and left the man with a smile in his throat to bleed out.

She watched three agents storm the lawn behind the oval office. They opened fire and must have realized it wouldn't penetrate the bullet-proof glass, but they might have also known it could have given her pause to question why they would have been so absent-minded.

It was in this pause that a bean bag hit her in the head, and she stumbled sideways. Before she could return to her feet, she was restrained by enough bodies and their combined strength to break her neck if they so chose. Her tired breathing did very little to repel any of her subduers.

Then the phone rang.

It kept ringing. The secretary's phone in the next room rang. The agents were more interested in Kola than in the phone. A phone farther down the hall began ringing.

Then all the phones rang, and in case they didn't hear that, a missile struck the White House lawn where the three agents had previously been standing. The agents restraining Kola tumbled down, upon her.

One of Kola's arresting agents picked up the phone from the oval office desk.

"Agent Kinsey," he said.

"Please hold for the president of United States," Chelsea's voice said.

"The president," Kinsey asked. "How?"

"Agent Manny Kinsey," Riley's voice came over the phone next. "Do I have your attention now."

"Who's this? You're not the president."

"I tried to do this so no one had to die, but now I'm about to target where you stand and where you live with a lot of nasty boom unless you tell me what I want to know, do we understand one another," Riley replied.

"This is a government line," Agent Kinsey said hatefully.

"Let me try another number then," Riley said.

"Yeah," agent Kinsey said, as the phone started ringing in his ear. "You do that."

"Hello," a woman's voice that Kinsey immediately recognized entered the conversation.

"Charlotte," he asked.

"Manny," she asked in return. "Oh, thank god! What's going on?"

"He's about to let you die," Riley replied, and the static click in the background told Kinsey that Charlotte was no longer on the line.

"Yes, I have your address," Riley said. "You wouldn't believe what information I have at my fingertips at this moment, and I'm about to launch one bonafide human soup maker to your house that you can't stop, because my satellite is bigger than yours. Now how's my mother? I know you know who I'm talking about. She's there in the oval office with you. Is she dead?"

"And if she is," Kinsey replied.

"Then so are you," Riley replied. "And everyone else within 40 miles of you. So, I'd choose your answer wisely."

"You've got some balls," Kinsey said.

"No, I have missiles. Lot's of giant, fucking missiles. Don't believe me? Listen!"

Fifteen seconds later, the far side of the white house exploded. Five seconds after that a second and third missile hit the exact same target.

"Where is she," Riley yelled.

"She's alive," Kinsey said.

"Prove it," Riley said. "Take her to the south lawn, or the next thing to hit the white house will be what's left of your wife."

"Take her to the south lawn," Kinsey instructed.

"And she better not be cuffed or have a single scratch anywhere when she gets there," Riley ordered.

The agents pulled at Kola and continued to do so until they had all stepped onto the south lawn with its new crater. Here, Kinsey removed Kola's handcuffs. The field began to fill with more agents, all that remained and many that had been loyal enough to respond to the attack on the White House in their off-hours from their various departments.

Kinsey's cellphone rang now. He answered.

"Put it on speaker," Riley ordered.

Kinsey did.

"Mom," Riley asked.

"I'm here," Kola said, while her suit announced once more that her engine had a malfunction, but her suit was still sealed.

"Now, instruct your men to let her go," Riley demanded.

"Not a chance," Kinsey said.

"You're not getting this, are you," Riley said. "I am God. Let her go or—

"I hear one more explosion and I put a bullet in her head right here," Kinsey said, and he held his sidearm towards Kola's face enclosed behind her clear mask. "Threaten my family again, and I put a bullet in her. You have my family, I have yours."

"Agent Kinsey," Riley said. "Boy, did you pick the wrong family to bluff."

"I don't think so," Kinsey said. "You may be able to touch my family, but you won't drop a bomb on your mother, and I'll keep her safe and put her somewhere that our best interrogators can keep her breathing just for you. So, we're done talking."

"Riley," Kola said. "Listen to me."

"Yeah, Mom," Riley answered.

"It's okay," Kola said. "You're safe."

"You're not."

"This was always for you," Kola said.

The phone magnified Riley's sobbing.

"That was never a place for someone like me," Kola said.

"It's not going to be a place for any of you after today, you bitch," Kinsey said, and he suddenly drew his hidden blade and buried it in Kola's thigh, pleased with himself, but suddenly not when Kola's brow tightened into hatred rather than pain. She should be screaming.

Kola's first impulse was to snap his neck, but she had enough guns on her to end her before she could try. She had no opening. Still, no one called her Riley anything less than perfect.

"Riley," Kola said.

"Yeah, Mom?"

"Target me."

She watched that familiar fear of realizing Kola was a monster cross Kinsey's face.

"I already have," Riley replied.

This rumble in the sky was different, faster, deeper. Kinsey saw what made it, and, in that moment—like the other officers and agents who also looked up—realized that one thing that was most important about life. It could end whether you were an asshole or not.

Kinsey watched the trail of afterburn arc downwards, while Kola simply held her glare on him.

"Why," he asked.

"Why," Kola asked, incredulously. "You people picked a fight with God."

Kinsey's eyes filled with fear and regret, and felt Kola drive his own knife into his throat.

"And now God is pissed."

No bullets flew at her. Instead, Kola felt the impact of the nuclear warhead dig into the ground behind her and she watched Kinsey's face surrender to his fate. She laughed as the agents around him had already taken to flight from the impact of the warhead and the waves of dirt that now crashed upon them. As the explosion erupted, she felt herself thrown upward above them all. No, not thrown but launched, and not stably either. The engine lifted her straight up. She reached back and smacked the topside of the engine to her frontside as it was designed to do, but the drag made it much more difficult than it she would have thought it would.

She stabilized. The angry brain of the orange, red and black mushroom cloud chased up after her, licking at soles her golden suit, unaware that this outfit had decided not to take any shit from this explosion.

She rose higher and higher, faster than the blinding orange light beneath her.

Kola didn't know how it happened, didn't realize that, at that very moment, Chelsea, in orbit, clenched her command post railing so tightly that her hands, had they not been hidden beneath her own golden gloves, were completely white. Nor was she aware that Riley and Shauna, like everyone else in the marble, were watching an image of Kola's speck in the atmosphere outrunning the nuclear blast. She couldn't hear Shauna scream, "Fly, you magnificent bitch!"

Kola wasn't stupid, she closed her eyes and awaited her face shield to turn into the golden plastic that would defend her from the sun's rays, which were far stronger than that wimpy nuclear weapon.

Only now, did she come to the realization that she wasn't alone. Someone was attached to her, hugging her from behind. The force of the missile and the take off was so strong, that Kola hadn't even felt that one of the agents, the only one not caught up in the sudden surrender to imminent nuclear death, had snapped a new engine onto her belt. It was the agent's engine, not Kola's, that raced her to the heavens.

"Suit seal is complete," the suit told Kola.

The agent's grip began to fumble, and Kola realized the woman was falling only when she finally had the full understanding of what had just happened. Kola watched one agent Trinity Opeikans flail back towards the earth. Kola knew her only as the agent from Alabama Nation. She had known that Trinity had been forged into a system where she could serve and protect Max. She did not know that Chelsea had secretly helped Mince deliver one last order to her, which was to ensure that Riley above all others launched safely, and that, in the event she did not, the agent was to surrender her own flight suit and await a replacement for a later launch date. In her efforts to smuggle Kola her own engine, Trinity hadn't time to pull her own hood over her face without compromising her actions to her fellow agents, and her own strength could simply handle no more of the acceleration and loss of oxygen as they rose higher into the atmosphere. She used the last bit of what she had in her to cut a piece of the plastic, sticky strip that should have sealed her own hood to her flightsuit, and then slap it over the hole in Kola's leg where Kinsey had stabbed her.

Agent Trinity fell ethically into nuclear mushroom.

Soon, all was quiet and black. Kola succumbed to the weightless lack of power that she suddenly held in the universe, much like the sun's rays that were everywhere, but had nothing to grasp, so all seemed dark. The engine shut off and the propulsion jets within oriented her with orbit and then sped her away for retrieval.

Kola floated with thousands of satellites, watched even more sail high above her. Space modules floated farther away from earth, safe and out of reach of those measly fools that had failed to realize what an oppressed people could do.

For nearly an hour and a half, she held pressure against her knife wound, and she felt alone enough to cry. This time, she knew that she was, and why she was. She felt it. Her family was coming. When she drew near to the command module, a gold suit exited it and drew towards her on a tether.

"Mom," Riley's voice came through the hood speakers, and Kola cried some more, this time with an entirely different emotion, something pleasant, relieved, proud, if she knew what any of those words meant.

One left

Chapter Thirty-seven

President Zaxxon stayed in her shelter for three weeks. Chief Justice Maybe swore her in virtually. From her bunker three hundred feet below the Mississippi River somewhere between the Gulf of Mexico and "Sir, you're going to have to turn your car around now," she was able to work with congress to fund a counterstrike against those who attacked American soil and trapped her military beneath it.

Local rescue workers had to be dispatched to begin bringing soldiers back to the safehouses, and they came out in droves. Those large holes in the earth that had once housed Salvo's modules remained empty, and security doors resealed them. So far, government leaders decided it would take far more resources than they had to try accessing them while there were still military personnel in need of being rescued every day from underground. Through this, a second and even third group of launches of people were able to enter orbit and continue towards the construction site of the space station.

Between the counsel of General Hayden and Clinton Myers, President Zaxxon, unlike Munger, had decided an aggressive approach was the proper action of retaliation.

ASP expedited the construction of six rockets. Three were armed with nuclear warheads. ASP armored the other three and made them capable of steering a kamikaze course straight into the space station, which was now in control of geosynchronous orbit.

The station had become cylindrical in shape with solar arrays capping each end. The modules had extended, opened wider and curved to form four rings, around an axis, with the command component and its marble room in the very center. According to analysts in Florida, the length of the axis alone, without the solar panels, was roughly a mile and a half long and each of the four rings was three miles in diameter.

While the new space station had spent two weeks constructing itself, it taunted the elected leaders of the United States. ASP studied its construction, and President Zaxxon approved launching two armored craft through the axis. Two would be enough to stop the rotation of the space station, killing its artificial gravity. Destroy the gravity, and the inhabitants, if they should happen to survive the attack, would die slowly from bone and muscle loss in the months and years to come. The third armored rocket was meant solely to be a demonstration of U.S. strength. The three nuclear-armed rockets were intended to establish defense measures preventing such migration from ever happening again. The U.S. wanted all to know that no one would dominate space, except them of course.

Meanwhile, the new White House had already begun its construction in Chicago, and scaffolding had turned its work to reframing America from within.

The American people, now aware of a space threat, unified in purpose of destroying Salvo's space station. They cried for vengeance, blamed the mentally unstable and began at once to implant tracking chips into every person who could potentialy show signs of mental disability or ailment. Each chip had one dose of cyanide in case any person with one should stray from an approved schedule.

Zaxxon then authorized the full internment of all people who had ever been convicted, suspected or even had a complaint from a neighbor for having some sort of behavior that should prove too creative or educationally inept.

After three weeks, Zaxxon decided she was safe to walk among her fellow peoples. Then she went home. She wanted to look like every other average American who lived in a ten-billion-dollar estate.

On launch day, ASP had only to load the pilots, run checks and ignite rockets from six launch sites. Russia, China, North Korea and Iran orchestrated their own missiles aimed on space, each with weaponry of its own.

Zaxxon had sat down with a chocolate-chip cookie to watch the rockets begin their respective pre-flight checks. Canaveral's rockets had just been cleared to launch when six, five-inch marbles, aimed towards the United States, punctured into the earth's atmosphere, turning into red, hot fireballs that no one even noticed.

As the rockets neared the end of their countdowns, the six spheres struck the rocket fuel tanks. All six appeared to simultaneously burst into flames. The four other ships from around the world mysteriously disengaged their fuel tanks and first-stage rockets, spilling fuel across launchpads and causing all sorts of crew to flee before it could accidentally ignite.

"What was that," Zaxxon said, dropping her unfinished cookie and picking up her ringing phone.

"Let's be clear," Kola said plainly. "Space is ours. Any attack on it, is an attack on its people and we will defend against it. When your communication satellites see something, I hear about it before you do. You launch an attack on us, and I will end it. You attempt anything to enter this sovereign nation without approval from its government and I will dismantle your satellites and send you back to hula hoops and poodle skirts."

"Who is—

"Shut," Kola interrupted, "up! Look. I can drop shit on your house all day long. There's no shortage of natural resource up here for me to do that. So, do I start lobbing space debris at you? Or do we have a conversation where you shut up, and I don't have to smash you with a space station toilet seat?"

Zaxxon didn't know how to reply, and the secret service assigned to listen in on her phone calls were still too wounded from the loss of their fellow agents to dare invite a similar fate. She found herself a seat in the couch that cost her $40,000 from her last visit to New Manhattan. The sun had already warmed it and made it comfortable for her.

Outside, she watched the secret service agents who stood alert before her house, and she realized just how useless they were.

"I'm listening," she said.

"Oh, I know you are," Kola said. "First you're going to recognize us as a sovereign nation and stay out of my tunnels beneath you and my space above you. Salvo built them. Salvo owns them. You will treat them as foreign soil or I will treat yours like a nuclear battleground with your own weapons. You will then release all interned prisoners and people who wish to leave their communities and direct them to a safehouse, and you will remove their chips. All my safehouses will be granted diplomatic protection."

"I have to say, I don't see what the American people get out of this," Zaxxon replied.

"You get to learn what consequence is for stifling freedom. I'm going to make your country wealthy again," Kola replied. "I'm willing to open trade routes with the United States. What you do with your citizens is up to you, but I will offer asylum to any who wish it from your oppression. They will find it in my tunnels, and you will stay out."

"Why not just take them all with you?"

"And reward you? No. You need to be reminded what it means to live with other people. We will continue to build our nation. My soil in orbit, my cities beneath your feet, and my safehouses will be our embassies. Up here, we will open our borders from time to time when we are ready to expand, and we will open trade with the United States."

"What could you possibly have to trade?"

"Besides the obvious satellite maintenance and sharing of space data so you don't have to bloat yourselves with space travel costs you can't afford, I now own an entire solar system rich with resources. I am prepared to put artificial intelligence on Mercury that can start gathering minerals and balloons that can begin harvesting gases from Venus. I can finally put the successful module on Mars that you've continually failed to. I can put one on the moon, as well as mining operations, then open tourism. I can start the construction of an entire space defense system, so you never have to worry about asteroids or comets or anything hitting earth ever again. I will give you an edge that will make you the envy of the world once again and offer you the ultimate defense system. In return you'll open trade with us for the odds and ends that we wish to have."

"Just like that," Zaxxon asked. "I'm supposed to go to the American people and tell them, after all you've done, that we're supposed to enter into a trade agreement and become, what? Allies?"

"That's exactly right," Kola's voice replied. "You get in front of your people and you tell them that when they took what used to be the nation of freedom from oppression and turned it into a nation of bullies, that you lost your claim to being the pinnacle of liberty, so we'll take that burden away from you right now."

"So, you get to oppress us now," Zaxxon said. "Must make you feel whole."

"Save your antagonizing righteousness for your cookie," Kola replied. "I put you in that proverbial White House, and I'll take it away."

"How did you—

"Who do you think saturated the political field with so many opponents," Kola replied. "You started this, and now you're done. We could have developed this technology together, but you people just had to have a villain so badly that you couldn't see it was you. Now it's time to face the consequences. Rob people of rights if you want but stop killing imperfect babies and locking people in orchards. If your businesses can't afford to pay employees, then they shouldn't be trying to produce product they can't make. Break down your geographic offense zones, and maybe someday, we can discuss opening the skies to your country once again. For now, you stay on the ground."

"Our economy can't take that," Zaxxon said.

"Ours can," Kola said. "And whose fault is that, by the way? What I know is, if we work together, we can make better days ahead, and you can go on and continue being the assholes you were bred to be, while the people you sought to destroy are going to make you untouchable. With our domination of space, no one will dare conspire against the U.S."

Zaxxon was silent for some time and had to tell Kola she was thinking. Finally, she came back with, "I'll have the treaty drawn up at once and present it to congress."

"Good," Kola said. "You have 48 hours before I take my offer to China and negotiate all that I've offered you for an exchange of all the debt you owe them, and I will collect."

"How will I contact you," Zaxxon asked.

"You won't," Kola said. "President Munger will speak for his people until his term is up."

"Munger isn't the president anymore."

"Maybe not there," Kola replied.

"He's a traitor," Zaxxon said.

"Again, not here he's not, and how wonderful is it that I'm talking to the one person who can pardon him on your soil."

"Then why am I talking to you?"

"The people and their government may be here, but I own the sovereign soil they live on and all the technology and operations to establish my claim over space."

"You can't claim space, it's unlawful."

"So, come take it from me," Salvo replied.

*   *   *

Riley wore white, not because it was virtuous, but, because she had grown up with so many drab colors, she wanted something bright. The fabric had been packed into one of the warehouse modules specifically for Riley prior to the launch. She modeled it after a doctor's graduation robe. It didn't matter that it was ugly, Riley felt beautiful, her mothers knew she was.

Out of spirit of tradition, Riley wanted her mothers to give her away.

The cathedral was filled. Unlike the other parts of the constantly turning rings that had three or four levels, sometimes up to 20 of floorspace, the cathedral was open and reached the full height of the 250-foot tube. Here, sharp, white spires reached all the way to ceiling, which appeared clear from within the chamber but would look gold from outside. The sky was starry black. The axis of the space station spun much more quickly than the outer rings.

When Riley said she wanted an official wedding, she had already made up her mind about who she wanted to conduct the ceremony. The person she had decided had become like a grandfather to her in place of the one she had lost at a young age, a man who had come to treat her almost as protectively as her own mothers, yet not as capable of death as Kola, not anymore anyway, and a man whose actions to protect her, saved her mother's life and proved himself.

Argyle Mince stood wearing his military dress, but not the same as he had worn when he came to these people. Riley had asked that a new one be made for him, after he had finally resigned himself to retire from his military existence, as he knew it, and began a new one as Kola's private General of station security. His new suit was a light gray, something that allowed him to see himself a bit brighter than he had in a uniform before.

Kola had suggested he keep his medals, pins and other commendations since he had truly earned them, and they were a testament to the kind of leader he was. However, Mince knew it was to ensure he would never forget what he'd done, failures as well as accomplishments. She had, however, consulted with Riley to create another medal for him. Munger agreed to the purpose and the cast and adopted it as the official seal of this new government's presidential award. It would be reserved as the highest honor a president could give. It was a purple lilac with the words "Honor Memory." It was a simple award and Mince hung it around his neck today, not because he was proud of it nor deserved it. He wore it because he must, and he would wear it every day until it was too heavy for his mortal neck to carry.

He had passed Kola's test and brought the final piece required to save this people, but he had destroyed far more than he could ever atone for. Perhaps, in the future, people would wear the medal in pride, but he wore his in shame. However, not today.

"Who gives this woman to this man," Mince had asked.

"Her mother and I do," Shauna and Kola both replied.

Kola didn't quite like saying it. No one said it for her when she married Shauna. Yet, Riley wanted it.

Mince said his words. Riley married Jim. They kissed, and Kola's finger tapped the side of her pistol through her own dress, which she couldn't believe she was wearing. Shauna took her hand and kissed it.

Later, Riley's moms swayed with each other on the dance floor, something Kola had felt more than self-conscious about as she'd never danced before. Kola wondered how she'd gotten here, with Shauna, with Riley. This wasn't supposed to be her adventure, and yet, it was.

"What changed your mind," Shauna whispered into Kola's ear as she watched Riley and Jim move together on the other side of the dance floor.

"I love her," Kola said. This time when her eyes watered, so did Shauna's. Kola could feel her wife's tears on her neck. "And I love you. I know that now."

Shauna smiled and kissed her head. As the music ended, they both pulled apart and decided they should take a break from balancing in the strange new gravity, then they took two seats at a nearby table. They watched Riley dance, until Severus interrupted their scenery. He handed the box with its strawberry paper and white ribbon to Kola.

"It's easy for the night to get away from you," he said. "Better do it before they run off."

"What is that," Shauna asked, cocking her head at the surprise. "I thought we put it all in their apartment already. Chinese checkers too."

"Not this," Kola said, and she waved for Riley to come over, just as Jim's sister stepped in to ask a dance with her brother.

Riley bounded over, "Yeah, Mom?"

Kola handed Riley the box.

"What's this," she asked gleefully and dropped into a chair next to Kola, plopping the box onto the table.

The box whined.

Riley's face suddenly froze, and her own eyes glistened at once. She tore off the paper and crowed in child-like awe at the little, black, pug-nosed puppy. She hefted it up under his armpits, and his tail wagged his fat caterpillar-like body in excitement to see such a pleasant and beautiful woman. She hugged him close and he squirmed in her arms, licking at her chin. She suddenly hugged Kola into her and the puppy.

"Thank you," she said, and she cried.

"Okay," an older woman announced from behind a microphone on a stage. She was a wedding planner on the Denver module and an excellent one at that, it turned out. Gertie, Kola thought her name was.

"Okay," Gertie said again. "I think we have a bouquet that needs throwing."

The young, single women all began to gather on the floor. Riley set the puppy in Kola's lap and rushed off before suddenly turning and running back to her mothers' table to take up her bouquet. She rushed off again.

That was when Shauna finally saw it, and she wondered how she'd not noticed the small decoration before, tucked into the heart of the blue ribbon around the bouquet. It was square and still as bright red as when they'd found it the night this entire journey together began.

"Is that what I think it is," Shauna asked softly, yet sternly.

"What," Kola asked.

"What do you mean what? That," she pointed to the bright, unopened condom wrapper inserted into Riley's bouquet made of white roses from one of the greenhouse modules.

Kola looked more closely, unsure of what should upset Shauna. "Oh! She said she needed something old."

The puppy licked at Kola's face, and memories flooded her brain of another puppy, happy to see her, before anyone had taught him "bite" or her "stab."

Meanwhile, Riley climbed a one-step podium and stood before a group of young women, or at least women with youthful dreams still, and Kola watched her toss her bouquet over her head. The young woman turned laughing, not because something funny had happened, but because she was where she wanted to be and where she should be. She was on top of the world, in a better place, alive and herself. She was perfect.

Suddenly, Kola was happy.

Thank you for reading the
The Exodus.

It is an honor to share this story with you.

Please leave a review online.

Visit
davidfairchild.com
to learn more about the author, his
other works and news regarding his
forthcoming books.